I0822319

PASSAGE TWO OF THE DIVINE GODSQUEEN CODA

BILL ADAMS

Willow Wraith Press
Visit our website at willowwraithpress.com

The characters and events portrayed in this book are fictitious. Any similarity to real persons, living or dead, is coincidental and not intended by the author.

ISBN-13: (ebook) 979-8-9899405-7-8
(paperback) 979-8-9899405-8-5
(hardback) 979-8-9899405-9-2

Cover Art by: Felix Ortiz
Cover Title Design & Interior Art by:
Dewey Conway
Character Art by: Puos

Printed in St. John, IN, of the United
States of America

It’s still for me…

Fair friends, the Passages of the Divine Godsqueen Coda are not for the faint of heart. So be warned, within these pages are scenes containing blood by the gallonful, violence & death by the plenty, profanity by the metric shit-ton, haunting past off-page sexual & emotional trauma, explicit sexy times (both wondrous & darkly themed), alcohol use, misogynistic assholes, as well as scenes of intense torture using blood magic.

Table of Contents

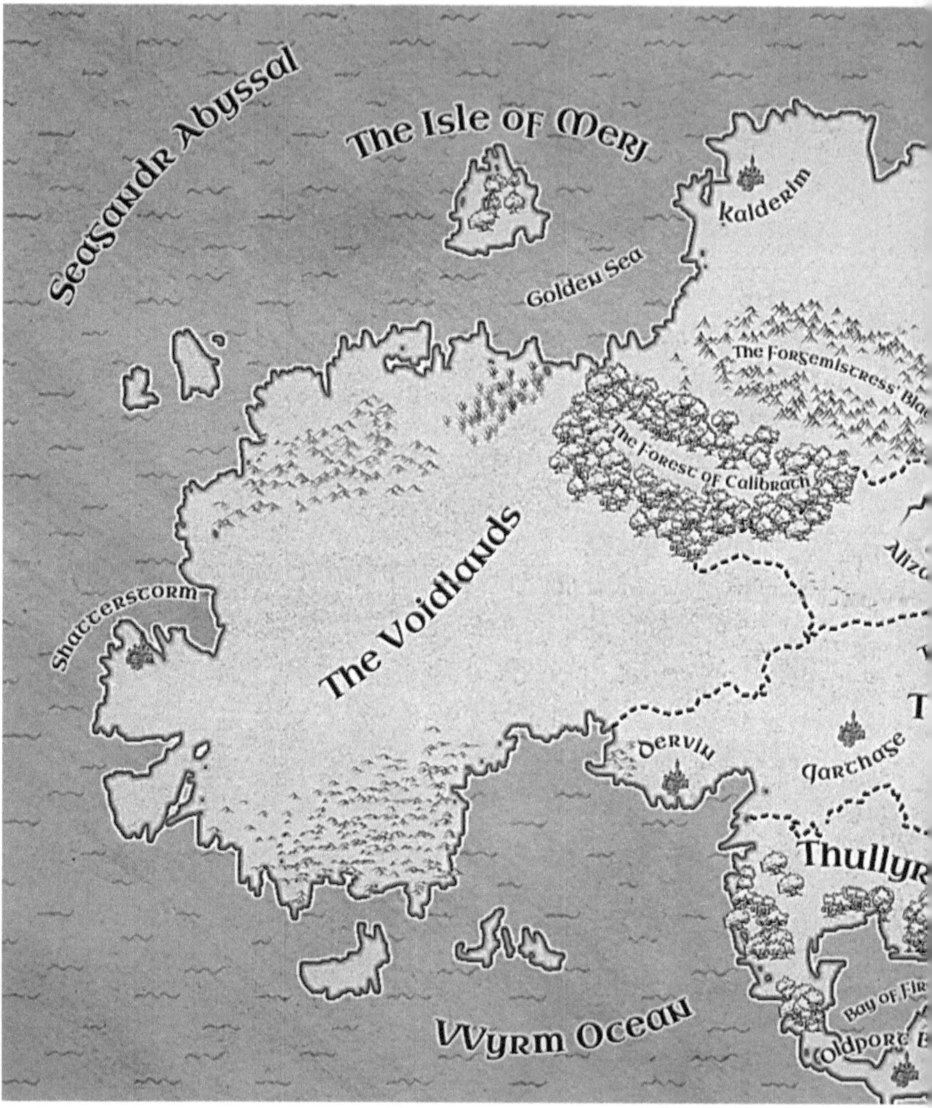

Seasandr Abyssal
The Isle of Meri
Golden Sea
Kalderim
The Forest of Calibrach
The Voidlands
Shatterstorm
Dervin
Jarthase
Wyrm Ocean

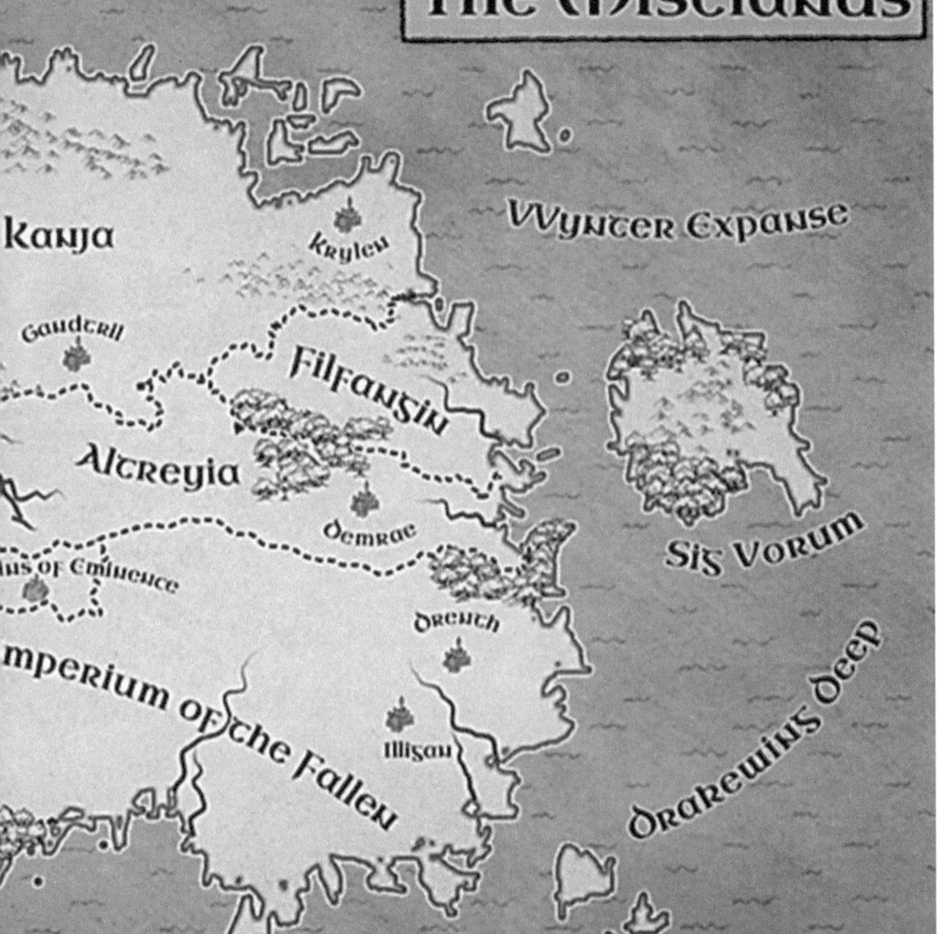

The Mistlands
Wynter Expanse
Kanja
Krylen
Gaudtrill
Filfansin
Altreyia
Demrae
Sig Vorum
ns of Eminence
Drenth
mperium of the Fallen
Illisan
Drakewins Deep

IMPRÎMÎS

(ADDITIONAL APPENDICIS IN BACK OF BOOK)

Aether [**ee**-ther] – magical essence of all existence, borne of the Great Crystals, Eminence & Noctis; bequeaths the Four Tenets of Aether: *Ignis*, *Aquis*, *Terris*, and *Aere*.

Aethecite [**ee**-th-e-sahyt] – pressurized & condensed aether into an ore-like manner; its essence has been derived into a potent & valuable fuel, technology, and weaponry. Becoming a rarity after the events in Drenth.

Aetheurgy [**ee**-th-er-jee] – the art of burning aether into one of five forms of the Pentax Gods & the God of the Void; **Soul Form, Vision Form**, **Burn Form, Shard Form**, & **Void Form**.

Draconem [drey-**koh**-nem] – Greater & lesser orders of drakes

Firedrake – Greater order. The smartest, as well as the cruelest, grand of size, & notoriously violent. As such, these savage beasts tend to lair on fiery peaks far from the races of man. Their scales are near impossible to breach, thus are used in body armor manufacturing.

Seagandr – Greater order. The bane of every sailor, for they possess multiple heads & rise from their gloomy depths only when cargo ships are bulging with drake essence or aethecite. Their oil offers an alternative fuel source to aethecite, as well as a suitable machine grease.

Aerovern – Greater order. The smallest in size, with a wingspan half the size of their firedrake cousins but possesses a healthy dose of claw & lightning breath. Their scales drip poison & frost, but once past their exteriors, they make for excellent food seasoning.

Terrisvvyrm – Greater order. All have perished during the destruction of the aethecite mines & Temple of Mother Marrow. The largest drake, but simplest of intelligence. These subterranean behemoths had slimy scales & no eyes. Instantly after death, vvyrm corpses become fetid & rotten, making a perfect source of fertilizer.

Drakken – Lesser order. Anthropomorphic, these drakes live amongst men. Renowned for their warrior-heart, some become wardkeepers, or counselors & generals to rēgis & rēginae.

Blooddrake – Lesser order. Cunning & secretive, most owing allegiance to the Divines. These loathsome drakes utilize aether to wear the flesh of men, stealing their identities to further the Divine's endeavors. Wily & hateful.

DRAMATIS PERSONAE

AS DETAILED BY F. DUNLEITH, RĒX OF KALDERIM

YEAR 20 A.R.O.E.

Brynn Benld *[brin ben-*uh*ld]* – also known as Ashe, Lilia, Camilla, & Snow Eyes. Godsblood & snarky heroine of this Coda. Left with Cyan the Defiant of the Scattered Shards by Valeria Dunleith as a babe after the invasion of Drenth. Trained in Shard Form aetheurgy, but also possesses the mysterious Soul Form. Dying by the nigrum pulmonem. Carries the daemon blade Strix & the Hammer of Mother Marrow. Bound upon her wrist is the Eye of the Soul, a golden bangle with a diamond eye in the palm & said bangle will lead her to her unwanted destiny: the Seals to Eminence. She has already broken *Terris.*

Cadrianna Benld *[kad-ree-**an**-uh ben-*uh*ld] née* Nightingale – deceased mother to Brynn. Taken prisoner by the Fallen. Thinking Brynn captured & tortured, she allowed herself to be bound with Void Form aetheurgy to the sentient daemon blade, the Strix, to stave her child's punishment. As a scourge of the Fallen's Coven, she became his most valued assassin.

Canlon Carr *[**kahn**-lon kahr]* – the Last Godsking of Eminence. To save the Crystal of Life from the Fallen's clutches, he used his Soul Form to seal the great floating city from the Divine's attacks. He currently waits within the ancient city for a Godsblood to break the Seals & take their place upon the throne of the Gods.

Cyan the Defiant *[**sahy**-an the dih-**fahy**-uhnt]* – a titillatingly handsome vicar of the Scattered Shards. A devout believer in the Pentax, especially Justice. Was given baby Brynn by Valeria Dunleith after the invasion of Drenth, told to train her into a warrior for Eminence. He knew nothing of Brynn's history, nor her Godsblood heritage, only knowing she was incredibly strong in aetheurgy. He is stubborn & determined.

Elian *[eel-lee-****yuhn****]* – deceased gang leader of Drenth's Slag's End. A wily ne'er-do-well who took Brynn Benld in upon her arrival in the desert mega-city. Secretly worked for Solanine but tried to double-cross the Fallen's number two & deliver Brynn directly to the Fallen.

Emre Benld *[eh-****mrah*** *ben-*uh*ld]* – deceased father of Brynn, heir to regency of Drenth. He knew of the location of the Seal of *Terris* & by refusing to give its location, his throat was cut before his wife's eyes (luckily Valeria Dunleith was able to bring him back to life). Harboring a deep hatred for the Fallen, he sowed rebellion in Drenth, aiming to bring war, & reclaim his homeland. He sacrificed himself to save his daughter from the Fallen's clutches, finally receiving forgiveness from Cadrianna, but also breaking yours truly's heart in the process.

Evander *[ee-****vahn****-der]* – a deceased street rat of Drenth's Slag's End. Brother to murderous felon Elian. Taken by one of the Divines, promised power & wealth. Trained by the nefarious (and smug) Solanine, his body transformed under the pall of Void Form aetheurgy & was killed by Cyan the Defiant's Sharded Gauntlet at the Temple of Mother Marrow in retribution for the vicars' torture & murder of Amaranth the Pure. Had an unhealthy desire for Brynn Benld.

Finnus Dunleith *[****fin****-uhs* ***duhn****-leeth]* – the best looking elfir in all the Mistlands! Third son of the Dunleith family in Kalderim & in line for the Golden Throne. Mischievous, debonair, & perfect in almost every way, especially a keen fashion sense. Borne with a rēx's blood but became a rebel after meeting the love of his life, Emre Benld. Heartbroken, at this time, but it all worked out in the end (no spoilers seen here).

Harlequin the Resolute *[****hahr****-luh-kwin the* ***rez****-uh-loot]* – formerly Harlequin the Bloodless & Tista. A young vicar of the Scattered Shards & acolyte of Cyan the Defiant. This fire-haired young woman was with Cyan & Amaranth the Pure as they hunted for Brynn Benld in Drenth. Was tortured by Solanine & remains traumatized by Amaranth's murder & subsequent alteration into a daemon.

***Lojen Tevunson** [**lo**-jen tae-**vuhn**-suhn]* – a drakken hatchling borne to Tevun, former wardkeeper of the Regents Benld & friend to Canlon Carr. A sweet roll bound in drake scales. Loyal friend & massive shoulder to mourn upon. Current wardkeeper without a ward as Brynn abandoned him after the events in Drenth.

***Lu Har** [**loo** hahr]* – also known as the Fallen. The Divine's agent in the realm of Life. Kin to Canlon Carr, grew jealous the Pentax chose Canlon as Godsking. Began turning Canlon's confidants to his side & tried to take Eminence as his own. After the Fall of Eminence, the lands surrounding the ruins became his Imperium. Daemon horde master & all-around evil man (but loathe to admit, he is impossibly beautiful).

***Neenah LeFleur** [nee-**nah** le-**flœr**]* – a smuggler, thief, & narcissistic (there's only room enough for one dashing & beautiful personage around here) captain of the airship *Marrow's Lover*. Her swashbuckling crew consists of one-eyed Roland, dvergir Tris, giantess mute Doll, hobgoblin twins (who she can never tell apart) Zig & Zag, & young orphan Alexina. Was the captain who had brought stowaway Brynn Benld to Drenth, setting the girl up with Elian. Gave the girl the name Ashe, adding the 'e' because it sounded more stylish (have to agree).

***Ruane Tevunsdotyr** [**roo**-an tae-**vuhn**-s-dot-teer]* – younger sibling of Lojen & hatchling of Tevun. Quick to temper & has a visible distaste toward the races of man (as witnessed by yours truly on multiple occasions). Has an unquenchable desire to prove herself a worthy drakken.

***Solanine** [**soh**-lah-nahyn]* – a blooddrake. Second only to the Fallen in the Imperium. Was present at the Fall of Eminence. Quite the abhorrent & sadistic drake, they taught (and taunted & coveted) Cadrianna in the dark arts of Void Form aetheurgy. The self-stylized god of the floating fortress of Gargantua in Drenth. Was a confidant of Canlon Carr during his reign & one-time lover to Valeria Dunleith, but was one of the first to turn to the Dark Divine after being recruited by the Fallen. Mercilessly hunting for Brynn Benld.

Tevun *[**tey**-vuhn]* – former friend of Canlon Carr & former wardkeeper of the Regents Benld in Drenth after the Fall of Eminence. Helped revive Emre after the destruction of the desert city & guided the young heir in his quest for vengeance against the Fallen. Father to Lojen & Ruane.

Valeria Dunleith *[**vah**-lair-ee-uh **duhn**-leeth]* – youngest child of the Dunleith family & only daughter. Borne a bikrome, with one black eye & one white. Her Vision Form aetheurgy is nearly unparalleled in all of Kanja. Was a close confidant of Canlon Carr, one-time lover to Solanine (truly never approved of this relationship, but alas, siblings…) & eventually turned to the Dark Divine prior to the Fall of Eminence. Forsook her dark oaths after the Fall (thankfully), revived Emre Benld after his murder at the hands of the Fallen, & planted the Eye of the Soul for Brynn Benld to discover, thus setting the Godsblood upon her destined path.

Wick *[wik]* – a lapin survivor of the obliteration & subjugation of Dervin. With shredded ears & a fickle chip on his shoulder, he joined the rebellion in Drenth with a button-shaped eye toward seeing the Fallen burn. A combustible & competent pilot (and a very genial chap, but don't tell him this). Mate & Bonded to lapin spy Ancantha.

Wren *[ren]* – a deceased scourge & spy for Solanine in Drenth. Her first assignment was infiltrating the Slag's End gang to spy on Elian for Solanine, but pressed her nefarious luck when Brynn Benld came to Drenth. Became Brynn's first lover before immediately trying to kill her (trust me, she got what she deserved).

How things went down in Drenth

As told by Esteemed Captain Neenah LeFleur

Wait, you're telling Neenah LeFleur, the greatest smuggler in all the Mistlands, that you don't recollect what happened in bloody Drenth? Well then, don't I have a little tale for you!

A year's turn after arriving in the desert mega-city of Drenth to find more about her past, little bint Ashe (not her trueborn name, that was what she was trying to find out. But truth told, I gave her the name Ashe, using 'e' to give it flavor, hear?) crossed a threshold she hadn't expected to bloody cross: killing someone. Now I'm no stranger to a murder, mind, but even if it was by accident, something changed in this poppet, something that had to do with her innate connection with the poisonous mist that covered the land. You know, the mist of the Mistlands? Yeah, that prick-sucking stuff. It was killing her from the inside, the pulmo, that's what it bloody well does.

Anyway, this little bint was voidbent on completing a thievery job with Evander (a sadistic bastard who was infatuated with her) and Wren (a pretty young thief with whom Ashe was infatuated with). And as Ashe had called upon her magic, a golden, gemstoned bracelet affixed to her arm and released a spectral entity that called her 'Godsblood' before frightening the ever-living void out of her. Upon fleeing the job, the entity showed up in the flesh, and it was Solanine, an aetheurgist who was second only to the Fallen in power over Drenth. Trust in me, this bint was as mean as a cu… you get my drift. Literally over Drenth they ruled from a floating fortress anchored above the City of Sands, you might recollect that at least, right? Also in attendance was Ashe's former taskmaster of the Scattered Shards, a vicar named Cyan the Defiant, a man so interesting, so handsome, so elusive… but I digress. Cyan and his two acolytes—Harlequin the Bloodless and Amaranth the Pure—chased after Ashe, eventually catching her, and tossing her in prison to await their return to their sect in Kalderim. Not to mention a reunion with yours truly. I swear I hadn't stolen a thing!

Meanwhile, a scourge of the Fallen's coven, Cadrianna, killed one of the Fallen's associates. Not that I bloody well care about it, but Cadrianna was a proper prick-sucker, a dark one, her. Bonded to a daemon blade called the Strix, Cadrianna killed in the name of the Fallen because she believed he had her daughter in captivity (you'd think she'd bloody well doublecheck that stuff, eh?). Cadrianna was married to Emre Benld, the former heir to Drenth's regency. The Fallen came to Drenth because the aethecite mines are in the surrounding desert and you know how greed follows the source of fuel. Little did they godsdamned know, but one of the great Seals to Eminence—the holy city where the Last Godsking protected the Crystal of Life or some such belief—resided in a temple to one of the goddesses of the Pentax. In her pissing wretched state, Cadrianna had reluctantly fallen in love with the Fallen, and she hated herself for it. I mean, wouldn't you, too? The bloody Fallen!

After being brought back to life after the invasion seventeen years prior, Emre Benld had started a rebellion against the Fallen like a proper man, brave and self-serving, hear? With his wardkeeper, Tevun, a lapin pilot named Wick, a bikromi seer called Valeria Dunleith, and her brother, the new love of Emre's life, Finnus Dunleith (never trust a narcissist like this bugger, he's not egoless like a certain smuggling captain, no he is not!), Emre's plans to bring down the floating fortress were finally close to coming true. He just needed his daughter to become the warrior she was meant to be. Guess who that bloody daughter is…

Drakken siblings Lojen Tevunson and Ruane Tevunsdotyr, had arrived in Drenth looking for Tevun's wardkeeper horns, a holy relic of the drakken race. Never had the cause to meet a drakken, hear, but they are some godsdamned great folk once you sit down and have a mug of ale with them. They had received a mysterious communication to come to Drenth (it was that tricksy bikrome who'd sent it). As they fell in with

Emre's rebels, they had seen their father for the first time in almost two decades, only for a scourge to murder him before their eyes (Rest in Peace, Tevun. Didn't bloody know you, but heard you were good folk and bugger those who would give Lojen and Ruane a false hope. Bastard…). Agreeing to help Emre, the drakken scaled the giant anchors to the fortress to plant bombs while Emre, Valeria, Finn, and Wick attended the annual party aboard the fortress in celebration of the conquest of Drenth (Worry not, I was the best-dressed guest).

Ashe fled after meeting Emre, where she learned her trueborn name is Brynn, only to take matters into her own bloody hands. She attended the party but was attacked by a scourge on the way because that's what craven pricks do. After defeating the scourge, Ashe demanded to see Solanine like a boss bint. While waiting, Wren was somehow aboard the fortress. Ashe and Wren did the lovin' deed (Ashe lost her virginity, mind) and her magic began to grow stronger (see, she came to learn it is Life and Death within her, killing a man equates to Death, becoming a woman means Life, good thing my first wasn't that special because he lasted less than a minute…) only for Ashe to find out Wren was a spy for Solanine all along. Yeah, it's true, Wren was a bloody spy. I would've known better than to trust that bint. Ashe and Wren fought, and Ashe killed Wren. I taught her well. What, doesn't matter we only spent a couple of days together.

Pissed like a godsdamned harpy and bleeding, Ashe stormed into the party and confronted the Fallen. She also saw her father and Cadrianna, whom she realized was her mother. Emre's bombs blew the bloody anchors, releasing the floating fortress from its restraints. In the confusion, that elusive, handsome Cyan the Defiant entered into my debt for saving him and his acolyte Harlequin from becoming a daemon like his other vicar Amaranth. Don't worry, he'll pay his tithe with his hands…

As all converged upon the godsforsaken temple found within the desert, Ashe was confronted by Evander (who had sold his soul to Solanine in exchange for access to aether like a pissing fool). Cyan and Harlequin, after being tortured by Solanine, killed Evander and helped Ashe reach the Seal of Eminence. Solanine tried to trick Ashe, but she did not give in because that poppet has some intelligent brain meat if I do say so myself.

As this is happening, Lojen took his father's wardkeeper horns, attached them, and became a berserker against the Fallen's soldiers after they shot Emre. Cadrianna tried to save Ashe from the Fallen after Ashe defeated Solanine, but was impaled by her daemon blade under the Fallen's aetheurgy. That's why you should never bloody trust a daemon, hear?

Knowing she had no other choice, Ashe summoned her aetheurgy, and in the process, summoned a giant terrisvvyrm, one of the largest underground drakes ever. I've seen a number of vvryms in my time and this bugger was enormous. I shit you not. Ask anyone. The vvyrm swallowed the Fallen like a plump date, broke the Seal, and erupted skyward to destroy the floating fortress like it's a godsdamned clay mug. But this little bint's victory was not a happy one as both Emre and Cadrianna died in her arms. Shame, that.

Ashe decided to return to her training with Cyan. But in darkness, that evil, bloody whoremonger Solanine was revived, revealed to be a blooddrake who can wear the flesh of man, learning that the Fallen had also lived. Both vowed to break the other three Seals and take Eminence.

Now that's the godsdamned truest story Neenah LeFleur's ever bloody told!

Fire begets, Fire taketh.
Water rears, Water recedes.
Earth sculpts, Earth razes.
Air breathes, Air stifles.
Scales ward, Scales break.
Scales are All. Scales are Nothing.
Immortality does not come from the proliferation of Life,
But upon the wave of Death.

Atop Mount Bastard

UPON ENTERING THE firedrake's ruined lair, the first thing Grand Quaestor Owl noted was the stench.

It smelt like charred meat left on the spit too long, and based on smell alone, Owl knew the firedrake was dead. Firedrakes were clever, but not clever enough to act perished while quaestors of the Scattered Shards raced into the beast's lair with weapons drawn and aetheurgy at the ready.

"Cadoz, you fool, where you at?" Owl called.

"Here, m'lord. O'er… um… here," replied the hobgoblin servant. The grotesque voidspawn—with his flat face, hooked nose, and sizable hairy ears—had his eyes cast down as he scuttled up beside the grand quaestor.

"On with you, then." Owl shooed the creature ahead into the cavern. "Don't forget my chair. My knees ache something fierce."

The hobgoblin lugged the ornate wooden chair he had dragged throughout the mountain like it was the most precious thing in the world. For the aged, grey-skinned, withered body of the grand quaestor, it would be.

The cavern was grandiose enough for the tavern-sized firedrake to fit comfortably three times over. Smoothed rock was underfoot from decades-long entrenchment, while stalactites resembling a pup's teeth protruded downward from above. Recent scorch marks left blackened, still-smoking stone in multiple places. Piles of dusty bones were strewn about, some charred. Only one entrance, the one in which Owl now stood. Well, except the gaping hole toward the southern end of the cavern where the rock had been shattered outward over the mountainside. Nightturn shone through the gap in a reddish tint as the southward sky bled garnet, a stark contrast to the eastern emerald.

From the look of it, this aperture was new.

They were high atop Mount Bastard, a treacherous volcano on the southern shores of the Mistlands. Difficult to reach by airship or glider, boat even harder still. It was no wonder why the ornery drake had chosen such a place to guard the invaluable Seal of *Ignis*.

Dozens of quaestors milled about the cavern, many pointing or gesturing excitedly. The tainted warriors of the Scattered Shards each had sunken and stretched skin from the aether within the corrupted mist. Clad in crimson cassocks and glass breathing masks, their red-iron maces remained sheathed on their belt loops while wheellock rifles were slung across their backs.

The men and women of the rank circled around something, and it wasn't until the grand quaestor shuffled through, did Owl finally see the corpse of the firedrake. Owl whistled, casually stroking a waist-long white beard. There was still some awe left in this world to tingle old bones.

The draconem was immense. Easily pushing one hundred feet from the tip of the snout to the point of the tail, nearly twice the size of every firedrake ever recorded, larger even than the Fallen's daemon drake Cinder. This drake's head was the size of a fully mature auroch. The snout was beak-like, with teeth forearm-long. Tiny spikes grew like eyebrows and formed an intricate pattern over eyes as big as dinner plates. A sloping neck possessed a single row of progressively larger spikes. Scales the size of a man's head covered the body, garnet in color. Four dynamically built legs as big as wagon beds ended in clawed talons as long as Owl was tall when not stooping. Leathery wings coiled about the body, so thin, almost transparent. The tail ended with a stinging barb sharp enough to pierce nigh on anything.

There were burns all along the drake's flank, gossamer wings pocked with seared holes. The scales on both legs were blackened and wisps of smoke curled from beneath, the char of flesh strong and cloying.

Owl took a step closer, something crunching underfoot. A bright red shine in the muted nightturn glowed under Owl's boot. With a whisper of *Aere* aetheurgy, the glimmering shard lifted under the spell of air. Owl stared at it intently.

A garnet crystal shard. Hundreds lay around the dead firedrake.

"The Seal of *Ignis*?" Owl asked as the shard was slipped into a cassock pocket. A nearby quaestor stared dumbly as if the grand quaestor had asked him to calculate winter storage sums for each mega-city across the Mistlands. Owl breathed a frustrated sigh into the bushy white beard. "Where is Cyan the Defiant's acolyte?"

"Lady Drakeslayer… er… mistress vicar… Ashe is over the…" The quaestor's words died on his lips as a dark shadow and whoosh of wings filled the cavern's opening.

Owl smiled as a colossal bird winged into the firedrake lair, coming to land upon the back of the deceased draconem. An owl. Owl's owl. A strix. A rare predator found in the orcirish homeland of Sig Vorum. The huge bird preened its feathers as its yellow saucer-shaped eyes scrutinized the lair.

"Any bodies?"

The quaestor nodded in response, a whisper of the word *'drake'* from another nearby quaestor. "Another one of those…"

"Speak up, man, one of those what?"

The man gulped, found his voice, yet his gaze never strayed from the strix. "One of those… blooddrakes, grand quaestor. Like the one we found after… you know, outside *The Arbiter's Axe.*"

Like the strix with its feathers, Owl preened the waist-long beard in contemplation. "What of the Seal?" The quaestor shook his head. "I want everything recorded before returning to Oldport."

The man saluted over the insignia of the Scattered Shards brandished on his ankle-long, cassocked breast—the symbol of the Pentax Gods in the form of a fist holding a sword, a five-pointed star above the crossguard. The soldier hurriedly moved away, glancing nervously at the strix.

Leaning heavily on the staff of office, Grand Quaestor Owl shuffled farther into the firedrake lair. The quaestors had set up some aethecite lamps, and they filled the cavern with an unnatural, piss-tinted glow. It was unbearably warm as Mount Bastard had been a violent volcano in ages long past, dormant now since the Fall of Eminence, but still the fires burned deep in its belly.

A few quaestors huddled over some corpses, these ones recent. Nearing, Owl noticed they were indeed blooddrakes. One of the lesser orders of draconem, the two-clawed, snake-like drakes.

Beyond was ring of quaestors surrounding a midnight blue-cassocked vicar, injured by the look. Badly, even. A second person—a female elfir with long silver hair and bi-colored eyes—sat chained beside the vicar.

"Why are they bound? Unchain them."

"We thou—" started a woman in a red cassock.

"Unchain them," Owl demanded calmly with the smack of the staff in hand. Always calm, always under control. The way of the hunter. "What's the delay, quaestor? You would hold in contempt Valeria Dunleith, fourth child of the Golden Throne? And one of the Shards' vicars? Well, vicar-in-training, that is."

The quaestor hastily moved to comply. The seated warrior of the Scattered Shards looked a proper mess, as the young acolyte of Cyan the Defiant was burned and covered in blood, hers and purplish draconem blood.

"Grand Quaestor Owl," the girl started, "I always enjoy it when the lazy ones show up after all the dirty work is complete." She smirked as the heavy manacles etched with aetheric runes fell to the cavern floor, resulting in a dull thud. "But then again, you needed me to get this far. The Seal…" The girl shook her head as if meaning to say something else, but instead she fingered the grip of a multi-barrel wheellock pistol at her belt. The letter 'B' was engraved upon it.

"It was a long climb, child."

The girl laughed. "Too old, these days, grand quaestor? Bet you feel as old as the Fall of Eminence, eh? What's that, Val, five hundred years now? Zenith's cock, probably even older than that, I'd surmise. Don't you think?"

The bikrome appraised Owl with those eerie eyes; one all black, one all white. "Older." Her words were barely more than a whisper.

The grand quaestor held the calm façade, but inside was seething. "You look terrible, child."

The vicar-in-training lifted her left hand, which was coated in purplish ichor. A gold-braided bangle wrapped her wrist and a diamond in the shape of an eye was nestled in her palm as thin, braided links fanned to gemstoned rings on each of her fingers.

The fabled Eye of the Soul, a relic of Eminence. As her sleeve fell back, the girl's runic tattoos peeked through the ichor and ash.

"O, this?" She indicated her face with her bangled hand, a grin. "I bet I feel better than I look."

The entire righthand side of her youthful face was covered in layers of bloody gauze, with intense burns underneath. Her raven, shoulder-length hair was singed. Her all-white left eye was bright, while her right was milky as if blinded. Her right arm below the shoulder was missing, the cassock sleeve torn to shreds.

And yet, she was grinning like a madwoman.

"Aether," she said, "you know what it feels like inside. The burning and all."

"Cadoz."

The hobgoblin was lingering behind. The girl winked at the skittish servant with her good eye.

"Cadoz!" The little voidspawn jumped, bringing the chair forward. "Now, then," Owl said as a quaestor set a writing table down and took Owl's staff, ancient knees cracking upon sitting. "I, Grand Quaestor Owl," the scratch of quill writing, "am oathbound to lead the depositions of the suspects found at the scene of the theft, and… apprehended near the corpse of the last firedrake. Due to the sensitive nature of this case in relation to the Scattered Shards itself, care will be taken by myself to painstakingly avoid criticism, and only requisition the detail of the depositions of the suspects to determine their culpability in the theft of the Seal of *Ignis*, if any."

"Funny," the girl studied the surrounding quaestors, "I can smell the aether about them. And not because of their canisters of mist. I mean, I can actually feel the aether inside each of them. In you. It's fucking weird. But so it goes. We are but children meddling with the Four Tenets of Aether. Stupid we all were. We wouldn't have understood the nuance of aether if the All Father slapped us in the face with it." She glanced toward the corpse of the firedrake, hesitating before sighing. "I wasn't ready for it. Even Drenth…"

There was a wariness in the young woman, a maturity within the famous Shards acolyte many called Lady Drakeslayer. The girl wasn't even twenty years of age, and yet, she spoke of things a centuries-old elfir might when telling their grandchildren of the bygone eras before the Fall. The good ol' days as those nearing the eternal slumber of the Meadows might say.

"Brynn, put your faith in Them," the bikrome said softly.

"Even now you reproach me, Val," she responded. "Is this my punishment for failing to heed my father's wishes? For being such a little cu—"

"Your father had only one wish, Brynn Benld, and that is for you to claim what is yours."

"Half of Oldport Basin is destroyed," Owl said, feeling the investigation slipping. "From the Beggars Chain down through the Guild Politic. Hundreds, if not thousands are dead. A slew of high-ranking Guild members are missing, presumed dead. The events at *The Axe* were a sorry affair."

"And you want to pin the blame on me?" The girl callously laughed. She sat up straighter, the empty sleeve of her fire-scorched cassock hung limply at her side, her bangled hand forming a fist. "An aerovern, grand quaestor, how such a harboring escaped your knowledge is… regrettable, to say the least." The unburnt side of her mouth quirked, curling upward. "Luckily for you, I'm no longer in investigating conspiracies. Or Scattered Shards business."

"You would presume to threaten me?"

"Let's cut the bullshit, shall we? You owe me that courtesy after everything. You wanted the Seal of *Ignis* all along. Thinking to boost your rank within the Shards if you became its savior. You just needed someone with… more skill to find it. A Godsblood borne from the line of Nightingale." She shook her head before cocking it to the side as if she was listening to someone. But no one had spoken. "Void, I knew this would've happened. I can't escape it, can I?"

Owl was bemused. The Owl of old would have risen to this petty child's recriminations, but there wasn't time for such mummery. "I know you're involved in the theft of the Seal of *Ignis*. It couldn't have gone missing while we followed. Why deny it?"

"Who said I was denying it, you old bugger?"

"You were here, at the scene, when Mount Bastard exploded in a bright red flame."

A nod. "Wouldn't be elsewhere, would I? Zenith's cock, you're dense, grand quaestor."

The explosion had resembled Zenith taking a fiery blade to His southern sky and leaving behind a crimson gash of emptiness. No cloud crossed the expanse, no star filled the red.

"What do you know of it?" Owl continued, ignoring the attempt to goad. "Was this the work of Brio? Or Nocturne Himself?"

The young woman released the white-knuckled fist. "You know, I hear my mother had a saying about the gods."

Owl leaned forward, ancient, wrinkled elbows on the writing table. "O? What did Cadrianna Benld have to say? Or should I say Cadrianna Nightingale? The word of a scourge of the Fallen's Coven might not be the most respectable quoting. His greatest, they say. An evil woman, I hear it told myself."

"My mother was a Nightingale, as you know. But before the Fallen murdered her in front of me, she was wont to say: 'Never trust the gods.'" The girl coughed, her body doubling over as she spat nigrum pulmonem tar all over the ground. Then she grew businesslike as she wiped away the tarry blood that dribbled from her lips. "You would think, grand quaestor, seeing as Eminence is bound by three Seals now, not four, maybe the gods aren't actually the problem. Maybe we are. Man. Not many have the seedpods to challenge such an ideal. Except for one."

"And who would that be?"

The girl grinned as she glanced with one all-white seeing eye toward the bikrome. The girl called Ashe. The child who once carried the name Lilia while training under Cyan the Defiant. A woman borne with the blood of Nightingale. "Me. Brynn Benld."

Smiling, Grand Quaestor Owl drew out a folder and laid it on the writing table and dipped the tip of the quill into an inkwell. Owl readied it over a blank piece of parchment. "Tell me, Lady Drakeslayer, where is the Seal of *Ignis*?"

I

Ashe

WHEN THE SEA of Mist unveils a grisly murder scene, most people would blanch or potentially dry heave. Some might even relieve the contents of their stomach in a goodly effort to fertilize the surrounding wheat field. Others might curl into a ball and cry mercy to the Pentax.

But for Ashe, it was just another codex report to be transcribed.

Ashe waded through the crops that exuded the faint aroma of crisped flesh, the coppery tang of spilt blood in the air, and freshly burned boles. A homestead was ahead, but no slanted roof or bricked chimney toppers poked above the fruitage.

"ARSON'S NO REASON FOR THE SHARDS TO SEND IN THE FAMED LADY DRAKESLAYER TO INVESTIGATE," said the Strix. The daemon blade, with its outstretched wings of an owl and garnet-gemmed eyes, was sheathed at her belt, but it tsked as if it was humir. *"THIS MEANS ONE THING AND ONE THING ONLY, DEAR BRYNN. DRACONEM."*

"Such a master of the obvious. How was it possible to have survived nineteen years without you? And stop calling me Brynn."

"THAT'S YOUR NAME. OR HAVE YOU FORGOTTEN?"

"A name of the past."

Zenith's cock, why couldn't she just accept who she was? It ate at her, would devour her if she allowed it. That was why she couldn't claim the name Brynn yet. It was hard enough with the name Ashe.

Wren. Evander. Elian. All the others of Slag's End. All dead because of the name she chose to live by.

She wasn't truly ready to adhere to the path the name she was born with, as that path led to Eminence. Not yet. Perhaps not ever. Not after losing everything in Drenth a year prior.

Mother… Father…

Ashe fit her because she left nothing but ashes in her wake.

"O, HUMIR CHILD, YOU ARE TRULY STARTING TO SOUND LIKE YOUR MOTHER."

"What's that, bored?"

"YOU WOUND THIS OL' DAEMON'S HEART."

"You don't have a heart, or did you forget that?"

"POINT CONCEDED."

Two vicars stood outside the burnt farmstead, hidden slightly in the grey haze of the Sea. They both wore the standard-issue breathers of the Scattered Shards. Ashe didn't wear one, as she didn't need it to access the aether in the mist like the untainted warriors did. Pulmo be godsdamned.

Harlequin the Resolute's glass breather fogged as she spoke, "Four in the field, Ashe. Running most like."

The Resolute had bouncy curls the color of fire and had grey-green irises surrounding yellow pupils. Despite a smattering of cute freckles across the bridge of her nose, she was a few years older. Ashe liked her, though, always had while they grew up under Cyan's tutelage when Harlequin had been called Tista. It also didn't help that Ashe found her quite alluring, something that never would have crossed her mind if it wasn't for her time in Drenth with Wren.

"Five," the other vicar corrected with a sneer. His name was Phlox the Faithful, and he was a man she didn't care for one bit. "You've tainted Harlequin with your drink, Ashe. Her brain has turned to mush. Why Vicar Cyan allows it, I'll never understand."

A humir, Phlox was one of the ugliest sods to ever walk the Mistlands, and that was saying something. He had shallow eyes of bland brown with puke-green pupils. His whitish hair was shorn close to the scalp and his body was all sorts of ill-fitting, long of arm and short of leg. He was about half a decade short of fifty and was as devout to the Arbiter as they came.

"Because he likes me better than you, Phloxy," she said as she entered the burnt remains of the home, the grey haze parting for her. "Maybe if you pulled Justice's finger out of your as—"

"Ashe, you're not funny." She could almost feel Harlequin's eye rolling as the Resolute cut off her attempted snide remark.

"NICE PLACE, THIS," the Strix said before she could launch a comeback.

To say the ruin had once been a home was generous to the term. In fact, shack, lean-to, or a pest-ridden shithole of a shanty might constitute a better name of the scorched pile of kindling in the middle of the Sea of Mist. Only the doorway and one of the walls were standing, and the wall was smoldering where it was rent in thirds. There had been a roof once, but nothing remained, not even a stray crossbeam. The other walls were heaps of charcoal. Of furniture, those were also fried. A solitary firepit still stood, singed marks of black soot streaked the grey stone.

Hunched in front of the firepit was a lump of cinders in the shape of a corpse.

"Gross," she said as she flicked the bottom of her cassock aside to kneel beside the powdery corpse.

Ashe burned her aetheurgy and the mist around her surged with a joyous desire to do her bidding. The ruin erupted in a colorful spray as the pyre of aether raged in her blood. A piercing wail from beyond the veil of Life and Death accompanied her summons of her Soul Form, that mysterious Form none but she possessed.

She lifted her bangled left hand and pulled the sleeve of her cassock back to expose the intricate runes of aetheurgy tattooed onto her arm. The rune of *Ignis* blazed upon her bicep, her flesh tingling as a ball of flame sprung into life. Not flames of true fire, but that of aether. Ashe quelled the aetheric fire by cradling it above her palm, over the diamond of the Eye of the Soul.

The bangle glowed like liquid fire as she whispered, "Guide me."

The corpse burst with elemental colors of reds, greens, blues, and yellows. Tiny wisps formed misty, smoke-like fingers that stretched forth from the Eye to the scene before her. A lace crisscrossing, reforming the hunk of ash into a rainbow haze, stitching the once-existing lifeform back to what it once was: a person contently tending a cooking pot.

Fiery crimson aether danced across the emerald ground to the firepit. Flames crackled and spit to a time before being snuffed by whatever had destroyed the home. Earthen-infused greens shot upright in the form of timber used to construct the walls, translucent pines and firs strapped together. Smokey yellows of mustard billowed upwards from the firepit and bounced off the reformed roof. Bluish drips trickled down from a waterpot that once hung along the wall, collecting rainwater.

But it was the larger droplets of yellow-blue all along the western wall that caught her attention. Light azure splayed out like drying puddles or snowflakes melting. Only one thing made tinted golden sapphire appear that way.

"FROST," the Strix said. *"THIS WAS NO DAEMON."*

Interesting, to be certain. *But this far south?* That was improbable.

"EVERYTHING BECAME UNSTABLE WHEN YOU KILLED THE MOTHER LAST YEAR'S TURN. KILLED THE VVYRMS."

"Quiet, Strix. I need to think."

"DON'T HURT YOURSELF, DEAR BRYNN," the daemon said anyway.

In moments, Ashe's aether had rebuilt the shack, a tapestry rewoven in the misty spells. She glanced around the small hut and examined the lines of aether pulsating with colorful hues. Reading the magical auras like she was reading a book, taking in everything. Still, her gaze wandered back to the frosty blues.

"Withdraw," she spoke softly, her aether blazing anew as she snapped her fingers.

Instantly, all that she'd reconstructed broke as the aetheric mist heeded her command, as the heartbeats thumping within the latticework of colors became the last of this poor person's life. Like watching a scene upon an aerescreen, the magically-rebuilt person stirred the pot, the lines of aether along their arms oscillated in the mundane movements of cooking. Dark cobalt drifted throughout, a contented serenity at the joyous peridot from the meal to come.

A dangerous crimson warning pierced the outer walls of the shack. The person looked up, aura shifting from light yellow to hardened gold in growing fear and confusion. The walls burst from potent violence created by frost and lightning. Planks exploded by vicious claws. The fire in the pit winked out in a gust created by heavy wings. The person's body burned violently as snaps of electricity torched them.

The magic of Ashe's aetheric spell concluded; the smoke dissipated. Then came the pain.

Intense hurt wracked her body as she coughed so hard, black goop spewed all over the ashy corpse, causing it to disintegrate. Her insides burned as the corrupt aether in the mist claimed its tithe. Stomach clenched, stars behind her eyes. Sweat poured down her face as she sought to control the slow death. A losing battle.

Soon the pulmo would kill her. And soon, she would join her father and mother in the Meadows. Maybe, just maybe, their souls will forgive her.

Mother… Father…

Gathering herself, she smoothed her cassock, her hands trembling in the attempt. Combing a hand through her ebony locks, she dug out a golden flask etched with filigree from her belt pouch. She brought the flask to her lips and downed the spirits within, her pain receding.

"YOU ARE PUSHING YOURSELF TOO FAR, TOO FAST, DEAR BRYNN. I PROMISED CAD I WOULD WATCH OVER YOU. I DON'T THINK I'M SUCCEEDING."

Ashe took a deep breath, then exited the incinerated hut. "The others?" she asked of Harlequin, ignoring the bleating daemon blade and side-eying the baleful Phlox.

The vicar jutted her breather-covered chin toward the east. "'Bout ten paces. Digging for something. Before… you know."

Ashe swam through the scalded wheatfield that smelt of overbaked bread. Four bodies lay where they had burned, torn to shreds in vicious bites from a jaw too large to be anything else than a draconem. Daemons in the Sea could be large, but not this large. The stalks were splayed outward as the fire had been blown by the torrent gusts of wind brought by the bearer of death and doom. The fifth was hidden under one of the other burnt corpses. A child.

"What did you see, Lilia?"

Turning, Ashe found her taskmaster, Cyan the Defiant, standing over one of the corpses, his breather hiding his dark eyes with crimson pupils. She couldn't stop herself from staring at that stupid crest of blue horsehair atop his breather. It really was fucking ugly.

Touching one of the few standing wheat stalks, Ashe felt the undercurrent of aether within. "Aerovern," she said.

"A 'vern? Here?" Cyan the Defiant shook his head, the hideous dyed blue horsehair bristle on his helm whipped back and forth. "Getting bold without the firedrakes about. Rare to see a wild 'vern below the Blades." Cyan hunched over the grey ash of the largest corpse, penning notations in a small notebook. "Queer tidings, this. I want th—"

A wicked screech filled the air, cutting Cyan off.

In the empty sky above, a golden-hued shadow swooped, electricity crackling like lightning across the expanse. Thunderclouds formed from nothingness as the current drew convection, the air pulled condensation. The sky darkened, darker even than the Sea of Mist below.

The aerovern was still in the area, a drake in its claimed territory. Hovering over its kill.

Ashe crouched and burned her aetheurgy, her body humming with aether, wails piercing the veil. Death filled her.

Lightning flashed across the blackened sky. The beat of the aerovern's wings snapped, like twigs underfoot in a silent forest.

The mist canisters on his belt geysered as Cyan burned his Shard Form. He summoned a six-foot, double-bladed crescent axe of pure aether with his Gauntlet of Justice. Harlequin and Phlox appeared in the periphery, their canisters whistling as they burned, drawing their dual, blue-iron crescent axes from their belt loops.

High up, the aerovern circled, elongated tail slithering through the air like a snake in the grass. Powerful back legs tucked close as it banked this way and that, screeching over the wheatfield before disappearing into the thunderclouds. Brilliant flashes of electrical luminescence danced within the darkness overhead.

Her aetheurgy spun like a tornado, her senses expanding and enhancing. Her sightline grew like staring into a looking glass layered in a silver sheen. With her Four Enhancements aglow, she spotted the drake in the growing clouds, coming directly at them now, no longer content to skate through the sky.

Flat of snout, bony spikes ran in rows from the tip to the rounded part of its head over the eyes, where the spikes fanned out more than three feet in a beard-like pattern from the cheeks to under the jaw. Every inch of the head was covered in golden scales, gleaming under a coating of frost. Wings spread wide, sharpened talons. Twenty-five feet of death incarnate.

"Don't even think about it, Lilia." Cyan stepped closer to her. His aetheric axe humming with power borne of Eminence.

"Wouldn't dare," Ashe said through a lying grin.

The smallest of the greater orders of draconem dived, shrieking like a gale, lightning striking from its open mouth. The wheatfield lit up by the blasts all around them in a frightening show of nature.

Ashe set her feet and waited. Her body thrummed with anticipation, seeking release.

"I'm not joking, Lilia. Hold the formation." And then came the prayer of the vicar sect, "Take thy blood, the blood of man. Take thy heart, the heart of man. The fire in the soul, the forge it bequeaths. Show thy soul, let it burn in the pyre. Molded when white hot. In thy name, the vicars are yours. My soul is yours."

She hated that prayer.

"O, HERE WE GO AGAIN..."

The drake was nearly upon them when she uncoiled the tense muscles in her legs and shot up into the air using a spell of *Aere* mixed with a reverse spell of *Terris* to spear herself upward. *Aere* to make her light as a feather, *Terris* to give her purchase of an anchor. The surrounding wheats stalks flattened and the ground cratered, sending Cyan the Defiant, Phlox the Faithful, and Harlequin the Resolute to their knees from the force.

Under the aetheric sway of Soul Form, Ashe unhooked the three-foot Hammer of Mother Marrow from the loop on her belt. Green iron flashed with aetheric runes along the haft as she gripped a weapon equal to that of the diving drake. A holy weapon of the Pentax goddess she had slayed. The Hammer's head burned bright with white-hot flames licking emerald.

Down came the drake, its natural lightning sparking all around her as she cut through the air, meeting the beast mid-dive. The veins in the gossamer wings rushed with draconem blood in slowed beats. Its breath smelled of offal and flesh, no doubt the poor souls from the farmstead.

The aerovern's mouth opened wider, its yellowed eyes narrowing. Almost as if smiling. Draconem were the smartest creatures alive. Crafty, even. And were egotistical assholes because they knew it. No man was stupid enough to leap into their path. It was suicide.

But she was no simple soon-to-be vicar, no mere mortal. She was Lady Drakeslayer. She had killed Mother Marrow Herself.

She screamed, aether ripping through her throat, her voice carrying her aetheurgy alongside the fever pitch of wails. Ever since Gargantua, the scream and the wails sung with her aether in a never-ending hymn of Death. She knew naught what it meant, only that this coda was not normal. Something inhumir.

The lightningsac pulsated inside the beast's maw, ready to release electric death. She had only a few heartbeats before the creature's element would be released upon her in a maelstrom of energy. Reaching the apex of her jump, Ashe pulled upon the currents created by the diving drake's mass to cast a spell of *Aere* that swerved her out of the draconem's path. She then swung the fiery Hammer of the Forgemistress as the aerovern's teeth dripped with frosty saliva, pummeling through the polished gold scales, rending the magnificence with a sizzle as *Terris* from the Hammer quaked through the *Aere* of the drake. Frosty blood blasted across the front of Ashe's cassock as she completed her swing, screaming at the top of her lungs, the wails of the Meadows a full chorus. The draconem's head whipped sideways as pent-up electricity fizzled. The great body shuddering as the lightningsac exploded, sending sparkwaves across the sky.

Time slowed as she drifted back down on a cloud of *Aere*, the drake crashing into the wheatfield, half of its snout falling twenty feet away. Wings folded in on themselves, bone and sinew snapped, the earth of the field trembling. Her feet settled into the destroyed field; midnight blue cassock covered in drake blood. Her aetheurgy quelled; the onslaught brought on by the pulmo overtook her. She hacked and heaved.

In the void, she thought she heard the Strix cry in mourning. Odd, that.

"Lilia, that was far too brash for a vicar," Cyan said as he moved toward her, ever teaching, ever preaching. "You could've killed yourself, and worse, killed me, Harlequin, and Phlox by such use of aetheurgy. You may've spent an entire year in Drenth on your own, but I did not take you back under my tutelage only to be killed by your stupidity."

Ashe put up a hand as blood dribbled down her lips. There was no point in arguing, her body hurt too much. "Finish… the case."

"I will handle the remainder of this codex, acolyte."

Ashe turned at the sound of the newcomer's voice, but then stood rigid, wiping the blood from her mouth, shoving the pain as far down as she could.

Cyan tapped a hand to the Shards insignia upon his breast, bowing the bristle-topped helm in a sign of respect. "Grand Quaestor Tallow."

Harlequin edged behind their taskmaster like the cute, nervy bitty she was. Phlox stood plank-straight, his long arms folded behind his back, head bowed.

Ashe inwardly groaned as the pulmo pain fighting her aetheurgy finally took the hint and backed off. For now. *Bloody Nocturne, what is she doing here?*

"THERE IS SOMETHING I CANNOT PLACE ABOUT HER. SHE… SMELLS WRONG."

You're a daemon, Strix, all you smell is the blood of the dead. I've been in the Meadows, there isn't anything there besides the dead. And Tallow is like a hundred years old, pretty much dead on her feet.

"I SUPPOSE THIS IS TRUE. ANOTHER POINT. I NEED TO UP MY GAME. CAN'T LET YOU WIN THIS DAY."

Grand Quaestor Tallow took in the dead drake with a rheumy gaze. "An aerovern? Down here, this close to Alizarin? Hmm. Not the greatest of news, yes?"

The farmstead wasn't but an hour east from the mega-city of Alizarin. The capital of Altreyia was northwest of the ruins of Eminence and south of the Forgemistress' Blades. Once fiercely opposing the Imperium of the Fallen as its border-sharing neighbor, Altreyia was now the bustling hub of the nascent Guild, none so more than the city of Alizarin.

A month prior, Cyan was assigned to Alizarin's Shards stronghold due to the influx of daemon sightings within the surrounding Sea. Daemon hunting wasn't a normal endeavor of the vicars, but increased daemon attacks meant frightened lowborn, and frightened lowborn tended to bring panic.

So, Ashe and the others came south. Little did she know, increased daemon sightings also went hand in hand with increased drake sightings. This farmstead was merely the first violent attack by the draconem in the area.

But for the ancient grand quaestor to travel this far from the Scattered Shards stronghold, Ashe knew this was no simple joyride in lush farmlands surrounded by the dank, poisonous mist of the Sea. No, this told Ashe she wasn't going to like the tidings Tallow brought in her gnarled hands and easygoing smile.

The grand quaestor raised a skeletal finger toward Cyan. "I'll send word to the harvesters to clear this place. Waste not, they say. A 'vern carcass will ease the minds of the Guild, if only until the next tax is collected. Walk with me, Cyan the Defiant." To Ashe, "If you can manage, child of Drenth, follow and listen. I can see you've spent too much of yourself presently."

She wanted to hurl as the pulmo fought to come up. Yet, she would stand strong. That's what her father and mother would have demanded of her. Probably. What her taskmaster expected, her father in all but name. Definitely.

Cyan stared at her, and in her estimation, was deciding between reprimanding her further in front of Tallow, or worried about her deadly illness. Ashe nodded to her taskmaster as she dropped the Hammer into the loop on her belt, her fingers brushing upon the wheellock pistol she kept tucked opposite the holy artifact. Her father's wheellock.

"I'm at your service, grand quaestor," Cyan finally said. "Harlequin, Phlox, remain with the beast."

The red-haired woman nodded solemnly. "As you command, Vicar Cyan."

While the ugly Phlox merely grunted something not worth hearing.

Grand Quaestor Tallow rested her knurled hand upon Cyan's forearm as the three members of the Scattered Shards moved away from the scene, Ashe a few steps behind as required of her rank as acolyte.

Silence hung heavy before Ashe unthinkingly cleared her throat.

"You were always the impatient one, young acolyte," Tallow said over her shoulder while patting Cyan's arm. "Ever since the day we took you into our arms. Poor dear Cyan the Defiant. He had his hands full with you. Still do by the looks of it."

"You don't know the half of it, grand quaestor," Cyan said with a lilt chuckle.

"Patience was never a virtue of the Benlds, I hear told."

"Truer words, truer words."

Try as she might, Ashe was never one to mince words, even after what happened in Drenth. Maturity had yet to claim her. She stopped, the mist circling her waist clawed up her torso in love, in hate, in need. "What do you need of me, grand quaestor? You wouldn't come for me without dire need. Especially out here. Guild High Seat business?"

"Ashe, respect," Cyan hissed, that stupid horsehair bristle bristling same as he.

Tallow stopped, the garnet cassock of her sect swished slightly in the evenfall breeze, the bronze studs along her side glinted in the fading sunlight of pink-emerald. She cracked a maternal smile, one in contrast to the seriousness plastered over Cyan's ebony-skinned face. "I'm old, my dear, but not that old I can't leave the warmth of Alizarin to rough it in daemon-infested lands. Imagine the chronicles written should I take up the hunt again."

The grand quaestor was a wizened old hag. In terms of age, she was grandmotherly, but because of her prolonged use of the aether in the mist, she looked like a goblin's skull covered in grey, desiccated flesh pulled taut. All misshapen and ugly. Her tundra-white hair was sparse, and her lips were constantly chapped like the sand dunes surrounding Drenth.

Tallow had been an acolyte augur in her younger years, but one lecherous elder augur had devious intentions for the unassuming girl. After cornering her in a temple, his intentions had led to his demise when the not-so-unassuming girl deftly defended herself by a double knee to the groin, one to his nose, and an upward kick into a wall of burning candles. That lecherous augur had died horribly by burning to a crisp. Because of this murder, she was conscripted into the quaestors the next day, where she requested the name Tallow for her penance to Zenith and Mother Marrow for taking a life so heinously.

Ashe held high admiration for the tainted warrior and mirrored the old woman's grin. "Never said the like."

"Remember that, child." The grand quaestor's face turned sour. "A case has arisen, one that is near and dear to the High Seat. You've guessed that correctly, acolyte. Astute, you most are."

Sighing, Ashe grimaced. "The last firedrake, finally?" Cyan made a show of throwing his hands up in the air. She heard him murmur *'when will she learn, Justice?'* under his breath.

"You've heard, child?"

"O, yes. Would have to be deaf to not, grand quaestor. Despite what Cyan would have you believe, I'm most definitely not deaf." Her grin died as she saw Cyan's aura turn fiery crimson.

"YOU GOAD HIM, DEAR BRYNN. WATCH YOUR NEXT STEP CAREFULLY, LEST HE PUT YOU ON PRIVY DUTY AGAIN."

He doesn't scare me, Strix.

"THAT'S WHAT WORRIES ME. WHAT DOES SCARE YOU?"

Spiders. Moldy cheese. Pretty women in baths.

"I should have guessed," Tallow said. "A secret such as this would not remain secret for very long."

Rumor ran rampant throughout the Mistlands that the firedrakes were on the brink of extinction for years now, but most paid it no mind. It didn't seem plausible that such a creature could die out. But then again, unless one was at Drenth and saw all the terrisvvyrms willingly destroy themselves in protection of the Temple of Mother Marrow, it stood to reason the draconem were unending.

A shrug. "Like I said, you wouldn't come for a nothing-to-do codex. I just figured…"

"She'd make a sterling member of the Conclave someday, wouldn't she, Cyan the Defiant." The older quaestor coughed a laugh, but Cyan frowned. To that, Tallow patted the vicar's arm again as if to say *'she'll learn one day.'*

"Not interested, grand quaestor."

"Indeed, other tasks await you." Tallow urged Cyan to walk anew, this time the venerable grand quaestor strode on her own, without the help of the vicar. Ashe followed dutifully. "The High Seat has received word from Grand Quaestor Owl in Oldport that a firedrake has been spotted upon Mount Bastard. I want your team to go investigate."

Ashe was about to speak, but Cyan cut her off with a glare. "As you wish, grand quaestor."

The Strix made its feelings known. *"THERE IS MORE TO THIS, DEAR BRYNN. YOU CAN FEEL THE PULL, CAN'T YOU? THIS IS NOT ABOUT THE FIREDRAKES. THIS IS ABOUT THE SEAL OF* IGNIS*."*

She did feel that pull south. It was as if her entire soul was being directed that way, soul and all. *Zenith's cock, of course. The Seal of* Ignis. *Can't get away from this, can I?*

If ever there was a moment to groan, grimace, or throw a childish tantrum, now would be the time. But Ashe stored that emotion deep inside the vault where she hid the emotions from her past. From the day her father was murdered before her eyes. From when her mother died trying to stop the Fallen. None could see her break, none ever would. Until she met her father and mother again in death, only then would she be free. Free from the guilt. From the hate. From the desire to join them.

All because of the Seals to Eminence.

"Vicar Cyan, a moment alone with your acolyte, if you will?" Ashe's taskmaster reluctantly nodded and moved aside, facing north toward Kalderim. Tallow regarded her curiously with those rheumy eyes of hers. "Never the slightest hint of what brews inside you. But I understand you better than you know, child." The grand quaestor gave a heady scratch to the grey-skinned chin with a shriveled finger that reminded of a sharpened talon. "You ache for closure. This case may give you that."

"O?"

Tallow pushed through the throng of destroyed wheat, stopping at a carriage. It was a finely crafted thing, the carriage, like a traditional horse-drawn wagon, but it had an aethecite engine at the rear. Even though aethecite was becoming rationed due to Ashe's father's exploits in Drenth, it was an amalgamation of metal and coils, a pipe to release the grey haze that powered the transport.

Quaestors stood nearby, eyes scanning the Sea for danger, maces and wheellocks a breath away. The idiots thought another drake about or even a daemon, but Ashe knew better. Aeroverns may sometimes hunt in packs, but once one was killed, they scattered like craven pricks in a battle's massacre.

Before reaching the carriage, Tallow placed a desiccated hand to Ashe's cheek. It was cold as the void. She fought the shiver at the base of her spine. "You hide behind what happened in Drenth. Don't. Remember and use that knowledge. Dredge it up from the depths in which you have buried that day. You are all that is left of the Benld and Nightingale lines. Closure may yet be within your reach. Learn the truth about your father and mother in ways you never would've fathomed."

Closure to that day?

"YOU DO HIDE THAT PAIN, DEAR BRYNN. RELEASE IT."

Tallow's knees popped as she dragged her aether-riddled bones into the carriage. She peered out the carriage's window. "Use the memories, child. Don't hide them anymore. Release them and become who you were meant to be. The Pentax has holy ambition for you. As do I." The grand quaestor slapped the side of the carriage. "Until we meet again, Lady Drakeslayer. Be who you were born to be. And don't trust anyone in Oldport. Even those whom you think you might. Betrayal is a common currency there. O, before I forget. There are other rumors. Rumors that your parents are still alive. Stay your heart and seek the truth."

Ashe couldn't stop the gasp as the aethecite-powered carriage rumbled down the uneven dirt road away from the wheatfield crime scene, black smoke mingling with the stench of the Sea. The red-cassocked quaestors trotted alongside to keep pace. Ashe stood motionless in the growing darkness, her hands at her sides. Aghast.

Father? Mother? Alive? How?

II

ASHE

OLDPORT BASIN IS the sort of place only two true outcomes exist:

Either you are fresh to the City of Sin, pockets full of quadrans ready to be spent at the nearest gaming hall or brothel, only to end up lying bloodied in a ditch, pockets empty, ruin to your name. More often than not, death is also likely in your future.

Or, you are the rapacious scoundrel relieving said fresh meat of their bounty.

Which is why it was somewhat surprising when they found themselves held at wheellockpoint a few leagues out from Port Sin.

"HALT, DEAR BRYNN."

Ashe killed the spell of her gyroscope at the Strix's unexpected warning, her single-wheeled vehicle screeching to a stop, sliding in the mud. The forest trail around them was eerily silent except for the pitter-patter of rain through the trees and the slowing of the others' gyroscopes. The mist was only up to their ankles and was a transparent grey.

What is it, Strix?

"DANGER."

Helpful, very helpful.

"What is it, Lilia?" Cyan asked as he drew his gyroscope beside her, the outer rubberized wheel kicking up mud. He turned toward her, rain rivering down his hood. "See anything out there?"

"I don't know, Cyan. A feeling?" Cyan knew about the Strix, but it made her uncomfortable to openly speak of it to him, with his beliefs toward the Pentax and all. "And stop calling me Lilia, for the love of Zenith's cock."

Cyan kicked the stand out of his gyroscope and dismounted the vehicle, a geysering of mist from one of his canisters as he burned his Shard Form. The cloud-hidden sun was descending in the gaps of the trees above, as they were pelted with rain. "I see nothing."

"How far until Oldport?" said Harlequin as she came close. The red-haired vicar was shivering within her cloak, and impulsively Ashe felt her heart quicken as she could think of a way or two to warm Harlequin up. The mist below her feet churned with desire.

"I think this sucks," said Phlox. The man fingered the steering wheel of his gyroscope, leaning out of the inner ring and yet not falling over, although he made every attempt to.

It was a feat, the gyroscope, of intelligent craftsmanship not seen since the Fall of Eminence. They were faster than horses but not as fast as aethecite burning machines. Two rings were along a set axis; the outer ring was coated in thick rubber, capable of traversing all types of landscapes without fear of cracking or bursting, while the inner ring stayed stationary as the outer rotated, driving forward. A curved seat was placed upon the axis toward the back of the wheel, allowing the driver to sit upright within the inner ring. A simple steering mechanism was covered in runes of the Four Tenets, thus only one capable of burning aetheurgy could drive a gyroscope.

Ashe was about to reply with a zinger when a man stepped into the trail a few horse-lengths ahead of them, slicing through the falling drizzle.

"Hail, lords and lasses," the new addition called, one hand on the pommel of his sword, the other on a wheellock pistol shoved into the front of his belt. Barely visible was his face, but he had a nose pronounced like a pig and did not have a breather on.

"HOW MANY TIMES DO I HAVE TO TELL YOU TO BURN YOUR AETHEURGY AT THE SLIGHTEST HINT OF WARNING, DEAR BRYNN?" the Strix asked in the back of her mind as the overwhelming fire of red warning pulsed from the daemon blade.

Shut up, Strix. To Cyan, "You've got to be shitting me." Ashe pinched the bridge of her nose. "You said nothing. Eyesight going, old man?"

Cyan shrugged; precipitation drops bouncing off his stupid horsehair bristle. "Sorry?"

Is this my penance for being a little shit of a teenager? "We are going to have to work on our communication."

Her taskmaster tsked. "You're the one who stopped, Lilia. Haven't I taught you to mind your aether when it warns you?"

"SEE? SLAYING GODDESSES BUT STILL LACKING THE BASICS."

Ashe grumbled a curse while pulling back the hood of her cloak, the rain immediately soaking her hair. She squinted, lifted her left hand, and forced her aetheurgy to come alive through her tattooed runes and the golden Eye affixed to her wrist.

The forest trail erupted in a colorful dash of aether.

A greenish haze of *Terris* arose in her vision, covering the entirety of the forest with emerald tints of life as the poisonous mist circled like vultures. Of nature and healing, of growth and perpetuity. A billow of blue *Aquis* as each raindrop tinted serenity. A few throbs of yellow *Aere* shades, most likely animals alerted to their presence. A faint red stain of *Ignis* warning, she could imagine pointed little teeth bared.

But with her aether in full burn, she saw the others waiting in the drizzle. A cadre of men with dark crimson auras, some swirling with yellows and greens. Crouched and standing by, nervous, eager, guilty, ready to wreak violence.

"BE WARY," the Strix said, that ethereal vocalization that was distant sounding, like someone speaking from the bottom of a well. *"DO NOT HESITATE. THEY WON'T."*

O, thanks for the heads up.

"I ONLY AIM TO PLEASE."

"Ease, friend," Cyan said to the pig-nosed man down the trail. A standoff would mean blood, and her taskmaster apparently wanted none of it. "A bit wet out here and we have someplace to be. We intend no quarrel."

"I don't think so, *friend*." Pig Nose's aura raged bloodred. He whistled and three shoddily armored men jumped from tree branches, six or seven others popped up from the brush along the trail. All armed with steel and bows, a few crossbows, and one had an old wheellock rifle. Aetheric hues shading green with greed. "Gird your loins, boys, we're gon' et like rēxes tonight."

"You don't want to do this," Cyan said calmly.

Inside, Ashe felt a surge of desire to do violence. She hadn't felt such a desire since she had killed that servant in the Guilder's villa in Silk Circle. Everything had changed that day for her. Had set her on a path she dared not traverse.

She tried to tamp down the feeling, but the mist clawed angrily at her boots, churning black.

"THE CALL OF NOCTIS GROWS, DEAR BRYNN."

No shit, Strix, how do I turn it off?

"YOU CANNOT QUELL DEATH ANYMORE THAN YOU COULD STOP THE SUN FROM RISING."

Great, violence it is, then.

"QUELL IT YOU CANNOT, BUT HARNESS IT AND MASTER IT, YOU CAN."

"You've the wrong of it there," Pig Nose continued, drawing his weapons. The sword was a notched thing and was rusty. But the wheellock appeared well-kept. "It won't end well for you."

Appears we don't have time for lessons, Strix. To her taskmaster, "What a comeback, eh?"

"I'D WAGER THEY WERE PAID. NOT THIEVES. THEY AREN'T PACKING ENOUGH HEAT FOR A TRUE THREAT."

"Thieves." Harlequin said. "Of course there are thieves waiting in the rain for those coming to Oldport. Opportunists who don't want to pay the Guild's tax, I say."

"AS EVER, SOMEONE TAKING ACCOLADES FOR MY DISCOVERIES. CURSE THIS LIFE OF BEING BONDED TO ONLY ONE PERSON."

"Thieves would be too simple, Vicar Cyan," Phlox the Faithful said. The gaunt vicar glanced up to the treetops, beads of water streaming down his breather. "Is it too much to ask for a clear day? Zenith must be upset with me for some reason."

"Probably because you touch yourself at nightturn," Ashe sniggered as she took out her flask and took a sip.

"HE DOES THAT... ALL... THE... TIME."

Phlox was incredulous. "No more than you do yourself. At least I'm quiet about it."

"You are quite loud, Lilia," Cyan added as he plucked the flask out of Ashe's hand, "hard to sleep sometimes with all that moaning." He raised his breather and took a long gulp.

Ashe smiled, ever since Drenth, Cyan was more playful and allowed indulgences that were heavily frowned upon, even outlawed by the Scattered Shards. Such as liquor. He was still the harsh taskmaster when it came to her training, but he was far more enjoyable to be around when he gave the ribbing right back. Ashe preferred this Cyan to the one she'd left two summers ago. If only he'd stop calling her Lilia, she had always hated that name, never thought it fit. Guess she was right about that.

"Don't lie, Ashe," Harlequin winked at her, which set Ashe's heart fluttering again, "you enjoy it."

"THAT IS ALSO TRUE. AND I KNOW WHO YOU THINK OF."

Shut it, Strix.

Harlequin had also changed after Drenth. Ashe had always thought of the girl called Tista as a stuck-up, hem-kisser while growing up under Cyan's tutelage. After Drenth, the young woman, now named Harlequin after attaining the cassock, not only seemed far more likable, but became someone Ashe might even consider a friend, if only because she also enjoyed targeting Cyan as the butt of jokes. But aside from the bickering, Ashe, well, did have a few lewd thoughts about her now and then.

"FROM THE DEPTHS OF YOUR MEMORIES, YOU'VE ALWAYS HAD A THING FOR HER, DEAR BRYNN."

I said shut it, Strix.

"They would dare harm one of Zenith's creations?" Phlox, though, was still as dull as she remembered him from their training before Drenth. She hadn't cared for the older man then and still didn't now. Phlox the Faithful was like a lecherous uncle, the one everyone put up with at holiday time but felt the need to bathe immediately afterwards.

"Why don't you lads join us?" Cyan offered to the thieves, trying to keep the topic at hand, on hand and becoming serious. "Perhaps we could buy you a bottle instead of you leaving us without our rides in this lovely rain."

Pig Nose smiled yellowed snaggled things he called teeth. "Tempting proposition, that. But a job's a job. The Kraken's Cabal never fails. Even if ya are of the Shards." He pointed his pistol toward her, "And that there lassie be Lady Drakeslayer. 'Sides, I thought ya got et by that seagandr over off Merj winter last. Fancy you survived that, ya?"

"AH, SO THE MAN ISN'T STUPID, DEAR BRYNN."

Ashe realized this would-be-thief wasn't just serving a plate of ignorance but had ordered a side of stupid to complete the meal. "Kraken's Cabal? What kind of preposterous name is that? I've heard better names for children's toys."

"A sellsword group on the rise," one crossbowmen chirped.

While another holding the wheellock rifle echoed, "One of the best in the Mistlands!"

"Sellswords?" A fiery edge saturated her voice. Ever since one ill-timed training mission that nearly got her drowned in a spriggan's boggy cairn when she was twelve, Ashe had harbored a healthy distaste for sellswords. "I. Fucking. Hate. Sellswords."

"O, THAT MIGHT HAVE DONE IT."

"Lilia…"

But she was already vaulting off her gyroscope, unlodging the Hammer of Mother Marrow. She barreled into one of the crossbowmen, the bolt flying off into the forest. She was up in an instant and swung the Hammer at another, hewing the man across the chest. The man's aetheric aura went from shaded-red to shaded-yellow in a matter of heartbeats as his heart was obliterated. Then he died.

Arrows, bolts, and bullets whizzed through the mist. A bolt ripped through her cloak and the sleeve of her cassock, a tingle of pain jigging down her arm as the bolt embedded into the flesh of her shoulder. All warriors of the Scattered Shards wore firedrake scale vests under their cassocks, but they were sleeveless. A stupid design and now she was paying the price for it.

The mercenaries of the Kraken's Cabal began to reload their crossbows, drew steel-tipped arrows, readying to nock. The one with the wheellock rifle was nervously pointing it everywhere and nowhere at once.

Ashe cursed and lifted her palm, the bangle on her wrist glowed like Zenith's sun. Calling upon *Aquis*, the tattoo of three blue wavy lines that resembled crashing waves on her inner forearm blazed. The raindrops became her magic. Drawing the rain toward her like a river being diverted by a dam, each droplet froze in the air between her team and the mercenaries. The rune of *Aquis* on the ring of her middle finger was bright blue as royal sapphire burned in her palm, above the diamond eye.

Arrows loosed; bolts fired.

The impending death was stopped by the magical wall of raindrops, concaving inward. Then the spell broke, the arrows and bolts dropping to the muddy ground, followed by a clacking boom like thunder.

But the mercenaries of Kraken's Cabal were undeterred by her magic. They raised their weapons and charged. Idiots.

There was a cry of agony, and dismembered hand landed in the mud beside her, shorn in a jagged tearing of flesh, the wheellock rifle fell from its deadened grip. The sellsword howled and fled into the forest, cradling his bloodied stump. Ashe turned and saw Harlequin holding one of her blue-iron axes.

"You owe me one," the pretty, fire-haired vicar said with a devious grin. Then she charged into the nearest sellsword.

"BRYNN!" It was the Strix sending warning.

Ashe backpedaled as Cyan leapt by, his aetheric axe cleaving into the neck of a brute of a man. The dying man's mouth burbled as blood rushed out, and Ashe was hit in the face with it. Gross. There was no time to wipe the blood-spittle away as another of the bastards came at her with sword aimed for a kill. Ashe flung her cloak aside but winced as the bolt in her shoulder flared with hurt. With her left hand, she lifted the Hammer of the Forgemistress.

The sellsword lurched with his sword, the rusty blade coming down. Ashe ducked the haphazard swing by burning aetheurgy, bringing the green-iron hammer into the man's unprotected gut. Ashe was a head shorter than the man, but she was burning the Four Enhancements plus wielding a holy artifact, and as such, her blow lifted the rogue clear off his feet. The battered man flew backward with a gasp and clattered into the hireling crossing weapons with Cyan, who had summoned a warhammer with his Gauntlet instead of an axe. Both would-be-thieves went down, and the vicar clobbered once, twice, and thrice with his hammer of pure aether, killing both.

"Hey, that one counts as mine!" she yelled to Cyan.

Before Cyan could retort, more sellswords appeared. Ashe drew the mist upon her in a wave of black and sent it toward the oncoming enemy with a beard like a giant's. Like a wave, it crested over the hairy man, dragging him under angry black fog as the wails of the Meadows sung. Of Cyan and his opponent, all she heard was the devastating curse of a vicar still learning how to blaspheme—meaning it was swears followed by taunts followed by more swears, ending with a barb about a small manhood for good measure.

Her Hammer shattered a man's dented sword like the snapping of a twig. He threw his broken hilt to the ground and proceeded backward twenty paces to fumble with the crossbow strapped around his torso. It gave Ashe a much-needed moment to yank out the crossbow bolt.

"Bloody Nocturne!" The head tore apart the flesh of her shoulder, blood gushing after it. Her Enhancements were already at work sewing up her wound, albeit slowly. Blood dribbled down her arm and cassock.

"HOW MANY TIMES DO I HAVE TO TELL YOU NOT TO CALL UPON THE NAME OF NOCTURNE LIKE THAT? YOU DON'T UNDERSTAND ITS TRUE MEANING."

"Shut it, daemon!"

"WHAT IF I SAID 'ASHE, THAT MAN IS SETTING ANOTHER BOLT.' WOULD YOU STILL WANT ME TO SHUT IT? WHEN WILL YOU RELEASE ME TO DEVOUR THEIR SOULS?"

The man opposite had the crank turned on the crossbow, a bolt settled in the groove of the wooden-and-metal weapon of death. Then it was loose.

Reacting on instinct, Ashe called to the aether within the mist. A thin, elegant line sliced through the mist and the veil between the realms of Life and Death. Wails of ungodsly tenor rose with it. It was a gateway to the Meadows. The bolt entered the gash in the veil, and Ashe called forth her aetheurgy once more, creating another slice right behind the sellsword. Out came the bolt and it slammed into the mercenary's back. He lurched forward as he died, the wails of the dead crowing.

"GOOD TRICK, DEAR BRYNN. BUT CAN YOU DO IT ANOTHER TIME SO QUICKLY?"

The Strix was speaking about another hoodlum who had stepped into view, a crossbow aimed at her. Ashe charged, lifting the Hammer as her aetheurgy began to wane. The other's aura was yellow in dread. The crossbow raised slowly, Ashe's Hammer ready to bludgeon the ever-loving piss out of him. But she was still too far away, even while sprinting faster than a normal man, and the other was now ready to fire.

But the grace of the Pentax—the deceased Mother Marrow to be exact—shone down on her for the briefest of moments because a tremendous tremor rattled the forest with unyielding fervor. Ashe found herself pitching forward, face planting into the muddied trail, the bolt fizzing overhead as the ground quaked. Ashe pawed the mud from her eyes.

"NOW?"

She scrabbled to her feet after the tremor subsided and resumed her charge, crushing the sellsword's ribcage with a monstrous blow to the side, mangling his innards, and the man's mouth turned to a silent 'O' as revolting breath was expelled, followed by bloodied spittle, which so happened to blast all over Ashe. Again.

"IF YOU HAD JUST USED ME INSTEAD, YOU WOULDN'T BE BATHED IN BLOOD AND SPIT, DEAR BRYNN."

She stood over the dead sellsword heaving in anger, blood staining her cassock, mud-caked and spittle-covered face glowering. All the colorful hues in her aetheric vision began to fade back to normal as the high of aetheurgy died.

"FINE, WE CAN TALK ABOUT THIS LATER WHEN YOU AREN'T MAD. JUST LIKE YOUR MOTHER..."

The nigrum pulmonem doubled her over as she hacked her lungs up. Her body was drained, hunger gnawed at her gut, legs weak, head full of drowsiness.

Soon, she thought as she fought back the coughing.

Harlequin was wiping blood from the crescent of her axe with a cloak that suspiciously seemed like the one Pig Nose had been wearing.

Ashe saw the corpse a few feet behind. "He was mine, Harlequin."

The woman smiled. "That's two you owe me, now. We'll figure out later how you'll pay me back." And she winked again, her aura a fiery crimson.

Ashe returned the knowing smile, continuing their forever dance around the subject of their relationship. Or lack thereof.

"There's something wrong with you two." Cyan poked through the bodies, a sad expression upon his face, as he always had when he took the life of others. Somber the vicar was around death, even when one like Cyan was constantly courted by it. There was a slice in his cloak, but otherwise he didn't appear wounded.

All told, there were eight dead sellswords from the group called Kraken's Cabal, and the hand of the one who had fled. Muddy tracks in two other directions meant another pair of survivors.

"If this is the type of welcome we can expect this far from the city," Ashe said, "then who's to say what happens when we meet with Owl." She found her flask in the mud and slapped away some of the grime. She took a long pull. "Not likin' our odds on this case, Cyan. Something ain't right here."

"We proceed as planned," Cyan said as he hopped upon his gyroscope.

Ashe went to retrieve her aether-powered gyroscope, ready to be out of the rain. Hopping into the seat, she grunted from the pain in her shoulder that was still far from being knit by the faithful mist.

"I don't understand who'd send sellswords to meet us here." Harlequin combed her unruly, fiery locks. "Something's not adding up. They weren't just a bunch of hacks trying to pick off travelers. They called you by name, Ashe. Nickname, that is."

"Icterine has probably grown tired of your ass, Harle-bub."

"You try too hard to be funny sometimes. Besides, you know you like my ass."

"So?"

Cyan shook his head as his gyroscope kicked into gear, the outer wheel rotating as he took off down the trail toward Oldport Basin, Ashe muttered under her breath about how nobody can take a joke these days. They left the bodies of the Kraken's Cabal for the crows.

"BY THE WAY, WHAT'S A KRAKEN?"

III

ASHE

AN HOUR AFTER the scrap with the Kraken's Cabal, they emerged from the forest and before them sprawled the fabled port mega-city of Oldport Basin. However, that fable was now more like a daemon story told to children on the yearly holiday, the Eve of Nocturne. A scary and blood-filled story at that.

On the furthest peninsula of southern Thullyr, Oldport Basin was a latticework of land and tributaries that flowed from the high peak of Mount Bastard down into the bowl-shaped bay. Once an active volcano, the mountain bordered the coast of the VVyrm Ocean all along its western shelf and the mega-city grew from the fertile lands below where the last explosion of the volcano had created the Bay of Fire.

"THE SEAL OF IGNIS *IS HERE, DEAR BRYNN,"* the Strix said in the vast emptiness between Ashe's mind and that of Nocturne's Pit. *"TRY NOT TO LET IT GET TO YOU. THIS TIME MIGHT TURN OUT DIFFERENTLY. I HAVE A FEELING IN MY BONES."*

A cruel shudder washed through her thinking of the Seals to Eminence, that phantom destiny she constantly ran from. And yet, she could feel the pull of the Seal of *Ignis*. It was leading her directly south into the mega-city.

Mother, Father, why now, why here? You cannot be alive, can you? "You're a daemon locked in the Pit, Strix. You have no bones."

"O YEAH, GOOD POINT. WELL, I DID ONCE, SO THAT STILL COUNTS IN MY BOOK."

"You don't have books in the Pit either."

"HOW WOULD YOU KNOW? I MIGHT BE READING A GRAND TOME RIGHT NOW."

"Thank the Pentax, the rain finally stopped," Phlox said, scratching his leathery neck roughly like he was trying to rip his flesh off as they slowed their gyroscopes. "I'm tired of being wet."

"I'm tired of you complaining all the time." Ashe gave the lank vicar a glare.

"The same could be said for you, Ashe," Harlequin said as the outer wheel of her gyroscope stopped spinning.

"You'd be lost without me, Harle-bub. You're full of shit and you know it."

"My mother used to say I never walked through shit but rolled in it." Cyan chuckled to himself as his gyroscope rolled ahead. "You fit her words just as well, Lilia."

Ashe gave her taskmaster's back a rude finger gesture. "Your mother was a wise woman."

"I should have left you in Drenth." Cyan's stupid horsehair bristle dripped with water. "You know, as a babe."

"O, now that's low."

The gate loomed ahead. Oldport Basin had been a beautiful place once, all of Thullyr had been according to the elfir in Kalderim. Now, it was a place of sin and death, and not necessarily in that order. A radiant locale in generations long past where the Sea of Mist barely flowed but knee high all around after the Fall.

But those days were long gone.

Unlike the sky rising complexes of Drenth, Port Sin was a hodgepodge of buildings no more than ten stories smashed together. But what made Port Sin stand out from other mega-cities was the fact that city permeated everything and everyone. Once gripped by the vices aplenty, one never left alive. Those who did, were never the same.

It was a wonder Cadrianna Nightingale had ever escaped to marry her father.

Starting from the northern wall down to about a third of the way into the City of Sin was the market called the Barter Yard. All sorts of dilapidated shops stacked upon each other, hawking their specific wares by way of aethecite-lit signs proclaiming *'Come one, Come all'*. Stalls from the many mega-cities around the Mistlands, fishermen with iced tubs of scaly food from the ocean hauled up from the Harbor of Thieves—an apt name for the current iteration of Guild owners. Random farmers not of the Guild Houses with bushels of grain and barley, or cereals and oats. Greedy and ambitious, these Houses. Each mega-city had their own Guild buildings, their own leaders, but all Houses sold their loyalty to a loose-fitting body called the Guild High Seat out of Alizarin.

The people of the southern Mistlands had exchanged one ruler for a handful, and to be fair, Ashe wasn't sure which was worse.

A rotten apple came flying out of the crowd as the multitudes moved out of their way, hitting Ashe in the chest. There was a callous curse also flung her way. It wasn't the first time, nor would it be the last, she'd been pelted with something or other. The Scattered Shards were not welcomed fondly in Port Sin. Or in many cities or nations outside of Kanja, and those were still tenuous at best.

Her eyes wandered toward a small stall that sold hay-stuffed dolls surrounded by a low brume of black mist. Aether surged within. She blinked and envisioned a taller man with a child sitting upon his shoulders. A memory. But it wasn't her memory.

Blink.

What?

The man in the memory carried that smiling, little girl toward the dollmaker, the authentic happiness on the girl's face was so pure, so gentle. The man's smile was great, his own joy evident. The girl's fingers pointed toward a singular doll with dark twine for hair, big eyes painted lifelike. She squealed when the dollmaker put the stuffed toy in her hands. The father laughed and laughed, the girl hugged the doll tight.

Blink.

The memory ended with the doll burning as the girl's home burned to ashes.

What the void was that? Strix?

"ONE OF CAD'S MEMORIES. THAT LITTLE GIRL WAS HER. THIS CITY WAS HOME ONCE TO THE NIGHTINGALE LINE."

Why show me this, why now?

"YOUR SOUL FORM IS GROWING. THE EWER OF NOCTIS HAS TIPPED AND YOU HAVE SIPPED AT IT. WHAT IT BLOOMS INTO, IT REMAINS TO BE SEEN. BUT MEMORIES SUCH AS THESE CAN HELP YOU. REMEMBER IT. REMEMBER WHAT YOU SEE. THERE IS NOTHING TO FEAR FROM NOCTIS."

Lingering images of her father and mother flashed in her mind as the black haze purled about the stall. She couldn't shake them since Tallow had told her. It shouldn't be possible.

"THE FIRE BURNS WITHIN YOU. DO NOT QUELL IT. THAT'S WHAT MAKES YOU, YOU. A GODSBLOOD. WHAT BROUGHT ME TO YOU. ALLOW THE FIRE TO BURN. YOUR PARENTS, CAD IN

PARTICULAR, BROUGHT YOU TO THIS MOMENT. DO NOT SHY FROM IT. YOU RUN, BUT YOU CANNOT ESCAPE YOUR FATE. SUCH AS WE CANNOT."

"I'm trying, Strix. But if they are alive…" She couldn't finish the thought.

"I hate this time of evenfall." Phlox was warily watching the many street urchins wandering through the crowds, most of them cutting purses, snatching unsupervised goods, or just downright picking fights with barterers.

"Probably because they got a glance at your ugly mug."

"You know, Ashe, your jibes are not appreciated. Mother Marrow would not approve."

"Mother Marrow's dead, Phloxy."

"Blasphemy! You are offensive…" Phlox's words faded as Ashe stopped listening, preferring to ride through the city without trying to think about that day.

It was easier to forget than to remember.

The Barter Yard's shops began to close as the sun went down, the doors shutting. With aethecite stores dwindling, Port Sin grew shadowy. Without the brilliant aerescreens of Drenth, the darkest of sinners could stalk the City of Sin unseen. The few remaining shoppers left the market and filtered their way toward the many inns, taverns, and casinos to spend the remainder of their quadrans. The rest made their ways to the buildings of the sin of the flesh.

"YOU'RE BROODING AGAIN. WANT ME TO PUT ON A SPOT OF TEA AND WE CAN COMISERATE TOGETHER?"

No.

"I LIKED YOU BETTER AT FIRST. YOU WEREN'T ALL THAT FUNNY, EVEN THOUGH YOU THINK YOU ARE. BUT NOW ALL

YOU DO IS WALLOW WHEN YOU'RE NOT THINKING TANTALIZING THOUGHTS ABOUT THAT REDHEAD."

And you know all there is about wallowing, Strix. And if I wallow, it's because I have to listen to you all godsdamned day. No wonder my mother decided to jump in front of Lu Har at the Temple of Mother Marrow. And leave Harlequin out of this.

The Strix laughed in the void.

Adjacent to the Barter Yard in the northeastern section was the quarter called the Red Moon District—though there had not been a red moon since the Fall of Eminence, so none knew where the originator of the name got the idea. The Red Moon District was the center of sex. Massive wooden boards hung between the uprights of unlit aerescreens, and on these boards were lewd, artistic renderings of men and women in various stages of undress, all provocatively beckoning would-be fornicators to their doors.

The Harbor of Thieves typically held dozens upon dozens of cargo ships. Since the mega-city was on a peninsula, air transport landing was quite difficult, but despite airships grounding in greater frequency in the last few months without aethecite, Port Sin was still as lively as ever. A gate existed between the District and the shipyard anchorage of the Bay of Fire. The buildings in the Harbor were all made of plank and mismatched stone, fishline and netting, pressed smack up next to each other, all dozens of stories with single room apartments.

All along the western cliffs was the Beggars Chain. These slums were essentially shacks or massive apartment complexes, somewhat like Stanktown back in Drenth, only shorter. The poor and destitute hunkered there. The stink alone kept many away from the sector, but there were plenty pulling rank amongst the hovels. The remnants of a tramline similar to Drenth's lay in ruins throughout the Chain, and those who couldn't afford the complexes resorted to the broken-down tram cars for shelter.

The Hangman's Hex occupied the epicenter of the peninsula, as it's where most of the city's hangings took place. The Hex had arched gates to the prime districts, though, like the Bay and the Red Moon, most were poorly guarded. Here, the tramlines worked as designed, another symbol between the haves and have nots.

Between the Hex and the Barter Yard was an acclaimed arena affectionately called *The Arbiter's Axe*. A colosseum of sorts. Three tiered with seats, awnings hung over the open sandy arena in the middle. Gladiator fights and prisoner executions when the Hex wasn't spacious enough, horse and chariot races, and other games of death and death-defying endeavors held.

On the journey south, Cyan had told her that Cadrianna's father used to own *The Axe* before her marriage. Although she knew nothing of her Nightingale line, it was a surprise because she hadn't expected her family to be purveyors of bloodsport. Perhaps that helped explain her mother's turn toward the life of a scourge and her own path of death.

South of the Hex, the Guild Politic was the home of everything pertaining to the Guild. Their council chambers, the treasury, their personal offices, their homes. The northern districts callously called the entire section the Swindler's Den, an indubitably fitting name. A stark contrast to the Beggars Chain where it smelled like mountains of human feces, the Guild Politic was cleaned regularly and guarded by elite soldiers who weren't open to bribery like the numpties of the city watch. The Scattered Shards stronghold in Oldport backed up to the Hex.

And beyond the Guild Politic, further onto the peninsula tip, some many leagues away, circling the bay was Mount Bastard. Its shadow cast a heavy curtain across Port Sin like a debaucher throwing an arm around your shoulder and beckoning you to forfeit your soul.

The place where the last firedrake supposedly laired. Their quarry, their codex, her path to the Seal of *Ignis.*

"Well now, what do we have here," Ashe said as they came upon the Hex, their path forward blocked. "Must be a hanging."

In a densely populated Hangman's Hex, people pushed and shoved to get closer to the raised platform at the east end that stood ten feet above the crowd and had a single rafter above the planks of the belvedere. Five hempen nooses swayed in the slight breeze of evenfall.

The Hex was filled to the brim, bloodlust a strong taste on the tongue, palpable and eager.

The crowd began to murmur in excited whispers. A massive steel gate opened from the building behind, and many stumbled into one another as a bevy of the city watch marched through with wheellock rifles. Each wore helmed breathers, and their drake scale armor was bone white, the blazing symbol of the Guild brandished on their cuirasses.

Amidst the city watch came a man, a woman, and three youths aged between eighteen and twenty-five, all hunched as thick chains weighed them down. The male prisoner was older, and from the look of it, he had been a lord of a Guild House. Each prisoner's aura was blazing cowardice honey, a glaze of jaundice showcasing the fear of what was to come.

As they were dragged toward the nooses hanging from the rafter, behind them, an older figure took the stairs to the stage.

Grand Quaestor Owl.

The grand quaestor was a humir on the short side. Hair kept short, stark white, with skin that sagged like a corpse brought back to life twenty years prior and was somehow still functioning. A beard hung long, was as white as snow and as fine as silk. Dark eyes with red pupils hid behind a pair of spectacles. Dressed in a red cassock that stopped above the ankles, and in hand was a gnarled staff, topped with the symbol of the Scattered Shards. A breather was perched on the canistered belt and surrounding the grand quaestor was an aura of tinted blue posterity.

"OWL! OWL! OWL!"

It wasn't so much the grand quaestor the crowd crowed for, but the huge bird perched upon the tainted warrior's shoulder. Owl's namesake. The strix was a massive thing with a rounded crown and flat disc of a face, of grey feathers, and yellow eyes with dark black circles around them. Its beak pointed downward in a wicked curve. The wings, when extended, exceeded five feet from tip to tip.

"THESE PEOPLE KNOW NOT WHAT A TRUE WINGSPAN CAN INSPIRE. THIS WINGSPAN IS TREASONOUS TO MY SOUL."

"I really dislike the look of that bird," Ashe said.

"You dislike lots of things," Cyan shot back, thinking she was talking to him.

Harlequin sniggered.

"Justice guide them," Phlox said as he ran a cassocked arm across his nose, his breather sitting atop his forehead. He glanced at Cyan. "I can't watch this. I'll meet you at the Shards stronghold, Vicar Cyan." Cyan nodded and the skinny vicar turned his gyroscope and disappeared down the street.

"Sissy."

"Not everyone is as heartless as you, Ashe."

"And not everyone is as boring as you, Harle-bub."

"You say such loving words."

City guards pressed the crowd back. Taunts rose from the assembly as projectiles in the form of throwable vegetables rained down on the prisoners. The strix flapped his mighty wings and a hush fell about the square, one so silent, one could hear a quadran drop—although, that was a weak analogy as no coin has ever been dropped undetected in Port Sin.

"People of Oldport Basin," the grand quaestor started, leaning heavily on the staff of office. "The Scattered Shards presents a man who has tarnished the name of the Guild in this fine city. Florin Tified has been arrested under the suspicion of conspiracy to overthrow the Guild and to sully the Scattered Shards."

The crowd erupted in angry boos and hisses, a berry-colored haze drifting from onlooker to onlooker. Owl slammed the staff, urging quiet, but a rock struck Tified in the face, which sent him tumbling, and that, in turn, dragged Lady Tified and their children down along with him. The audience roared in laughter while the guards pulled them to their feet, Tified's face dripping blood from a rent nose.

The black mist circled the walls of the Hex, only Ashe seemingly noticing. Instantly, another memory flashed before her.

Blink.

A crowd like this, but another House, and one of the women on the platform, noose around her neck was grandmotherly. Her grandmother. Talthanian, that was their name, the House. A whole House wiped clean by decree of the Scattered Shards, by their own blood, Owl. As the people demanded blood, the little girl named Cadrianna watched it all from the window in the Scattered Shards stronghold, her father's hands on her shoulders while her mother wept silently behind, not willing to watch.

Blink.

"Strix?" she whispered.

"REMEMBER IT, DEAR BRYNN. LET THE MEMORIES FREE."

"Quiet!" Owl bellowed, ripping her from the memory. But Owl's demand didn't stop the crowd. One cannot quell the quest for blood when it was demanded. "Good people, bear witness! These people have confessed their crimes against the Guild before the vaunted honesty of the Scattered Shards. Confessed directly to me, your grand quaestor."

"Owl's got some hefty quadrans below the cassock," Ashe said. "How do we even know that this Tified is guilty of anything other than being a poor dresser?"

Cyan smirked. "Guilty of being born, Lilia. Some of us consider that guilt enough."

"But don't take my word for it," the grand quaestor went on, "you deserve the truth. To hear their treason from their own mouths!" The crowd went wild anew as one city watchman pulled the lord forward. "Florin Tified, you have served the Guild, and your family has been loyal to Oldport for nearly a century now. Upon that loyalty, what words do you have?"

Tified, hunched as he was by the chains, drew up as tall as he could and puffed out his chest. His voice was measured. "To the Pit with the Guild. May the Fallen wipe this voidhole clean."

Ashe had to give it to him, not all in the Guild or the Houses were as strong-willed, most would sell their own mothers to curry favor.

"Very well," Owl said. "Such is the nature of traitors. A grave for them all. It's upon my title, as Grand Quaestor to Oldport Basin, I hereby declare Florin Tified, and by association, the entirety of House Tified, guilty of treason. The penalty is death by hanging. May Zenith guide your souls to the Pit to pass into the hands of His reverent Twin, Nocturne."

"DEATH! DEATH! DEATH!" The crowd whooped and hollered as the guards steadied the treasonous Guilder and his family under the hempen nooses, looping the rope over their heads. The red of passion and the green of greed and want weaved a fitting tapestry over the crowd.

A man wearing a black cassock and a hood with only the eyes cut out ascended the stairs, chanting a hangman's prayer. People started singing along with him.

Grand Quaestor Owl tapped the staff, and the crowd went silent. The old quaestor gave a nod, and the hooded man fired the mechanism to the trapdoors built into the platform. Down the House went, rope pulled taut. Lady Tified died instantly; her neck broken in the drop. As did two of the children, the third died moments later. But Tified kicked and spun in tight circles, dying slowly, agonizingly.

It was long minutes after the House was declared dead did the crowd begin to disperse, their bloodlust quenched until the next time, which in this city, could be as soon as nightturn.

And for Ashe, all she saw was that little girl who was her mother in the black misty memory. What was she trying to tell her?

Cyan
the Defiant

IV

CYAN THE DEFIANT

CYAN AND HIS acolytes waited until the Hex was empty, which took the better part of a quarter hour.

Their gyroscopes' wheels were silent on the cobbled stones of the recently raucous square as they traveled toward the stronghold of the Shards in the center of the Guild Politic. A black marble behemoth, the singular tower rose well over a hundred feet, jagged lines of grey squirreling the stone. There were no windows. A single stone entryway atop a dozen stairs circling the tower base.

"Now, there's a woman after my own heart," Lilia said with a wide grin.

Upon the steps was a woman clad in a scarlet firedrake scale cuirass. Her hair was the color of spun gold, and it cascaded down her shoulders, her elfirish ears poking through the tresses of streaming aurelian. Face the carved art of masterpieces, young, maybe thirty, lips painstakingly delicate amid a gentle cocoa brown skin tone. Irises bright, a light brown in color. Behind the woman were two green goliaths. Orcirish bodyguards most like.

"She's waiting for something or someone," Harlequin noted.

"Seeing that finely honed cuirass covering those ample baps, I hope me," Lilia answered, and when Harlequin gave her a quizzical look, the girl grinned mightily. "Jealous, are we?"

They weren't, were they?

He was loathe to admit it, but Cyan saw far too much of himself in Lilia, and not his better qualities. Cyan's upbringing in Qarthage under the harsh rule of the Fallen had been rough, and every acolyte he'd ever trained, he'd sought to make each better than he. Hard he was on his acolytes, but they were the closest he would have to children, and he loved each and every one just as fiercely as a father would. He'd largely been successful over the years, Harlequin being one of them, but Lilia was one who teetered on the edge of failure.

Upon the events in Drenth last year, he had redoubled his efforts with them both. Harlequin was the easier of the pair, although she still harbored the trauma of Amaranth the Pure's brutal torture. He would forever hold Amaranth's death close to his heart, a piece of him ripped away violently. A daughter taken from his care.

But the young vicar formerly known as Tista, was strong and resolute, which was why when they had returned to Kalderim, he had petitioned the Conclave to award her the name 'the Resolute'. No longer was she 'the Bloodless' acolyte. He felt sorrow for the path trod by his curly-haired, faux daughter.

Lilia—or Ashe as she wanted to be called—was another matter. One he wasn't certain he'd succeed with. He had raised her from babe to maturity, naming her after his late mother, and she was more than daughter to him, she was him. Cyan had put more effort into raising her, training her, guiding her than any other acolytes because she was the chosen of the Pentax.

He wouldn't fail her, wouldn't let her fail. She was far too dear to him, a daughter in all but blood, and she needed him far more than she would ever admit. And he needed her, too. Even though it was still hard for him to call her Ashe instead of Lilia.

By the Arbiter, I'm growing soft… "Helpful," Cyan said with the shake of his head. The girl never knew when to mind her tongue.

"Probably High Seat," Harlequin said.

"A keen eye, you, Harle-bub."

"You are quite annoying sometimes, Ashe."

"That's why you love me."

"Enough, you two." Cyan was on the verge of slapping both upside the head. A good ear boxing might do the pair good. At least it would make him feel better.

The woman studied them as they climbed the stairs at the base of the tower after passing their gyroscopes off to Shards servants to be rolled away. "Vicar Cyan," she said, her voice melodious. "Vicar Harlequin." To Lilia, who was grinning stupidly, "Lady Drakeslayer. A pleasure to meet the famed vicar who claimed the largest terrisvvyrm ever recorded. Cadrianna Benld would have been proud of you."

"She is not yet a vicar, milady," Cyan started, "and on—"

"Did you know her?" Lilia spoke over him. "My mother?"

Cyan took a deep breath, seeking calm. The girl was growing more headstrong by the day. Soon, he figured, his teachings would truly fall on deaf ears. He feared that day, not just for his pride, but also for the world's.

"After a fashion," the elfir replied gracefully. "You could say we shared many commonalities."

"I fail to understand how you would know a scourge of the Fallen unless you were in league with Lu Har. In his Imperium, perhaps?"

The woman laughed lightly. "You don't miss much, Brynn Benld, do you?" To Cyan, "I suppose this one's a handful?"

Cyan nodded. *Nigh on impossible, even.*

"Cadrianna, she bore the blood of the gods in her veins, just as you do. Nightingale blood. Don't think her suffering under the Fallen was the only thing known about her. There was much more. To many of us. Rest her soul in the Meadows."

"If you say so, milady." Lilia bowed her head in respect of the Guilder's words about her deceased mother. If there was anything that silenced the girl's tongue, it was a mention of her parents. Drenth had changed her in several ways; he only wished the Pentax had seen it fit to quell that sarcastic tongue of hers as well. "But my mother supposedly never believed much in the Pentax."

"You needn't be so formal for my sake, Brynn. I've been around soldiers all my life. I'm no spoiled sprat fluffed up in an ivory tower waiting for a glory-seeking hero to rescue me with a marriage proposal and a kiss. Like Shon and Solly here." The elfir thumbed toward the big orcir.

The aforementioned Shon and Solly were enormous beasts with black-green hides bulging with muscles and had long topknots atop their heads. Their faces were flat and full of underbite teeth. They had enough armaments to stock a small army strapped across their gargantuan frames.

Lilia choked out a laugh that brought some pulmo tar to her lips. "I like her," she said as she wiped the black away.

"I'm glad for you, Lilia." To the Guilder, "Milady," Cyan said with the proper respect to a Guilder, regardless of what the woman had just said. "I'm afraid I know not your name."

"You may call me Maja Carr."

"As in Canlon Carr's, I mean, the Last Godsking's wife?" the girl asked.

Maja scoffed. "You think me that old? I am of Canlon's line, yes, but merely named after his beloved wife. However, my history is for another time. We have more pressing discussions ahead." The elfir motioned for one of the orcir to open the steel gate. It squealed on its hinges as the bodyguard drew the ten-foot-tall entrance open. The High Seat Guilder proceeded inside, expecting them to follow. "This will be a dangerous case."

"Have you tried sellswords?" Lilia elbowed Harlequin with a wink. "They like danger if you pay them enough. Couldn't these two louts do the job?" She was talking about the massive orcir shadowing them.

"The task in which you are needed is much more than what simple muscle can accomplish," Maja responded.

Their boots smacked loudly on the marble of the grand foyer. Unlike the radiant rouge aethecite lighting put on the dreariness that was Oldport Basin, the Shards stronghold was sterile. Cold.

The inside was a single rotunda with a winding stair upwards to landings, which fractured off into offices and studies. Down at the base, other doorways led below into other functional spaces needed to sustain a small garrison of tainted and untainted warriors of the Shards. Small aethecite globes perched atop the railing of the staircase sat at regular intervals. High up into the apex of the tower was a thick glass opening, but it was so high up and the glass so thick, not much light filtered into the building, even during midday in summertime.

Quaestors in their scarlet cassocks ringed the rotunda, reddish-iron maces ready at a moment's notice. One by the entranceway nodded to Cyan, bowing deeper to Maja Carr in utmost respect.

Phlox the Faithful stood near the stairs, waiting for Cyan and the others before falling into step with them. Cyan heard Lilia say something under her breath, but he couldn't make it out. She had an innate distaste for Phlox. The Faithful was a pious man, bland of personality, a valued member of their team, but nowhere near as worthy as Amaranth had been.

O, Amaranth… forgive me.

"Why us?" Cyan asked as he unhooked his breather and placed it upon his belt. Harlequin and Phlox did the same. It was protocol for a warrior of the Scattered Shards to remove their masks in buildings unless on duty.

"Because Brynn Benld's parents have been spotted this side of the Meadows," Maja said as they took to the winding staircase.

"My parents are dead," Lilia responded flatly.

"Emre and Cadrianna Benld perished last year," Cyan added, "by the Fallen's own hand. It was unto Lilia to defeat him." Cyan still found it hard to not think of that day, for it was the day he was in the presence of Mother Marrow. He would never forget being so close to such holiness, a culmination of all his prayers.

Lilia had told him what Tallow had said about her parents, and if he was being honest with himself, he couldn't bring himself to believe it. The Pentax did not allow such things, which made him fear Nocturne was involved with Lu Har's impossible return. Just as He had done fifty years prior.

"Indeed, both the scion of Drenth and his lovely Nightingale wife died in the fight for Drenth," Maja said. "And yet, the truth is they aren't. At least any longer."

"My parents are dead," Lilia repeated with more heat lacing her tone. "They were buried at the ruins of the Regent's Tower in Drenth. I was there, I saw them entombed."

"To where they are memorialized. But when a sighting of Emre Benld was reported, questions began to arise. It wasn't until a Cadrianna Benld appearance did the Guild step in to investigate.

Their tombs were exhumed, and their bodies were gone. As if never buried."

"That cannot be," Harlequin breathed as Lilia cursed. Phlox choked out a gasp.

Cyan let the rebuke die on his tongue.

Maja paused on one of the landings. The aethecite globe reflected off her drake scale armor, leaving eerie shadows on the wall that reminded him of a roosting firedrake. There was pity in her eyes meant for Lilia, but she addressed Cyan, "What do you know of the blooddrakes?"

"A lesser order of draconem, if memory serves." Cyan plumbed the depths of his training and tried to recall what was written in the Book of the Scattered Shards. "Sold their souls to Nocturne during the Fall. Caused untold amount of damage to the land. After the Fall they disappeared."

"The blooddrakes didn't disappear," Maja said, continuing her ascent. "They merely went into hiding."

"How's that any different?"

"Maybe you should try reading it instead of using it for target practice for that wheellock you carry, Ashe," Harlequin snorted.

No vicar carried any weapon other than their holy axes unless Sharded with a Gauntlet of Justice, such as he wore. Yet his prized acolyte carried a daemonized blade and a pistol. Both were keepsakes of her parents, so he had allowed it after what she'd gone through. Not yet raised to the cassock, she also carried the holiest of hammers, a Hammer gifted by the Mother Herself.

"Enlighten me, O masterly philosopher."

"Lilia, Harlequin, knock it off," Cyan admonished. At times like this, he wished he could put an aetheric muzzle on them both to keep them from speaking. Lilia had been a scurrilous teen prior to fleeing Kalderim, but Harlequin was nearly just as bad after

Drenth. Dull as he may be, at least Phlox didn't constantly badger him. "Lady Maja, if you please?"

"The blooddrakes are still the Pentax's children," Maja said. "And thus, they have the power of the aether. And with their aether, they have the ability to wear the skin of man. They call it wearing scales."

"Wear the skin of man? That's fucking gross," Lilia said through a gag. "Who would do such a thing?"

"Sinners against Zenith," Phlox uttered in disbelief as he picked at a scab on his non-tattooed forearm.

"The sort of people who would take on the Pentax, Brynn Benld," said the elfirish Guilder as she plunged into the hallway toward the grand quaestor's office. "Not to mention destroying the underlying beliefs of the Scattered Shards."

Maja leaned in to speak to a servant just outside the door of Owl's office. A hobgoblin. The voidspawn was barely up to the woman's waist, his long arms nearly grazing the floor. His clothing was designed for a standard-sized man, so they were insanely baggy. He spoke in excited bursts; his ears perked the entire time.

Cyan recalled his name as Cadoz.

A race most looked down upon, hobgoblins were simple creatures trying to eke out a life different from their more warlike, larger brethren, the goblins. Hobgoblins were adequate servants, especially for doing odd jobs around an estate, such as hunting rodents in cellars (which they found as gourmet eating), cleaning the privies (they were not much cleaner than pigs if left in the wild), and guarding a kennel of hunting hounds (they had an odd affinity for hounds). Carrying messages wasn't their greatest of strengths since they forgot most of what was told to them immediately after.

Cadoz opened the wooden door after a series of knocks. "Lady Maja… uh Carr… re-re-req… um, O yeah," said the sheepish hobgoblin as he stuck his head into the office, trying to remember why he had knocked in the first place. "Asks per-per-permis… wait, I think, yeah, that's it, asks if she can enter."

Inside the office, the grand quaestor sat behind a sizable desk with mountains of codex reports stacked for review. The old, bent warrior of the Shards hunched over a report, a quill in crooked fingers, ink staining the grey flesh. The strix perched upon a stand behind, slumbering, though one coin-sized eye measured up the hobgoblin and the new guests.

"Grand quaestor?" The hobgoblin shifted uncomfortably. "Sh'll see 'em in?"

Owl glanced up, rubbed red-pupiled eyes behind the spectacles precariously hanging from the bulbous nose. "What's that? O, Cadoz, is that you?"

Cadoz cupped his hands, his fingers like spider legs around his mouth, "Lady Maja and Vicar Cyan and his… um… friends are here!" he yelled, as if thinking a raised voice might work better.

"Praise Zenith," Owl said. "I'm old, but not deaf." The poor messenger scuffed his hairy foot against the stone ground in an apology. "Go on, see them in."

"Shon, Solly." Maja motioned toward the orcir, and the two bodyguards took up station outside.

One of the highest chambers in the tower, the grand quaestor's office was shaped like a sickle: narrow and curved. The grand quaestor's bed and personal effects were in a far corner. Most of the room was filled with excessive stacks of codex reports, a few maps and other case drawings affixed to the walls. There were cabinets and shelves filled with evidence. A chair set to the side of the desk was covered in papers and reports. Order, there was not.

The Guilder took the only other seat in the room, which was a lounging couch, and that left Cyan and his acolytes to stand before the grand quaestor's desk. Normally, a slight to a Sharded vicar such as Cyan would have irked him, but he was in no mood for a minor squabble. He wanted to learn the true purpose of their case.

The grand quaestor tossed the most recent codex report aside. "I know you are yet to be raised to the cassock, acolyte, but I find your disrespect of uniform appalling."

Lilia tensed next to Cyan. "I don't follow."

"You forego the breather of your order," Owl said. "It is disrespectful to the untainted warriors of the Shards. A vicar, and more importantly, an acolyte, should maintain the line set forth by the Conclave. What Icterine sees in you, I'll never understand."

The man who would later be named Owl was the younger brother of the late Lord Talthanian of Oldport Basin. A gambler in his younger years, Owl had been as wily a card-player as there was. After accruing considerable debt, collectors had come after him. Turned out, the normally mellow strix Owl kept as a pet, was still a deadly predator when it came down to it. And although Owl was the beloved brother of one of the most authoritative lords in Thullyr at the time, an owl-pecked corpse had condemned the young Talthanian to the quaestors.

And Cyan, unfortunately, had the pleasure of working with the quaestor years ago before Owl had been transferred to Oldport. Needless to say, Cyan held little respect for the grand quaestor because Owl was as surly as a famished minotaur caught in a bramble of thorns housing a nesting fowl.

Cyan grabbed Lilia's wrist, squeezing hard enough to infer it would be unwise to speak. So, he did for her. "The Pentax has already seen fit to punish her with the pulmo, grand quaestor.

And as her taskmaster, if you plan to reprimand my acolyte again, it's best you speak to me alone first."

Owl's face twitched.

"What you are about to hear stays in this room," Maja started from the couch, speaking before the grand quaestor could further assault his pupil or him. "The High Seat is not concerned about the firedrake lairing upon Mount Bastard but is instead concerned about what the drake is guarding. Something of dire importance."

"The Seal of *Ignis*," Lilia said, her all-white gaze upon Owl, apparently unconcerned speaking out of turn. He would need to have a word with her later.

Of course, Cyan thought. He should have seen the reason right away, but he hadn't. Sending Lilia on a case for the Guild High Seat could only involve her Godsblood. He *was* getting old.

"You have the right of it, Brynn Benld," Maja replied as she crossed her legs. "As was at Drenth with the Seal of *Terris*, now is the time for the Seal of *Ignis* to be found."

"How?" Cyan asked, curious. "Forgive, but the Shards have long sought the locations of Seals. None have ever been found on Mount Bastard."

"It wasn't until Lu Har and his soldiers uncovered the Temple of Mother Marrow in Drenth's aethecite mines did we ever believe the Seals to be anything but legend," Maja continued. "Even the Book teaches the Seals were the Pentax's greatest spell of aether wielded by my kin. But never did the Book discuss an actual Seal. The truth of the matter is that veritable proof was uncovered during the discovery of the Seal of *Terris* by—"

"Don't even say it," Lilia muttered.

"By Emre Benld and his rebels. This truth was verified by a bikrome, one Valeria Dunleith, the daughter of the Golden Throne. I believe you know of her?"

Know her? The bikromi daughter of the Golden Throne had been the very person to put the babe into Cyan's arms some eighteen years ago. She had set both their paths, the girl's and his, that day.

Lilia absently brought a filigreed flask to her lips, ignoring Owl's frown. Drink was forbidden in the Shards; another fight Cyan had given up after Drenth. "We've met."

Owl stood, back cracking in so many places, Cyan wondered how those old bones weren't dust by now. Grabbing the staff of office and shuffling toward the strix, the old quaestor produced a tin stinking of lard and fed the bird of prey. "I know what it feels like to be abandoned by your family, acolyte, but duty still remains to us. And there is no duty higher than that of the Pentax. Icterine the Unfettered has allowed you back within the Shards after your disgraceful flight, thus she saw your path. The Seal of *Ignis* is but one rung further on yours."

Lilia appeared on the verge of speaking, but Cyan saw Harlequin reach for her hand out of the corner of his eye. The younger vicar's touch seemed to quell the fire in the girl. Relief washed over him. *They couldn't be… right?*

"The rebirth of souls is a boon by the Divines, both Zenith and Nocturne," Maja continued. "You, Brynn, may have seen him killed at the Temple by the guardian vvyrm, but Lu Har has been given another chance by one of the Divines. And he has brought with him someone you know quite well. Someone who you knew as a short woman with a heart-shaped face and all-onyx eyes. But this woman was no woman, this creature is a blooddrake."

"Solanine," Lilia hissed around the flask's lip, sending clear spirits spraying.

"Bless the Pentax," Cyan whispered, his heart racing.

It was racing because Solanine was the evil creature who had killed Amaranth the Pure and gave him a scar on the back of his hand that had yet to fully heal. If he were to peel off his right glove, his bones were still visible through the flesh. Killing Solanine's bodyguard in the Temple had avenged Amaranth the Pure but had not satiated Cyan. He had prayed daily since for atonement and forgiveness for having such dark thoughts.

He could almost sense Harlequin also growing uneased. He went to touch her, but her hand was already entwined with Lilia's behind their backs. *Maybe they are…*

"The same," Maja Carr confirmed. "Solanine is a hateful creature, but they have returned, Lu Har and Solanine. This Divine has seen fit to bring His warriors back into the fold. We must do the same if we are to win this coming war. They have stolen your parents' flesh, Brynn. Their scales as the blooddrakes call them. Whatever they plan to do, we don't know, but we can surmise they are after the Wayward Son's Seal. That, my dear vicars, is why you have been summoned here to Oldport Basin."

"Which Divine," Lilia asked, pocketing her flask.

The elfir's face went blank, almost as if she wouldn't answer. But she spoke, "That is for you to determine, young Godsblood."

The old quaestor gave the big strix another chunk of lard and combed the bird's feathers. "If the Fallen has indeed returned to do the Divine's work, the Seals are at risk once more. You couldn't fathom what he would do if the other three fell. We were lucky with Drenth. Lucky that the hateful spawn of Nightingale realized who she was." Red-pupiled eyes bore into the girl.

Surprisingly, Lilia didn't rise to the taunt, she just stood there biting her lip, staring off into the void, nodding as if she was having a conversation with someone not there. Cyan knew she was communicating with the daemon blade at her hip, for she had told him of it after returning to Kalderim. A strange thing, that.

But Owl's words were meant to sting because Lilia's maternal grandmother, Jensa Nightingale had once been Jensa Talthanian, Owl's sister prior to the House being cleansed.

Shifting his feet, Cyan spoke, "I'm going to assume this conspiracy cost House Tified their lives and is mixed up in this mess?"

"Indeed." Owl rifled through the codex reports on the desk, finding one to the quaestor's liking. "Tified brokered a poor deal. But after interrogating him, he gave us Dil, Ranhold, Hobb, and Klander as names connected with a deal between contacts in Drenth. Tified and Hobb are the ranking Guilders of the Harbor, that means trade of something. That is what you must deduce before they can find the Seal of *Ignis,* Vicar Cyan."

Owl fingered the tip of the staff, and Cyan noted a symbol engraved into the wood. It was a semi-circle facing east with a slash of zigzags going northeast to southwest, ending in an arrowhead. He had never seen that symbol before but made a mental note about it for later.

"There is more, vicar," Maja said.

"O great," Lilia said.

Have you forgotten your birth, child? O, but you haven't, have you? You act as if you don't care. "What else is demanded of us, Lady Carr?"

The woman's face was hard to read, but Cyan noted the slight twinge of her lips, which told him she was about to tell them less of everything she knew. Withholding knowledge because she didn't trust those within the room. Interesting. "Not only have the blooddrakes infiltrated Oldport in view of finding the Seal of *Ignis*, but we believe they have wormed their way into the Guild, perhaps even the High Seat."

"As well as the Scattered Shards," Owl added.

"Even better," Lilia grunted.

"If Nocturne's servants have taken root in the Shards or the Guild," Cyan started, "then the war for Eminence is truly upon us and we are leagues behind." His mind raced with thoughts. "What do we do?"

"Survive, vicar."

"Lady Carr?"

"We all have to do whatever is necessary for… survival." Maja reached behind the molded cuirass and pulled forth a folded piece of parchment, handing it to Cyan.

"What's this?" The parchment had fine brushstrokes in fancy lettering. Lilia leaned over to read but Cyan nudged her away. "Tickets to *The Arbiter's Axe*?"

"Some are saying there's to be some sort of big announcement in a few days," Maja answered. "Ifant Klander now runs *The Axe*, bought after your grandfather was murdered in Drenth, Brynn Benld. And Tified names him as co-conspirator. Coincidence? Find the blooddrake here in Oldport and they will lead us to the ones within the Guild or Shards."

Lilia was none too discreet with her feelings, as always. "Really?"

Cyan's emotions quirked. Tallow was correct, maybe this would be the closure Lilia needed to finally accept her fate. A case to set things right, not just for her, but her parents as well. "What's the matter, Lilia, you frightened?"

"You suicidal?"

He smiled at the girl who he had raised. He might not be the perfect father figure, but one thing he knew for certain, he wouldn't fail her again. "Only at dawnbreak."

V

LOJEN

MEN SIMPLY DIDN'T go into the Sea of Mist other than necessity. Nor any right-minded drakken worth their exoscales.

A delicate breeze blew through the thin stalks of the hard, dull-colored grass. The packed earth was cracked with finger-length ruts. Above, a few carrion daemons swooped and swerved through the grey. One shrieked but didn't dive.

It wasn't a true sea, but the mist covered everything south of Kanja not built upon stilts, behind walls, or into mountains like most mega-cities in the Mistlands. In snow-covered Kanja, the Sea flowed, but not like this. Not this dense. Not this dangerous. Death stalked the land like an unwanted mistress. Daemons claimed the once fertile marshes. Remnants of the old world before the Fall of Eminence poked through the bog and mud. Few called the Sea of Mist home, and those who did were stubborn to the core. But it also made the wary soul lose their mind.

Lojen Tevunson had no choice but to creep silently. Luckily, drakken were as silent as could be.

His prey was on the other side of the closest brush. Lojen sat back on his haunches, debating what to do about the other while he ran a taloned claw over his two-foot-long, sloping keratin horns—his wardkeeper horns, gods above, they were his horns weren't they?—as if touching them would give him an inkling of what to do. Lojen then eased his grey-blue, exoscaled claw through the thorny bush to find the man sitting cross-legged in the minuscule sunlight that pierced the Sea. The man was huddled under a cloak as he rocked back and forth, whimpering unintelligibly.

Should the man spook and run, the Sea could bring death swiftly to them both.

Lojen moved and a branch snapped underfoot. "Broken shells," he hissed knowing he'd just cocked it up.

The man bolted into the darkened marshland. Crashing after, thick thorns snagged Lojen's sleeveless vest, tearing it, leaving imperceptible scratches on his exoscales. Though the man ran at breakneck speed through the low tangle of trees, Lojen kept pace, ignoring the muddy pools, as dark muck splashed in dung-colored arcs. Thick moss and heavy sludge soon caked his boots, slowing him, but Lojen stumbled after the elusive man.

Even though drakken had near perfect vision in the dark, caution was still necessary despite the growing darkness of evenfall. He was losing ground, and he didn't want to break a leg on the treacherous marshlands. Daemons would be on a wounded victim in heartbeats.

After a quarter hour, Lojen lost track of the man, the mist swallowing all his signs.

"Broken shells."

The man couldn't have gotten that far ahead, could he? Drakken were supposedly excellent trackers, but he was showing his inexperience. Years spent away from the Isle of Merj had blunted his skills. Skills that should be second nature to one blessed by the Forgemistress as he. Skills his father had long ago taught him.

Some wardkeeper he was shaping up to be, though he was only a year into the role and didn't possess the one thing a wardkeeper was supposed to have…

There were gouges in the moss, but nothing to indicate it had come from an elfir. Even crazed, there was no way the man—a Kanjan legionnaire named Tonns—could keep up the hurried clip. Eventually Tonns would succumb to fatigue, for no humir, dvergir, elfir, or any race of man had the stamina of a drakken.

Lojen was about to take a quick drink from his waterskin, but his claw froze when he heard a noise just ahead. Creeping like he was some daemonic beast of the Sea with his long tail parallel to the marsh, Lojen spied Tonns leaning against a short, branchless tree, breathing heavily.

Sensing his opportunity, and tired of the chase, he stepped through the thicket.

Tonns' eyes snapped toward him, but he didn't look to be in any condition to flee. "I can't take it anymore, drakken. The howling. It's driving me mad." The lank legionnaire put a trembling hand to his head, breather fogging as he huffed. "It'll be the death of me."

"It doesn't have to be that way, Tonns. The Legion needs men like you."

"He's coming." Tonn's breather hissed as he wheezed, and his silvery tangle of hair hung limp. "He's coming, and I can't be here when he does."

Lojen lifted a calming claw toward the frightened legionnaire. He could almost hear his father lecturing him on how to keep a panicked man from overstepping the edge. Lectures that ran through his mind on never-ending repeat. Lectures that became mantras.

'Fear has a way of turning the most sane inside out, Lojen. Never question one's fear. Instead, lean into it. Help them fight it. Be their guide, my hatchling.'

"Who's coming, Tonns?"

Tonns threw his head back, hands pressed to both pointed ears, screaming into the night. "He's coming. Aghhh! I can feel him now. Soon, drakken. Soon." The elfirish legionnaire went to his knees, breathing strained from the scream.

"Come back with me. The primus pilus will—"

"No! The captain'll have me hung for running. You know the laws. The laws are clear as Eminence. I've failed the Golden Throne. There is no return for me. I cannot. Not with him coming. We cannot stop him."

Underfoot, the marshlands began to quake. Lojen set his feet to stop himself from falling, but Tonns tipped over, almost as if he didn't care. The Sea's mist groaned as if inconvenienced. Dead trees toppled, swallowed by the muddy ground. The quake ended, muddy pools of water surrounding them sloshed like filled mugs being cheered.

Ever since Mother Marrow's demise, the land cried as if missing its parent. Perhaps it was. The world was forever changed since the destruction of the terrisvvyrms and the Forgemistress.

"We can figure this out, Tonns," Lojen said. "Landra knows your heart. Even Praetor Rignork knows you. You've served the Legion and the Golden Throne with loyalty for centuries now."

Tonns' demeanor softened as he regained his feet, if only somewhat. Lojen might be making headway, but he wasn't much of a skilled negotiator like a wardkeeper should be. He was still learning. "You do me such kindness, brother-friend. You may have the ear of the drunken princeling and his bikromi sister, but you know the truth of it, you'd be better served by killing me now."

The Legion's rules were strict, but Lojen had to hope they would show mercy. By the Arbiter, he would go to the Golden Throne if he had to.

"Come now, Tonns, you know I won't kill you."

"That's what I was hoping for." Tonns sprung at him, bringing Lojen down into the wetness with a thick slurp.

The legionnaire rolled atop him. Tonns was smaller, three hundred years his senior as elfir age versus that of drakken, and wiry strong for a man. But Lojen Tevunson *was* a drakken, seven feet tall and bulging with muscle underneath his grey-blue exoscales. Tonns' arms tried to lock around Lojen's chest, but he was able to squirm through the other's grizzled grip like a toddler trying to snare their parent. He grabbed Tonns' wrist as he shimmied, twisting it. Tonns kicked and punched at him. Lojen ducked as they both regained their footing.

Lojen was no seasoned warrior like most legionnaires, but the mismatch of strength between elfir and drakken weighed heavily in his favor. He merely had no intention of hurting the man. The half-crazed elfir reared back and Lojen sidestepped the swing deftly, but he placed his foot wrong, and it went straight into a muddy hole. Lojen fell into the marsh.

Tonns was on him with a dagger at his throat. "I won't go back. He's coming and there's no stopping him. I can't live like this anymore. My heart has gone weak. No one can avert this. Death follows him like a wave."

A low growl reverberated in the thicket of muddied bog.

"Tonns, please. Why run?"

"Dark tidings come. The Sea is going to run red with blood. Lu Har, he comes."

Lu Har, the man once called the Fallen. A man killed the previous year in the Temple of Mother Marrow near the aethecite mines in Drenth. Lojen had been there, had seen the magnificent terrisvvyrm of the Forgemistress rise from the center of the earth and swallow the Fallen whole before the vvyrm tore into the floating fortress of Gargantua. Nothing and no one could have survived such a death.

"Come back with me," Lojen repeated against the pressing dagger. For as strong as exoscales were, a dagger to the jugular still meant death. "Gandtril needs to know what you know. What you fear."

"It's not the Fallen I fear. I fear no man. Something comes with him we cannot fight. I've seen his presence in my dreams. Haunting and howling, all-black eyes. They're driving my mind to madness."

"You saw this in a dream?" A line of purplish blood streamed from under the blade. All-black eyes meant only one thing: Void Form aetheurgy.

More growling, closer now. Predatory.

"Too old, yet I fear the night. The Fallen is the night." Tonns did something Lojen didn't expect, he laughed. "It's too late for me, drakken. Remember these words: Only a Godsblood can rekindle Eminence. Blood of Nightingale must bloom or aether will kill us all. Ever shall the world be broken. The protectors of the Gods have been named. The Golden Sword will bear the Crown. The Aegis will sing the Hymn of War and stand against the fire. The Mantle of the Void shall merge the rift. And the Breath will breathe the Crystals into one."

Godsblood? Brynn? Protectors? Gods above, why did I ever allow her to leave my side?

'It was the correct thing to do as wardkeeper, Lojen,' his father voiced his own thoughts. Lecturing. Always.

To Tonns, "You know I can't let you leave."

"I know, drakken. But I shan't go back alive. Call her." The dagger pulled back.

Lojen's heart tightened, the elfir's body sagged before he whistled. Sad smile from behind glass as a great, black shadow crashed into Tonns in a vicious rush. Body lying nearby, unconscious and unmoving, ghastly apparition hidden within the mist, dark and foreboding.

Sitting up, Lojen sighed. "You didn't have to pulverize him."

Ruane Tevunsdotyr padded out of the fog. The setting sunlight above the Sea danced along her light blue exoscales, upon the rounded protrusions above her purplish eyes, on her angled snout. "The man nearly skewered your throat, Lojen. You may wear the horns of our father, but by the Arbiter, you make a lousy wardkeeper sometimes."

Lojen shook his head, restraining another sigh. He had hoped she would return to the sweet younger sister she had been before their father's murder in Drenth, but he had been sorely mistaken. Ruane had only grown surlier, more eager to prove herself worthy of the Pentax. He once thought Lu Har's death would sate her desire for revenge, but that fire had merely grown tenfold.

"The man was crazed, Ru."

"As is half the Legion. This place drives the stoutest to madness." She crouched beside him, helping loosen Lojen's boot from the muck. "But he's more a fool if he thinks Lu Har is back."

Lu Har was dead, he couldn't be back. Tonns had to be wrong. But Lojen had been wrong before. And Val had divinations from the Twins, she'd never been wrong. *Gods, Finn, we need you…* "I know that," he said as he dug the mud from the sole of his boot with a stick. "Lu Har's dead. But that doesn't explain the daemons massing in the Sea."

"Broken shells, Lojen, you would sit on your tail and let the world fall apart around you just so you can see the destruction from all angles. A Scurred Hatch, you."

"You were there, Ru, when Brynn summoned the vvyrm that killed the Fallen. You saw the Seal of *Terris* break with your own eyes. No one can survive that. None. It shouldn't possible for Lu Har to be back."

Ruane rose and kicked an overturned log into the grey haze. "You're a fool then, brother. Nocturne has the realm of the dead at His command. You think He cannot rebirth any soul bound to the Pit? He did it before with Lu Har and Solanine. He also allowed Emre Benld to breach the veil and return to the living. Once done is once opened."

"Since when have you been so keen on the Pentax and the Master of the Pit? You been speaking with Augur Puce again?" He chuckled at the thought of Ruane reading the Book of the Scattered Shards under the teachings of the dvergirish augur. Truth told, the thought of Ruane reading anything was a funny thought.

His sister apparently didn't see the humor in his jest. "For such a believer in Zenith's honor, you do fall short. Augur Puce knows much more than you could ever imagine, brother."

Picking up the dagger and sheathing it at his belt, Lojen checked the legionnaire's vitals. Still breathing. Looking to the sky, the incandescence of the moon pierced the mist in a pale orb.

"Maybe someday you'll be able to show me what I lack, sister-friend."

"Now you are starting to speak like these Kanjans. Father must be molting in his grave."

Hefting the man onto his back, Lojen began the long trek back through the wetlands toward Gandtril, Ruane loping alongside him.

The return was relatively easy through the many pools of stagnant water and vats of mud, and as the great city rose out of the night-bound bog, the ground became slightly more compact.

Gandtril lay at the southern border of Kanja, nestled in the lowlands between the Forgemistress' Blades to the west, Altreyia to the south, and the goblin highlands of Filfangin to the east. Built upon the only solid foundation for leagues, Gandtril possessed twenty-foot-tall walls with aethecite-powered vacuums and gates of waist-thick steel. Runes of aether were carved into the walls to ward against the daemons without. Attached to the turrets were gears and pulleys, and each moved rotating cannons capable of rapidly firing hundreds of aethecite bullets in minutes by a single operator. Legionnaires lined the walls with grim faces, weapons held in fists.

"Hail!" he called as they neared the gate, and when the legionnaire on the other side saw the pair of drakken, the heavy doors groaned inward.

"Got 'im, did ya?" asked a legionnaire as they passed into the mega-city. The man's bald head shone in the moonlight above his breather, his elfirish ears poked straight out like someone had jabbed a stick through them.

Though there were mist-vacuums along the walls, all legionnaires on gate duty wore breathing masks because the rationing of aethecite meant the vacuums were now on rotating schedules of downtime. No one knew how long the supply of aethecite would last, and so far, the Guild leaders in Drenth had yet to make a breakthrough in reopening the mines.

And based on what he'd seen with Mother Marrow and Her vvyrms, it might be centuries, if not epochs before the mines were accessed again. That's even if the rumors weren't true that aethecite came from the tunnelling vvyrms themselves. He wasn't certain he believed those rumors, but only the Pentax knew the truth.

"Wasn't easy." Two others from within the guardhouse took Tonns from him as he shrugged the inert elfir from his shoulder. "Bastard's heavy."

The first legionnaire laughed. "Growing soft, drakken?"

"He was always soft," Ruane grumbled, looking away. "Too soft for a wardkeeper."

Sensing the unease building, the soldier gulped. "We'll take care of Tonns. Spit might be aflamed by now. Mutton on the menu."

Lojen's stomach growled, but he was too concerned about the tidings Tonns spoke of. "Where's Finnus Dunleith?"

"Do I look like the princeps' attendant?" the man harrumphed. "You may be sworn to the Dunleiths, but down here in the asshole of Kanja, we all have our own duties, drakken. The princeps is most likely lost in his cups again. You'd have a better chance of seeing a sober Brio than a sober Finnus Dunleith these days."

If only that wasn't the truth. Drenth had destroyed the man, had destroyed much more than Gargantua and the Fallen's Imperium. He was left without a ward, but Finnus Dunleith had lost his soul.

"Come on, Ru. Better find Landra, then."

Shaped like the typical Kanjan fortress built around the base of mega-cities, Gandtril had three sets of walls, the first two were separated by fifty paces, the second and third by near five hundred. The outer two walls were the first and second lines of protection, and the final wall separated the citizens from the soldiers of the Legion. Simple in design, hardy to the core. Between the innermost two walls, a main road led to a towering spire called the Obelisk.

In most Kanjan mega-cities, there were four cardinal entrances, supported by four gates and four bulwarks, regiments of the Legion on hand at each.

But not Gandtril.

Since Gandtril was the southernmost Kanjan mega-city, and due to this strategic location, the main hub of the city and that of the Obelisk faced south. Gandtril was built around a singular mountain peak. Not as tall as those in the Blades, but tall enough to support an entire city built into its cliff face. The curling tower of Obelisk was formed of black granite blocks and was almost as tall as the second tier of the city where it butted up against the mountain, a good fifty feet buffering the stone of the mountain from the blocks of the tower. Blocky walkways supported by large metal girders crossed to the four corners of the fortress and had gears capable of lifting and retracting in case of attack. All traffic from the south into the city went through the Obelisk.

Sixty thousand men, women, and children of all races called Gandtril home, almost five thousand fighting soldiers strong. The brave legionnaires kept the daemons of the mist out of the mega-city, as well as the Fallen's Imperium the last fifty years. A high honor for any born-and-bred Kanjan.

"You worry too much about these elfir, brother."

"And you worry too little," he huffed as they made for the Obelisk. "Finn is our friend. If the rumors are true and Lu Har is alive, the Golden Throne is at risk. He wanted the Seals to Eminence and Kalderim is home to the Peridot of *Aere* according to Val. Men like Lu Har don't abandon such pursuits."

"Spoken like a wardkeeper. You are without a ward, or have you forgotten?"

How could he possibly forget? It was the solemn duty of a wardkeeper to protect their wards until the grave; theirs or the wardkeeper's. Family lines became wards, not just individuals. The Benld line had been Lojen's father's ward for decades before the invasion of Drenth. Upon Tevun's death, Lojen had sworn his honor to protect the line. With Emre dead, that duty fell to his daughter, Brynn. But Brynn had forsaken that oath of protection, something Lojen had never heard of back on the drakken homeland, the Isle of Merj.

He was wardless. And lost because of it.

One year, while a raindrop in the lake that was a drakken's lifespan, without a ward was like a death sentence to the proud wardkeeper. How was he ever to prove his worth to the Pentax if he failed to protect his holy ward? Mother Marrow had given him courage and honor, and he had repaid Her gift with failure.

So much failure, his life. He had tried, and failed, to be like his father.

With nothing resembling a prideful plan, he had done the one thing he could do to continue his service to the Pentax, and that was to submit to the Golden Throne. If he couldn't protect the daughter of Emre and Cadrianna Benld, then he would do the next best thing, serve the rēx and rēgīna of the Seal of *Aere*. And by extension, the love of Emre, Finnus Dunleith.

As the rumors of Lu Har's return had gained steam these last months, the rēx had sent his third son down to the mega-city of Gandtril as the official advisor to the praetor of the Legion. And as such, Lojen and a reluctant Ruane had followed, and she had not let him forget it since.

Father, how do I get her, and myself, out of this? Show me the way. The way to appease the gods…

Lojen noted the praetor upon the battlements of the Obelisk.

A flurry of activity stirred the hard-packed earth when recruits hustled into file, assembling in perfect columns of eighty apiece. Backs straight, daemon-killing spears held in front. Cloaks of earthen brown fell over their right shoulders, pinned by a broach—the outstretched wings of an eagle, the sigil of the Legion. Polished drake scale cuirasses reflected the aethecite lamps that ran along the walls, glinting steel spear points bright, wheellock sidearms holstered upon belts, wheellock rifles slung across their backs. Stern faces under half-helms, breathers hanging loose.

"Fine looking legionnaires you've given us again, Emont," the Legion general said as Lojen took the stairs behind the assembled soldiers and eavesdropped. Ruane lingered behind.

For all her bluster, she was wary of Praetor Rignork, making Lojen wonder if the taciturn general reminded her of their father.

In fact, Tevun and Eran Rignork hadn't been the best of friends since long before Lojen's hatching. He had never known why, but he suspected it had to do with the Dunleith reclusion as the Last Godsking had unleashed his final spell of aether and sent Eminence crashing from the heavens.

"It's my honor that you praise me so, my lord," Primus Pilus Emont Landra said. The captain stood behind the praetor, sharp eyes scrutinizing every move below. His self-dyed, jet-black hair was slicked back over his elfirish ears with oils, and he was bedecked in a drake scale cuirass and sword befit for a prideful Calibrathian elfir, not a soldier of Kanja. For no proud Kanjan would dye their pale locks nor wear a bejeweled weapon.

Rignork waved the comment aside. Lojen had learned him to be a hard man to please. Shrewd, but honorable. Made a solid wardkeeper had he been born a drakken. Maybe that's why his father held distaste for him? "You've done time and again."

Nearing two thousand summers, Eran Rignork was aged like a sun-drenched melon despite his pale skin tone. The praetor's face was deeply lined, and his snowy white hair receded at the temples. Icy-grey eyes surveyed the recruits in the yard below. He leaned upon the crenellation, his cane gripped in one gnarled hand, gout corrupting his once prim posture.

"I serve as by your grace," Landra said.

With help from the primus pilus, the praetor drew his sword. Three feet of sharpened steel raised high, pointing to the dim pale moonlight shaded by that eerie emerald gash across the eastern sky as he addressed the assembled legionnaires below.

Rignork's voice carried above, "You have given your lives over to the Golden Throne. A harsh and demanding life. Molded from young, wide-eyed youths from all over Kanja, honed into legionnaires who will not break upon the blood and bone of our enemies. You hold the strength within to guard the Golden Throne. Each of you part of a whole. Siblings unto death. When one of your siblings falls, you will not allow them to fall in vain. What befalls one, befalls the entire Legion. You must not waiver before any foe. The Golden Throne only demands two things from you. How do you serve?"

"With Honor and Blood!" came the resounding call in perfect unison.

"These foolish children know nothing of honor," grunted Ruane. Lojen turned to shush her, but she had already looked away.

Rignork raised his sword as high as his aged arm could go, the new legionnaires thrusting up their spears. For a brief heartbeat there was silence, but then a roar of cheer erupted in the yard. Hoots and hollers of jubilation, joined by their siblings of the Legion on the walls watching the ceremony.

For once, the dreary sounds of the Sea of Mist became awash with celebration.

A smile broke the hard plane of the praetor's stoic face. But the smile withered when he saw Lojen standing nearby. "Fine legionnaires. They will test their mettle soon enough."

Odd the words were, a portent perhaps? Did he know about Tonns and the tidings he spoke? Was there more to the daemons than they were led to believe?

A pair of worn-looking stewards came to help the praetor depart for his chambers. Long cloak fluttering in a sudden gust of wind, earthen brown snapping taut as a bowstring, sending a shiver down Lojen's spine to the tip of his tail.

Emont Landra turned to leave as well, but Lojen reached for him. "A word, Landra?"

The primus pilus spun on his heel and yanked his arm from Lojen's taloned touch. "What word is that, drakken? I've got pressing matters to deal with. Traitors to hang."

"It's Tonns I wanted to speak to you about."

"The man broke the laws. He must reap the consequence."

Landra made to leave once more, but Lojen slid in front. The man looked most displeased. "I know he did. But the things he's told us. The things he's seen. Don't you think that would be useful? He saw something."

"The law is the law. No family name, no special commendation supersedes the law. Desertion equals death. You aren't of Kanja, drakken, so your ignorance is forgivable. But the rules are crystal. I'm a primus pilus of the Legion, I know that which I serve. You'd best remember that before I have you whipped for insolence to your oaths to our rēx."

"Didn't you see the look on the praetor's face? Something is coming. Maybe Tonns saw it. Only those blessed by the Pentax could foresee it. Valeria knows the truth. Seek her, she's a bikrome. She knows something comes and will need every soldier for it. You know it. I know it. Primus Pilus, you have to give mercy. Stay the command unt—"

"Until when? Until the Pentax shines down on us with Their holy gaze and free the land of this mist? No, whatever comes, will come, regardless of what the daughter of the Golden Throne sees. The Pentax sent us the Fall for our arrogance, for our disobedience. If the Pentax sought to punish us then, why should we forgo punishment of our own laws? The laws of the Legion are meant to hold our legionnaires to their oaths. Oaths they swore in the name of the Golden Throne. Oaths you swore as a drakken wardkeeper. Tonns was a Legion man once, he swore those oaths."

"He still is," Lojen insisted. "Tonns is broken and defeated by what he saw, but his heart still beats with the Legion inside. Don't take that from him as well."

"Some fires must be quenched to make the fields sow, drakken."

If Lojen had been humir, his brow might have risen at the odd comment, instead he leaned forward. "Primus Pilus, please."

"Lojen, let it go," his sister broke in. Landra sneered at the younger drakken, but Ruane didn't budge, in fact, she showed the elfir her teeth. "Men like him don't listen to reason. Men like him are weak and easily swayed. You cannot trust men like him."

"It doesn't matter," Landra said, ignoring the harsh words of Ruane, glaring instead. "The man's fate is sealed." With that, Emont Landra marched away.

Lojen's mood sank. He had failed Tonns. Just as he failed so many others.

VI
FINN

THE LAST PLACE an elfir like Finnus Dunleith wanted to be was with a bunch of Guilders discussing mundane governance, but that's exactly where he found himself.

He was bored. Ridiculously, annoyingly, achingly bored. His head rested lightly upon his thumb and forefinger as he weaved in and out of listening to the ongoing discussions. They had been at it for hours now, and nothing to show for it other than he had almost fallen asleep a handful of times.

But this was his existence now, and truth told, he didn't know how his parents did this day in and day out.

For near twenty years when he had been gallivanting down in Drenth, building a resistance alongside Emre Benld, he had a purpose. Finn had a reason to think, to act. For Drenth's freedom. For love.

Godsdamn you, Emre. Why, love, why?

He knew why, of course, but that didn't make it any easier. The hurt of Emre's death would follow him for centuries. It would be a slow, sorrowful descent into madness. Depression had already settled in for the long haul.

"We need something to stimulate the economy without putting a major burden on the commons," said one of the Guilders. He was a tall man who cut a striking figure despite a boyish face. "The Fallen's soldiers crippled nigh on every village in Altreyia as they fled Drenth."

After Emre's victory in the City of Sands, the army of the Imperium had been left bereft of leadership. Solanine and all the Fallen's scourges had been killed at the aethecite mines, and with the floating fortress of Gargantua a smoldering sarcophagus, it had left the body without a head. The Imperium soldiers had fled, sacking every village and shanty town in the Sea of Mist for hundreds of miles in all directions. Most had eventually found employment with the Guild, but bands of rogues still ran rampant.

A problem the High Seat out of Alizarin grappled with but had yet to produce a solid plan for.

"Could increase our trade output," a slight Guilder said. The man was wrapped in a plethora of silks that made Finn wonder how the man's spouse could possibly have allowed him out in such attire. *The gall to wear that…* "The only thing you want to avoid is rising taxation."

"Trade what?" asked a grandmotherly hag of an elfir. She was so old, a summer breeze might atomize all her bones into dust. "We have nothing to trade. The dvergir hoard their gems, the goblins prefer war over all else, and Alizarin wants to play kingmaker."

"Then we send another delegation to help Drenth reopen the aethecite mines," said a swarthy Guilder with a mop of red-gold hair. He might be considered handsome if not for the fact the man always stank as if his mastiff had pissed on his pillow before slumber each nightturn.

"With what money, I ask?" The speaker's gaze surveyed the whole table before settling upon Finn. "I won't spend the Golden

Throne's coin on frivolous attempts. The mines are closed by the grace of Mother Marrow Herself. Let the cities in the south swerve to the word of the High Seat. Kanja will remain strong and will not fall prey to greed when the Pentax demands penitence."

The speaker was Titen Dunleith, the heir to the Golden Throne of Kalderim and bearer of the Golden Sword, the kingdom's fabled blade as well as royal title. And Finn's eldest brother.

None of the Guilders offered up any retort, which didn't surprise Finn. To him, they were nothing but flies swarming a pile of shit, the shit being Titen.

"Well said, brother-friend," Finn mumbled while he drew circles upon the parchment he was meant to be taking notes on, "glad to know the rēx wants to remain steadfast upon his throne. Not the first time this millennia, either."

There were five Guilders sitting at the table, and Finn didn't much care to recall whose House each belonged to. They all stared at him; dumbstruck that the thirdborn son would badger the firstborn of Kalderim.

He would admit that it was curious his parents had put up with the Guild worming their way into Kanja, but if his eldest brother's words carried any truth, it seemed the rēx and rēgīna cared only about Kalderim and less about the rest of the nation.

During Drenth's occupation, trade of the life-supplying aethecite had become a delicate dance. Lu Har would never willingly trade with Kanja, so Finn's parents had resorted to a mediary: the Guild. And the Guild charged thrice what aethecite was worth. It had nearly bled the Golden Throne's coffers dry these last eighteen years. And it hadn't stopped with Lu Har's demise, for the Guild still charged an exorbitant price, rationing and hoarding.

There were other free cities in Kanja, such as Krylen in the northeast, so he supposed Gandtril might one day claim that status if the Guild had its way.

Gandtril was a hundred leagues south of Kalderim. The vast swathe of Kanja was covered with snow nearly a full turn of the year from the Golden Sea to the VVynter Expanse, only a few short months where green pocked the hard earth. Only the lowlands in the northwest by the floating mountains where Kalderim resided had anything remotely close to what the lands of Altreyia possessed in terms of greenage. Well below, some thousands of feet below, those floating mountains, down below the heavy mist of the Sea colloquially called the Gloom.

But Gandtril had none of that.

With the Forgemistress' Blades to the west, the ground was mostly stony outcroppings of the great mountains where the dvergir holds flourished underground. But Gandtril was built around a lonely mountain a few leagues from the Blades, and the city was crafted from the very stone and bluff of this relatively small, singular peak. Root crops their main source sustenance.

A lonely peak for a free city.

"Finn?"

He glanced up from his scribbles, blinking a few times before he realized it had been Titen speaking to him. "What?"

His brother was a ball of barely controlled annoyance. Titen was a goliath of an elfir, tall and built like a prizefighter. His silvery hair was receding, so Titen kept it trimmed short. He was near three centuries older than Finn, and his bearded face bespoke of a man clinging tightly to their parents' coattails. The only thing Finn couldn't begrudge was the three-piece suit his brother wore, it was, he had to admit, an excellent ensemble. Dark grey with peridot stripes, quite the trend.

"I asked what you suggest? Gandtril was named your jurisdiction by the decree of Rēx Vitus. So I ask again, what should we do?"

The Guilders looked his way, their eyes calculating, their gears spinning. Finn was under no illusion that he brought anything to this mega-city other than the name Dunleith. He knew his father had only sent him south in attempt to get him out of his mourning.

Grabbing his winecup, which was nearly empty, Finn's face split into a grin. "Why, dearest brother-friend, you know I'm only here because someone needs to sit around and look glorious."

Titen's left eye twitched. The others in the room might not have caught it, but Finn did. It was a tic his brother possessed when he was livid. Outwardly, the Golden Sword showed nothing. "Thank you for your… impeccable input, Finn. As always. I'll be certain to have the stewards mark the minutes carefully."

Finn raised the winecup. "See that you do, brother-friend." But then he looked down at his circle drawings, "O Bloody Nocturne, it appears I've gone and messed up the minutes." He angrily tossed the badly written notes overlaid with unending ink circles toward the overly dressed Guilder. "Here, maybe you can pick up where I left off."

With that, Finn pushed his chair back and wobbled to his feet, for the wine had gone directly to his head it seemed. After a haphazard bow, Finn shuffled toward the exit, ignoring the gasps of surprised Guilders and the annoyed scoff from the Golden Sword. Once through the door, Kanjan legionnaires stiffened into proper posture.

Finn tossed the empty winecup to one, who fumbled the unexpected projectile, dropping his daemon-killing spear in the process. "Take care of that, will you?"

"Princeps?"

Finn waved the legionnaire off and exited the building. It had some sort of important name, the building; something to do with governing and such, but Finn seemed to have misplaced the name.

Caring about anything seemed like it wasn't worth it anymore. Not since Emre.

Gandtril opened to him as evenfall labored toward nightturn. The setting sun was a pinkish blob on the western horizon, saying a fond farewell to the queer, never-ending emerald tint of the east. Another lingering memory of Drenth.

Drenth.

By the Pentax, why did he still dwell on it? They had won. Emre had freed his city from the shackles of the Fallen. Seventeen years of oppression, the desire of revenge reaching a fervid crescendo. His love had done it, and yet, Finn couldn't seem to let it go.

Perhaps it was because he felt betrayed.

He wasn't so stupid to think the Meadows might call any of them during their fight for freedom. Death had courted them like a gaggle of spinsters in a sewing club from the moment they had vowed to bring down the Imperium. He had lost so many friends in the fight. Siblings to the core.

But to not even be told the truth, that hurt him the most.

Tevun's murder, the scourge-wife Cadrianna, the Godsblood-child Brynn, Val's betrayal and subsequent lie to Lu Har. All of those were means to an end. He knew Emre had planned it all, some with his help.

In the end, Emre hadn't told him it all.

"Sacrifice, eh, Em?" he said to himself as he ambled through the upper level of Gandtril. Gods, he needed another drink to drown out the memories. "See what good that did? And look where you left me!"

Gandtril was a two-tiered mega-city, and the Upper City was a manmade disc that jutted over the lower and was held up by building-thick steel trusses, creating a plateau a mile in diameter around the mountain peak, the fortress of the Legion surrounding the mega-city's base. Facing northward into Kanja, extravagant villas with surrounding gardens brushed shoulder to shoulder with stunning architecture resembling the old world before the Fall. Fluted columns held peristyles, while balconies vomited flowers of all colors. Statues lined paved roads as deep green trees reached over. Spires protruded from manses so vast, it was a wonder how such a construction wouldn't topple the trusses supporting the Upper City.

Before Emre, before tasting true power that was aetheurgy, Finn had always enjoyed the galas and balls thrown upon Gandtril's upper tier, had marveled at its wealth. Unlike Drenth's aethecite aerescreens, neon *Aere*, and sky-scraping buildings, Gandtril was a more classic city, one that focused on theater and music. Of the arts of old. Parties and dances.

That Finnus Dunleith, third in line for the Golden Throne, had been a regular at all the fancy to-dos throughout Kanja. A guest with endless wit, a link to the royals who wasn't unapproachable. A lover who could put in the right words when necessary. A thrill-seeker who brought a smile to all.

But now, after Emre's death, everything in Gandtril carried a bitter taste.

Ahead was a corkscrew road sarcastically called the Ceveo. The Ceveo wrapped around the squat peak, conjoining the upper and lower levels, separating the dregs and commons behind the outer walls and the Obelisk from those of the Guild above. A single car tramline paralleled the road, a sleek metal egg that could carry upwards of fifteen people was reserved for inhabitants of the Upper City only, not the lower tier folk. While the Lower City was dirty and bathed in the shit that was life in the Mistlands, the tiptop was pristine and clean, privileged beyond reproach.

Hence the locally coined named road between levels: the lowborn were being passively buggered in the backend by the Guild highborn.

And to Finn, it wasn't far off to how he felt about himself.

Down in the Lower City he figured he'd find a nice place to drown himself in wine and gamble away Dunleith fortunes. It was the only way to kill the pain inside.

"Emre, you should have told me."

"Talking to yourself again are we, needle dick?"

Finn slowed to a shaky stop and found a lapin leaning against an aethecite light post, flipping a dueling knife in his paw. The short creature's long, shredded ears were pulled back and tied off like man might with a tail of hair. His button-sized black eyes danced with devilry. The lapin smirked, showing his elongated front teeth.

"I'm not in the mood, Wick."

The lapin pilot snatched the dueling knife midair by the blade's tip, stuffing it away in his belt. "When are you? We've been here for months, and I've barely seen you without a cup in your hand. I could be anywhere but here, but no. Ancantha is in Alizarin. I should be with her. She's my mate, you know?"

"Leave me alone."

"Lojen needs to talk to you. He's been bugging me for days to find you."

"Well, I don't want to talk to him." He made to saunter past the lapin, but Wick hopped in front of him. Finn grunted as he was forced to stop. "What do you want?"

"I want to slap that stupid face of yours, needle dick," Wick said, staring up at him, admonishment in his voice. The lapin was barely up to Finn's waist. "You can't keep this up, Finn. Em wouldn't want this of you."

"What do you know about what Em would want?" His voice rose and some highborn folk stopped whatever it was they were doing and looked over at him. *Bugger them.* "Emre died in Drenth, Wick. And he never even told me!" His hands balled into fists. "My godsdamned sister didn't tell me."

Wick's already lowered ears drooped further, his snout dipping. "He may have been sharing your bed, but Emre Benld was my friend. One of my only true friends. His loss eats away at me because I allowed him to send me away before Lu Har appeared." The lapin shook his head. "But we swore an oath. Remember? An oath to destroy Lu Har. To burn the Imperium to cinder. Regardless of the outcome. And guess what, we fucking won! Emre knew this. That was everything he died for."

Finn's body suddenly felt heavy, so he dropped right there in the middle of the street, caring naught that his expensive pants ripped at the knee. His hand went to his pounding head, wine and heartache waging a bitter war. He couldn't stop the sobs. "I miss him, Wick. I miss him every waking day."

The smaller lapin neared and put furry arms around his neck, pulling him close. "I know, Finn. I know. I miss him, too."

"I should have stopped him."

Wick chuckled into Finn's shoulder-length silver hair. "Nobody could've stopped Emre Benld when an idea got into his head. Not even that thing dangling between your legs you both enjoyed playing with." That elicited a smile, a snotty smile. "Emre was single-minded. He believed in taking Lu Har down. He believed his daughter will right the wrongs of this world. What he did was the only thing he could do. Don't allow his actions to shape yours."

Wiping the ugly from his face, along with the tears and snot, he gave Wick a grin. "When did you get so sympathetic?"

"When I realized kicking your backside up and down the Ceveo wouldn't get you out of your doldrums." The lapin, while half his size, was stronger than most realized, and he pulled Finn to his feet. "Besides, I'm getting mighty tired of you and Lojen trying to out-mope each other. It's driving me mad."

"Lojen's mopey?" Finn's trousers had dust on them, so he began wiping it away, hoping they wouldn't be ruined any further.

"By the Ideal Daughter, needle dick, are you too lost in your own misery to notice your friends need you?"

A hand ran through the silver waves in thought. "I guess I have been a poor friend, haven't I?"

"To be honest, I don't think you have any friends."

"Ouch, now you're just trying to hurt me."

"Princeps Finnus?"

O Zenith, what now?

Finn turned to see an augur standing to the side. The dvergirish man wore the standard white cassock of the Scattered Shards, the insignia representing the Pentax adorning the breast. The augur's craggy face was bereft of beard, unlike most dvergirish men, but had plaits in his brown hair.

"Yes, Augur Puce?"

"The Golden Sword wishes to see you," Puce said as he nervously fingered the Beads of Aether around his wrist. The gemstones of aether glimmered in the moonlight, some bright, others dull. The augur's magic.

Finn blew raspberries with his lips. "Of course he does. In his reception room I take it?"

"Yes, Princeps Finnus. I am to escort you forthright."

"Guess I better see what he wants," Finn said to Wick. "I don't suppose you want to join?"

Wick grunted. "Not in a thousand lifetimes. Good luck, needle dick. See you afterwards. If Lojen and her are back, maybe I'll see if Ruane is up to swaddling that reamed asshole you're bound to bring back. She's been reading the Book of the Scattered Shards you know." His button eyes moved toward Puce. Contemptuously, Finn realized. Augur Puce must be the one teaching the younger hatchling of Tevun. "Trying to be a better drakken. Lojen's been beside himself with worry over her."

"Tell Lojen only I'm allowed to mope. But I'll come see him afterward, hear what he has to say." To the augur, "After you."

They left Wick standing at the Ceveo and the dvergir nervously skittered across the Upper City, walking fast enough for Finn to stretch out his strides to keep up with the smaller dvergir.

Upon coming to Gandtril, Titen had taken over a House villa, which House, Finn couldn't remember. It was a nice villa, one that the old Finnus Dunleith easily would've attended an expensive function or two at. Now, it was just another stone façade that housed a false sense of entitlement.

These Guild Houses knew nothing of sacrifice, of reaping the fruits of difficulties overcome. They were nothing but leeches. He hated them all.

Puce ushered him through the villa's front doors and up a set of circular stairs. The augur knocked at a door and after the muffled response, stepped to the side so Finn could enter.

"Why do you insist on goading me, Finn?" Titen said irritably as he loosened the knot of his tie. His brother stood in the center of the room, anger marking his face. "I swear you do it because you know you'll get away with it."

"Isn't that the greatest part about being the youngest son," Finn responded as he moved across the room and plopped into a chair, crossing his legs. A fire burned in the brazier; the heat made him start to sweat immediately. *Godsdamned wine has left me parched.* "I get to say whatever I want, and Mother and Father barely bat an eyelash. I don't envy you, brother-friend. Too much responsibility for a man of my tastes."

"Tastes of what? Wine? Men?" Titen sat behind his Calibrathian redwood desk and on it lay the Golden Sword of Kalderim. Titen fingered the crossguard idly.

The Golden Sword of Kalderim—the actual blade, not the title—was four feet of golden steel, sharper than any blade ever created. Forged by aether upon Eminence, the blade was more than five thousand years old and had never seen a dull edge. Within the fuller were runes of the Four Tenets of Aether. A braid of gold formed a crossguard into the shape of a semi-circle over the blade, and in the center was a brilliant peridot shard. In the pommel was another gemstone, but it appeared as if broken off.

A gift to Kalderim in the time of peace, only to be drawn in the time of war. The Golden Sword had only been drawn once: by Vitus Dunleith during the Fall of Eminence.

Finn's gaze lingered on the sword. *Was this what you sought to avoid, Em?* "We all need our vices when the heart lies in twain."

"It wouldn't have lasted, Finn. You're elfir, the Benld heir was humir. You had already lived forty-five of his lifetimes before meeting him. And Zenith willing, you'll live one hundred more."

"What would you know of love?" *If only you knew the truth, Titen, you'd know that was wrong to say.* "The only thing you've ever loved was that stupid sword!" It was a low blow and Finn instantly regretted saying it. Titen was unmarried, but that was because his beloved fell during the war with the Fallen.

Titen frowned, but instead of answering, he moved toward a nearby cupboard and pulled out a bottle of Calibrathian red. He poured a full glass for himself and downed it, quite unlike him. Pouring another, he took a sip before drawing one for Finn.

"We need to talk." Titen sat upon a couch near to Finn's chair, gulped the wine, then stared a long time at the half-empty glass.

"I've never seen you like this. Drinking, that is," he added when Titen glanced up.

A log crackled in the brazier. "Two nightturns ago, a legionnaire named Tonns deserted." Finn had heard. *Maybe this is what Lojen wanted to speak to me about?* Finn nodded, to which Titen continued, "The man, he h—"

His words were cut off as the door opened. In walked their sister and Augur Puce.

Although most of the nation of Kanja was, for all intents and purposes, a tundra, Gandtril and the surrounding area was more temperate. A chill still permeated the northern air, but Val wore a buttoned tunic with sleeves that ended above the elbows and a simple, yet current style of pant one might see amongst the Silk Circle of Drenth. Her mid-back, shining silver hair hung loose in slight waves as her bangs were pulled back behind her elfirish ears, braided intricately, framing her bi-colored eyes and pale cheeks. On both wrists were a number of gold and silver bracelets.

"Brother-friends," Val said in a low whisper. When Finn had been but a lad, he had wondered if she feared to raise her voice because the Pentax might not speak through her otherwise.

Titen stood and greeted their sister warmly, then motioned for Val to sit beside him on the couch. "We were just discussing the issue down in the Obelisk."

Wine to his lips, "I bet she already knows everything."

His bikromi sister smiled. "One of us must keep abreast of the happenings in this city. Especially when they concern the Divine."

"Forgive me, but I don't recall Father insisting you come here."

"I go where the Pentax sends me. Not our parents."

After the rebel victory in Drenth, there was nothing to keep Finn in the City of Sands. Had Emre lived, he would have stayed, but with his beloved's death, there was no reason. So back to Kalderim he had gone, along with his sister, the drakken of Tevun's brood, and, more importantly, Emre's daughter Brynn. The girl had gone to the Shards to complete her training.

And while Finn had kept tabs on her for Emre's sake, it hadn't kept him from succumbing to depression.

Vitus had decided to send Finn down to Gandtril, the thinking was to get him out of his funk if he had something of value to do, a task to perform. But it hadn't. And because of the daemons growing more and more adventurous in the Sea, the Golden Sword had been sent to shore up where Finn had failed.

Failure, always failure.

"It must be exhausting having the gods force your feet to move to Their dance whether you want to or not."

"You will not profane the Pentax like that, brother-friend," Titen cut in. "We are family. Much as it pains me to say, Finn, this family needs you. Kanja needs you. You've tasted aetheurgy, the Golden Throne can use that. This self-pity and lashing out needs to stop. We have a problem. This Tonns, from what Praetor Rignork says, is special. He's not a bikrome, before you ask. But the man had experienced dreams before."

"So do I, should we sit around and discuss my dreams as if they are true? Some of them aren't made for pious ears." He winked toward the dvergirish augur.

"Be serious for once in your life. What would the Benld heir say if the man you thought you killed last year had lived?"

In his blood he could feel his unused aetheurgy stir. He hadn't taken a hit of parch since Drenth, but the aether in his body threatened to rekindle nonetheless. Burn Form, ah, he remembered the first time tasting the fire of aether. It had been after meeting Emre. After their first kiss.

"Don't you dare bring Emre into this."

"Emre is," Val whispered, her bi-colored eyes lowering.

"What?"

"Your drakken friend and his sister brought the deserted legionnaire back barely more than an hour's turn ago."

"Good for Lojen, he needed something to do. Poor drakken is bored senseless. Shame he refuses to join me in the Lower City taverns."

Titen fought to keep his sigh in, his eye twitching. "Augur Puce spoke with Tonns before his punishment was meted," Titen interjected as if Val was moving a step ahead. Then again, Val was ever two steps ahead. To the dvergirish augur, "Puce, tell my brother what Tonns said."

Even though Puce was an augur of the Shards, he had become a sort of advisor to his brother. Finn had never known his brother to be a beacon of the Pentax, but times had changed. While it wasn't unheard of for a member of the royal family to rely upon the Shards for guidance, it was rare for a simple augur to have such a closeness, usually it was the Conclave who had the ear.

Not to mention that Puce was a dvergir. While dvergir and elfir were cordial, it wasn't often one left the Blades to become an augur.

Puce cleared his throat. "The man was distraught over the dreams he had experienced. Some say the Pentax speak through dreams when They wish to communicate outside of Vision Form, mainly to those who…" he stuttered when Titen motioned for him to get to the point. "O, yes, forgive me, Princeps Titen. This Tonns told me word for word his dream. It was unlike anything I've ever read about in the Book. Direct words are rare."

"Puce," Finn said, while the dvergir was harmless, the man had a talent for rambling, and he was running out of patience. As was the wine in his glass. "Please spare me the Good Book stuff. I've a headache already and this will only make it worse."

"He said, 'Only a Godsblood can kindle Eminence. Blood of Nightingale must bloom or aether will kill us all. Ever shall the world be broken. The protectors of the gods has been named. The Golden Sword will bear the Crown. The Aegis will sing the Hymn of War and stand against the fire. The Mantle of the Void shall merge the rift. And the Breath will breathe the Crystals into one.'"

"That's not subtle, is it?" Titen's brows shot up. "What," Finn continued, "we already know all this. Brynn Benld is the Godsblood and she wears the Eye of the Soul. That means she can use the Breath of the Soul. But she ran from her duty. She's out there doing codex cases for the Guild. Slaying drakes or so I hear."

"Did it ever occur to you, brother-friend, that her shunning the path we think she must walk is exactly what the Pentax designed for her?" Val asked. "She is the Godsblood, and she is the only one who can bring Eminence, the Crystal of Life, not the city, back to prominence. And Noctis from the Pit. But she wasn't ready. Perhaps still isn't. Lu Har forced her to act in the Temple of Mother Marrow. The Seal of *Terris* was broken just as it was always meant to. But who are we to say that she was prepared to seek the others. Maybe she needed to grow, and not only in aetheurgy, but her in her soul."

"Sounds like you have this all figured out then."

"The path to Eminence was never a straight line. You remember Canlon Carr. He always said he wished he hadn't been chosen so young. The same could be said about Brynn."

"Then why don't you go find her and let me be?"

"Brynn Benld is not our problem, Finn." Titen straightened in his seat, appearing uncomfortable even voicing such a thing. "We have someone keeping eyes on her."

"I've heard the rumors in the Lower City."

"Rumors these aren't, Finn," Val said, "Lu Har has returned. It's not just daemons. It's the Fallen himself."

He supposed he should be shocked, but Finn wasn't. "I'd say that is a problem for the Golden Sword to handle, don't you think, Titen. Better find this Aegis to sing the Hymn of War, just like this Tonns said, eh?"

But Val wasn't finished, "He has raised Solanine from the Pit."

"Or maybe a problem for you, Val. That one's not going to let your betrayal sit idle. Never should have shacked with that blooddrake."

"And they have stolen the bodies of Emre and Cadrianna from Drenth."

Finn spit out his wine.

VII

THE MOST ALLURING & DASHING NEENAH LEFLEUR

AN ALARM SOUNDED and Neenah LeFleur cursed. Quite loud, too, not giving a damn if anyone heard or not.

"Bloody godsdamned Nocturne! I told those boot-licking sons of whores to keep their pissing wits about them. This is the last time I trust those bloody dullards to do something I should have done myself! Pissing voidspawn!"

Finally quelling her verbal assault on the hobgoblin twins of her crew who promised there would be no alarm, Neenah peered over the crenellation of the massive citadel's upper wall and was explicitly shocked to barely see a soul moving in the courtyard. She had expected dozens, if not hundreds of guards to be pouring from every doorway the aged fortress had to offer, but instead, maybe six or seven stood within the bailey glancing around like soon-to-be milked cows.

She was disappointed. A smuggler of Neenah LeFleur's renown demanded better. She had rules she lived by, and one of them was: don't get caught because your godsdamned crew mucks it up!

Pressing the button on her *Aere*-spelled communication device at her ear, she barked, "Tris, get that godsdamned alarm shut off!"

"Aye, Cap'n," came the dvergir's voice in the comm.

Moonlight of the dullest red shone down upon the citadel; shadows of pitch blanketed the fortress as the everlong nightturn approached. The citadel was a behemoth of stone; all keeps in Qarthage were. Qarthage had outer walls like most mega-cities in the Mistlands, but they were so short and broken, the Sea flowed freely as if they were rocks along the shore during high tide. Crenellation atop ten-foot walls led to parapets and spires, arches of steel and stone. Courtyards of stunted cypress, gardens devoid of all colors, tainted by the lack of sunlight in the Sea of Mist. Battlements lined with rotating guns.

The keep was ominous to behold, even in the greenish shade of a day's light. The sun barely cleaved through the black mist with its eerie emerald tint in the city of Qarthage, and on nightturns such as this, where the moon was fully hidden, the keep felt like a tomb. The non-working aethecite generators left the stone fortress in murk. It was eerily silent and desolate.

The perfect cover for a thievery job.

"This is ridiculous," Neenah said through gritted teeth, waiting impatiently for the blaring alarm to stop. *Godsdamnit, where is Tris?* Glancing between the crenels, Neenah ran her tongue over her golden teeth. "Better not get bloody shot out there."

Neenah LeFleur, the brave and magnetic captain, took a deep breath and vaulted over the crenellation, landing smoothly upon the gatehouse's stone roof, shaking her shaggy brown mane and straightening her ascot as if she were being watched in aerescreen glory. Two steps and she leapt to the ground, rolling into a crouch. A guard from within the gatehouse came out to investigate but Neenah was already moving, clobbering him with a log she grabbed from the firewood pile next to the gate's mechanisms.

The man dropped unconscious, nary a sound escaping his chapped lips, but she was perturbed. Doll had missed one.

Sprinting across the small courtyard of desiccated trees and black mist, Neenah took umbrage behind a low wall. Peeking over, she noted the dithering guards from before, but instead of looking around like wide-eyed toddlers, they were on the ground, lying in odd angles. In one of the moon's lucky streams through the dark haze, Neenah saw darts sticking from the guards' exposed necks under their breathers; the darts contained non-lethal sleep poison.

Jumping the low wall, Neenah checked the cuffs of her puffy-sleeved tunic before moving toward the door at the far end of the bailey—the one that would lead her into a storage cellar and the holdings of her next big score.

But as she readied her lockpick, a guard pulled the door inward. The man's eyes widened behind his breather.

Before the man could draw his wheellock pistol, Neenah slammed her open palm into the lower part of the breather, shoving it upward into his jaw. The glass shattered under the blow and sent the man careening backward. The nimble Neenah LeFleur kicked the man's legs from under him and followed up with a punch to the temple. Like the first guard at the gatehouse, this man's eyes rolled back into the void.

The alarm finally stopped thundering. *About bloody time…*

With Tris dallying over the alarm and Doll neglecting that fool in the gatehouse, Neenah wondered if her crew was up to the task ahead. They godsdamned better be, otherwise she was going to kick that dvergir and giantess clear off her ship, so help her.

Slipping into the door and locking it behind, Neenah pulled a crumpled sheaf of parchment from her tailored waistcoat of checkered green and purple silk. Turning it right-side up, she examined the hand-drawn map in the aethecite lights that flickered lazily in dusty sconces. Besides the door was a small three-legged table and a stool. Upon the table was a half-eaten leg of chicken and a metal goblet of wine. Grabbing the goblet with bejeweled fingers and lifting her filigree-emblazoned breather, Neenah took a swig before shoving the sheaf back into her waistcoat. She dropped the goblet on the table then proceeded down the darkened hall.

"Thanks for the drink, friend," she said to the unconscious guard.

Her supple leather boots made no sound on the worn stones underfoot, which was good because they cost a pretty quadran up in Kalderim and she had been promised they would be silent as a feline's paws in the dead of nightturn. Neenah's gaze darted left and right as she searched the arched branches off the hall, most were darkened, not a light in sight. There were no guards either. According to her contact, the owner of the citadel was supposed to be out at some fancy party at a Guilder's villa in northern Qarthage, but truth told, she had expected more guards for a supposed important fortress formerly of the Fallen's Imperium.

A light appeared down one hall, causing Neenah to become a statue. A pair of muffled boots smacked lightly on the stone. She drew a thin-bladed knife from the sheath in her left boot, readying it should it be another guard. It wasn't.

It was Tris.

The dvergir skidded to a stop. "Cap'n, all clear. Alarm's deactivated."

Tris was a solid crew member if Neenah had to tell it true. The dvergir was stout and full of muscle, quick with a wheellock and quicker with steel. His face was as hard as the Forgemistress' Blades and he was tattooed from fingertip to neck like those of the Shards, except he didn't possess any aetheurgy. He had a bald head and shorn face of dark sable, the only bit of hair he curated was a silly tail at the base of his neck.

"Not quick enough, you squat prick tease," Neenah said. She was ready to let the dvergir have a lashing of the choicest of words, but another set of boots from yet another hallway made her eat said words. Doll lumbered into view, towering over both. "Clear from back that way?"

Doll nodded.

The giantess had the face of a cherub, was pushing nine feet tall, had curly blonde hair cut like a child's ragdoll, and a terrible scar wrapping her neck from an attempted hanging. She was also mute—which Neenah approved of because it was one less crew member capable of backtalk.

"Fine, let's get this done with. I'll deal with you bloody sods later." The three smugglers reached the end of the hall where it branched in only two directions. Neenah pulled out the crude map and stared at it in the dim light. "Fourth door on the right."

Tris scuttled up to the predetermined door and tested its handle. It opened without a fuss. "Half figured we'd have to pick it."

"A win's a win in Neenah LeFleur's book, hear?"

They filed into the room and discovered it wasn't an actual storage room, but a room filled with books. There had to be thousands of them in stacks so tall, they could topple at any moment, on silverstone shelves, in crates propped against the walls under the shelves. Thousands and thousands of books. The ceiling rose into obscurity but there was a window somewhere above and in filtered the wane reddish light from the moon, bathing the odd assortment of books in a crimson glow.

"What in Mother Marrow's skirts is this?"

"A library, Cap'n?"

"In here?" It made no sense, but then again, Neenah LeFleur was one who went with the punches. "Fan out. Supposed to be a fireplace in here somewhere."

"A fireplace? In a library?" Tris ran his hand over his bald pate. "What the void is this citadel built upon?"

"An old temple," Neenah said as she wriggled around a precariously stacked tower of books. If she brushed one the wrong way, the whole thing would go down, probably dislodging the four towers nearby and thus burying all three of them under leatherbacks and parchment. That would be an awful ending to her growing legend. "From before the Fall. To some god or another."

"'Some god or another'? There's only six gods, Cap'n. Which one is it?"

"What you bloody getting at, Tris?" She would have glared at him but the dvergir was somewhere in the maze of book stacks and with him barely four and a half feet in height, he was truly lost from view. So, she glared at the books instead.

"This doesn't look like a temple 's all I'm sayin'. Looks more like a library of some sort."

"Temples have libraries, hear? Stop talkin' 'bout libraries. And who cares what godsdamned god this was a temple for. Doll, you best keep those ungainly mitts to yourself, you're big enough as it bloody is." The mute woman grunted from somewhere in the forest of books. "Good, make sure you keep it that way. Check along the east wall. Tris, the north."

After a search that took far too long in Neenah's opinion, not to mention the copious amounts of dust sprinkling her fine tunic, Tris pipped, "Think I found it, Cap'n."

She found the dvergir hunched down beside a stack of crates he had pushed aside. "Am I blind, or do I not see a buggering fireplace, Tris?"

The dvergir adjusted the breather on his face as he ran a finger in the dust below the crate, his finger came back grey. "See?"

"No."

"It's ash, Cap'n." His fat, stubby fingers roamed about the stone wall. It was blackened, the stone, as if a large blaze had kissed the rock. "And the stone bears the marks of fire."

Neenah leaned closer and whistled through her teeth. "Now how in Zenith's trousers did you see that?"

"Been 'round lots of blacksmiths in the Blades. Know ash when I see it."

"Then where's the godsdamned fireplace?"

Tris shrugged. "Does it matter? Here's where one was, though. You said this was a temple at one point before the Fall, shouldn't expect a modern fireplace. 'Sides, what sort of temple has a fireplace. My guess 's this was a sacrificial brazier." He reached forward and pressed one of the stones. A hidden door slid inward. "And here's your secret staircase."

A smile broke her perfect cheekbones. "Good job, Tris. But when we tell this story, it was Neenah LeFleur who bloody found the secret stair, hear?"

"Anything you say, Cap'n." Tris gave Doll a smirk, but the giantess just shrugged her massive shoulders. "But I don't like this."

"What's that, now?"

"If this is a temple, and, if I'm correct, this was a sacrificial brazier." He pointed toward the ash and scorched stone. "The Pentax would never allow for sacrifices to Them. At least that's what the Vird in the Blades say."

"The bloody Vird know nothing the Shards don't, hear? You said it yourself, those pissing shard workers care only for the stones, not the Book."

"I knew a dvergir woman, she turned to the Book. Took her son to Kalderim and became an augur."

"So?"

"Just sayin', Cap'n. This don't feel gravy, see? This feels like the work of Nocturne."

"Hsst, don't be saying that name, you blowhard." Finding a torch in a sconce near the hidden door, Neenah coaxed a flame to life as there didn't seem to be any aethecite pipes in this stretch of the citadel. The wayward reddish mist danced down the stairs. "Let's get this over with before those guards wake up. Temple or not, Neenah LeFleur doesn't suffer a failed job. Not when a cache of aethecite is at stake."

Tris found another brand and made himself a torch, but there was unease about the dvergir. Tris was as stolid as they came, and he wasn't no religious man. She wondered what could possibly have spooked him. It was just some soot and old burnt stone, not like that cave monster from that one job on Sig Vorum…

The tunnel smelt of cadavers as she began to descend. Her contact said there would be a room or two at the base of the stairs, and when they reached the bottom, she found two.

"Tris, Doll, check that one," she indicated toward the left, then went into the righthand room with the shin-deep mist as company.

The room dripped with shadows and the torchlight didn't do much to persuade them to hightail it out of there. There were a few empty wooden crates and what appeared to be a large freestanding mirror covered by linen. To ensure it wasn't a portal to the Meadows or some such daemonry, Neenah pulled back the linen.

She tussled her shaggy hair and ran a finger across her rather perfect jawline before readjusting her filigree breather, letting the cloth fall back into place over the mirror. "Tris, anything?"

"Not yet, Cap'n. Just a stone altar and some statuary. Most faded with time. I don't have a good feeling about this."

"Keep looking, you ninny." *Where is it?*

Sitting on one of the crates, she took off her breather to bite at her manicured nails, chipping the purple lacquer. Was the contact's information wrong? Couldn't be, the old bastard wouldn't have played her for a bloody fool just for spite.

No, Neenah was missing something. And that irritated the pissing void out of her.

Getting to her feet, she walked along the walls, searching for any irregularities like the secret door above. Tris wasn't the only bugger able to glean things from nothing.

Nothing, that's what she found, though.

"Bloody buggering godsdamned bloody prick-sucking coin-juggling shit!" In anger, Neenah kicked one of the crates and it shattered into pieces and sent the mist splitting. Within the remains was a circular rung. "Well call me a 'vern's whelpling. Can you believe these people? Always in the ground with these safes, seems bloody lazy curation."

Pulling the rung, a stone slab gave way to a safe buried within the ground, a simple padlock design she knew she could pick in less time it would take for people to tell her how dashing she was; she wasn't a master at her craft for nothing. Part of her wondered why there would be a new, modern lock on a safe in an old temple from before the Fall. But the other part of her was focused on the job, and that took precedence.

Lockpick in hand, she set about springing the mechanism. Within moments, she had the safe open, gave the lockpick a victorious kiss and shoved it into her boot. With the safe open, Neenah brandished the torch and whistled her good fortune. Gold and silver quadrans glinted, diamonds and other precious gemstones reflected.

"Someone must've stashed all the sacrifices to the gods. Ha!"

Any other day, she would have shoved them into every pocket and bag she could manage, skip outside and gloat at the nearest tavern about how much of a master thief she was.

But this job was special.

She had to stop her hand from pilfering the wealth, and instead sought a hidden latch within the bottom of the safe. Finding it, she heard a click, causing her to freeze. *Godsdamn you, old girl*, Neenah cursed her foolishness.

At the base of the safe was a pressure plate.

Neenah bit her lip as she thought. She was a blathering dunce for not thinking about that possibility, now, it could mean her death if she didn't release it properly. There just was no telling what type of spell, poison, or projectile that might have been placed upon the safe. As if mocking, the mist of red-black churned faster.

An eerie silence fell over the room, unnatural even. She looked around, but there was nothing, just a growing chill.

"Tris, get your dvergirish backside in here!" The dvergir came rushing in, the giantess nearly stepping over her shorter lover. "Empty your pockets, need something to take the bloody weight of this pressure plate."

"Didn't you check it first?"

The chill in the room grew and her breath became visible, which caused Neenah to shiver. Tris nervously scanned the small room while Doll rubbed biceps as large as Neenah's toned thighs. Prickles formed along Neenah's spine, almost like something was probing her. She could almost feel the desire in the mist.

All in your bloody head. She shot Tris a heated glare. "Don't question me, hear? Empty, both you."

All Tris had in his pockets were knives, a few quadrans, and a crumpled rose, which he gave to the giantess with a loving smile. Gods they were vomit-inducing. Doll had a hunk of hard bread, a pair of wheellock pistols, a phallic-shaped rod—which made Tris blush—and a two-inch marble horse.

"Give me that horse." It looked comically tiny in Doll's enormous fingers, but the horse was carved immaculately; it truly was a fine piece, and solid stone.

A soft sound echoed in the eerie silence, like a nail dropping. Three heads snapped toward the sound, but nothing was there, only the shadows. And the cold. Neenah blew out a breath, sending ice crystals up her breather, as a reddish light bloomed in her periphery. So soft, when she looked again, there was nothing.

"Where'd you get this?" Doll shrugged shoulders twice Neenah's well-shaped hips. "I'll buy you another one." Doll nodded appreciatively. Neenah's hand upon the plate began to shake with the cold.

"Cap'n," Tris said through puffing breaths, his eyes never straying from where the red light had bloomed, "I don't like this."

"You don't like nothing that isn't stone, flying, or this giantess' baps."

Doll grunted but Tris didn't budge. "Uh… Cap'n, you might want to hurry."

Neenah glanced up and saw that Tris was pointing toward the far corner of the room. The shadows were now glowing dark crimson. A mist of pure ink seeped from the walls, rolling down the stone toward them, the cold seizing. Neenah made to curse, but before the words left her mouth, the red glow formed eyes in the shadows. Daemonlike in the dark.

Carefully, Neenah replaced the weight of her hand with that of the horse, then found the release lever, deactivating the pressure plate. The red-black mist and the eyes winked out, the cold retreating, the mist bleeding into the stones of the room's walls.

"What in bloody Nocturne was that?"

"Cap'n, we best get out of here."

Hastily, she pocketed the statue and pulled back the false bottom of the safe, where a small metal box lay amongst the dark. Within the box was the item her contact had sent her to find.

A queer chill overtook her as she stared at the object, a chill so cold it pierced her entire being. It felt as if the cold had wrapped around her heart, drawing out her life's essence. It pulsed, this chill, against her beating heart, latching on, taking hold. Queer, indeed.

Then it was over.

Shaking her head, she drew out one of her kerchiefs and wrapped the item carefully, put it in her waistcoat pocket, replaced the box, the false bottom, took a wistful glance at the wealth, then closed the safe.

"Let's go." But Doll crossed arms that could rip an orcir limb from limb, frowning down on her, even the noose scar around her neck frowned. "O, yeah, sorry." Neenah gave Doll the horse statue. She was a hard captain, but she wasn't a prick-sucker like many she knew. At least in the asshole sense of the term.

They retraced their steps through the citadel's storerooms, back through the bailey of still unconscious soldiers, then were jogging through the red-black mist of Qarthage.

Overcast and dreary, the city was clouded in red, hazy darkness. This close to the tomb that was Eminence, no matter the time of day, there were shadows upon shadows. The murk was the city's mother, and the Fallen's father while he had ruled his Imperium. Black-red mist filled the mega-city to the knee, vacuums along the walls of each citadel never drawing it clear. Even within the buildings, the mist followed.

Imperium-wrought automatons stood like forgotten statues on the streets. Powered by aethecite, the metal beasts, with their dome-like heads, gears and metal limbs, posed uselessly since the destruction at Drenth by that little bitty of a stowaway. Spikes and weapons protruded from their chasses, dangerous, they had been in their use during the Fallen's reign.

Now, were but a remembrance of a time better left in the past.

Before long, Neenah and her pirates were deep into the Sea. It was another few minutes until they came upon Neenah's airship. Her sleek vessel, her babe. And one of the few ships still taking to the air that wasn't on Guild business, because Neenah LeFleur didn't do jobs for mere money, no, she did jobs for aethecite. Anything to keep her airborne.

Her ship, *Marrow's Lover*, was narrow and curved at the bow, seventy feet in length and twenty-five from starboard to port. Two aethecite engines amidships, low of keel. It was the prettiest ship Neenah ever did lay eyes on. A rope ladder hung affixed to the rail as two mooring lines held the ship twenty feet off the ground. The hobgoblin twins, Zig and Zag, stood by the ladder.

"Get those lines ready for takeoff, Zig." She thought it was Zig, but she could never tell the two apart. "Scurry up and get that one-eyed bastard Roland ready to fly. And you did a sorry job on that alarm."

"I'm Zag, Cap'n," the hobgoblin cackled, punching his brother. Gods, they really needed to do something to separate them from the other.

"Then get your hide up topside!" The twins were incorrigible, but they were solid flyers, so she put up with them.

Neenah climbed the rope ladder, and moments later they were clear of the Sea, the engines spewing scree of burnt aethecite. She made for the pilotbox where Roland was behind the wheel.

The big first mate gave her a curious look. "Get it?"

"Godsdamned right I got it. Wouldn't be back otherwise. Almost lost a bloody hand, too." She hadn't, but Roland didn't need to know that. Stories that would enhance her legend needed some panache now and then.

"Lost a hand, Neenah?" Roland's rotund gullet rose and fell as he stifled some laughter.

"That's right you bloody son of a whore. It was Nocturne's work, for certain."

"Off to Krylen then?"

"That's the plan Neenah LeFleur outlined, wasn't it?" Neenah didn't expect an answer. Roland was a good man, a greater friend, and one of the best godsdamned pilots this side of Eminence. Neenah wouldn't think of going anywhere without the burly, one-eyed bastard. "Yes," she said in a more even tone, "to Krylen to get our aethecite. And get pissing drunk afterwards. And your mother was no whore." That was as close as she'd get to apologizing.

Roland's whole body shivered with a glass-breaking laugh. "Aye, Cap'n. You're getting soft, Neenah LeFleur. Must be that vicar you took a liking to last summer. He turned you into a lady, didn't he."

"The bugger most certainly did not, hear?" But she couldn't keep her mind from replaying a dirty thought about the vicar. "And bugger you for insinuating elsewise, you bastard."

"Aye, Cap'n, if you say so."

Neenah slapped the first mate on his shoulder and left the pilotbox, heading toward the cabins belowdecks. *Marrow's Lover,* while not the largest private airship, had four cabins, two aft and two forward. Her cabin was toward the bow. Once inside, Neenah undid her waistcoat and hung it upon a peg on the back of her cabin door. She pulled off the puffed-sleeve tunic, leaving her in only her sleeveless undershirt while she examined the dirt upon the tunic. Annoyed. She'd have the twins launder it.

She dug into her pocket and went to the small writing desk that was built into the hull. Atop the desk sat a wooden ship within a glass bottle, a token from her brother when she'd left their home at fifteen to try her hand at sailing. It was the only thing she had from her childhood. If only Merrick hadn't been such a brat, she might have been happy when he joined the Shards a few years later. Siblings were buggers at times.

Sitting upon the three-legged stool, she unrolled the kerchief and stared at the object for quite some time, licking her tongue over her golden teeth.

What in the bloody name of the Pentax could that old bastard want with a bloody bracelet?

VIII
ASHE

ASHE WALKED ALONE through the Harbor of Thieves toward the Beggars Chain to seek an old friend.

The City of Sin was lively. The multitudes of fishermen and sailors coming in from the harbor filed into the Red Moon District in vast numbers as the sun waned, dropping off hauls before heading for drinks and tosses. Singers in scant clothing on street corners crooned bawdy tunes, leading the would-be-sinners toward tavern and brothel in droves. Fire breathers and other acrobatic showstoppers urged men and women to part with whatever precious coin they could spare, all the while cutpurses ran amok pocketing quadrans not intended to be parted with. Without the aethecite aerescreens, seagandr-oil lights led the way with dreary shadows and through onerous alleys.

There was even a billboard freshly papered with a declaration of invite to *The Arbiter's Axe*. A grand affair the people of Oldport Basin would truly enjoy. A spectacle of the ages.

Blink.

A memory of running down the halls of arena before games Efan Nightingale announced. Games to the Pentax. Honor in bloodshed. Holding Jensa's hand while Efan spoke to the crowds.

A memory of Cadrianna, her mother as a child.

Blink.

"Why am I having all these memories of my mother?" She had had another three since getting the case from Maja Carr. All of them were her mother and her grandparents within Port Sin.

"WE WERE BONDED FOR MANY YEARS, DEAR BRYNN. THEY TOOK HER WOMANHOOD TO BIND ME IN ITS PLACE. YOU CAME FROM HER. THAT IS HOW WE ARE BONDED WITHOUT THE RITUAL."

"Was it painful, the ritual?"

"YOUR MOTHER, SHE'D NEVER TALK ABOUT IT. BUT I KNEW IT DESTROYED HER. EVERYTHING THAT WAS GOOD ABOUT HER DIED THAT DAY. EXCEPT YOU. YOU WERE ALL SHE COULD THINK ABOUT. HER DAUGHTER. HER BLOOD."

"And these visions?"

"YOU CARRY HER BLOOD, THE BLOOD OF NIGHTINGALE. THE FIRST WIFE'S BLOOD IS STRONG. I SENSE THIS IS WHY YOU SEE HER. TO HELP YOU UNDERSTAND HER BETTER, PERHAPS."

To better understand Cadrianna. She didn't really know her. But why now? Too many unanswered questions. "Who is the First Wife?"

Silence spanned in the abyss between her mind and that of the daemon blade. She almost asked again, but the Strix finally spoke. ***"NIGHTINGALE WAS THE FIRST WIFE TO ZENITH PRIOR MOTHER MARROW. SHE WAS THE RE—"***

"Listen sinners! Listen to the words of the Pentax," crowed an augur on a street corner, breaking the daemon's story. "Repent your sins or face the wroth of the Gods! For the Pentax sees all. Zenith does not condone your actions upon His hollowed earth.

Mother Marrow condemns your sins! Repent! Or you will become Nocturne's servant."

"THESE LOUTS PRETEND TO HEAR THE WORDS OF THE DIVINES," the Strix's daemon voice sounded strained. *"NOW BACK IN THE DAY, THOSE WERE TRUE AUGURS. THIS SO-CALLED SECT OF YOUR TIME IS A FRIVOLOUS SPARK FROM THE FORGEMISTRESS' ANVIL. A SCRAP THAT TWISTS AND FRAYS THE VERY FABRIC OF THE WORLD. LETTING THE THREADS UNRAVEL."*

"Don't change the subject."

"Sinners, you must repent!" Standing atop a rickety box, the man was clothed in the mundane cassock of the Shards that at one point must have been white, but the robe was in tatters and was barely held together by a hempen braided belt. His face was pockmarked by common disease, his hair as greasy as if he'd been baptized in cooking oil—which wasn't too far removed from the seldom, but highly profiled purification via seagandr-oil popular some twenty years prior. A lot of people died, hence why it was seldom used.

The augur's Beads of Aether were all shattered, which meant this particular holy man was no longer part of the Scattered Shards.

"I'D PURGE THIS WORLD OF THESE AUGURS. REPLACE THEM WITH TRUE PURVEYORS OF TRUTH. AND I'M NOT TRYING TO CHANGE THE SUBJECT, THANK YOU MUCH."

"You seem agitated. Feeling the pressure down there in the Pit? And it sure sounds like you are, Strix."

"TO QUOTE YOU, 'GO BUGGER YOURSELF.'"

The augur yelled at anyone who came close enough, pointing aggressively. He reminded Ashe of the pontifex maximus, a man named Merrick. A very zealous man. A harsh man.

"You, maid." The augur's focus was on a young woman in a pink dress, bosom propped up by a tight bone corset over a short skirt, no coat and no protective companion. The skirt wasn't in the greatest of shape, and she looked haggard, presumably after a long day performing acts which gave Oldport its namesake. "You spoil the very ground Zenith crafted with your brazen openness of sin. 'Til marriage should you wait. A whore, spreading your legs for truthless souls!"

The woman hurried by and the augur moved on to another target. This time it was an overweight man dressed in a fine overcoat, a plumed hat, pristine boots without mud or shit caking the bottoms. A low-ranking Guilder most like, heading toward the Bay of Thieves.

"You there, Guilder! A glutton filling your belt, becoming fat off the backs of the Pentax's working children. Eager to fill your mouth with food while many others go wanting every night. Judging and condoning from your houses on high. This is not the way of the Forgemistress! For the Forger of Life favors those who work for their livelihood, not growing complacent and content."

"HE SOUNDS LIKE PHLOX."

"Phloxy is worse."

The Guild member, fat and hoggish, and about as junior on the Guild's ladder as he no doubt was, quickened his pace. He pulled the bill of his plumed hat lower, skedaddling like a crab scuttling from a bird of prey.

The augur's rangy arms held aloft; face pointed toward Zenith's sky. "Sinners all, everyone who partakes in the spoilt fruit in this city!" Eyes lowering, he noticed Ashe waltzing by slowly, like a newly hatched turtle braving the monastic seacoast for the ocean. "You, vicar! A sinner amongst sinners."

Ashe stopped, staring at him stupidly while the man ranted.

"O GREAT, DEAR BRYNN. GOOD JOB DALLYING LONG ENOUGH FOR HIM TO TURN HIS ZEAL ON YOU."

"You're the worst of the lot in this city! Nay, on all of Zenith's earth! The Pentax's aether is not your plaything. Not yours to steal Their aether and use it to perform your black magic. Magic is the realm of the Pentax. Man is not meant for Their gifts. You aren't worthy of Their nature. Of Their powers. Steal it, you do. Unwarranted and undeserved! Your presence is an affront to the Pentax. Nocturne should have long taken you down to the eternity of the Pit. Sinner, I say. Sinners, the lot of you!"

Ashe didn't respond, she didn't have a mind to care about the diatribes of a madman, especially since he had once used aetheurgy via his Beads. She had known many like him over the years, losing themselves to their zeal. Like the augur's other targets, she resumed her path, the augur moving on, still raving about sinners.

"YOU SURE TOLD HIM."

Truth told, augurs without the Beads of Aether would not last long in Port Sin, far too much damnation for them to handle. Some caved and turned to sin themselves. Or, they were murdered in their slumber, which was far more common. Drunkards spewing garbled shit was one thing, but most in Port Sin couldn't tolerate an idealist.

Besides, Ashe had other things on her mind. Like trying to figure out if she could trust the word of Maja Carr. "Was she lying, Strix? About my parents and Solanine?"

"SHE WAS NOT. SOLANINE HAS BEEN REBIRTHED FROM THE PIT. I SENSED THE PASSING OF THE VEIL. BUT BELIEVE ME WHEN I SAY THIS, THIS IS NOT NOCTURNE'S WORK. THIS SMELLS OF SOMETHING ELSE."

"Of something else? Who but Nocturne would dare bring back Lu Har and that cu—"

"I'M NOT CERTAIN ENOUGH TO SAY. THERE IS MORE A-WING THAN THIS DAEMON CAN SEE."

"Don't you mean afoot?"

"I HAD WINGS ONCE. GREAT BIG WINGS. POWERFUL EVEN."

"Bah, don't lie, I bet you were nothing bigger than a thrush."

"WHO SAID ANYTHING ABOUT LYING? I ENJOY OUR BACK AND FORTHS. IT REMINDS ME OF YOUR MOTHER. CAD... SHE WAS ONE OF A KIND. TORTURED, TRUE, BUT MOST OF THAT WAS SELF-INFLICTED. YOU HAVE SOMETHING ABOUT YOU THAT DRAWS ME TO YOU."

"O yeah? What's that?"

"YOUR SUGARY PERSONALITY." Ashe groused a laugh as she pulled close a black cloak around her cassock, pulling the hood up and covering the Hammer and the Strix. *"BUT HONESTLY, I CHOSE TO BIND YOU. FOR CAD'S SAKE. REMEMBER THAT."*

"How could I ever forget?"

"AND YOUR PENITENCE WILL BE RETURNED FIVE-FOLD."

"You promise such pretty things," she said in a mocking tone as she pulled out her flask and took a sip.

Ashe walked down a gravelly alleyway between the shack-like homes of Barter Yard's shopkeepers and the rundown hovels of the Beggars Chain. Only an ill-kept wall separated the two districts. Nobody seemed to pay her mind, which was better than the usual acrimony the presence of the Shards caused amongst the locals.

The Beggars Chain wasn't truly filled with beggars, but more closely followed the saying '*beggars can't be choosers.*' Essentially, the Guild, like the Fallen before, bled citizens dry, whether by the various means of vice or by the exorbitant tax placed on the buildings in the Barter Yard. Thus, the cheapest rent was in the Beggars Chain by the vagrants who never fully left Port Sin's sins.

The hovels were so rundown, it was a small wonder they were able to stand, let alone the tenets be certain of four solid walls and a roof over their heads. If one happened to have a window still with glass, they were the cream of the crop in this part of the city. None had running water, none had fancy aethecite lamps, and not a single building had anything remotely resembling a bathhouse. People were lucky if they were even able to purchase firewood or seagandr-oil, therefore most resorted to petty theft of anything capable of burning for heat during the cold winters. And that included cow chips and dead bodies.

This back alley had the type of enterprises that were not considered prestigious for the Barter Yard, yet profitable enough for those in the Beggars Chain. Such as homemade drugs or backdoor apothecaries specializing potent poisons. The quadrans flowed in these alleys, but the passing hands typically didn't show face or use names that could be affirmed. Information was held at a premium in these alleys, a district within a city of vicious nights.

Shadows between buildings and in creaky doorways, the mist swam over the loose rock of the street. Most of the windows were boarded up, a few stray candles peeked through the slats. Overhead were awnings of moldy canvas, blocking out the moonlight. Trash and refuse littered the walk. Uncouth thugs leaned against walls sharpening knives or practicing with wheellock pistols, watching leerily. Others crouched beside those doorways, guarding the unmentionables inside with muscle and grit.

"Fuckin' vicar butcher," one grungy-looking ruffian spat as she passed.

More taunts followed.

"Gut her like she deserves."

"Not after we take her first."

"That witch'll suck you dry. Kill her fast and quick."

"Fuckin' gutter trash."

A normal man might be quaking in his boots, and an unarmed, unaccompanied woman frightened worse still, but Ashe had been in areas like this before. Slag's End in Drenth was barely a knot above this voidhole.

The building that was her destination was a four-story narrow thing that was missing mortar between the bricks in more than one place. The doorway was crumbling and had some of the rustiest hinges Ashe had ever laid eyes on. The door also didn't fit the frame, a gap at least two inches wide at the top and the base. Faint light trickled from within, but beyond, voices. And the heavy aroma of pipeweed.

A drug den.

As she pushed her way into the den, she came face-to-face with a couple of eager youths ready to prove their worth. One was all beef, his eyes as narrow as a blade's edge, his hair mussed. The other had a face full of pimples, a hooked nose, and a mean mouth. Both carried cudgels, clad in sleeveless jerkins and stained trousers.

The inside of the den was barren of furniture, devoid of anything but mats covering the decrepit floorboards, and a gaping hole in the center of the foundation. A rickety stairway led to the second floor, where a simple cloth drape hung between the doorframe.

Men and women, plus a few teenagers and wayward children here and there, were scattered about the floor of the den, eyes glazed over as they stared at nothing. Most were half-clothed, predominantly from the waist down. For those who ingested the intoxicating weed of the pipe not only made one extremely horny, but also rendered them on the canvas a few hours later when the high came down. The entire place was an overflow of yellowed auras in her aetheric-vision. A conglomeration of peridot joy, happiness to be put on their asses.

"A SHAME, THIS." Ashe could almost picture the Strix shaking its daemonic head at the scene.

One of the hoodlums—she dubbed him Narrow Eyes—put up a hand. "What you want?"

"I know you," the Pimple-faced one said. "Youse that Lady Drakeslayer, ain't ya?"

Narrow Eyes frowned. "The 'un who done kill't that vvyrm up in Drenth?"

Ashe smiled at the pair like they were old drinking buddies, though by their age, both struck her like they had just sprouted their first hairs on their coinpurses. "Evenfall, gents. I'm looking for Evzen."

"Gots 'n appointm'nt?" asked Pimple-face.

"I repeat, I'm looking for Evzen." There was a squeal upstairs as if someone had pushed back a chair. "Heard he runs here."

"Yeah?" The narrow-eyed man narrowed his eyes even further. They were essentially closed at that point. "What's Lady Drakeslayer doin' here?"

"Ashe. My name's Ashe. And I want to see Evzen."

Wrong choice of words as there was a plethora of swears from behind the curtain upstairs and a crashing of overturned chairs.

"Zenith's cock." She burned her aetheurgy and brushed past the two would-be-guards before they knew what hit them.

The upstairs room was a shaded yellow hue, a complete opposite color to the joy of the addicts downstairs. Fear. A square table sat in the center of the room, a single aethecite lamp overhead. Bottles, iced glasses, piles of quadrans, and some playing cards atop. Four chairs were akin, three thrown to the ground.

The two goons recovered and followed her up the stairs, swinging their cudgels like they knew what to do with them. She ducked under one, letting it crack against the other. A sprig of aetheurgy enhancing her strength, Ashe bashed Pimple-face in his pimpled-face with her elbow, breaking a few teeth and popping some of those pimples by force alone. She smashed her fist into Narrow Eyes' temple, briefly widening his narrow eyes before the guy flew into the table, knocking bottles and quadrans all over.

Both pathetic guards went down and did not rise. Served them right for attacking her like they could best her.

"DON'T GET COCKY. YOUR MOTHER ONCE TOOK OUT A FULL BUNKER OF YOUR FATHER'S REBELS. THEY WERE TRULY THE PERFECT COUPLE, WEREN'T THEY?"

There was another crash further in the building, this time it sounded like broken timber. Ashe cursed and raced through the doorless hallway where those playing cards had fled. At the end, a window, slats on the ground before it.

Ashe hopped through the window and saw three shapes climbing up a ladder across the alley. She took the ladder's bottom rung moments later. Her Soul Form coursed through her veins like fire licking the sides of a brazier as she climbed. Her marks up higher began swearing as they realized she was gaining on them.

One reached a landing and shattered the slats of another window. A frightful scream from the room inside indicated there were tenets within, but Ashe had caught a glimpse of the figure as they went through the boards, and it was not who she was seeking. The other two continued to climb, disappearing over the roof's edge. Ashe reached the top barely half a minute later.

Typical roofing style in the Mistlands was a terracotta shingle system, with a slightly downward slope. In mega-cities like Port Sin, running water was a luxury, so catching rainwater in huge barrels was the way to go. Usually, there was a balcony below the roof to catch the drainage. This building was no different, except this edifice had about one terracotta shingle row for every five holes in the roof, the barrels in rooms instead of on the balconies. And that made footing precarious.

The fleeing pair bounced across the missing rows of shingles, carefully, yet quickly. Ashe ran after, her aetheurgy guiding her steps as the aether of the terracotta shone brightly, illuminating emerald the stronger parts where she could put her feet.

The bigger of the two had reached the end of the roof and leapt. He cleared the ten-foot gap between this building and the one next. He turned briefly toward his companion, but thought better of waiting and kept running, disappearing across, probably down another ladder.

Clambering to the edge, the smaller runner took the same jump, but unfortunately, this one did not have the distance. A grunt came as the runner struck the ledge of the opposite domicile, struggling to find a grasp. The drop was forty feet to the ground below.

Ashe burned more aetheurgy and her muscles coiled as she prepared to jump, releasing aether as she sprung. The runic tattoos on her left arm flared as the Four Enhancements propelled her across the distance easily, landing five feet deep onto the building's roof. The shingles shifted underfoot, but Ashe caught her momentum as there were curses filtering through the hole as people below were pelted by falling terracotta.

Turning back toward the ledge, and seeing ten fingers clinging to it, Ashe peered over. Gripping with the determination of two cyclops fighting over a beautiful damsel was a boy, no more than fifteen. He had a round face, dark brown irises under thick eyebrows. His black hair blew in the wind, blinding him as he struggled to hang on.

"Hey, Evzen." Ashe planted a boot on the ledge between the boy's hands. She leaned with arm resting on her knee, considering the ground below, whistling, then coughed roughly. "Long drop down there," she said after catching her breath.

"Help me, you wench!"

Ashe's cloak flapped about as she snuffed her Soul Form. "I don't know. I'm feeling a bit disrespected here. Running from me?"

"Ashe!" The boy's left hand flagged, and he let go. "Help me! Please?"

"I don't know." She shook her head, prolonging the boy's agony. "I'd never run from you. That's just… shameful. Don't you think?"

"Godsdamnit, Ashe, we're friends!"

There were tears streaming down Evzen's face, left arm swinging, legs kicking. "You look pathetic."

"Ashe!"

"O, all right."

Ashe reached down and grabbed Evzen's weakening hand, lifting the teenage boy clear of the ledge with the help of aetheurgy. Evzen was a tiny thing, still not yet grown into manhood it seemed since she had seen him last. A little more than a year on the streets of Port Sin hadn't been overly kind to the kid. Though he was taller than her, he was essentially a stick wearing an oversized shirt and saggy trousers meant for an adult man.

After Evzen's feet comfortably settled on the roof, the boy punched her with all the strength his teenage arm could muster. "You wench! I could've died."

"Nah, I wouldn't have let you." He punched her again, but Ashe barely felt the blow while her aetheurgy burned. But the mist wasn't a fan of the assault, it swirled darkly around her ankles. "Glad to see you haven't changed much."

"And you're still a bitch," he shot back. "Why are you here?"

"HE'S NOT TOO NICE, IS HE?"

Lifting her bangled hand, she whispered, "Light." Instantly the diamond in the center of her palm flashed with *Ignis*, a small flame held aloft. Her aetheric rune of *Ignis* on her left bicep scorched as the aether summoned the spell. She bore the pain of her pulmo until it quelled.

"That's a nice trick." Evzen slid down the ledge, sitting with his back to it. "After you left Drenth and became famous for killing that vvyrm, I heard you got crisped up by a 'vern in Kanja like a seagandr-oil lit tree on Zenith's Day."

Evzen had once picked pockets back in Drenth for Elian, his bastard father. He was a sickly thirteen-year-old when she had first joined up with the Slag's End gang, his mother some unnamed whore working for the young, up-and-coming gang leader. And even though he was the son of the leader of Slag's

End, Evzen was treated no differently. She had always liked Evzen, even if he was a little bastard, a bastard in blood and in behavior. Evzen had a violent streak in him, and while one would think that would endear him to a man like Elian, it had the opposite effect. Elian was hard on his only son, and Evander had teased the little runt to no end.

So, it had not surprised Ashe when Evzen had run away from Drenth a few months before she had gutted Elian on Gargantua.

It was not long after she was back under Cyan's tutelage did Ashe learn Evzen had gone to Port Sin, having seen him while during a codex case in the City of Sin. It was as good a place as any for someone like him, bastard that he was. But now, it seemed a godsend for Evzen ran with Danma Dil's crew, so if there was anyone who could give her information on the Guilder who claimed the Beggars Chain, it would be the son of Elian.

Further still, she was lucky he didn't know she was the one to kill his father. Even if he thanked her, some people were just predisposed to seek vengeance for that sort of thing.

"Special case," she said, sitting next to Evzen, keeping the flame low. "I'm seeking rumors regarding your boss. And, no, not dead yet. Still trying though."

"I've heard those rumors. That's all they are. Danma Dil's shiny. Besides, why would she tell a grunt like me her grand plans."

"Humor me. What have you heard about the Guild? Any rumblings of discontent?"

Evzen picked a stray black hair from his mouth and flicked it away. "There's always discontent. Blogard had a business deal go sour because Derry fleeced him in a trade. Flubar's plantations have yielded shit-all for the past two harvests, blames it all on Kyllan. Klander sent some of his associates up to Drenth for

Pentax-knows-what. Nothin' came of it apparently, as they came back empty handed. Hyrro's wife filed for divorce, turned out she was fucking some guard. Hyrro challenged him to a duel. He won, but lost use of his arm in the process. Claims he should get special treatment down in the Swindler's Den. Ranhold's raking in the cash at *The Wheel* but feels like it's not enough. Hobb is off being Hobb, you know? Heard she's been doing some gutting down in the Bay, and not fish, mind. Heard she and Tified smuggled something interesting in a few days ago."

Klander sent people to Drenth? Why? Strix, what do you think?

"IF THE FEATHER'S THE SAME COLOR, PERHAPS THERE IS TRUTH TO MAJA CARR'S WORDS."

You and your bird analogies… "Interesting." She thought a moment. Ashe was hesitant to push further, but if one of the Guilders could be linked to Drenth and her parents. No, not her parents, Solanine. *Fucking bit—* "Guild up to any big jobs?"

Evzen wiped his nose on his shirtsleeve. "Nah, nothing pretty. Simple jobs trickle down, you know the lot. Ain't seen a big job in ages. Barely getting by, we are. Hey, for the trouble, you got any quadrans to spare?"

"That's all you want from me, Evzen? Coin?"

"Come on, what am I supposed to tell the others? You're a vicar, I need to tell them something. Grease palms, you know."

Ashe dug into her belt pouch and pulled out two quadrans, gold ones at that—the highest denomination of coin in the Mistlands. Much more than Evzen probably made in six months. The young boy coveted the coins greedily, his aura green with jealousy.

Holding them out, Ashe paused, fisting the coins. "Fine, but I need you to keep your ears and eyes open. Find out about any Guild jobs. The more whispered the better."

Elian's bastard held his palm out, waiting. "What kind of jobs?"

"Draconem type. I have reason to believe someone in the Guild is trying to find the firedrake lair." Evzen's gaze lifted toward Mount Bastard that pierced the sky some miles down the peninsula. "Get me some details, Evzen."

Ashe dropped the quadrans into his expectant hand. Evzen stood. "'Tis good to see you, Ashe. I'll see what I can find out. And don't trust no one. Ain't nobody you can trust in this city."

"You know me."

"Good." Evzen jogged across the terracotta shingles but stopped at the edge of the roof. Turning back, "O, I forgive you for killing my old da. Wish I coulda plunged the knife into his fat gut, but better to know it was you and not someone else." With that, Elian's son disappeared down the ladder.

"THAT WENT WELL."

Did it, Strix? Him knowing makes me question how.

IX

SOLANINE

AGITATED VOICES BURGEONED from around a corner, closer to where Solanine waited in the shadows created by spells of Void Form aetheurgy. The blooddrake was upon the upper floor of a gambling den of man flesh called *The Endless Wheel* in the mortal city called Oldport Basin.

"You don't thin—"

"Hush, little dove," a man said in a forced whisper, shushing the other with him. They rounded the corner, just two of them. "Not yet. You must be patient."

"To throw your lot in wi—"

"Elena!" the man growled. "Not here."

The man—one of the Guild who had taken up power after Lu Har's defeat in Drenth—was a girthy humir by the name of Olum Ranhold. He wore a bright blue half-coat with a bone white shirt underneath, gold trimmed blue trousers, and knee-high boots of cocoa brown leather turned below his kneecap. Long, greying hair was pulled back into a tail under a hat curved upward on one side, ending in a liberal plume of royal. A fine-looking sword with a jeweled hilt at his belt.

Fixated arm-in-arm with Ranhold was the humirish woman called Elena. She had loose auburn hair down her back over a laced corset and was about half the age of the man, late thirties as humir age at best. The skirts of her dress flowed a few feet behind her, a light purple in color. Her pale skin shone in the glow from the seagandr-oil torch sconces nestled into the alcoves of the hall.

"Fine," Elena said, voice oozing with irritation. A coveting prickled Solanine's exoscales, not one of mortal desire, but one of wanting the scales of this young humir. A longing. "You must be mad, Olum. Mad indeed."

"You knew that the day you consented to this marriage," he said, attempting a little bit of repartee.

But the jest fell on deaf ears. "If I'd known what that consent would drive me toward, I wouldn't have agreed to the union."

Ranhold grabbed her by the arm. "All will be fine, little dove. Trust in me. Trust in what I do. I do this for us."

For us.

Those had been the words Lu Har had used seven centuries prior when he moved to bring Solanine to his side against the Godsking, Canlon Carr. He had needed Solanine then, just as he needed the blooddrake now.

To hunt.

A memory flickered from across the void. Solanine had been there, but this memory was not the blooddrake's, but a memory borne of the scales Solanine now wore.

"Rinkhal is in Port Sin," Solanine said around a mouthful of wine. Port Sin was the local sobriquet of Oldport Basin. "Finally, you send me to a place I deserve. Rinkhal will be pleased we are prepared to move for Ignis. *Long has Rinkhal waited. What of Bliss'* Aere*? Will you now move on Kalderim? Or of Justice's* Aquis *in the Voidlands?"*

The Fallen turned toward her, his lover, "The time has come. The Gutter King would rend Drenth further than it has already gone. You know what to do."

It was almost a question, like the scales was some two-bit trollop sharing his bed, not the Imperium's most deadly scourge. All because of the blood in her veins. Nightingale blood. She wanted to scream. Strong as stone. Give nothing.

The memory returned back to the void and Solanine snarled.

"FEED IT, MY DISCIPLE. THIS IS THE KEY TO FINDING THE SON'S TEMPLE. SHE WILL LEAD YOU TO IT."

Solanine was not the ideal hunter because blooddrakes are light of foot and quick as a fae in flight through the Forest of Calibrath. Nor was it because of the aether Solanine could wield. No, what made Solanine the ideal hunter was because of the revenge burning brightly inside.

Revenge was a potent tonic to fuel destruction against those who had undone all they had worked for.

For centuries, Solanine had plotted with the Fallen to bring Eminence to their Divine. To free Noctis from the Pit and place the obsidian crystal in the heavens where it belonged beside Eminence. The Fall of Eminence was the first step to bring it from the shadows into the light, it mattered not that the Last Godsking had ended the war by thrusting the city from the sky, forever sealing the ruins behind the Four Tenets of Aether, the only entrance being a Godsblood. Eminence had been shattered, the Crystal of Life broken, the corrupted aether filling the land.

A victory for the Fallen, and ultimately, for Solanine.

The Fallen may have been the chosen of their Divine in the fight for the heavens, but Solanine was His fiercest warrior. Glory had been promised. The only need was to find the Godsblood. Though only rebirthed the first time four decades ago, Solanine had to wait half of that time for the child with the blood of the Pentax and Nightingale to be born. Two decades consolidating power in the Mistlands, readying for the end battle between the gods in the desert mega-city of Drenth. A place that served multiple fronts for their Imperium, for the Fallen to begin his final conquest. Atop Gargantua, they had ruled with an iron fist. The aethecite mines were theirs, the people defeated, the Godsblood born. All Solanine needed to do was to bring that child into the Fallen's hands.

Another memory sprung from the depths of the scales' abyss. A hated memory that had guided the scales in the years to come, the memory driving her to seek vengeance.

The elfir snapped his fingers, and the orcirish torturers cut her beloved's throat. Blood spotted her face. Tears of blood and salt went unchecked down her cheeks as she howled.

Then came a woman, a shade within the arches, holding her child, Brynn. Pale as a Kanjan blizzard, the woman's hair silver, pointed elfirish ears, dozens of bracelets affixed to her wrist.

"Master Lu Har," the woman said. Her gaze moved toward the chained Cadrianna, and she gasped despite herself. The woman had two different colored eyes; one entirely white, the other black as pitch. A bikrome, a seer of Bliss. A marked contrast to the darkness all around them. And the blood. Vision Form she'd later learned. "What of the babe?"

Brynn, no, not her daughter.

And Solanine had put the child in the Fallen's hands, only for the Godsblood—with the help of that same Kanjan elfir—to defy them all and send the blooddrake's soul to the Pit.

Revenge was the only thing that would quell Solanine's ever-present guilt. The guilt of failure toward the Divine and the obsidian crystal. Of believing in the virtues of the heart, of trusting that bikromi elfir for a second time.

Solanine would see the Godsblood and the bikrome dead, it was the only thing that drove the blooddrake now. No matter where, no matter how, the Godsblood would submit on her knees to the Divine, would break Eminence and restore Noctis.

For Solanine possessed the one thing the mortal child sought: her parents, their scales.

A similar memory drifted upward, another one that Solanine shared.

As her babe was taken from her, Emre's body not yet cold in death, a blooddrake slithered from the shadows. Snout elongated like a firedrake's but without the curved beak, finger-length pointed teeth. Grey-blue interlocking exoscales, larger on the breast and belly, smaller like a snake's along the limbs. Rounded protrusions covered the crest from nostrils to above the irises, morphing into a pair of two-foot long, keratin horns sloping backward and upward to a point.

"Master Lu Har," the blooddrake said, "what of this one?" The draconem's eyes turned on Cadrianna, a chill running through her.

"She's to be trained, Solanine," the beautiful elfir had responded. "Bathe her in Void Form. I want her for the Strix. Break her."

"Can I have her scales instead? They are so pretty." The Fallen said nothing. Head back, sighing as a taloned claw combed over the keratin horns as a lady might run her hand through her hair. Deviousness in those all-onyx irises. "As you wish."

Victory was once again within grasp, only then would Solanine's revenge be complete.

Promise me, master. Promise me I get her soul.

"You don't think I don't trust you," Elena said, snapping Solanine back to the present. "But I don't trust those… associates of yours."

Olum shushed her again. "Don't say that aloud here. You know they have ears everywhere."

"In our own casino?" Elena sounded surprised by such an admission as her eyes moved frantically around the hall.

It was a singular hall atop the establishment of coin-letting. There was nowhere for spies to hide, no branches, no balconies beyond the windows. Practically impossible to climb. Unless one had aether to command, or a blooddrake.

In a mega-city full of quadran-draining establishments, *The Endless Wheel* stood out amongst the other casinos in Oldport Basin. Whereas most of the gambling halls in the City of Sin were a new design, *The Endless Wheel* harkened back to the sprawling architecture of old Thullyr. The previous owner before Ranhold had been of a line dating back centuries before the Fall, and after, became one of the premier Houses of the Guild in the nations not of the Fallen's Imperium. Although the Fall had destroyed most everything, somehow—some say by divine intervention—the villa that would eventually become *The Wheel* had survived almost intact.

A multi-story villa, the walls were shaped like a series of steps, like a ziggurat. The outer step, with a gatehouse and House-paid guards, was done-up with graffiti like every other building in Port Sin, but every six to twelve feet of steps was a landing which was covered with colorful awnings. Each landing below was geared toward different types of gaming pursuits. Card games, high stakes larks of chance. Blood was even a source of bets; a boxing ring, knife throwing, and animal fighting. Bars situated on each. The villa itself was rectangular, and the terracotta roof was slanted. Like most Guilder's homes, Ranhold's rooms were at the top level, a grand room opening into a garden.

It was from this garden that Solanine was able to enter Ranhold's chambers to lie in wait.

Olum nodded glumly. "Even in our own casino. The Guild hears all." He grabbed the door handle and escorted his wife inside.

Letting go of the black cloud of concealing aether, Solanine shot from the shadows into the closing door, a mirror beside the doorframe showed a lithe humir with shoulder-length raven hair and all-onyx eyes dressed in a drake scale cuirass.

O yes, Solanine wore the scales of the scourge once called Cadrianna Benld after slithering from the Pit into the world anew.

Once, Solanine had sought a set of scales and kept them until they withered with age, cherishing the beauty that was the flesh of man. Using the scales to build imperiums, using them for desire and lust. But no longer. The Godsblood had changed everything.

Now, Solanine switched between scales as necessary to draw the girl out. Three sets of import; two humir—the Godsblood's parents no less—and one orcir from the free city of Krylen. But this set Solanine had craved since the invasion of Drenth. To good use, Solanine would put the scales of Cadrianna Benld.

To access the memories locked within of the bloodline of Nightingale.

"They say the Guild has turned an eye upon the city."

"There's nothing we can do about it now, Elena," Olum responded, speaking freely now they were inside their chambers, away from prowling ears about the casino below. Except for Solanine, of course. "The Guild will do what they will."

"They knew this would come to pass," Elena said, her face scrunched with annoyance. "Nightingale warned us. Before, you know, the Fallen cleansed his House."

I waste time playing with these… fools.

"SOON, MY DISCIPLE. LU HAR MOVES IN THE NORTH. THE DAEMONS ARE RISING. SOON HE WILL HAVE REGAINED THE OCULUS OF APATHY."

We dally, master. Lu Har, he promised me. I…

"THE GODSBLOOD IS COMING HERE, SOLANINE, TO THIS CITY. I CAN FEEL THE CHILD'S AETHER," the ethereal voice of the Divine said. ***"WHAT YOU MUST FOCUS ON IS IGNIS. FIND THE TEMPLE. FIND THE WAYWARD SON'S MANTLE, FOR TO PASS INTO EMINENCE, IT IS NECESSARY. FOR FLESH WILL ROT OTHERWISE. EVEN A BLOODDRAKE'S."***

Yes, master. After Your return, I get her. You promised me her.

The 'her' was not the Godsblood, no, but another soul Solanine had craved once before the Fall. Not anymore.

"DO AND SO SHALL YOU RECEIVE. THIS HAS BEEN PROMISED, MY DISCIPLE, FEAR NOT. BRING HER TO ME, BRING HER TO EMINENCE. SHE MUST BREAK THE SEALS. ONCE RETURNED, VALERIA IS YOURS."

Yes… Valeria Dunleith's soul will be mine to forever torture. You will rue treading on me, Valeria.

"We must be wary, little dove, we cannot go the way of Nightingale." Ranhold pulled off the many jewel-encrusted rings from his fat fingers and moved toward the fireplace. "Tified and Hobb have done their part." He pressed something upon the mantle, and the painting above swung open on silent hinges, revealing a safe.

"From the shadows!" Elena threw her arms up in exasperation. "Why do they not see the truth? Nightingale's sprat is going to bring ruin down upon us. Praise Zenith, Olum. Not only would the High Seat send the vicars in, but to fool the Scattered Shards is treason. We'll all get nicked for greed. They won't save your head this time." Elena turned away from her husband, throwing a fit like a wailing babe ripe off the suckling teat.

Ranhold grabbed his wife by the wrist and spun her around. "Which is why we need to continue with our plan. Klander is certain of this path."

"Are *you* certain of this? Klander was the one who stabbed Nightingale in the back." Elena's big doe eyes were wide with fear. "The Guild doesn't mess around, Olum. The Fallen didn't. Remember Drenth? Almost ruined all of us because of that man's grandchild."

The lord leaned in and kissed his wife. "Of course, Elena," he said, lip to lip. He moved up toward her temple and kissed both sides of her forehead. "Klander is on our side in this, he killed his closest friend. Besides, the Fallen is dead." He kissed her ear, running his tongue along its edge, she murmured with a pleasurable shiver. "This plan will work. You know what they said was found in Drenth's desert. Should we be successful at finding a Seal here in Port Sin, we will be rich beyond belief."

Elena pulled back, "They'll kill us, Olum. You know that."

"I have a bargaining chip." He kissed her. "Trust me." His flabby face crushed into his wife's.

These paltry humir were such fools. They knew not what power drove them like cattle. Aether coalesced around Cadrianna Benld's left fist, the right useless because of the fight in the Temple of Mother Marrow. Ire fueled the call of Void Form. Blood dripped from the runes carved into Cadrianna's breastbone and spine, and Solanine's entire body shook, the near translucent haze quavering as aetheurgy came alive.

The windows of Ranhold's chambers trembled, the stone around the glass shuddering. Dust poured from the creases. Solanine wanted to scream, but refrained, instead bellowing internally. With enough aether, Solanine could tear the casino down, brick by brick. Level the city if such a need was warranted.

"QUELL IT, MY DISCIPLE. SOON YOU WILL BE ABLE TO RELEASE IT."

Solanine let the rage reluctantly subside. A hunter had to be clear, had to be free of fault.

"A quake?" Elena asked, breaking off the kiss from Ranhold. The woman glanced at the window. "You think a vvyrm is nearby?"

"No, little dove. They are dead. In Drenth, they fou—"

Solanine had enough, the blooddrake moved from the shadows and grabbed Ranhold by the scruff of the neck, claws extending from the humirish flesh that was Cadrianna Benld, nay Cadrianna Nightingale. A gasp escaped the Guilder's lips as he went stiff. Elena screamed at the sight of Solanine's talons constricting around Ranhold's generous neck.

"Silence this whelping before I slit her throat," Solanine hissed.

Elena continued to scream bloody murder.

Void Form grew from Solanine's useless right arm in a blackened mist of corrupted aether, and the blooddrake sent wave after wave of the corruption toward the cowering woman. Aether of *Aere* borne from the air gusting through the open window silenced the woman's screech. *Aquis* birthed from the perspiration of a wine decanter swallowed her like a cresting surf. *Ignis* called from the brazier warmed her blood, making her sleepy. *Terris* from the stone of the villa shaking in a soothing motion under their feet.

Elena slid to the ground as a hammering came at the door, asleep. The pounding was incessant, demanding. Voices on the other side yammering for their lord to open, demanding if everything was okay.

Solanine leaned close to Ranhold's ear. "You've broken the rules. You were supposed to tell no one of this deal."

"But… I… she's my wife," blabbered the older, overweight man. "I cannot lie to her. Please… please don't kill her."

"That depends on you." Solanine's claws dug into the fleshy neck, blood drawn. Olum stifled a cry. "They are on to us. On to our plan. Should you wish your loving wife to escape such a fate, you'll need to stop the Shards-trained rats who are on their way to Port Sin. Especially the one they call Lady Drakeslayer."

"Lady Drakeslayer is here?" Olum gasped. "You said… that she…"

"It matters not what I said, you fool. Have you found the book?"

As the voices beyond the door grew more forceful, Ranhold nodded best he could toward a desk in the far corner of the room. Atop the desk was a thick tome, ancient by the mottled, worn cover, its pages browned with age.

A smile crossed the face of Cadrianna Nightingale, a predatory smile from the draconem lurking within. "The Temple of Brio will be mine. She mustn't discover the truth. She is the Godsblood."

The first time Solanine had interacted with the child Brynn Benld after she'd claimed the Eye of the Soul, the blooddrake had realized the Godsblood was nothing like the men Solanine had interacted with before. No, this young woman was different. A youthful vibrancy behind those all-white eyes, a luster that only came from one with the blood of Nightingale within. And seeing this scion of the First Wife in the flesh had brewed an odd concoction of wonderment and absolute desire.

It reminded Solanine of being in the presence of Canlon Carr.

All living creatures, plants, soil, and inanimate alike, radiated with aether. An aura of the colors of life borne of Eminence. It surrounded everything. The very spark, better yet, the bare essence of all existence. A single blade of grass was a minute green, but a field was a blinding sea of emerald. A drop of water glowed a molecular blue, while the ocean was a sheen of sapphire.

People, all races, even the voidspawn, were an infinite jumble of colors, their auras forever changing. All based on their mood. This is how the Scattered Shards described the use of Soul Form aetheurgy. Those learned men and women clinging to a concept a draconem fully understood from the first moment of hatchhood. Barely scratching the surface of what aether is.

But this humirish mortal, the Godsblood, was a beacon of aether, as blinding as if Solanine were directly staring into Eminence. Aether leaked from her flesh like tiny little wispy cirrus of smoke, a rainbow of mist. Anger, wisdom, joy, sorrow, fear, everything the race of man described as trains of thought, of feeling. The Godsblood should have been drowning in the swarm of essence, and yet, she was halcyon. No man since Canlon Carr had been able to withstand so much essence and not buckle under its weight.

Only draconem. Only a Godsblood.

It had reminded Solanine of the regal crystal of Zenith: Eminence. The magnificent crystal, the source of all aether. The Crystal of Life. The beginning and the ending of all things. The pinnacle of draconem ethos, the underground throne of the Hatch of Nightingale.

The prison of a god. Solanine's god.

"What do you want me to do, mil—" Solanine silenced Ranhold with a squeeze. The man almost went limp.

"Silence, swine. You know what I want for her."

Solanine released Ranhold and slunk back into the shadows of the room, waving Cadrianna Nightingale's left hand, drawing more aether. A pitch-black mist formed between Olum and where the blooddrake stood, enveloping, disguising. The wails from beyond the veil of Life sang their misery.

Olum slowly turned.

"Kill her," Solanine whispered from behind the wall of aether as the blooddrake ghosted toward the desk.

The foolish man could not kill the Godsblood, no. But Solanine had a plan, one even the Fallen knew nothing of. A prison made of aether, inscribed with the Four Tenets in the language of the void. It would house the Godsblood until the moment to break the Seals.

Solanine could almost taste the girl's pain.

"I… I sent people who can do it," Ranhold said. "Just like you ordered me."

But Solanine didn't care. Any thug Olum would send could never kill the Godsblood, but instead they would serve to waken her gift further. Only then will revenge be satiated. "And they failed to do so. Send more."

"I'll see it—"

The door crashed open, casino guards spilling into the room. One came forward, averting his gaze. "Milord, are you… do you need assistance?"

Ranhold regained his Guilder composure. "Whatever for? I was just showing my little dove a good time. As you can see, I tuckered her out."

Solanine grabbed the ancient tome and slid out of the broken door, aether hiding. But not before seeing the image of an object on the cover that would be their key into Eminence.

The Oculus of Apathy.

X
LOJEN

TRY AS HE might to avoid it, Lojen found himself glancing toward Tonns' mutilated corpse as it swayed in the feeble dawnbreak breeze.

The body of the legionnaire dangled from a wooden beam just outside Gandtril's southern wall, his arms held outward by thick coils of damp rope pulled tight. He hadn't known the elfirish man personally, but for Lojen, it felt as though he had failed another person in his growing list of failures. He knew he shouldn't feel that way, but seeing Tonns' corpse only served to remind him that he was not living up to the standard a wardkeeper was held to.

Father, did you ever lose a soldier because of your weakness?

'Soldiers die, son,' his father had once said when Lojen was a young hatchling. He had asked his father what it felt like during the war with the Fallen. *'Friends, comrades, enemies, brothers and sisters. That's what soldiering is all about. But every soldier knows that the life they chose to live might one day lead to their end. It is loyalty to a cause that makes them. That tests their limits, their mettle. Only then, will the Pentax deem their sacrifices worthy.'*

Lojen wasn't certain he could believe that; he hadn't then and didn't now. Death was too final of an outcome, especially when it could have been avoided. As was the case for Tonns.

The penalty for desertion in Kanja had been created after the Fall, when the Kanjan Legion was formed to keep the mist daemons out of the northern nation, and military law had become the bedrock on which the Legion was built. Breach it and your life was forfeit.

As both of Tonns' wrists were pulled taut, Primus Pilus Emont Landra had recited the epithets of the Legion, harkening no quarter for the disgraced legionnaire. The old elfirish legionnaire had stayed quiet, paying the price for his actions solemnly. A legionnaire's ordered death rarely ever got as far as starvation.

Tonns hadn't even come close. His screams came a few hours after nightturn, as the daemons and willowy wraiths of the Sea of Mist preyed upon an easy meal.

Lojen had stood upon the nearest crenel the entire night, a silent figure, pained on the inside. No matter how much it hurt him to watch, he endured. He may not have known Tonns the man, but Lojen knew duty, and duty demanded he stay. It was what his father would have done, what any wardkeeper would do for those honorbound to their wards.

Ruane had stood beside him for some time, but eventually she had wandered off to slumber, leaving him alone. After reading the edict, Landra had returned to the Obelisk. A few legionnaires lingered long enough to see Tonns cross over to the Meadows, comrades until the end. Praetor Rignork made no showing, neither did any of the Dunleiths.

By dawnbreak, Tonns' body had been picked clean, head torn away by some dark hunk of daemonized flesh borne of the mist.

As the green-orange sun pierced the dense fog of the Sea, Lojen was uneasy, his heart and soul filled with concern. Tonns' words had stayed with him, and he felt sure if he'd be driven to the same folly as the legionnaire. How did that fit for Honor and Blood?

Father… I don't know how you did this for all those decades. Living with the fear of failure…

'Failure is a part of life, son,' he could hear his father saying. *'Failure is what makes us stronger, what makes us grow. Do not fear failure. And do not let it rule you.'*

I can't…

The Legion encampment surrounding Gandtril was eerily quiet since dawnbreak, only the mundane sounds of the soldiers' daily pursuits giving serenade. Routine continued as if nothing mattered. Only military law and justice. Legionnaire training, the constant hammering of metal in the armory. All was regular. The mega-city itself was coming alive with the prospect of a new day. Beyond the Obelisk, the sounds of life met his earholes, people and aethecite-powered machines churning.

He needed to find his sister. Or Finn. The elfir had been as scarce as Lojen's cheer.

"Still moping, are we?" came a voice from behind.

Without turning, "I'm not Finn, Wick, I don't rise to taunts."

A paw patted the small of his back, for the lapin could not reach his shoulder. "You've nothing on that needle dick, Lojen. At least your moping has value."

The two, drakken and lapin, shared a laugh.

But Lojen cut it short. He glanced at his friend. "Still nothing?"

Wick shook his head, his frayed ears waggling dejectedly. "The man is killing himself. And there's nothing I can say or do about it. He drinks himself stupid. All day, every day." Wick tapped a paw to his heart, where his Bond rune lay. "I miss Ancantha..."

The Bond, a lapin form of aetheurgy. A rare rune of aether only those in Dervin used. Mates or siblings binding their bodies and hearts, gifting each other their abilities. It was like Shard Form and the Enhancements, but on a lesser scale. More personal.

Lojen had seen the Bond in action, back in Drenth aboard Gargantua. He hadn't known Wick was Bonded at the time, but he now knew that Wick and his mate Ancantha could call upon each other's strength if need arise. No matter the distance. It must be hard for the lapin to be so far from his mate, looking after a man who wanted nothing but the next glass of wine.

"Then leave," Lojen said. "You've done what you could. Ancantha is all alone in Alizarin."

"She's fine, drakken," Wick responded. "She spent years upon Gargantua, alone. She doesn't need me to bugger her schemes. I just miss her, that's all." Wick's button-sized eyes found his as the lapin sighed. "Besides, you know I can't."

Lojen nodded. *All too well, my friend. All too well.*

The two of them stood in silence for long heartbeats before Wick broke it. "Come, walk with me. Resande wants to see you."

Bowing his head, Lojen turned away from the deceased legionnaire and stole down the battlements after the lapin. His hubris was low as he was swallowed by the hustle and bustle of the fortress. Curling, black smoke filtered out the armorer's foundry, large gears turning rhythmically against the ringing hammers, the great forges' heat was stifling. Other legionnaires clashed steel under the watchful eye of other hard-nosed veterans. Hand-to-hand combat and wrestling. Beyond the walls in the city itself, he heard the continual vibration of thousands teeming with the morn. A melody reminding him of his duty.

As they neared one of the training arenas, a group of young children saw them and ran over, in their small fists were wooden practice swords. They all wore the colors of the Legion, but they were far too young to be full recruits. Squires, perhaps.

"I'm gon' be a hero just like you, Wardkeeper Lojen!" exclaimed a straw-haired Kanjan boy of two hundred and thirty as elfir age—or about a ten-year-old humir. The boy slashed the air with his wooden sword.

"Me, too!" cried another, this a girl with silver hair down to her buttocks, maybe a fraction older than the first.

The rest all piped up, confirming their eventual hero status.

Despite the dearth of promise within him, he couldn't help but smile at these children. Hope was always the strongest with the young. A shame he felt that these children would be faced with a shattering of dreams all too soon. His smile faded.

"You'd best keep practicing then," Wick said, coming to his rescue as the children eagerly awaited Lojen to formulate words, "because that stick looks like it needs a new master."

The straw-haired boy harrumphed. "It's only a toy. But I'm real good with it. Watch." He jumped around, slashing and hacking like he was in a raging battle. But then he caught his foot on the other, tripping to the hard earth.

The other children hooted.

Lojen scooped up the wooden practice sword, showboating with a vicious cut, then flipped the weapon, catching it by the tip before spinning it across his talons.

He could already hear his father's voice, *'That will not suffice in combat, son, but you already know that, don't you? A show for the children to ease their mind, that is the way it should be. And that is the way of a wardkeeper. Know thy friends, know thy foe. Protect where needed, show warmth where there is none.'*

Lojen helped the boy back to his feet, handing him back the wooden sword. "I've no shortage of faith that all of you will be heroes one day. But stay a child for as long as you can."

The children promised him they would and then ran off to practice their swordplay.

Wick was watching him closely, somber as it was. "You sound like him. Tevun."

Lojen was about to speak but a clash of metal drew his attention. Thankfully.

Three legionnaires danced back and forth, their daemon-killing spears swishing through the air. The trio wore the cuirass of the rank; both had their helmed breathers on. Eight-foot lengths of solid metal clanking against one another as the combatants moved. From their rushed movements, Lojen could tell the three were excellently skilled with spear and fight. A low hum filled his being, one that made him pause.

"Wardkeeper, how good of ye to join us!" a man shouted from across the arena. A muscular man with sweat beading his creased brow as he circled the combatants to join Lojen and Wick, his elfirish ears poking through tresses of wispy silver waves. His beard had a reddish tinge to it, uncommon for elfir of Kanjan. "See ye've got my message?"

"What message is that, Master Resande?" Lojen asked of the optio, or the primus pilus' second in command.

The optio's lips dipped into a frown as he turned toward the lapin. "Master Wick?"

"Don't look at me." Wick shrugged. "This drakken is impossible to move when he's brooding."

Brooding?

The elder legionnaire burst out laughing. "'Tis the truth, innit, Master Wick?" The man clapped Lojen on the bicep, for he towered over the man, though his bicep was robust. "We need ye eyes, wardkeeper. Ye keen eye for ones who 'ears the Hymn of War."

Lojen glanced at Wick, but the lapin was busy watching the pair of duelers. "Uh, sure, Optio Resande."

"Pssht, none of that 'optio' shit, wardkeeper. I ain't Landra, aye? Titles mean nothing to a man as old as me."

"Lojen, then."

"Aye, Lojen it is. Come, brother-friend." The man tried to encircle his muscled arm around Lojen. To Wick, "Ye be joining the practice this eve, Master Wick?"

The lapin snorted through his whiskers. "Not likely, Resande. I'm still sore from the beating I took yesterday."

The elfir grinned. "If only that were the case, Master Wick. Despite your size, ye've got the gift of the blade. Were I a younger man, I reckon I'd give ye a good run. But in the end, ye'd still best me, aye. Eamonn's arm is all black and blue, 'e could barely lift it last evenfall. Nothin' a few ales can't fix, though."

"I appreciate the lie," Wick grunted.

Resande guffawed. "Humph, cocky now, are we?" But then he pulled Lojen closer to the arena. "Tell me what ye think."

"Think?"

The optio laughed, his belly jiggling his cuirass. "Just watch, wardkeeper."

The trio of legionnaires moved about the arena, their spears moving faster than their feet. The one further to Lojen's left had long, almost white hair pulled into a tail. He was smaller than the one on his right, more lean, more narrow of shoulder. The legionnaire on Lojen's right was taller, and behind his breather was a bushy beard of blond. The third moved between the two, and he was also lanky, his arctic hair trimmed short over his breather but had a slight wave to it.

"I don't know…" His thoughts drifted as the low hum within his breast began to rise. Something about it he knew.

The bearded legionnaire strafed to the right before bringing his spear whirling around, attempting to catch the long-haired one off-guard while sliding the butt toward the shorter-haired legionnaire.

But then something strange happened.

The hum became a tenor within him and Lojen's vision wavered. Not so much blinding, but he flinched nonetheless. And in that flinch, his eyesight sped up, or so it felt. He saw the jab of the spear before the bearded man had completed his juke. Almost like a hazy shadow of the man performing the action before the real him did. In a counter, the long-haired man moved, his spear coming up to knock the other's away. And yet, the legionnaire was still on his back foot, his body contorting, not yet in position to be able to do such a maneuver. The third legionnaire darting forward with his own spear. Clash. Spears flying from all three soldiers' hands, spinning into the arena.

He blinked and the haze disappeared as the humming cut off. The song that filled him gone. *What?*

Before him, the three legionnaires fought, their moves happening exactly as he saw them with the shadowy forms. Their spears clashed, sending sparks as their weapons were flung from their grips, clattering into the dusty arena ground.

How? Father…

"So?"

Lojen shook his head as Wick elbowed him in the thigh. "I… what?"

"What do ye reckon, wardkeeper?" Resande asked.

"About what?"

The optio looked toward Wick. "Is he always like this?"

"You've no idea."

A grin. "The Golden Sword is worried about the princeps, goin' into the Lower City as he does, I reckon."

"Skirting his duty, you mean."

"Aye, Master Wick. Aye. Anyway, the Golden Sword wants some shadows for the princeps. Keep him out of the gutter, so to speak. Some hands to protect 'im from the scum of the Lower City. A few of the best, ye know?"

"Scum? Those are people," Lojen said, suddenly annoyed. "Same as you and… well the princeps."

The man seemed abashed. "Of course, no disrespect intended, wardkeeper." Nervously, the elfirish optio called a halt to the trio of fighters. "Alyx. Jaterral, Davel, here." The legionnaires hustled over, stopping on a quadran and saluting the optio. "These lot are my best, some of the best we've got to spare. What do ye think?"

Lojen was at a loss. He had no idea why Resande was asking for his opinion. He was a failure of a wardkeeper, barely able to keep his own thoughts together. He wasn't worthy.

'A wardkeeper who doubts is a wardkeeper who can be bested by a hatchling, my son,' he could hear his father speaking. A lesson from the past. *'You must be true at all times, for if you aren't, every truss falls. You are the foundation, they will look to you, your ward. Guidance is what you give, but stalwart and unmovable is what makes you. Give them reason to doubt and you are broken.'*

"Uh… yeah, I think they are good."

Resande's brow rose, beading with sweat. "Alyx. Jaterral. Davel. Off ye go." The legionnaires saluted once more and returned to the ring, picking up their fallen spears.

Silence hung between the optio, the lapin, and the drakken. What did they expect of him?

It was Resande who broke it finally. "Well, better get back to these recruits before they skewer themselves, aye. Before they can test themselves against a mist daemon. Wouldn't want to send word to Kalderim and their mothers they couldn't hack it in the Legion due to some daemon's tears. My thanks, wardkeeper. Master Wick. I'll send Alyx, Jaterral, and Davel to ye shortly after they get washed up. Don't want 'em to stink worse than the Lower City, eh?"

"We wouldn't want that now, would we?" Wick smirked with his buck teeth.

"No, Master Wick, we wouldn't, aye?" To Lojen, "Ya don't think ye could talk to ye sister into coming out here for a show?"

"Ruane?"

"She's been out here, Lojen," Wick said. "You'd know that if you'd ever get your snout out of your ass."

Lojen ran a talon over a horn. "I can try, but I don't think there's a man here who wants to deal with her. Void, even I don't sometimes."

The optio clapped his hands. "I'd give my left arm, I reckon, to see that drakken lass down here against our brave boys."

"You might want to keep that arm, she's a mean one."

"Aye, Lojen, aye she is." Optio Resande bowed his head and left the two of them to their devices.

After he'd gone, Lojen turned to Wick. "What was that all about?"

"You're a fool, Lojen, you know that right? You might consider trying to listen to your heart first. Tevun said he taught you right. Find it. There'll be your answers." Wick began backpedaling, "Best go find that lout Finn, see what trouble he's up to now."

The lapin left him standing like a dunce in the center of the fortress.

What was all that about, Father?

By the Pentax, he needed to find his sister.

Dozens of legionnaires filled the mess, raucous with laughter, even though the sun was fresh, the day had already started for most in the Legion. The banner bearing the Legion's sigil hung from the beams, illuminated by soft aethecite lamplight. He scanned the legionnaires within the mess, looking for his sister. Elfirish soldiers stuffed food into their maws, those off duty guzzled ale and mead, others slapping comrades on their backs, telling stories. Friendship and companionship evident.

But he didn't see Ruane.

Landra sat at the far end, an aide with him. The primus pilus' dyed black hair was ever slick with oils and his eyes narrowed when he noticed Lojen dawdling in the entrance, a contemptuous sneer curling his lips.

Lojen turned from the mess.

What am I doing here, Father? This place will be the death of me. Finn is lost. Wick is listless being stuck on the ground, being cryptic. Resande and those legionnaires. Ruane, who knows anymore with her. She blows hot and cold, ready to seek revenge, yet ready to throw down her longknife and take up the Book. And Brynn…

'Stay the course, my hatchling,' the voice of his father danced about his mind. A lie that built up his hope, the hope he'd regain his path.

But I shouldn't be here, he argued with the specter of his father. *I should be by her side. I promised. I should leave this place and find her.*

But would they do to him what he did to Tonns? He had sworn his oath to the Golden Throne. A somber thought told him they would. Most would skin him to save their own hides, but there were a few he trusted.

'You know what you must do, my son.'

"You look like a daemon has rattled you boneless, brother."

Lojen found Ruane sitting atop a barrel of water in one of the halls that led to the barracks, scraping the edges of her talons with the tip of her drakken longknife.

"Perhaps that is what the Pentax has set for me."

His sister cocked her head to the side. "Is that an attempt at humor? Because it wasn't very funny."

"No, it wasn't," he said, walking away from her. He suddenly felt the need to be alone, not with Ru.

Ruane hopped off the barrel and started after him, grabbing him by the arm. "You sound like a defeated prizefighter losing for the first time. This isn't you, Lojen. The Pentax has gifted you the honor of wardkeeper, don't step off the path because your faith has faltered. It is only through your faith that y—"

"Not the Book, Ru," he cut her off. "I don't want to hear it."

She puffed her exoscaled cheeks. "Maybe you should. Augur Puce has questioned why I harbor anger against you for your hatching before mine. And the more I thought about it, the more I realized I don't have an answer other than my pride. The Pentax chose you, Lojen, to be the heir to Father's horns, not me. It is not unto me to challenge Their choices. The same goes for you."

He spun on her, ripping his arm from her grip. One of his talons came upward like a parent pointing toward their misbehaving child. She was, in a way. This was not the Ruane he knew. "You weren't there in the Temple when the Forgemistress blessed me. You didn't hear Her words. She told me the Seals… broken shells, just forget it." He turned and stomped off.

Gods, why was he angry with her? He had no right to be, this was the Ruane he had wanted to see after the conquest of Drenth and their banishment from Merj. He had wanted the caring, carefree sister he had known for decades, not the angry, revenge seeker she'd become.

So, why now? Was it because of what Tonns had said about Lu Har's return? Was it because she had turned to the Shards for hope instead of trusting in the direct words of Mother Marrow?

The Forgemistress' words ran through his mind, flitting ahead of him as if taunting his failure. The words She had spoken to him after blessing him with the wardkeeper horns. Words that haunted him to this day.

'NO OTHER WARDKEEPER BEARS RESPONSIBILTY TO EMINENCE AS DOES YOU. EMINENCE IS WEAKENING, WITH IT, THE WORLD WE HAVE SO VALIANTLY FOUGHT OVER REMAINS BROKEN IN ZENITH'S JEALOUSY. WITHOUT A GODSBLOOD ASCENDING TO EMINENCE, WE WILL ONLY FEAR THE END. A GREAT TASK IS NOW AT YOUR FEET.'

What task, my Goddess? Anything for you and Zenith. If it is in my bones and soul, it shall be done.

'THE SEALS TO EMINENCE MUST BE SHATTERED.'

No! They mustn't. We cannot allow the Fallen into the city.

'THIS IS THE ONLY WAY, LOJEN TEVUNSON. THE GODSBLOOD HAS THE POWER TO BECOME GODSLAYER. IT MUST HAPPEN. SHE MUST BEAR MY HAMMER BEFORE SHE CAN WIELD THE AXE, MANTLE, AND CROWN.'

I can't. That goes against everything a wardkeeper stands for.

'HEED US. THIS IS THE ONLY WAY. THE SEALS MUST BREAK. AND THE DRACONEM GUARDING MUST ALSO PERISH FOR THEY ARE THE TRUE SEALS.'

The draconem? Those are Your favored children, my Goddess. How can I do this?

'YOU MUST CALL THEM FORTH. THE GODSBLOOD MUST SING THE SONG OF WAR. ONLY THEN WILL THEY KNOW THE GODSLAYER HAS COME FORTH. IT IS WHAT THEY GUARD FOR, LOJEN TEVUNSON. THEY AWAIT THE GODSLAYER. SEE IT SO.'

He had promised to see the Godsblood, his ward, do what she must to save Eminence. And yet, she was not doing any of it. Ran from it, even. He should have counseled her, stood beside her. But because she had shunned her destiny, he had stepped aside, letting her go.

No, he had failed as a wardkeeper. Had failed to uphold his promise to the Forgemistress.

"You're just being a Scurred Hatch," Ruane shouted after him, causing him to stop. She hustled up but he didn't turn to face her.

He couldn't. She didn't understand. She couldn't. Ever.

"Just like me with my rage, you must learn to control the warring of your soul. It will cripple you, Lojen, if you don't. It nearly crippled me. If it wasn't for that stupid humir, Emre, I… I would have been lost."

Father, what do I do?

'Remember who you are, my son,' he could envision his father responding. *'And she is your sister. She needs you just as much as you need her. This is just a phase.'*

Lojen barked a laugh, to both his father's perceived guidance and to Ruane. "By the Arbiter's bloody axe, you've really taken to the Book of the Scattered Shards, haven't you?

"You've said it yourself, brother, we are where the Pentax demands us. I was too blind to see it, too caught up in my need to destroy what destroyed our family. Who killed our father. Emre's sacrifice changed everything."

He glanced upward toward the greenish glow in the eastern sky as if seeking answers from the Forgemistress. From his father, even. "Near twenty years I tried to make you see reason, and all it took was a dvergirish augur…" He shook his head. "What is this world coming to?"

"I'm still your sister, you big dolt. I've just… what does man call it… matured."

Lojen could hardly contain himself, he roared with laugher. "If this is maturity, then I cannot wait to see what old age brings you. Besides, I thought you despised man."

Ruane's spikes over her eyes quivered, which if she were man, would mean her brows drew together in a curious manner. She grabbed his arm and began pulling him toward the southern gate. "Come, brother, we need to get you out of this place and do something even a useless wardkeeper can do."

"Where are we going?"

"Into the Sea with Augur Puce."

He skidded his boots to a stop. "I'm not going back out there. Besides, I need to see Finn, and te—"

"Don't be such a Scurred Hatch, Lojen," she cut him off. "The Dunleith princeps is lost in his own sorrow. I'll not have you follow after him."

"I'm not, Ru, it's just…"

"I'm bored of this mood you carry behind you daily," she said angrily, a little of the old Ruane bleeding through. "You need to get off your tail and do something worthwhile. There are people in the Sea in need of the Pentax's grace, maybe even the help of a lost wardkeeper. Who knows, maybe you'll find your place out there."

Lojen made to argue, but then realized he had no reason to do so. He had been floundering against the earth like a fish drawn from the ocean, lost and slowly dying. By the Pentax, she was right.

Am I truly worthy, Mother?

Of course, there was no answer, Mother Marrow was gone when the Godsblood had become the Godslayer. One fifth of the Pentax was gone, and so were Her vvyrms, Her guardians.

Perhaps there was something to Her final words, but he wasn't going to find out sitting around like a bole on a tree trunk.

XI
THE BEAUTIFUL SMUGGLER, NEENAH LEFLEUR

AS FAR BACK as Neenah LeFleur could remember, she always wanted to be the most famous smuggler to ever grace the Mistlands.

Let it be said, regardless of her status, she *did* know she was the most fearless smuggler in the Mistlands, that much was certain. And egoless. No one bloody enjoyed hiring narcissists for jobs.

An hour after dawnbreak—and a three-day slow flight from Qarthage to Krylen due to the rationing of aethecite—Neenah and the crew of *Marrow's Lover* entered a flower shop where a tough-looking ruffian stood near the door of the front and gateway into the underground of City of the Matriarch. The flower shop was in the far west end of the upper Kanjan free city and was a secret entrance only the matriarch and her top brass knew about, a refuge for the dregs governed by the bint in charge. The true leadership of Krylen. Those pompous Guilders knew naught of the underground. And if they did, then they bloody kissed the matriarch's orcirish ass just as well.

Luckily for Neenah, she *was* considered top brass, a well-earned respect if you asked her. Now, she just needed to become tippy-top brass, then the world would be hers.

Neenah paused in the doorway and dusted off the light snow from her shoulders. From floor to crumbling ceiling were flowers, saplings, and shrubbery not found anywhere else within the Mistlands. Greenery was a rarity in the southern mega-cities near the tomb of Eminence, for the Sea of Mist made natural life nigh on impossible. And Kanja was mostly ice and snow, so these flowers were specially grown right here in Krylen's greenhouses. Her nose drank in the scents of flora and herb in an attempt to drown out the odious stank of the mist forever burned in her nostrils. Pleasing, it was.

She adjusted the collar of her heavy woolen jacket and admired her image in a vase. Dashing, indeed.

"Mistress Neenah," the stout florist started. Even though it was the early hours of a creepy greenish sunlit morn, the dowager was awake and at work, plucking and trimming various flowers miraculously green and not dying. She was short, hunched, and had a coiled bun of grey hair fraying every which way. "How good of ye to grace us again. Will ye be needing a single or a bouquet?"

"A bouquet of black roses." The passphrase of the matriarchy. The old florist nodded appropriately, the tough at the door mimicking her affirmation. They both knew Neenah well enough, and it didn't make the need for a passphrase in her estimation.

Protocol, she thought. *Bloody, buggering protocol. Always, these bints.*

Roland stood beside the tough at the door chatting congenially as he shook off the snow mounding on his shoulders. The one-eyed bastard was friendly with all the doormen in Krylen; probably because he'd been one in his younger years. Doll and

Tris had their heads together, well, Doll had to squat since Tris was barely up to her waist. Young Alexina skipped straight toward the old florist, who beamed at the girl like a granny lighting up at the sight of her grandchild. Finally, the pair of hobgoblin twins skulked inside, trouble dancing in their yellowed eyes as their wispy tufts of hair were frozen solid like icicles.

Neenah grabbed one (Zag, she thought) by the cuff of his patchwork jacket. "Don't touch nothing, hear?"

"Yes… uh… Cap'n," the voidspawn responded. The other, Zig (yes, definitely Zig), nodded so thoroughly, Neenah swore she could hear the creature's teeth rattle in that misshapen skull of his.

"Good. Keep it that way."

"Fine day, Mistress Neenah?" The old florist handed Alexina a pair of shears and the girl began chopping away at stems, handing the flowers back to the elderly woman to arrange in vases. "Heard of a kerfuffle in Qarthage some nightturns past."

"Kerfuffle? Bah, nothing that greasy. A fun night dancing, I suspect." *Why's this bloody milkmaid bringing up Qarthage? She's not supposed to know of my job…*

The old woman's gums aped a smirk, a detestable sight if Neenah was any judge. "It was all over the aerescreens. Vicars showed up," she shook her head, the frays of her bun frolicking, "never 'xpected the Scattered Shards to go all that way, hmm? She's not pleased, O no, she's not."

Vicars in Qarthage? What the void was I sent in for? Involuntarily, Neenah patted the kerchief-wrapped bundle in her pocket. "Is she here?" Neenah didn't have to explain who 'she' was, for they all knew of whom she spoke. Invaris the Matriarch. If Invaris wasn't pleased about Qarthage, that meant the old man wasn't either, her contract holder.

"No," the florist replied in such a grandmotherly manner, the one laced in disappointment in the younger generations. "Hasn't been here in a month. Word is she's meeting with the Guild in Alizarin. The man's been runnin' in her stead."

"Alizarin?" One of the hobgoblin twins (Zig maybe?) was sniffing a bluish flower. Neenah slapped the back of voidspawn's head. "I said don't touch nothing!" The other hobgoblin twin cackled. She shot the pair a heated glare, but that didn't stop them from their amusement. Back to the florist, "She's not mentioned that to me."

That wasn't surprising as Neenah was only a smuggler, not one of the tippy-top brass members of the matriarchy like the old man who advised Invaris. But Neenah could be should she finish just one more job. By the Pentax, she was so close she could taste the honor. The quadrans would rain from the heavens and the name Neenah LeFleur would live on in legend. She'd be humble in acceptance, though.

Truth told, it didn't matter if Invaris was in the city or not, the old man had the orcirish matriarch's green-skinned ear regardless, and completing this job should get her on Invaris' schedule book whenever she returned.

"The man's been up twice this dawnbreak, yet." The florist had narrow eyes hidden amongst her many wrinkles. "Best not keep him on tenterhooks."

Neenah frowned. "Better not."

"This way." The pleb shop owner motioned toward the back of the building. She chuckled before taking the shears from Alexina. "Kindly thank ye, little one. Ye've an eye for the trade. Maybe I should take ye under my wing instead of leaving ye with these scoundrels. Hmm?"

Alexina glanced toward Neenah with big doe eyes, but then shook her head to the florist. "But I like them."

The woman laughed louder, her apron swishing as she shuffled away. "'Course ye does, my child. 'Course ye does."

Zig (Neenah was dead certain it was Zig) pushed his brother—both grinning ear-to-ear with those ugly hobgoblinly lopsided smiles—after the rickety woman, who pressed a plate beside the aethecite-powered cooler with her gnarled fingers and a hidden door slid open, revealing a circular stair. Neenah nodded to the hag after the rest of her crew began to descend, and the doorway sealed up behind them, leaving them in total darkness. The stairs were smooth and well-known to all. At the bottom, was another trap door, this time, instead of a dark passage, the door led to a city beneath Krylen.

Krylen above, was a free city in the northeast of Kanja. One of the furthest cities in all the Mistlands from Eminence's ruins, Krylen owed allegiance to no one, not even Kalderim. It was a city built on cliffs of ice all along the great ocean called the VVinter Expanse. The Expanse held no bounds, and the ocean was as violent as the land Krylen was built on, ice and glacier.

Most who called Krylen home were exiles of other mega-cities, those seeking asylum, or just about anyone who enjoyed blistering cold and frostbite. Farming was impossible within the ever-present tundra, the only means of survival were fishing and the dangerous hunting of seagandr in the Expanse. It was a deadly trade, but highly profitable. Law was upheld tenuously by a council of Guilders, but quadrans ran free because the matriarch was the true ruler. Anyone willing to brave the snow and the ice was welcome within Krylen. A free city in name and in virtue.

Below the snow was a city within the city. The underbelly was a series of interconnected caverns. Seagandr-oil lamps clung the cavern's ice walls, pipes wormed about the glacial stalactites dripping downward, and even during the era of aethecite, seagandr-oil was preferred, as it didn't burn hot enough to melt the glacial caverns like the ore containing aether.

A single street carved through the middle of the lower city of ice, with warehouses and taverns on both sides. Brothels and pipeweed dens. The lowest of the low made their home under the ice. Whether it be getting a toss in, dicing, or addling of brains, pleasures were abound for all the thugs, thieves, whores, assassins, and other dark denizens of Krylen. Deals made in quadrans and blood, lives and slaves. All in the name of Invaris.

It was a haven for people to make a name for themselves. A place where someone like Neenah LeFleur could thrive, where her name might become infamous, no doubt about it.

"Best not keep the old man twiddling his prick any longer," Neenah said. "You know the gist, be accounted for prior to evenfall. No show, you rat finks, and your backsides will be left behind. Got it?"

"Aye, Cap'n," came the half-assed reply from her crew.

They were eager to be off to find what pleasures they could, though Roland would stay with her, as would Alexina as the little bint was too young for a place like Krylen.

"Good. I've business to attend tonight, no fouling this up. I aim to leave first thing in the morn. Ain't got no time to waste on you sorry lot. Roland, you even-keeled bastard, let's go."

Roland was the closest thing Neenah had to a brother. Well, Neenah did have a brother, Merrick was his name, but Roland was more like one than her trueborn sibling. She liked Roland better by far too, mainly because her trueborn brother had unbearable morals, like becoming the pontifex maximus of the Scattered Shards and all. Merrick could preach all he wanted, no skin off Neenah's hide, but that type of thing wasn't for Neenah LeFleur, she cared only about quadrans and fame.

The first mate of *Marrow's Lover* was a few years Neenah's senior and kept a close cut on his grey hair, much greyer than Neenah's own, but that's because unlike Roland, hers blended better in the dark brunette, and it made her more distinguished. Sometimes gruff, but quick to joke, Roland was an honest and loyal man. Without the one-eyed bastard, Neenah probably would've long ago met the end of a hangman's noose.

But she'd never tell Roland that, lest the gratitude spoil her reputation as a hard captain to please.

"Don't forget to fetch the rations," Neenah said to Tris before the dvergir could disappear with Doll. "Especially the whiskey." That was another of Neenah's rules: always have enough whiskey aboard to drown out a bad contract.

Tris nodded, his unshaven dvergirish face grimaced, which made the crags and valleys of his cheeks more pronounced. He tossed that silly black hair tail over his shoulder and grabbed Doll by the monstrous lump she called a hand.

Doll had been a semi-famous arena fighter down in Port Sin, most giantesses were. But Doll wasn't as ugly as a daemonized mammoth like most giants, and her pretty face had led her to the noose, which was why she was mute and had that scar around her neck. Neenah had been present at Doll's hanging and was, in fact, the one to save her. Truth told, Doll's only curse was that she wouldn't bed some Guilder's sadistic son, which, to Neenah, didn't resort in the girl needing to end up feed for the crows.

Tris and Roland had already been part of her crew when Doll became in need of rescue. And, if she didn't say so herself, Doll's rescue *was* one of Neenah LeFleur's better stories.

Tris knew the Sea of Mist like he was born to it, even though most dvergir tended to stay underground rather than fly over it. But the prick-sucker was also the one to bring aboard the hobgoblin twins. They'd been servants to some distant cousin of his in the Blades, the dvergir had said. *Marrow's Lover* had been in good need of some cabin boys, but if Neenah had known at the time what irritation Nocturne had bestowed upon her with Zig and Zag, she would've kicked Tris in the seedpods right then and there.

Her attention turned toward the hobgoblin twins. "You two better mind your bloody business, hear? Last time I let you loose down here, half that job's quadrans went to paying for a new bartop. You keep your smarmy mitts off anything relating to fire. Do I need to godsdamned repeat that?" Zig and Zag both beamed with their voidspawn grins. "I mean it. I'll drop you both off in the Sea with naught but your hairy backsides and swinging peckers if you cost me more coin. Now be off 'fore I change my mind, hear?"

The hobgoblins cackled and skittered over the uneven stones of the road toward a building proffering cock fighting.

I'm too good to those bloody fools, she thought, figuring they wouldn't be heading for the cock fights to see roosters tussling to the death, but instead to test their mettle against one of the fighting cocks.

"You think we'll get to see Kalderim soon?" the young bint Alexina asked. "Roland promised he'd take me one day."

Alexina was a nervous thing, small and ill-suited for the life of a smuggler. She looked almost like she would break in a strong wind. Smaller even than the Benld girl who had stowed upon the *Lover* two years past. Alexina was brown of skin with soft, curly, short-kempt hair. Eyes the color of cocoa. Neenah had brought the girl onboard *Marrow's Lover* after Alexina had tried to steal her coinpurse in Alizarin. Neenah's soft-heartedness for orphan girls had gotten the better of her. Alexina wore a golden broach in the shape of a thrush attached to the lapel of her tunic. It was the only thing the girl never removed, polishing it whenever she'd a chance. Where she got such a fine bauble of jewelry, Neenah hadn't a clue.

But Neenah had a mind to keep Alexina out of trouble, whereas that Benld girl had brought no end of it.

"Never know, little bint." Though Neenah wanted to stay as far from Kalderim as possible. A lot of bad vibes, Kalderim. Mostly from her brother and the Scattered Shards. *Godsdamn, Brynn, girl, you could've stayed with us…* She sighed. "Bugger it, let's get this over with and get our pockets filled."

Neenah passed through the broken doors of Invaris' main roost and nodded a greeting to the reed-thin barkeeper. He slapped a perspiring goblet of ale on the bar and Neenah slid him a silver quadran. "He upstairs?"

The wafer-thin man nodded. "As always. I hear the old man's in a giddy mood today."

Neenah grabbed the goblet and took a long swig as she ascended the staircase to the second floor, tossing her heavy jacket toward her one-eyed first mate. A balcony overlooked the tavern, and it had a few small tables that were filled with shifty patrons. Roland and Alexina took up station at a nearby table, the young girl curled about the big man like a loving daughter out with her papa.

A tough stood next to the only hallway leading into the back of the tavern. The man had a wheellock pistol stuffed into his belt; a cudgel strapped to his hip. He eyed Neenah as she approached, but said not a single word, letting the smuggler pass before resuming his vigil. Neenah left the empty goblet with him.

Seagandr-oil lamps clung precariously to the plastered ceiling and threatened to fall from their moldings at any moment. The hallway was empty of souls, only her footsteps made any sound. A portal surrounded by shadows rose from the blacky depths of the hall, so dark, it felt as if the void itself had sprung from the gloom.

The door drew inward on hinges without a touch, and Neenah could see a shadow-filled room, only two lighted seagandr-oil table lamps forcing back the murk, a soft hum surging along the walls.

"LeFleur," whispered a voice that once might have been melodious but was now aged as if the owner smoked a daily dose of pipeweed.

Neenah strolled into the dark room as if she hadn't a care in the world. She shouldn't, care that is, but no matter how many jobs she did for Invaris' advisor, meeting him always gave her a queer twist in her stomach. She dared not show her weakness, though, hence the confident gait.

The old man sat behind a desk that had seen better days but was still probably better off than the man himself. He was Calibrathian elfir, or at least Neenah thought he might be based on the shade of his complexion and the slight upwards tilt of his ears, but she wasn't too certain as the tip of said ears were missing and most of his face was burned to a pulp. Perhaps by the acid of a dead vvyrm, perhaps by aetheurgy of *Ignis*, maybe just some bad luck in his younger years with a bad contract. Black-grey hair peppered the burnt scars of his face in what might have once been a full beard but was now patched. The same-colored locks spilled from his head in luscious waves on one side, the other barren behind a mass of scars. His eyes were hidden behind a bloodred cloth, no doubt burnt away when he had suffered whatever it was he had suffered.

In fact, Neenah didn't even know the man's name, only that he was the advisor of the matriarch, joining the orcir's inner circle some half a year's turn past. Invaris had many advisors over the time Neenah had pulled jobs, and the old man was merely the latest. He just happened to be the oddest of the bunch.

She found a chair in the shaded corner near the doorway and pulled it toward the desk. Straightening her ascot and daintily plucking at sleeves of her embroidered silken shirt, she sat, folding one leg over the other.

The blinded man titled his head, "Did you retrieve what you were sent to retrieve?"

"Yes, I godsdamned got it," Neenah snapped, letting her annoyance show. The old advisor always spoke down to her, like he was someone better than she. Neenah LeFleur was a proper smuggler, one with a reputation to boot, he was just an advisor, a new one at that. "Nearly got skinned for this bloody job, too."

"Always a way with words," the matriarch man said, his burnt mouth quirking as if it pained him. "Give it to me."

"Not without pay," she said carefully. Her boot began wagging nervously and she cursed her visible show of unease. Even if the man was blind, he had a way of knowing things he had no business knowing. "You remember the bloody deal."

The old man snapped his crippled fingers and a figure materialized from the shadows behind, hauling a heavy crate. Gods, Neenah hated when people appeared out of thin air. Especially with Invaris' new advisor, and especially when she thought they were alone. Weirded her right out. No way on

Zenith's green earth was this not the work of aetheurgy of some Form.

"Paid in full. Now give it to me."

Neenah stood, casually lifting the crate's lid. Inside were tiny, diamond-like pellets that reflected the meager seagandr-oil lights. Thousands of them. Aethecite. The ore that had ruled the Mistlands for over a century after the Fall of Eminence. Based on the size and depth of the crate, she calculated the aethecite within would power *Marrow's Lover* for a solid four months. A sizable bounty for such a straightforward job. She reached into her tunic and pulled out the bracelet bound in her kerchief, handing it to the old man, who greedily received it with trembling, singed fingers.

The old man unwrapped it, smiling, his scarred lips stretching taut. "A beauty it is. Drinks on Invaris tonight, LeFleur."

"Now that's what I call a bloody bargain." Neenah watched as the old man carefully lifted the blackened chain, turning the obsidian stone with an indent in the center toward him. There were four black steel rings affixed to the center stone by thin chain links. It was the godsdamnedest bracelet Neenah had ever seen, but it reminded her of something she'd seen before, she just couldn't place where. "Mind if I do some business here while we drink?"

"The Oculus of Apathy," the old man said, but then realized he spoke aloud, so he waved her away. "Do as you will, LeFleur. I treat my friends well, you know that."

"Aye, and I thank ye for it." She made to leave the darkened room with her payment under her arm.

"While you do your business," the man said while fingering the obsidian stone. To Neenah, it reminded her of an eye, except that the multiple facets of shorn stone distorted its appearance. The bloodred blindfold shifted as if the old man was staring at her. That queer feeling in her gut reappeared. "I've an offer for you."

"What kind of offer?" She paused, her hands gripping the crate of aethecite. Maybe this would be Neenah's break. She felt the thrill rise within. "Better be a big one, hear?"

The old man put down the black bracelet. "Biggest one yet, LeFleur. For you and yours. Do this, and Invaris will approve you."

By the Pentax, it was everything Neenah had always desired. Being made a matriarch woman would be the first step in her name going down in legend. She'd be remembered forever.

She couldn't contain herself. "What's the job?"

"Transport to Gandtril, followed by Kalderim."

Neenah's face fell, as did her hopes. "Bugger me with a sword tip."

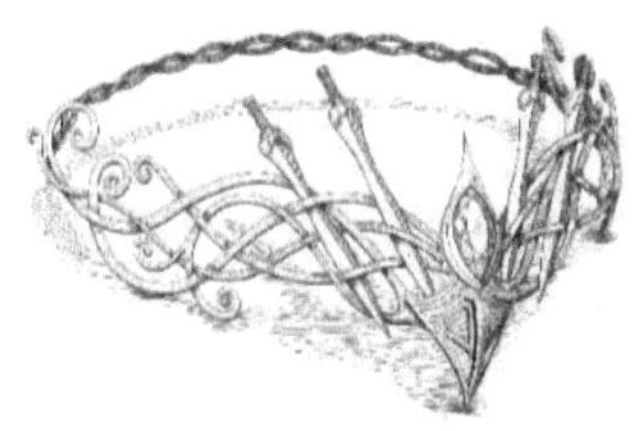

XII

FINN

"ON WIT'T, MEATBAG," the goblin garbled in broken common speak. "Ain got all ev'fall."

Finn lifted the throwing knife by the tip, held gingerly between his forefinger and thumb, his tongue sticking askew as he closed one dreamy eye and focused on picking out the correct target of the drunken three in his spinning vision.

He'd been in the Lower City for most of the day and he was well deep into his cups, at the level of drunk that makes one do some fairly stupid things. Such as bragging about leading a victorious rebellion against the Fallen, or more presently, trying to swindle a pair of gnarly goblins out of their coin purses.

The Cracked Pot was one of the Lower City's dozen of inns, all sharing the same look of faded timber and perfume of ale. The place wasn't special, none were in the Lower City, but that mattered not to Finn. He wanted to get drunk and drunk he had gotten. But *The Cracked Pot* did have some excellent baked apple tarts.

The inn's tavern was hellishly busy this evenfall. Lowborn of all shapes and dress crammed elbows to assholes downing the swill the rotund barkeep called ale and spirits aplenty. A place of debauchery of liquid. Serving girls in skimpy corsets, lots of legs showing, poor ensembles to be fair, made for coin from lecherous men. Not for men like Finnus Dunleith.

The mugs never stayed empty for long, that's what a man like Finnus Dunleith preferred. That and bladed sport.

Paint of stark white outlined a center dot on a wooden slab ten paces from where he stood. The goblin's previous toss had stuck just outside the dot, whereas Finn's first throw had barely clipped the outer ring, a fingernail closer to the center than the goblin's first wayward toss.

A second grotesquely-featured voidspawn slammed his mug of ale down on a nearby tabletop with a guttural laughter that sounded like pigs rutting. "Git 'em, Silantiv. This dandy elfir ain got what 't takes to beacha."

"Sell 'em to Nocturne!" someone yelled from behind, using one of the oft-stated phrases of selling one's soul to the Dark God of the Pit. Finn hadn't a care who said it but agreed with the sentiment. "Send 'em back to Filfangin broke as a virgin in a whorehouse!"

Finn wobbled on his feet, the throwing knife dropping to the ground. Nausea crept up his throat as he bent to retrieve the uncooperating blade. "Whoops," he gave the goblin one of his most handsome smiles. "My… bad…"

Silantiv eyed him with those beady yellow orbs he called eyeballs. His skin was a putrid grey-green. A dozen or more copper rings dovetailed between his nostrils and the bridge of his curved nose. His ears, pointed and parallel to the ground, were hairy, and one was notched from a scarred blade wound. Garbed in the traditional goblin armor of Filfangin, a bone-like breastplate, greaves to match, and a serrated sword at his hip.

"Come on!" Silantiv roared in irritation. The creature's quashed nose twitched above wickedly pointed teeth within black lips. He held his own throwing knife menacingly, pointing it at him as if to say *'get your ass in motion or I'll take pleasure in guttin' you, boy.'* "Git goin', dandy man."

He ran a hand through his shoulder-length, silvery hair trying to think of a zinging retort for a voidspawn speaking to him like he wasn't a princeps of the Golden Throne, but all he could come up with was, "Fuchshh off."

To be true, Finn believed he had a distinct advantage over the foul-smelling goblin, with his being practically a professional knife thrower and all, having been the rebellion's resident champion. Then add the Four Enhancements of his Burn Form still to fall back on. Despite not using them for months, he still felt the dam holding the parch back, ready for him to unleash the burn.

But when drunk, that *feel* didn't account for much when there were three godsdamned targets, and each blurrier than the next.

A tad brash, his first throw had been a ploy, a goad to let Silantiv think he had the better of him. As the goblins were jawing at one another, Finn released his burn.

A pyre filled his veins, a violent burning of all that he was as the parch reduced the dam into nothingness. A raging inferno that billowed within his body, within his soul, filling him with a fire borne of the Pentax. A searing of blood and flesh alike.

A memory of Drenth he quite savored, missed even.

The target came into clarity as the three became one in a silver glow, his eyesight focusing like looking in a spyglass. Growing as if he was standing directly in front of it, blazing in a sterling sheen. This was the Four Enhancements in all their aetheric glory.

Finn raised the thin-bladed throwing knife, uncorking a solid throw despite his inebriation, the burn of his Form rendering it null. Blade over tang over blade as it hummed across the tavern, smacking with a dense thud of splintered wood, embedding itself square in the center of the target, glimmering in his Enhancement as the knife shivered.

Turning, and nearly losing his balance in the process due to the parch running out, his Enhancements disintegrated as the parch ran its course, little as it was. He found Silantiv with fetid-smelling mouth agape, anger rising in those beady yellow eyes.

"Ya sandbagging sumbich. Ya che't me, ya did!"

"O shit!" Finn muttered as the goblin threw down the game knife and drew his sword. Jagged teeth of the saw-like blade portended doom for the would-be-sly princeps.

"Look out!" screamed an elfirish serving girl with a pixie voice, but before the girl's words settled into his liquor-addled brain, Finn tumbled violently backwards as another tavern goer thrust out his arm, shoving the third son of the Golden Throne to the ground.

Overhead, a second serrated sword whooshed, narrowly missing Finn's exposed back. Silantiv's drinking companion had drawn his own blade with the thought to skewer him. Opportunistic bugger.

The second goblin—whose name Finn couldn't recall, nor cared to—amid a hellish sneer, swung his sword at Finn's rescuer, a brutish half-ogre by the looks. And even though the half-ogre had a single arm and was drunker than a sky pirate celebrating a commandeered airship laden with rum, he was still a formidable fighter. And that meant the dumb voidspawn had overestimated his chances of victory. In fact, it was downright asinine of the unnamed goblin. For it meant his untimely death by the squeeze of a stout hand. Neck twisted as one-armed half-ogre held the limp goblin by a pointed ear and growled.

By that time, the entire tavern had erupted into a slaughterhouse fracas as a quake hit Gandtril. Drinks spilled on others, curses arising over said spilled drinks. Swords rattling out of their scabbards as dreg after dreg name-called, boasted, and stuck out chests in bragging taunts all while trying to keep their footing through the tremor. Punches thrown and tables overturned. Drinkers of all races, genders, and age screeched not in liquid pleasure but frustration, slamming whatever they could over the heads of fellow clientele.

An all-out brawl, the type of brawl a common occurrence in the Lower City. One that stirred memories of a fight in a desert mega-city.

Silantiv watched his brethren go down with a neck nearly spun clear from his torso. He unleashed a squeal undoubtedly designed to frighten, but to Finn, it sounded like he just stepped on something sharp while barefoot. Piss-yellow eyes glared at him while he sat dumbfounded on the ground.

The goblin dove at him, driving the serrated sword toward his gullet. Instinct roared to life because he was bereft of parch, but also accompanied said instinct was a pitiful squeak he would omit from the tale later. Finn rolled under a waist-high table, putting an overturned stool between him and the angry goblin. The beast's sword struck the ale-slick, wooden ground of *The Cracked Pot*, slamming into it, forcing Silantiv to struggle it free.

Finn crawled away from the snarling voidspawn who continued to rage about his cheating during a friendly knife throwing game.

A trio of shrewkin were battling the tavern's hobgoblin floor cleaner, as he wormed across the ground, trying to shake the liquor's effects from his brain. The hairy little bugger—who was a normally level-headed and congenial chap who Finn enjoyed drinking with after his shift—had cracked a broom over one of the shrewkin's head. And shrewkin weren't ever ones to back down from a challenge, especially a hobgoblin dumber than them.

Finn stumbled to his feet as Silantiv had apparently won the battle with the floorboards over his sword and flung the table aside, roaring some battle cry from Filfangin. The table crashed into some fist-fighting humir, throwing the men off-balance, who then pulled each other into an embrace to soften their blow against the ground.

Ducking, Finn was then attacked by what appeared to be a married orcirish couple. One could never tell the difference between the male and female green goliaths; all muscle, slimy hides, and smelling of weeks' old goat's milk sitting in the sun. Finn ducked a fist and kicked his boot into the one of the big orcir, then slipped between the two, and jabbed away with elbows and knees while the pixie-voiced serving girl leapt onto the other orcir's back, biting at its neck like a godsdamned harpy.

The goblin jumped toward him, sword arcing through the dim light of the overhead aethecite lamps that intended to lighten the mood, not bathe the melee now within. The sword in Silantiv's clawed fist came down, and Finn sidestepped the swipe deftly despite his alcohol-infused brain, giving him the opportunity to kick the goblin in the back of the knee just above the leather wrapping of the voidspawn's bone grieve. There was a snap of cartilage, the creature howling as his shinbone protruded from under the grieve made of another's bone, momentum taking it into a nearby booth. Mugs clattered to the ground, spilling ale everywhere as Finn properly set his feet in a fighting stance.

But as he continued about face to pummel the voidspawn goblin into tiny little pieces, a gunshot echoed throughout the tavern, followed by a loud, booming voice from up above the barroom, "Who the fuck started this fight?"

All eyes turned upward as one, including Finn's, a sigh escaping his lips.

Titen Dunleith stood with arms crossed, a smoking wheellock held in one white-knuckled hand. Wick peered out from behind Finn's brother's wake. Swords, daggers, and table-leg cudgels lowered, others clutching bleeding wounds. One drunkard downed a mug before coughing up bloody phlegm all over the tavern's floorboards.

Titen's voice carried above the silence. "Finnus…"

Finn straightened his tunic and took a step forward, but something slammed into the back of his skull. Down he went, down into the darkness of unconsciousness of the Pit.

When the ringing in his ears, and the varying shades of black in his vision had finally cleared, Finn swore he felt worse than being trampled by a rag of centaurs.

A metal goblet sloshed down in front of him. "Buck up, needle dick. Ain't nothing but a scratch." Wick sat across from him. The lapin's whiskers quivered.

"Feels like I've been hit with an aerovern's bloody tail," Finn grumbled. A tremor ran underfoot, not a terribly intense one, but enough to cause mugs to topple off tables. Finn grabbed his and foam spilled on the back of his hand, soaking his tunic sleeve, causing him to swear.

Finn was slumped like a sack of grain in one of the rear booths of the tavern, holding a dirty rag to the back of his head, staunching the blood that had come from the vicious blow the godsdamned Silantiv had given him. Striking from behind like a coward with a glass pitcher. He could feel the stickiness of blood dying his hair a gummy red; it would take ages to clean out, and that irritated him like no other.

All bravado, goblins were, until challenged, then they became nothing but craven pricks.

His half-ogre rescuer from earlier was dragging the dead goblin by the legs, for someone must've gutted him after he gutlessly clobbered Finn. Greenish-black blood streaked the floor as hobgoblin followed behind with a wet mop. It would probably take a few good deep cleans before the stain of that blood came out.

Finn spat blood in the dead goblin's direction, earning a glare from the hobgoblin servant and his mop.

The Cracked Pot had quickly settled back into the revelry that had pre-dated the brawl. Tables that had been the unfortunate casualty of drunken braggadocios were turned upright, the chairs not broken returned, and those in need of replacement found in the backroom somewhere. Patrons who were just beating the bloody snot out of another sat back down with mugs brimming with ale and spirits, forgetting all their bluster. Laughter roared as some wheat-stalk thin man struck up a chord on a battered lute, singing through a few newly missing teeth. The pixie-voiced serving girl, who had a bruise forming upon her cheek, swerved through the crowd with ale and apple tarts.

The lapin took a long pull from the mug, froth dribbling down his furred snout. "Spilled milk at this point, needle dick," Wick said, "they're both seeking passage to Nocturne now. The Master of the Pit will sort them out. Besides, you have bigger problems at hand."

Of course, brother, O brother. Come to keep me out of trouble, eh? Finn took a sip of warm ale, wishing it were wine instead. "Where's Titen? Cleaning up the mess, I take it?"

Wick pointed behind, where Finn noticed the Golden Sword wore a sheepish look as someone yelled at him, gesturing wildly with gold-banded arms. The tavern's owner, his whiskered cheeks ruddy as he yelled.

Near to where Finn and Wick sat, three legionnaires stood stoically. The trifecta wore the standard cuirass, but instead of watching the Golden Sword, they were staring directly at him in the booth. One had a long tail of white hair, one a bushy beard, the final one short, wavy hair. Weapons strapped everywhere. Alert.

"You might want to take it easy from here on out, Finn," Wick said. "See those three? Yeah, they're gonna hound you from here out. You gotta wipe your ass, they'll be there to help. Jaterral, Alyx, and Davel, them. Get used to seeing their mugs. Titen's not happy, needle dick. Not happy you've been spending so much time down here in the Lower City. They're gonna keep you from it. Three of the best, according to Resande. So get used to hearing the word 'no'. I know it's not a word you're familiar with."

Finn's brother finally finished his conversation with the tavern owner, a bag of quadrans exchanging hands. The Golden Sword's glare found his, a single twitch of an eye.

A withering glare, the twitch saying all the words necessary.

Finn grunted. "It seems I've no choice. Lovely."

XIII
LOJEN

RUANE SAT CROSS-LEGGED opposite Augur Puce and another augur named Indigo while they tended a sick man deep in the Sea of Mist. Lojen squatted nearby, trying to be supportive of his sister's newfound interest but his patience was waning.

The augurs—on a mission proclaiming Zenith's word—and the drakken siblings had happened upon this small hamlet in the Sea between Gandtril and the lower slopes of the Filfangin highlands, one of many such villages down south of Kanja in the nation of Altreyia. The untamed marshlands threatened to swallow the handful of huts built upon stilts at any moment. They had come upon this village an hour's turn ago, the sixth such village since they had left Gandtril, and they had quickly discovered the poisonous pulmo raged unchecked. They were swiftly succumbing without remedy, without Zenith's light shining upon them. These people's plight reminded Lojen of Brynn Benld.

But to the pair of holy augurs of the Scattered Shards, these people needed help.

Augur Indigo, a Kanjan elfir who appeared older than dirt, put a hand to the sick man's forehead, the beaded bracelet of the

Shards dangled from his bony wrist. "Ease, brother-friend. Zenith will watch over you. Augur Puce will help guide you to the Meadows."

The ill man mumbled incoherently.

Ruane leaned close, whispering none too softly for she had no knowledge of quiet, "Watch this, brother."

"Watch what?" Lojen rolled his eyes.

He was a loyal servant to the Pentax but even he knew how hopeless the augurs' attempts would be. He had seen plenty with the pulmo in Krylen while they had lived there, and this man was far and away worse off than those. And those poor souls in Krylen had not lasted long. Besides, the augurs had tried, and failed, to heal similar cases in the previous six villages.

To Ruane, he kept his tongue firmly behind his sharp teeth lest he bite it in half.

Augur Puce's plaited brown hair hung limply over his breather's glass shield, tiny rays of yellow representing He Who Fathered the World's sun fogged the glass with each exhale as he drew back the sleeve of his robe, showing his own bracelet with the Beads of Aether. It was looped around his wide wrist multiple times, fifty Beads in total. Shards of crystal—garnet, peridot, sapphire, and emerald—were round, many of them bright and colorful, others darkened with visible cracks in them.

"That's his Beads, Lojen," Ruane said excitedly. His younger sister was nearly one hundred and fifty years old, which was considered a fully matured drakken. In humir years, she was almost twenty-five, so it was humorous to see her light up like a child beholden to a nightturn story told by their father.

"Yes, Ru, I know." She scowled in his direction. "I've read the Book before, you know? And we've been out here for days…"

While the aetheurgy of the untainted warriors held no bounds, an augur's Shard Form was far more restrictive, meant to heal and protect only, not to be used elsewise. Although the Four Tenets of Aether fueled all four cadre of the Scattered Shards, it was the augurs who promoted the benevolence of the Holy Couple, shunning the darker arts associated within the realm of Life.

Like the inked runes on a vicar's flesh, the binding of aetheurgy to a person resided in the Beads. But unlike the inked runes, an augur did not need a deep connection to the aether in the mist and did not need to rely on the poison within to make their aetheurgy burn. All an augur needed was the devotion to the Pentax as the prayers became their spells, the Beads Their physical manifestation. This was an augur's Shard Form, crafted by the Holy Order of the Vird. Once a Bead is cracked, its aether was gone forever.

Augur Indigo hovered his hands over the sick man, Puce doing the same. There was a pop of gemstone, a soothing essence of aether washing over both augurs and the ill man as one of Augur Indigo's Beads splintered as the spell of healing within came to life.

Ruane jumped like a little child seeing fireworks for the first time. For Lojen, he could taste the growing aetheurgy; the warmth of Life itself enveloping them. A soft song sung within him, no words, just a delicate hymn. He had used the wardkeeper horns, he knew the touch of aether, had heard this melody before. His sister, however, leaned forward, wonder filling her lavender eyes, her mouth gawping.

Of all the things for her to show interest in, this was the last I'd expected. He glanced through the haze toward the greenish glow in the eastern sky. *Is this what you want me to learn, Forgemistress?*

Sweat dripped down Indigo's aged forehead, his knowledgeable brown irised, sapphire-pupiled eyes flashed; same with Puce's slate grey, ruby-pupiled eyes as one of his own Beads broke, releasing the aetheric spell to combine with that of the elder augur.

Lojen looked upon the sick man as the aether draped him, a clear-ish sheen just above his flesh, pushing back the dark grey mist of the Sea. The song of aether grew in Lojen's mind, a sweet sound, almost mirroring the taste of a freshly plucked mango back on Merj. The sweat that had perspired upon the ill man's face was gone, and the flesh was not pulled tight in pain as it had been moments ago. The fever he was suffering appeared to have broken.

Even Lojen had to admit the aetheric use of the Beads was breathtaking to behold, regardless of the outcome.

"Is he healed?" Ruane asked of the augurs after their spell faded, their warming aether dwindling, leaving Lojen feeling empty as the song died, like someone stealing a security blanket from him. The Sea of Mist grew darker once more.

"Only the fever," Augur Indigo answered, examining the Bead that had broken. It had been an emerald shard, and the gemstone was blackened, a crack across its surface. "I'm afraid the pulmo has drawn him too far from Zenith's light. Soon he will enter the Meadows." Indigo glanced toward Puce. "Recall your training, Augur Puce, about the nigrum pulmonem."

"The mist is our punishment for Canlon Carr's betrayal against the Pentax," the dvergirish augur recited rote words from the Book of the Scattered Shards for the umpteenth time. So many, in fact, Lojen could recite it alongside him. "Breathed long enough unhindered, the aether within the mist will bring upon the nigrum pulmonem. Even those borne of Zenith's light are at risk. Many years can transpire before the mist eventually breaks down the body's natural resistance. Those who stay too long in the mist will all succumb to its nature."

Augur Indigo leaned over to pat Puce's stocky shoulder in congratulations. "Very good, dear Puce. The pontifex maximus was correct when he said you were advanced beyond your age. Very few dvergir become augurs."

Lojen could sense in Puce the power of the praise. From what little Lojen knew about the non-warriors of the Shards, most fully-fledged augurs were half Puce's true age. Puce being dvergirish and not even fifty, he was still considered a young pup, barely more than a matured man when compared to a humir. Perhaps that was why the augur and Ruane got along, they were both looked down upon by their respective races due to their immaturity.

"I just want to help people, Augur Indigo. It is what He wants of me."

"It's what all those who are called to His service want."

The man lying between them took in a shuttering breath, a cough escaping as blood dribbled from his chapped lips. His eyes opened wide, staring at nothing as the cough abruptly cut off. The man's chest deflated. Dead.

"Now, we must say the final words over this man so his soul can rest easy in the after," Indigo said as he closed the man's eyes with skeletal fingers. The elder augur spoke to Ruane, "I hear Augur Puce has been teaching you the prayers on this mission, young drakken. Join us in the power of our prayers if you feel ready."

The augurs' voices joined together in prayer, Ruane's guttural tone chipping in with the words she apparently had memorized. Lojen kept silent. "Guide him, O great Zenith. Take thy child unto Your breast. Lead him unto Your holy realm. Forever to be by Your side."

With the prayer complete, Augur Indigo pulled a raggedy blanket over the dead man, whispering further prayers before taking an eon to get to his feet, practically cracking every bone in both his legs. The elderly augur shuffled over to a small hut where another sick person waited patiently against the wall of the dilapidated home.

"Why didn't you join the Vird, Augur Puce?" Lojen asked as the short dvergir straightened his white cassock. He did not know why, but he was suddenly interested in Puce's story. "You don't see too many dvergirish augurs."

"Every dvergir worth our weight in ore aims to serve the Pentax, Lojen," Puce started, his craggy face flushed behind his breather. "Most are content honoring the Forgemistress under Her Blades, and the highest honor is to join the Holy Order of the Vird. But I wanted to guide, not create."

The Holy Order of the Vird were the most renown smiths in all the Mistlands. Living upon the tallest peak in the Blades, the Vird took the gemstones mined in the mountains below and crafted the holiest of treasures using aether. Most importantly, the Vird smithed the tools used to ink Shard Form aetheurgy into the tainted and untainted warriors of the Scattered Shards, as well as the Beads of Aether. And other implements for the ingeniators.

"I hail from the hold of Vermillion. My father died in a tunnel collapse when I was but a boy," Puce said. "My great-great-grandfather worked in the Maw, believe it or not, when he was a young lad. Before you know. Was one of those lost to the xillianth beasts before the Fall and the Broken Quarry became no more." Puce sighed heavily. "But my father followed in his greatgrandpap's footsteps anyway, even after migrating to the Blades after the Fall. Rest his soul in the Meadows."

"The Maw?" Ruane asked, her interest in this nightturn story grown even stronger.

"You know of the Maw, Ru." She glared at him and he rolled his eyes. "The famous story of Durm Moonblade and the xillianth queen in the Broken Quarry? The one Father told us many nightturns as hatchlings. The one you kept asking for because the legendary moonblade was lost for all ages, as were those drakken broods."

"O… that Durm Moonblade?"

"You're incorrigible, Ru. How many drakken do you think are named Durm Moonblade?" He shook his head.

The story of Durm Moonblade going into the Maw to fight the xillianth queen was one of legend amongst the hatchlings of Merj, mainly because the drakken broods in the Broken Quarry were forever lost as they were swallowed by the Voidlands; near half the population of drakken at the time of the Fall, plus entire dvergir holds. A lesson, the story of Durm, as well. One to always be on your guard, for betrayal could be the downfall you least expect. Even from those you think are allies, for they are the silent betrayers you don't see coming. They are the ones that bring you to your knees the quickest.

Ruane grumbled something under her breath that sounded familiarly vulgar.

"A month prior," Puce continued, "my father had found a rare amethyst in an abandoned mineshaft. He claimed that Mother Marrow intended he find the stone to help turn our family's fortunes around. We were paupers, never knowing wealth. Most in Vermillion, including Queen Cattal Oastlar, live but humble lives. We were no different. My father, after finding that stone, had gone back into the same tunnel, believing he would find more. But on that fateful day, the tunnel caved in. They dug and dug, but we never recovered his body.

"My mother was beside herself with grief and she turned to the Book. The glories of He Who Fathered the World consumed her, as it did for me. Grief closed in around us, but through the Book, I learned that living by Zenith's grace, that is the true path to happiness. I moved to Kalderim as soon as I was old enough, for the Golden Throne is the barbican of Zenith's light. I didn't want to remain hidden in the depths of the Blades like my father. Helping the unfortunate, such as him," he motioned to the dead man they had failed to heal, "is the only way to truly serve Zenith. A repayment for His belief in me."

Hearing Puce's story, Lojen realized he had judged the dvergir all wrong. They had more in common than he could have ever envisioned.

"Before I left Vermillion," Puce said, "I went down to that tunnel, to pay my final respects to my father. And you know what I found there, aside from the closure I felt toward him, I found that amethyst." Puce dug into his belt pouch and produced a small purple stone, part of it was a dark burgundy. Dried blood, Lojen realized. "I chose the name Puce to honor my father, for he was the one to truly set me on the path to the Pentax."

All those raised to the cassock were given a new name, Lojen knew. The renaming not only declared all previous titles, roles, and heritages null, but inferred that only the Scattered Shards mattered from there on out. For vicars and augurs, their names were derived from one color of the Shards. And a vicar was also given a moniker which best represented them. For the quaestors, their name change was also as a way for the criminal to draw penance for their crime to the Pentax. A constant memory of what they've done to displease the gods.

Lojen had never understood the practice of the Shards renaming, but now he supposed he did.

There was a thunderclap in the distance. Lojen and Ruane shared a look, his pulse beginning to race. The song within his breast began to sing, low at first, but then rising. Then there was screaming, high pitched and fearful. It was no ordinary thunderclap, it sounded like a massive cracking of Beads, as if a thousand breaking all at once.

"WARDKEEPER!"

"Augur Puce?" he asked, confused by the call of his title from within the Sea. The dvergir gazed off into the distance. Face darkened within the breather, knowing more, knowing the unseen.

A whoosh of wings circled in the Sea above them. Lojen ducked reflexively. The wings flapped, sending the mist reeling. A great roar accompanied the maneuver. A drake's call.

"Firedrake!" Puce screamed.

"No," Indigo said as he came close, squinting into the mist toward the shadowed bulk above them. "A daemon."

Lojen felt dread creep throughout his body. A daemon firedrake. *O Zenith, that means… it can't be, that drake is dead.*

"WARDKEEPER! I FEEL YOU!"

"Go, drakken. Back to Gandtril. Hurry you must. This place is no longer safe under Zenith." Indigo shifted on creaking knees riddled with arthritis. He was panicked now; scared Lojen could see. "Hurry, you must go now!"

"Augur Indigo?"

"Daemons rising at last. We've long awaited this."

"I'm staying with you," Augur Puce said, thrusting his satchel into Lojen's arms. Within were all Puce's earthly possessions. Except the amethyst, as the dvergir held it tight in his fist, of which he handed to Ruane carefully.

"Come with us," Ruane begged.

The augurs—at first panicked and scared, now were beacons of calm—turned, serenity in their posture.

"WARDKEEPER! YOU CANNOT HIDE FOREVER FROM LEMURES! AEGIS!"

Lemures? "Augur Indigo?"

"Noctis has risen, Lojen," Puce said instead. "Sending daemons bound from within the Pit. I know of this Lemures from the Book. A hunter until the end. Go, warn the men of the Legion, for if they cannot stall this tide, then all the Mistlands will fall. I must stay and fight them off, to give you time."

Ruane rushed forward. "But Augur Puce, you're an augur, not a vicar."

A smile. "I wasn't always an augur, dear Ruane." He cracked his knuckles, then adjusted the Beads of Aether at his wrist. "I enjoyed our time together. I see the light in you. Zenith has chosen you, remember that." To Lojen, "Let's see if I can cause any disruption to the Fallen. Go, Lojen. Go with Zenith."

And then the pair of augurs plunged into the Sea of Mist, the crack of Beads filling Lojen's earholes.

"Lojen, what do we do?" Ruane asked. She teetered on the edge of wanting to run after the augurs and turn tail like they commanded and retreat back to Gandtril.

Before he could answer, he heard a shout from the village, followed by what Lojen could only describe as swords clearing scabbards. *Can't be…*With nary a glance at his sister, Lojen bolted toward the sound, the rhythm of the song building within.

The village was a tiny hamlet, maybe less than a dozen shacks all built upon stilts in the marshlands of the Sea. There were dead trees surrounding the small encampment and out of the heavy ocean of mist, a woman clad in a brown shirt and leather skirt burst into view. Right on her heels was a girl dressed similarly, and both were running as fast as they could.

Behind came twenty or more black-painted, drake scale armored soldiers in black breathers outlined with crimson skulls atop the glass. The mist a whorl of black and anger.

No... Tonns had spoken true...

Soldiers of the Fallen.

Ruane snarled beside him as she drew her drakken longknife, going to all fours as she redoubled her effort to reach the women before the soldiers. Lojen drew his own longknife, but as he did, he felt a surge of power ignite within his breast, the song reaching its pinnacle. The wardkeeper horns atop his head gleamed and grew warm, his muscles surging with essence borne of draconem.

The women saw them in the obscure haze and Lojen yelled out, "Don't stop!"

They didn't, and they ran past him and Ruane, disappearing into the Sea.

A large, heavily muscled man sprang upon him with a wickedly curved axe, the blade a blackened steel crescent moon, and a gap-toothed smile broke the plane of the soldier's face as he closed on Lojen. A wide arc swept his way, but Lojen veered to the left, causing the axe to whistle past unharmed. It stuck in the boggy earth and the man lost his balance, tumbling feet over head. Lojen thrust his longknife into the soldier's scaled middle, the sharpened blade from the Isle of Merj piercing drake scale and soft flesh alike, pinning the man to the ground. Jerking it free, Lojen twisted the longknife, severing the man's intestines.

Another blade came at him, but Lojen spun, bringing his longknife to block, twisting his arm and blade to slice across the soldier's arm. The man squealed and dropped his sword and Lojen rammed his horns into the man's face, killing him instantly.

Aether swelled his breast as the chorus of the Arbiter's drums sang the Hymn of War in his heart. Lost Lojen became in the artform of wardkeeping, lost in the berserker dance.

"THERE YOU ARE! MINE YOU SHALL BE, AEGIS!"

He leapt after two soldiers who tried to veer around him, catching one by the pauldron. Lojen upended the flailing soldier and used him as a club to slam into the second. Both went down and Lojen slammed his taloned claw into their sanguine-painted breathers, smashing glass skulls and real skulls, killing them.

Behind him, he could hear Ruane's guttural roars of defiance as she battled soldiers of the Fallen's army. Death cries echoed in his ears as aetheric spells unleashed by the augurs' Beads sizzled across the Sea of Mist. The rhythm of the Hymn grew fierce.

A soldier came at him with a sword, but he side-stepped the attack and landed one of his own with his longknife in the man's flesh just below his chin. But a searing pain erupted in the soft underside of his right arm, breaching hardened exoscales. The sound of claws scraping. The Hymn faltered. Lojen spun, but his footing was off, and he went down to a knee. A foot, not a boot like he expected, connected to his chest and Lojen fell backwards into the soggy marshlands, mud splattering everywhere.

In agonizingly slow motion, he watched as a daemon his size, perhaps larger, snapped at his arm with teeth the length of Lojen's talon. He pulled his arm back as he rolled, narrowly avoiding the clamp of jaws. The daemon, a sneer borne of the void emblazoned upon the rictus grin of serrated teeth, swung at him again. Down the blackened claw came, and Lojen saw the end of his life nearing.

Father, he thought. *Forgive me.*

But then the daemon went tumbling as Ruane barreled into it. She landed atop the creature of the void and brought her longknife down, stabbing it over and over. Black blood as dark as night rose in viscous arcs as she roared.

Ruane helped him to his feet and gave him a lopsided grin of pointed teeth. "Saving you once again, brother. Seems to be a common thing these days."

He looked around and counted eleven dead soldiers in addition to the daemon. The mist crawled over the corpses like grey maggots as the wetlands claimed them. Moving in the direction the two women had fled with a claw to his wound, he found them not long after. Both were dead, cut apart.

Lojen went to his knees besides one, touching a talon to the blonde tresses. He then glanced skyward at the muted sun, Zenith's sun. *Why? Why this, Zenith? I couldn't save them… Father, I failed again.*

More aetheric spells crackled across the Sea to the south, more daemonic screeches and men shouting war cries. His heart raced. He knew he should have stood beside Augur Indigo and Augur Puce, but he hadn't. And these women had paid the price.

The ground trembled violently as Mother Marrow's death rattled underfoot. Something large landed within the marshland not far from them. A bulk bigger than anything Lojen had ever seen rose from within the Sea, blazing red eyes searing through the grey, honed on the drakken siblings.

"WARDKEEPER!"

"Lojen," Ruane whispered from behind, pulling at his sleeveless vest. "We have to go. We need to warn Gandtril."

"I failed them, Ru." Purple blood flowed over his talons, the wound in his side painful as the daemon stalked closer.

"Nothing can stop this tide, brother. Lu Har has returned. It has to be him. These are scourges. And he has an entire army marching north. We have to warn Gandtril."

He looked at his sister; his hotheaded, brash, and vengeful sister. She glared at him. Gods, she was the logical one.

Standing, a dejected Lojen took one last look at the dead villagers and balled his claw into a fist. And he shook it at the oncoming daemon with red eyes. *I will not fail again, Father.*

Then they ran, the sound of the daemon laughing echoing in his earholes.

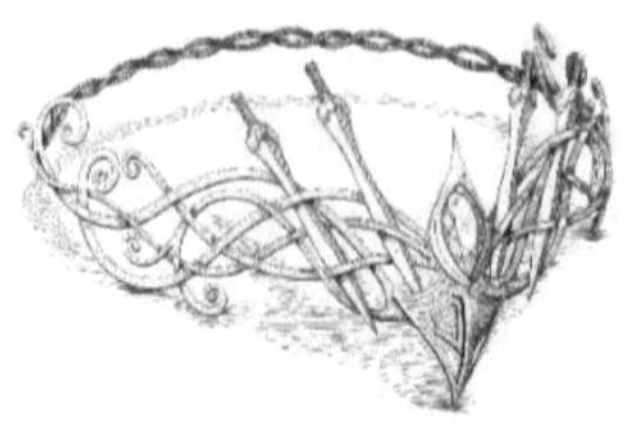

XIV
FINN

ON A BALCONY upon the upper tier of Gandtril, Finn's gaze crept over the Lower City toward the black granite tower of the Obelisk, wine spilling from his decanter as he gripped the rail, the hairs on the back of his hand submerged under the red wave.

If he squinted, he could just glimpse the fortress that kept the daemons of the mist from entering the mega-city in the small hours before dawnbreak. Burning his fleeting aetheurgy, the hustle and the bustle of soldiering from within the fortress filled his sightline in a silvery sheen that threatened to banish his drunk. Duties being performed in militaristic perfection in the order of the Legion of Kanja despite the early hour. Nothing ever finished, always alert. Duty to perfection.

Duty, he smiled with the thought. *We all have our duty, don't we, Em?*

Of course, there was no response from his beloved, why would there be? Emre was dead, but his body was not. Wasn't that the case per his sister-friend?

Finn brought the glass decanter to his lips, as he quelled his Burn Form, swallowing the sweet, O so sublime fermentation of grape as the Four Enhancements faded. "Remember, Em, that time at the mines? We were but fools, coming together to fight Lu

Har." He shook his head ruefully. "Fools... O, Em... why did we ever start the fight?"

Again, no answer, but he knew what Emre would've said. It was for more than just them; it was for all who couldn't stand on their own against tyranny. It was for everyone who needed a symbol of hope. For those who wanted to rally behind a cause.

Even if meant death.

He smiled bitterly because it reminded him of a time when Gandtril was nothing more than a ramshackle collection of huts after the Fall, some four hundred and seventy-five years in the past. Back when the world was still reeling from the wrought horrors that was the Fallen's war against Canlon Carr.

He was there when Gandtril had become more than a smattering of survivors and had become a bastion of hope, and that memory played out before him now. He took a large sip of wine and blinked.

At the behest of the small village, soldiers assembled into columns of fifty men apiece. Near two hundred Kanjan soldiers ready to give their all to the newly formed Legion. Townsfolk, the ragged survivors of the Fall, huddled behind, partially hidden within the Sea and their own shabby hovels.

Finn stood with his brother Titen, the Golden Sword of Kalderim was resplendent in his polished armor, even with a face hardened by the war with the Fallen. Beside them was Praetor Eran Rignork and a number of other high-ranking soldiers who'd survived the war.

The young soldiers of the newly christened Legion stood rigid with backs straight, swords on their hips, long spears in their grips. They wore earthen brown cloaks that were pinned to one side by a sigil that would soon become their standard: an eagle with outstretched wings. The soldiers wore boiled leather armor and linen masks to help keep the Sea from destroying their lungs with the nigrum pulmonem borne of the corrupted mist. Some held the new sigil upon flags, others held burning torches, for fire was the only thing that pushed back the darkened mist that threatened everyone and every blade of grass for hundreds of leagues in every direction from the ruins of Eminence.

Finn glanced at his brother; it appeared the Golden Sword seemed to be content with the rank and file. Their father, Rēx Vitus Dunleith, had wanted a force to protect southern Kanja trained quick and presented even quicker. And it seemed Praetor Rignork had done a fine job.

It was a shame these soldiers would be faced with a daunting task, one that terrorized even Finn's nightmares: mist daemons. For the war with the Fallen may have ended, but the man's terrifying horde still roamed free. Kalderim was protected by the highest peak of the floating mountains, but even in the Gloom did daemons fly. Mist daemons cared not whether it was marshland or the opacity of the Gloom.

"Fine soldiers you've given us again, praetor," Titen said, his hand clenching the pommel of the Golden Sword.

Rignork bowed his ancient head, he was older after the war. They all were. "It is my honor that you praise me so, Lord Sword. I serve by the grace of the Golden Throne."

Titen waved the comment off. Titen Dunleith was a hard man to please, even harder after all the misfortunes during the war with the Fallen. Especially after his beloved betrothed was murdered by the vile blooddrake who was Valeria's lover.

O, Finn hated that creature for turning his sister-friend against Canlon.

The Golden Sword's long peridot cloak flapped behind him, unpinned. Hands clasped behind his back, Titen walked toward the new soldiers of the Legion, and even the largest Kanjan amongst them seemed small in relation to his commanding presence. Finn understood that feeling far too close for comfort, being the third son and all.

But Finn remained two steps behind the Golden Sword, as per his rank demanded.

Titen scrutinized the soldiers, his face betraying nothing of what he thought. And then, his booming voice pierced the opaque Sea, almost pushing it back. "How do you serve?"

"With Honor and Blood!" came the reply in unison.

"What is thy Honor and Blood?"

"That which the Golden Throne demands!"

"What does the Golden Throne demand?"

"Praise to the Pentax and nothing of Nocturne!"

Finn's brother stood before the soldiers of the Legion. "Kanjans, today you are soldiers of the Golden Throne. Today we start a new world. These lands, these misted lands, were once our home. That home is no more. Thanks to the Fallen and his daemons, this land has become an infested voidscape. But the Golden Throne remains!" All the legionnaires began tamping their spear butts on the cracked earth in a steady rhythm. "Today we forge a new Kanja. A new home."

Titen spread his arms out, gesturing to the collection of buildings and then to the people behind them, the lonely mountain peak muted in the distance. A wall had begun construction, one that would eventually keep the daemons at bay, but until then…

"This world is still ours. Never has Nocturne claimed the Peridot, and never shall He!" The spear tapping became faster, rising in crescendo. "This will be a new city. A new home for Kanjans and others alike." His hand rose toward the mountain peak. "We shall call this city Gandtril. In the old tongue, it means 'the unbroken'. Gandtril shall always remain. Steadfast," Titen spun as he spoke, facing the soldiers anew, "we must remain. Keep the daemons from taking what is ours. This is our city! Our home! How do you serve?"

A roar filled the lowlands between the Forgemistress' Blades to the west and the goblin plateaus to the east. Hundreds of voices all bellowing as one. "With Honor and Blood!"

As Finn blinked away the memory, he couldn't help but feel this was history repeating itself, only this time, he was the one who was meant to lead, to inspire. Even if Titen was here.

And yet, he still was unsure if he was able. After Drenth…

Em… I'm sorry. He took a long pull from the wine decanter as his Burn Form snuffed, leaving him lethargic and out of sorts.

Two days has it been since Val had told him about Emre and Cadrianna. Two days of wondering what if he had been still in Drenth, would this have happened. Two days of him wallowing in his cups, begging for it to end, for it to be not true, for anything to happen to snap him out of it.

Two days added to the scrap heap that was his heart for the last year's turn. And he couldn't even go into the Lower City to forget.

Wick had tried to make him see reason, but Finn had wanted nothing to do with the lapin unless he was open to following him to a tavern to drown his misery (which Wick wasn't). Val was as aloof as ever, and Titen wouldn't see him unless he sobered up (which Finn wasn't). Lojen and his sister had gone into the Sea with that bothersome Puce, so Finn found himself alone. Alone with his three chaperones who shadowed him everywhere he went within Gandtril. Even to the privy. He was truly and utterly alone.

O, Em…

Finn shuffled toward the untidy, smelly bed that had been his own self-stylized fortress for the past months and plopped down upon it, drinking deeply until the decanter was empty. It fell from his fingers and clinked upon the floor, it didn't shatter, but if it had, Finn probably wouldn't have noticed as there was broken glass all over, the tiny shards resembling his shattered heart.

He stared at the ceiling, his eyes unfocused, lost in the ocean of liquor that clouded his mind, no lifeboat in sight. He let his mind wander listlessly like a limp sail without wind, let his body grow tired. Nothing mattered any more.

In the haze of rolling waves of disillusion, a faded light grew, irregularly pulsing. At first, he almost missed it, too drunk to care, but the pulse became brighter, a beacon in the distance. His brows drew together, and Finn realized it was not a light, but his soul. His fractured and broken soul.

Seeing it up close, almost able to touch it, really, Finn felt something inside. And with it came a figure he knew; one he missed more than life itself.

Em?

The spectral figure stepped forward from the light within his soul. Light brown complexion, a darker hue of curled hair, a narrow nose with a slight hook, dark stubble upon his jaw. Lean of body, broad of ambition.

By the Ideal Daughter, he was just as beautiful as that first time Finn had laid eyes on him after the destruction of Drenth. From the Meadows Val and the wardkeeper Tevun had raised him. Gods above, he was more beautiful.

Finn reached for him, *Em…*

But the figure moved naught an inch, stood there just beyond his touch.

Em, why do you haunt me like this?

Nothing. Hands at his side, the specter watching with empty, yet somber eyes.

I'm not strong enough! I can't do this without you!

Emre's gentle lips parted slightly into a serene smile. A knowing smile. That smile that melted Finn's aged heart, the one that brought him to his knees.

What is it you want of me?

The light haloing around Emre pulsed, a vigorous yellowed tint.

Gods, Em, I can't! I know what you'd have me do. But I… I… what do I do? I can't without you. The pain… it hurts so much…

The light grew so intense, Emre disappeared in it, Finn's own vision a blaze of peridot. A giant crystal filled his vision, a pillar of Life, yellow with essence. It pulsed so bright, so fierce, Finn was drawn to it, lost in it.

When he blinked again, Emre and the light were gone. He was staring at the ceiling once more.

Clarity found. Decision awaiting.

He decided right then and there, that today would be the change he needed. For Emre. Gods above, Emre was right. He had to stop from turning away from the truth. Why hadn't he seen it earlier? He didn't want to, that was why.

But not anymore.

Grabbing a pillow from under his head, Finn smooshed it into his face and screamed as loud as he could. With the bellow, he burned every last bit of aetheurgy in his body, all the parch that lingered in every nook and cranny of his insides. Aether, in its liquidated form, exploded, a pyre so intense, every nerve caterwauled, every muscle conflagrated, every pore burst with natural fire of Burn Form.

The drink that had wrapped and chained him to his misery evaporated in an instant, bringing with it a lucidity, a clean mind, an unsullied soul.

Breathing heavily, but free of the hurt at last, Finn sprung from the bed and tiptoe-ran past the glass pitfalls, yanking open the door and startling the trio of legionnaires stationed outside. He stuck his head out and yelled, "Find Wick! Send him up immediately." The trio of dunces glanced at each other with bewildered looks. Finn held his hand waist high. "A lapin, this tall, shredded ears, poor attitude and worse dresser. That Wick. Go find him."

"But, princeps, it's before dawnbreak," one said. He had a long tail of hair. A lingering of a name surfaced, Alyx.

"Just find him."

The trio fumbled a salute and raced off.

Grinning like he was about to waltz into a tavern on a two-for-one pint of ale night, Finn moved toward an on-suite bathing chamber that had a sink with running water. He drew a sinkful and began to hastily shear away the scraggly fuzz that had grown in all patchy in the intervening days since Val's revelation. Dunking his hands, he washed away the grime and drool of days lost to alcohol. Cleaning his person as well as his soul.

He was giddy, feeling determined. A plan. Finally, he would show his face in a place he should have been in for months. Doing the duty tasked to him by his father. A gift from the Peridot. He still didn't know if he was prepared for it, but something had to change. Something must change.

Em, why did you take so long to make me see the truth?

Finn pulled off his wine and sweat stained shirt, balling it before tossing it to the side. He did the same with his soiled trousers before dancing across the room, careful to not step on the broken fragments of past poor life choices. He hummed a jaunty tune whilst he opened his wardrobe, digging through his clothing.

He had just shoved a leg into a new pair of smallclothes when the door to his room opened and he heard a sharp inhale.

"By Zenith, needle dick, you've been sleeping with a vvyrm carcass?"

"Wick, ah, my friend, there you are. Come in, come in."

"I'd rather not. Why the fuck am I awake?"

"Quit being a kitten," Finn said as he lifted a pair of pants from the wardrobe before peering around the door at the lapin standing in the bedroom's entrance. He held out the pants for Wick to see. "What do you think about these? Will these be appropriate?"

The lapin's button-sized eyes stared blankly while he rubbed one with a paw. "For what?"

"I need them to see I mean business." He tossed the pants back into the wardrobe, unimpressed with the selection. He would need to send for more season appropriate clothing. Something more fashionable. "I want them to be inspired."

"Who?" The lapin rebel had made his way to the bed but did not sit, instead he glowered at all the broken glass and disgusting linens.

"Who was the man who had that dreamer hung?" Finn asked instead of answering. "The one Lojen was placed under?"

"Emont Landra. The man is dogmatic and harsh. Why you ask?"

"O, this is perfect." A few frantic minutes later, with Wick peppering him with questions, Finn closed the wardrobe and spread out his arms with a grin. "What do you think?"

Finn donned his best suit jacket—a dark burgundy with thin, yellow stripes—over a drake scale cuirass that his mother, Faye, had given him just prior to the Fallen's war, the armor a perfect mold to his frame. Under the cuirass he wore a bone white shirt, and he wore matching burgundy, slim-cut trousers that tucked into drake scale coated boots. He tied his long silver hair back into a tail and wore a Dunleith family rapier sheathed at his belt, the hilt made of *Aere*-infused gold to make it lighter than a normal rapier but also stronger.

"You look a proper sod, needle dick," said Wick. His paws were crossed and his perfectly round eyes were endless pools of black glare. "You ever going to tell me why you sent those fools banging on my door so godsdamned early?"

"I'm going down to the Obelisk, and I want you with me." He shifted the rapier, putting his hand on the pommel like Titen always did with the Golden Sword. Distinguished, he felt. "It's time I visited it."

"O, you mean like do something useful for once?"

Glass crunching under his drake scaled boots. He placed a hand upon the lapin's shoulder. "I'm sorry, my friend. I cannot atone for what grief I've caused you."

Wick slapped his hand away with a furry paw. "What's gotten into you?"

A sigh. *Em, please tell me I'm right in this…* "Nothing, Wick." He shook his head. "No, everything. I'm done with it. Come, let me set things straight with this Landra fellow."

As they left his room, Wick grumbled under his breath, "What sort of Nocturne-spawned drink has you under its spell now?"

XV
CYAN THE DEFIANT

CYAN WARMED HIS hands by holding a steaming cup of Oldport's finest as he sat with Lilia, Phlox, and Harlequin at a small teahouse right inside the Guild Politic.

"Do you remember that drink," Lilia said as she sipped her tea, "what was it called? You know, the one the Shards swear by? The one that tastes like a bitter cup of vomit. Here I was, raised that nothing tasted better. Ha! I can't remember what it was called. Isn't that sad?"

"What on Mother Marrow's once green land are you talking about?" Phlox the Faithful asked, his craggy brows knit together.

"Nobody asked you, Phloxy."

Harlequin the Resolute, who was sitting next to Lilia, snorted. "Why do you continue to lie about how much you love Phlox, Ashe?" she said playfully before she began scratching her neck vigorously like she was uncomfortable in her skin. "Did he hurt your feelings or something a long time ago?"

Cyan's eyebrow rose. *No, don't go there, old man…* He glanced at each of them in turn, going over Maja Carr's words in his head.

'…they have wormed their way into the Guild, perhaps even the High Seat.'

And Owl's.

'As well as the Scattered Shards.'

Worry had seeped into Cyan's heart like that of the teabag in his cup. It could be anyone, these blooddrakes. Dare he question the loyalty of his acolytes? Were they even his acolytes any longer? Gods above, he didn't know what to think.

"She has no feelings," Phlox muttered. "Except being rude."

"Go bugger yourself."

The gangly man frowned. "My point exactly."

They had been camped close to the center of the Guild Politic for an hour, near to the main administration buildings unlovingly referred to as the Swindler's Den. They had sat in late midday, prior to the rush before evenfall, and had clear visibility to the two central thoroughfares a Guilder may come from.

It wasn't a terribly cold autumn yet in Port Sin, but Cyan felt the chill in his bones. Not the chill of weather, but rather the change riding the wind. Change was coming, for him, easily, but something struck him that this change would affect all. Lilia especially.

He could not shake the perception something bad was brewing and it all stemmed from Nocturne. Bloody blooddrakes.

"Lilia, you have something else of dire importance to add before we get underway?" Cyan asked, trying his godsdamnedest to remain calm, to keep focused on the case before him. *But if any were…*

"Yes, yes, I'm getting to it," Lilia said, all-white eyes glazed over, her face going slack.

She was speaking to the daemon bound within that owl-shaped blade of hers, not to Cyan. He was losing her, he could see. Time was trickling far too fast. *Perhaps, I should tell her…*

"No," Lilia mumbled finally as she fiddled with her teacup, but she did grumble a low complaint about there not being any booze at this establishment.

"It's called kiathra," Cyan said, studying the girl. Ever since waking that dawnbreak, she had been eerily sullen, and when Lilia was not her usual sarcastic, guileless self, there was reason for concern. She had left the Shards stronghold and where she had gone, Cyan was certain it was the reason for her downturn in attitude. "Lilia, your hand is shaking. You're going to bust that mug in half."

Lilia must not have realized. She calmed herself with a steadying breath, taking a sip of the warm tea. Her pulmo was growing worse for her to have the shakes already, it meant the end was ever closer.

I'll help you stop this, Lilia. I promise. She will always be Lilia to him. *There's no way she can be one. Can there?*

"Remind me again why we're here?" The girl dunked a biscuit into her tea aggressively as she coughed lightly. "I'm not particularly fond of waiting."

"That she's not."

Cyan gave Harlequin a frown before continuing, "We need details about our suspects, Lilia. Patterns of transit, who they dine with, what other members of Port Sin they entertain. What brothels they prefer. Especially their soldiers and business partners. You know, the things I've spent a lifetime teaching you."

"You believe all that slag from the High Seat Guilder?"

Cyan nodded. "I do."

"As you say, Cyan, you're the boss," Lilia said, "but spies are supposed to blend in." She glanced at Harlequin with a shy smile but with a frown toward Phlox. "We're vicars, not exactly shipshape for that, eh?"

"To be sure. But we need to dig our fingers in deep here if we are to find our blooddrake. Or drakes."

Lilia leaned close to Harlequin. "Not sure I'd want Phloxy's fingers digging anywhere, if you know what I mean?" She covered her mouth to block a cough while Harlequin chortled.

"Hey!" The skinny vicar showed his offense, to which the vicar-in-training mumbled incoherently as she chomped on a biscuit.

"Sounds like a start," Lilia said after swallowing. "Though, these Guild folk have a mighty high opinion of themselves. Every one of them are rotten." Lilia said the last part loudly enough for the pair of nobleborn next to them to hear. When they peeked over, she smiled broadly.

"Could you be any less annoying?" Phlox asked while he tugged heartily at his earlobe.

Why is every little tic making me question? I'm getting too old for this shit…

On cue, Lilia leaned back, patted her stomach, and declared, "Too many biscuits, gonna need to see a man about a horse in a few minutes." One of the occupants of the table nearby gave the girl a questioning goggle. Lilia cackled. "Shit, man, gonna need to shit." The man raised his hand to his mouth in disgust and tried his best to ignore her.

No blooddrake would be this uncouth. "Hobb, Ranhold, Dil, and Klander are our marks," Cyan started, trying to reel Lilia back in, troublesome as it was. He was certain he was right about her. Lilia is too unfiltered, always has been. No drake could be like her. Besides, she was a Godsblood, blessed by Zenith Himself. "I'll take care of Klander. If anyone knows anything about Solanine and Lu Har's return, it'll be the bikrome."

At the mention of the Fallen and his pet blooddrake, Lilia's face became a blank slate, locking her emotions inside. A façade all too familiar when anything relating to Drenth came up. Her all-white eyes blinked. "Speak of the daemon."

Cyan gently turned, so it was not obvious. Out of the corner of his eye, he saw a procession coming from the Guild Politic.

The carriage was open faced, almost like a palanquin, pulled by a pair of horses. A driver stood on a single axle, holding the reins of the black fillies. Expensive creatures, the horses. Four posts rose from the carriage bed, topped with an intricately woven covering. Ifant Klander rode within the open carriage.

When Ifant's father went the way of Nocturne, according to Owl's files, he had supposedly intended for Ifant to be the heir of House Klander, not his elder brother as was custom. Although the lord's death wish was overseen by an augur, Ifant's brother had dismissed the claim, taking the mantle for his own. He died not a month later from one of Nocturne's deadly poxes. Some believe to this day the pox was actually poison.

And based on their current case, Cyan was of a mind to believe the rumors. Conspirators knew no bounds.

Long after the carriage had passed, Cyan stood. "Let's go."

The four vicars left the teahouse, heading toward the Hangman's Hex, but not before Cyan made his apologies to the nobleborn couple on Lilia's behalf.

Passing the open forum where Tified had been hung and his House purged, Cyan turned toward the Faithful. "I want you on Neron Hobb to start, Phlox. I want to know what it is they brought into the Harbor. Hobb has double-crossed enough Houses that the Guild eventually raised her to Lady of her own

House just so she would stop undercutting them. That means she's dangerous. Grand Quaestor Owl's files say Hobb doesn't get to the Swindler's Den much. Says she holes up in the chambers above her tavern, *Nocturne's Bounty.* Nobody but Guilders are allowed up. Heard told she has an army of goblins running protection for her. Meet me at the stronghold by evenfall. I want initial canvasing reports of Hobb. Be wary, Phlox."

Phlox nodded and turned toward the Harbor of Thieves. The skinny man quickened his pace and disappeared in the crowd.

"Hobb sounds like my kind of bitty." Lilia's shoulders twitched as she laughed. "What's the files say on the others?"

"You'd know that if you'd read them."

"Tell me anyway."

Cyan suppressed a groan. Seventeen years under his training and still she skimped on the easiest of tasks. Guess that's what he deserved for being so hard on her when she was younger, he had inadvertently pushed her away.

"Olum Ranhold's top dog in the Barter Yard, his place is called *The Endless Wheel.* House Ranhold's a young pup barely off the Guild's teat. Olum's House rose to prominence after striking it rich in a card game from the previous owner of *The Endless Wheel* about three decades prior. Ranhold's a man who thrives on pocketing more coin than he loses. I want you on Ranhold, Harlequin."

"We'll make that wheel end."

"Wow, that one's bad, Ashe," the Resolute said with a laugh. "Stay up too late last night?"

"You could have just invited me over instead, Harle-bub. You know you wanted to."

Harlequin's brow arched. "You've never tried."

"Maybe later."

"Lilia, drop it." She gave a poignant 'go bugger yourself' look, but Cyan continued, "Danma Dil has run the Beggars Chain for years now, ruling with an iron fist. Information's hard to come by from within the Chain. House Dil's been around since Oldport Basin was but a fledgling little town climbing out of the remains of the Fall. They're renowned for their tenacity, the Dils, and Danma's no exception. She's killed all those willing to challenge her rule, even her own family."

"Don't worry about Dil," Lilia said flatly. "I've got a mouse working on her."

Cyan gave her a skeptical look. "That were you were off sneaking last nightturn?"

"Maybe." Lilia smiled. "This is exciting. Most of the time, we just beat the Pit out of suspects. Or kill drakes now that they're attacking people in droves. I quite enjoy being able to try something new."

"And I enjoy you being sober for once." Cyan returned the smile. To Harlequin, "Be wary of Olum Ranhold, I've heard he's got one of those faces that will draw you while he skins you dry. Be safe."

Harlequin bowed. "And you, Vicar Cyan." She gave Lilia a grin before lowering her breather and heading off toward the Barter Yard, bent over like a prowling drake.

Gods above, why am I so skittish about my own team?

Lilia watched the red-haired vicar before she spun toward him, her all-white gaze narrowed. "I don't see why I have to play Guilder tagalong in the Beggars Chain when you get to go to *The Parlour.* That's just rude of you."

"What's that supposed to mean?"

"When was the last time you ogled a pair of legs?"

Cyan merely shook his head. The girl never seemed to be far from her true self, even when down. Maybe the winds of change were not going to be so bad after all. "Fine, you can accompany me, but one drink, Lilia. Then you are to head to the Chain."

Lilia clapped her hands and giddily quickened her step toward the Red Moon District, leaving him behind. The mist that always trailed her danced.

Nocturne's everlasting torture in the Pit seems far more ideal than the headache this girl brings daily.

As one of Oldport Basin's oldest establishments, *The Parlour of Innocent Sirens* was a staple for a nightturn of debauchery. A massive building, *The Parlour* stood four stories tall, terracotta tiled roof burnished in red, multiple balconies along the façade, with dozens of opened windows bedecked by stained glass. Trailing down the columns holding up the balconies were vines dotted with roses. Golden chains dangled between the fluted columns, a well-trodden walkway to the Calibrathian redwood doors. Atop the awning was a scene of painted stone to resemble water. In the center was a raised 'reef' where a thin girl sat, singing a soft song, her shoulders swaying with the melody of her impeccable alto, her lower half the tail of a fish. A siren singing her song, beckoning the wayward.

Lilia examined the siren singer with a careful gaze. "This is new. Looks like there's been a makeover since we've been here last."

A young buck of a boy in pink livery rushed from a small stool beside the door. A dvergir, dark of hair and iris, maybe ten at the most, his cheery face ruddy and pale under a thick brow and the markings of a pre-puberty fuzz atop his thin lips. "Welcome t' *The*

Parlour, where all yer fantashies ish fer but a coin," the boy said with a heavy lisp.

Cyan the Defiant nodded, dropped a silver quadran in the dvergirish boy's palm, and passed through the redwood doors into the brothel.

Lilia's face lit up. "A'right hard drinkers, let's drink hard."

"One drink, Lilia. Remember that." He didn't know why he had allowed her this vice. Part of him knew it was because he had missed her while she was in Drenth, and the Lilia who had returned from the City of Sands was not the girl he had raised.

She waved him off and dove into the brothel with too much impish glee.

The outside of *The Parlour of Innocent Sirens* was decorated like a fine keep, but inside was something akin to a slaughterhouse. One filled with rowdy drinkers and whores of every race, all genders and none, young and old. All lounged, sashayed, bounced, or danced. Scantily clad in enticing gowns and garb of their homelands. Dainty men and masculine women, and vice versa. Every size, every shape. From elfir to goblins. Nocturne's Pit, even a centaur was on hand, and those sorts of things were frowned upon, especially by the Shards.

In Port Sin, anything went.

Amongst the pleasure workers were the pleasure seekers, all ranging from simple farmers to the wealthiest of lords, from sellswords to city watch. Shy and brash brushed shoulders together with ale or spirits in hand. Unlikely virgins and experienced trollopers. Music bumped from a gregarious band on the stage. Ale overflowed mugs. Spirits tossed back in single shots. Stories and laughter told. Arguments and whispers between the payers and payees.

A few of the heavy drinkers glanced Cyan's way, some giving him scowls and hisses upon seeing his cassock and horsehair-topped breather.

Two toughs lounged near the door, all biceps and steel. Dark leers took him in but returned toward their perpetual watching of the workers and keeping impulsive lushes under control. They each had steel rings on each of their thick fingers; excellent for punching the piss out of people should they get rowdy—which was probably a nightly happenstance.

A narrow stair beyond the stage led to the rooms on the second, third, and fourth floors, separated from the main rooms by a single doorway to each as few people had the pleasure of passing without the proper payment of quadrans. At each floor was a steel portal with a sturdy lock. Most of the establishment's patrons only wanted their tosses, but Ifant Klander had not gotten to where he was without being extra cautious. In Port Sin, a knife to the back was just as common as one to the front.

Behind the main bar was a giant of a man; an actual giant because he was half giant. There was a mirror behind the halfblood, liquor bottles and wine decanters reflecting, the man towered over the mirror, so the only thing visible was a broad back twice Cyan's shoulders.

Cyan made for the half-giant. "Clague. How goes?"

"Vicar Cyan, you crafty ol' bastard." The wild-faced halfblood smiled behind his bushy beard. "To what do we owe the pleasure?"

Clague had inherited the best of both his parents' races. The halfblood had a face and head of hair resembling a mammoth, brown and coarse but was more humirish than giant. He soared well over eight feet tall but could have been larger if the giant blood on his mother's side had been any stronger. His shoulders were as broad as a cart bed, and his arms as thick as a man's waist.

"Is Lord Klander in?"

Clague's woolly forehead furrowed. "Aiming high are we, vicar? New fancy for ya? Didn't know a Shards man such as you to seek out the finer desires of the flesh."

"Not yet," Cyan grunted. Only once had he given into the temptation of the flesh since donning the cassock. A certain smuggler captain he had met in Drenth… she had some legs to ogle… no, he would not fall into that trap again. He had work to finish in the name of the Pentax. "Need some information."

Clague had worked with the Scattered Shards over the years, garnering information. After his fateful encounter with the giantess, Clague's father had turned to the good Book. And when the giantess returned with his halfblood son, the newly discovered religious man had brought the babe up to Kalderim for blessings. The man had died destitute, but the halfblood son was already enthralled by those in the Conclave, especially Icterine the Unfettered, which, truth told, was shocking. Cyan had known Clague until he up and left Kanja some ten years ago. But the halfblood still maintained some loyalty to the Shards and Icterine, and secrets came out in places like this, secrets told between the sheets. Secrets that might affect the Shards and the Pentax.

The half-giant glanced toward the fourth floor, and Cyan's gaze followed. There, standing at the railing was Ifant Klander.

Klander was over six and a half feet in height, thin as a barstool leg. His pointed ears poked from underneath hair that was a blend of silver and blond and he bore no facial hair on his Kanjan porcelain skin. His eyes were set wide apart and because he was a bikrome, he had one black eyeball and one pure white.

He surveyed the landscape of the brothel before disappearing back into his chamber.

Cyan noticed a person standing on the balcony, one he didn't recognize. "Who's that?"

Clague began cleaning a mug with a stained rag. "That's Roqanth. Ever heard of 'em?"

Cyan nodded. He had never met Roqanth person to person. Only knew of them from a distance. And the reputation. "Name's been around the Shards since I was an acolyte. A courtesan and advisor, depending on the need. When'd they get in with Klander?"

"Been here awhile now," Clague answered. "Working with the lord on some business. Say close t' a year now, I think." That was about the time of Drenth and the Fallen's defeat. *Interesting.*

Roqanth was handsome, Cyan noted, about the age of fifty to fifty-five if they had been humir, but since they were Calibrathian elfir, Roqanth was probably closer to fifteen hundred. Tall and whip-thin, delicate shoulders and demure of posture. Roqanth's gentle brown skin and blonde hair were quite a comely combination, but their hazel irises and pupils were hard and weary. The elfir's flaxen hair was kept short, mused into a flop. A flowing gown of rose held daintily between fingernails that were lacquered a vibrant purple.

The elfir saw him standing at the bar, and then did the oddest thing, they winked. Then, Roqanth too, disappeared into Klander's chamber.

"Business, eh? Perhaps something to do with Drenth?"

"Ah," the half-giant said. "The lor—."

A screech came from the balcony of the second floor, the slapping of feet on the wooden slats. A moment later, a half-naked woman bounded down the stairs, struggling to not trip over her sheer robe. She was horrified and beelined straight for the halfblood behind the bar. The room full of hard drinkers all began laughing.

Clague cursed into his beard. "I got t' handle this. I'll let the lord know you're here t' see him."

Cyan saw Lilia sitting upon the lap of a woman naked from the waist up. She glanced his way upon hearing the screams, so Cyan held up one finger to reinforce his rule on drink for the evenfall.

Back to the halfblood, "Of course. Thanks, Clague." He leaned closer, whispering, "Keep your eyes peeled for anything suspicious. If you see anything you think I'll want to know. And that girl over there, she's to have one drink only. Got it?"

If he had not been looking for it, Cyan never would have seen the grin within the tangle of Clague's bushy beard. "You got 't, Vicar Cyan."

XVI

ASHE

ASHE DUNKED HER head under the warm water of the bath, her raven hair floating above like churned waves of foam after a thunderstorm on a lake.

She was still in *The Parlour of Innocent Sirens,* in a private bathing chamber paid for out of her own pocket. It was long past time to head into the Beggars Chain, but rarely had she done what was expected of her, especially when *The Parlour* had much more enticing accommodations than that of the Shards stronghold. Even if Cyan would be mighty pissed that she lied and said she was going straight to the Chain but instead snuck back into the brothel while he met with the owner of said brothel. She needed this relaxation.

She was here, in this city, not on her own volition, but on that of the Pentax.

Her mind wandered, the warmth in the water soothing her body, easing the strain on her soul. If it was indeed possible, she wanted some time for herself before she was escorted to the gods' dance once more.

Guild conspiracies weren't her typical foray, she was Lady Drakeslayer, after all. But if a rebirthed Solanine did indeed sprout a scaly head back from the Pit, then maybe she was best for this case. She did have a vision of battling the witch in different forms.

She just never would have guessed it'd be as a draconem. Or her mother…

Not much was known about the blooddrakes, and most of what she did know, she had just learned from Maja Carr. Aetheurgy could do a number of interesting things, its magic extraordinary, but taking the flesh of another and wearing it like a dress to a ball was not something she had ever heard of, let alone thought of.

No, this case wasn't a normal drake hunt nor a conspiracy. It was far worse.

Didn't help that she couldn't get the elfirish Guilder out of her mind. She kept thinking about the beauty, and in lewd fashion, too. She fought with her hands from making a move down below. Which is why she submerged her head and held her breath.

"YOU MAY BE AIMING HIGH, DEAR BRYNN." The Strix, along with Mother Marrow's Hammer, were on the other side of the room, atop a stool. The daemon's voice was strong as if still sheathed on her belt. ***"BUT I ADMIRE YOUR AMBITION. SUCH IS FITTING FOR A GODSBLOOD LIKE YOU."***

Shut up, Strix. And fuck off with these desires.

"AND HERE I THOUGHT YOU HAD TURNED A CORNER WITH THAT RED-HAIRED WHELPING. YOU TWO HAVE GROWN MIGHTY CLOSE. I JUST DON'T UNDERSTAND WHY YOU HAVEN'T CONSUMATED YET."

Because I can't. Not yet.

Could she? She hadn't gone to that brink with anyone since Wren. She remembered what it felt like, the pure aetheurgy that had come alive alongside her passion, her desire. It was so hard to resist, even in a place like *The Parlour*, where the women flowed like wine, all to be had for the right amount of coin.

She talked a heady game, but she was afraid to go that route again. She hadn't with the whore downstairs. Hadn't with Harlequin, Zenith's cock, even though she wanted to. She didn't know if she could face that touch of aether again.

Killing was something altogether different. Ever since that first servant back in Drenth last year, taking the life of another did not bring forth that feeling of initiation. That feeling of being one with the void.

Of Death.

The dregs of Slag's End always said it got easier with each kill, and they hadn't exaggerated. The servant was unlucky to be her first. Wren had been her second, and because of her betrayal, the guilt had been washed away. Elian's death had almost created a wall between her emotions and her soul. Solanine and Lu Har had shuttered that vault. She was numb to it all by now.

But of Life, part of her was scared to open that door anew. Afraid to let anyone else in lest they betray her heart again.

Mother… Father… is this what it was like for you as well? Betrayal being all that you knew?

"THAT WAS ALL THAT DROVE CADRIANNA, DEAR BRYNN. EMRE'S BETRAYAL, WRONG AS SHE WAS TO THE TRUTH, IT WAS HER FIRE. HER VENGEANCE. CADRIANNA WAS A FORCE STRONGER THAN A GALE, BUT NOT MANY SAW IT FIRSTHAND AND LIVED TO TELL THE TALE. AND YOUR FATHER, I KNEW HIM NAUGHT PERSONALLY, BUT I CAN SAY WITHOUT A HINT OF DOUBT, THE MAN WAS LIKE STEEL AND STONE, UNBREAKABLE."

And yet you—

Her head poked above the water when she heard the door to the bathing room squeal open. She was supposed to be alone, the halfblood giant called Clague had ensured she would remain so. Cyan was in a meeting with Klander, and who knew how long that would take, but he had no inkling she was still there. Harlequin was probably being a do-gooder and patiently spying on Olum Ranhold. And Phloxy the Ever-Faithful-Boring-Vicar would never step foot in the brothel without just cause.

In walked the mysterious Guild advisor Cyan had told her about before he had left her thinking she was soon to be up to her ankles in the shit of the Chain. Roqanth their name. Following the elfir was a handful of nude figures.

"Why, the famed Lady Drakeslayer," Roqanth started, "all alone in my benefactor's establishment and not a body to keep her warm. Tsk. Tsk. We should rectify that."

The elfir glided into the room. Unlike earlier when Ashe had first laid eyes on the advisor, Roqanth now wore naught but a bone corset adorned with a brooch in the shape of a thrush and skintight trousers tucked into knee-high leather boots. The gentle brown of Roqanth's bare arms and shoulders glittered in the seagandr-oil lamps along the bathing room's walls. Hair was combed to one side, slick with floral oils. A golden chain wrapped thrice around the elfir's neck where a pendant hung down into the concavity of their sternum, the pendant also in the shape of a thrush.

Ashe eyed those standing behind the Guild advisor. Three women and three men. One each of humir, elfir, and dvergir. All were attractive physically in their own manner, the elfirish woman in particular caught her eye, made her think again about Maja Carr, to which the Strix chuckled in the void. Each smiled coyly, the women demurer in their nudity, while the men flexed their vigor in bulging displays.

But that elfirish woman… She forced the thought aside as a lustful pang ran up her spine. She could feel the layer of mist clawing at the tub's legs. "Very nice, but I'm busy."

"My friends call me Ro. Everyone needs friends, Brynn the would-be-vicar. I'd like to be yours. Seems like you need one. With no one to wash your backside." Roqanth smiled, painted lips curling, aura glowing mischief. "Not expensive for such a highly thought of guest."

"The last time someone visited me in the bath, they tried to kill me." The ground began to tremor, the water sloshing over the lip of the tub. Mother Marrow's lasting memory.

"That sounds an intriguing story."

"Not exactly," she said as she forced the memory of Wren to the far reaches of her mind. "I'll pass. Call me disenchanted."

"I highly doubt that daemon blade vibrates enough when speaking to you from the void. Everyone can use a release now and again. A shame." The Guild advisor clicked their tongue. The six naked figures hurried from the bathing room, leaving the pair alone. The elfir sat upon the rim of another brass tub, leg draped over the other. "Clague tells me your taskmaster has asked for an audience with my benefactor. Might I enquire the need of such a meeting? And before you ask, he does not know you are here. A sneaky one, you."

Part of her tensed, and the mist grew surly below the tub. But the other part of her was curious at this advisor's reasons for being here. She wanted to understand this elfir's shifting aura. "Shards business. Forgive, but that is all I can say."

"You know," the Calibrathian elfir said, all-hazel gaze taking in the runes tattooed on Ashe's left arm, then down the length of her body under the water. The aetheric mischief grew brighter. "There are plenty of stories relating to the exploits of Lady Drakeslayer since her rise from the sands in Drenth. I should like to hear some, free of charge, of course."

"BE WARY OF THIS ONE, BRYNN. ROQANTH WAS ON EMINENCE DURING THE FALL."

With Canlon or against?

"HARD TO SAY FOR CERTAIN. THEY ARE A TRICKSTER AND CON ARTIST. A LIAR AND THIEF."

"I'm afraid those stories are nothing more than a bard's exaggeration," she said. "Nothing more than blood and dead draconem. The kind you'd see on aerescreen newscasts."

Roqanth smiled again. "So, you say. I don't know if I believe you. The killing of Mother Marrow's vvyrms would tell otherwise." The elfir motioned to a large scar across her right thigh, a scar Ashe received on her first hunt after being tattooed with her Shard Form runes. She had been foolish on that hunt, foolish and prideful. She had learned much from that aerovern, especially about herself. "Particularly nasty, that one. I've heard told the Guild believes the last firedrake is up on Mount Bastard. And the Shards are investigating."

"SEE?"

How does Roqanth know this? Klander, perhaps? "You know I cannot tell you that information." Ashe frowned apologetically. "But I wouldn't put much faith in rumormongering."

"Rumors are all over this place, my dear," Roqanth said with a wave of lacquered fingers. "It's what we come to expect in places such as this business. The only currency of value. It's why Clague still passes along of what he hears to your taskmaster."

"Cyan's never mentioned him before." But it made sense, she always had an inkling the Scattered Shards were never what they seemed, especially the Conclave.

"That doesn't surprise me, young Brynn Benld. Only what little that halfblood himself tells others is what they know. That somehow his father was able to gather the seedpods to copulate with a giant. Not exactly a tall tale, nor exciting." Roqanth smiled devilishly. "One of those right place right times sort of things." The advisor's aura shifted through so many shades; Ashe was having trouble keeping track. "A goat herder, Clague's father. Caught in a nasty rainstorm, where he sought shelter in the nearest cave he could find. Turns out it belonged to a very lonely, and very horny, giantess who instantly took a liking to the simple humirish herder. And the rest, they say, is history."

A brow arched. "Why tell me this?"

The handsome elfir grinned. "Clague is a friend to your taskmaster. They share a story, the two of them. Not everyone comes to *The Parlour* looking for a ride."

If the Strix could nod, the daemon blade would be nodding right now. ***"I'VE SEEN THE MANHOOD OF ONE LIKE HIM BEFORE. EVEN NOW IT GIVES ME THE SHIVERS. I BET HE GETS ALL SORTS OF CURIOUS PEOPLE WANTING TO KNOW WHAT SHAGGING A GIANT WOULD BE LIKE. BUT THEY PROBABLY LEAVE MORE SORE THAN SATISFIED BY THE EXPERIENCE."***

Where do you come up with this stuff?

"ETERNAL SLUMBER GIVES YOU PLEEENTY OF TIME TO THINK ABOUT THINGS YOU'VE ALWAYS WANTED ANSWERS FOR."

And this is something you wanted to know about?

"COLOR ME INTRIGUED ABOUT SUCH MATTERS."

Consider yourself colored then.

Roqanth was still speaking, "Stories are what bind us, Brynn Benld… forgive me, you like to be called Ashe of the Scattered Shards. And friends are the ones we either tell our stories to or the ones who experience them alongside. So, I ask you again, are you in need of a friend?"

Ashe didn't know how to answer, instead, "What is your business with Lord Klander, might I inquire?"

"Guild business." The elfir smiled. "Forgive, but that's all I can say."

Ashe felt herself smirking. "Wouldn't be much of an advisor otherwise, would you, Ro?"

"Ah, see there, you've named me as a friend." Roqanth stood and straightened the thrush brooch upon their corset. "I've lived long enough to see rumors start, come to fruition, then die into legend. I've also learned to decipher what is rumor and what is truth. You may think me beholden to my duty to the Guild and those who pay for my services, but I would suggest you worry about my benefactor. He remains the man who he was when Eminence fell. Myself, I haven't changed in a millennium."

"I highly doubt that. I've changed a lot in the last year's turn."

"O, no doubt, child of Emre Benld and Cadrianna Nightingale. And in more ways than one, I surmise. Which I have to ask, why do you not claim your name, the name borne to you? Brynn Benld."

For the young woman who had forsaken the Benld line, she had kept the name Ashe, the name bestowed by a self-absorbed smuggler, one Neenah LeFleur. But upon her return to Kalderim, many had inferred it was because of her all-white eyes, from sclera, iris, and pupil, but she had stuck with the name because her actions in Drenth had left ashes that was her family heritage. She had scoured the tracts that were her blood, her history.

Icterine the Unfettered—the vicar who led the Conclave—hadn't asked questions, merely frowned as she had knelt before them. She could see them now, the Conclave. Could see their scowls when she'd returned, sitting upon their raised chairs in the Proving Chamber. Zaffre. Mindaro the Blind. Icterine the Unfettered. Randol. Tarpaulin.

Ashe had cause to remember them all. They were present the day she swore her oaths to the Scattered Shards, was inked by Cyan the Defiant, bound to the Pentax.

And then she had run away, a thing the Shards didn't abide very much, prostrating herself before them in an effort to be allowed to resume her training. She'd been prepared to beg, to plead even, but they said nothing. Only nodded as Cyan was granted his role once more as her taskmaster. She recalled the relief within her, then.

At the time, it had felt right, but now, a year later, she didn't know if she had made the correct choice.

Blink.

The Conclave of the Scattered Shards in Kalderim.

An augur, Zaffre had light blond hair streaked with grey, middle-aged and was a cool-headed humirish augur.

Mindaro was the longest serving vicar in the history of the Scattered Shards, the elfirish bikrome alive centuries before the Fall.

Icterine the Unfettered was the highest rank in all the Scattered Shards. Strong and stone-cold, her shoulder-length grey hair coiled around her stern elfirish face, eyes wrinkled and alert.

The ingeniator Randol was a dvergir from under the Forgemistress' Blades. Flat face was craggy under bushy brows, his beard and braided hair curly-grey.

Tarpaulin was a feisty, hot-tempered giantess and her hair was a short wispy white and the same pallor and desiccated flesh of a quaestor, which meant she looked like a massive, angry zombie.

"You've denounced your oaths, child," Icterine the Unfettered said as Ashe knelt before them. "And yet, you've seen fit to return." It wasn't a question, merely a statement.

"I have," Ashe said, head bowed. "To finish what was started by… by Cyan the Defiant." She glanced up. She wanted to say so much more but couldn't find the words. "I… my parents… I…"

Icterine looked toward Cyan. "See it done, vicar."

Blink.

"I see you don't want to share," Roqanth said in her silence. Those delicate lips parted with an upward twirl. Roqanth winked under elongated eyelashes rimmed with kohl. "I would very much like to hear your stories someday, Lady Drakeslayer. Especially your exploits in Drenth. That story truly does intrigue me. The Seal of *Terris*. I imagine that tale to be truly exceptional. I wish I had met your parents."

I bet you would. Just as Klander would. Wonder what he could possibly be up to? Bedding with Solanine?

"But to ease your mind on if you can trust me as a friend, know this, one amongst you is not who they say they are." Ashe inhaled, but the Guild advisor smiled. "You see, Brynn Benld, I am more than this face you see, too. I very much hope one day we can be friends. Until then, I suggest you watch with whom you treat."

The soft soles of Roqanth's fine boots danced as the elfir glided from the bathing room, the door closing behind.

A spy within my circle?

"THE FACE YOU SEE IS NOT ALWAYS THE FACE OF A FRIEND, DEAR BRYNN. IN THAT, ROQANTH IS CORRECT."

It can't be Harlequin or Cyan, right, Strix?

"THE FALLEN AND SOLANINE HAVE LONG SINCE BEEN DECEITFUL. YOU'D BEST REMEMBER THAT. EVEN ONE YOU HAVE LOVED ALL YOUR LIFE CAN BE TAKEN."

It can't be either of them. Could it?

Ashe pushed from the bronze tub, water sluicing from her flesh. There were mirrors all around the room and her reflection stared back at her in the seagandr-oil lighting. Left arm ringed in multi-colored tattoos, from shoulder to wrist. Each rune inked with spells of aetheurgy, of the Four Tenets and Four Enhancements. The Eye of the Soul affixed to her left wrist and fingers.

The rest of her body was a mishmash of scars, the heaviest in her heart. The biggest wound was one none could see: the death of her parents.

Is this my penitence, Icterine, to forever be questioned, and to question myself?

XVII
THE GROWING SULLEN LEGEND, NEENAH LEFLEUR

AT THE AFT railing of *Marrow's Lover,* Neenah brooded as Roland circled the sightless vastness of the Sea of Mist near the highlands where Filfangin met Altreyia.

She held a looking glass to her eye, scanning the impenetrable fog for godsdamned-knows-what, searching for any sign of bloody movement. She'd been at it for most of the day, not exactly the type of task a captain of her renown should be performing, but the pissing old matriarch advisor had scared her half-cocked about not being made by Invaris if she didn't do as he commanded.

So, she searched the Sea but found nothing.

It had been three days since getting the contract, and she wasn't exactly pleased with the details. In fact, she might consider it a damnable contract. At first, she had jumped at the opportunity, for it would only grow her legend, but as they flew south—not west, mind, to Kalderim like the old man had said was the destination during negotiations—her enthusiasm began to wane.

And it had to do with those the old man had brought with him.

It was one thing to have a full squad of soldiers file onto the *Lover* with their grey-painted firedrake scale and breathers clearly bearing the mark of the Imperium of the Fallen, but it was another to see four black scaled warriors. And if Neenah was any judge, she knew without a shadow of a doubt, these four were scourges.

Bloody godsdamned scourges. If only she kept to her own rules: stay the fuck away from the Fallen.

South they flew, the soldiers and scourges crammed together on the *Lover*. The old man had taken Neenah's cabin, so she was stuck with the lot of them. The soldiers sharpened their blades, cleaning their wheellocks with precision, chatting and cavorting as they geared up for some sort of battle. The scourges were aloof, staying in the cramped hall belowdecks outside the advisor's pilfered cabin, not letting anyone close, especially an irate captain. A wary presence carried throughout the airship. Assassins and killers all.

"Bloody buggering Nocturne," she swore to herself as she continued her stupid search of the stupid Sea. "What the pissing void are we even looking for?"

"Cap'n?" one of the voidspawn hobgoblin twins asked as he skuttled nearby, a dirty mop bucket in his gnarled digits.

"Get back to work, you pond scum prick." She didn't even try to figure out which twin it was, and that, in itself, showed her frustration was bubbling to the surface. "Now!"

The voidspawn jumped and ran off, spilling dreggy water all over her beauty. She cursed the creature's mother for whelping such a useless bag of bones.

Neenah took a breath to settle herself, getting worked up solved nothing. It would only stress her out and she didn't need any more greys. Her gaze drifted toward the pilotbox where Roland was at the wheel, the big one-eyed bastard trying to keep the *Lover* in a steady drift through the highland wind. The rest of her crew worked hard to keep the airship in top shape, fixing and repairing, swabbing and cleaning. Working around the squad of Imperium soldiers that should no longer be Imperium soldiers. A pleasure cruise it was not.

Her thoughts became a reality when the airship lurched as a highland current collided portside. Curses and shouts came from the soldiers abovedecks. Another ebbing mistral struck aft from below, then another stern above. The *Lover* buffeted from all sides. It was as if Zenith didn't know heads or asses which way He wanted His wind to blow in this cursed country.

Gods, she hated the bloody highlands of Filfangin. Awful gusts and worse denizens.

On cue, a wailing lilted out of the Sea, high pitched and grating. It was abruptly cut off by a snarling snap. A mist daemon preying upon another. Predator and prey.

"There!" one of the hobgoblins shouted from the bow portside. "Cap'n, 'ere!"

Neenah raced front; her feet steady under the vicious swaying of her beauty and found the voidspawn (she was fairly certain it was Zig) pointing down at one of his homeland's highland bluffs toward a depression in the Sea. With the swirling wind gales, the heavy fog was pushed back to reveal dozens, if not hundreds of crimson tents.

She didn't know if that was what the old man had them searching for, but it was the first sign of life they'd seen in the Sea all day. That and the daemons crying and keening.

Grabbing Zig by his knobby shoulders, she shoved him toward middeck. "Get your bloody ass down there, Zig, and get the man up top, hear?"

The hobgoblin skittered off while cackling, "I'm Zag." His annoying laughter echoing from belowdecks.

Moments later, the old man emerged. His peppery hair caught in the gust, flicking across his linen-covered eyes, his crimson robe's trail fluttered and snapped. The scars across his face were tight as he walked across the deck, the four scourges shadowing him in their black firedrake scale cuirasses and tinted breathers.

He leaned over the rail as the tents disappeared in the reforming Sea. His hidden eyes turned upward toward her, and she froze in place. There was no way on Zenith's green earth he could have seen them. "Put this ship down, LeFleur."

"Where? The highlands are buggered three ways from the Arbiter's bloody axe. Ain't nobody can land here, hear?"

"Land or I'll have your hide for a blanket."

Neenah threw up her hands. "Fine. You better get Invaris to make me, you buggering old prick." She spun and yelled toward Roland, "Bring this bint of a ship down right this bloody instant, you one-eyed firedrake tit. Gird your loins, boys!"

As Roland swung the wheel around, everyone abovedecks sought a hold on whatever was closest. Except the old man. He merely stood calmly; face honed on the Sea of Mist as it swallowed them up. Covering her nose from the stank of the mist, Neenah grumbled under her breath and pulled on a glass breathing mask.

All she wanted in life was fame, drink, and a quick quadran, but no, all she got was pissing trouble!

Marrow's Lover came to a stop near the base of a bluff, some twenty feet from the cliff face and ten feet off the ground. The rocky outcropping—at least to Neenah's keen eye in the hazy mist—overlooked what was once a lake but was now a cracked and dead patch of milky brown dirt. Tris lumbered toward the bow, tossing over a mooring rope, then raced stern to do the same, fighting his way through the throng of Imperium soldiers before disappearing over the rail. Doll gave hand signals to Neenah to indicate the dvergir was tethering the lines.

Invaris' advisor—who Neenah was growing ever more suspicious of—stood at the rail while the scourges leapt over. He wore no breather and didn't seem inclined to put one on when offered. Rope ladders were dropped by the hobgoblin twins and the grey-scaled soldiers began disembarking, only to disappear into the Sea. Before long, the old man and Neenah's crew were the only souls aboard.

With a finger deadlier than a wheellock pistol, the old man beckoned her. To her surprise, he wore the strange black bracelet and rings. "See that your ship stays here, LeFleur. Should it flee, you'll regret the day your mother spread her legs."

Neenah licked her plump lips nervously. "Won't be goin' bloody nowhere, hear?"

"I know they won't, LeFleur, because you're coming with me."

Jaw dropping. "What's that now? You want me to bloody go waltzing through the Sea like a bleating donkey ripe for some mist daemon to rip my pissing heart out. No buggering thanks."

The man twisted his finger, and a gust of blackened mist swept Neenah from behind, dragging her the span between them. The ring on his finger blazed bright crimson. She hung suspended, his burned face rife with anger. He removed the crimson cloth over his eyes, and she found her reflection staring back at her in his all-onyx gaze. The man had void aetheurgy! "Don't test me, LeFleur. I won't hesitate to end you and your crew."

She swallowed the lump in her throat and nodded.

The mist dropped her, and Roland rushed up to help. The old man moved his fingers again and the blackened mist cradled around him, lifting him off the deck and over the rail like he was floating on a thundercloud. He disappeared in the Sea but the mist all around the *Lover* crackled with aether, sending shivers down Neenah's spine.

"Cap'n, you shiny?"

"Do I look shiny, you big dumb oaf? I didn't come all this way to get my perfect ass magicked by a bloody aetheurgist and his dung-eating assassins!"

Roland scratched his fleshy chin under his breather. "Something isn't right about him, but I can't put my finger on it."

She rounded on the one-eyed mate. "No bloody shit, you fire-gobbling drake ass. Gon' get my hide skinned by that bugger. Godsdamnit, how does Neenah LeFleur always find herself in these situations?" Neenah glared at her crew. "You leave without me, and I'll bloody come back from the Meadows to haunt you, hear?"

The hobgoblin twins laughed but the waif Alexina smacked them both upside the head. The little bint was finally coming into her own.

With that, Neenah took to the rope ladder and descended into the Sea.

Although she could barely see her own hand in front of her face, the old aetheurgist led the company of soldiers, scourges, and her godsdamned self through the Sea until they came upon the camp.

They hadn't gone more than a hundred paces before they were set upon by firedrake scaled sentries carrying wheellock rifles, all pointed in their direction. The not-blind aetheurgist calmly walked ahead, his scarred hands parting the Sea, leaving an emptiness in the fog like being under a dome. The sentries quickly lowered their wheellocks, letting him pass, as did the squad and scourges.

Neenah swore softly.

What was she getting herself into here? And who was he? Definitely was no simple matriarch advisor. Why would Invaris bring an aetheurgist into her confidence? Neenah decided to make it a point to ask the matriarch whenever she returned from wherever she was at. And if Neenah survived this trip.

To her mild surprise, the camp was well organized and not a gaggle of people meekly surviving the horrors of the mist. No, it was a camp of soldiers and their followers. And as they neared, she saw they were all wearing the drake scale armor of the Imperium of the Fallen.

Bloodred tents were lined up in equal rows, spaced evenly apart. Cooking fires pocked the space between every five tents. How many, she couldn't begin to guess as the mist swallowed the encampment in muted greys and crimson. Soldiers not on duty milled around the fires telling stories and joking with their comrades. Camp followers, such as cooks and blacksmiths, worked in solemn silence, performing their roles as necessary to keep such a force functioning. The soldiers on duty ringed the tents with their rifles and blades, grimly fierce crimson skulled, breather-covered faces alert toward the surrounding Sea, the airs of an army ready for anything.

Barely visible at the far end of the camp were three massive lumps jutting over the tents. She couldn't make heads or asses what they were until the mist parted with a breezy gust and the bowsprit of an airship became unhidden.

Three warships? Here, of all bloody places? What is this godsdamned camp?

The elfirish aetheurgist moved toward a larger tent, one that Neenah supposed was camp's captain's. The scourges took a flanking position next to the flap as the man entered. The squad who had been passengers on *Marrow's Lover* melded into the encampment. Thankfully.

Neenah stopped in front of the tent, wondering what to do. "Bugger it," she breathed as she pushed inside. She was a captain herself, as it were.

A man sat at a large table, a captain by the red-painted firedrake scale cuirass. Surrounding him were dozens of officers also in red scale and tinted breathers. On the table was a detailed map of the Filfangin and Altreyian borders. Small figurines lay scattered across the map, one was a castle-like model to the northwest. If she had to fathom a guess, that represented the mega-city of Gandtril.

The captain had short, dark hair, slight stubble on his chin below his breather, and eyes of grey-green with pupils of red. The man was an aetheurgist. He rose so fast from the desk and down to a knee, Neenah barely had time to process what came out of his mouth. "Master Lu Har." The other soldiers also went to knee.

"Rise, Captain Agir."

As the captain stood, his words finally seeped into Neenah's brainmeat. Her mouth opened with a gasp. *Lu Har? No, it couldn't be. Could it?*

She stood stock still as she re-examined Invaris' advisor. Calibrathian elfirish tone, the full beard that was once black, the build, the flowing hair. Even through the scars and the burns, she would never have guessed it was the man known throughout the Mistlands as the Fallen. But now, she was clever enough to know she had been stupid to believe otherwise.

"You were supposed to have reached Gandtril by now."

The red-scaled captain visibly grimaced. Sweat beaded his forehead above this breather. "We've… forgive me, Master Lu Har, but we've had issues keeping the uh… daemons in check."

The Fallen—Gods above, he was the bloody Fallen, and Neenah found herself involuntarily taking a step back—was displeased by the response. Lu Har flicked his bangled wrist, and the captain was dragged over the table by a current of blackened mist, toppling the figurines over, scattering them all over the ground. The other soldiers moved backward. Red-pupiled eyes wide in fear, Lu Har pulled the frightened Captain Agir through the tent and out into the Sea.

Neenah fumbled with the flap to avoid him. One of the scourges pushed her aside like she was a child. She fell to the cracked ground with a curse.

Outside, Lu Har swung the captain around, the pitch-black mist thrusting him high into the air as he yelped. Hundreds of eyes looked up all at once, silence settled the once thriving camp, bathing it in surprise. And fear.

"Failure is not an option." The Fallen spoke softly but the words carried throughout the mist in amplified waves so that all could hear him. For Neenah, it felt like someone had just cranked up the volume on an aerescreen right next to her head. "My horde is finally re—"

A screech of ghastly intensity cut the Sea like a blade.

Sentries screamed from beyond Neenah's sightline, but she saw the source moments later as a massive bulk barreled into the camp, soldiers scrambling for weapons or to get out of the way. The bulk was covered in coarse hair, and as it careened into some tents, Neenah saw it had four arms and six legs.

Bloody buggering Nocturne, a mist daemon!

The daemon skittered backward, one of its legs piercing a crimson tent. Its body, while covered in hair, had a bug-like carapace on its belly, its arms ending in pinchers. The head was all misshapen and only little red dots indicated eyes lost within the hair. But the maw was unmistakable.

Skewering a nearby soldier, the daemon roared.

Neenah scrambled to her feet as Lu Har closed his eyes and spread his arms out, palms toward the daemon. All four bejeweled rings on the bracelet blossomed with aetheurgy. The captain fell to the earth as the black mist swept up the creature, raising it up like a hapless doll. The daemon screeched as its ten limbs were wrapped by the angry mist that electrocuted with lightning. Its bloodcurdling shriek echoed throughout the camp, causing Neenah to cover her ears like a frightened dunce. Luckily none of her crew was there to see her like this.

As the daemon fought the mist prison, Lu Har spoke to his army, "We leave at once for Gandtril. My horde will obey. If not," he twisted his hands, and the daemon squealed as the lightning-filled mist systematically pulled the creature's limbs from its body.

The arms separated in a gory crunch as the hairy carapace splintered in twain, the bones popping out of joints. One by one, the legs were torn free as green ichor rained over the ground. When the daemon's body sagged against the misted restraint, Lu Har snapped his fingers and the ugly head tore free, flying into a group of unblinking soldiers, who backed away as it rolled to a stop.

Neenah fought the urge to vomit.

Lu Har glanced at her before his all-onyx gaze fell upon the captain. "It seems, Captain Agir, your life was spared. A lesson is learned?" The disgraced soldier nodded and saluted. The Fallen gathered his robe and strode toward the tent, fingering Neenah to follow. "To Gandtril, LeFleur. Get it done."

Neenah looked at the captain, then the dismembered body of the daemon, then the rustling tent flaps.

Being made a matriarch woman isn't worth this…

Finnus

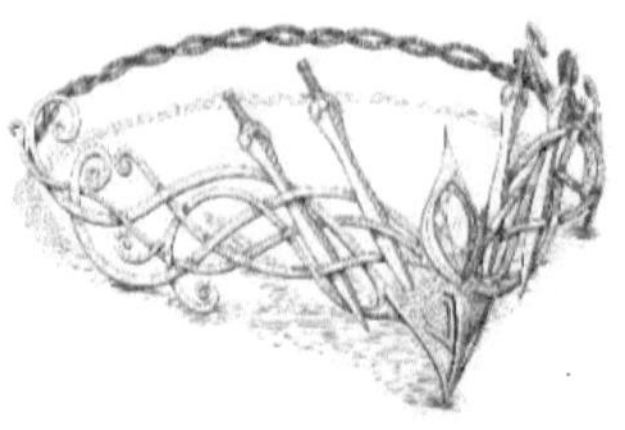

XVIII
FINN

THE COBBLESTONE STREET led them to the egress of the Obelisk.

The base of the sprawling spire was constructed of black granite blocks that weighed near a thousand pounds apiece. And unlike the utilitarian design of the tower on the southern side, the mega-city side had stone porticos that held carved statues of proud Kanjans in their Legion regalia.

The first set of gates were inch-thick steel bars and were inscribed with golden runes of aether, the spells hard as stone and practically unbreakable. Legionnaires stood on both sides of the first gate, daemon-killing spears in hand, wheellock pistols at their belts, breathers on their faces. They saluted when they noted who he was. Finn's three shadows weren't far behind.

The second set of gates down a granite hall with kill holes along the walls and above were far more formidable than the first. Not only were the bars five times as thick, but the number of inscribed runes tripled. A heavy steel, rune-etched door just beyond in case of breach. Half a dozen Legionnaires stood ready.

As the gates opened to allow Finn and Wick inside, he felt a wave of aether tickle his skin. It was an alarm of sorts, one made of *Aere* and *Aquis*. It warded against those who would enter the

Obelisk with malice. Finn remembered the number of augurs it had taken to set the ward when the Obelisk had been completed some hundred years ago.

"I'll never get used to that," Wick said.

"You know Kanjans, Wick, ever cautious."

"Except you, needle dick?"

Finn snorted as he turned a corner toward an open foyer where a man sat behind a carved stone desk. The soldier wore the eagle sigil of the Legion but was more an administrator than grunt.

"Princeps Finnus," the soldier stood and saluted hastily. Gods above was the man twitchy. "I didn't know you wer—"

"None of that, now," Finn cut him off. "I'm here to find Emont Landra. Know where he's at?"

"Uh… I think the primus pilus is down by the Crows." The Crows were rows of hay-stuffed bags in the shape of daemons for the Legion to practice their spear thrusts.

Finn nodded, but before he turned from the nervous legionnaire, "How many new recruits lately, soldier?"

"Only four… uh… this week, princeps." The man's voice was deep, and Finn could detect the hint of shame behind it.

Four, my word, Em, remember when we couldn't get four in a bloody month?

"The numbers are dwindling," Wick said, irritated, "you'd know that if you stopped dipping your prick in a vat of wine each day. We've only thirty-one in the past six months. With the Imperium of the Fallen imploding, Rignork figures the people think the threat over. But you stubborn Kanjans refuse to see the truth. Nobody wants to fight for the Golden Throne any longer."

It also didn't help that children of elfirish descent were also dwindling. Ever since the Fall, elfir—both Kanjan and

Calibrathian—had seen a sharp decline in their populations. The augurs of the Shards believed it had to do with the corrupted aether in the mist, for outside of draconem, elfir possessed the most aether in their bloodlines. And despite being long-lived and never prone to over-procreate prior to the corruption, elfirish women were now lucky to birth more than a single child in the five centuries since.

"You tryin' to pin this on me? Fair enough." He glanced at the three legionnaires, "Onward, my friends."

Because Finn didn't rise to Wick's jibe, the lapin glowered, which made Finn smile all the more. He enjoyed grinding Wick's gears. Always had, always would. The three chaperones exchanged looks but said nothing.

But Wick wasn't wrong.

Rēx Vitus harbored the belief that Kanja was the greatest nation of all and should help everyone in need, even before the Fall. It was a noble ideal, but it lacked the essence of sanity. Kanja was indeed the largest nation, and was the first to recover, but it was foolish to think the elfir in the northern cold were anything but disconnected to the comings and goings of anything south of the Forgemistress' Blades, let alone any other race beside elfir. It was easy to remain ignorant to those below the floating mountains of Kalderim, even their own nation.

The rebellion in Drenth and the Golden Throne's inaction to help was indicative of that very fact.

Ahead as Finn marched down a southern corridor, the inner gates of the Obelisk slowly opened. As he passed under the gate, he looked around and saw that legionnaires were positioned at the kill holes with wheellocks drawn.

Odd.

The inner fortress was a flurry of activity. Soldiers trained, marched, and guarded the outer walls of Gandtril. The foundry was ablaze and black smoke plumed. The Legion in full swing.

Wick pointed toward a man with lengthy, jet-black hair slicked behind his pointed ears. "That's Landra."

The man stood with his hands on his hips as he watched legionnaires stab away with their daemon-killing spears at the hay bags. His voice was rough and annoyed as he barked orders.

Something about the man told Finn that all was not right in Gandtril, and it set his nerve on edge. He was dressed in too fine a garb to be a Legion soldier. Finn's scale notwithstanding, he was royalty. Landra most certainly was not, and the man wore a tailored doublet instead of the uniform of the rank.

As Finn approached, the tall elfirish primus pilus turned his way, a scowl deepening. "By Honor and Blood, what has taken you so long to get here, Princeps Finnus?" the man practically spat his words, the annoyance etched in furrowed skin upon his thin face.

"I've been busy, Emont. I beg your pardon for negle—"

"Primus Pilus to you, boy." Landra was indeed as harsh as Wick had said. Finn let the comment slide because he had no intention of arguing, he had other things on his mind. Instead, Finn tapped his fist to his heart in salute to Landra. The man huffed. "The Golden Throne sent word that you would be here months ago, but we've had to do with Lord Titen in your place."

"I'm sorry, Primus Pilus Landra, but I wasn't prepared to lead the Legion. I had… other things to attend to." Why was he acting a blubbering fool to a lowly Legion captain?

A specter filled his vision, one doused in yellow light. Emre. It was as if his beloved was there, by his side. Maybe he would always be. Hopefully.

Emre, silent, gave him a look.

Guilt, ah, yes, that was why.

"Don't make excuses, boy." Landra's contempt was deep.

"Primus Pilus, you shouldn't talk to a child of the Golden Throne like a common soldier," Wick growled, then added *'even if he is an ingrate'* under his breath.

The man gave the lapin a deeper scowl than the one he'd given Finn. "Who the fuckin' void do you think you are to talk to a primus pilus of the Legion as such?"

"He's my personal pilot, primus pilus." The man turned back toward him, so Finn smiled pleasantly. One to reel Landra into his confidence by showing respect, but two, he felt the need to pester Wick after months wallowing in depression. "My lice-ridden friend here has an uncouth mouth. But he's good in the air."

"You'd be better served with a pilot who kept his mouth shut."

"Yes, he certainly should," was all he replied but could feel the daggers Wick was shooting into his back.

A runner, a young elfirish boy maybe no older than ninety came rushing from one of the buildings along the walls. He skittered to a stop and saluted the primus pilus, then his eyes went wide when he saw Finn. He gave the boy a wink. The boy's mouth dropped.

"What is it, boy?" Landra said. Apparently, he had a thing for calling all people younger than he 'boy'.

"The… um… umm…"

"Spit it out, son. Close that yap, the princeps doesn't need you gawking like a milked goat at him." Landra side-eyed Finn. "Even though he likes being the center of attention."

Finn heard Wick snort. "He's not wrong," he said apologetically to the young boy.

That seemed to loosen his tongue. "Word on the aerescreens, the praetor wishes to see you, primus pilus."

Landra nodded to the boy and walked away from them, but stopped and turned back, glaring at Finn. "If you're ready to serve with Honor and Blood, princeps, you'd best come along, too."

Were we ever this demanding, Em? The specter of his beloved said nothing, of course. *I suppose you're right. We had to be, otherwise we never would've won.*

Finn motioned to Landra, "Lead on, good captain. I shall follow and be of service. With Honor and Blood, and all that mummery."

Landra scowled yet another scowl but marched toward the Obelisk

Wick came close and kidney-punched him, eliciting a grunt of pain. "You're a bloody fool, needle dick. That man will be the downfall of this city. Be wary of him."

"Whyever for, Wick? The man's of the Legion. I can't believe he will throw us all to the wolves. Or daemons, you know. I think you're scared of what's outside these walls."

The lapin stroked his whiskers. "If what Val says is true, Lu Har will destroy men like him without second thought."

Finn stood tall, looked at the wraith of Emre in his mind's eye, hand on his rapier hilt. He gave the lapin his most sincere, confident grin he had in his arsenal, the same one he had given to Emre the nightturn before their botched attack on the mines of Drenth that almost got them sent to the Meadows prematurely.

"Please, Wick, you think my intrepid sister-friend is the only one who can see the future? Bah, you're a fool if you think otherwise. Trust me, I wouldn't place my faith in a man like Landra any further than I could toss him full burn."

"Now you're starting to sound like Kephren," the lapin said with a pinched frown. "You recall what happened to him, don't you?"

Of course, I do, my friend. What do you think, Em, will it happen once more? Don't answer that question, I know the answer. "You seem to have forgotten who was the handsome elfir who fingered Keph for a spy, my friend."

An alarm rose, causing Finn and Wick to share a glance.

Landra turned back, head raised as the alarm blared. "The southern gates."

The six of them took off toward a thick set of stone steps, climbing up the middle wall before racing over one of the narrow stone bridges that spanned the middle wall to the outer. It groaned under their bootfalls as other soldiers of the Legion scurried into positions, weapons clutched, facing outward toward the Sea.

The primus pilus stood above the gated bulwark, hands clutching the smooth stone of the wall. Nearby, on both sides of the gates, giant aethecite-powered vacuums regurgitated the mist back into the Sea. Finn and Wick neared, eyes searching the haze for the alarmed threat.

Then came a cry, someone, no, someones running through the mist. A drakken pair. Arms flailing, yelling as they ran.

Lojen and Ruane.

"Open the gates!" a legionnaire near the portcullis yelled.

The gates squealing open, Finn watched as the drakken siblings raced into the fortress, disappearing.

Long before they reached the war room within the Obelisk, they heard the voices. Raised voices. Worried voices. Arguing voices.

Finn, with Wick and Landra on his heels, entered into a heated discussion. Titen leaned over a table in the center of the room. Praetor Rignork sat in a cushioned chair to his left. A number of stewards, augurs, and other ranking members of the Legion all surrounded the table, including Optio Resande. Some were expressing opinions, others were taking copious amounts of notes, presumably correspondences to be sent to Kalderim. Lojen and Ruane filled the other side, their broad, scaled backs and tails facing the entrance Finn and company entered. Their gravelly draconem tones lost within the cacophony of elfirish. Finn's shadows remained outside.

Only Titen glanced his way, his brother's eye twitching, telling Finn he wasn't going to like the news the drakken siblings brought from their sojourn in the Sea.

"Here," Lojen was saying as he pointed a thick talon toward the table. "This is where Augur Indigo and Augur Puce made their stand. Where we… we fled. Where the, broken shells, I still can't believe it. Where the scourges were."

Scourges? But that's impossible. Em?

His beloved said nothing, his somber green-pupiled eyes focused to where Lojen was pointing.

Upon the table was a map of the Mistlands rendered in three dimensions, about twelve inches at the highest peaks of the Forgemistress' Blades. It was massive, the map, and was as detailed as the finest sculpture in all of Kanja. All Legion fortresses had a similar map as it was designed in Kalderim, commissioned by the rēx not long after the Fall. As the world grew from the ashes, so did the detail of the maps.

The drakken was pointing to a village marked in the middle of the Sea down southwest, near to Filfangin. It was a small village, one that wasn't even named as far as the map went. Probably nothing more than a handful of homes, a few families willing to brave the mist.

"The Fallen's army," Lojen continued, "I swear it by my honor as a wardkeeper."

"The Fallen is no more," Praetor Rignork said, shaking his aged head. "You shouldn't believe in the rumors, drakken."

Ruane puffed out her chest, going to her full height of half plus six feet. Her teeth protruded from her jaw as she snarled. "You question a wardkeeper's word, elfir? Dare you go against the word of one of Zenith's chosen? Man always think they know better."

"Blasphemy," Landra hissed besides Finn. The man's posture was tense, his demeanor tenser. The other soldiers of the Legion bristled behind their primus pilus.

"Rumors they aren't, praetor," Titen said, remaining calm amongst the growing tension.

There were audible gasps from the soldiers of the Legion, none louder than the praetor himself. For apparently Titen and their intrepid sister hadn't told the old warrior.

Why?

"My sister has heard directly from Bliss," Titen was saying as if to calm the murmurs. "The Fallen has been rebirthed anew."

"Fuck," Rignork muttered. "And why haven't you informed me of this, Titen." Very few people outside of the Dunleith family called Titen anything other than 'Lord Sword', Eran Rignork being one of them. "If the Ideal Daughter saw fit to bequeath this knowledge to Valeria, I should have been the first to know of it as the head of the Legion." It was almost a rebuke. He glanced toward Lojen and Ruane but said nothing, his lips a tight line. Finn knew of the tension between Tevun and Eran Rignork.

Titen's eye twitched again, but he bowed his head. "'Tis the truth, praetor. I stand before you asking your forgiveness, but I thought it prudent to await further word from the Virtuous One. She promised She would speak further to my sister-friend."

"And She will," Val said with a whisper as she entered the war room. All the murmurs and grumbling silenced as she came to a stop at the map. "She will speak now."

"O bugger me." Finn hated this part.

Val's bi-colored gaze turned upon Ruane, holding out a pale hand adorned with gold and silver bikromi bracelets. "The augur's amethyst, Ruane?"

In the drakken's grip was a satchel. Finn vaguely remembered Puce wearing such a satchel, but it was fleeting as he had been too busy lost in his wine. Ruane dug into the weathered leather bag and pulled out a light purple gemstone that was half stained with blood, handing it to Val.

He opened his mouth to say something, but Wick jabbed him in the hip bone. The specter of Emre shook at the shoulders as if laughing, for it was the Gutter King of Drenth who had the usual pleasure of staving off Finn's protestations in Val's process.

Bloodstained gem in both hands, Val held it before her, leaning forward in an unnatural angle for a normal person, her forehead touching the gemstone while her spine was pliant. The bracelets on her pale wrists gleamed fiercely. Then her body went completely stiff, her sterling hair—which was braided in dozens of plaits—fell across her face and the amethyst. The air within the war room rippled as if a short-statured bard plucked the string of a magical lute in preparation for a performance.

Then her head snapped backward, a silent scream streaming from her as her breath became visible, her bracelets burning like aethecite. She rose, then. Arms clutching the gemstone to her chest, her entire rigid body inches above the floor. Hoarfrost coated her arms, which were bare from mid-bicep. Braids now sticking out in static.

Her head lowered, her bikromi eyes settling upon all those within the war room, specifically Titen. One black eye, dark as the void. The other white, pearlescent. Black bound to the past, white to the future to come. Both glowed with aether. Vision Form.

"HE COMES. HE COMES," Val spoke as snowflakes dripped from her body. But it was not his sister's normal whisper, no, it was the voice of Bliss. The Ideal Daughter of the Pentax.

Titen went to a knee, as did everyone else in the room aside from Rignork (too old), Ruane (too shocked, probably), and Finn (seen it too many times to care). "My goddess. You praise us with your presence."

"SCOURGES REVEALED. DANGER TO KALDERIM."

"No void," Finn uttered. Titen's head rose. "What? Lojen and Ruane were there, brother-friend. We don't need Her for that information." He waved a hand at the prone Val hovering like a children's parlour trick. "Call me a heretic if you want, but She hasn't exactly given us anything we don't already know."

The specter of his beloved gave him a sad frown. A disappointed one.

An odd choking sound filled the silence of the war room, and Finn soon realized it was coming from Val's open mouth. It wasn't choking, it was Bliss laughing. ***"THE PRINCEPS SPEAKS SENSE FINALLY. MY BROTHER ALWAYS KNEW HE LIKED YOU. I NEVER UNDERSTOOD UNTIL NOW. YOU SHUN SUBTLENESS.***

SOMETHING THE PENITENT VEER AGAINST, WHERE THEY POCKET THEIR LIES."

Finn was stunned. Actually stunned. In near ten centuries, Bliss had never spoken in unbroken, full sentences through Val. In fact, She had never spoken more than a handful of words at a time. "By the Pentax…"

"INDEED, PRINCEPS OF MY GOLDEN THRONE." The goddess laughed once more. Queer it was, that sound coming from Val without her body moving. But then it stopped, the Ideal Daughter's voice growing stern. ***"THE DIVINE HAS SEEN FIT TO RAISE THE FALLEN. LONG HAVE WE SEARCHED FOR HIM IN THE VOID, BUT NOW HE MAKES HIS PRESENCE KNOWN. HE HAS TAKEN HOLD OF THE OCULUS OF APATHY."***

"No, that cannot be," Rignork said from his chair, his eyes facing away from Val as if she were the goddess Herself. Respect given. "That was destroyed by Canlon Carr."

"IT WAS NOT," Bliss said through Val. ***"OUR GREATEST FEAR HAS ARISEN, THE FALLEN HAS THE MEANS TO ENTER EMINENCE. A THIEF FOR HIS DREAMS."***

"But the Seals still hold," Lojen said. Though on his knees, his keratin horns glimmered as aether swirled within their hardness, visible. "Well, three of them. Brynn has abandoned them."

"NO, AEGIS, SHE HAS NOT. SHE CANNOT ABANDON HER FATE. FIGHT IT, SHE WILL, BUT SHE WILL BREAK EACH SEAL. THE MISTRESS OF THE FORGE TOLD YOU TRUE BEFORE HER SACRIFICE. THE DAUGHTER OF NIGHTINGALE WILL BREAK THE SEALS, SHE WILL DESTROY THE DRACONEM GUARDIANS. HER BLOOD IS WOVEN TO THIS PATH. SHE WILL FIGHT THE DIVINE AND BRING EMINENCE BACK TO THE REALM OF LIFE."

Wait, what is an 'aegis'? Em?

Nothing but a blank stare.

"What must be done, my goddess?" Titen gripped the Golden Sword tightly. Finn could tell his brother was struggling, they all were. Except Ruane, of course.

The Oculus of Apathy was the one weapon they all should fear. For that had almost been how the Fallen had won five hundred years prior. The antithesis to the Eye of the Soul. The weapon of the Pit. Of Noctis.

"ENDURE, PRINCEPS OF MY GOLDEN THRONE. ENDURE WHAT THE FALLEN WILL BRING. HIS HORDE WILL FLOW LIKE THE TIDE. THE HYMN MUST SING AGAINST THE FIRE."

"The words from the dreamer," one of the stewards said. Finn tried to pick out the speaker, but the man had gone silent afresh.

Tonns, that was the dreamer's name, the one who Lojen had brought back from the Sea.

"THERE IS BUT ONE WAY TO EMINENCE, PRINCEPS, THAT IS THROUGH THE VIRD. SEEK THE VIRD."

The Vird? Finn thought. Why would Bliss want his brother to go to the Forgemistress' Blades to seek out the Vird?

"NO, PRINCEPS OF MY GOLDEN THRONE, NOT HIM," Finn looked at his sister, her bi-colored stare was squarely upon him, ***"THE GOLDEN SWORD WILL BEAR THE CROWN. SEEK MY TINES. IT LAYS RENT, AWAITING YOU IS THE PATH OF BLADES."***

Me?

Val's mouth began to close, but not before her head turned back to Titen. ***"FEAR NOT WHAT COMES. IT HAS BEEN SEEN BY NIGHTINGALE. THE END MAY LIE BEFORE YOU, BUT THE STRENGTH IN YOUR HEART WILL CARRY ON. MYSELF, I AM***

WITH YOU ALWAYS." To Lojen now, ***"AEGIS YOU ARE. THE MISTRESS OF THE FORGE CLAIMED YOU SUCH. DON'T HIDE IT, EMBRACE IT. SEEK THE VIRD FOR THEY WILL GIFT YOU THE PATH TO TREAD. HONOR TO BE SOUGHT, HONOR TO BIND."***

A spasm overtook Val's body; the frost filming her arms and bracelets evaporating into a sizzling steam, puddles forming under her. Her boots touched the floor, and she pitched forward. Both Finn and Lojen lunged for her, catching her by the arms before she fell completely. Finn took her in his grasp and lowered her to the floor as her breathing became deep, sucking in the air.

She searched his eyes. "What did She say?"

Val barely remembered what she said during the throes of Vision Form unless Bliss wanted her to, which was rare. The Virtuous One would overtake her completely. Finn could only recall a handful of times since her birth that Val knew word for word what Bliss had said. Such a barren gift.

"That we're fucked," Finn said around a grin. "And apparently I've got a task to complete."

Ever serious, Val gave no smile. "Then do not disappoint Her."

"You're talking about needle dick," Wick said, "he's nothing but a disappointment."

In his periphery, Emre shook his wraithly head in disagreement. At least someone was on his side, didn't matter if they were dead and dancing about the Meadows.

"So now what?" Ruane asked the question upon everyone's tongue.

All eyes were upon the Golden Sword. The big elfir, Finn's stalwart, loyal brother-friend, sighed. "We prepare for war."

"Great," Finn started, "from the frying pan into the kettle. What do you say, Wick, you ready for this?"

A dueling knife quickly appeared in the lapin's paw before disappearing again. Show off. "For Dervin. For Drenth."

"For the Golden Throne," Rignork said as he pushed his gout-ridden body upright. "By Honor and Blood."

A chorus repeating by all those of the Legion, except Emont Landra, who just shook his head ruefully.

"For Brynn Benld," Lojen said.

Val's cold hand cupped his cheek. "For you, brother-friend. Always for you."

What could she possibly mean by that?

XIX
SOLANINE

LAUGHTER FILLED THE tavern called *Nocturne's Bounty*. An apt name for what Solanine had in mind.

From the shadows of the tavern's beamed ceiling between the first floor and the second, a steady drizzle pelted the dirty pane of glass Solanine had just slithered in from. Loud and boisterous was the barroom below.

O, how these mortals crow.

The Solanine of old would have cared about the bleating sheep by forcing them into line, so they could eagerly await the slaughter in the Divine's name. Would have sought the stage to be in the light, to have the adulation of those underneath. Would have pined for the world to remember the name Solanine. For a beautiful mortal face to be plastered on every aerescreen across the Mistlands.

But that was the Solanine of old. Now, Solanine preferred the shadows. Preferred the hunt, reminding the blooddrake what it was like before the Fall. What it was like being the apex hunter.

Nocturne's Bounty was a three-story building that was a mash of warehouse and storefront. The first floor where the bar and its drinkers frivolously pounded alcohol, was an elongated rectangle filling multiple building fronts to create an exceptionally large drinking establishment. So large, it was difficult to spy the far wall while standing at one end, even for a blooddrake's aether. The second and third floors were of the original building, thus it was almost like a tower smashed atop a warehouse. Only a single stair led upward to the top floors.

As the laughter and drunken cheer raged undertail, Solanine moved across *Nocturne's Bounty's* trusses toward where the second floor met the first by the stair, rainwater dripping from the blooddrake's obtained clothing. Body leveled like a prowling cat, Solanine leapt from beam to beam, claw within mortal flesh gouging into the rotted wood, sending shavings down into the revelers' drinks. One glanced upward but would see nothing but shadows, not even a smudge within, for Solanine burned Void Form aetheurgy, drawing the blackness around in an invisible cloak. A void walk.

A pair of goblin guards watched with putrid yellow eyes narrowed upon the drinkers, scowling at anyone coming too close to the stairs. They carried serrated bone swords from Filfangin and had wheellocks shoved into their belts. Fully armored in bone and full of snarl. Guards protecting the woman upstairs from being bothered. There were other goblin guards, three on the roof, in fact, all dead from Solanine's claw.

Unhurried, Solanine unwound from the beam above the stair, mortal legs of man swinging silently before letting go and dropping soundlessly behind the unwitting goblin guards and climbing the stair. At the doorway at the top, Solanine placed a mortal left hand upon the portal, drawing upon natural aetheric magic underneath the flesh. To the exoscales of a lesser order of draconem beneath. To Void Form.

The metal of the door radiated under Solanine's claw, sending a glow of green aether vibrating all along the door's edges, filtering between the hinges. Emerald tinted *Terris* drained from the metal and into the floor. Solanine spoke a magical chant in the language of the void as blood oozed from the scars upon the scales' breastbone, sending aether forward like a jade smoke under the portal into the hall beyond. Healing of nature, a sense of calming drawn from the earth itself.

Not all aether was tainted by Noctis, nor was all aether used by Solanine that of Eminence. No, the fools of this world only thought in binaries. Aether was neither, aether was all. One soul.

Glancing down the stair, the goblin guards had yet to turn, had yet to discover the blooddrake. Waiting a heartbeat, a soft thump came from beyond the door. Solanine cut off the aetheric magic, its glow returning to flesh like a goblet's contents being poured in reverse and opened the portal. Two goblins leaned against the wall; their wheellock rifles held loose in the crooks of their arms. Their faces were a gruesome green-grey of stretched leather, dozens of rings protruding from the things they called noses and ears.

A memory dredged up from the well of their scales' stolen mind.

A fortress within a city surrounded by desert. Drenth. The scales slipping through the fortress home in the dark, clinging to the shadows with Void Form. Two goblins blissfully talking about one's sister becoming fecund with child. Painfully dying as the scales released a blackened steel daemon blade.

Solanine hated the voidspawn, so the memory of Cadrianna Nightingale killing was not an unpleasant one. Unreliable and lazy, goblins. Give a horde of daemons over the voidspawn from Filfangin. The goblin guards snored softly through crooked noses. Knocked out for only a few minutes, but long enough for

Solanine to pass and not long enough they would actually recall falling asleep on the job.

The blooddrake moved toward the tavern's rear, sliding through the gloom of the second floor, keeping to the shadows, avoiding any man or goblin—which only seemed to be the staff working in the kitchens. Sweet aromas of baking bread and aromatic soups. Solanine could distinguish the scent of aerovern mixed with the hints of cinnamon and clove. Men seemed to enjoy the taste of aerovern for some reason. Solanine thought it tasted like a dead beast that had decayed in the sun and was covered in its own feces. A goblin guard stalked the halls but was unaware of a drake in its midst.

A thin set of stairs ran upward to the third and final floor. Solanine quickly ascended and found a locked door. No guard nearby, but Solanine heard a barbaric belch, which indicated a goblin had wandered into the kitchen for a late nighttum snack.

Fools… Using a combination of aether comprised of *Terris* and *Aere*, Solanine made short work of the lock, pushing it open.

Grunting.

"Fuck m—"

More grunting.

A naked woman rode a man.

Small seagandr-oil lamps were alighted upon a desk, a cracked mirror on the wall overhead. It had surprised Solanine upon rebirth nearly fifty years prior, some five hundred years after the Fall, to see those detestable multi-headed beasts boiled down to such a simple luxury. Aethecite had been one thing, but draconem essence, that had bothered Solanine.

"Fuck. O fuck."

The woman was Neron Hobb. The man was some unlucky sot used for his prick before being tossed into the Bay of Fire when

Hobb moved on to the next willing shaft. Hobb was a firebrand, taking what she thought was hers by right. Mostly by violence. But Hobb had served her purpose in Solanine's hunt for the Godsblood and the Seal of *Ignis*. Hobb also possessed something that the Godsblood would also require to find the Seal. A ship.

The woman—as well as the man she was riding—had not heard the door open, nor had they noticed Solanine standing bedside.

Claw nestled under the olive-skinned flesh of the daughter of Nightingale, Solanine grabbed Hobb by the back of the neck, shoving the Guilder to the bed with enough force to shatter the bedframe. The man Hobb had been humping scrambled, his mouth opened to emit a scream, but Solanine shoved drake scaled greaves into the man's throat, sound muffling like a muzzle. The naked man struggled and kicked, suddenly flaccid prick flailing wildly. But Solanine held him tight.

Men were weak.

Hobb gurgled into the bed under Solanine's tight grip on her neck, face down into the linen, legs thrashing, arms fighting. The man's brows pinched together, focusing on the face of the scales Solanine had bonded, knowing the face of a scourge of the Fallen's coven. The famed face of a woman once of Port Sin.

"For the love of Nocturne," Solanine hissed.

With a useless right hand, Solanine released aether. A greenish glow fled from the scales' benumbed fingers and encapsulated the man's face. Suffocating him, going down his throat with an earthy force, filling his lungs with aetheric sand of *Terris* pulled from the splintered wooden bedframe. The man's eyes rolled back, and he died. Blood dribbled from the Void Form scars upon Cadrianna Benld's breast, down the runes carved in the woman's spine under the cuirass of firedrake scale.

Leaning toward the Guilder, Solanine spoke into the woman's ear. "You've served Nightingale well. Served me well. Your talents in smuggling have worked, the trap has now been set. The Godsblood has been summoned and sent." Hobb screamed into the linen sheets for her guards. Solanine smirked as men are wont to do when amused. "But I'm afraid your purpose has run out, for only the blood of Nightingale can access the volcano. Humir like you cannot pass its magic. But you possess something I need."

Solanine called upon Void Form. Alive the power of the gods came, firing tiny little wisps of a glowing mist down Cadrianna Benld's hand. Blues, reds, yellows, and greens danced over the drake scale accompanied by a chant of voidspeak. The blooddrake's own scales, etched with runes of the Four Tenets of Aether, blazed under the flesh of man. Aether became a river of haze encircling Solanine's body.

And the scales of Cadrianna Benld peeled away. The flesh that was man folded upon itself like a scroll. No blood, no bone, nor muscle. Just flesh. It fell from Solanine like the dropping of a gown to reveal red-black interlocking exoscales.

The true scales of a blooddrake.

Long had it been since Solanine breathed freely, a year's turn almost. Always wearing scales since being rebirthed by the Divine's grace and guile. Taloned left hand roamed the hard exterior of exoscales as Solanine slithered into a S shape, for no legs did the blooddrake have. Solanine's right claw ended above the elbow joint, maimed by that infernal Godsblood. Muscular tail flicked about, for too long had it been forced to hide in those tailless scales of men. Head back and sighing in relief.

"Praise the void!"

Solanine's singular claw tightened into a fist, devolving into the painful memory locked tight in the vault that was the past of Noctis, of the Hatch. Of Lu Har's war with Canlon Carr.

When the call to mobilize had been issued, Solanine had gone to war with the other orders of drakes. Willing to sacrifice a place amongst Zenith's spawn so the firedrakes, aeroverns, terrisvvyrms, and the seagandrs would all understand the might of the blooddrakes of Nightingale and Nocturne. Especially the favored drakken and wardkeepers. Solanine hadn't hesitated in adding aether to the cause.

It had been a costly calculation.

Deadlier than any disease, the war between Eminence and Noctis was. Deadlier than Nocturne's forever assault on His Twin's heavens. Thousands upon thousands of the Pentax's chosen had died in the fight for supremacy. Firedrakes suffering immense blows as their skies had become black with smoke from their corpses. The very soil of the Forgemistress' earth had become caustic from the disintegrating carcasses of vvyrms blasted by aether and flame alike. Many of the floating mountains that soon became the Voidlands fell from the sky bearing the dead of the Twins' aerovern and firedrakes. Seas, rivers, and all collections of water polluted and dammed by the shorn heads of the seagandrs.

And yet, for all the deaths tolled by the four higher orders of draconem, the grandest losses had been totaled by the drakken. The smallest and craftiest of all the drakes in Zenith's brood suffered the most. Now, there were hardly any left.

Same with Nocturne's blooddrakes.

Solanine's own brood had been killed in the war, destroyed by a scarlet firedrake raining brimstone down upon the battlefield.

Reliving it constantly, trying to keep it locked in the vault of memory. But the vault of regret was never fully secure.

But little did any of them know the truth about the First Wife, of who Nightingale was, and who had fathered the draconem and why. It wasn't until Lu Har had shown Solanine the truth of the Hatch, shown the truth of their history, did the blooddrake change allegiance.

And soon, once the Godsblood and the Seal of *Ignis* were in claw, Solanine would be one step closer to revenge.

Hobb cried uncontrollably into the bed; the gritty, tenacious woman who ruled the Harbor of Thieves became nothing more than a sobbing babe. Knowledge known that her life was over and now wailed in sorrow.

Scaled lower half pressing into the woman's back to keep her contained, Solanine slammed a taloned claw that shone brightly with aether into the back of Hobb's head, piercing through the woman's mouth into the bedding. Hobb went limp. Lifting the Guilder, Solanine turned her around. She wasn't dead, not yet, but soon. Neron Hobb's pupils dilated. Horror gamboled within.

"This is the face of your gods, mortal. Savor it because the Pit awaits you. Tified has already beat you there, although his death was stolen from me. Yours will not."

Blood streamed around Solanine's talons as Hobb died. Retracting the claw, the Guilder slumped to the base of the bed, crimson pooling on the floorboards. One loose end clipped, three others still to cut. And then the Godsblood would be prepared to lead the way to the Seal.

Reaching for the fleshy blanket of the daughter of Nightingale, Solanine began to chant softly, speaking the ancient spells of the void. The bond forming. A rancid stink of an overgrown swamp rose from the scales, leaving the room smelling of a terrisvvrym's cloaca.

Holding the scales like a cloak to be worn, Solanine's arm disappeared into the body, replicating the cocoon of aether that melded the two of them together. Flesh combining with scales. The runes etched into Solanine's exoscales radiated with the Four Tenets. Instead of a cloaked hood pulled up and over, Solanine's snout wormed into the back of the formless head. Then body, the other useless arm. Finally, Solanine's tail, pulled close.

The voidspeak chant died, aether wavering. The mortals called it Void Form. For Solanine, it was the essence of Death.

In moments, Solanine stood, re-wearing Cadrianna Benld's scales, knitted together like new. Solanine flexed the scales' hand, the bond now cemented fresh. Memories flooded into Solanine's mind, heated memories of Efan Nightingale and his wife Jensa. Of a daughter named Brynn. A husband named Emre. A lover named Lu Har.

Of unfiltered memories wrought in the blood of Nightingale. Memories to be parsed. Memories for Solanine to uncover, for they would lead to the Seal of *Ignis*.

At Solanine's feet was an empty husk of flesh which resembled a snake's scales when shed, the magic of a blooddrake's aether leaving behind its gory spell. But instead, this was an outer layer of man's skin, discarded by the new set of worn scales. A gift to the Godsblood to know who hounded her.

Close they were to the Seal of *Ignis*. The other blooddrakes, Rinkhal and Ialtris, had found the way here in Port Sin long before the plan had been set. Entrenched in the game they were, the pair setting the stage for Solanine's ascension.

Come to me, Godsblood. Come…

XX
CYAN THE DEFIANT

"LU HAR WAS A soulless man. Never did care for him," Ifant Klander said casually, a wine glass sloshing around in blasé hand movements while talking. "I've heard it said that your acolyte has a strong connection to aetheurgy. Quite the Form, I hear, to have slain the Fallen. Forgive if I assume too much, but as her taskmaster, I bet you swell with pride?"

"I appreciate the sentiment, Lord Klander." Cyan grimaced at the droll attempt at sincerity. It was meetings like these that made him yearn for codex cases in the field and not those of politics. "My pride is but a gift by the Pentax, for it is unto Them all I have comes. I appreciate the audience, as well, it was kind of you to see me on such short notice. I know your business… endeavors must keep you entirely too busy."

Cyan sat in a cushy chair in front of a fireplace so plentiful, it could practically warm the entire city. He was sweating in his woolen cassock and the chilled water he was sipping did nothing to cool him. Klander sat across. He held a cup of wine in his delicate hands, drinking occasionally, the dozens of bikromi silver and gold bracelets about his wrists clacking softly when he did.

"Nagnoz, bring that tray here. Good man. Anything for the Scattered Shards," Klander said as he plucked a square of chocolate-covered something from the tray held by the hobgoblin servant. "You know, Vicar Cyan, I must confess as to the confusion of our meeting." He popped the sweet into his mouth. "I've no qualms with the Shards enjoying the… fruits of my establishment, but I have to ask, am I in trouble?"

If you are a blooddrake under that pale visage, then yes, yes you are. "You're not under any investigation, if that's what you're thinking." *Do you bear the stain of Nocturne under there? Show me true, Justice.* "To be honest, I wanted to speak to you about the aethecite mines in Drenth. I heard you commissioned an excursion up to the City of Sands with Danma Dil's backing."

The bikrome fingered the sweets, pushing them aside until he found one to his liking. "Didn't find much in there. Danma thought it'd be a smart business deal. Aethecite is soon to become a curio, Vicar Cyan. Drenth has gone through so much, what with the Gutter King's war and the destruction of Gargantua. Aethecite has driven the world for a long time. Without it, we are helpless, just like after the Fall. But if you want my honesty, we thought our help might fill our pockets afterward. Wealth such as this doesn't come because of some prayers to the Pentax. Forgive the offense."

Wealth, Cyan assumed, was the main reason Klander got up in the morning.

Klander's personal chamber on the fourth floor of *The Parlour* was the very definition of ostentation. It was one of the most lavish rooms Cyan had ever seen. Every item was of the finest make imported from all over the Mistlands. The Blades' masterful dvergirish stonework for the desk. The bedframe clearly from the Forest of Calibrath's elfirish artisans. The linen drapery from

Dervin's lapin tribes. The back of the hand calculation of cost alone signaled how deep the Guilder's coffers were.

"Was there anything in there?"

"Yeah, bone." Klander stuck another chocolate in his mouth, licking the smudge left on his fingers. "Nothing in there but bone and sand. Whatever it was your acolyte did with the help of the Forgemistress, nothing could penetrate the old mines. They have been sealed shut with the acidic corpses of the vvyrms. Not even blasts of raw aethecite could pierce the ruins. Or the draconem carcasses. Appears the Pentax want the mines to remain so. Danma was beyond livid, her reaction was magnificent, even for her."

"I have heard of Lady Dil's, shall we call it, vigor from Grand Quaestor Owl."

"Ha! Now, that's putting it nicely for the old flower. For the most part, I'm not too keen on Danma, we tend not to agree on many things. Especially when it comes to running profitable businesses. But this venture was solid. Or so we thought."

"What made you decide to help Drenth reopen the mines?"

"Bliss gave me a vision," Klander said, tapping a golden bracelet around his wrist. It was through those bracelets a bikrome would trigger Vision Form. They were like the runes tattooed onto Cyan's right arm. A link between aether and the gods. "When the Ideal Daughter proclaims, I listen."

Bikromi were essentially seers, their dual eye color representative of the Pentax Gods. The black was of the past that was, the white of the future unwritten. Bliss and Brio were the patrons of Vision Form aetheurgy. Seeing a bikrome in the throes of Vision Form was a sight Cyan was not too keen on, for he believed the veil between Life and Death was not meant to be breached, regardless if the Pentax deemed it so.

Besides, Cyan found a bikrome to be an odd companion, crazier than an ogre and giant trying their hands at ice dancing during the First Snowday Competitions of Krylen's end of summer.

"What was your relationship with Emre Benld? Back before the conquest of Drenth, that is. I know you had a friendly rivalry with his wife's family, House Nightingale." Cyan proffered a weak attempt at humor. Humor had never been his strongest attribute, stubbornness held that title. But he was trying to change; he could blame Lilia for that. "Most Houses I hear in Oldport like to one up each other whenever they get the chance."

"Nagnoz, would you be so generous and get me another glass of wine?" Klander said to the hobgoblin. The creature's sharp face scrunched up as the poor thing tried to figure out what to do with the tray of sweets and be able to comply with his lord's request. "Here, give me the tray, Nagnoz. Now, go fetch me some wine."

The hobgoblin was in a finer set of trousers than Grand Inquisitor Owl's Cadoz, but it essentially meant Nagnoz's were tailored to fit him. The little voidspawn was slightly taller than Cadoz, a browner shade of greyish skin, and his head a tad more bobble-y. Nagnoz also had a huge overbite when he smiled and was far less enjoyable to talk with. All in all, a proper hobgoblin punching well above their weight.

The voidspawn scrambled to where a litany of beverages in decanters waited atop a silver three-legged table. Cyan heard the slosh of liquid and the hobgoblin scuttled back into view, carefully holding a nearly overflowing glass of red vintage. Klander took it from him and handed back the tray of sweets, trickles of sweat beading on the hobgoblin's wrinkled forehead.

"Ah, much better. Now, where were we, Vicar Cyan?"

"Before the conquest of Drenth, did you have dealings with Emre Benld?"

"Thought this wasn't an investigation?"

"Humor me, Lord Klander." Cyan shifted in his seat, slightly perturbed by Klander's unsubtle attempts at changing the subject. He truly hated putting on a front of civility with Guilders. "You see, the Shards recently learned some things about Emre and Cadrianna Benld. Things that have come to light after the happenings in Drenth last year. You and Danma Dil sent a delegation up to Drenth. I'm just trying to understand."

"I don't dabble in rumors. That sort of thing isn't for me. Efan Nightingale and I were friends. Rivals majority of the time, but still on friendly terms. I wouldn't say I could expect him to bail me out with a loan should my endeavors go bottom up, but we always exchanged pleasantries and coin when the time necessitated it. Jensa was a lovely lady, as was his daughter, Cadrianna, before the conquest of Drenth. I don't care for what happened to her under Lu Har's reign, but I hear she redeemed herself in the end."

"So it goes."

Klander motioned toward the hobgoblin again, "Nagnoz, stoke the fire, will you?" The simpleton went to kick the logs with his oversized, bare, hairy feet. "No, Nagnoz, not your foot, you dunce. The poker. The metal rod in the stand over there. Bah! I'll get it."

Constantly changing the subject, O, Klander, don't think I haven't played this game before. With far better players, too.

Annoyance was within Klander, and it wasn't aimed at the poor hobgoblin. No, Cyan had struck a nerve. The man knew more than he was trying to let on.

Klander stood at the fireplace, dwarfed by the magnificent mantelpiece, using a thin poker to churn the logs. Affixed above the mantle was a yellowed skull of an aerovern, the blunted snout permanently opened to show its magnificent teeth and was easily as wide as Klander was tall. Within the center of the mouth was an inscription in a runic script Cyan didn't recognize. The largest of the runes was a semi-circle facing eastward, a slash of zigzags north to south, each point ending in an arrowhead.

A tremor caressed *The Parlour*, one that shook the 'vern skull above the fireplace. The death of Mother Marrow had forever changed the world, and it seemed like everything was balancing on the edge of a blade, just waiting to be cut apart.

Justice, did we do the right thing in Drenth? Did Lilia?

The Guilder gazed at the flames for long moments after the tremor quelled before speaking again. "Jensa didn't deserve to be married off to Efan." His voice was low. "Talthanian wanted an ally, a capable ally. Efan was that." He turned toward Cyan. "To answer your question, Vicar Cyan, yes. Yes, I had dealings with the Gutter King. Not before the conquest, but with his war against the Fallen."

"What sort of dealings?" *Now we are getting somewhere, Justice. Keep him speaking, I'll get to the bottom of this.*

"The Gutter King needed help with his little rebellion. To be frank, he needed money to finance what he couldn't steal from the Imperium. Early on, his wardkeeper, the drakken Tevun, came to Port Sin, seeking aid." Klander paused; a flame crackled. "Other Houses turned down the request for aid, for many thought helping the Gutter King meant future ruin should the Fallen win. And the odds were stacked heavily in the Fallen's favor. Most in Port Sin, forgive the gambling reference, don't like to play the odds."

"And yet you still helped Emre Benld? Why?"

"Nightingale was one of us. The House, that is. We in Port Sin protect our own, even traitors like Efan Nightingale."

"Traitor to whom?"

"House Talthanian, of course. Jensa was the only daughter of the House, and by her marriage to Efan, she forsook her family name. She was no longer of House Talthanian but of Nightingale. And when old Owl got sent off to the Shards for murdering that debt collector, that left only the elder brother. And he died before he whelped any children. Legitimate ones, at least. House Talthanian went the way of the blooddrakes once the Fallen slayed the House."

"From what I understand, House Klander and House Talthanian weren't the closest of allies, so what difference does it make if you decided to help Emre Benld's rebellion?"

"Benld's rebellion stained what legacy House Nightingale sought to create after the Fall. We in Oldport Basin all sought to build a new city, a better one, from the ashes of Eminence." Klander's bikromi eyes turned toward him, the fire reflecting in the all-onyx orb, the one representing the past. "You know who their line traced back to, yes?" Cyan nodded. "Of course, you do. But does your acolyte? Based on the look you're giving me; I'd say she doesn't. Why is that, hmm?"

"Because her parents were murdered right before her eyes as Mother Marrow claimed her. Too much has been laid upon her shoulders." *And because I cannot bear to see her suffer any further. I've failed her once; I cannot do it again.* "She should stand on her own, not be tainted by the first of her blood. She was saved from that once. She doesn't need me to guide her feet to a path she doesn't intend to walk." *Curse the bikrome who told me who she was. Who made this decision for me.*

"A child's duty is to pay for the sins of their forebears, isn't it?" Klander asked. "Alas, Vicar Cyan, there was no lie about Emre Benld's loyalty. He wanted to save Drenth from the Fallen. The same couldn't be said about most here in Oldport."

"Where would you place yourself, Lord Klander?" The man's eyebrow rose. "A jest. A poor one at that."

"I'm afraid my sense of humor is touchy these days. After the venture with Danma in Drenth, things have hit a downturn." He stuck his hand into a pocket, drawing forth something small and rolling it in his fingers. A bead of aethecite. "Hopefully my interests will encounter an uptick soon while I wait for what Bliss has in store for me." Klander handed the poker to Nagnoz and found himself another chocolate sweet to concern himself with. There was a gentle knock on the door. "Come."

The door eased open and Roqanth's head popped in, their hair slicked straight back, ends curled around the nape of their neck. "Is this a poor time?"

"No, no." Klander waved the Guild advisor in. "What is it?"

The Calibrathian elfir floated across the room, the trail of their robe flowing behind. A single button held the plunging robe closed over the elfir's taut abdomen. Something skimpy covered the advisor's privates, their long legs bare. As were their feet.

Cyan ogled; he could not help it even though he knew he should look away.

Roqanth leaned close to Klander's ear, whispering. The bikrome nodded. "I'll see to it." There was mild amusement upon Klander's face. "I have matters to attend to. Is there anything else I can help you with, Vicar Cyan?"

Roqanth glided from the room, closing the door behind.

"One last thing, Lord Klander," Cyan said as he rose from his seat. "I heard you had also purchased *The Axe* after the

Nightingales were cleansed by the Fallen's order." Cleansed was the nicest way Cyan could say murdered. Every last one of them. He doubted a man like Ifant Klander had a care of which words he used, but to him, it meant everything, this was his surrogate daughter's family he was speaking of.

"Indeed, I did. Efan Nightingale may not have been my closest of friends, but I didn't want the House's hard work to go to the highest bidder, only to see it crumble. I had the opportunity to honor a friendly rival, so I took it. From one Oldporter to another. That, my dear vicar, is why I chose to help Emre Benld's cause. Because of my love for House Nightingale of Oldport Basin. Luckily for me, the Fallen was stopped at Drenth and I wasn't given a traitor's death as they had."

"I certainly understand. You've helped me quite enough, Lord Klander." There was no lie in Cyan's words, Klander had indeed given him something, even if the Guilder hadn't intended.

"Nagnoz, please show the vicar out, if you will." The hobgoblin grabbed Cyan by the hand and started to yank him away. "It was a pleasure to entertain you, Vicar Cyan. I should hope our paths cross again, but in happier circumstances. Until then, enjoy the fruits of my employees should you be so inclined. I know what rules the Shards live by, but I do possess a fine stock to choose from."

"And you as well, Lord Klander. Until then."

Roqanth stood in the hallway outside of Klander's chamber, one hand dancing along the rail of the stairs, the other fingering the button holding their robe. A thrush emblazoned upon it. All-hazel eyes finding Cyan's, a bite of the painted lip. "Sorry to bother you, vicar, but I was wondering if you've seen your young friend? I was so very hoping to speak with her again."

His suspicion rose. *When did this advisor get to speak to Lilia?* "About what?"

The elfir straightened their robe with a flourish, beckoning him to descend beside them. "O, just a small request of her. I merely want to be her friend and hear her story. Ask her if the art of a story would sharpen the axe after a stone long since buried? Would the telling reveal a history unbeknownst to even the most knowledgeable? I eagerly await her answer."

What riddle do you speak, advisor? "I will ask her when I see her next, Roqanth."

They stopped at the third floor. A door opened and one of Klander's working boys ushered out a larger man. But once the trick spotted Cyan, he quickly spun and grabbed Klander's worker and scampered back inside the room. The nervy man must have been a Guilder or a proponent of the Shards for how he reacted.

Roqanth tittered behind their hand. "I just love the shame of these men sometimes. They deny what the Pentax has gifted them." The elfir smiled toward Cyan. "This is where we part, vicar. Please do bring my questions to your young friend. She is quite the interesting humir."

"Interesting is a strong word. But I will. Thank you, Roqanth, for your… assistance."

"And you, vicar. Ah, there she is now." With that, the elfir bowed with a flourish and disappeared down the hallway of the third floor, laughter accompanying them.

Cyan turned to find Lilia exiting a room, alone as she buttoned up the brass studs along her cassocked side. She saw him glowering and cast down her gaze.

To say he was livid with her was an understatement. By the Pentax, why was she so dismissive?

Instead of berating her like his taskmaster would have, Cyan motioned her over with a curt, pointed finger. She skulked over, still not meeting his gaze.

Anger seething inside, Cyan was descending the stairs to the first floor while trying to parse through Klander's words when the doors to the brothel burst open. Phlox the Faithful spotted him and rushed over.

The Faithful skidded to a stop, breathing heavily as if he'd run through every alley of Oldport Basin twice over. "You aren't going to believe this, Vicar Cyan. I was scoping out *Nocturne's Bounty* like you commanded. Lots of voidspawn soldiers, and lots of commotion at the tavern. Don't know what happened. I didn't get too close. Could've used my Shard Form but too many people around. Anyway, it sounded like some sort of fight upstairs. Lots of banging and hammering. Breaking doors and such. I'd say you might want to check it out. I thought I heard whispers of Neron Hobb being dead!"

XXI

ASHE

ASHE SQUINTED IN the faint light that streamed through the window, the glass reflecting a prism of early morning dawnbreak sun into the room. "That is one ugly godsdamned painting."

Cyan made a face, so Ashe took it as a sign of agreement. Or it could be him trying to hold back from yelling at her about still being in *The Parlour* instead of the Beggars Chain the nightturn prior. She decided to go with the former.

The painting in question was an unsettling portrait of a woman holding a pointed fin on one of a seagandr's multiple sleek, black heads while wearing a flowing gown that highlighted perfectly toned leg and arm muscles. Hair curling at the nape, the woman grinned ear-to-ear with sword arm raised in some grand taunt. The seagandr spewed acidic oil, heads arched and angry.

Ashe had to assume it was a literal interpretation of the famed phrase *'to grab the seagandr by the fins'*. They were in the personal chamber of Neron Hobb above *Nocturne's Bounty*, so Ashe assumed the woman in the painting was supposed to be Hobb herself.

"Sure had a high opinion of herself, yeah?" Ashe's question received an unclear shrug from Cyan as he was too busy with the crime scene. Thankfully.

On the enormous, mussed, bed, two bodies lay. One was Hobb, the other, an unknown man. Both nude, both clearly deceased. Hobb's face was split nearly in twain, dried blood all down her breasts and abdomen. The man's tongue was out, almost as if he had been choked to death, but there were no wounds about his neck. Although sand piled beneath his tongue and dusted his lips.

"Wonder what happened here?" Phlox asked like the master of the obvious that he was.

Ashe elbowed Harlequin and made a universally noted hand signal: a circle formed by her forefinger and thumb while penetrating said circle with the forefinger of her other hand.

But Phlox being Phlox, didn't grasp the signal's meaning. "I think Ashe is implying something about a game… O wait… ewwww. You have issues."

"SOMETIMES I WONDER, DEAR BRYNN, HOW YOU EVER SURVIVED THE FALLEN'S TRAP." If the Strix was not a blackened steel blade, it would probably be shaking its owl's head at her while its ghastly voice moaned.

I could've left you impaled in Lu Har. Then you'd be melted into ore in that wyrm's gut."

"MIGHT BE WORTH IT."

Psst, you like me, don't lie.

"Lilia, knock it off," Cyan admonished while Harlequin covered her wry smile with the sleeve of her cassock. "Tell me, what do you see?"

"Two dead bodies," she said flatly. Cyan's green-pupiled eyes shot her way, his frown wiping the grin from her face. "Fine, fine. Be that way. And stop calling me Lilia."

Ashe had seen an ample number of deaths, but something about the pair here did not seem natural. Hobb wasn't an overly athletic woman, so even if she was supposedly as aggressive as an angry goblin and the painting over-emphasized, without aetheurgy, no way in Nocturne's Pit was she strong enough to choke out this man during sex based on his sheer size. And, even if Hobb *was* able to suffocate him, it seemed highly unlikely he would destroy half of her face before succumbing to his own untimely demise.

That did not explain the sand. This crime scene didn't add up.

For whatever reason, she found herself thinking about her last days in Drenth. Perhaps it reminded her of the times in Slag's End, of the good times she had spent in *The Colosseum* before everyone she had known went the way of Nocturne in vicious ends like Hobb and this man. Of Olaf, the fat bartender who had treated her like a daughter. With that murderous wench Wren and even creepy Evander. Both had tried to kill her, sure, but they had been friends before that. And Wren had been her first.

That stupid cu—

"NECESSARY EXPERIENCES, DEAR BRYNN. WITHOUT THEM, YOU WOULDN'T BE HERE NOW."

Perhaps that would be for the best, Strix.

"SO MACABRE, YOU."

Besides, Wren was such a lying cu—

"Is it often your suspects end up dead like this, Vicar Cyan?"

Maja Carr stood in the doorway, her two orcirish bodyguards, Shon and Solly, in the stairwell behind. The Guilder studied her with a soft glow of blue-tinted aether around. Trust and wisdom.

What wisdom, Ashe could not decipher. The constant dancing mist about her ankles probed her flesh with a desire she nearly kicked at. The tempest in her body surged with carnality.

Zenith's cock…

"DO YOU ALWAYS GO SO WEAK IN THE KNEES AT SUCH WOMEN?"

"All the time," Ashe answered, both to Maja's question in Cyan's stead as well as to the now chuckling sentient daemon blade. Her taskmaster in the world of Life gave her a scowl that she ignored. "Makes the job easier, don't ya think?"

"You would think, Brynn Benld, you'd want to question a suspect before they were offed. At least I would've assumed." But Maja's aura seemed to counter her words, ever shifting of sapphire. Peculiar.

"You know what they say about assuming?"

"I do not," Maja conceded. Her bearing was respectful and cautious, her aura a mix of green and blue.

"Well, it mak—"

"Enough, Ashe." Cyan appeared to be in no mood for her today. "Dead does no good to the case. Why don't you make yourself useful and tell me what happened here?"

Laughing to herself, Ashe funneled the aetheric magic raging inside her toward the bodies, and the misty aura of the tavern came to life in a blast of color, recreating the scene. The fiery red of *Ignis*. The pulsing blue of *Aquis*. The wispy natural yellow of *Aere*. The rumbling green of *Terris*.

Bit by bit, the intertwining aetheric hues in the mist became little threads of color as a darkened shade of yellow mingled with the faint tint of garnet. An outline of figures blended into the linen bed. A rebuilding of what had occurred, using only aetheurgy. Limbs and torsos reforged. Two people—a smaller female and a male—coalesced, one atop the other. It was almost like a painting, a singular moment in time. The pair frozen within their misted forms, but inside swirled the aethers both had felt when the moment of death had occurred.

"So, tell me, Maja," Ashe said as she waited for her aetheurgy to finish. "Why did the Guild send you here to Port Sin? And don't tell me the Seal is the sole reason. I know there is more to it. What about you, in particular?"

Maja Carr regarded her, her aura shifting toward caution. *Caution of what, hmm?* "Interrogating me now, are you, Brynn Benld? Going to drag me back to Kalderim in chains?"

"In a way. Part of my job description is to read people."

"Your job is to learn," Cyan corrected, "and you've done a poor job at that." He was writing in a small notebook as he examined the corpses. "Sometimes I feel like you've listened to nothing of what I've said."

"True enough."

"And don't think because I've not said anything on it, you are off the hook for *The Parlour*."

Shit…

"The Seal is truly the most important thing," Maja said. "You may not believe me when I say this, but it is. The Seal of *Terris* was broken, and that weakened the bonds of Eminence. The world is on the edge of change and the City of the Gods must not fall into the wrong hands. The Pentax chose you, Brynn Benld."

"RIGHTLY OR WRONGLY, I'VE NOT YET DEDUCED WHICH."

Shut up, you dumb owl. "I've not forgotten, trust me," Ashe said under her breath. "What? Don't give me that look, Cyan, I'll knock it right off that mug of yours."

"O, THAT WOULD BE FUN TO WITNESS. I'VE A FEELING HE WOULD ENJOY GIVING YOU A WHACK OR FIVE."

Cyan's aura blazed crimson but he said nothing. It was not that she was mad with him, but he was an easy outlet to vent her rage. She hoped he understood.

"If Solanine finds the Seal of *Ignis* before you do, the darkness will grow." Maja's smile was off-putting, even though it was pretty. Gods, she was alluring. And that scared her, for Wren had been similar. There were few she truly trusted and this Maja Carr was not yet one of them. "You say it can't just be about the Seal, well, Brynn Benld, it is just about the Seal. Without the Forgemistress to balance, the world leans toward the darkness. It grows stronger. And that weakens the rest of the gods."

"PERHAPS THAT WOULD BE FOR THE BEST. THINK ABOUT IT, DEAR BRYNN, WHY WOULD NOCTURNE GO TO SUCH LENGTHS?"

Because He is the Lord of the Pit, this is what He does.

"THEN YOU HAVE YET TO LEARN ANYTHING. THIS IS ALL ABOUT NIGHTINGALE. YOU'LL SEE IT SOON."

I am of Nightingale, apparently, and yet, no one seems to want to discuss what this actually means!

"The Wayward Son and the Ideal Daughter remain in balance," Phlox said as he scratched at his arm. "The Arbiter is strong. Justice wouldn't succumb that easily either."

"The Children are indeed strong, but They cannot battle the darkness without the guidance of the Mother. Cut one limb and the entire body is off kilter. It is the same with Them."

"I hope you don't fail then, Lady Carr." Ashe squatted next to the bed, trying to parse the fiery red aether from the rest of the swirling mist of other colors. To learn who these people had been. To avoid talking further about the Pentax and the Seal. "I'll try my best not to fail."

"I know you won't, daughter of Nightingale. But to answer your question, the Guild sent me because of my connection to Canlon Carr. Like a drakken wardkeeper, I've sworn oaths to Canlon. Oaths I will see upheld, even if it results in my death." She glanced up and Maja gestured toward the bed, smiling. "Since I don't understand what it is you are doing, throw me a bone? I may understand aetheurgy, but what Soul Form does, is beyond me, Brynn Benld."

Why does she keep calling me that?

"BECAUSE THAT IS YOUR NAME. NOT EVERYONE RUNS FROM THEIR NAME, BRYNN BENLD. NOT MANY WOULD HIDE FROM IT, LIKE YOU DO."

All that name brings is death. Every name carries pain along with it.

"IMMORTALITY DOES NOT COME FROM THE PROLIFERATION OF LIFE."

But upon the wave of Death, yes, Strix, I know this.

"THEN REMEMBER IT WELL."

"Aether is simple," Ashe said to Maja, "it just takes time to get used to. Like Phloxy."

"I'm getting really tired of your meanspirited jokes, Ashe."

She guffawed. "Meanspirited? Me?" Harlequin snickered, her red curls bouncing. The mist prodded, again.

Cyan cleared his throat in annoyance. If looks could kill, Ashe would have long taken the one-way trip to the Meadows.

Ashe coughed, then motioned toward the misty figures. "Aether is dynamic. Sure, aether can change based on a living creature's moment-to-moment emotion, and meld into a combination of pigments the more complex the creature is. A mixture, a blend of color borne of nature. That is what I see with my Soul Form, the colors of everything. But therein lies the power of aetheurgy. That combination shows me the final moments of these two before they died. Shows me their thoughts, their feelings. Their fears."

Maja crouched beside her. "You sound like Canlon." She paused. "From what I hear, anyway. Only the Godskings could use Soul Form aetheurgy. I guess Canlon described the use of Soul Form as reading the auras of a living being or object."

"I see every aura, even when not burning."

"Can you now?" Maja's fingers hooked a lock of golden hair behind her ear. The Strix tittered in the void. First Harlequin, now Maja Carr. Gods, the war inside was growing harder to quell. "What am I showing you?"

Ashe was assailed by tints of all four colors, a swirling mass of love, wisdom, fertility, and joyous youth. Coloration radiated from Maja inward toward her heart, where it collided into an arrayed rainbow. "I… uh… a lot."

The Guilder of the High Seat smiled. "Good." Toward the misted crime scene. "And them?"

Trying her best to stay on task considering Maja's magnetism, Ashe concentrated on the bottom, male figure. It was not that she was drawn to High Seat Guilder like some teenage girl fawning over a beautiful woman. There was that, truth told, but also because she was mystified by the woman. There was something about Maja Carr that made her uncomfortable and protected at the same time. A need to understand aether in a deeper way. Teacher-like, almost.

She looked toward Cyan, but he just gave her a satisfied nod, his aura was amused. *Godsdamn you, Cyan. I should have just kept my trap shut.* "Here, let me show you what I see within them." *Strix, give me something.*

"YOU MAY NOT LIKE THE ANSWER, DEAR BRYNN."

Breathing in deep, Ashe summoned more of her aetheurgy. Her entire body felt on fire, but she funneled it into the bangle wrapped around her wrist. The Fire of *Ignis* blazed a bright red on her forefinger. She channeled it into the diamond eye in the center of her palm.

Snap.

The air in the room crackled like a fire burning in a brazier. Maja Carr was startled as Ashe's hand burst into a fiery gout. But there was no heat, just the aetheurgy of *Ignis*. Focusing on the network of aether in her own vision, Ashe sent the non-flames toward the grid of mist. The flames of *Ignis* drowned the hues, igniting them. Leaving behind an ash-like filter over the pair's remaining aura.

Like a sculpture brought to life, Maja could now witness what she was seeing. The Guilder gave her a slight nudge of approval with her shoulder.

"This man's aether, these colors here," she pointed to the green shades building inside the male figure, "shows a frosty lover, an ambitious man. A man so filled with greed, he wanted power and was willing to do nearly anything for it. Like sleeping with Neron Hobb. And yet, he hated Hobb," she continued, pointing to the dark pine green which built the foundation of the man. "The burning of desire yearned." The diamond eye of her bangle hovered over the bodies. "So much so, he had only suffered Hobb to further his own ambitions." A tiny nugget of juniper green radiated jealousy. "I wonder if he'd been contemplating having Hobb whacked and taking her place in the Guild."

"I'll have Guild ears find out for us." Maja whistled. One of her bodyguards stepped into the room, leaned down, spoke in orcirish—which was a rasp that sounded like a blade crooning a ballad about a whetstone—then left the room. Ashe couldn't tell the two apart, and now fully understood Neenah LeFleur's trouble with the hobgoblins Zig and Zag. "Please proceed, Brynn Benld."

Ashe's hand stopped above where the man's heart would be located in the lattice of aetheurgy, the mist palpitated with an underpinning of emerald sickness shades, though at the center was a smidgeon of dark honey. "There was fear within him. This man was fearful of being discovered."

"Perhaps he was working with another Guilder?" Harlequin stated. Ashe glanced Harlequin's way, but then the vicar's gaze fell toward the base of the bed, and she lifted the edge of the bed's linen, only to stagger back. "What in the Pit is that?"

Piled below the bed was something appearing like a body, but it lacked the musculature and bones of a body and, instead, was folded up haphazardly upon itself. Except the skin. Just flesh. Transparent. Like a single layer peeled off the body.

"I think I'm going to be sick," Phlox said as he turned away, his face gone pale.

Cyan, who gave no outward reaction, scratched some more in his notebook. "Never seen anything like that before." He used his quill to lift it. "Reminds me of a snakeskin after molting."

Maja, undeterred physically and with her aura, leaned closer and touched it with her hand, flattening out what might have once been a face. "Blooddrake shedding their scales." Her voice was cold. "Look closely. You must."

Bile rose in her throat, but Ashe looked at the face. Though flat, there was no mistaking the shape of the nose, the delicate curve of cheek, the slightly angled brow. A pulmo cough surged past the dam of her lips. Tar and blood. When it was finally quelled, the tears came.

"Mother."

The flesh was that of Cadrianna Benld, there was no denying it.

"Yes, Brynn Benld, your mother. Brought back from the Meadows by a blooddrake. This is a message for you. They knew you would be here. Schemes within schemes."

Strix, is this truly my mother?

"I CANNOT SAY FOR CERTAIN, BUT I'VE NOT SEEN CAD'S SOUL IN SOME TIME."

What? Why haven't you told me this?

"I... WELL, I SUPPOSE I DIDN'T NOTICE IT UNTIL WE NEARED THIS CITY."

So glad I am bonded to you. To Maja she hissed, "Solanine."

"I TOLD YOU THAT YOU WOULDN'T LIKE THE ANSWER..."

She quickly shoved the blanket back down and stood. "I need to finish this." But more pulmo tore through her and she bent double, hacking black goo onto the floor.

"Ashe," Cyan said softly as he rubbed her back. "We ca—"

"No, Cyan," she straightened and wiped the tar from her lips. "I must finish this." So she could kill Solanine for good this time. "Solanine has killed Hobb. You might want to bring Ranhold in, you know, before the same can be done to him."

"Unless he's our blooddrake," Phlox said as he gagged into his cassock sleeve.

"It's clear that Hobb wasn't our blooddrake," Cyan started, "which means one of the others killed her. We need to find out who, and fast, because we don't need more Guilders' corpses lining the streets."

"This is only a diversion," Ashe said. "A game played by Solanine. That cu... blooddrake wanted me to find my mother's skin. Wanted me here, specifically to see something. This entire case is nothing more than a game. They're taunting us, Cyan. Taunting me."

"Your young acolyte speaks wisely, Vicar Cyan," said Maja.

Worry and confusion played across Cyan's face like a dramatic show upon an aerescreen. But then he was nodding, "Phlox, you and I shall bring Olum Ranhold in for questioning. Even if he has nothing to do with Hobb, he is a suspect. It's high time we tightened the noose. To even the playing field." To Ashe, "When you're done here, meet me at the Shards stronghold. I'm not playing, Ashe." Ashe grunted. To Maja, "Lady Carr."

"Vicar Cyan."

After Cyan and Phlox had gone, Ashe returned her attention to Hobb's grid of aether. Like the man's, Hobb's aetheric aura was predominately shaded green underneath the lusty red. In it was the jealousy and greed all Guilders seemed made of. But deeper, Ashe noticed a mossy patch of selfishness. That, in itself, was not odd, but the fact the green was edged with a darkened blue made her pause. Almost as if the green was layered over the blue.

"Hmm, what's this?" she said more to herself than anyone.

Something about the way the woman was sitting on top of the man. His head turned the other way, eyes closed, no emotion on his face. While probable for a lover not interested in the act, Hobb, on the other hand, was still in motion, head thrown abaft, face permeating a cry of pain, eyes rolled back into her head. This was not the moment of the sexual act, no, this was immediately after their deed finished. This woman was dead, yet not.

This was foreign, even in the static display of a moment in time. Ashe had never seen a layering of different hues such as this. She would expect to see the colors bleeding into each other, shifting as emotions changed. This was different. Far different.

Something familiar. A memory. But not her memory, her mother's.

Aetheurgy rarely reached the other senses, such as smell. But smell she did. And there was a subtle hint of sulfur. A gaseous stench she had only ever smelt once before.

Blink.

The young girl, Cadrianna, stood upon the bow of an oceanic ship. Nearby was the volcano that had once been active, now just a beacon that overlooked the Bay of Fire. It smelled, the volcano, as if it had just spewed. But it had not blown in an age.

"Father," the girl who was Ashe's mother said, "what's that smell? Smells like rotten eggs."

A larger man, one with a kindly face, turned toward the girl. Ashe's grandfather, she supposed, Efan Nightingale. "It's called sulfur, my lovely child. It's of the earth. See there," he pointed toward the volcano's base. "There are natural caves down there, it's said. Made a long time ago, from when the mountain was alive. It is in there, the smell forms."

"It smells like the mist of the Sea."

Efan laughed. "That it does, that it does. And that's because the mountain is made of the same aether that is in the mist. Magic, you know what aether is, right?"

Blink.

The memory faded.

"No," she whispered. Fear started to rise. She felt woozy in the head, a dull ache forming behind her eyes.

"Brynn?"

Ashe trembled, worry starting to build inside. "Fucking Nocturne," she said matter-of-factly, snuffing out the aetheurgy. She stumbled to her feet. "I've underestimated what we're dealing with. Now I understand why you chose me, Lady Carr. These memories, from my mother, are how you plan to find the Seal.

And this is why Solanine stole my parents' bodies? Cadrianna knew where the Seal was located?"

Harlequin looked like she had been bludgeoned with her axes while the Guilder merely nodded. The orcir by the door subtly frowned behind his massive overbite.

Strix, why didn't you tell me?

"I'M SORRY, DEAR BRYNN, I COULD NOT. YOUR MOTHER DIDN'T EVEN KNOW. WHILE WITH LU HAR, AFTER YOUR FATHER'S MURDER, CAD BURIED EVERY MEMORY IN THE DEEPEST REACHES OF HER SOUL. BURIED AND LOCKED THEM AWAY. THAT WAS HOW SHE WAS ABLE TO MAINTAIN HER SANITY. TO KILL IN THE FALLEN'S NAME. HER ONLY THOUGHTS WERE OF YOU. THE KEY TO HER MEMORY IS ME. I AM THAT VAULT. AND IT IS UP TO YOU TO FREE THEM. FREE HER."

Anger inside, Ashe punched the mattress, and kept on punching it until her pulmo took over and she had to bend down to stifle the coughing. Harlequin stepped beside her, placing a supportive hand upon her shoulder, she grabbed at it, holding it tight to her cheek. Harlequin's calloused hand was rough, almost like the scales of a crocodile. The older vicar said nothing, did not need to.

"I'm sorry, Brynn Benld," Maja said. "I told you; our paths were meant to cross. It is in our blood."

"Of course," Ashe said dryly. "Everything comes back to this bloody Nightingale." She needed to turn off her brain. "You expected this to happen, didn't you?"

"A likely scenario," Maja confirmed, willingly moving from the topic of her mother's memories. "Hobb and Tified are the only ones who can get anything into Port Sin undetected. But what?

That's what we need to know. And Solanine must have concluded Hobb was expendable."

"Thanks for the vote of confidence." Ashe pulled out her flask, guzzling down half the spirits before wiping her mouth.

"Ashe, see that?" Harlequin reached under the dead man's limp hair, and as she straightened, Ashe noted the small diamond-like bead in her hand. "And the Pentax has given us our answer."

"Aethecite," Ashe said. "I think we've found our clue as to what Tified and Hobb smuggled in."

But for what purpose?

XXII
CYAN THE DEFIANT

IT WAS QUIET in the casino, no constant trilling of music, no raucous laughter, or shouts of anger at empty purses. Only those in Ranhold's employ.

Standing before the gates, Cyan the Defiant released the contents of his mist canisters upon his belt, his Shard Form roaring to life as he surveyed the casino in a silvery sheen of aetheurgy. He was nowhere near as skilled as Lilia was with her Soul Form, but within the enhanced aetheric sight, he could sense the many heartbeats inside, their rhythmic pulses. Minute, they were, but like beacons. Counting, there were over fifty. A large number. Voices inside, growing ever stronger on the wisps of *Aere*. Louder and more purposeful as midday rapidly approached.

"Well, Vicar Cyan," Phlox the Faithful started as he drew his pair of blue-iron axes from his belt loops, "shall we?"

Why did Phlox draw his weapons? "Now's as good a time as any."

"You think that the old bastard knows what's coming for him?"

Cyan shot the Faithful a stunned smirk. "Been hanging around Lilia too long, have you? Speaking like that, you sound just like her." Phlox shrugged. *Justice, we are all changing, aren't we? Even one as ardent as the Faithful. The future cannot resemble the past, can it?* "This *old bastard* probably knows far more than we do, Phlox. Don't tread lightly around him. Ranhold may seem odd, but many know it's a façade. I've met him before, personally and in private. There is a dastardly presence about him. Especially if he is our blooddrake."

"Sounds like my kind of bastard."

Cyan shook his head as they approached the gatehouse of the first set of steps. *That girl will change us all.*

For all his life, Cyan had prided himself on never being one to succumb to pressure. He had held his nerve for as long as he could under Solanine's torture before finally breaking. It had cost Amaranth the Pure her life.

Now, as Cyan and another of his acolytes stood before *The Endless Wheel*, he felt sapped of all energy, his soul bled dry.

He was sweating in his cassock, and it wasn't from the codex that had kept him up most of the nightturn worried about Lilia. It was as if the world fell around him. A heavy pall of failure.

And he didn't want to lose her. Couldn't lose her.

Drenth had been a colossal failure on his part to save not only Amaranth, but to right a wrong placed in his hands eighteen years prior. He shouldn't have been so hard on Lilia, nay, on Brynn Benld during her upbringing. He should have tended her more carefully, less strict, and demanding. Icterine the Unfettered had issued a strict regime for all vicar trainees, for it had been since the beginning of the Shards, prior to the Fall of Eminence.

But Brynn Benld was no ordinary would-be-vicar. She was the Godsblood. The chosen of the Pentax. You cannot cage a god and expect to be in control.

Despite losing Amaranth, Cyan had been victorious at Drenth, for Brynn had decided to come home. To finish her training. It should have been his absolution.

He had changed, for the better he had come to realize. Not so strict, not so hard. He had allowed the girl to become the woman she was meant to be. She had found her place again, it had seemed.

Cyan the Defiant had come to realize, the Godsblood walked a path none would ever begin to understand, he included.

But Cyan knew Phlox wasn't becoming more akin to Lilia, instead he was harkening back to his past, a life not normal of one of Justice's flock. No, Phlox should have been one of Brio's quaestors but was spared that fate because he was untainted.

Unlike Lilia who had been placed directly in Cyan's hands by Valeria Dunleith, nor like Harlequin or Amaranth who'd been tested by members of the Shards seeking out untainted children who could wield aether, Phlox had come to Kalderim much later in life than was normal.

The man who would become Phlox the Faithful was as devout as most augurs, especially to Zenith. From a small woodland village in western Altreyia, not far from the Forest of Calibrath, the eventual vicar had been a holy man. Zealous at best, fervent at worst. From a shaky memory of the event, one nightturn after a severe indulgence of sacred wine, the man claims to have witnessed Zenith in the flesh, the glorious divine bequeathing glory upon him. It was then Phlox's aetheurgy came alive.

None had discovered the truth of that nightturn, but the man who would become Phlox was the only survivor of that small woodland village, for all others had been massacred, blood splattered everywhere, including upon Phlox. Some think it was Phlox's aether that did it, but others, like Cyan, believed it was the man himself who did it under the sway of the wine.

But Cyan was a man of the Scattered Shards, and if the Conclave deemed Phlox free of guilt, then who was he to say otherwise? They were all killers, weren't they?

A pair of guards stopped them, each armed with a wheellock rifle and pistol, a cudgel looped on their belts.

"What business does the Scattered Shards have here?" one asked as they took in the cassocks of their sect, Cyan's horsehair bristle. "Vicar," added with respect.

Cyan dug into his belt pouch and brought forth a piece of folded parchment. "I have a warrant for the arrest of Olum Ranhold, signed by Grand Quaestor Owl."

Phlox gave him a sidelong glance from behind his breather.

"Let me see th't," the second guard said.

"You dare question the Shards, boy?" Cyan demanded. He hoped his bearing and rank was enough because he did not, in fact, have a warrant. Owl hadn't given him such authority.

The folded parchment was blank.

"Watch your tone, indweller," Phlox added for affect, "you are in the presence of a vicar of the Scattered Shards. A man chosen by the Pentax to be Their warrior."

Their bravado must have worked as both guards stiffened. "Alright, alright. No need to get frisky here, vicar. The Shards are always welcome." The first guard turned toward his compatriot. "Go send for Aris, he'll bring this news to Lord Ranhold."

As the gate groaned open, the second guard raced up the steps, the first bowing while Cyan and Phlox began their ascent.

Phlox leaned close to whisper, "You've a warrant for his arrest?"

Cyan shushed him. "Let's not let him know it."

"Lying is against the wishes of Zenith, Vicar Cyan."

"I will serve my penitence later, Phlox. We need Ranhold before the blooddrake can get to him."

"Aye. I will attest to the All Father that you will seek His forgiveness."

This codex case has us all on the edge of a blade. Trust is but a wish. A dream, Cyan, you old fool. Got you doing things all askew.

The ten-foot tall-carved doors to *The Endless Wheel* swung in on command from the guards as the breathless soldier from the gate explained their presence. Cyan and Phlox passed through to the central atrium of the casino. A sweeping open space where gamblers typically met and socialized before fracturing off into their choice of amusement. With a domed ceiling, a center ocular above allowed the green-tinted dawnbreak to fill the atrium. A recessed pool with a fountain trickled with clear arcs of reed-thin water under the oculus dome, five stairs of marble coated with plush carpet separating the two levels.

A man was giving orders to an army of staff, arms all herky-jerky as he spoke, he was likely the maior domus. Typically, the head servant for the Houses of the Guild, but according to Owl's files, the maior domus of *The Endless Wheel* was also Ranhold's casino floor manager. He displayed the colors of Ranhold: a tailored doublet and striped, white sleeves mingled with gold. His name was Aris, Cyan recalled from the grand quaestor's files. And from said records, he was found to be an honorable Guild man.

Aris hastened over. "Vicar, this is hardly the time for such a visit. Word of your coming just now reached my ears. If you would've sent wor—"

"I'm here under official Shards business. When and where I choose to be, you are not to question. Understood?"

The man hung his head as if scolded like a child. "Yes, of course. Anything for the Guild. And the Shards. Of course."

Cyan lifted the folded piece of blank parchment and waved it toward the maior domus. "See to it that Lord Ranhold is alerted to our presence. I don't want to make a big spectacle here. The man has been loyal to the Guild in the past; thus we'll keep this, shall we say, discreet."

"Thank you, vicar. I shall see to it." The maior domus was about to rush off but saw the portly figure of Olum Ranhold descending the short stair and trotted over, frenzy alighting the servant's face. "Milord!"

"Gamblers, Aris? Isn't it a tad early to open the doors?" Ranhold said, rubbing the sleep from his eyes. "I don't recall any invitations for dawnbreak card games. I hope you had the staff prepare those cinnamon rolls I like. A hungry gambler does not stay at the tables long. You did make them, right? You know I cannot start my day without those rolls. And some tea. Hot, but not scalding. With orange peel. O, eggs too, Aris. Yes, eggs sound delightful."

Long had it been since Cyan had interacted with Ranhold, it was before he had been given Lilia to train, to be frank, but Ranhold's mannerisms were acknowledged widespread within the Guild and Shards. Although greedy, Olum Ranhold had been prone to be forgetful at times. Most in Alizarin believed senility wasn't far off in his future, and that was the thought eighteen years ago. It was a wonder of the Pentax the man still functioned.

"Milord! Please. It's the Scattered Shards," Aris responded with unheralded gusto. The poor maior domus was trying to assert a level of modicum but couldn't retain his stead. "They've come with a warrant!"

"A warrant? Pray to Zenith, whyever would they need a warrant? We've all the proper paperwork filed, no skimming off the top here. No sir."

It reminded Cyan of the tragedies and comedies actors played upon the stage. Ranhold was a comedy genius with his penchant for forgetfulness mixed with an undeniable thirst for advancement. It was no wonder he progressed up the chain in the Guild as he had. Cyan had always assumed forgetfulness was but a veneer.

"Grand Quaestor Owl is always most welcome at my table," Ranhold continued. "I enjoy taking his, well, the Shards' coin."

"But, milord, Grand Quaestor Owl is not at the door."

Ranhold harrumphed, slovenly jowls jiggling. "Well, that doesn't make a lick of sense, Aris. I do declare I can't recall inviting any other to my table. But see them in anyway. I shall have to change if I'm going to work a good game." He glanced down at the silken pajamas he was wearing. "These won't do at all. Unbecoming, yes?"

Cyan and Phlox exchanged glances. It was not as if they *weren't* standing there in full sight of the old Guilder. If Cyan wasn't in such a hurry, he might find the entire ordeal amusing. Instead, he began tapping his foot and put his hands on his hips. Waiting. Thank the Pentax Lilia wasn't with him, she would've lost her tongue many times over already.

Aris was beyond flustered, his cheeks red. "Milord, the Scattered Shards are here with a warrant. A warrant for your arrest!"

The eventual-to-be-senile Guilder grabbed the maior domus by the arms. "Godsdamnit man, why didn't you say so?"

"But, milord, I tri—"

For the second time in mere moments, the maior domus was cut off, this time by an ever-impatient Cyan. He'd had enough. "Olum Ranhold, the Guild believes you've conspired treason with

Lord Tified and Lady Hobb and have requested the Shards intervene. What say you?"

Now, most in Ranhold's political position would throw a fit or deny the charges vehemently, but the Guilder's shoulders slumped, almost as a relief. And it was probably because Cyan may have saved him a different fate than Hobb. Which meant the man had much to tell about the blooddrake, clearly not within Olum's flesh.

The maior domus blanched. "Surely, vicar, there must be some mistake."

There were sounds of heavy boots smacking stone. Cyan turned, several red cassocked quaestors marched through the front doors of the casino.

What are they doing here? Perhaps Maja Carr had gotten word to the stronghold in the Politic?

But Cyan couldn't worry about that now. "Sorry to say it, Lord Ranhold, but no mistake." Tendrils of aether drew his attention in the silvery sheen of aetheurgy. He glanced upward toward where Ranhold's rooms were situated. His eyes narrowed slightly. He couldn't place the feeling, but he had sensed it while in *Nocturne's Bounty*. "I have questions for you. Will you oblige?"

The lord's head bobbed. "No need for pomp, vicar. I'll surrender and answer your questions."

"If you'll follow my acolyte, Lord Ranhold, he'll escort you to a safe location where we can talk more privately." Again, the aetheric tendrils drew his gaze toward the Guilder's chambers. *Justice, what is this feeling?* There was so much about this Guilder that needed uncovering. He wanted to examine his room, but time was of essence. "I know all too well the amount of ears lingering around here." He motioned to Phlox. "Lord Ranhold, if you will?"

Ranhold didn't fight it. Head held high, hands at his sides. It was a grand affair, the escorting of Olum Ranhold from his casino.

His wife clutched at the sleeves of her nightdress, hair quickly brushed and braided, face hastily painted with rouge and makeup lest she appear below her station. She stood crying, muttering false promises of *'always standing with him'*, *'I'll seek out the Grand Quaestor'*, and Cyan's personal favorite *'I'll fight this tooth and nail'*. Cyan was too well versed in the games of Guilders, and he knew the woman would be in another's arms in no time, forsaking Olum in hopes she and her children don't get wiped out by the Guild.

The three children of House Ranhold watched with bleary restlessness of sleep, barely awake and barely comprehending what their father was going through. They were young, hardly more than whelpings. They cried, too.

The entire staff of *The Endless Wheel* watched the tainted warriors of the Scattered Shards lead their lord away. The women sobbed into their aprons or on another's shoulders. The men shied away in shame, trying to hide their tears. Aris, the head of the casino, stared at the back of the Guilder with sorrow, lip quivering as he struggled to hold back his grief.

Even Olum's trusty hounds were there, growling or barking at the transgression.

Cyan dipped his head toward the maior domus, "Stay a moment. After I see to Lord Ranhold's escort, I want to examine the premise." He didn't wait for an answer before following the procession out the casino. "Phlox, go with Ranhold. I need to see Ranhold's chamber, then see Owl."

XXIII
ASHE

OUTSIDE *NOCTURNE'S BOUNTY* a crowd had formed, held in check by a handful of quaestors. Word of Hobb's death had obviously spread throughout the City of Sin.

The tavern was smack dab in the center of the Harbor of Thieves, and unlike most taverns in the Barter Yard, *Nocturne's Bounty* was a sight to behold. A four-story building with multiple turrets, topped with carved sculptures of a seagandr's many heads. Painted black as nightturn, the tavern was a go-to for Guilders while they conducted business at the Harbor.

Neron Hobb's twin warships were docked opposite the tavern. Two majestic pieces of oceanic construction. Both had been her pride and joy during her smuggling days it was said, stolen from the Guild and refitted to sail faster, to outwit any pirate or Guild naval vessel. As part of her rise to the Guild, she was allowed to keep her prizes. The ships were called *Peerless* and *Dauntless.*

Seeing those ships made her replay the memory of her mother from earlier. The smell. The volcano. Her mother and grandfather. What did that memory mean to tell her?

Ashe shook the memory away; she would figure it out. Eventually. "Hobb won't need those beauties any longer."

Maja gazed upon the warships. "We've long wanted to requisition those ships back to the Guild's navy, Brynn Benld. I suppose now is the only chance we will have." She motioned toward her bodyguards. "If you'll excuse me, I have business to attend. I look forward to hearing more about your investigation. If you should have need of me, you know where I'm to be found."

"Lady Carr." Ashe dipped her head, raven hair falling across her face. When the Guilder was out of earshot, she turned to Harlequin. "She sure got here fast. I find that hard to fathom."

"You find many things hard to fathom," Harlequin said with a wry smirk. The young woman's aura was a playful yellow red.

"It should've taken twice as long to get here. That's fishy smelling."

"You sure it's not just fish you smell? This is a harbor."

"ACTUALLY, THAT'S NOT A BAD ONE, DEAR BRYNN. SHE IS GETTING BETTER."

They walked the water-soaked planks of the Harbor. The quaestors in their red cassocks held the jostling crowd back. Many of them were sailors, others were traders. Many hurled questions, others insults. Lots of curses.

"No," Harlequin said after some silence, while also ignoring the vicious abuse from some within the gaggle of Port Sinners, "you're right. It doesn't add up. If Hobb brought in aethecite, then where would it go next?"

"I'd wager Danma Dil. She's got a warehouse in the Beggars Chain under tight lock and key." A small cough rippled up her insides, escaping. "Then Ranhold does what?"

"Ranhold would be an ideal way to funnel the money after selling. Good thing Cyan's bringing him in. Maybe he will cop to sending those sellswords. One of them sent those bastards. The coin leads back to Ranhold, in my estimation."

Or Klander, she thought.

"Ashe, what's got you so quiet?"

Before she could respond, her pulmo burst forth, the mist at her feet turning the black of oblivion. Her eyes watered and she coughed so hard, she pitched forward. Harlequin reached for her, and Ashe found herself gripping the vicar with everything she had.

"We need to get back to the stronghold," Harlequin said, hugging her to keep Ashe upright.

Jeers came from the surrounding crowd as they surged. Weakness was preyed upon in Port Sin and an injured or dying member of the Scattered Shards was seen as a boon. The army of quaestors struggled to hold them at bay. Ashe heard more than one canister of mist geyser into Shard Form.

Her hacking subsided; she pushed free of Harlequin. Reluctantly. "I'm alright. I can walk."

But that was a lie.

Ashe struggled to put one foot in front of the other. Her growing exhaustion was starting to wear her down and her pulmo was not letting her off an inch. She needed a long sleep.

They left Hobb's tavern, and the crowd had dispersed for the most part. Some still gave hard stares, but most went back to whatever they had been doing.

Except one figure standing across the way, wearing a dark cloak, face partially hidden by the cowl. The figure stood surrounded by the passing crowd, not moving, staring at her, black mist gusting around them.

Ashe stopped dead in her wobbly tracks. "What the?"

"Ashe?"

Burning aetheurgy, the swirling colors around the lone figure erupted. Emerald greed. Crimson danger. Peridot fear. Sapphire knowledge.

"BRYNN, YOU'RE BURNING TOO FAST. IF YOU DON'T STOP THIS USAGE, YOU'LL BURN YOURSELF OUT." There was extreme caution in the Strix's warning, but also worry. Yet, she couldn't stop just yet. *"I CANNOT LOSE YOU, TOO. NOT YET."*

Stay with me a bit longer, Strix. "Who?"

The cowl lifted slightly. A chin exposed, indiscriminate height and body type. Perhaps male, perhaps not. Ashe squinted, using Soul Form to build a face of aetheurgy across the distance of the Harbor. To pierce the cowl. The misted colors jumped in her aetheric-vision. She gasped as the face came into semi-focus.

A familiar one.

"Father?" She rubbed her eyes. It couldn't be. The face in her aetheurgy shifted, no longer resembling her father's, but instead a face more like her own. "What?"

A wagon drawn by a burly fisherman passed between Ashe and the cloaked figure. She stepped toward where the figure was standing, but as the cart went by, the figure was gone. As if they were never there.

"Ashe, are you alright?" The concern in Harlequin's voice was unmistakable.

She shook her head, searching the surrounding area, but the cloaked figure was nowhere to be seen and the mist of pitch also. The jumble of colors faded as she snuffed her aetheurgy with another painful pulmo cough. She was tired, hungry, and sore. Maybe her eyes were playing tricks on her. Hallucinations were common during towards the end of one's life with the nigrum pulmonem.

But it *had* looked just like her father. Just the way she remembered meeting him in that prison cell back in Drenth.

"Yeah," she said. "Thought I saw a ghost."

It couldn't have been him.

Could it?

Father?

"Bad memories, Lady Drakeslayer?"

Ashe turned and saw Roqanth leaning against a wall, dressed in a suit as magnificent as Ashe had ever seen. Bangs combed to the side, the rest in a tight bun. Kohl-rimmed makeup and subtle pink nail polish.

"What are you doing here?"

"I heard the news about Neron Hobb, and I wanted to see if they were true." The elfirish advisor moved closer, elegant and with an unreadable aura. "It's never easy to return to the place of our greatest sorrows. This city, I mean, for your family. Your mother, I heard was such a precocious young child."

Curious statement. "What do you want?"

"Have you thought about my request? Did your dearest taskmaster relay my words?"

"He did."

Cyan had pulled her aside, telling her of Klander's Guild advisor's questions.

'Ask her if the art of a story would sharpen the axe after a stone long since buried? Would the telling reveal a history unbeknownst to even the most knowledgeable?'

At the time, Hobb's face split like firewood had been the most pressing, but now they bubbled up to the surface.

Strix, what in Pit could this elfir be talking about?

"A STONE LONG SINCE BURIED, COME NOW, DEAR BRYNN, YOU SHOULD GLEAN WHAT THAT MEANS."

Yeah, the Seal of Ignis. *I'm not that stupid. But the rest of it?*

"THINK HARDER. YOU'LL FIGURE IT OUT."

Some friend you are, Strix.

"I CAN'T DO EVERYTHING FOR YOU, DEAR BRYNN. A DAY MAY COME WHEN I WON'T BE HERE TO HELP GUIDE YOU. YOU NEED TO BE READY ON YOUR OWN."

Gee, thanks.

"And?"

"Not a fucking clue. Why don't you just tell me and stop with the riddles?"

A hand reached out to stroke Ashe's hair. Intimately. "Such a lovely black color, Brynn Benld. And those beautiful all-white eyes. To know what they've seen or where they come from, hmm? I know a great many things. But until you name me friend, secrets shall remain mine. Beware of those around you." A glance toward Harlequin. "Have a good midday, Lady Drakeslayer."

Roqanth sashayed away, leaving Ashe confused. "That one's a queer one."

"I'll say," Harlequin said. Why did Roqanth look her way? She couldn't be a blooddrake. Right? "What game is being played, I wonder."

"I have no idea."

"ROQANTH GIVES YOU WARNING. THOUGH THE WORD OF A CON IS TO BE TAKEN WITH DISTRUST, A SOUND WARNING I CANNOT DENY."

You don't think Roqanth is talking about the spy in our midst, do you?

"FAIR ASSESSMENT. KEEP A WEATHERED EYE."

Who is it, Strix? Do you know?

Silence in the void. Then, *"SOMEONE CLOSE."*

Ashe side-eyed Harlequin. The woman's aura was a calming sapphire with a tint of garnet. *I don't… not her. Right?*

"IT'S HARD TO SAY FOR CERTAIN."

It can't be her. That would be too much like Wren. Nor Cyan. I don't believe it.

"JUST BE CAREFUL, DEAR BRYNN. THAT IS ALL YOU CAN DO UNTIL THE TRUTH IS REVEALED."

There were drunkards passed out in alleys, others fighting over the last of their shared bottles, another thieving from a corpse lying in the dirtied avenue. Unregistered whores tossed tricks in the shadows of the alleys, their pimps eagerly awaiting the coin relieved of those idiots who paid for sex outside the finer establishments like *The Parlour*. They dovetailed through a labyrinth of small apartments and ramshackle buildings all cobbled together by sheer grit and gravity.

"Youse cocksure," came a voice, "to be sneaking 'round. E'en for a pair of vicars."

Five men wearing drake scale cuirasses stood in the mouth of an alleyway ahead of them. Each held a blade and a small buckler shield. No wheellocks or crossbows. Just blades. Four bore firedrake scale helms, while the final—presumably the leader and the one who'd spoken—wore nothing adorning his noggin.

"Don'cha think, Lady Drakeslayer?" the man finished.

In the shadows of the alley, she appraised the man. His face was flat, and he had a thick, greying mustache over cracked lips under a thin-bridged nose. His hair was kept short and there was a jagged scar across one cheek. His aura shaded red. Danger.

The four behind the mustachioed leader hefted blades, ready to rabble rouse. These weren't soldiers of the Guild Politic. The army of the Guild sported full drake scale and carried spears or halberds in addition to their wheellock sidearms. No, these were hired thugs.

Ashe's first thought was a turfland bully wanting tithe. Her second was, *not again.*

"Figger'd you'd come crawlin' back, once they learn't youse was here," the leader said. "Surprised me, though. Heard youse was bit in half in the Abyssal by a seagandr." He put his hands to his hips like he was politicking before a crowd of listeners instead of threatening a member of the Scattered Shards, who was way above his normal paygrade. "Heard from some 'f ma boys youse was good. Real good."

"Has anyone ever told you that you sound like shrewkin gnawing on its own lice-filled foot when you talk?" Ashe asked.

Harlequin was like a coiled snake, the flash of a bluish iron as her dual double-bladed axes appeared in her hands.

"Was paid to silence youse, lassie. Regardless of yer reputation. R's paid us real good to end youse."

"Wait, don't tell me you are part of that sellsword group?" Ashe rubbed her chin. "What was their name, Harlequin?" She may be playing up her stupidity, but in reality, she had already stepped to the precipice of unleashing the Pit on these sellswords. Didn't bode well for them on account of them being, well, sellswords. "O yeah, the Kraken's Cabal. Right?"

The leader with the mustache pointed his short sword at her. "Karloc said one of yours kill't my brother out on the road. And another took Karloc's hand, they did."

"Sorry, don't know any Karloc. But I do recall being held at arrowpoint by a bunch of prickless bandits."

"The Kraken's Cabal ain't no bandits, lassie," Mustache growled. "We do what's we paid for. And that means youse life."

"You do know who I am, right?"

"WILL YOU FINALLY LET ME DO WHAT I WAS FORGED TO DO, DEAR BRYNN?"

"That we do, lassie. And 't don't matter much how big your britches is. R's tired of your prattling and primping."

"Who sent you?"

"Time for talk is over."

Harlequin sprang toward the group of men, the vicar striking one ill-prepared thug with her axe, his neck cleaved in twain. Chaos followed.

Ashe was barely able to unhook the Hammer of Mother Marrow in time before Mustache swung. She deflected the blow haphazardly, but the impact left her arm tingling. She tried to burn her aetheurgy but her pulmo raged inside instead, causing her to lose touch with the aether in the mist. Fuck.

Shoving the leader with her offhand, Ashe coughed and spat tarry blood as she attempted to parry one of the other sellsword's attacks. Spinning, she brought a crushing blow with the Hammer into the fourth thug's cuirass, smashing through the drake scale like it was nothing. The man dropped dead.

She doubled over and hacked black goop, sucking breath after breath in, desperately trying for her aetheurgy. *Why… Strix?*

"NO TIME FOR QUESTIONS, RELEASE ME! I CAN PROTECT YOU!"

Mustache stabbed her way, but Ashe doggedly knocked the short sword to the side. The mouth of the alleyway wasn't large, so she shouldered into another of the helmeted rogues, who'd avoided Harlequin's swing and tried to clock her with the buckler.

Stone from one of the nearby buildings exploded in a spray of dust as Harlequin's hand axe struck it.

Both she and the Kraken's Cabal-man tumbled to the cobbled stones, Ashe punching and elbowing the other, taking a similar blow to the chin. She bit into her tongue and the metallic cruor and tar from her pulmo had a battle of their own in her mouth.

A shadow passed overhead, and Ashe realized it was Harlequin. The woman collided with Mustache, raining down a flurry of axe swings fueled by her Shard Form, her canisters geysering like a tea kettle. The man fought her off, but the vicar was clearly faster, and better, than he due to her aetheric advantage. Harlequin leapt and ran sideways up the nearby wall some four feet and swung around, kicking the leader right in the face.

Rolling atop the unnamed bandit hacking angry tar everywhere, Ashe dropped the Hammer and grappled with the hand holding the sword. The man struck her with the buckler, sending sparks behind her eyes. Fighting to stay conscious, her fingers wrapped around the man's own, and Ashe began to pry the blade free all while trying to fend off the wayward punches of the shield. The man didn't want to give up.

So, Ashe did the one thing she tried to never do to a man unless absolutely necessary; she kneed him in the groin.

The Kraken's Cabal-man grunted and the sword fell from his grip, but he kept slamming the buckler into her face. She was blinded by the black nothingness building in her head and the pulmo in her lungs. A hand went to her throat and squeezed.

Fumbling weakly, Ashe pulled the daemon blade from its sheath and stabbed the man in the apple of his throat, piercing flesh as a cacophony of wails from the void roared in her ears. The man squealed and died.

"AHHHHHHH, FINALLY A SOUL TO PLUNDER. TOOK YOU LONG ENOUGH."

She wobbled to her feet and as her vision came into focus, she saw Harlequin cleaning the blood from her axes' crescents. The mustachioed leader of the Kraken's Cabal lay dead at the vicar's feet with a head resembling a smashed melon.

Harlequin gave a toothy grin from behind her breather as she smoothed down the folds of her cassock over her hips, the axes sliding back in their loops. The desire in Ashe rose like a blaze. "That's three you owe me. Really racking up the debt here, Ashe. Gonna have a hard time paying up if you don't start soon."

Ashe spat a full mouth of blood and tar on the dead rogue, her pulmo finally subsiding. "This better be the last time I hear about this sellsword group," she grumbled as she finally was able to burn her aetheurgy, the magic of the Pentax coursing through her, tending to her wounds and sores. She was definitely *not* trying to think about how she would pay Harlequin back. "Tired of them."

She felt woozy and put a hand to the wall of the alley, feet feeling heavy under her. The grey mist—that was curiously probing the dead sellswords—curled around her legs, dancing upward.

"Ashe?"

Pitching over, Ashe heaved the contents of her gullet all over the cobbled stones. She hadn't eaten much the last few days, so it was mostly tea and liquor, which stung coming up. Her stomach felt like it was about to run up her throat and wish her a happy life, waltzing off into the sunset. It hurt so bad.

"Ashe?" Harlequin came near and put her arms under Ashe's pits, helping her stand. The woman's aura was a dark yellow.

"I'll be fine. See if there's anything on them." She wiped her mouth on the sleeve of her cassock. There was blood on it.

Father, Mother, almost.

"NOT YET, DEAR BRYNN. NOT JUST YET. THANK YOU FOR THE SOUL, BY THE WAY. I'M GOING TO NEED MORE FROM YOU IF WE ARE GOING TO CONTINUE THIS RELATIONSHIP."

Harlequin, who kept watching her with worried eyes, finally bent down and frisked through the leader's outfit, searching the pockets in his trousers, his belt pouch, and eventually in the collar of his shirt, where she found a crumpled piece of parchment.

Frowning, she handed it to Ashe. In smeared ink was descriptions of both her and her team, instructions telling the Kraken's Cabal to kill them on sight. It was signed with a fancy-looking 'R', and there was a symbol drawn under the directions. It had a semi-circle facing east with a slash of zigzags going northeast to southwest, ending in an arrowhead.

That symbol.

"Hmm, something about this feels familiar." She held it toward Harlequin. "Know what this symbol means? I swear I've seen it before." The woman shook her head as Ashe stuffed the note into her cassock pocket. "If I had to fathom a guess. 'R' would be Ranhold. Olum Ranhold."

"A SYMBOL OF NIGHTINGALE."

Harlequin laughed mirthlessly. "Gutless prick couldn't even try to kill us himself."

"Psst, Ashe."

Harlequin spun, drawing an axe while Ashe lazily turned, drained from her pulmo. Standing next to a termite-ridden post holding up an even worse-off balcony was Evzen. Ashe couldn't tell which was thicker, Elian's bastard's waist or the rotting post. Her money might be on the post.

She put a hand over Harlequin's fist. "Ease, Harle-bub. I know him. Seems like everyone and their brother-friend are out in the Harbor today."

The young boy was wearing a loose pair of miner's overalls with a threadbare overcoat. Evzen's dark hair fluttered in the wind. "If you're done canoodling, I got something for you." His smirk was catholic and his eyes alight with mischief.

"You've gotten better at sneaking about, Evzen. Always said if you put your mind to something, you'd be good at it. Shame your pops didn't see it in you."

"Gah, you sound like my old man," Evzen said. "You wanted me to keep my ears open. Well, they were."

Harlequin gave her a questioning look. "I'll explain later. Find anything worth my while?"

"Depends, how much coin you got for me?"

"Evzen."

"Fine, fine. You can be a lousy friend sometimes, Ashe." Evzen harrumphed and shoved his hands in to the overalls' front pockets. "I'm sure you've heard about Hobb seeing as I find you here behind the *Bounty*?" Ashe nodded. "Well, I've heard she was seen with Dil and Klander the day before she turned up driftwood."

"Where at?"

"Over at *The Arbiter's Axe*."

Ashe tapped her finger against her lips. *'Sharpen the axe.'* Roqanth's words. *Could that be the elfir's meaning?* "Any word as to what their meeting was all about?"

"Nothing doing, from what I've been able to find out. Haven't been any games since the turn of the year. By the Pit, there haven't been too many hangings either. They always save *The Axe* for the good ones. Maybe they've got their pantaloons all twisted for a hanging. But that's not all, Ashe. Dil's up to something. She's got a warehouse, see, and well, I saw some of her goons smuggling in some heavy-looking crates. Tried to get a peek, but wasn't able to. Pretty secret-like if you ask me. Don't live long in Port Sin without covering your backside. Either way, Dil's up to something."

"And you've learned from the best. But thanks, we have an idea what Hobb and Tified smuggled in."

"I'm sure you do. Being Shards and all." Evzen made to leave but turned back. "O, haven't confirmed, but word is your Grand Quaestor Tallow is also driftwood."

"What?" Now that was a slap to the face while sleeping soundly. "How?"

Harlequin turned away, her face in the shadows of the alley, but Ashe noticed her mouth quirked and her eyes brimmed with tears. Things had most certainly taken a turn in the wrong direction.

Evzen rocked on his feet. "Like I said, don't know much. But some of the guys are whispering it so. I'd be willing to bet it as true. Has something to do with Gandtril, from what I hear told."

"Up in Kanja?" Evzen nodded. "Zenith's cock. Any other surprises you have in store for me?"

"BE WARY, DEAR BRYNN. LIES UPON LIES. READ THEM AT YOUR DISCRETION."

I'm not that naïve, Strix. Especially from a sprat of Elian's. What's going on in Gandtril?

"JUST A FAIR WARNING, SEEING AS YOU TEND TO JUMP WITHOUT CONFIRMATION OF WATER BELOW. AND I'VE NOT A CLUE. MY KNOWLEDGE DOES NOT REACH THE LAND OF THE

LIVING OUTSIDE OF YOU AND WHAT I CAN SENSE IN THE VOID. AND THERE IS NOTHING OF SUCH IN THE VOID."

Evzen stuffed his hands into his overalls. "You sure you ain't got nothing to spare? I brought you some good gossip."

Ashe dug a coin from her belt purse and tossed the bastard son of Elian a gold quadran, who snatched it clear from the air. "Thanks, Evzen. Who knows, maybe you could've been a scholar if your father hadn't gone and screwed things up."

"And die with ink staining my fingers and still starving? Count me out. Later, Ashe." With that, the lithe urchin melted between the buildings and disappeared back into the streets of Port Sin.

She sighed. "So much for a decent night's sleep. Guess we better check out Dil's place."

"Cyan wanted us to meet him at the stronghold."

"Afraid of him, Harle-bub?" The red-haired vicar frowned but her aura told a different story, the young woman wanted to defy the Defiant, which caused Ashe to smile. "You know I can tell you think otherwise. You can't hide it from me."

The woman's aura shifted to a dangerous red, and not one that meant she wanted Ashe's blood, but instead wanted something else. "I suppose you can sway me."

"YOU TWO ARE BECOMING UNBEARABLE."

"But you're right," Harlequin started as she worked her jaw in an unnatural way. Maybe she had taken a hit to the face? Ashe didn't see any bruising beginning to form. Her aura hadn't changed but it still struck Ashe as odd. "We need to warn Cyan."

Ashe tried to keep her face blank, lest distrust settle back in. *It can't be her… right?* "I'm going to Dil's. You do what you must, Harle-bub."

The vicar seemed conflicted. After a handful of breaths, she steadied, but she tugged at the collar of her cassock. "I'll see to Cyan. Then I'll meet you in the Chain."

Ashe nodded, but inwardly, *Fuck*…

XXIV
LOJEN

"HERE, LOOK AT this, wardkeeper."

Lojen craned his neck to look at what Titen Dunleith was pointing toward and grimaced as the motion tugged at the wound in his side that had breached his exoscales in his fight with the Fallen's daemon. He had put a bandage upon it, but the flesh was still raw.

Scourges. Alive. Daemons en masse. It shouldn't be possible.

Father, do you think we are doing what is right? Is this the tactic you'd have endorsed, or would you have us leave?

He thought he knew what his father would do, but now faced with the choice, he didn't know what he believed anymore. Everything had been turned on its head. Or he was just too blind to see past his own two claws.

The Golden Sword stood upon one of the stone archways that bridged the gap between the Obelisk and the upper tier of Gandtril. The jutting disc that surrounded the mountain's peak was not fully centered, instead, the vast majority of the tier faced northward towards Kanja. Only about a third of the level faced southward and though massive stone and metal struts held up the tier, there was still a fifty or so feet gap between the edge and the start of the Obelisk. It reminded Lojen of an upside-down top that had been broken on one side.

Spanning the distance were half a dozen bridges that were barely wider than Lojen was tall. For a drakken, it just wide enough for him to walk alone, maybe for men, two abreast. Each bridge was fronted by a stout gate, thick bars of steel coated in aetheric runes and guarded by a quartet of legionnaires, two behind the gate and two in front cityside. Another pair of soldiers stood at the entrance of the Obelisk.

Titen motioned for Lojen to cross the bridge and despite the fact there was a rail on both sides, it was still a narrow path, and he couldn't help but think of the tethers of Gargantua. The Obelisk and the upper tier of Gandtril were nowhere near as tall as the base of the floating fortress had been, but with the wind swirling around him from the peak's apex, it didn't stop the memories from arising. He had never had a fear of heights, but that climb had stuck with him. It was something he wouldn't ever forget.

"See these anchors?" Titen indicated a wrist-thick steel rod that was inset between a stone divot. The top of the rod was tapered with a flat head, almost like a nail with only half a head on one side. There were four such anchors, one at the top and bottom of the bridge's rails. Titen motioned toward the pair of legionnaires. "If you will?"

The legionnaires saluted and squeezed past the Golden Sword and the drakken, swapping places atop the bridge. Titen stepped closer to the rune-covered doorway and reached for something hidden in the alcove of the entrance that led into the upper floors of the Obelisk. It was a thick-headed sledge, the haft nearly four feet in length. The head was made with the same green iron that the Hammer of Mother Marrow was forged of. And across the slabbed face were runes of all Four Tenets.

Titen handed Lojen the sledge. It was practically weightless for its size. "It's spelled." The elfir pointed to the anchors. "And so are these. The inscriptions and order are the same. Meaning they are paired. This is the only way to knock the anchors free and drop the bridge. This sledge cannot be moved to another bridge, only this one. This is why they are guarded at all hours."

Lojen looked over the rail and realized the bridge spanned over an empty space between the Lower City and the Obelisk's inner fortifications. If knocked free, the bridges wouldn't fall upon anything of value, including the living of the city. Of that, he was mildly grateful.

"Makes it difficult for some street gang to give it to the nobleborn," Lojen said with a light chuckle.

Titen's face was blank. "Gandtril is not Drenth, wardkeeper. Despite what my brother-friend would have you believe; the Lower City holds no seagandr candle to the gangs of the City of Sands."

"No, that's not… nevermind." Lojen snapped his snout shut. He glanced nervously toward the legionnaires behind him, but they weren't paying attention. Perhaps they hadn't heard… He never was good with a joke. Instead, he hefted the sledge. "Have these ever been used?"

"Never in four centuries has Gandtril or the Obelisk been breached," Titen said, taking the sledge back from Lojen and replacing it within a hammer-shaped crevice just inside the alcove. A greenish glow bloomed around it for a moment, holding it in place with a spell of *Terris*. "Never has the thought crossed my mind that it ever could be, but with the words of Bliss and your encounter in the Sea, I fear we might not be able to withstand the Fallen this time."

"It shouldn't be possible," Lojen whispered.

It seemed like those words were all he could muster at this point. He knew what his own eyes told him, what his own earholes heard via Bliss' divination. The Fallen has returned to the land of the living, and his army was greater than ever. All done in secret.

Nocturne had rebirthed Lu Har for a second time. He had seen the man swallowed by the terrisvvyrm at the Temple of Mother Marrow. There was no way to escape those magnificent jaws. No way for anyone to survive that. It had to have been Nocturne who dug Lu Har's soul from the Pit once more.

His claw went to the wound at his side just thinking about the small village in the Sea. He winced as he touched the tender flesh under his exoscales. He had felt the kiss of sharpened claw from an enemy that he'd thought they'd defeated last summer. An enemy bested by his fallen ward, by Emre Benld.

It shouldn't be possible, but it was.

"As you've no doubt seen since coming to Gandtril, the only way to get to the upper tier is through the Ceveo. There are gates at both ends and the Legion holds them at all times."

"Have to keep the lowborn from the nobleborn, right?"

The Ceveo, as naughty as the term was, was essentially a pinch point, one that could serve as another means of defense. The quality and strength of the Obelisk was never in question, but the Lower City was still a weakness should the walls to the other three directions ever be breached. And while the mountain possessed a number of caverns and tunnels, the fastest and safest place behind the fortress behemoth was the upper tier.

The struts that held up the manmade disc were as strong as the mountain itself and reinforced with aetheric runes. Thus, if necessary, falling back to the Ceveo was the next best option.

But it also created a natural barrier between the upper caste and the lower. A physical representation of social standing.

Titen glanced his way. "It seems you are no stranger to the hierarchy of the haves and have nots, drakken. It is no different here. Gandtril has and will always be a city of the Golden Throne, but I fear my parents may have given it too much freedom."

"You mean with the Guild?"

"I do." Titen's hands rested upon the railing. "The Guild has only grown stronger since Drenth's emancipation. Fatter in the gullet and in the purse."

"I've noticed."

"And it doesn't go unnoticed up in Kalderim. There are many within my parents' court, including in my own family, who think we've allowed the Guild too much authority. Others think we should leave Gandtril to them, for Gandtril brings nothing of value, especially now since Drenth had defeated the Fallen. Well… was defeated." The Golden Sword shook his head. "Even still, these people here, this city, they are Kanjans. And it is my duty to see them home. Whether that be here at the front of a siege to come, or back in Kalderim."

Duty. Lojen knew all about duty, even when it ended in failure.

"How fares the evacuation?" he ventured, his gaze taking in the crammed Lower City.

People by the score filled the streets, all carrying their livelihoods in arms and on backs. All headed toward the northern exits. It was an orderly, yet chaotic mess. Thousands of souls streaming through the streets. The few legionnaires spared to help police the flight were invisible within the mass, only a stray sigil-emblazoned flag here and there. Sixty thousand called Gandtril home, it would take days for the mega-city to empty.

"Steady as can be in such short order, wardkeeper," replied the Golden Sword. "Word has been carried upon the aerescreens, and as you can see, most of the people are taking the warning to heart. But others…"

Immediately after their meeting with Praetor Rignork, the Golden Sword declared a state of emergency. The Legion began to fortify their defenses. Word spread quickly of the impending army, of the need to flee to Kalderim and the other mega-cities within Kanja. Panic set in not long after despite the message for calm.

And Lojen knew it was because the army coming at them was the deadliest in the entire history of the Mistlands. Even greater than that of the time of the Last Godsking, for even the Pentax had taken most of Their valiant warriors to the Meadows.

For centuries, the Legion had been the spear defending Kanja from the daemons in the mist, but never have they gone against a horde rumored within the Fallen's grasp. In fact, no one truly knew the extent of Lu Har's daemon horde, for it hadn't been unleashed since his demise five hundred years, from before the Fall. The threat had arisen when he had been rebirthed fifty years prior, but none had seen its true might for Drenth had fallen with only the need for men and metal soldiers. By scourge and Predator automatons. By Gargantua. The daemons were held in reserve.

And if Lojen's fears were true, then even the stalwarts of the Legion might not be enough.

'WARDKEEPER! AEGIS!' The words of the daemon filled his mind, even now he could hear them. That ghastly voice from beyond the void. Calling for him.

While the others—including Finn, which was a sight for sore eyes, and a major relief to see his friend finally out of his self-inflicted grief—began to formulate their plans for evacuating the mega-city, Lojen had pulled Val aside. Hoping that maybe Bliss had given her anything else. Anything relating to his eerie pursuer.

But Val had no additional insight into what or who was after him. Nor why.

It couldn't be a coincidence, could it? He didn't think it that simple. No, there was much more to it than being an unlucky wardkeeper in the same location as one of the Fallen's daemons.

His father and Lu Har had been close to Canlon Carr before the Fall, had great agreements and even greater disagreements according to Tevun. Lojen hatched near three hundred years after the war for Eminence, but his father had told stories of the time when he was the wardkeeper for the Last Godsking. Stories about the man who'd become the Fallen. Stories of the arcane arts the elfir studied with Void Form. The dangerous use of blood and twisted runes.

This was no mere coincidence, this strange voice had to be after him.

"...many of whom are nobleborn, are refusing to leave," Titen was saying, breaking Lojen's thoughts. "Most of the fools think they are safe on the upper tier. What's worse, is they think if they leave and Gandtril should stand strong, those in the Lower City will have free reign of their villas. That they'd storm the Ceveo and run rampant. Pillaging their wealth."

Lojen had been too preoccupied in the intervening hours to have noticed that the bustle was all within the Lower City, not on the upper tier. "They're worried about being plundered? With what we've told them?"

"You are a drakken, Lojen, not man. Man cares about their family and wealth in equal measures. More often than not, their wealth comes first. I've seen plenty over my centuries who would trade their own souls to maintain their power, their purses full."

While the masses moved like ants down below, out past the gated and guarded Ceveo, people went about their daily business as if what was happening around them meant nothing. Richly dressed folk walked lazily, chatting without a care. The roads were filled, yes, but not with panic, not with chaos, but with carelessness.

It irked him to see.

"Fools."

"Indeed. No matter how much we present this threat, they will see and hear what they want to hear. As much as it pains me, this is why we cannot abandon the city, even if that is what Bliss might imply. She said the tide will come here, and we must be here to stem it. Any Kanjan soul who remains must be protected. Even the fools. Maybe the fools most of all."

An airship rose out of the docking bay in the west. It was a barrel-shaped transport, one typically used for cargo hauling, specifically aethecite in trade with Drenth. But Lojen figured it was now hauling refugees.

Since the entire mega-city wrapped the mountain peak, the docking bay had been carved out of the western slope. Once a natural cavern, it had been sculpted to house and land airships. Gandtril was a fraction the size of a mega-city like Drenth, and because there weren't any natural sources of trade, Gandtril's docking bay was relatively small by comparison. Whereas a city like Drenth or Kalderim might berth hundreds of airships of all sizes at any given time, Gandtril could only hold upwards of fifty.

Most were personal crafts of the nobleborn or Guild. Small to medium sized at best.

That singular transport might have been the biggest Gandtril could offer. Hopefully it was filled to the brim with women and children. Hopefully saving those worth saving. Hopefully those not of the Guild.

"We don't even know what is coming," Lojen said dejectedly as he watched the airship disappear into the evenfall gloom, heading northward. "Soldiers, scourges, yes. And daemons. But they've broken before. You fear for the Legion?"

Pride rippled across the Golden Sword's features. "Never would I doubt the Legion, nor the hearts of Kanjans. But people are easily misled, wardkeeper."

Lojen's angular snout crept into a smirk. "If my sister was here, she'd tell you that men are weak. That the Pentax were the ones who were misled when They made you. For why would They gift the races of man skin and not exoscales?"

Titen's lips quirked. "You give your sister too little credit, Lojen. She hides behind her fierce exterior because she is just as lost as you are. She just doesn't know how to express it."

"The same could be said about Finn."

The Golden Sword sighed. "You may be right about that. Finn has always been a man of conviction. We just never knew which way the wind would blow that sail of his. It seemed that all it took was a man in Drenth to capture his heart. But look at where he is now?"

"Finn is a good man, Lord Sword."

"Titen, Lojen."

"Titen, your brother is and always was a good man. Nothing can change that, even Drenth. You just need to give him the space to grieve."

“And here I thought we were discussing your sibling, not mine.”

“Seems we are both underestimating our siblings.”

XXV

THE BUGGERED CAPTAIN, NEENAH LEFLEUR

IF THERE WAS one thing that frightened Neenah LeFleur, that was dying without being remembered.

But bugger all the pissing gods and Their creations if dying meant being brought back as a daemon.

For near a full day's turn, Neenah had been witness to Void Form in all its perverted glory. Its corruption that many feared. Its impurity that permeated the land, its stink, its decay. If there was anything that was ever more unholy than Void Form, Neenah had yet to uncover it. And that was saying a lot because Neenah LeFleur had seen a thing or two in her life, things that would make a stalwart person spew the contents of their gullets.

Void Form was just about the worst thing in all existence.

The army of the Fallen had marched toward Gandtril after Lu Har had bloody surprised the piss out of her and decided to be the Fallen instead of the matriarch's advisor. The burnt bastard, who by all rights should be vvyrm shit, had pushed the grand army fast and fierce. The daemons in his unhallowed horde marched side-by-side with scrouges and soldiers. Corrupted souls beside the derelict.

It was a sight the Mistlands hadn't seen in half a millennium.

While his army marched through the Sea, Neenah and crew had become the personal pleasure airship of the Fallen. Not that it hadn't been bloody so before when she was under the impression she'd be made a matriarch woman and he commandeered her godsdamned cabin. His forces were shrouded in the Sea's grey while the other airships—three buggers that were some of the largest warships she'd ever laid her pretty brown eyes on—sailed high above the corrupted haze.

The warships were weapons of destruction that were unparalleled by anything Kalderim could boast. Even those in the Imperium's employ during conquest and subsequent occupation of Drenth had been near half the size of these behemoths. The amount of aetheric firepower aboard these bitties rivaled that of Gargantua but lacked the true magnificence of the floating fortress. Neenah had heard rumors of such warships under construction, but those tall tales went silent after the Fallen's death last summer. Apparently, they had been completed in the shadows while this army mustered.

And yet, all that might, all that fear-inducing rhythmic marching, the majestic warships in flight paled in comparison to what the Fallen subjected her and her devoted crew to the entire trip.

At the bowsprit of *Marrow's Lover,* the Fallen sat cross-legged, facing the stern. His robe lay opened, revealing dark-toned flesh marred by the acidic burns of terrisvvyrm blood. His patchy hair fluttered in the breeze, the salt-and-pepper locks cracking like auroch whips. His all-onyx eyes were glazed as his mouth never seemed to close, chanting in the language of godsdamned Nocturne.

Despite the burns that crisscrossed his chest from naked waist to ear, there was no mistaking the Void Form runes carved into his breast, almost as if the acid had feared to go near the depraved runes. The runes bled in a steady stream, smoking whenever it dribbled to the deck. A blackened mist circled his body, dark lightning crackling within.

On the decking of her beautiful airship, marring its perfection, was a six-pointed star drawn in blood. The Fallen's blood. Within the points of the star were runes, also in blood. Neenah had seen enough aetheric runes in her day, and she knew these were corrupted forms of the Four Tenets. Those of the Pit.

To top it off, a pair of scourges had dragged two crystalline vessels from the cargo bay toward the bowsprit, which truth told, irked Neenah to no end as they hadn't given a godsdamn about the gouges they left in the planks of her beauty. Within these man-tall vessels was a burgundy liquid, thick and syrupy. At first, Neenah hadn't a clue to what it was, but the odor was worse than when the hobgoblin twins had a contest to see who could forgo a bath the longest. That had been the longest three weeks of Neenah's life. But those vessels had tubes, and they pierced the Fallen in various places. It wasn't until the first abomination had been summoned, did Neenah realize those vessels were full of blood.

It didn't matter to a woman of Neenah's caliber that the man rolled in the hay with the Master of the Pit, using His dark arts of Void Form. No, her own brother Merrick had dabbled in aetheurgy of the void for a spell before committing himself to the Pentax and the Scattered Shards, so she was used to aetheurgy of the blackest kind. And she never begrudged a man or woman their due if that's what got their privies worked up.

But summoning souls from the Meadows to augment your already frightening and famished horde of daemons, that was pure blasphemy in Neenah's eyes.

And she was the last to be used, her crew already drained of their memories. Of their loved ones. Of their friends. Now, it was her turn.

She made to move, but the dark-haired Imperium captain clamped a drake scaled palm upon her shoulder, rumpling the already past its rumpled stage tunic, shoving her back into the kneeling position she'd been assuming since the *Lover* took off from that camp some hours ago. From up near the pilotbox midships. Neenah wanted to bite at the hand and hop over the portside railing and disappear into the Sea. But if she did, her crew would be flayed alive, a stain she didn't want tarnishing her reputation. Flayed crew didn't exactly make new potential crewmembers come a-runnin' to sign up.

Instead, she glared up at the man. "Ain't goin' nowhere, you prick-riding hog. No need to mess this tunic any godsdamned more, hear?"

The captain's breather fogged as he snorted, those grey-green, red-pupiled eyes gleamed with daemonish intent. "You're lucky the Fallen has need of you, LeFleur, otherwise you'd long since fed the horde."

"Pfft, I know these baps are a handful for a bugger like you, but I'd much prefer not to end up bloody daemon feed. Thank you very much." She raised her left wrist, jiggling the heavy manacle encasing her arm, the rubber tube that had been inserted into her flesh slapped at her forearm. "Zenith will strike you down for this pissing rape, captain, for that's what this bloody well is."

The aetheurgist captain said nothing, just stared forward toward his dark master. "It begins, LeFleur. Brace yourself."

Neenah sucked in a breath when the Fallen's all-onyx gaze flashed crimson, face turning toward her instead of upward. A shiver danced along her spine. With a grunt, the Imperium captain grabbed her by the pits and dragged her closer to Nocturne's agent in the world of Life. She fought and kicked but the man's aetheurgy crackled around her and she knew she was helpless, a feeling she knew all too well while growing up with Merrick, for her brother could only best her when using aether.

Roughly, Neenah was thrown a body's length away from the seated Fallen, the man never flinching. The ghastly tubing of burgundy flapped between them. She sent the bloody captain her best glare as she delicately smoothed her tunic sleeves. Say what you will about Captain Neenah LeFleur, she would always look her godsdamned best if she was about to meet the Pentax. The captain grunted that annoying grunt of his and stood behind her with his arms at his sides.

"You fight what you cannot, LeFleur," the Fallen said, his voice coarse as if he'd been screaming for hours on end. But with all that voidspeak chanting that sounds like wailing, perhaps it had. "The Divine is in need of warriors if Kalderim is to fall."

"But to bring back the dead. That's godsdamned… bloody fuck, that's just evil."

"Evil is but a word you mortals live by when you disagree." His burned face turned to the side; the raised scars caressed by the blackened mist. "You know nothing of what the Divines are capable of. Your gods, your Zenith and Nocturne, They are but constructs your feeble minds conjure to make yourself understand. But you cannot ever understand."

"And you bloody do? Buggers, man, you've broken Divine will. Don't think Neenah LeFleur doesn't know what the rules of Life and Death are."

The false advisor laughed, a dark sound. "Rules? You speak to me of rules? She who has flaunted them all her life? Tsk tsk, LeFleur. Those rules you speak of are the rules of mortals, of those who would shackle you to this plane of suffering. Life is nothing but suffering. But rules? The Divines live by the rules of the Crystals, the light and the void. Not those of your world."

"What are you pissing blathering about, prick-sucker? The All Father will bloody smite you for such."

"I offer you the truth upon a platter, LeFleur, and yet you still hold dear to beliefs you don't even believe yourself."

"Bugger your words, Fallen. I know the truth. Merrick has told me. I believe him, you bloody well know, hear?"

The Fallen shook his head. "Kin can be destined for a greater purpose. Or they can be the chosen ahead of you. It matters not, we all get what is ours in the end." Lu Har popped his neck, sighing as he closed his eyes. "Come, LeFleur, it is time for your history to fuel my army. Do you know why it was so easy for you to find the Oculus?"

She'd thought the job was too simple, too few soldiers. It was Qarthage, the home of the Fallen's Imperium. It should have been a stronghold if this godsdamned bracelet was that powerful. "I assume you'll tell me. But just know, Neenah LeFleur prefers to be wined and dined before she's buggered, hear?"

"I like you, LeFleur, always have. Don't think I haven't followed you since your brother was but an augur with the Shards. O, yes, LeFleur, I've watched your rise for that long. You've flaunted it, sure enough. But no, the reason why I chose you to bring me the Oculus is because of your ties to the

Godsblood. That child is but the key to my victory, a blade in need of a whetstone. As she is honed by breaking the Seals, the gate to Eminence awaits me at Kalderim. To break the Golden Throne, I need the strongest rebirthed from the Pit. And do you know who the strongest are?"

"Neenah LeFleur don't care much for riddles, Fallen."

"Soul Form is the source of Life, but it is also the bridge to Death. You've been in the presence of the Godsblood. Your crew has eaten with her, lived with her. Her aura has bled into you. It has seeped into this airship, into these boards below our feet. Her aether is all around you, LeFleur. This ship, your crew, you, all have her essence touching you. And the memories you share. The souls you both have touched. Those are the ones who will sharpen the blade that is my horde. Those who were slain by her. Those who loved her. Those who knew her, wanted her. That is what the Oculus of Apathy is used for. To bring forth those souls from beyond the veil of the Pit, to bring them back so they can fulfill their hatred for the one who wronged them. To hound the Godsblood and all who worship her. To slay her Aegises."

Neenah was about to speak but the air all around her went as cold as the blizzards constantly pummeling Krylen. She pitched forward as Lu Har's voidspeak settled over her like a cloak. Pressure from within built, working its way out of her, like every vein, every atom, every essence was depleted of warmth, sucked away and into the void. A piercing, she felt it worm its way through every facet that was Neenah LeFleur.

She screamed. There was no holding back. No stopping it in the name of saving face. Of being strong. There was nothing but the pressure and piercing. The famed captain of *Marrow's Lover* was nothing but an ant being smashed.

Neenah's face smacked the planking of the *Lover*, jolting stars behind her eyes, which were squeezed shut as she bellowed. And then she vomited, blackness that wasn't liquid, wasn't solid, just blackness. It spooled under her body like she was an unraveling loom as the pressure kept building. It hurt, O, there was nothing but hurt.

And then it stopped, receding. With it went her soul. Or at least that's what it felt like.

Ripped from her in a torrent of black aether, it was like her soul was being torn in twain, drawn from her forcefully. Behind her closed eyes, she watched as her soul took form in the black, like a shade of her, reaching for her as it screamed silently. Violently pulled and drawn down the tube piercing her wrist, slithering in the viscous red blood that was not hers, upward toward the Fallen. Into the agent of the Pit, through the tubes in his flesh.

Then the black mist surrounding both went still, crinkling like parchment, a horrid sound in her ears. The voidspoken chant overtook her and she fell completely forward, the black mist pushing her down. Neenah cranked her neck to witness, for she vowed to see who it was. To see who the Fallen would pull from the Pit, which soul in need of vengeance toward the little bint.

The mist quirked, a crimson light blooming within its center between her and the Fallen. Then it sliced open, for that was the only way Neenah could describe such a thing. Like the world of Life was split by an unseen blade. Ungodsly wails arose from the rent, ghastly sounds only meant for Nocturne.

Out of the slice came a hand, well not truly a hand, more like a scaled version of a hand. It was oily, this hand, each pudgy finger ending in a claw. Another clawed arm protruded, followed by both wide arms, each dark as the void. Then a head emerged, a pate bald but scaled like that of a draconem. The face was turned away from her, but Neenah could see the scraggly wisps that once was a beard over bulging cheeks. As the bald head flung backwards as it wailed, the daemon dragged its bulbous body further from the Pit, collapsing at the Fallen's sitting form.

It rose, the daemon, upon thick legs that were covered in coarse hair and wide scales. Its body was rotund, but within its center, where the gullet met spine, hardened keratin had replaced the skeleton that had once existed within the gaping hole. Black ichor dripped from the open wound, as if the man had been impaled before his death. His body, while decayed and pallid under the scales, pulsed like its beating heart. But it pulsed in aether, not in Life. Corrupted aether. Dark aether. Void aether.

The daemon turned toward her, finally. The crimson eyes within the scaled, portly face finding hers. And Neenah sucked in her breath.

It was Elian, the former gangleader of Slag's End.

Bugger me…

"My pet," the Fallen said calmly, his all-onyx eyes glazed as if it had taken a toll on him to summon this creature from the Pit. It must have, for his chest bled bright crimson over the runes inscribed in his flesh. Neenah had lost count on how many summons this had been. The man should be bereft of blood by now.

The daemon housed within the corpse of Elian smiled at her, wicked teeth serrated and sharp. Then it took a bounding step that belied the man's former girth and leapt over the bowsprit, disappearing into the Sea. She barely heard the beast hitting the marshland below.

Neenah lay panting as she forced herself to look at the Fallen, watching what was to come just as it had for the last few hours to her crew. This was only the first. The first of many to come, as it had been for her crew.

Glancing to starboard, she saw the giantess Doll holding Tris in her large arms. The poor dvergir had been the last before her to be bled of the souls in their memories, for that is what the Fallen was doing. Reaching into their souls, taking the memories of those who had died and gone to the Pit and the Meadows. These were the souls of friends, kin, and acquaintances. All drawn from their memories of them, ripped from the eternal slumber, and brought back to feed the army of the Fallen's horde.

But not like the one just stolen from Neenah. No, if what Lu Har just said was true, these were the special souls meant to hound that snarky girl named Brynn Benld.

Doll caressed Tris, the small dvergir like a babe in the giantess' arms. Dozens, if not hundreds of souls ripped from the pair's memories. Hours it had taken, the toll too heavy a tithe for the taciturn dvergir. He wept in his lover's arms as tears also fell from Doll's sockets. Pain, that's all there was. Pain and sorrow.

Poor Alexina, that little bint who was nary older than her first moonflow, had cried herself into a stupor. There was nothing that broke Neenah's stout heart quite like seeing the young girl go catatonic upon seeing her mother and father returned to the world of Life in daemonic form. Even though he was also burdened by the soul-sucking memories of his loved ones, only Roland was able to stay strong. The big bastard had cradled Alexina and took her belowdecks, an allowance of the Fallen as mercy.

Only the hobgoblin twins had been spared such a fate, for they were already voidspawn. And voidspawn held no such connections to the realm of Death, they just were. Zig and Zag were left to steer the ship, and prior to Elian, Neenah was afeared they'd crash, but so far, they hadn't. Maybe there was a glimmer of hope for the twins.

Neenah pushed herself upright, the lingering pressure in her body was fleeting, but she knew the respite wouldn't last. "This… this is…"

"Say it, LeFleur. Say that this act is an abomination. Guilt yourself into believing you know what happens in the Pit. What happens to the souls who must remain in agony because the Divines quibble." He raised his wrist, the one wearing the obsidian bangle she'd retrieved in Qarthage. "Apathy is what befalls all those who believe. It matters not the belief. The longer one believes, the deeper the apathy. The world changes and your beliefs remain. Why is that?"

"You're speaking in godsdamned riddles again, Fallen. I don't know what it is you want me to pissing say, hear?"

A smile. "Because you yourself don't believe, do you, LeFleur."

"I believe just fine."

"Is that so? Then why do you loathe your brother? O, yes, LeFleur, I can feel the loathing within you. I can feel the hate you harbor. It is deep within, anchored. Is it because he left you when you were but children to the throes of Zenith? Because he renounced you, and your family, for a Divine? Left you to rot on the streets of Alizarin? Where the hands of evil men took you, took your body? Left you to the stain that is humanity?"

Memories crept out of the darkness that she had strove to keep hidden. Memories of hands. Of reeking breath on her face. Memories of… no, she couldn't go there. How could Zenith on high allow such a thing? His creations.

"Ah, there it is, LeFleur, you let it fester. It consumed you. Forced to hide in the shadows, you let it fester. Let it grow. But then you sought to change your misfortune. To seek a way to forget it, to leave it all behind. To change the path the Divines set for you. And in that wake, you turned toward apathy to help you forget. To bury the belief that Zenith would never allow such things to happen. A just god would never let His flock suffer. See where that led you?" Neenah looked at the Fallen with such hatred. "It led you to me. Just as it was unto Merrick, it will be unto you. The void cares naught for your beliefs, LeFleur, only your apathy. Come, we have more memories to pull from you before you are broken. The Godsblood awaits the sins you carry, for that shall be her demise."

Neenah made to move, but once again, the hand of the Imperium captain forced her back down. Chest heaving, she defiantly faced the Fallen.

That was until the pressure came again. Down she went, face to the planks of the *Lover*, the blackened mist cracking with the void.

This time, Neenah LeFleur, the most dashing, the most daring smuggler in all the Mistlands did not hold her scream. Couldn't. Dare not.

XXVI
THE DAEMON

KEENING.

O Nocturne, he heard nothing but the keening of the dead locked within the Pit. They, the souls, were in pain, just the same as he. O, they hurt. O, he hurt. It was a pyre.

A pyre where it was his soul which blazed.

Dead, that's what he was. In the never-ending abyss that was the void. He didn't even know how or when. It mattered not. Pain and suffering were all he knew. All he would ever know. Time meant nothing in the Pit, and eons passed like heartbeats.

The very essence of his being was ripped asunder, tormented until it was ground to a pulp. Life was nowhere to be seen, not to be had. Death was his mistress, his god. His Divine.

Every shred of him was destroyed. A wave of Death. Over and over, never ceasing.

Then, a pressure engulfed him, his soul. A stabbing pressure through the veil that protected the Meadows from Nocturne's Pit. That thin barrier of elemental essence that warded souls like his, the damned, from those in eternal slumber. O, how he wished for that sleep. But it will never come for him. Never.

The pressure grabbed at his lifeforce, a direct grab, meant for him and him alone. The veil pulsated, pestering his torment like a pebble in a boot, digging ever deeper into flesh. Flesh, he had that once. Right? A memory breaching the hurt.

It pulled at his essence, at his very soul. The veil convexed as he was dragged from his prison, elemental tendrils fraying. From the Pit he was pulled, snapping the veil's tethers, the wails of the other souls piercing his essence like blades.

His soul didn't 'see' but rather sensed. And from within the Pit was a crystal of obsidian so large, it was the only thing he felt. Crystalline black with facets, a linking between his soul and that of the Crystal of Death. Noctis. A final binding, a prison known all too well, for not only was it his, but his Divine's.

And then, the Meadows spanned before him, heaving in a non-color, non-light. A heartbeat almost. The wails of the hateful blared, but beyond, he heard a voice. Not his Divine, no, but that of the living. How, he hadn't a notion, all he knew was he was no longer in pain. It was glorious.

He reached for it, his soul latching on to that voice. The words incoherent as they seeped into his lifeforce. Clawing, he began to regain himself. Thoughts billowed, returning in a drip. But they weren't clear, weren't understood. Fractions of knowledge, broken and busted like a clay pot put back together without all the pieces.

He was whole, yet not.

More pain ripped through him, but not like his soul being frayed. This was physical, if such a thing could be done to a soul in the Meadows. Fire burned within, hurt like no other, reminding this wayward thought of a woman with reddish-blonde hair and bee-stung lips. Carved flesh upon a bleeding breast.

A memory of walking the Meadows. Aether, that's what it was. Yes, aether.

Aether tore apart his soul, physically breaking, then mending. Had he a voice, he would have screamed. But there wasn't sound for him. No, nothing like that existed. Why?

The pressure drew him onward through the Meadows, the wails singing his passage. And then Life reached for him, glorious and bright.

Life.

His eyes, no, wrong, his eye opened. Only one, where the other was, he felt emptiness. Not as in blind, but gone, simply gone. The memory of always having two was a strange one. Just odd.

He reached up, remembering what it felt like to control a body, for it felt like millennia since. His limbs were heavy. What a feeling. Heavy. His gaze drifted toward his arms, taking in the organic flesh that he slowly remembered from before. But he did not recall the claws that were on the end. Vicious and sharp, black as Noctis was, jagged protrusions piercing his flesh up to the crook.

Gingerly, he touched his face. That's what it was called, a face. Yes, he remembered that word. A claw touched the side where his eye should be and felt nothing but gumminess. Looking at the claw, it was covered in crimson, a liquid thick and syrupy. His claws clacked as he touched it, feeling nothing of the thickness, no feeling at all within them. The red ran down the black claw.

Blood, that's what it was.

His face bled, it dribbled down his neck, tingling flesh. Missing, he was missing part of his face. Why? Was that how he had died?

Died, why did he remember that word? Was that what Death was?

Then he realized what was before him. A man, seated with legs crossed. Yes, a man, remembering. Scarred with all-onyx eyes. Two eyes. A red covering, the word escaping his memory. Lips within a blackened hair on his face curling. Smile, that's what it was called. The man was smiling.

A gasp from behind.

Turning, he saw another, this time a person unlike the first. Prone upon the wood below his feet. Yes, feet. Another word recalled. Wood, he knew that, too. This person was lying on the wood, hair damp. Why did he remember the word 'damp'? Sweat, that's why. O, yes. This person's hair was damp.

He couldn't place why this person was different other than their looks were softer, fairer, less severe. He took this person in, the swell of a chest that was unlike the man's. Larger. O, yes, breasts, that's the word. A tingle within him at the memory. Why? Desire, was that it?

"Fucking bastard… you…" The woman was in pain, breasts heaving as she sucked in air. That desire within rose with every gasping breath she took. Want, he wanted her. Tingling in his flesh between his legs.

He knew this person. This woman. Memory anew. This woman was someone from his past. What was the word she said? He made to ask, to speak, that's what he used to do. But nothing came forth. No sound.

Reaching with the claw, he went to his face again, out of his sightline. Nothing but the bloody flesh. He roamed, experimentally touching. No lips like the woman or the man. No mouth, just gaping flesh, blood dribbling where it should be. Just a mess of flesh.

"The buggering void happen to you?" the woman asked, her eyes wide in emotion as she caught her breath, face slick with sweat. Horror, that's it. Horror. He remembered that feeling.

No words would come, but what would he say anyway? Dead. He had died, but how?

"FEAR NOT, MY DISCIPLE, FOR I SHALL GUIDE YOU."

He tensed. That voice, he knew that voice. His Divine. Yes, it was his Divine.

Master. A word he knew all too well. *Master?*

"RETURNED YOU'VE BEEN. ANOTHER CHANCE AT OBTAINING MY GIFT. DO NOT SQUANDER IT AGAIN."

Gift? What was a gift?

"IN TIME YOU'LL UNDERSTAND. IT WILL ALL RETURN. BUT YOU'VE TIED YOUR FATE TO MY AGENT, MY FALLEN."

He turned back to the seated man. Fallen? The man's name, there it was, the memory returned. The Fallen. With its recollection came the name 'Lu Har'. Yes.

Tied, master?

MY DISCIPLE YOU REMAIN, BUT MY GIFT IS FINITE. MY FALLEN OWNS YOU, SOUL AND ALL. WHAT HE COMMANDS IS MY COMMAND. DO NOT FAIL ME AGAIN, FOR WHAT YOU ENDURED IN THE PIT WILL BE A PITTANCE TO THE TITHE YOU WILL SOON PAY."

Pay? What is this meaning? He couldn't remember.

"MY FALLEN WILL STEER YOU TRUE. NOT ALL IN HIS HORDE WAS TRAINED IN AETHER IN LIFE. THE MEMORIES OF THAT TRAINING WILL RETURN. BE MY WARRIOR AT MY FALLEN'S SIDE. BRING ME THE GODSBLOOD. SHE CAN AND WILL BREAK MY PRISON."

Godsblood? Why did that word sound so familiar. He knew of it, from before.

"CORRUPTION FEEDS YOU, MY DISICPLE. YOUR AETHER WILL ONLY BE AS STRONG AS YOUR WILL. UNTIL YOU RECOVER, YOU WILL BE HALF FULL."

"You," said the seated man, his voice melodic, "were Solanine's pet. Become mine and reap what was stolen from you."

Pet? The word 'companion' rose from the depths of his empty memory. He thought to voice this word, but again, couldn't as his mouth was gone. This was becoming straining and difficult.

"What our Divine says is the truth. The Godsblood is the means to free Him, and free Him we must." Toward the woman, "Your help has concluded, LeFleur." To someone else, this one a man behind the woman, "Take her below with the others. We are close to Gandtril. This ends tonight."

The other man, he had red flesh that appeared hard. No, that wasn't it. Armor, another memory dredged. The armored man reached for the woman, grabbing at her damp hair.

"Bloody prick-sucker!" the woman screamed as the armored man dug his fingers into the brown shag, pulling none too lightly. LeFleur? He felt like he should know that word.

Dragged across the wood, the woman kicked and screamed. Yes, tantrum, that was the word. Tantrum.

Back to the Fallen his gaze went, other words rising from his memory like a beast from the… water. He couldn't remember what either were called. It mattered not.

"A task awaits you, daemon child," the Fallen said. "Until he is dead, you will hunt Finnus Dunleith. He cannot take up the Crown of Bliss. Hunt him and send this Aegis to the Pit."

Aegis? A word that meant nothing to him. No memory sprung from the well that had been his mind.

"The Godsblood will come to us. You knew her well. This Ashe. Once the Aegis is dead, she can be yours."

Ashe? Who was this 'Ashe'? A name he tried to remember but nothing came forth.

The Fallen closed his black eyes. Black, the opposite of white. He knew that, why? White… white… a color of the falling objects from the sky. Snow. Something about snow triggered him.

And then a name reared. One that meant something to him, that tingle of desire. That want. The need to own.

Snow Eyes.

Solanine

XXVII

SOLANINE

THE BRITTLE TOME lay open before Solanine.

It was ancient, perhaps older than any creature living, over thousands of years. Perhaps even as old as the first rise of the races of man under the divine crystals of Eminence and Noctis. It held knowledge long since lost, knowledge of aether. The pages were brown with age, the runic script barely more than a faded scribble. The binding was falling apart, and pages were missing.

But it fascinated Solanine nonetheless, for the secret to Noctis and Eminence lay within.

"USE IT, MY DISCIPLE. GAIN IT. IT IS THERE FOR YOU TO TAKE. YOUR RIGHTFUL PLACE IS AT THE TABLE OF THE DIVINES WITH ME AT THE HEAD."

Two figures emerged in Solanine's peripheral. The all-onyx eyes of Cadrianna Benld rose from the page and a snarl of lip graced the scales' face. "Ialtris, Rinkhal, I've awaited you."

Ialtris' scales' frowned, "I came as soon as the word was sent, Solanine. Not all of us hide in the shadows."

"Some of us must drive your prey to the trap," said Rinkhal while scratching at the humir flesh under the scales' cassock collar. It was the cassock of the Scattered Shards. Solanine's gaze leveled upon the five-pointed star adorning the cassock's breast from within the fist holding the sword. A pitiful emblem. "I assume you've found something within the Benld's memories?"

"I've kept my end of the plan," Solanine gestured toward the tome, "and this scales' memories have led me to the gateway to Brio's Temple."

"We had a hunch when House Nightingale was cleansed. Hence our purchase." Rinkhal's scales' head surveyed the room, a personal office on the third floor of a much larger building. "Master Lu Har was wise to claim *The Arbiter's Axe*."

Solanine placed Cadrianna's finger on one of the more legible runes. It was an eastern-facing semi-circle with zigzags and arrows. "It was under our snouts the entire time. Not only was it the symbol of your faithful Guilders, but also of the Shards. The symbol of the House Nightingale. Their home."

A memory welled from within Cadrianna Benld's depths, one that had shown Solanine the way. A memory of Cadrianna's pushed to the fore.

A girl skipping along, this girl was her, was Cadrianna. And she was headed toward a place of her childhood dreams and the lows of her nightmares: The Arbiter's Axe.

Built upon a small hill smack between the Hangman's Hex and the Barter Yard, The Axe *was pure white marble, surrounded by fluted columns and burnished metal, the paved road she skipped upon was lined with tall, twisted trees. Three levels of balconies, aethecite lamps lighting up the façade. The highest pinnacle of the arena rose, the flag bearing the crest of House Nightingale—a black thrush on a field of white snow slashed with red—snapped in the wind.*

Servants, dressed in solid black waistcoats who stood along the cobbled pathway, inclined their heads, not toward her, but toward her parents who trailed behind her. They were lapin. The fuzzy creatures reminded her so much of a bunny she'd once owned. They wore white gloves and held aethecite-powered lanterns. She smiled and they smiled back with buckteeth, the rabbit hopping through her mind again at the sight.

There was a grand evenfall planned, that was why they were there. She wouldn't be able to watch, of course, but that didn't bother her. She enjoyed roaming the darkened halls of The Axe *while her parents played host.*

The arena was the main draw of The Arbiter's Axe, *but the place wasn't only an open-air colosseum, but also a homestead, just as every heir of Nightingale blood had before. So, tender little Cadrianna had grown up in the theater of death.*

Shaped like a giant bowl, the arena's seating went upward at an incline, thus the atrium was the largest of the three floors. The second floor had always been offices, seating rooms, balconies, and dining halls. Each room led to the arena, where guests of House Nightingale could sit in lavish individual suites.

The smallest floor was the third, was where her family lived.

But the basement below the arena was her favorite play area, for there were so many rooms, so many places to hide, to explore. Especially those guarded by her father's loyal swords.

There were all sorts of curiosities in the basement vaults. Doors she hadn't explored. Some were even guarded by her father's soldiers. Especially one deep in the pinnacle tower, the one covered in runes and her family's crest.

Solanine smiled at the memory. "The Wayward Son was borne at the feet of blood and revelry. It's no small secret that this arena should house the entrance to His Temple."

Ialtris ran a hand across the scales' face, a jingle of jewelry upon the pale wrist. "I've searched high and low of this arena, Solanine, long before the Godsblood slipped from your claws." Solanine growled low but Ialtris continued unconcerned, "Every room, every hall, they've all been searched. I've used aether to read the Earth. I've even gone into the void. There is nothing here."

"But you've not had this," again tapping the tome, "and without the rituals, you never would have sensed it." Ialtris didn't appear pleased, but Solanine cared not. "And you aren't me, Ialtris. Strong you may be in claw and aether, but I am our Divine's chosen warrior. Don't forget your place." To Rinkhal, "What word of the Godsblood?"

The blooddrake-in-the-scales-of-the-Scattered-Shards yawned. "They circle the trap we've set, Solanine. Tallow revealed what was necessary, and the girl believes it as truth."

"ALL PART OF THE PLAN," the voice of Solanine's Divine cooed in the blooddrake's mind. ***"HEED AND REMEMBER."***

"Tallow is ours, Rinkhal. Datura remains firmly entrenched in the Shards of Kalderim, pulling the strings as we await Lu Har's conquest of the Golden Throne. Cauda is on the way with the manacles. The Fallen has regained the Oculus of Apathy and is on his way to Kalderim as we speak. Once the Golden Throne topples, the Mistlands will be ours. Datura is nearing completion on the gateway in Alizarin. The plan has been set; we have but to walk it."

"You seem unfazed," Ialtris said. "The Godsblood can undo everything we've worked for. Drenth was your fail—"

Solanine slammed a humirish fist upon the table, the ancient tome shivering. "Finish not that sentence!"

Rinkhal laughed. "Your threats are toothless. The Divine speaks to us just as He speaks to you. Whatever He's promised you, He's promised us the same."

Lies! I'm the chosen one.

"YOU PANDER TO PETTY SQUABBLES. WHAT MUST COME IS MORE THAN WHAT IS DESIRED. YOU SHALL HAVE YOUR DESIRES, MY DISCIPLE, AS SHALL THEY. FALTER NOT."

You promised me!

"AND SHALL RECEIVE."

Regaining composure, Solanine leaned back in the chair that had once belonged to House Nightingale. "We fight for the same goals, Rinkhal. What I want, you want. But don't cross me, for I am not the Solanine of old."

"Alizarin sent Maja Carr," Rinkhal said, the insignia of the Scattered Shards glinted in the seagandr-oil lantern as the small flame flickered. "Datura couldn't get to Carr in time."

"Does the Godsblood suspect?"

A shake of the scales' head. "I think not. But the girl knows more than she lets on. She hurts."

"Her Soul Form is growing, yet she holds it in check," Ialtris added. "Her taskmaster worries for her. The corruption will take her soon. We must act, Solanine. That man is getting closer to figuring it out. He must be dealt with."

Solanine nodded. "I've set the bait with Hobb as her use was ended. The box is almost done. And with Cauda bringing the manacles, we now know how to bind the box. I want to grind the girl into dust. The loss of her parents," the blooddrake tapped a finger-covered-talon to the side of Cadrianna Benld's head, "torments her. It's time for her to see their specter. I'll handle her taskmaster. It is time we finish what we started on Gargantua. But first, we find the Temple of the Drunk God. Come."

Tucking the tome under an arm, Solanine called upon Void Form and snuffed the seagandr-oil lantern, plunging the study into darkness. Rinkhal let out a clipped barking laugh, but all three blooddrakes left the room.

The blooddrakes moved throughout the underground rooms of the arena, sliding through the hazy gloom as black mist seeped from the walls.

Deep down into the basements they went, down sets of stairs carved into the very stone of the basin, down into the earth itself. At the bottom of the stair was a cellar of dust and rot, crates full of spice and wine stacked. Beyond was a darkened hallway but a piss-yellow bloom of light pushed away the shadows at the far end, where four soldiers sat at a small wooden table, gaming with dice as they quietly joked.

"These are mine, Solanine," Ialtris said. "I can handle this. But there is nothing beyond them." The blooddrake paused, tilted the scales' head. "At least nothing with which you must be concerned. Some business of mine, if you will."

Before the blooddrake could take one step toward the soldiers, Solanine scoffed and ignored the passage. Instead, Solanine placed Cadrianna Benld's left hand upon the wall of mortared stone, the useless right hanging by the side. Speaking softly, Solanine drew the black mist upwards and channeled it into the stone wall. A rune formed in a hazy emerald of *Terris*.

A rune in the shape of a semi-circle facing east.

Speaking again in the language of the draconem, Solanine's aether rippled along the wall, forming a smoky green doorway around the rune in the unbroken mortar. Then the wall shimmered and disappeared, leaving a yawning opening for the three blooddrakes to walk through into an earthen tunnel. The wall glimmered and closed behind with nary a sound.

"Showing off now are we, Solanine?"

"I grow tired of you, Rinkhal." Solanine called forth a spell of *Ignis* and instantly the tunnel illuminated a soft red, revealing a warren of stalactites and stalagmites, caves and fissures worn smooth over the ages. Solanine released the spell, and the reddish mist danced ahead with a swell of light.

The trio of lesser draconem traversed the dank spider's web of burrows, it smelt of long dead cadavers mixed with the dried scent of fermented grape. Rough-hewn the walls were, as if ancient aether had carved them in haphazard fashion. Perhaps it was Brio Himself. Solanine wouldn't put it past the Drunk God to falter with aether such, nor the stench of His bacchanalian followers.

A large chamber opened within the burrow, and it stood before them, a large underground building. The Temple of Brio.

It rose into the shadows of the cave, disappearing from view. Solid quartz and shiny travertine reflected the *Ignis*-generated light, with interlocking stones set in six-feet-long blocks. The front portico jutted out, its awning held up by eight columns, each as wide as a blooddrake's shoulders in draconem form, some fluted with ornate moldings on the crown and base. The top of the temple was a rounded dome, the very apex hidden in the darkness.

It was awesome, it truly was, and even Solanine felt that awe.

"SOLANINE, 'TIS TIME TO GO ALONE," said the voice of the Divine, all three heard, two growled their discontent. ***"ARGUE NOT, MY DISCIPLES. THE PATH IS FRAUGHT WITH THE STAIN OF THE PENTAX. EASY, THIS WILL NOT BE. SOLANINE, FORWARD."***

Solanine glanced at the two blooddrakes, each glaring under their scales' mortal eyes. "Should I fail, the Godsblood must still reach the Garnet."

"The Garnet should never have been separated from the Seal," Rinkhal said.

"Blame Canlon for that, Rinkhal." Ialtris nodded the scales' head toward the Temple of Brio with a swish of silver. "If you don't return, I'll see the girl there myself."

Taking a deep breath, Solanine marched to the portico, the reddish mist-light guiding the blooddrake's steps. The awning stretched above; a commanding presence held up by the pillars as if stretching from the very earth. The mist stopped. Solanine urged it forward with Void Form, but it struck against an invisible wall, rippling like a pebble dropped in a stream.

Aether of the purest form. Solanine was a trespasser here.

"FEAR NOT, MY DISCIPLE. THE SON WILL NOT STOP THE WARDS OF THE FATHER."

I fear nothing!

Dismissing the *Ignis*-infused mist, Solanine held out Cadrianna Benld's arm and stepped through the aetheric veil. But no more than a step inside, Solanine went to a knee. Power, borne of aether, shook to the core, rendering the blooddrake's Void Form null.

Solanine pitched forward, and for the first time in a long existence, tears of contrition streamed down the scales' face.

Blood, draconem blood, coursed through veins at a sickening pace, essence of nature igniting aether under true exoscales. Heart palpitated as if a spark was intending to explode. Arms and legs and tail felt heavy, as if attached to a stone thrown in the Abyssal. Try as Solanine might, draconem head wouldn't move more than a fraction. The drake's breath struggling to escape.

"WHY HAVE THOU COME TO MINE TEMPLE, DRACONEM?" The voice shot into Solanine's mind, scattering the presence of the Divine, leaving only this eerie replacement. ***"DO THOU NOT***

connecting the Four Tenets of Aether represented by the gemstones, the remaining two points not touching any of the gemstones.

"ONLY THRU ME CAN NOCTIS BE RESTORED, THE SEAL MUST BREAK AT THE HANDS OF THE GODSBLOOD. THE GUARDIANS DESTROYED."

Solanine hesitated on the precipice of the room. Unsure.

"THE SEAL OF* IGNIS *CAN ONLY BE BROKEN BY THE BLOOD OF NIGHTINGALE. OF OUR MOTHER," Brio said. ***"OUR MOTHER, THE FIRST WIFE AND THE HOLY WIFE ARE ONE IN THE SAME THOUGHT ON THIS. THE END MUST COME, OTHERWISE WE WILL ALL FALL INTO DARKNESS OF THE VOID. THE END MUST COME AND A NEW DIVINE TO RISE, BUT NOT FOR THE DIVINE THOU FOLLOW, DRACONEM. COME AGAIN INTO THE FOLD. JOIN WITH THE HATCH. TAKE MINE MANTLE TO EMINENCE, RESTORE THIS WORLD, RECLAIM IT FROM THE LIAR ON THE THRONE."***

I don't understand, Solanine pleaded, wavering in commitment. Voidbent, the blooddrake was. Revenge was necessary.

Valeria… you are mine…

Solanine's Divine broke through, ***"AND I SHALL GIVE HER SOUL TO YOU, MY DISCIPLE. ONCE EMINENCE IS MINE."***

"THOU CANNOT ALLOW HIM TO RECLAIM WHAT HE DESTROYED."

"I DESTROYED NOTHING! YOU STOLE IT FROM ME. THE CHILDREN OF NIGHTINGALE DISOBEYED ME!"

"WE WERE SPAWNED TO STOP THOU," Brio argued back. ***"THOU BANISHED THINE BROTHER FOR LOVING THE MORTAL THOU CRAVED. WE WERE TO RIVAL THINE HATRED. WE***

WERE ALL MORTAL ONCE. MINE SKIN WAS SHED LONG AGO TO TAKE MINE PLACE IN THE HEAVENS. ALL BECAUSE OF ZENITH'S HATRED OF NOCTURNE. NIGHTINGALE IS OUR TRUE MOTHER."

"DON'T LISTEN TO THIS DRIVEL, MY DISCIPLE. THIS PALTRY EXCUSE OF A GOD DOES NOT UNDERSTAND. TAKE THE SEAL TO THE GODSBLOOD, SLAY THE GUARDIAN AND UNLEASH EMINENCE!"

And what of my revenge?

"IT IS LAID AT YOUR FEET."

Solanine looked up at the statue's face, searching those carved eyes for a reprieve. There was expectation of Brio trying to tempt from the path set upon, but devotion kept the blooddrake true.

I pledge to see the guardians destroyed and Eminence the truth revealed.

Reaching toward the Seal with a working left hand, Solanine thought a deep sigh filled the air, but it wasn't clear if it was from the Divine or Brio. With the Seal of *Ignis* in hand, Solanine called aether to take the Mantle of Brio, but the cloth moved not.

What's the meaning of this? Your gift was taken and pledged.

"MY GIFT WAS TO MINE MOTHER, NOT MINE FALSE FATHER. THE WILL OF THE HATCH HAS BEEN DENIED THEE. THE SEALS MUST BREAK, FOR THAT, NO FIGHT WILL STOP THEE. BUT THAT ENDS MINE GIFT. GO, DRACONEM. JUSTICE WILL NOT BE SO FORGIVING, FOR SHATTERSTORM REMAINS GUARDED BY MORE THAN THE ARBITER'S AXE. MINE SISTER WILL SEE TO THEE'S DESTRUCTION FOR MINE DEAREST TWIN HAS FORESEEN THEE'S FAILURE."

The red aether slurped from the Temple's room, removing all emotion of desire within. Solanine felt the void.

The Divine whispered in Solanine's mind. ***"CATER NOT, MY DISCIPLE, FOR IN MY TRUTH IS POWER. IT HAS ALWAYS BEEN SO. DO NOT DEVIATE. BRING ME THE GODSLAYER."***

XXVIII
CYAN THE DEFIANT

CYAN'S DESTINATION APPEARED in the alley ahead, and the only source of life was the vociferous sound of carnal relations coming from a window overhead.

To say Cyan the Defiant was irritated was like telling someone the sun would still rise on the morrow. Lilia and Harlequin had not yet returned to the stronghold, and there was no word of where they were. He had waited for two hours for them. He'd been lax with their training and now they were taking advantage. It would not happen again.

But a tendril of hope filled him. Hope that he had figured out who was the blooddrake.

After Phlox had taken the Guilder, Cyan had Aris take him to Ranhold's chamber. Elena Ranhold had voiced objection, but the word of a Guilder's spouse only went so far, and a vicar superseded anything but the High Seat.

The first thing Cyan had noted was the new door set between the hallway and the chamber. With his aether, he had sensed the freshness of the paint. Asking Aris, he had learned the previous door had been destroyed some nightturns prior when Ranhold and his wife had been under some duress that forced the House guards to break it. When asked of her duress, Elena said she didn't recall anything of the sort, contradicting the maior domus' story. Suspicion was sufficiently raised.

However, the room bore no clue to the naked eye, not like Hobb's had with the molted skin of Cadrianna Benld. But Cyan had been a vicar for a long time, he knew something wasn't right, and after burning Shard Form, he sensed the use of aetheurgy. It reminded him of the aether used by Solanine when torturing him aboard Gargantua. The same texture as the spell that had raised a murdered Amaranth the Pure as a daemon. The stink of the void.

He was close to solving the codex, he could almost taste it. Solving the riddle of who was the blooddrake would spare Lilia, and that was what drove him.

At the mouth of the alley was a building, the vague outline of a stone doorway barely visible, even as a faint green and yellow haze emanated from the insignia carved into the stone. The insignia of the Scattered Shards.

He glanced around, verifying he was alone. Only the rays of Zenith's sun greeted him, an emerald shadow in the east. The sun over the alley's buildings but a sliver. The moaning of the fornicators strong, causing Cyan to grin as he turned from the alley.

But he stopped when he saw movement atop the opposing building top.

Flicking his right hand out, his Sharded Gauntlet brimmed with aether, ready to be summoned, searching the tops of the buildings as he burned. The silvery sheen of the Four Enhancements sung alongside his geysering mist canisters. Every corner, every nook. The moaning grew tenfold in his ears. A cat mewed somewhere in the distance, but he saw it not. Nothing was there.

You're getting jumpy as you age, old boy.

Shaking his head, Cyan snuffed his Enhancements and smacked a palm to the glowing insignia on the building wall. The fragile green-yellow haze intensified as his Shard Form burned and his mist canisters blew afresh, releasing the spell of *Aere* and *Terris* binding the door. There came a shudder like a quake and a clap like thunder, both miniscule, and then the door groaned inward as one might push aside the entrance of a sarcophagus sealed for ages. Dust cascaded into the black portal, and the stale scent of death filtered out.

Although the building's façade was a typical drinking establishment in Oldport Basin, below was a dank tunnel deep into the earth of the basin, one built for a specific purpose: Scattered Shards secret gathering.

Not gatherings in secrecy to discuss politics or assassination, no, this tunnel into the underground bunker was a soundproof locale for the Shards to draw out secrets. Secrets against the Guild, against the Pentax. And none of it was done with gentleness, like offering a steadying arm to the elderly or helping a wailing child find their lost dog.

No, this bunker was the den of bloodletting.

Only a single spitting torch in a sconce many steps below illumined as Cyan plunged into the dark, the doorway grating back into place behind. As he passed, runes carved into the walls bloomed like lamps, the tunnel stretching in waves of light silver translucence. His shadow followed like a hulking beast, twice his size.

Another shadow flickered across the glowing runes, one that wasn't his. Turning, Cyan burned. But like before, there was nothing there, only the runes and his shadow.

By Justice, this codex has you jumping at your own shadow…

At the bottom was a door, the torch beside it brandishing the insignia of the Shards. *Terris* and *Ignis* bound within it.

Cyan called upon his Shard Form to unbolt the metal gateway. The ground shook as it swung, a small room beyond. The room, well-lit by a dozen or more torches, was full of flickering smoke melding with the haze of the mist. A man sat upon a chair at the wall opposite. The man was old and had a wooden crutch leaning against the chair. Eyes clouded with grey. Blind. Hair greasy as if not washed for years, thin and sparse. Head cocked to the side as Cyan approached, listening like a bird sensing a threat.

"Now, there's a sight for sore eyes," Cyan said in jest, with full knowledge the man wasn't truly blind as aetheurgy allowed the old man to 'see' Cyan standing before him—a great trick when alone with a maiden in a dark room, the old-timer had once told him, even though at the time, Cyan hadn't a clue as to what that meant.

"Cyan the Defiant," the man said with the thick accent of those born in southeast Altreyia, "I see you've found humor in the time since last we spoke. Must be from that acolyte of yours I keep hearing about. Silver tongue they say."

"Quaestor Bucket, how's the leg?"

To question a fellow of the Shards on their disability would be considered taboo, but Cyan and the old man had a deeper bond.

Quaestor Bucket—who'd gotten his name after rage-killing an adulterous man using a tobacco spit pail after discovering his long-time sweetie had cheated on him, even though vicars were supposed to abstain from carnal desires—had lost his leg to the rot some years prior after a tedious case involving some boisterous ogres drunkenly pillaging all along the coasts of Sig Vorum. A cocky vicar at the time, he'd recklessly thought he could kill the ogres by himself. The pompous bastard hadn't restocked his mist canisters before heading after, and he had drained his stock tracking them. And since Sig Vorum was completely bereft of mist, his body went into blazing withdrawal, falling before the ogres in convulsions as if his skin was melting.

Luckily, his earlier bravado had roused some local toughs, and they'd followed the vicar, killing the ogres, and saving young Bucket's life, though not before one of the dumb brutes had taken a huge bite out of his leg.

The old-timer lifted his stump. "Hurts all the godsdamned time." He licked his chapped lips. "Bugger's been gone for thirty-some years, and I still feel the phantom of it." His clouded eyes softened. "'Tis good to see you again, lad." Bucket leaned toward Cyan and gestured him closer. "That Phlox, he's a dark one. Too reckless, by Justice." He lifted the stump again. "But so was I, once upon a year's turn. But be wary, lad. Keep your eyes peeled and stay safe. Don't want you limping in my footsteps. Or lack thereof." He cackled.

It was not that Cyan didn't approve of the Faithful's methods, who was he to deny one of Justice's chosen. The Shards had need of every warrior, even ones like Phlox, tainted or untainted.

The untainted were a motley lot, consisting of the most devout of believers in living in Zenith's grace and those like Cyan, people who had grown up in difficult situations. Temperament was not necessarily the deciding factor. Instead, the key driver of the vicar recruitment was the ability to withstand the poison of the mist.

The same couldn't be said for the tainted warrior class, and the reason why murderers and criminals were recruited by the Scattered Shards was twofold.

One, most criminals tend to have a certain innate ambition that pushes one to commit the ultimate crime against the Pentax. An instinctive drive to hunt, and ultimately, a desire to follow a tortured path to the ugliest of conclusions. And since most codex cases revolved around the unsavory aspects of life, it made sense to have those who already thought like a criminal on the side of the Shards as to the opposite.

Second, due to the inevitable death by the nigrum pulmonem, it was still a better alternative to a quick noose. Also, besides the impulsive would-be-heroes amongst the vicars, with the influx of draconem wielding death in a thousand different ways, it was easier to send those already destined for the Meadows.

Except Cyan and his acolytes, it seemed. Especially Lady Drakeslayer.

"I wouldn't dream of it, Bucket. Besides, my acolytes keep me on my toes."

"I've heard lots about this Lady Drakeslayer of yours. Great power, she has." Bucket leaned back, crossing his arms. "Heard of her growing up, even down here. She's got that Nightingale blood in her."

Seems like everyone knows of Lilia's line. "She never knew it prior to last summer."

"I'd have kept it from you, too, my acolyte. Better to not know the stain of one's line. Still, she's the strongest of us, I hear it said."

"She is quite strong in aetheurgy. Still learning, though."

"Good, good. I'm certain you've taught her well enough. You always were one of my prides, Cyan."

"I'm grateful."

"I remember the first time you came to Kalderim. From Demrae, wasn't it?"

"Qarthage."

Bucket had been Cyan's first teacher when Bucket was not called 'Bucket' but was instead a vicar of the name Carob. And for a child of the harsh streets of Qarthage, the former vicar had taken a sort of father-figure role in his life before his failed case, almost like how Cyan had taken to the babe Lilia. Cyan had recently been raised to the cassock, and therefore wasn't present when the man had gone against all the teachings of a vicar of the Scattered Shards.

"Ah, yes, that's right. Mind's getting so buggered these days. Anyway, enough prattling like old hags, best get on with it. Your Sharded now, official. Don't wanna keep you from your official business."

Bucket tapped the wall with his crutch, it flared the green of *Terris.* The wall shivered and shook, accompanied by piercing screams. Cyan gripped Bucket by the shoulder and proceeded farther into the underground bunker.

Beyond stood a beast of a goblin, almost as big as an orcir. Both ears were missing, crooked nose glinting with rings and thin chains. The goblin wore traditional Filfangin bone grieves, but instead of the usual bone armor, the voidspawn sported a leather apron caked with blood, brittle and hard as baked clay.

Seeing the bristle atop his helm, the unnamed goblin flicked a fist toward the back of the room, into a den filled with screams of pain and terror. Cyan was no stranger to torture, having used it himself in previous cases, but it didn't mean he enjoyed what he did. It was his job. While a necessary evil, he was much more appreciative of the work involving investigating above ground than the hurting below it. A proper beating often yielded the same results. Especially after what happened aboard Gargantua and to Amaranth. Rest her soul in the Meadows.

Phlox stood next to a table wearing a leather apron over his cassock. Sleeves rolled to the elbow; his hands were red-tinged.

"Vicar Cyan," the man said, noticing his approach. "I've got some information for you."

On the table was a fat, naked man. Cyan hoped it wasn't who he thought it was as the Faithful had a blood-stained towel covering the man's face. There were strips of skin missing on the man's side, starting from the armpit down to the groin. The feet were blackened and badly burned; the stench strong. A gruesome sight, indeed.

Choking back a hard swallow, Cyan glanced back up to the Faithful. The vicar drew the towel from the man's face, and sure enough, it was Olum Ranhold.

To say Cyan was incensed was an understatement. He was livid.

Phlox slapped the Guilder awake. "Up and at 'em."

"Please," the Guilder whispered through parched lips. "No more. I can't do it anymore. Zenith protect me."

"The Pentax don't like liars. And you, sir, have been a liar." The Faithful lifted a bloodied knife and waved it in front of Ranhold's face. "Remember our discussion on lies. Zenith will receive your penitence." Phlox bent closer to the man, the blade now only an inch away. The man squealed.

Cyan didn't care for the cruel delight emanating from Phlox. He grabbed him roughly by the arm. "What is wrong with you?"

The Faithful yanked his arm from Cyan's grasp. "He's a suspect against the Guild. He'll answer anything you want of him." He waved the knife again near the man's face. "Won'cha? Why don't you tell Vicar Cyan about your meeting at *The Arbiter's Axe*?"

Ranhold blubbered nonsense as he watched the blade in Phlox's hand, nodding furiously. "Please, don't hurt me anymore."

The tortured man would tell him anything he wished, even if he insisted the sky was red. Cyan wouldn't get answers like this.

Calling upon his aetheurgy, his mist canisters flared, the fire of aether raging through his veins like a hurricane of *Aquis*. His hand whipped out faster than the eye could move, grabbing the knife from Phlox's grip, and he slammed it into Ranhold's side. The blade bit into flesh, piercing ribs, and into the older man's heart. Ranhold shuddered, glazed eyes finding Cyan's as he spasmed. Thankfulness in his death throes.

"What the Pit was that for?" the Faithful decried.

"Torturing Guilders is not what we do, Phlox!" Cyan unleashed his burgeoning wroth. *Gods, what have I done?* "I wanted him watched until I came back to question him! We need answers, not a trail of bodies. Especially bodies of the Guild. He was not yours to take."

The Faithful spread his blood-soaked hands. "That's what I was doing here. Doing Zenith's work as He called for me to do."

"This is Nocturne's work." Cyan thrust Phlox backward with a forceful, aether-enhanced shove. The man clattered into the torture table. "I asked for leads, vicar. This is my case. My team. We do it my way. Got it?"

Phlox's mist canisters hissed, the worst of humanity bellowing in a pyre of angry aether. "What do you think I'm doing?"

"Listen to me. I don't give an aerovern's tail what you've done in the past. I have a few rules for my team, you know them. But seeing as you ignored them, let me repeat them. One, never underestimate your suspect. Expect the unforeseen. Two, don't throw punches unless they punch first. And three, be nice." Phlox's face turned from anger to confusion. "Yeah, that's right. Be fucking nice. Until it's time to not be nice."

"And when will I know?"

"You won't," Cyan said with finality. "I'll let you know. Got it?"

The furor died in the Faithful. "I got it."

Forgive me, Justice. Haste, that is not what you preach. Forgive me… "Good. Now, what information did he offer you?"

The skinny vicar retreated a few steps and threw the towel over the dead Guilder. "Ranhold had been to secret meetings with Tified in *The Arbiter's Axe.* With Danma Dil and Ifant Klander."

"Go on."

"This poor soul, Zenith guide him to the Pit," the Faithful said as he reverently ran a hand above the toweled face of Ranhold as if he hadn't been the one to send him there, "said they have a gift for the Guild. And for the Scattered Shards. Something about draconem. But there was always another in attendance for these meetings. Ranhold hadn't give me a name yet." He gave Cyan a pointed frown. "I was waiting for you, Vicar Cyan." An impish grin spread across the vicar's face. "You *do* realize you just killed a Guilder, don't you? After arresting him without a warrant."

By the Arbiter, he was slipping. He could feel it. "Clean this up, Phlox. Dispose of him. Make it clean."

There was a grunt from behind, something heavy hitting one of the nearby tables, torture implements crashing to the bunker's flooring. Cyan was in half turn, half crouch when he saw the fallen body of the goblin. He summoned his aetheric axe, could hear Phlox's mist canisters whistling.

Out of the shadows and flickering torches a hand grabbed his throat. As it wrapped around his neck, the skin peeled back over the cassocked arm, revealing black and crimson exoscales and a taloned claw. Sharp keratin dug into his flesh.

Eyes wide as his breathing became labored, the claw crushed his neck. Up the draconem limb, past the cassock of the Scattered Shards, to the face of one Cyan knew all too well.

"You?" he choked out. *Justice, please…*

But his god did not answer.

The lips peeled back, an exoscaled snout tearing through humirish flesh, smiling pointed teeth. "Yes me."

Then the blackness overtook him, and Cyan the Defiant knew no more.

XXIX
ASHE

ASHE LEANED OVER the edge of a terracotta roof and burned. "Show me."

The wails from beyond the veil screamed in her head, spilling forth from the realm of the dead. The aetheric hues of the ground below exploded in color as the mist swept through the streets. Reds, blues, greens, and yellows all trimmed everything in a sheen of rainbow, illumining all life with the magic of aetheurgy, pushing back the virulent darkness filling the Chain.

It was the hour after evenfall, and she was crouched atop a six-story apartment building in the slums of the Beggars Chain. The dilapidated complex overlooked a sizable, rundown warehouse owned by Danma Dil on the western edge of the peninsula, near to the sea cliffs on a small jutting parcel of land. Below was the VVyrm Ocean. It was no wonder why Dil had chosen this spot for her warehouse, she only needed to keep an eye on one direction instead of four.

"How long she's been at it?" Harlequin asked.

The red-haired woman squatted next to her, so close that because she was burning, Ashe could smell her every scent: under the layer of sweat from their earlier fight with the sellswords was rosewater soap that was mixed with lavender and a smidgen of chamomile. It was intoxicating. And distracting. The mist swirling under the hem of her cassock needled her legs relentlessly.

Zenith's cock…

"I THOUGHT YOU STRONGER THAN THIS, DEAR BRYNN."

Bugger off, Strix. It's not normally this strong. And it's not Harlequin, before you ask it. No way it's her.

"IT'S THE SEAL OF **IGNIS** ***AND YOUR NIGHTINGALE BLOOD CALLING YOU BACK TO THE CRYSTALS. IT IS LIFE, DEAR BRYNN, THAT IS WHAT YOU FEEL. WHAT YOU DESIRE. BUT IT COULD BE HER. DON'T LET YOUR FEELINGS BLIND YOU. SHE COULD JUST BE USING THOSE FEELINGS TO MAKE YOU BLIND TO THE FACT SOLANINE RESIDES WITHIN."***

It's not her, Strix. "Little more than an hour," Ashe replied. "Dil's boys have been busier than plundering goblins for the better part of this evenfall. Most of them have been squawking about the Chain since you left me all alone at midday."

A pair of small drones flitted above the warehouse, cameras attached to purring aethecite motors, propellers spewing smog as they zoomed in and out of the alleys leading to Dil's. Aetheric spotlights scouring the Chain in a stark reminder of Drenth, only there were far less of them. Dil must be confident in her stock of aethecite, for Ashe hadn't seen any drones within Port Sin since arrival. Granted, the City of Sin wasn't much for spying on its citizens as Lu Har had been within Drenth, but still, the skyline was blissfully empty of the motorized buggers.

Which, truth told, made Dil more suspicious if she was brazen enough to waste valuable fuel just for the sake of secrecy.

"She's got a whole army of grunts throughout the Chain. You don't want to know how many I followed to the pipeweed dens while you sat up here," Harlequin's grey-green, yellow-pupiled eyes grew doe-like as her voice became sultry in its mocking, "all by your lonesome, you poor… lonely… woman."

Ashe shook off the taunt, "I can bet most of them."

"You'd bet correct."

Everyone in the Beggars Chain paid Danma by way of a tithe for her protection. Life was cheap in Port Sin, and it paid to have friends in high places. It also helped that the Guilder had a verifiable army of thieves, assassins, pipeweed addicts, and toughs. Should anyone move in on her territory, the ambitious personage would face the wrath of a woman with a harpy's temper.

"Did you miss me while we were apart?" Aura full of mischief.

"About as much as Phloxy boy." Ashe focused her gaze on the warehouse to avoid the desire growing inside.

Throaty laughter as one of the mist canisters affixed to Harlequin's belt let off a short hiss, the vicar burning. Her body shivered and Ashe noted her aura shift through many different tones and colors. The woman shrugged. "You must be bored to death out here being sober and all. Cyan was pretty upset you broke his one drink rule at *The Parlour* the other nightturn."

"UPSET IS AN UNDERSTATEMENT."

What's your point, Strix?

"ONLY THAT YOU HAVE YET TO LEARN MODERATION."

And you've yet to learn to shut your beak. "Admit it, you just enjoy seeing me squirm, Harle-bub." The mist clawed at her legs. "Almost as much as you rue your chance sharing my bath."

"Maybe." Harlequin's aura shifted to a dangerous shade of crimson. A glorious shade. "Maybe not."

Gods, they danced around the topic for far too long and it was slowly starting to eat at her. Vicars were a celibate lot, the Book of the Scattered Shards held strict rules about designs of the carnal flesh. Growing up under the tutelage of Cyan the Defiant, she had suppressed her inner desires, even after puberty had brought baser needs. It wasn't until she was in Drenth did she finally give into her pangs with Wren. But that time with Wren had opened a whole new world for her, one she struggled to keep tamed. Especially around Harlequin.

Life and Death, that's what Canlon Carr had told her in the Meadows after Wren's touch. Life and Death, that was the power of her Soul Form. Her aetheurgy. Her Godsblood.

She cursed the desirous mist in her head while the Strix cachinnated in the void.

To push images of Harlequin straddling her lap out of her mind, Ashe burned more aetheurgy. The fire felt like a stab in the gut and her body pushed to the brink. More wails accompanied the flow of aether through her veins of fire. The wails had grown louder since breaking the Seal of *Terris*. It was almost unbearable at times.

From six stories up, in her normal eyesight, the dregs below bore resemblance to hobgoblin children slinking about the warehouse. But under the sway of the full-bore Soul Form, the figures grew to the size of giants surrounded by a silver sheen, almost as if she were a young girl looking up at awe-inspiring adults. She could read faces, tell the colors of eyes, the laugh or frown lines around mouths, the gaps between teeth.

The warehouse was surrounded by a wire fence, a rarity in not only the Beggars Chain, but also the whole of Port Sin. Ten feet tall, there were coiled steel barbs all along the top, and each tipped with runed spells of *Ignis*. No doubt meant to give any brave soul willing to climb a quick pyre to the Meadows. Which meant whatever Danma Dil had inside, she wanted the scum of the city kept out.

From a spacious opening with a door on rails, those in Dil's employ lugged nondescript crates with no writing on the sides. The crates appeared heavy as two, sometimes three people were needed to lift a single box. Some thick-necked toughs held seagandr-oil lanterns and clipboards, marking off each crate. Ashe estimated there had to be at least a hundred or more crates. Other Dil soldiers walked the perimeter of the warehouse, wheellock rifles in hand, seagandr-oil lights flashing.

A flock of people came out of the warehouse, a woman in the front wearing a flowing cloak.

Danma Dil.

Tall for a humir and thin. Her hair was dark and kept short at the nape of her neck, with straight bangs. Her face was severe and sharp, and though they were hidden under her fringe, Ashe could see the piercing blueness of hard irises, black pupils indicating no Form of aetheurgy. The Guilder's aura was the darkest of greens.

Dil's arms motioned to the crates and her sycophants, speaking words Ashe couldn't hear from the distance. Aetheurgy could only bear so much brunt of the senses. But her movements indicated she was on edge, begging for urgency.

"Has to be aethecite in those crates?" Harlequin asked.

"Not a godsdamned clue," she started, cutting off the fire of aetheurgy. Her vision snapped back to normal as her stomach clenched in pain, bile rising in her throat. She leaned back to calm her racing heart and to stop her pulmo from tearing apart her lungs. "Bet's pretty good you're right, though. Wait, see that?"

There was a crash down by the warehouse, a splintering of wood. Ashe burned her aether, the wails returning louder, her insides wailing in concerto. On the ground was a broken crate, spilling out of it was hundreds, if not thousands of clear prisms of ore. In her aetheurgy, wisps swirled within those pellets. Her own aetheurgy was drawn to the diamond stones, as if pulled, wanting to join with it.

Ashe cut off her burn and coughed, her throat constricting. She wiped the sweat beading off her forehead. She was tired, but it didn't matter. "Cyan can wait. Come on, we need to get in there."

Harlequin's aura shifted. "O, sneaking is it? I like it."

Ashe's tattoo of *Ignis* came alive as she used a flame to cut through the fence surrounding Dil's warehouse with ease, slicing through the links as if she was carving a roasted hunk of meat. Little sparks spraying.

With her right hand, she carefully withdrew the small gap and set it aside. Harlequin crawled through, Ashe doing the same before she reset the shorn ingress. It didn't fit tightly, but unless a Dil tough was actively searching this particular spot for a sneakthief's entrance, it wouldn't appear disturbed to most.

They were at the back of the warehouse, where it butted up against rows of burnt-out buildings what once might have been villas on the small jut of rock, the coast beyond. Manses nothing more than outlines of timber and metal lined a narrow lane, scorched in ash and heaps of memories. Waist-high wooden fences lay toppled, once green trees nothing but hunks of charcoal.

She could taste the VVyrm Ocean on her tongue, hear it lapping against the cliffs of the peninsula. As they'd sneaked through the slums, Ashe had seen the jut was actually a broken plateau. It almost appeared as if a kraken had taken one of its almighty tentacles and attacked the cliff of the peninsula, shearing the cliffside, boulders dropping into the sea. It was jagged, and so was the accumulation at the base where the waves crashed. It most likely had occurred when the volcano of Mount Bastard spewed forth, creating the Bay of Fire, its deathly prominence hacking away at this end of the peninsula in angry retribution.

They'd watched the routes of the guards for the better part of an hour before heading in. The patterns were all the same, a trio of soldiers walked the perimeter, eyes typically peeled out the fence, not inside. With any luck, they'd not encounter any trouble.

Between the fence and the warehouse was precious little cover. All the buildings had long been razed. Here and there a strut or lone wall of bricks remained, but nearly all had been destroyed and removed from the area. There were hand-built watch towers every fifty steps, where guards watched from the wooden structures. Seagandr-oil spotlights lay dormant in midday, but now, in the a few hours short of nightturn, they shined their lights every five minutes. Most were solitary, but a couple had squat buildings below with some sort of machinery running, engines churning aethecite within. A pair of security drones buzzed overhead every handful of minutes, thin spotlights flicking back and forth as the motors purred and the drones beeped.

Dil also had lookouts plopped atop the warehouse, all with looking glasses and wheellock rifles on tripods. The Guilder had taken no chances, it seemed. Which made it nearly impossible to sneak in. With all these soldiers, no one would have the gall to do so. And it might make these guards complacent.

Complacency could be a generous friend for Ashe and Harlequin. They'd made it this far. She hoped since they were already inside the compound, it would be smoother sailing.

Hope was such a fickle bastard, though.

Ahead was a lookout atop one of the free-standing structures. Burning, her vision became enhanced, and the guard appeared as if she was standing right beside him. He was asleep. She nodded to Harlequin, and both bolted toward the warehouse wall.

"How are we going to get in?"

"Do you trust me, Harle-bub?"

Harlequin frowned, her aura darkening. "Are you kidding me?"

Ashe grinned as she grabbed Harlequin's hand with her right, while her left tapped into the aether bound within her runic tattoos, creating an elegant slice in the veil of the world. From waist to ground, the slice pulsed with aether. Beyond was a mirrored image of the warehouse and the wailing souls within the Meadows. Pulling the protesting Harlequin, Ashe plunged into the slice.

Aether of Life seeped from them as they entered the realm of the dead, Harlequin's hand gripping hers tightly. Cold prickled their skin. The warehouse in the Meadows vibrated and was almost transparent. Light of all colors and none, forms hazy.

She put her bangled hand upon the outer wall of the warehouse-that-wasn't-a-warehouse and summoned aether of Death. The wails grew louder, and lights flickered nearby as souls of the dead noted their presence. Aether burned in the Eye, the wall shimmered and parted. Ashe dragged Harlequin into the void.

Then she created another slice in the veil between the worlds and pulled the vicar through, back into the realm of Life. They emerged inside Dil's warehouse.

"That was queer," Harlequin said as she shivered. "Was that the Meadows?"

"It was. Best split here, Harle-bub," she whispered, trying to fight off the pulmo raging inside. "Take the western wall, see what you can find. If it gets sticky, run."

The vicar nodded, gripped Ashe's hand briefly, and then slipped into the darkness.

"YOU'RE BLUSHING, DEAR BRYNN."

I hope you choke on the next soul you eat.

The Strix crowed with laughter as Ashe headed east, plunging into the darkness within the warehouse. Getting in this easy felt off, it shouldn't have been this simple. In fact, it felt like a trap.

"IT IS A TRAP, DEAR BRYNN. BUT THE QUESTION NOW ARISES, WHAT ARE YOU TO SEE?"

Hopefully a vat of iron so hot, I can drop you in it and never hear your voice in my head again.

"OUCH, YOU WOUND ME SO."

Don't be such an owlet, Strix. Maybe, if you're quiet long enough, I might use you this time if things go pear-shaped.

The warehouse was cavernous and dark. There were some overhead seagandr-oil lights that illuminated the place in a bloodred phosphorescence due to filters placed over them. Some spices harvested in the far southeast of the old Imperium were temperamental in certain lights, especially direct aethecite or seagandr-oil, thus a red filter was used in many a storage unit such as this. Crates were stacked in neat rows, the fronts painted in various colors drenched in red shine, most likely to indicate what was inside. The entire warehouse smelt of spice, fabric, and death, and not necessarily in order of strength of stench.

One of the crates nearby was opened, the lid propped. She neared and aethecite sparkled garnet within, aether swirling inside. Instantly, her stomach clenched and she fought off a pulmo cough, but she noticed that the aether within the ore reached toward her, almost as if she was pulling at the wisps like the strings on a harp.

"IT BEGS FOR YOU. LIKE THE MIST OF THE SEA. IT WANTS YOUR COMMAND."

"Loose ends?" came a woman's voice from down the row of crates.

"Hobb was a danger," responded a raspy voice that sounded neither male nor female, but it did sound slightly familiar.

Strix?

"I CANNOT PLACE IT. THEY HIDE IT WELL."

"More money for my pockets," the first continued. "Never liked the bitty. All these upstarts trying to act like they run the place. Same with Ranhold."

"Ranhold is dead," a third, another raspy-sounding speaker. Sounded like the rubbing of two rocks together. This voice Ashe did not recognize. "His purpose came good at the hands of the Shards. He will snare the Godsblood."

Godsblood?

"YOU, DEAR BRYNN."

Zenith's cock, Strix. Do you really think me that obtuse?

"SOMETIMES. BUT IT DOES CONFIRM THIS BEING A TRAP FOR YOU. TREAD CAREFULLY."

Ashe peered between two sets of crates. Three figures stood beyond, huddling over one of the open boxes containing the aethecite. A tall woman with short hair and straight bangs had hands on her hips. Danma Dil. The other two donned dark cloaks, hoods pulled up. One had their back to Ashe and was of medium height, shorter than Dil by a whole head. The other stood sideways and was on the shorter side, perhaps bent by age or by design.

"Good," Dil said. "He cocked up the first attempt. Shouldn't have been so lucky to get another."

"Twice, Danma," said the one sideways to Ashe, the one with the familiar voice. A hand reached out of the cloak, going for the crate of diamond ore. A hand which was cassocked like those of the Scattered Shards. But because of the filter on the seagandr-oil lights, Ashe couldn't tell heads from asses what color the cassock was. It could be red, white, or even midnight blue. "Ranhold paid for his failure with his life. But he will still bring us the Godsblood. She is much closer than you think."

If the Shards were involved… *It can't be her.*

"THESE VOICES DID NOT RISE UNTIL SHE LEFT YOUR SIDE, DEAR BRYNN. DO NOT BE BLINDED.

It's not her, I know it's not…

"The box is done," Dil was saying. "Wasted eighteen crates of aethecite building it by your specifications. Will it work?"

Box? What box?

"You've done well, Dil," said the third unknown person with back facing Ashe. Something about the inflection gave her gooseflesh. *The accent...* "Finish here and riches will be yours."

"Godsdamned right, Benld."

Benld? Mother? It couldn't be… Strix?

"IT IS NOT YOUR MOTHER. BUT THE ONE WE SEEK."

Solanine, she hissed into the void.

There was a shout further in the warehouse, then an alarm began to ring. All three looked up. Danma growled. "Intruders."

Harlequin?

The three rushed toward the growing commotion, disappearing into the stacks of crates and it indicated that it was time for Ashe to skedaddle. And to make matters more difficult, the entire warehouse was plunged into darkness.

With the aid of her aetheurgy, Ashe found the outer wall of the warehouse but stopped short of calling forth the Meadows. A pull came off to her left, a pull that nearly dragged her away from her exit. The mist at her ankles pushed her toward it.

Zenith's cock, what now?

"YOU KNOW WHAT. THE SEAL."

A spiral staircase descending into the belly of Danma Dil's warehouse appeared. *Fuck it.*

Darkness as black as pitch accompanied her for long minutes as she descended. There were no branches or doors, only the stairs down. The mist happily danced downward, the pull within growing stronger with each step. At the base of the staircase, a door formulated as a slit of light peeked through an elongated horizontal slice in the metal. She put her ear to the door, hearing voices on the other side, two maybe three. Guards most likely.

Strix?

The daemon blade was silent for a moment. *"GONE. MOVE QUICKLY. LIGHT IN THERE."*

She carefully drew the door open a smidge and blinked a few times in the sudden light, and satisfied, she nudged the door open enough to slip through.

A small table with two chairs was nestled near the door. A jug of water, a pair of mugs, a bowl of half-eaten porridge. Sconces with seagandr-oil lamps burned low. At the fork beyond, the backs of two drake scale-wearing guards marched around a circular hall. And if there were guards down here, it meant Dil had something important in need of guarding. Their aether were joyful yellow, oblivious in their circular rounds. They disappeared around the curve of the hall, their voices fading to whispers.

What is this place, Strix?

"LOOKS LIKE A HALLWAY TO ME."

Funny.

"I TAKE MY CUES FROM THOSE I BIND. AND YOU, DEAR BRYNN, AREN'T THAT FUNNY. MORE OBNOXIOUS THAN HUMOROUS."

Pound sand.

She crept toward the forked path on silent feet, her aetheurgy ready to burn. The low level of mist circling around like a pack of wolves ready for a kill. The sounds of drake scale came closer from one direction, which meant if she kept standing there like a dunce, she'd be spotted in short order.

Ashe went the opposite way, and quickly discovered the entire circular hall was filled with niches and pedestals.

What in the void? And don't you dare tell me this is a museum or something snarky, Strix.

"ACTUALLY, I KNOW SOME OF THESE OBJECTS."

Ashe scanned each podium and its object. Books, jewels, blades, precious stones. Vases, small statues, instruments, carvings. Each covered by a glass shield. *"What are they?"*

"OBJECTS USED IN VOID FORM RITUALS."

Danma Dil is an aetheurgist?

"NOT THAT I AM AWARE OF."

Solanine, perhaps?

"OR ANOTHER BLOODDRAKE."

After doing almost a full circle of the hall, Ashe found a small door, the wood old and warped. She put her fingers to it and the door opened without much resistance. Sliding in, she shut it behind her, just as the guards passed by in another rotation, presumably on their way back to their meager meal of gelatinous porridge.

Instantly the room lit up in a strange reddish glow. Aetheurgy.

Small the room was, a circular one, and opposite the door was a plinth, fluted and had red fabric over the capital, fanning downward like dripping blood.

"What is that?"

"YOU KNOW WHAT IT IS, DEAR BRYNN."

Jaw agape, she moved toward the column. Atop the marble stone was a bust and wrapped around the bust was something resembling a cloak and a mask, but as she neared, she realized in horror it wasn't either. It was dried skin.

The skin of a humirish man.

Stretched like old leather but had the coloring of one born in the City of Sands. The man's eyes were gone, the nose wrinkled. Brown and flush with grey, curled hair clung to the flesh. The rest of his body's hide was wrapped around the bust, flappy, and grotesque.

Bile rose in her throat. The ground beneath her feet began to tremble violently.

No…

This was the skin of her father, Emre Benld. Like a trophy taken from the conquered.

A voice behind her. "I wouldn't do that if I were you." Blackened mist washed over her, and before she could counter the void, Ashe faintly heard the word: "Godsblood."

XXX

LOJEN

OPTIO RESANDE'S PALE corpse was bloated, giving the impression that the elfir was larger than he had been in life. Although his face appeared peaceful in death, Lojen couldn't think of it as anything less than what it truly was: murder.

Lojen sat back on his haunches. "This isn't recent," he said. "Resande has been bled dry; you can see his skin is already showing the signs. Aetheurgy was used here." He pointed to the wound near the base of Resande's neck, a wicked slice across the man's artery. But that wasn't why he said that, no, it was the cauterized flesh around the wound. Only *Ignis* did that. Or a rune-spelled blade.

Barely more than a night's turn had passed since Lojen and Ruane had returned to Gandtril with news of the Fallen's improbable return. The mega-city was still in the process of evacuation, but to have a body turn up in the fortress surrounding the Obelisk was jarring. Especially since the body belonged to the third in command of the Legion behind the praetor and primus pilus. A man who'd been at the same meeting with them the day prior, a man who was instrumental in setting up the defense.

It was disconcerting to say the least.

Resande's body was found near the Crows, those hay-stuffed dummies, not far from the entrance to one of the barracks, where the man's quarters were. The body had been found not long before dawnbreak by some legionnaires rising for their shift atop the outer set of walls. Lojen had been roused from his slumber because he had taken a room near to the optio's and he was the closest thing to a leader not housed in the Obelisk, despite his misgivings as a wardkeeper.

To Lojen, something seemed off, and it wasn't the fact that aetheurgy was also in play. No, it was because of the way the man's body lay.

The optio—who was the master-at-arms of the Legion, as well as the main trainer of recruits for Emont Landra—was left where he was found, his body appearing as if meticulously laid in his final resting place. Despite the neat slice across his throat, the man faced upward, not pitched forward. His arms were placed crosswise over his sunken chest, his feet also crossed. So unless he had seen his killer coming, allowed it to happen, and delicately laid down in death, it was an odd way to fall.

"Where's the primus pilus?" he asked the handful of legionnaires who lingered behind them.

"Been sent for immediately after we came for you, Wardkeeper Lojen," a woman said softly. "Same with the Golden Sword. Word's also been sent to Praetor Rignork and Princeps Finnus."

"Good," Lojen said. It was a strange thing he was the only one available. Lowly the failed wardkeeper.

"A clean cut," Wick said. The lapin was knelt opposite Lojen, the blade of his dueling knife pushing back the optio's reddish beard. "*Ignis* seared, too. Bet the poor bastard never even felt the blade touch his skin before dying. Cut right through the artery."

Wick had also taken up a room near to Lojen's. Same as had Ruane, but she wasn't in her chamber when the legionnaires had knocked on his. Strange, that. She'd been acting funny ever since they'd returned to Gandtril.

"There'd be a lot more blood for that," Lojen said. There was a small pool of blood near the man's head, but not enough from a cut throat.

Wick's whiskers wrinkled. "You're right, drakken. Seen enough bodies in my age, someone must've put him here. Expecting him to be found, I'd fathom."

"Doesn't make sense. Anyone check his quarters?" Lojen asked the legionnaires.

"Not yet, Wardkeeper Lojen," one answered. The man's face was ashen. He was a youngish elfir, and by his red-rimmed eyes, the optio's death weighed heavy upon him.

Lojen put his claws to his thighs and pushed himself upright, the wound in his side giving a jolt of pain. He was tired, exhausted from his flight back to the mega-city and subsequent attempt to help the people flee. The daemon-wrought wound burned something fierce. "I doubt we'll find anything, but I want to be certain. Better if we knew before reporting to Landra or Rignork."

"What are you thinking, Lojen?" Wick asked as the legionnaires led them into the barracks' militaristic hallway.

"I'm not ready to put words to it, Wick." How could he be, what he was thinking was insane. But then again, after all that befell him in the Sea, was it? He had been hoping to speak to Ruane about it, she had a way of determining if what he thought was true or not. *Where is she? Perhaps still mourning Augur Puce?*

The pair of legionnaires stood outside Resande's private quarters, waiting for the drakken and lapin. With a nod, one tried to open the door, but found it locked. He looked back at Lojen, who only nodded. The guard put his shoulder into the door, a squeal of bent metal as it rocked on its hinges, the handle falling to the floor. The guard stepped into the room with a wheellock pistol in hand.

"Wardkeeper… you may want to see this…" The guard then gagged before exiting the room with a hand to his mouth.

Lojen's claw went to his own snout in disgust as he entered into Resande's quarters. From the bed to the walls, blood painted everything in crimson. It dripped from the mused sheets, coalescing into a puddle. The smell was so intense, Lojen wondered how none of them had smelt it from within the hall, especially a drakken's keen sense.

"Praise the Pentax," Wick whispered through distressed whiskers. His button-eyes eyed the room, the doorway in particular caught his eye. He put a paw to it. Under the furred pad, Lojen noticed a rune cut into the wood. One of *Aere*. "Spelled to hide the smell. No wonder. Coulda been hours it's been like this."

A crowd formed in the hallway, legionnaires half dressed, most likely having heard the breaking door. Lojen turned toward one of the guards who had found Resande. "Get them back, no one but the primus pilus, praetor, or Golden Sword gets in. Finn too if he decides to show up. Or my sister for that matter."

They nodded and began to order the rest of the milling onlookers away, the sound of dry retching accompanying.

"Who the fuck could do such a thing?" Wick said.

The dim aethecite-powered lights in the small room did nothing to keep the shadows from making the room appear anything less than sinister. Streaks of crimson all across the walls and floor, blackened round the edges as the fiery spells consumed the cruor. The very thin layer of mist that filled the mega-city was prowling the puddle like a cat lapping their milk bowl.

But there was no blood near the doorway, nor was there any in the hallway. If Resande had been dragged or carried to where he was deposited by the Crows, there should have been some blood, droplets at least. Yet nothing.

It was the godsdamnedest thing Lojen had ever seen.

"Lojen, look at this."

Wick bent near the head of the bed. Lojen peered over the lapin's shoulder and saw, written in blood, a name: Eran Rignork.

"We need to warn the praetor," Lojen said.

"Wardkeeper Lojen," one of the original guards said, poking her head back into the room, "Princeps Finnus is asking for you."

"Now is not the time."

"But… they found another body."

Lojen's eyes snapped up. "Who?"

"One of the princeps' guards. Jaterral."

He exchanged a look with Wick. What in the void was going on? And where the void was Ruane?

The body of the young elfirish legionnaire was like Resande's, face-up, staring at the ceiling of the villa. Jaterral's arms were crossed, his ankles too. Face already sunken from loss of blood.

Lifting the man's arm, he noticed the shattered links of drake scale from the Legion-issue cuirass. But that didn't bother him, no, it was the flayed skin showing underneath.

A gaping wound, flesh shorn clean off, bone poking through. Like with Resande's neck, the edges had been cauterized, the blood vessels burnt closed. And yet, there was no blood anywhere to be found, only a smear upon his scale. But under the man's body was a name written in blood: Emont Landra.

Finn leaned against the doorframe of his room, biting one of his fingernails. "So?"

They were on the second floor of a villa in the Upper City. It had belonged to a Guilder, but now was the residence of Finnus Dunleith. A grand staircase filled the foyer behind them, the body at one of the branches that led away from Finn's chosen room. A glass chandelier shone aethecite-drenched light on the corpse.

Lojen shook his head. "Makes no sense, Finn. First Resande, now one of your personal guards. Something isn't right. Both the praetor and the primus pilus named."

"You think?"

"Now's not the time, needle dick," Wick growled. "Can't you be serious just once in your life?"

"But, Wick, whenever is the time to not dig at you?"

Normally Lojen wouldn't get between the bickering elfir and lapin, but two dead bodies made the case for him. "Finn, Wick, enough." They both looked at him like he had cream all over his snout. "This is serious."

"Never said it wasn't," Finn said with a grin.

Just then, Titen Dunleith appeared climbing the staircase, Landra on his heels. The Golden Sword marched with purpose, his hand firmly upon the sword at his hip. Landra, his hair slicked back as usual, glared at Lojen before sneering at Finn, finally his eyes settling upon the dead legionnaire at their feet.

Titen knelt beside the corpse, lifting the man's arm just as Lojen had. He took in the name stoically, showing Landra, who grunted. "Who found him?"

"Who do you think?"

"Finn…"

Finn stiffened, if only slightly. "Fine, fine. It was those other two louts you've saddled me with, brother-friend." He jerked his thumb toward the pair of legionnaires standing at the head of the staircase, eyes drifting back and forth between the princeps siblings.

The Golden Sword motioned for the pair; they came close. "Report."

The one Resande had named Alyx spoke, "I found him, Lord Sword." He glanced toward the other elfir named Davel. "As we've done since being assigned to Princeps Finnus, we three have done a full sweep of the princeps' floor at regular intervals while one stays to guard the princeps' door. Davel and I were following this routine while Jaterral remained."

"We check each room, Lord Sword," Davel added. "I went down the west hall. Alyx the east hall."

"How long are these rounds?"

"No more than ten minutes, Lord Sword," Davel answered. His bearded face was flushed, nervous almost. "We're thorough in our checks, but we don't dally."

Ten minutes, thought Lojen. *That's more than enough time for a killer to take out Jaterral. But like this?* It didn't make sense. None of it did. How could someone flay a man's backside in under ten minutes without being heard or caught in the act?

"You heard nothing?"

"No, Lord Sword," nearly in unison.

"Did you move the body? Exam it in any way?"

"No, Lord Sword," said Alyx, who was nervously toying with the chain of a necklace peeking above his cuirass.

"Very well. And where were you?" Titen asked of Finn, who was still gnawing at his cuticles.

The elfir shrugged. "Curling this luscious hair of mine." Titen's eye twitched. "What do you want me to say, brother-friend? I was in my room sleeping. It was nightturn. I heard nothing."

"Sleeping." A statement more than a question.

"As hard as it is for you to understand, some of us need sleep, Titen." Finn seemed on the back foot for some reason, but they all were. Lojen knew Finn wouldn't ever murder one of his own. The Fallen was doing more to unnerve them without needing an army. "With the news my drakken friends brought, the city soon to be under siege, Emre's bloody body stolen. It's been a long fucking week, don't you think?"

Titen chewed his lip, anger simmering in his jaw. His attention went back to both legionnaires. "You heard nothing? No commotion? No visible use of aetheurgy?" Both soldiers shook their heads in the negative. Titen gauged their answers. Lojen saw nothing but shame. "Dismissed, legionnaires."

The two slunk away, taking up station at the top of the staircase.

"Well, that didn't tell us much."

"Finn… gah, you grate on me at times, brother-friend."

"You have no idea," Wick mumbled under his breath.

A quirk of Titen's lips. "I expect nothing less at this point."

Landra, who had all been but forgotten minus his sneer, cleared his throat. "Two bodies, Lord Sword, two of mine. Few knew of your assignment to the princeps."

"What are you implying?"

"Ten minutes is not enough time for a surprise attack without knowing their schedule."

"You think this is an inside job?"

Lojen wasn't sure if Titen was acting or if he was that surprised. There was no way the Golden Sword couldn't see what was before him. It was clear as midday. This was murder and it was someone inside the Legion.

"It's nothing but conjecture, Lord Sword," Landra said as he ran a hand over his greased hair. "But if my name's in blood, that means someone's after me next. I don't like the idea of being in the crosshairs."

Hand gripping the pommel of the golden blade, "Question all who were on duty, Emont. I want all there is to know about Resande's whereabouts last nightturn. I also want half a dozen legionnaires with you at all times. And a full squad outside the praetor's door. He can question it all he wants but tell him I've demanded it."

"As you command, Lord Sword. With Honor and Blood." The primus pilus grimaced as he brushed past Lojen, barking orders to the pair of guards at the staircase then descending.

Titen turned toward Finn. "I don't trust what my eyes are telling me. What do you know that you aren't telling me, Finn?"

"Ask your wardkeeper, he knows what I'm thinking," Finn replied with a wink. The man certainly had an irritating streak.

Lojen inhaled. *Father, is this what it's like to have a ward? Always on the receiving end?* "I'm not certain," he started, "but this feels like scourges…"

"Tevun would be O so proud, Lojen, my friend."

"…and if I had to fathom, is to intentionally throw us off course," he finished, ignoring Finn's comment. He bent over and moved the body, uncovering the written name of Emont Landra for all to see. Titen's face showed nothing, so he continued, "If Lu Har has indeed returned, then his goal is to take Kalderim, and the only way is through Gandtril. But the Fallen is nothing if not smart. He knows this city will tumble regardless, but why send in his horde if he doesn't have to. He wants us to flee. He no doubt has seen the citizens run, but he knows the Legion will never leave Gandtril behind. Unless he can create chaos within. Cut off the head, so to speak."

"That isn't far from the truth, brother-friend."

Val emerged from the stairs to join the conversation. She wore a woolen overcoat, long sleeved to hide her bikromi bracelets, and her long, silver hair was in an elegant braid. Her eyes hid behind a pair of mining goggles, but a peridot pendant hung from a chain on her forehead.

Behind her was Ruane. She was hunched over in an almost primal state as she crested the stairs. Her grip held her longknife tightly. In her purplish eyes Lojen saw the hunter inside, the draconem in its natural state. What did that mean?

"Going somewhere, sister-friend?" Titen asked

"I've a vision from the Ideal Daughter," she whispered, "The Seal of *Ignis* has been found."

Titen looked like he took a knife to the heart. "By whom?"

The bikrome shook her head. "She would not say. But I fear it is not Brynn who discovered it. I must make haste to her side. My eyes in Port Sin sent word that the girl is close, though."

"Why would Bliss not show you the truth?" Finn questioned.

Lojen had to concur. He hadn't known Valeria Dunleith long, but with her Vision Form, it was unlike the Virtuous One to withhold information of such magnitude.

"I know not, brother-friend. But She did show me something… peculiar." Val held her braid, stroking it. Lojen had seen men do similar tics as a way of working through their thoughts. Or worse, nervousness. To see her like this now, something was very wrong.

"What is it, Val?" Finn asked, he too shared that confused and caring look.

"It's about Nocturne and Zenith. Somehow, we've gotten Them w—" She stopped speaking, glancing down at the dead legionnaire. At the name of the primus pilus. To Finn, "Brother-friend, the time is nigh for you to take control," whispered Val. "Bliss has seen your future, it does not end here. But sit idle you cannot. Not any longer. Take the lead. They will follow."

Finn nodded his head toward their elder sibling. "You think Titen won't have a say in all this?"

But she shook hers, braid slapping against her overcoat. Cool, collected, sure. Eerily sure. "Our brother's path is separate from ours, Finn. I must go to Brynn Benld's side. Lu Har has recalled the Oculus of Apathy. She must be warned." She pulled him close, hugging him tight. Then she did the same to Titen.

"Godsdamnit, the Oculus?" She nodded as Titen reluctantly let her go. "You be safe, Val. You were always the best of us."

Her head cocked, goggles reflecting the hidden sunlight. "And you, brother-friend. We will meet once again; Bliss has shown me."

The Oculus of Apathy? What was that? *Father, do you know?*

Ruane was nearly frothing at the mouth, bouncing from boot to boot, her tail swishing angrily. She was antsy about something. But what?

"Val," Wick started. "Should I fall, send word to Ancantha? She will sense my death through the Bond."

"I will, Wick. But as with my brother-friends, we shall meet again someday soon." Then she turned toward Lojen, gazing up at him with her bi-colored eyes. "Bliss has given you strength, wardkeeper, do not loss faith. Do not let faith blind you either. What you seek will not be what you desire. But let not your failure show you the wrong path. Sing the Hymn. Find the Vird and learn the truth." To the body at their feet, "This is only the beginning. Fear it not, for in the darkest nightturns, we shine the brightest."

Yeah, but will we survive to see the dawnbreak? And what the void is up with Ru?

XXXI

THE CRESTFALLEN PRISONER, NEENAH LEFLEUR

ONE OF THE hobgoblins (Zig, Neenah thought?) was smacking the back of his lumpy head against the hull of *Marrow's Lover.* The other voidspawn drummed his gnarled fingers upon his leg while humming some ungodsly out of tune song.

"You know, hit your godsdamned head hard enough, you might knock some bloody sense into your shit-eatin' brain."

The twin (maybe it was Zag after all?) glanced over at her and grinned lopsidedly. "Can't be showin' youse up, Cap'n. Youse the ones wit the brains 'ere."

The two voidspawn cackled in unison and Neenah cursed.

She was bored sitting belowdecks of her beautiful airship. Her hands were shackled, and her expensive, fine woolen overcoat was now dirty and torn in a few places when that bastard Captain Agir had dragged her by the scalp from the harrowing Void Form summoning session. By the gods above, her head still hurt from his bloody fingers nearly tearing her beloved shag free. Bastard.

Things were not going well for her and her crew. Worse, this would be a stain upon her legend when all was said and done.

Part of her felt betrayed by Invaris, working for the Fallen, but the greater part of her—the important part, mind—was angry at the fact that she hadn't deduced the old man's true self much sooner. Someone of her stature and ability was not prone to such obvious missteps. She should've seen it from the off, and the fact that she hadn't, that truly gnawed at her soul.

And she hated that. Much more than her current appearance and horrible daemons brought back from the Pit.

Her once-white sleeved tunic underneath was anything but pearl and Neenah LeFleur could only imagine how flat her painstakingly cared for lustrous, shaggy curls might be. Neenah tried to straighten her outfit the best she could. No one could accuse Neenah LeFleur of not looking her best, even as a prisoner.

A stuck pig, she felt, wallowing in its dying misery.

"Cap'n, tell that one tale about that time youse gots knicked in Mersen," one of the twins said.

"Ya, that one wheres youse was caught tossing that brothel madame in the middle of the job," the other piped.

"I love that one," the first hooted. "That's my favorite."

"*'Never drop your pants when a pretty bint smiles at you, boys,'*" the second bugger quoted one of Neenah's famous smuggling rules.

Both hobgoblins roared with laughter.

Neenah glared at them, but a smile fought through her deepening scowl. That *had* been a fun contract if she did say so herself. "She was something special," she said, remembering her long blonde hair and the swell of her bosom pressed against her face. "Special indeed. The softest of hands, Carlena had."

That got the two hobgoblins rollicking even harder, if such a thing was possible.

On the other side of the voidspawned twins, Roland was snoring softly as his chained hands lay across his girth, sleeping soundly against a stack of crates that held their aethecite reserves. The small, waifish Alexina lay cuddled in Roland's crooked arms, the orphaned lass Neenah had grudgingly adopted as part of the crew was never far from Roland's side. Tris and Doll had their heads pressed close together opposite the big one-eyed mate as per usual for the pair. Neenah never understood the allure of a dvergir tossing a giantess, but hey, each to their own, even if there was some climbing involved.

At least her crew all seemed to have forgotten about the harrowing experience from earlier. Well, all but the hobgoblins.

"How's 'bout the one when Stray Cat joined us."

That bloody girl, she thought.

Always a problem that girl was, ever since she allowed Ashe to stowaway aboard her ship. If it wasn't for that bloody girl and the sorry affairs in Drenth last year with a burnt-up Fallen, Neenah might have long been counting her quadrans as a made woman instead of being cooped up with the hobgoblin twins bugging the everliving piss out of her. All because her own orphaned upbringing made her soft on such girls.

Truth told, she should have told that bloody bikrome to bugger off when the bint was but a babe. That's when all her trouble started. Nothing but trouble for Neenah since.

"Leave off, you buggers, hear?" Neenah swore, trying to not think about Ashe any longer. The girl was off on her own, building her own legend, Neenah heard told. Killing gods, draconem, and some such. Didn't matter she was the cause of Neenah's current predicament, she liked seeing other women succeed in this world. "I'm tired of you hemming and hawing like gossip-sharing old bitties around a knitting circle."

That didn't dissuade the voidspawn from continuing. "Or the one wheres youse almost gots another asshole by a dropped wheellock pistol."

"Or how about the one wheres youse wound up with the grey fever o'er some blankets."

"No, that one's boring. Tell the one when Roland had to snatch youse by the baps when that propeller almost took yer head off."

"She always tells that one. I likes the one wheres she almost gots her backside bitten off by that daemon basilisk in the Sea. Busts my gullet that ones."

"How about the one she tried to be a war envoy but gots seduced by that infuriatin' dandy with the bicorne hat."

"Bah, that one's nowheres near fun as the snakelady one."

"O, that one's good, aye. But how about that oddyllic stone and the postmaster's sprat?"

"Idyllic," Neenah grunted, then slapped her thigh. "Enough! Bloody Nocturne you grate on me."

Roland opened his one good eye before going back to sleep grinning, while Tris and Doll glanced up. Alexina remained asleep, thankfully, for the girl had not been told many of the stories the hobgoblins brought up. Some legends about Neenah LeFleur needed to remain vaulted. The twins continued laughing despite her outburst, offering further anecdotes of Neenah's more embarrassing contracts. They were good stories, she had to admit, but she didn't want her legend to be chock full of missteps and potential anatomy altering myths.

"O, lighten up, Cap'n," Zig started.

"We might be heres awhiles. Need to pass the time," Zag finished. At least she thought they were the correct twin; she never did know.

Luckily for her sanity, the door leading abovedecks opened and shut the voidspawn up.

A soldier in Imperium firedrake scale pulled open the portal, big and burly with a frown to match. Dark hair with greying temples over his breather. Behind him were two more drake-scaled soldiers. "Let's go, LeFleur."

Neenah stood, taking her time to dust off her overcoat and trousers best she could with manacled hands. "Why, good sire, how grand it is to see you. How fares the Fallen's war with Gandtril?"

"Shut yer trap, LeFleur."

"Speak to a woman captain like that?" Neenah put her hands to her breast in feigned shock. Sometimes men had a soft spot for stricken dames. A charade that had gotten her out of her fair share of sticky situations in the past.

"No games, LeFleur." The man backed out of the room where other soldiers stood on the *Lover's* deck. "You've been summoned before Captain Agir. Your herd of smugglers can wait for your return should the captain not take your head."

"The Fallen just letting me go, then?" Neenah glanced down the hatch at her crew, but Roland hadn't opened his eye this time, snoring away. They'd be fine without her for a few moments. Unless the twins got themselves shivved in her absence for being too annoying—which, to be fair, Neenah wasn't so sure was a bad thing. Following the soldier, one of the Imperium brutes pushed her with the tip of his wheellock rifle. "Bloody buggering oaf! That isn't godsdamned necessary, friend."

But the guard shoved her again, this time toward her cabin.

The red-scaled captain from the Fallen's camp leaned over the small table affixed to the cabin's wall, studying sheaves of parchment. At first, Neenah bristled, thinking the parchments were her maps and personal documents from contracts previous, but upon further survey, she realized they were maps of lower Kanja as well as written pages in a script she couldn't translate. Her eyes darted to the hidden compartment under her mattress where said contracts were kept. The bed hadn't been moved, so her documents were still safely hidden.

She relaxed slightly. Precious cargo, those papers.

And her miniature ship in a bottle was pushed toward the end to the desk, buried under the map's edge. Unbroken. Thankfully.

The captain's breather was pushed up to the top of his head, his stubbled cheeks were hollow, and he had a hook of a nose. When she was pushed inside her dimly lit cabin, his grey-green, red-pupiled eyes bore into her, making her feel uncomfortable.

He motioned for her to sit on her bunk. The soldiers left, locking the door behind.

She didn't hold back. "Why in the godsdamned Pit have you been holding me and mine in the hold of my ship? I was promised to be made by Invaris, hear? And Neenah LeFleur deserves better accommodations, not you taking mine, you prick-sucker. Lu… the Fallen, aside from giving me the shivers since he's alive and all, dragging souls from the Pit through my memories, which, truth told, was pissing rude and disgusting in equal measures, said Invaris assured him. Now, I don't have any skin in this bloody game, mind, but I demand some answers. Look at me when I'm talking to you, captain. Captain to captain, I'm not a fan of your methods. Godsdamnit, look at me!"

Ignoring her tirade, Captain Agir shuffled through papers, reading aloud. "Smuggling of Imperium goods. Extortion of Imperium figures. Profiteering off of Imperium wares. Impersonation of a consul in Qarthage." Neenah grinned at that memory despite him ignoring her. "Destruction of Imperium cargo airships. Deep contacts with Imperium gangs such as Elian of Slag's End and Killian Ness of Stanktown in Drenth." The man put down the parchment and looked at Neenah with beady eyes of red. "For all the crimes I've mentioned, you should be hanged for your discretions against the Fallen. But the worst is alleged assassination of Imperium officials."

"That wasn't me." She lifted her shackled hands in protest. "Wait. Which one are you referring to?"

The captain sucked his teeth. "There was more than one?"

Neenah was shocked, actually affronted. "I've never in my years come close to murdering a bloody Imperium official. Not the type of work I agree to."

"No, the great Neenah LeFleur is not that type of smuggler. However, you may play the tragedy, your name does precede you. But that doesn't give you free reign of the Imperium. Crimes must be punished."

"The Imperium is no more." Well, that wasn't exactly true, seeing as Lu Har was still alive. "Right? Shouldn't you bloody be in Gandtril? Is that where the Fallen has gone?"

"It's in my power to order your body hung from the highest parapet in Qarthage and once the last essence of life flows from your corpse, have your limbs quartered and sent to the four corners of the Imperium." The man's smug refusal to answer her questions was starting to grate. She was a captain, after all, she deserved more respect. "While your head thrust upon a spike to be sent back to Kalderim to lay on the doorstep of the pontifex maximus."

Neenah's ego swelled, her self-proclaimed alluring face split into a golden smile. "Now that would surely get me remembered. Though you godsdamned better leave my brother out of this."

The man shook his head. "Is that all you care about, Neenah LeFleur? To be remembered?"

"Gods above and below, that's all that matters in this world."

"Even when the name of a smuggler is all you'll have?" Neenah nodded. "Then I suppose that depends on you, Captain LeFleur. Confess and reap your punishment. The Fallen is merciful. Or we could wipe your name from the hist—" The words died on the man's tongue, mouth hung agape, eyes glazed and staring at her, but not seeing.

Neenah reached forward, waving her chained hands in front of the frozen man's face. "Hail, you bugger," she snapped her fingers. Nothing, not a blink. The man was solid stiff.

A chill passed through Neenah, and not the chill of a Kanjan winter. No, this was the chill of aetheurgy, a specific form. The eternal cold, that feeling she'd been touched by only once before. Eighteen years ago to be true.

"To be remembered, that's all you care about, Neenah? Your legacy?" She turned, found a cloaked figure within the doorway to her cabin, the guards nowhere to be seen. Arms crossed, hands in opposing sleeves. Silver hair peeked through the cowl. "You always had a legacy. One that started with a babe."

"That voice," she placed it back a year, after Drenth, but then eighteen years back, too. The shadow-form moved, hands appeared from the cloak's sleeves, drawing down the heavy hood as dozens of gold and silver bracelets jangled. "You… Valeria Dunleith. But… how?"

The bikrome stood watching her, face tilted to the side, a pair of mining goggles hanging around her neck, a peridot within a circlet upon her brow. Then, she chuckled—an unexpected sound from one such as she, she was an elfirish seer, after all. And a principissa of Kalderim. "For once the great Neenah LeFleur is speechless." The bikrome ran a hand through the thick rivulets of silver in a very casual manner. "Never thought the day would come."

"Wh... why now?" For some reason, she couldn't form a string of words more than two at the moment. All source of thought vanished the moment the bikrome appeared. "You're supposed to be in Kalderim. Right?"

"We can never choose the time in which the Pentax demands our service. We must follow the paths They set us upon. We cannot question lest we falter."

"Bloody Nocturne."

"If only you understood how true those words are, Neenah LeFleur." The bikromi seer sighed. "But time we have naught to speak on such things. The Fallen has made his play. I cannot dally any longer. I'm here on behalf of the girl."

"Ashe?"

"A fitting name you chose for her with the ashes she has left in her wake. And will leave."

"Is Ashe in danger?" She mastered the slow churn of her brain and got to thinking. Hard. Neenah thrust out the shackles toward the bikrome. "Get me out of here, we need to bloody find her."

The bikrome curled her fingers, articulating them through the air with a spell of aetheurgy. The cold pall ran through her body once more. A click and the manacles fell from Neenah's wrists.

Neenah sported a quick glance toward the captain, who was still as statue. "What about him, he dead?" Say what you will about her methods, but Neenah LeFleur didn't leave corpses unnecessarily.

"He will wake an hour after we leave this place." Neenah began moving toward the door, but the bikrome reached out, snagging her by her tunicsleeve. "Now is not the time for you to be off running rampant."

"Whatever does that mean? You've bloody said yourself; Ashe is in danger. Wait, where is that bint anyway?"

"Danger she is in, yes, but that is not for you to worry yourself with. We must be wary, Neenah. The Fallen's soldiers are everywhere. Gandtril is about to fall. There are others still nearby. I can only do so much to hide us, so we must leave at once. In secrecy." A smile across the ageless elfirish face. "You care deeply for her, yes, I see it, Neenah. Or maybe it's that vicar teacher of hers? I saw how you looked at him. As well you should. That's why I chose you back then. But the girl's path has already been set. Walk it she must."

"What have you done, woman?" Neenah said threateningly. "If you so much as lay a finger on her, Zenith wouldn't even begin to fath—"

A thin finger pressed against her lips, the touch feeling of hoarfrost. "Quell that anger, smuggler. The girl is fine. For now. The inferno comes and she must walk through it. Brio awaits her. Your place alongside her still remains, as is mine."

Neenah threw up her arms and stomped around the cabin. "Just like a godsdamned bikrome. Stupid riddles upon riddles. I need to release my crew and get these Imperium rats off my ship. Where are we going?"

"Oldport Basin."

Neenah was at a total and—gods be damned—utter loss. She was stuck, and not like a stuck pig in misery this time. She was bled dry.

XXXII
ASHE

"ASHE! WAKE THE Pit up!"

Sparks flew in her head in brilliant white like the color of her eyes as she opened them, the pall of a hammering at her brain like a carpenter attempting to erect a house but repeatedly missing the nail. She tried to assuage the source of the pain, but found her hands tied to a chair's arms, legs also bound with a thick rope. Another rope around her chest multiple times.

"Praise the bloody fucking Pentax, she's awake," said an aggressively annoyed woman.

"Language, acolyte."

To one side, she saw someone squirming against their bindings. A young woman with fire hair and a horrendous gash of dried blood along her freckled forehead. Harlequin, and she was a ball of angry red aether. On the far side of the vicar was another, larger figure dressed similarly. Cyan.

But both were encased by a misty cocoon so black, she knew it had to be from the bottom—if there was an actual bottom—of Nocturne's Pit. Only their unbreathered faces were not enclosed by the inky mist.

"Zenith's cock," Ashe said through dry lips. "Where are we?"

Brain foggy, Ashe found her surroundings were all shadows. Rounded at the ceiling with bricks held on arches and plain, blunted columns. It smelled heavily of dried blood, a musty scent of lingering death. There was a faint thrumming all around, as dust trickled from the bricks above in small puffs.

She had a strong inkling of this bouquet. As well as the sound.

"Below *The Arbiter's Axe*," Cyan said, confirming her suspicions. "I see you've done it again, Ashe, gotten yourself captured, and us along with you, by the way, after being somewhere you weren't supposed to be." He sounded angry, but not angry-angry like he wanted to punch a wall or something, just that angry parent sort of tone.

"Sorry?" She offered him an apologetic smile to go with her bantering reply but received a frown in return.

Ashe tested the bindings, found them tightly cinched. She called upon her Soul Form, but instead of the wails beyond the veil that indicated her burning of aether, she heard nothing and couldn't conjure her aetheurgy. It was like staring into the abyss and searching for a bridge that wasn't there. Panic brewed.

"Don't waste your time." For one called 'the Defiant', Cyan was fairly relaxed, a bit tussled, but tranquil. "Void Form spell. It's the mist. See?"

Ashe didn't notice it at first, because why would she think to look at her feet? She wasn't encased like Cyan and Harlequin, but she tried moving her feet, and even though she was bound to the chair, her legs moved naught an inch, almost as if she was cemented in place. But worse, it felt as if all the aether in her body was being drained away, the black mist sucking it from her, just out of reach.

"How?" *Strix?*

"THIS IS NOT OF NOCTURNE, DEAR BRYNN."

Then who is it if not the Dark Divine? Doubt the Wayward Son uses Void Form for garnishes in his drinks.

"THE TRUTH HAS ALWAYS BEEN RIGHT IN FRONT OF YOU, DAUGHTER OF NIGHTINGALE. WHEN WILL YOU OPEN YOUR EYES?" The Strix's tone was less playful, more intense.

Eyes to what, Strix? Just godsdamn spill it already.

"TAKE WHAT YOU KNOW. WHAT CANLON CARR HAS GIVEN YOU. OPEN YOUR EYES TO THE TRUTH IN YOUR SOUL."

I hate you sometimes.

A laugh in the void. ***"DON'T WE ALL, DEAR DAUGHTER."***

"Wouldn't think it possible," Cyan was saying in real time as Ashe conversed telepathically with the daemon blade. "A few steps ahead of us, they."

"Where's Phloxy?"

"Right here, you sniveling little runt." The willowy vicar emerged from the shadows and the septic mist parted reluctantly with a hiss to allow the man to walk through.

"You fucking craven asshole." Harlequin was growling like a rabid dog, almost frothing at the mouth like one, too. Ashe was surprised by the venom in the woman's aura, but she couldn't lie, it intrigued her.

"Phloxy, you cu—" The words cut off from the sharp sting of someone slapping the back of her head, in the exact spot where she'd been bludgeoned into oblivion by the void mist in the super-secret blooddrake museum. "Fuck!"

"Calm down, Lady Drakeslayer, screaming will get you nowhere."

"ON THE CONTRARY," the Strix said. ***"RECALL GARGANTUA, THAT WAS YOUR TRUE VOICE. THE BREATH OF THE SOUL."***

Huh?

The speaker circled the prisoners. A Kanjan elfir with silver hair, wide set bikromi eyes. Ifant Klander. Another person appeared, short of hair with bangs over piercing blue eyes. Danma Dil. Phlox the Faithful, in his midnight blue cassock, lurked behind predatorily.

"Lord Klander, haven't had the pleasure," Ashe said, ignoring the lingering soreness in her scalp and the overriding feeling of being naked and weak without access to her Soul Form. Bravado often serviced well in times like this. "But based on the exorbitant sums of quadrans you charge at *The Parlour* for just a delicate tickle, I can only imagine you're overcompensating for something." She raised a brow toward his crotch. "Trouble getting it up?"

Harlequin cackled, even Cyan broke out a grin. Phlox lunged from the shadows and cracked the Resolute in the jaw with an aether-enhanced fist of *Terris*. The fire-haired vicar's head snapped back, which elicited a string of curses from Cyan, something Ashe had never heard before.

"That's all you've got, fucker?" Blood dripped from Harlequin's broken lip. She grinned, a rictus show of teeth. "I've had stronger monthly moonflows."

"O, THAT'S A GOOD ONE."

Yeah, it was…

"I thought this was the one with the mouth," Klander said as he ran a pale finger down Ashe's jawline. Her reflexive bite caught only air and the sound of jangling bikromi bracelets. Phlox punched Harlequin again. The vicar spat blood. The humirish bastard readied to throw another, but Klander put up a hand. "Enough, vicar, we get the point."

Phlox stared hatred at Harlequin as the woman's head lulled.

Cyan sat straight in his bindings. "Why capture us, Klander?"

"Small gesture of power in all reality, vicar." His bi-colored eyes turned toward Ashe. A wave of unease washed through her. "You needed a reminder of whom you serve."

"We serve Zenith," Cyan said, a vigor in his voice that surprised Ashe. Then again, this wasn't Cyan's first capture at the hands, or claws, of a blooddrake.

"Is that what you believe? How wrong you've got it. The Scattered Shards are tainted by their belief. In their servitude. You would be surprised at how far the rot goes. The Fallen has made many rise within your beloved Shards."

What is he talking about, Strix?

"THE SHARDS ARE CORRUPTED, DEAR BRYNN. THE FALLEN HAS INFILTRATED THEM YEARS AGO."

And now you're telling me this?

"SORRY?"

We are going to have a long conversation about communication after this. You, me, and Cyan. It's only funny when I do it.

Danma snorted, breaking her thought-fight with the daemon blade. "They aren't worth the effort, Ifant. You should kill them and be done with it."

"I see the apple hasn't fallen far from the tree, Dil," Ashe said, earning a glare.

"Who you calling a tree, bitch?"

"Ashe," Cyan started his usual three-step approach to keeping her silent. At least he called her Ashe instead of stupid Lilia…

But she didn't. "Has she always been this stupid?" Ashe shook her head. "No wonder you can't get out of the Chain."

Danma raged, fists balled, chest heaving. There was a dangerous glint in her eye. Murder. And Ashe didn't need to read Danma's aura to determine that.

Klander stepped ahead of Dil. "Regardless of my acquaintance's… propensity for violence, in some cases it is necessary. The only way to get through to some people, like yourselves, is through violence. You'll be impressed with what we have in store for you. For all of you."

"What are you after, Klander? The Seal of *Ignis* cannot be used by the likes of you."

"O, Lady Drakeslayer, how little you know of the world around you." Klander motioned toward his seething accomplice. "Danma, be a dear and go see to it our friends are ready for the vicars." Danma hesitated, most likely not used to being told what to do. "Go. Please? I'm certain our guests have all waited patiently for the main event. They'll not be disappointed by what's to come."

Danma Dil turned on a heel and marched away, grumbling under her breath.

"Take it she doesn't know what you are, blooddrake?"

"I'm curious," the Guilder's voice turned gravelly, almost like a rumbling growl. Yes, indeed a blooddrake. "How do you know what I am?"

"A professional never tells her secrets."

"Funny. Who else would know about a blooddrake except another? Or someone who's been told about us, which points to one of us spilling secrets. Which one is it?" He glanced at the Strix sheathed at her hip. "Cadrianna's bonded blade, I assume? The one you call 'Strix'. If only you knew its true name."

"Maybe, maybe not." Ashe shifted in her chair, which wasn't much. "And I'm the one who doesn't know who I serve?"

Klander let out a laugh sounding more like a big cat coughing up a hairball. "You think I'm the only blooddrake in this world? Please, you're smarter than that, child."

"What do you gain by turning on the Guild for the Fallen?" Cyan asked. "The Fallen doesn't offer freedom, he offers supplication."

"Isn't it obvious, vicar?"

"Don't let him get to you, Cyan," Ashe said. "Pretty soon he'll be boring us all to death like Phloxy over there. How long, Phloxy, have you been a blooddrake?"

She'd long established Phlox the Faithful was more than met the eye, for the glum man was too much of an asshole to not be considered a prime candidate to be seduced by the Dark Divine. She knew the type of man he was. Rotten to the core. And if what Klander just said was true, he had to be a blooddrake.

Phlox's aura blazed crimson. "I'm no draconem! I am Zenith's servant."

"Godsdamn." She whistled. "I figured you had to be one."

Klander chuckled. "Not as smart as you think, Lady Drakeslayer. No matter. Telling it true, we have many blooddrakes amongst your beloved Shards. Just not in your Phlox the Faithful. But loyal he is to us. There are others just as loyal to the Fallen and our Divine. Within the Conclave, even."

"NOT TO NOCTURNE," the Strix whispered.

"He Who Fathered the World does not treat with prickless cowards," a bloodied Harlequin said, slumped in her cocoon of black mist. "You soil the cassock worse than your bedsheets."

The Faithful unleashed a blow to the vicar's temple, another square to the face. Harlequin's nose shattered, blood draining as her eyes rolled up as she drifted into unconsciousness.

"What's that, Harlequin? Can't hear you now!" Phlox looked toward Ashe. "Always hated you two. Always with the comments." He raised his aetherically-enhanced fist, ready to pummel Ashe into the Pit after Harlequin.

"That's enough," hissed a newcomer in the shadows.

Cloaked by the black mist, a figure emerged. Shorter than the others, lean of build. Hair black but wavier. Eyes of all-onyx.

"Mother?"

"NOT CADRIANNA, DEAR BRYNN. BLOODDRAKE."

The Strix was right. This body had the appearance of Cadrianna Benld, a woman Ashe had barely known, little more than an hour to be honest. And although this figure had the same face as the woman who'd birthed her, there was differences about her. Harder, almost. Dangerous, even. Cadrianna's aura was all wrong, all Four Tenets blending as one.

"Solanine," she gnarred as the blooddrake approached. "How?"

"Why, might be the more pertinent question to ask?" The blooddrake within her mother's flesh raised a hand and it became a beacon of aetheurgy, the flesh of Cadrianna's forefinger peeling back to reveal a taloned claw sharp as any blade. The claw drew down Ashe's cheek, leaving a swelling of blood. "A child would never understand the whims of the Divines. The True Divine."

Although Ashe remained calm on the outside, she was a raging inferno within. A pulmo cough tore through her. "Don't matter, I'll just kill you again and again and again if I have to."

The claw sliced across her other cheek. A flash of aetheurgy, more blood. Ashe didn't flinch, instead spat tar and blood at the blooddrake. A gravelly bark of laughter. "Man does not understand the nature of the Pentax. Or the draconem. The bitter hatred between the children of Nightingale and their Father. You cannot even begin to understand what it's like to be the weakest of Nightingale's brood." Solanine patted her dripping cheek, blood smeared upon the reformed hand of Cadrianna's flesh. "If not for His prison in Eminence, we would be the True Divine's favorite. Once He is freed, I shall get what is owed to me."

Strix?

"LISTEN CLOSELY AND YOU WILL LEARN THE TRUTH."

"Nightingale hated us more than any other of Her children." In the gloom of the chamber under *The Axe*, Klander's bikromi irises flashed a purplish shade, drowning out the solitary black and the solo white of the elfirish flesh. "It was She who started the war over Eminence."

"But we," Solanine wheezed, scratching at Cadrianna's skin fiercely, "will finish it and free the True Divine."

"You would free Nocturne from His place in the Pit?"

"You are a foolish child if you believe such lies, Godsblood." Solanine's all-onyx gaze settled upon Ashe and she was transported back to that Guilder's villa a year ago, to her first interaction with Solanine. That secret knowledge that seemed depthless, unfathomable. Enticing. "You, Godsblood, will lead us to His Seals. You've broken one and slayed the Goddess of the Forge, ending Her power. Her guardians. *Ignis* draws you to it. Brio will wilt and His firedrakes will turn to ash. Ialtris, the tome."

Klander, or Ialtris the blooddrake apparently, disappeared into the black mist, returning with an ancient book in pale hands. Opened to a page covered with runes similar to the ones tattooed on her arm in the language of aether. In the center was a larger rune shaped like a semi-circle facing east with a slash of zigzags going northeast to southwest, ending in an arrowhead. It was the same symbol found on the dead man of the Kraken's Cabal.

"The symbol of Nightingale," Solanine said. "Not just of House Nightingale, your mother's blood, but of Her, the First Wife. The Mother of Draconem. The Seals are Her doing, Her Children's doing. One has broken under your hand, Godsblood.

Now you must break the others and free Him. Ah, Danma, is all ready?"

Danma Dil appeared out of the shadows, her face and aura still angered. "All is ready."

"Is she one, too?" Solanine's posture told Ashe that the Guilder was not.

"One what?" Dil pressed.

Klander-Ialtris surged toward the Guilder of the Beggars Chain, grabbing Dil by the neck. Sapphires dilating. "Afraid not," the bikrome-wearing-blooddrake said apologetically. His hand ignited in *Ignis* aether and seared Dil's throat. She screamed, then died. "A use she has now fulfilled."

Danma Dil's body crumpled to the ground where the black, hungry mist gorged itself upon her flesh.

"I suppose that's one less suspect to worry about, eh, Cyan?" Her taskmaster gave her a side-eye.

"You quip, Godsblood, even now?"

She shrugged best she could in her bound state. "I find it helps ease the situation. Harle-bub would be proud. If Phloxy hadn't found the psychotic need to knock her out. Especially when everyone surrounding us seems like they just want to be pricks." Ashe glanced at Solanine in her mother's flesh and realized the right arm hung limply. "How's the hand? O wait, that's right, I broke it using Mother Marrow's aether."

"It amuses me," Solanine said, "your attempt at goading."

"I wouldn't want to disappoint, blooddrake."

"As am I. We blooddrakes can find common experiences with one such as you. Not many men kill a draconem and survive. Especially one of Nightingale's Children. I admire you for it. But that still doesn't negate what strife you've caused me, Godsblood. He brought me back for a reason and saved the Fallen. And you will break the Seals and let Him free. Noctis and Eminence will be His. And then Valeria Dunleith will be mine for all eternity."

Ashe smirked. "You think I'd do such a thing for you? You'd be sorely mistaken if you think I'd do something like that." She coughed as she cocked her head toward Cyan. "Ask him how demanding things of me goes."

"A choice is not yours, Godsblood. The Seal calls to you, and will continue to call to you until you answer it. But you shy away from the true power of your Soul Form. I will enjoy watching your friends suffer." Lavender flashed behind the all-onyx eyes. "You see, the will of my Divine always has a way of working itself out."

"The time is getting late," Klander-Ialtris said. "Shall we?"

"Yes. Time it is." Solanine held out the humirish hand of Cadrianna Benld, but all Ashe could think of is the claw underneath. "It is time for you to serve the True Divine."

"I don't think so, blooddrake."

"Without your Soul Form, serving is the only way."

Ashe's lip quirked. "I was doomed the moment the Fallen killed my father and took my mother. I'd die before helping you."

"You say that now. But what about your precious Cyan? Or this whelping called Harlequin? If I must, I will destroy every person you hold dear. The drakken siblings bound to you. The lapin. The princeps who loved your father. Valeria. Every single person you've ever encountered. And I'll start with the one who betrayed Dil."

"No!" The faces of Lojen, Ruane, Finn, Wick, Val all ran through her mind. Of Evzen, poor Evzen. He deserved better than this after being borne of Elian's loins.

"Ah, there's the nerve you been hiding." Solanine-in-Cadrianna-Benld's-flesh motioned toward Klander-Ialtris. "Fetch the boy."

"You wouldn't dare."

"Ashe, seek the calm inside," Cyan said, trying to assuage her, "just like I've trained you."

It wasn't working. She kept seeing all their faces, all their blood drained by the blooddrake. Their flesh toys for Solanine. Their souls lost to the Pit.

Solanine twirled the fingers of Cadrianna Benld, and the black mist rose in a storm of crackling aether. Another twist and the black enveloped Cyan completely. Her taskmaster cried out and shook violently in his chair. He disappeared behind a jet curtain, his cry cut off as if he was being smothered.

Ashe raged, but her pulmo raged hotter.

"YOU ARE STRONGER THAN THIS, DEAR BRYNN. HARNESS IT. RELEASE THE BREATH OF THE SOUL."

"I allowed you to live once, girl. The Fallen may be the chosen warrior of my Divine, but so am I. I will not allow you to be unshackled any further. I have the means to bind you, aether and all. It is the use Dil brought me. If I have to spill blood, I shall not hesitate. You will serve or the one called Cyan will be crushed, bone and all."

The blooddrake in Ifant Klander returned with a small humir kicking in their grip.

"Evzen!"

"BE SMART. YOU ARE THE DAUGHTER OF NIGHTINGALE, DO NOT BE BLIND."

"I didn't do anything," Evzen shouted. Klander tossed Elian's sprat to the ground, the blackened mist gurgling in anticipation. Evzen scrambled to his feet, his gaze lingering on the body of

Danma Dil. "What in the actual Pit is going on here? Who? Ashe, that you? Why are you tied up like that? Ashe, say something?"

Solanine put a left hand upon Evzen's shoulder, they were almost of the same height. "Your dearest friend is going to help us. Isn't that correct, Godsblood?"

"Who the fuck are you?" Evzen shrugged off Solanine's hand.

"Evzen, don't listen to her," Ashe said, struggling in her bindings. "She's not even a she. She's a drake."

Ashe was sweating freely now, feeling the urge for aether more than ever. She wanted to burn through the bindings and sweep up her friends and take them away. Wanted to end these creatures, these daemons.

Most of all, she wanted it all to end. Everyone associated with her family to no longer be a nightmare she relived over and over. Wanted to be free of her Nightingale past.

Evzen glanced at the strange wall of black mist that hid Cyan, then to Harlequin, who was still knocked out cold, then to the body of Danma Dil. "I see ol' Danma got hers finally. Can't say I'm upset about it. Just give them what they want, Ashe."

Solanine's useless right hand became encased in *Ignis* flames.

"No!"

Elian's bastard threw up his hands protectively, mouth agape as he staggered back.

Hateful purple draconem eyes flashed toward her. Ashe fought with her entire flagging strength at the bonds, but she felt weak. Useless. "You can save him, Godsblood. Do what we wish. Serve."

Ashe slumped in the chair, defeated. "What do you want me to do?"

"The entrance, where is it?"

"What fucking entrance?"

Solanine tapped a finger to Cadrianna's temple. "The entrance remains hidden, even from her memories. You are the only one who can uncover its location within the base of the volcano."

"THE MEMORIES OF CAD, DEAR BRYNN. RECALL HER MEMORIES. THIS IS THE ONLY WAY TO THE SEAL."

Strix?

"THE MEMORY. YOU SAW THE ONE. THE SMELL."

"The cave?"

"Which cave?" Solanine pressed.

She remembered it now. The cave from the memory of her mother and her grandfather. "I… I'll show you."

"I know you will, Godsblood. But I'm not a fool. You will show me after you suffer, for there will be no other way."

The ebony mist curtain dropped, revealing Cyan. He was still alive. Klander-Ialtris and Phlox the not-very-Faithful grabbed Cyan and Harlequin from behind, dragging the vicars back, the chairs squealing across the blood-infused stones of *The Arbiter's Axe*. Behind her, Ashe heard grunts. Then silence.

Solanine quelled the flames of *Ignis*. "Their lives depend on you serving, Brynn of Nightingale blood."

Ashe was tired, her body deprived of life. Pulmo tore through her lungs.

"THIS IS THE PATH. THE SEALS CALL YOU. FEAR THEM NOT."

It's not the Seals I fear, but not getting the chance to kill Solanine again.

Evzen got to his feet and padded over, lowering his face toward hers. His aura was curious and all over the place. "Sorry, Ashe," he started, "but I told you not to trust anyone."

She coughed so hard, her stomach clenched and would have ended up on her backside if she wasn't tied down. But anger flashed as she glared at the boy she had known and trusted. "I should've known Elian's traitorous blood flows through you, too."

He patted the top of her head condescendingly. "And yet, you didn't. Shame on you, Ashe. My father, rest his soul in the Meadows, was a man of ambition. You think I came to Port Sin on my own volition? He played the long game with the Fallen. And I was but one of his pawns. You did me a favor by murdering him. It gave me further credence in Dil's confidence. So, I should thank you for that. But I am just as ambitious as he." He looked over toward Solanine. "Fortune favors the ambitious. You think all that aethecite was meant for money? No, you idiot, it's for the Fallen's war. A war in which I plan to be on the winning side."

Ashe smiled, black tar and blood painting her lips. "I'm going to kill you worse than your father."

Evzen slapped her already bleeding face, sending a stinging shiver through her jaw. "I think not, Ashe. I think not." With that, the bastard of Elian marched away, leaving her with Solanine.

The blooddrake watched her with a sapphiric aura of knowing. "I'm going to enjoy this, Godsblood."

"Not nearly as much as I will when I rip your heart out."

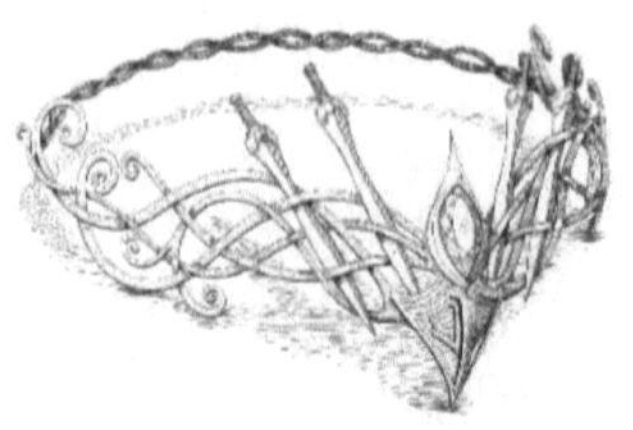

XXXIII
FINN

STANDING WITH HIS arms crossed, Finn leaned against the middle wall of Gandtril as he watched legionnaires train in the gloomy lambency of an emerald-tinted sunset. His chaperones, Alyx and Davel, were not far from his side.

Despite the threat of the Fallen's army and the death of the optio, the drilling never ceased. The soldiers of Kanja rotated in and out of drills, sparring and training with vigor and precision. Complaints were scarce and sweat by the bucket loads, even without the grizzled Resande to push them. There was a certain level of honor present that Finn found quite impressive. Ready the Legion was for what was to come.

But it still didn't bring him any semblance of comfort.

It was never like this in Drenth, Em, he said to the specter of his beloved. No response came. *It'd be nice to hear your voice instead of you just flitting around all handsomely in my addled mind.*

"Don't look so bored, needle dick."

Finn turned to find Wick sitting upon a nearby stair that led to the wall's parapets. The lapin was slicing chunks of apple with one of his dueling knives.

"Not exactly back breaking, is it? Now, Drenth and the rebellion, that was hard work."

"I'm not sure anything you did would constitute as work," Wick said as he popped a hunk of apple into his mouth. "Em did all the 'hard work', you just sat around and moaned."

Finn cracked a grin. "You remember when Kephren first joined us and we commandeered that shipment of aethecite heading to Alizarin? There we were, out in the Sea, just waiting, and that mist daemon attacked us just before the load got to us. Gods above, I thought Keph had pissed his britches right then and there." He laughed. "That was a sight. As gangly as he was, face all ashen behind his breather. He burned his parch so quick, I thought he'd burn out."

"I remember Em saving both your backsides." Wick tossed the core of the apple at him and Finn ducked. "Little help you were."

"Keph wasn't made for that life. No wonder he sold his soul to Solanine."

"None of us are made for this life," Wick said softly. "The Fallen forced us into it. We were all buggered the moment he showed up. But we were stupid enough back then to think we could fight back. Look where it got us."

"Now you're starting to sound like me."

Wick cradled his shredded ear. "Remember when that storm broke over Drenth? The night that rained blood."

Finn would never forget that night, try as he might. That was when the tide had turned in their favor. An omen from the Pentax. Still, he shivered. "It was as if the heavens opened with tears of blood."

"A lyrical genius you are."

"I've a way with words, what can I say?" A soft snowfall started. Fat white flakes a tad early in the season. It felt good, the snow, as did the banter. He needed it. Suddenly he smiled. "Ha, remember when Tevun tried his hand at singing?"

"By the Pentax, I wanted to murder hi—"

A deep, low-sounding resonance broke the air surrounding Gandtril, somewhere close outside the walls in the Sea of Mist. A horn, it sounded like.

He and Wick shared a glance as the alarm started blaring from the Obelisk. Davel and Alyx tensed, their weapons pulled up.

Finn pulled on a breather and rushed up the stairs as legionnaires raced toward the battlements with weapons drawn. Wick and his legionnaire shadows followed him up, as did the cacophony of noise from within the fortress. Moments later, they were atop the southern outermost wall, staring out over the Sea. Visibility was no more than a few hundred feet in the shrouding mist and snowfall, but even that was muted and unclear. The sky was overcast, the sun hidden within clouds of snow and fog as it was descending in the west. Drifting of frozen wetness nestled softly against drake scale cuirasses, white coating the hard earth below the walls.

Within the ocean of snowy haze, a continuing horn blew, soon joined by a rhythmic beating: drums and boots marching. The bass gradually increased, yet nothing appeared.

But then, suddenly, out of the grey-white came an airship.

The bow pierced through the foggy snowfall, moving forward until the entire vessel parted from the grey-coated flakes. It was at least one hundred feet from deck to the base of the hull. Tiny shapes moved about the railings; people so small in relation to the rest of the ship. A pair of ivory horns, curved like spikes of the legendary mammoths on the Isle of Merj were fitted at the bow, blowing the deep resonance. Two sets of twin metal fans attached to gears along the bottom of the hull, long, curved blades turning in steady motion. Gears ground systematically and were as large as a man was tall. Finn couldn't see the actual engines on the deck, but thick building-wide plumes of black rose from the airship and melted into the dense cloud-cover, sprinkling aethecite scree everywhere, melding black into the pure white of Kanja's winter.

Two additional airships of a similar size broke through the mist. And they all bore the red skull emblem of the Fallen painted upon their hulls.

"Zenith protect us," Finn muttered.

"No gods to be seen here, needle dick. The Pentax have left us to our own."

"How is that possible?"

"For Honor and Blood," Wick spat over the edge of the battlement. "Fuck 'em. The Guild never tallied them all. Had to be. Unless the Fallen built them in secret." Wick turned toward Finn. "Now do you believe, Finn? Bliss' words come true. The Fallen has been reborn."

Through the mist, came the army of the Fallen. Like ghosts rising from the grave, they came in a flood of apparitions in the grey. Line after line of Imperium soldiers, clad in black and crimson cuirasses, facemasks painted like skulls. On they marched, closer to Gandtril, unafraid with their numbers.

There were thousands of them, multiple times the size of the Legion. Interspersed throughout the army were creatures beyond imagination. Daemons. Horns and claws, twice the size of men. Teeth and tails. Bloodthirsty and death stalking.

Finn's heart jumped into his throat. But his tongue got the better of his mind. "Brace yourselves!" he yelled to the legionnaires all around him. "Ready weapons!"

The soldiers of the Legion looked his way, questions on many lips but none raised disagreement. Wheellock rifles came to shoulders, aim set on the incoming army. Soldiers of Kanja took position on the rotating cannons. Drones flitting above, bright lights pointing outward into the Sea, their cameras tracking the incoming army for the legionnaires below.

Weapons rang as the horns on the airship raised their pitch, blasting with intent. A crushing roar rose from the Fallen's army. The worst came from the daemons, unholy as it were. Then they charged through the suddenly heavier rain. Someone atop the battlements screamed for the Legion to hold strong. Finn saw calm men and women, but most held weapons with white knuckles.

"How far?" Wick asked.

Finn burned some parch, his aetheurgy coming alive. The Sea became transparent silver, clarity given under the Four Enhancements. "Five hundred paces."

"Where's Titen?"

"Meadows if I know. Haven't seen him since the body found outside my door this morning." Finn huffed within the breathing mask as he cast an eye toward Alyx and Davel. Both were tense as they watched the oncoming army. "Where the void is Landra?"

The primus pilus should be there in place of the Golden Sword or praetor now that the optio was dead. That left Finn the man in charge of the walls. A task he was not exactly suited for.

This is what Val meant before she took off, wasn't it? The specter of Emre nodded at him.

I bloody godsdamned know it, Em! Finn took control of the situation. "Cannons ready!" Snow coming heavier now as he yelled.

The gears of aethecite-powered cannons turned with a sharp groan, pivoting upwards toward the airships. Wheellocks clicked as legionnaires steadied them, ready to fire into the oncoming horde, particularly the daemons.

Then, before any defender knew what was happening, winged daemons swooped down between snowflake and spent aethecite, below the hulls of the massive airships. Down they flew with talons sharper than any blade, colliding with the drones. Smoke and metal squealed as the daemons ripped them asunder, destroying the lights and cameras. With the job done, the daemons banked toward the walls of the fortress, their wings flapping as they dove toward the Legion's, nay, Kanja's defenders.

Wick was right; they were buggered.

Finn covered his ears as the cannons fired. Snow streamed down his glass breather.

One of the airships sustained crippling damage from the cannons and it crashed into the Sea in smoke and fire, Imperium soldiers jumping to their deaths, killing dozens, if not hundreds below. The other airships took damage, swerving the best they could, firing down upon the Legion fortress with their own aethecite-powered weaponry. The deafening boom of aethecite ripping. Two defending cannons were destroyed, long barrels snapped from gearhouses, dropping useless to the now wet grounds, killing and maiming soldiers behind the walls.

"Mother Marrow's tits," Wick swore. "They brought siege machines."

Seven of them, to be exact. Tall structures on wheels, armored and slick with oil from the look of them. Hundreds of men piled within each. Slowly pulled by enormous beasts with flat, huge heads and rounded ears, long nose hanging to the ground, pointed tusks curving outward. War mammoths. But their eyes were blazing red with fury. Daemonized. Behind the siege machines were larger daemons pushing with arms the size of the mammoths' legs.

"Fire!" a legionnaire from along the outer wall screamed. Still not Landra or Finn's brother-friend.

Bullets flew from wheellocks. Grunts and screams of inhumanly essence echoed strongly as the aethecite ore hammered into the army of the Fallen. Blasts from the remaining cannons exploded in quick, rapid bursts as finger-wide bullets whistled toward the airships and swooping daemons. Airborne daemons screeching. Wheellocks expelled more aethecite bullets at the front raiders of crimson and black, aiming to rip apart daemons. Anything to slow down the oncoming horde.

With all the death filling the Sea, as every man and creature who fell, more replaced them. The wounded were trampled as the army pushed on, the dead turning to muddy pulp underfoot. Red stained the white snow. Daemons tore at the dead, ripping limb and flinging gore, snarling and bellowing.

Another volley came from the legionnaires, the sound deafening as muzzles flashed. The distance between the oncoming army and the walls of Gandtril was now down to only one hundred paces, and the invaders broke their controlled charge and sprinted, ladders and ropes in hand. The soldiers of the Legion rained death, but still they came. Enemy fire from wheellock rifles shot back, the protectors of Gandtril hunkering down from the barrage. Two of the mist vacuums exploded and thick grey poured over the wall with an odorous stink.

Dozens of winged daemons swerved and dove at the defenders. Blackened and misshapen bodies with clawed limbs forward, teeth snapping. Legionnaires were caught up by the daemons and lifted into the air, either to be dropped to their deaths far below, or torn apart where they'd been plucked.

Finn ducked beside Wick, Alyx and Davel diving to their faces as a daemon whooshed nearby, grabbing a woman of the Legion. Her scream filled the air as she was rent in pieces.

Legionnaires scrambled around, some falling to their deaths. Screams of pain, gore of blood. The battlements were slickery and dangerous, snow garnet.

"Where the void is Titen?" Finn growled. The Golden Sword needed to be on the wall with his soldiers. They needed to see their leader with them, to give them hope. "Fuck, I'd take Landra, too!"

He looked around, the walls seemed sparse. Even with the intense fighting, legionnaires wearing the eagle of the Legion were hardly to be seen. A skeleton force more like. Something was wrong; it trembled in Finn's bones. Lojen's words were ringing true. This was work of the scourges.

Fucking Nocturne. What do I do, Em? The specter smiled at him. *Gods above, that smile still makes me weak. And stupid.*

A bullet thudded next to the gap above Finn's head in between the ungodsly squawk of a flying daemon. "We need to destroy those ladders. And somebody take out those godsdamned fliers!"

"And those siege machines." Wick pawed flakes of snow from his button-shaped eyes. Drenched his fur was, ice forming. "Got any bright ideas, needle dick?"

The ground shivered as another of the airships crashed, closer to the walls now as fragments of the hull flew overhead, landing in the center of the fortress, sending the legionnaires scampering. But some pieces of the hull took out a pair of winged daemons. Thankfully. The ground groaned under the destruction of the airship. Cried more like.

"Oil!" Finn thundered down the battlements screaming, his footing unsure in the snow and blood.

Within heartbeats—as this had been one of Praetor Rignork's defenses planned—legionnaires carried multiple metal cauldrons that boiled with grease. Thick plumes of smoke filled the air with the fragrance of cooking liquid.

Finn thumbed over the walls. "Burn the bastards!"

The last Legion cannon went down in a maelstrom of Imperium-wrought bullets that sent debris flying, oil cauldrons spilling everywhere along the battlements, killing enemies at the base of the wall and legionnaires atop alike. Burnt flesh, charred and cracking. Finn gagged, even with his breathing mask he could smell it, and the added poison of the Sea made it worse. The steady snow did nothing to quell the flames or the mist.

The siege machines were now close enough that long metal planks crashed down upon the parapets, crimson-scaled soldiers of the Imperium raced across, weapons drawn as they entered Gandtril. The daemon elephants battered the walls, bodies riddled with bullet holes like red tattoos. Other daemons piercing claws into the stone and began climbing.

Men clashed. Daemons howled. Weapons sliced, pulling red streaks. Body parts and entrails wet the stones, slick with it. A river run red.

"We have to fall back!" Finn stabbed a crimson-cloaked enemy with his rapier, piercing drake scale. The soldier of the Fallen screamed as he died.

The last airship passed overhead, its thick metal blades whooshing, stirring up snow and death, sending Finn to his knees. A daemon topped the wall, its jaw nearly unhinged as it bit at Finn. He stabbed with his rapier into the open maw. The creature of the void gargled as spittle and black ichor sprayed as it fell backwards.

Wick grabbed him by the collar of his cuirass. "Move it!" The lapin jabbed an enemy through her breathing mask with his dueling knife, glass shattering.

"To the second set of walls!" Finn screamed, regaining his footing in the slick snow. "To the second set of walls!"

A legionnaire fell dead at Finn's feet and an Imperium soldier raised a bloody sword at him. Finn leapt as he burned his parch, his own blade stabbing at the man's side. With aether-enhanced strength, he tossed the soldier over the wall, sending him to his death fifty paces flung from the battlement. Finn pulled a wheellock pistol from the dead legionnaire's belt and fired at another enemy as his boots shifted along the wet stones. Between the snow and the blood, footing became tedious.

The ground under Gandtril trembled as one of Mother Marrow's dying quakes shook the world. Finn and Wick flew from their feet, Alyx and Davel too, as did everyone on the walls, friend and foe alike. Only a handful of daemons stayed upright, killing anyone near. This tremor was long, deep. Stones from the walls rattled, parapets tumbling, crushing unfortunate souls. The ground felt like it was going to swallow whole the mega-city of Gandtril.

Then it was over.

The dwindling number of Gandtril's Legion retreated from the outer wall into the fortress below, racing toward the gates of the second wall. Others ran across the narrow bridges that connected the two walls, legionnaires using thick-headed hammers to knock out the pins that held them up. The spanning bridges all fell into the gap between the two walls with hollow rings. The growing flow of crimson and black armor washed over the outer wall in a crest of flesh and hide, wails from the Pit accompanying.

A mountain of a daemon with a coarse beard bellowed at Finn as he vaulted the battlement, curved claws bearing down. He was a man, but also a daemon, Finn realized before the thing attacked him. Part of the rotund belly was missing, as if the spine had been shattered and somehow brought back to life. Something about the daemon man's face seemed familiar. Finn turned the attack aside, his rapier gashing across the daemon-man's leg, sending him… it to its knees. A quick thrust of the pointed steel into the daemon's body spilled the former man's lifeblood, dousing the stones of the wall in black cruor. But the once-man fell backward, yanking the rapier from Finn's grip. The Dunleith blade snapped as the man-turned-daemon died, again.

Finn picked up an enemy's curved sword from the ground nearby and ran.

Backing away as they hacked and cut, thrusted and swung, Finn and Wick fought on, keeping all attackers wary. Alyx and Davel used their daemon-killing spears, jabbing at man and creature of the void. Finn's arms were growing heavy as his aetheurgy began to dwindle, his parch running close to empty. He snuffed his burn to save what little he could. Wick was a tornado of stabbing blades, moving faster than he. The lapin thrived in a fight; the survivor of Dervin eager to attack. His Bond sapping Enhancements from Ancantha, even from the great distance between Gandtril and Alizarin. The lapin doe would know her mate was in peril for him to leech the Bond such.

Great fires sprung to life along the tops of the outer wall where timber lined the doors to parapets and towers, wet snow be godsdamned. The bridges on the ground soon caught flame, too. Tanned hide awnings sparked into burnt tatters. Few legionnaires held their ground, most dying under the press of enemy tide.

Finn's boots hit the bottom step near the gates of the middle wall; the hardened marshland dirt had turned to mud. Wick pulled his arm as he fought off an enemy with the curved sword, killing him. A daemon swooped toward him but Davel thrust his elongated spear with precision, piercing the coarse-haired hide. Down the daemon went, another stab with spear ending it.

There were pockets of fighting here and there between the two walls. Tevun's hatchlings and a unit of Legion defenders threw back the forces of the Fallen, purplish blood trickling down Lojen's exoscales unconcerned as the drakken wardkeeper was lost in the berserker rage. Lojen used his horns as weapons, ramming the two-foot keratin into soldiers and flinging them aside. It was almost like a dance, his rage. Ruane fought like a drake possessed, longknife and claws ripping Imperium soldiers to shreds. Daemons also died under their talons. They pressed, cut down some of the enemy, then fled toward where Finn and Wick waited, blades at the ready for the next attack.

Lojen's angry lavender eyes were glazed, and he was breathing heavily. He was terrifying to behold, something Finn didn't expect, for the drakken was one of the most kind-hearted creatures he'd ever met. "How were they able to get so many north without us knowing? We had sentries for leagues in the Sea."

"This was planned, Lojen," Wick said. The lapin looked tired, even with his Enhancements from his Bond with Ancantha. "Like you told Titen."

"Broken shells," the drakken swore.

"This gate's not held," Ruane said. She back kicked and it squealed as it flapped, opening inward toward the Obelisk. "By the Arbiter's Bloody Axe, I knew it!" She snarled.

Finn was at a loss. No member of the Legion would dare leave their post unguarded, especially the inner gate. He watched the enemy crawling over the battlements of the outer wall, but they didn't flow over now, and didn't attack any further. A few daemons tried to move further into the bailey, but they were called back by unholy screeches of other daemons. Almost like taking the wall was the goal, not the mega-city itself. The sanguine skull of the Fallen's standard rose atop the southern wall, whipping in the falling snow.

The final airship teetered in the sky, rent by cannon blasts and bullets. One of the propellers spewed flames as it disappeared back into the mist. Of the winged daemons, they dove and banked near the city itself, but didn't attack in force. Strange.

"Where's Titen?"

"The eastern wall was breached by a daemon," Lojen answered. "The Golden Sword is there."

"Something's not right."

Finn picked up a fallen wheellock pistol and raced through the gate at a sprint, flinging snowy muck. The others followed.

In the center of the fortress, the rest of the Legion stood, along with people from Gandtril beyond the Obelisk, those who hadn't fled with the rest of the mega-city. Mostly Upper City borne. None wore armor, none held swords or wheellocks. Men and women of the Guild dressed in their best Festival of the Pentax clothing, a few children with flowers in their hair. Singing in the falling snow.

At the head was Emont Landra.

Ruane grabbed Landra's tunic in a taloned fist. She towered over the elfirish primus pilus, that anger that had filled her in Drenth oozed from her voice, "You knew they were coming, didn't you? Resande, that was you? You tried to fool us, elfir. But not me!"

Lojen surged toward his sister, claw reaching for her, the throes of wardkeeping having had dwindled in his eyes. "Ru, wait!"

Landra gazed down on the drakken's claw with disgust. "There is no stopping him. No stopping them." He pointed back the way they'd come. "The Fallen will own the Mistlands. And he will plunge our world into darkness. We can only hope to join him before we are all carrion for the birds. His defeat at Drenth and rebirth is an omen."

Finn pushed up beside Lojen, suddenly as angry as the wardkeeper's sibling. "You threw away our lives. What about the praetor? What about the Golden Sword? You'll burn in Nocturne's Pit for this, Landra."

"Rignork is a fool who can't see reason. His own ego keeps him in check. Locked in his tower, hidden behind his sickness." Landra looked back at the Obelisk. "And that's where he'll die. Your brother is nothing more than a servant of the Golden Throne. Gandtril will fall, and so will Kalderim."

"You murderous bastard!" Ruane roared. She lifted Landra up, and for a moment, fear graced the elfirish captain's face. "You slaughtered your own. Tonns warned us all. Yet you killed him. Per the law, you said. But it was to hide your treachery, wasn't it! All men are weak like you, elfir. You sully this world the Pentax gifted us draconem."

"I did no such thing, Ruane Tevunsdotyr. You," he said in Finn's direction, "raised the call to arms. None of this death and bloodshed would've happened had you not. There wasn't supposed to be any casualties. Other than those before." He glanced toward Alyx and Davel briefly. "No one had to die here today. I saw to that. Resande wouldn't join me. He had to die."

But none of that made sense, Landra had no aetheurgy.

There were bootsteps from the outer walls, the army of the Fallen approached. Finn turned to see a man breaking away, an obvious commander. He hefted his stolen curved sword, Wick and many of the legionnaires who had survived the battle doing the same. Ruane dropped the primus pilus and set her feet, claws brandished, hissing murder.

"Don't be fools," Landra said as he straightened his shirt, frowning. "Throw down your weapons. Join us in taking back what was stolen from us. Help us take back what is rightfully ours before the gods gave this world a reaping. The Fallen will show us the way it should be. Gandtril and Kalderim must burn."

They couldn't fight off the invading horde with only a few dozen legionnaires, two drakken, a lapin, and a princeps of Kalderim. They'd be slaughtered to a soul and then the mega-city would follow. Hundreds of souls sent to the Meadows. The fools who wouldn't run, perhaps they deserved it.

"Obelisk," Wick whispered to Finn.

The Obelisk had never been breached since it had been erected. Strong and fortified to hold against any attack. Without taking the Obelisk, the enemy could never breach the walls into Gandtril. Too tall and strong the inner walls were. Siege machines and daemons would not be enough to destroy the runes of aether.

Without those airships, the only way into Gandtril was through the Obelisk and Landra was about to gift the Fallen that gateway.

Shit, he thought of Titen. The breach of the eastern wall. There were still people within Gandtril.

He looked toward Lojen, who was struggling. His drakken friend was bound by honor to his oath as a wardkeeper, to do as commanded. He could see Lojen's mind waging war on his heart. Finn didn't know which the wardkeeper would choose.

So, he chose for him.

With a distasteful glance to the apostate who dared call himself a man of Kanja, Finn whipped his arm toward the lone, crimson-armored man, wheellock clicking. The commander of the Fallen's army fell dead, a bullet embedded in his forehead under the fragmented skull-painted glass of his breather. Tiny shards of glass glinted in the droplets of heaven's tears.

Landra's face went red but turned to shock when Ruane stabbed her longknife into his shoulder. The man, his oiled hair and traitorous air slumped to the muddy ground, screaming after them.

The fortress erupted.

The unarmed soldiers who had been of the Legion but had turned heel with Landra shrieked as the crimson-clad army of the Fallen fell upon them. Guild and Legion men were brutally cut down, the women dragged off. The few children cried as they were culled.

Finn sprinted toward the Obelisk, with Lojen, Ruane, Wick, and the other legionnaires who kept their oaths closing around. Pushing through the heavy metal gates, they slammed them closed to the wails of death.

XXXIV

ASHE

ASHE CAME TO with a splitting headache caused by a boisterous din.

She lay on her back instead of sitting in the chair, arms unbound, a grainy earth under her fingertips. The ancient musk of dried blood filled her nose, but it was hampered by a mass upon her lower jaw. A hateful taste. Blinking a few times to adjust to the moonlight overhead, Ashe reached up and found a metal and leather muzzle. A familiar muzzle she knew was etched in aetheric runes, and yet different, as it didn't inhibit her mouth from functioning normally.

A muzzle to keep her from accessing her Soul Form.

This is not good.

"NOTHING GETS BY YOU, DEAR BRYNN."

Fuck off, Strix.

"Friends!" a voice boomed, slicing through the buzz like a sharpened blade through flesh. "My friends, hear me! Heed me!"

Ashe propped up on an elbow and found the speaker. It was Ifant Klander. Or, more correctly, the blooddrake Ialtris within the Guilder. His arms were spread wide, bikromi bracelets glinting.

"Good to see you finally join us."

Cyan was sitting in the sand next to her, as was Harlequin. Only Harlequin had a muzzle upon her face, Cyan did not. Why? The fire-haired vicar was rubbing the back of her head, her tresses gummy with blood, her face smeared with dried crimson from her busted nose, the front of the muzzle was grated like a mastiff's, the runes cleanly inscribed upon the grates. Cyan was toying with the Sharded gauntlet on his right wrist, his eyes downcast. Lying next to Ashe was the Hammer of Mother Marrow and the blackened steel daemon blade.

Still in *The Arbiter's Axe*, they were, she realized, but now in the heart of the arena.

Shaped like a bowl with a flat bottom, the stadium's base was covered with sand. Sand made for less sure footing during bouts of bloodletting, but also easier to clean up the aftermaths of said bloodletting. And there was always plenty to go around in Oldport Basin. No mist whatsoever.

Tiers of seats fifty feet above the sand ringed the amphitheater, currently filled to the brim with hooting and hollering fans hoping for a dandy of a spectacle. Seagandr-oil lights shone brightly on each level, illuminating the entire arena in the signature piss-yellow glow of the seagandr's lard. The lowest ring held individual suites separated by canvas bright with colors and crests, the suites leading to the second level of *The Axe's* front atrium. Many of the Guilders permanently purchased these suites and had them adorned with their colors. The remaining tiers were rows after rows of benches, the dregs of Port Sin squished in elbows to assholes. A separate entrance opposite the nicety of the atrium, another way for the separation of the haves and have-nots in Port Sin.

Above the highest row of seats and affixed to the outer wall of the arena were massive aerescreens, one at each corner of the compass. They were twenty feet tall and forty feet in width, their rune-inscribed posts aglow as aethecite ran within. Upon the misty screens was the center of the arena and the three Shards warriors, the screens facing both in and outward as *Aere* shimmered. It seemed despite the ration on aethecite, the blooddrakes wanted all in Port Sin to see and hear their end.

There were two gates on the northern and southern points, the only two ways in or out of the arena itself. The combatants were often lucky if one made it out from the bout alive, as most were to the death, the winner typically put to death in quick succession as a means of acknowledgement of their victory. Rarely were survivors on the bill at *The Arbiter's Axe*.

"Normally I'm the one who's constantly getting knocked out. What's that twice now, Cyan?" Ashe said sardonically. She lifted Mother Marrow's Hammer and the daemon blade. She glared at the postering Klander as he prostrated before the crowd. "I've been knocked out more times than I can count."

"Don't forget that spriggan?" Harlequin kept touching the back of her head and checking if her hand came away with fresh blood. Luckily, it appeared to be staunched.

"You're never going to let me live that down, are you, Harlebub? What's the last thing you remember?"

"Not much," Harlequin said.

"Little more than she," Cyan added, he still wouldn't look at her. Odd. He scratched irritably under his chin. *No…*

Ashe knuckled hers as she thought. "Void Form, Cyan. Can't you tell? We're cut off from our Forms."

"FIGURE THAT OUT ON YOUR OWN, DID YOU?"

I'm two seconds away fro—

"PAY ATTENTION, DEAR BRYNN, AND YOU'LL SEE THAT SOMETHING IS WRONG HERE."

"Great."

"Friends!" Klander shouted over the din. "I promised you a show. And you shall have it!"

Beside Klander in the owner's suite was his Guild advisor, Roqanth, and three others. The Calibrathian elfir was preoccupied, flipping through a folder of papers, probably the previous day's coitus tallies at *The Parlour*, and judging by the size of the folder, it must have been a strong input… output. They glanced up, locked gaze with Ashe, nodded slightly, and resumed their enumeration.

A cloaked figure sat behind the Guild advisor, soft purplish leer coming from within the cowl. Brazen the blooddrake, who was wearing the face of the deceased Cadrianna Benld in public. A child of the House Nightingale in her place of birth.

Next to Solanine was a diminutive youth Ashe wanted to stab aplenty. Evzen. The teenage boy lounged in his seat, legs buttressed atop Klander's armrest, twirling some sort of stick in his mouth, most likely from the tray held by the hobgoblin Nagnoz, who lingered behind his master's more important guests. The boy waved toward her, and she growled a curse in return for misplacing her faith with the urchin.

Speaking of faith, Phlox the Faithful stood at the back of the suite. The twitchy vicar scowled, watching the three untainted warriors of the Scattered Shards in the center of the arena.

The Guilder had his arms spread as he addressed the attendees. "Friends, before you are three members of the Scattered Shards. Three who've betrayed the trust of the Guild and the High Seat. Betrayed the fine people of Oldport Basin."

The seated spectators booed loudly, some tossing objects down into the basin of the arena; food, empty mugs, even some cow chips—which made Ashe wonder who might possibly have the audacity to smuggle in a dried-up disk of cow dung.

"Where *is* Owl and the Shards when you need them?" Harlequin asked, stretching her back. "Looks like a fight's on hand for us."

"Probably diddling with his bird. Mother Marrow's bane, those birds." Ashe began cracking her knuckles. Knuckles sufficiently cracked, she motioned with the Hammer. "There's Maja Carr. Four suites down from Klander."

The elfirish High Seat representative sat with her hands resting on the wall. Shon and Solly took up most of the space in the suite. Maja was staring directly at her, as if she was trying to communicate with her.

"Why is she just sitting there? She should be trying to stop this."

Only Zenith knew what the woman was thinking about all this mummery. Maybe she was complicit?

Complicit or infiltrated? The Guild and the Shards, Solanine had said. Were there more of these blooddrakes in positions of power? Did she believe who she thought it might be?

Please let me be right about this.

"YOU ARE, DEAR BRYNN?"

"The Scattered Shards think they can do as they desire," Klander continued. "Think they can investigate those in the Guild without a warrant. All on a nugget of rumor, no parcel of truth. One of our own, Port Sin, has been taken. Olum Ranhold was arrested just yesterday. No writ, no warrant."

"The seedpods on this bugger is amazing," Ashe said, her brow scrunched. "Wait, do blooddrakes even have seedpods?"

"Your mind goes in wonderful directions at the most inopportune times, my love."

She gave Harlequin a sidelong glance.

"The Scattered Shards hung Florin Tified for conspiracy." Klander-Ialtris' voice rose, pointing aggressively toward them. "But no word has come down from the grand quaestor as to what the conspiracy is. No truths given. Just a dead man and his family. A friend of mine until the very end! And now Olum Ranhold? The dearest of friends to me." He thrust his hand in the direction of the Shards tower in the Guild Politic. "And what of Neron Hobb? Her body was found in her chamber. Who was first on the scene?"

The crowd bellowed as one, "THE SCATTERED SHARDS!"

"Precisely, friends!"

Cyan stood. Many in the crowd jeered as he straightened his cassock and brought his Sharded gauntlet over his right wrist. Awkwardly. Her taskmaster's aura was all over the place, unsettled, he was.

"DEAR BRYNN..."

I know, Strix. I know.

"The would-be-vicar here," Klander said, referring specifically to her, "this scion of the corruption. This Lady Drakeslayer, the murderer of Mother Marrow if the rumors are to be believed. A Godslayer. Claims to have killed one of the Pentax gods. Her taskmaster was supposedly there as well. Who's to say they didn't orchestrate this entire conspiracy? They're clearly capable of such an act. Kill a goddess?"

The crowd went nuts, ate it all up like a hungry cyclops descending upon an apple orchard.

"This is ridiculous," she said. "How do these fools fall for such things?"

"Men are stupid," Cyan said calmly. Too calmly. "A single man can goad many falsities into truth. Especially politicians. Especially man. You are the fool if you think otherwise."

"But that's not all, dear friends," Klander snarled. Now that Ashe knew he was no man, but was a blooddrake, snarling was a good way to describe the vitriolic speech. "No, they weren't finished. We've just learned the death of another cherished friend of mine. It's with a heavy heart, Port Sin, I must tell you, Danma Dil has been murdered."

The audience let out a collective gasp as if the Guilder of the Chain was as saintly as an augur of the Shards, not a devious harpy devouring the souls, and coin, of pipefiends by the droves.

But why this farce? What was she still missing? How does this trial by public opinion fit into the blooddrake's plans for her?

What game do you play, Solanine?

"These servants of the Scattered Shards are liars and frauds," Klander said through the silence of the audience. "Zenith would have them punished!"

"Yes, punished," Cyan said. His aura shifting to dark crimson engulfed in a sea of purple.

O, Cyan…

The cacophony of applause shook the entirety of *The Arbiter's Axe*. "PUNISH THEM! PUNISH THEM! PUNISH THEM!"

The arena's gate shuddered as it was drawn open, sand waterfalling down the heavy steel beams. A shrill cry echoed from within the bowel of *The Axe*, a piercing wail freezing the blood of the spectators.

Ashe knew the sound. "We're fucked." She lifted the Hammer and the daemon blade. "We've got no aetheurgy. And there isn't any mist for me to call on. Only the Strix." She let go of the daemon blade and instantly it separated into six individual replicas, hanging in the air.

"You think this the only punishment?" Cyan growled under his breath, turning away from the noise and squaring up to them. His normally hard dark irises and red pupils flashed lavender. "You think this is all we have writ for you, Godsblood? Fool you are."

Harlequin gasped, realization dawning on her as Ashe merely grunted. Fucking blooddrakes.

"Why?"

"Why do you think, Godsblood?" the blooddrake within her former taskmaster said. It was Cyan's voice, but it wasn't him.

She wanted to scream, could feel it bubbling within.

"NOT YET, DEAR BRYNN. MOURN HIM LATER."

Easy for you to say, Strix.

"NO, IT IS NOT..."

"I told you, child," the drake wearing Cyan's flesh said, "you must lead us to the Seal. There is but only one way. Bring it forth."

Harlequin tensed; her pair of bluish iron axes raised. Tears flowed from her eyes. "You bastards."

The purplish drake gaze shifted toward the vicar. "You think the pain Solanine gifted you upon Gargantua was the last you would suffer, girl? I haven't even begun to bring you suffering."

Ashe realized now the blooddrake wasn't Solanine, but what of the one wearing her mother's flesh in the Guilder's box? Was that the real Solanine? Her anger rose, the desire to scream brewing even stronger. That meant three blooddrakes in Port Sin. And she didn't know which was which. Fuck.

A roar within the bowels of the arena.

The blooddrake grinned behind Cyan's face. "Watch, Godsblood, as we take everything you hold dear." The bloodrake in her taskmaster's body took many steps back as the crowd crowed in anticipation.

A massive bulk emerged from the darkness beyond the gate. A blunted head poked into the moonlight, snapped and wailed as it scanned the wall-to-wall living painting of flesh in the amphitheater's seats. A hushed silence settled over the crowd as the beast slithered into the arena, the aerescreens trained directly on it.

It was an aerovern.

The aerovern's snout was flat as if the beast had run directly into a marble wall and lost. Teeth longer than Ashe's arm protruded in almost a wicked smile as the creature examined them, its tiny nostrils flaring, breathing the prospective prey's scent in. From across the arena's sandy base, the aerovern's breath smelled like someone dunked a thousand pairs of sweaty socks into a gassy bog and left them to fester in the sun for a year. Little, bony spikes ran in three rows from the tip of the aerovern's snout to the rounded part of its head over the eyes, where the spikes fanned out more than three feet in a beard-like pattern from the cheeks to under the jaw. Every inch of the aerovern's head was covered in golden scales as wide Ashe's hand. They gleamed like polished metal, a shine only visible in nature. It was beauty in its purest form. And deadly.

It stalked around *The Axe's* arena basin slowly, this grievous draconem of the Pentax Gods. Twin wings dug into the sand silently, unable to take flight due to their shredded membranes, leaving it hobbled as it moved along the ground, yet still dangerous. It was deathly quiet, almost as if Ashe had stuffed wool into her ears during a thunderstorm. Unlike a bird's wing, affixed at the tips were deadly claws that could skewer a boar and his mate in a single swipe. Its body, while golden scaled, was covered in a layer of frost. It glistened on the twin wing muscles, down its sinewy belly toward the enormously robust hind legs. Its tail was as long as its torso but curled about like a piglet's, although this tail served a purpose in a hunt, whereas a piglet's just looked adorable.

The eyes, praise Zenith, were a crimson color and were as hard as any Ashe had ever seen. Normally an aerovern's eyes were honey-yellow, but since this drake's was red, that just made things far more difficult because this aerovern had the red eyes of a daemon. Of course.

"It's a bloody juvenile." Harlequin gripped her hand axes, the head milky blue in the nightturn moonshine.

"No shit, Harle-bub."

"Then why are you pissing your cassock?"

"We don't have our aetheurgy, you privy tease. A juvenile can still brochette us like a kebob. Not exactly how I want to die."

"You act like teasing your privy is a bad thing."

"Well… okay, true. You have a bloody point. Still, we're fucked. Proper fucked." She glared across the arena at the blooddrake within Cyan, his aura pulsating bloodred. "I'm going to gut that cu—"

The aerovern raised its flat snout and roared into the evenfall.

Ashe set her feet square to the juvenile daemonized drake, gripping the Hammer with a white-knuckled fist. She'd never fought a drake without the use of aetheurgy. Nobody was that stupid. Draconem were far too fast and too strong, no man could dance with a drake without aether. Then throw on the fact the beast was daemonized.

"What's the meaning of this?" bellowed a voice from the tiers.

It was Grand Quaestor Owl, along with a handful of quaestors. Ashe felt some relief that the warriors of the Shards were on hand, able to diffuse this farce. But the aerovern was already loose, it still had the potential for a full-on bloodbath.

Probably hers.

"This is your Lady Drakeslayer, Port Sin!" Klander's voice rang about *The Axe*, ignoring the grand quaestor's demand. "Let us see what this slayer of Gods is made of!"

As the crowd erupted, their bloodlust oozing, Ashe saw that the third blooddrake now knelt in the suite, cloak pulled back to reveal naked flesh on Cadrianna Benld's breast and abdomen. Dozens of thick scars wept blood as the drake within pierced the once living tissue with a black knife.

What was the drake doing?

A pitch-black mist seeped from the bloody scars on the aetheurgist's, nay, blooddrake's skin. It flashed red as blooms of light sparked within the mist.

"STEADY, DEAR BRYNN. THIS ONE IS NOT FOR YOU."

She glanced sideways at Harlequin. The woman was shaking, tears streaming down her freckled cheeks.

More wails rose from within the basin and not from the aerovern as the black mist poured over the walls, crackling with energy. Within the mist a figure materialized. Skin red like stained marble. Coarse hair with spikes of ivory within the mane. Face parting in serrated teeth under blazing red eyes. Limbs ending in claws. Lean and cruel.

It was Amaranth the Pure, but a daemon.

Leaning against the arena's wall, Cyan smiled. No, the blooddrake within smiled.

Ashe wanted to scream.

XXXV
LOJEN

"HOLD THE GATE!" Titen's voice carried over the babel of battle as Lojen and Ruane burst out of the Obelisk with a handful of legionnaires, crossing the bridge spanning to the Upper City.

A winged daemon shrieked overhead, diving. Lojen ducked instinctively but one of the legionnaires holding the bridge wasn't so lucky. The daemon—eight-foot torso with a barbed tail and no back legs—swooped down and plucked the unfortunate elfir from his post with forelimb talons longer than Lojen's forearm, piercing the drake scale cuirass like it was soft cheese. The man screamed as the winged daemon lifted him upward before dropping him unceremoniously into the gap between the two structures, his scream suddenly cut off with a thick squelch.

The daemon banked in the air and swung back toward the drakken siblings; teeth pulled back in a rictus grin as it dove. The Hymn of War serenaded Lojen's earholes as he braced for the daemon's impact, his wardkeeper horns radiating aether. He gripped his longknife, readying a thrust.

But before the daemon's outstretched claws reached him, a daemon-killing spear tip burst through its veiny wings, shearing the gossamer fiber, sending the daemon screeching into a fall where it hit the bridge. Its claws sought purchase, but another spear stabbed through its arm. The spawned nightmare of the void fell to its death between the Obelisk and the Upper City.

Lojen had no idea which of the legionnaires had saved him, but it mattered not, the group bolted the length of the bridge into the Upper City, which was cloyed with frightened nobleborn. Guilders and rich alike, huddled close together outside the bridges, begging for sanctuary within the great Obelisk. The soldiers of the Legion barely held them in check. Fools they'd been to stay behind.

As Lojen and his sister fought through the mass of men and women in their lush clothing and their lavish jewelry, a tremor shook the entire mega-city, one so vicious, the entire upper tier seemed to shake. The quake was accompanied by a collective screech of daemons, the yowls high-pitched and piercing. Some of the villas cracked, balconies falling under the weight of greed, columns and peristyles toppling. The people screamed in terror, pushing forward even more. Stolae and suits bloodied and torn as the mob pressed onward to safety in the Obelisk.

Despite the immediate threat, Lojen couldn't help but recall the fear in Drenth last summer, it was too similar. Eerily similar.

Once past the press of man flesh, they rushed across the open expanse of the Upper City toward the Ceveo. The once pristine upper tier had been trampled in the fright. Plants flattened and trees uprooted. Statues overturned. Bloody smears everywhere, so too were bodies and their parts.

The lone, corkscrew road connecting the tiers of the mountain was barely held by the Legion, less than fifty by Lojen's count as they skidded to a stop. The portcullis was still standing, but the gates were being bombarded by a slew of jagged teeth and sharpened claws. The gate was convexing inward while the legionnaires stabbed their spears through the metal bars. Wheellocks fired repeatedly into the void-wrought hides, pinging off hardened scale. The sound unbearable.

Winged daemons swooped downward toward the defenders while spears were thrust upwards. Twisted bodies littered the ground surrounding the gates, ungodsly shrieks crying in death. Men and women of the Legion were dropping like flies, their drake scale no match for the might of the Fallen's horde.

It was a losing battle.

The Golden Sword was amongst the legionnaires holding the Ceveo's gate. The fabled blade was a bright golden hue as *Aere* crackled around it with little flashes of lightning, peridot gemstone was brilliant. The heir to the Golden Throne was screaming for his soldiers to hold, his voice clear and strong. Blood trickled down his cheek, whether from one of his own wounds or from the dead, Lojen knew not.

Finn and Wick, plus other legionnaires, came from a full sprint down one of the other bridges connected to the Obelisk. Finn held a curved blade that must have been from an Imperium soldier, while Wick held his dueling knives in both paws.

"Look out!" someone yelled.

All eyes turned toward the greenish skyline. Something flew from above, not a daemon, but manmade. It took a few blinks for Lojen to realize it was the tram car that rode up and down the Ceveo. The metal carriage flew over the portcullis and crashed into the defenders, crushing many. Metal shards broke off and struck others, including the Golden Sword. Titen went to a knee as blood covered his face. Screams aplenty, both in death as they were buried under the tram and from those wounded. Dust and shrapnel filled the upper tier, forcing the too-few defenders back.

The gates buckled but still held. Somehow.

Lojen blinked away the soot that had gotten into his eyes, cursing the Fallen. It was too much, the attack too strong. They could never hold the Ceveo like this.

A pair of legionnaires hauled Titen away from the gates, where the big elfir shook away the pain in his ruined face, ordering them back into the fray. He glanced at his brother, before spinning back.

"Titen, stop," Finn said, reaching for the elder Dunleith. There was desperation within Finn's voice. One that Lojen hadn't heard before. One that might have simply been a brother trying to stop a sibling from throwing their life away needlessly.

The Golden Sword paused. "Finnus, now is not the time. You shouldn't be here."

"Are you fucking kidding me? None of us should be here."

Titen turned. "Go back to the Obelisk, Finn. That's an order." He hefted the blazing blade. "Go!"

"And leave you here?" Finn said. "You'd be foolish to think I'd do that, brother-friend. Not after Emre."

The gate groaned as the horde from the Pit pushed, the Legion barely holding on. Steel grated on stone. Claws slashed. Wheellocks kept firing. Bellows and screams. Death on both sides.

They crouched as another winged daemon descended upon them. It was an aerovern by the look of it, a smaller one. It swooped down and its back legs grabbed at a legionnaire while its barbed tail skewed another, lifting both into the air above Gandtril. The pair fell to the ground with such force, their bodies disintegrated upon impact.

Lojen turned from the sight but kept an eye upon the daemonized drake as it skated through the sky, diving down into the Lower City in another fell attack.

Daemonized draconem, how did the Pentax allow such a thing?

"We have to fall back, Lord Sword," an exhausted legionnaire said. The woman held her left arm as blood poured from a wound that Lojen knew would take said arm if not treated immediately.

"We cannot leave the gate," Titen declared, his face determined to hold at all costs. It was folly that drove him. "We lost the Lower City, we cannot lose the Upper. Stay, legionnaires. Fight with Honor and Blood!"

Lojen felt the need to say something, he was a wardkeeper, and wardkeepers were meant to advise. But he was at a loss. *Father, what should I say?*

"Titen," Finn started, "we have t—"

Before Finn could finish his plea, the gate shuddered as the biggest daemon Lojen had ever seen struck it. Multiple bars flew from their moorings, spearing legionnaires as they ducked, killing those precious few defenders. The beast—hairy and corded with muscles—struck the gate once again, the rune-enhanced stone of the portcullis crumbling. Another slam and the gate flew off its hinges, crashing into the defenders.

The daemon roared as it leapt onto the upper tier, landing upon the fallen gate, crushing those poor souls trapped underneath. With a howl borne of the Pit, the horde surged forward, claws and teeth seeking those still standing.

"WARDKEEPER! I SENSE YOUR AETHER," the humongous daemon howled, red eyes of fury searching the defenders. *"YOU CANNOT HIDE FROM LEMURES, AEGIS."*

Aegis?

Lojen dragged Ruane back by her sleeveless vest, nearly tripping over his own tail. She snarled at him but kept her footing. Lojen spun and darted toward a villa as a swarm of daemons came their way. Ruane was hot on his tail but he lost sight of the Dunleiths and Wick, no telling where the surviving legionnaires went. Chaos was all that existed for him. Chaos and death.

The drakken siblings cut across the open streets of the Upper City, half a dozen daemons closing in. Away from the safety of the Obelisk, unfortunately. The wound in Lojen's side ached as he ran. He could hear Ruane's labored breathing as they dashed between two large villas. The screeches of the daemons followed them as those claws met the smooth marble of the homes, slashing and destroying. Fear drove Lojen.

"WARDKEEPER! YOU CANNOT RUN FROM LEMURES! I CAN SMELL YOUR AETHER AS YOU FLEE!"

"Where are you going?" Ruane asked, her tongue lapping her snout. "And why is that daemon after you?"

"We have to get back to the bridges." He couldn't find the answer to her second question. Ever since the village in the Sea, he pondered that question.

"They're the other way, Scurred Hat—" she jerked forward as a daemon with six thin limbs had climbed the marble villa and dove at her. Teeth snapped as she rolled, bringing her longknife up into the carapace belly. It wailed as she stabbed it.

Another daemon, this one with a head like a misshapen boar, rammed into Lojen's gut. Fire burst in his wounded side, sending him to his backside with the daemon landing atop him. The Hymn of War sang in his soul, his roar joining the chorus. Aether rippled up and down his horns as he bellowed, lifting the daemon clear from him and tossing it into the other daemons circling them.

Lojen jumped to his feet and then into the oncoming void beasts. His claws met theirs. His lips drew back into a smile of teeth to match theirs. Lost he was in the dance of wardkeeping.

One struck at him with a limb that reminded him of a bone sword but was coated in pustules and sores. He backhanded the limb away with his longknife, jabbing his own claw deep into the daemon's chest, reaching for the beating black heart, if there was one. His claw rent straight through the creature, its spine shattering. Lifting the dead daemon, he threw it into the one beside it, both the dead and the daemon tumbled.

A claw grazed his exoscales, but no pain registered. He brought his own talons down on the daemon that had struck him, snapping bone and sinew in one ferocious blow. A parry with his longknife saw another attack thwarted. Within his breast, the Hymn blared, filling him with unbridled fury. Aether danced along his horns as he swirled into another daemon and swung his fist at the bifurcated jaw, rending it further.

Pushed back, he grabbed at the hanging vines attached to the wall of the nearest villa. Yanking them free, connected stones the size of his torso came crashing down, striking one of the daemons. He wrapped the vines around his wrist and began swinging the stones overhead, slamming the rock into another daemon, the explosion of dust and grit sending the daemon flying.

Ruane's roar echoed off the villas as she grabbed at a daemon, tearing one of its arms off with a sickening pop. She swung the dismembered limb like a club, knocking askew another daemon as Lojen rammed his horns into the gullet of another, skewering it against the villa's wall. A final shriek cut off as the drakken siblings stood amongst the dead daemons. The Hymn was crescendoing.

Lojen grabbed his sister's arm, and she growled at him, ready to strike, only to realize it was him. "Come on, Ru."

They took off, rushing through the once manicured yard toward the rear of the villa, hopping the waist-high decorative fence. Past a garden and through the yard of another villa before exiting into a street that would lead them back to the Obelisk.

The sounds of death filled the air, drowning out the Hymn. Gandtril was lost, there was no saving it.

"How do we stop them, Lojen?"

A gigantic thump landed in front of him, sending him to his backside once more. Ruane unleashed a healthy roar, leaping at the void-wrought creature before them. She was batted away like one shooed away gnats. Ruane crashed into a statue of a man holding a balance, destroying the piece of art in a blast of dust and rubble. She slid to a stop more than thirty feet away, balled up and not moving.

A daemon, the same that'd broken through the Ceveo's gate stalked toward him. It was massive, easily taller than he by three or more feet. On four legs it moved, gracefully like a feline hunting a mouse. From its forelimbs were chains wrapped around thrice, broken and covered in gore. It had black hair, coarse as frozen moss, all along its body. The lower jaw jutted out past the upper, rows upon rows of serrated teeth like a shark's. The neck was as thick as an auroch, bleeding sores where the jaw met neck. Its eyes, they were as red as a blazing garnet, unmistakable hatred filling them. Hatred for all things living.

"WARDKEEPER, THERE YOU ARE," the daemon gnarred, its jaw quirking in an almost smile. *"RUN, YOU CANNOT. THE FALLEN DESIRES YOUR BLOOD. AND LEMURES NEVER FAILS."*

Lojen backed away cautiously as the daemon prowled closer. He glanced toward Ruane, who was now twitching, a groan along with it. His back brushed against a ragged stump, the rest of the tree broken off to his left. There was nowhere for him to flee.

Beyond Ruane, he spied one of the entrance bridges to the Obelisk. Daemons and black-clad soldiers of the Fallen's army closed in upon the frightened people of Gandtril. Legionnaires struggled to hold them back. Down came the winged ones, plucking people at will. Spears flashed, cries echoed. Blood was spilled. Death the ultimate tithe.

The last bastion of hope was the Obelisk, but they were still too far from it. The daemons and enemy between them and safety. The chained daemon Lemures was the biggest threat of them all. It was fight this daemon or die. Odds he didn't exactly care for.

Ruane got into a crouching position, her body angled toward the daemon's back. He could see her reaching for her dropped longknife, reading her thoughts clear as a sunlit day.

"Ru, no!" he screamed at her. The daemon stopped, one majestic, clawed arm raised, the chain dangling against the cobbled stones. Head turning. "Run, Ru! Make it to the Obelisk where you can!"

Lemures turned back to face him, that grin of teeth and death freezing his heart, the Hymn the only thing keeping him from soiling his trousers.

The song of the wardkeeper filled him, his eyes nearly rolling back. There was only one way. He knew it now. This was where honor and duty met the inescapable touch of Death.

Lojen slowly stood, aether coursing his veins, the song of the Pentax raging within like a fire. He threw his head abaft and let out the loudest, deepest, most carnal roar he'd ever sung.

For Ruane. For Finn and Wick. For his father. For Merj. For him.

And then he charged.

XXXVI
ASHE

ASHE'S ASSHOLE WAS clenched so tight, even Mother Marrow's Hammer wouldn't be able to drive a spike up it.

Killing a solitary drake, especially a juvenile, wasn't the hard part. No, the hard part was to not get perished in the process by a godsdamned daemon version. Then throw in a daemonized Amaranth the Pure as a garnish to this tincture of bosh, without their aetheurgy to aid them, Ashe and Harlequin were swimming up a stream of shit.

And that didn't even include the blooddrake wearing Cyan's flesh. If the fucker decided to join the fray, there was no victory to be had here.

The daemonized aerovern tossed sand with every move, sizing them up. From furrowed winged claw to the highest point of the shoulder where wing met shoulder, was maybe six feet, and from snout to the beginning of the tail, maybe ten, thus telling Ashe this creature was barely past hatching, probably only a few months old.

But a newborn draconem of one of the greater orders was still a formidable opponent fresh from the egg even without being birthed by the Pit.

The daemon that was once an untainted warrior of the Scattered Shards glided across the arena like a cat hunting, silent where the aerovern was loud. Claws perked, ready to tear them apart, rending their flesh. Red eyes bearing ugly hatred, showing none of the woman Ashe had known. None of the gentle Amaranth.

She and Harlequin put their backs to one another, their weapons readied. The aerovern threw its head back and roared into the nightturn sky. Tiny lightning sparks shot out, electricity snapping and crinkling. The crowd jeered and jostled, sending agitating vibes into the arena, which only stoked the young aerovern further like a young buck's swagger in trying to prove itself to potential mates.

With that, the aerovern and the daemonized vicar attacked.

Shredded wings furled about the frost-coated body of the pouncing aerovern, an aerodynamism only seen in nature. Mouth of razor-sharp teeth snarling. Sand flew behind as forceful hind legs gave sudden propulsion. Tail whipping and straightening like a javelin.

The daemonized vicar bounded on all fours like a panther. Teeth snapping, armored body twisting and contorting in a haze of blackened mist.

Before they were crushed to a daemonized-draconem pulpy snack, Ashe shoved Harlequin out of the way. The daemon vicar collided with Ashe, both flailing into the sand. She grunted under the weight of the creature, a hammer blow ringing against the daemon's Pit-wrought armored flesh. Mother Marrow's boon sent the daemon flying across the arena. As all this happened, Ashe rolled head over ass, scrambling to her feet as the aerovern's tail lashed, pointed barb nearly skewering her like plump sausages over a campfire.

Wings folding under its body, the aerovern gracefully maneuvered like the apex predator it was. Frost fell from the creature's scales, sizzling into vapor as it touched the grains of earth underfoot. Instantly, it was upright, coiled tail cracking like a whip. The young draconem roared anew, lightning dancing across the sand in angry bursts as blackened mist curled around.

"I think we pissed it off," Ashe said through the Void Form muzzle. The black mist of the blooddrake's conjuring stabbed at her ankles, and she swore she could feel the aether within it reaching for her.

"Umm… you think?" Harlequin pawed sand from her eyes as she stood next to Ashe. "Where's that fucking blooddrake?"

Never taking her eyes off the aerovern, nor the now rising Amaranth, Ashe spied her taskmaster out of her peripherals. He, no, the blooddrake was still standing against the arena's wall, arms crossed, purple eyes gleaming, aura full of garnet.

The young draconem snarled and flicked sand, preparing another assault. Ashe rolled her shoulders. "Vertical pinscher."

Harlequin shoved a red curl from her yellow-pupiled, grey-green eyes. "You want to do what now?"

"You heard me," Ashe said, the fear coursing through her slowly becoming adrenaline. The longer they waited, the worse it would be. Draconem didn't tire as man did. They needed to attack now, attack for the kill before the beast could kill them. Simple as that. "Go left. Come at it with all you got. Strix, if you please." The daemon blade's six owl-winged replicas hung suspended. "To the right, good Strix."

"YES, DEAR BRYNN." There was a melancholy within the daemon blade's answer, but Ashe had no time to worry about what could possibly make the weapon so downcast.

"And you're going to take the middle? You're bloody nuts, Ashe. That daemon in the Pure is going to kill us both."

"Perhaps." She grinned. "On my first step, Harle-bub. And watch out for the tail."

"You've lost your mind, love."

"And that's why you love me, Harle-bub."

Ashe bent her knees, lifted Mother Marrow's Hammer over her head with both hands. Without her aetheurgy, the vertical pinscher was a rookie mistake designed to get them devoured or electrocuted to a crisp, but Ashe knew of no other option, limited as they were in both arsenal and space. It would have to suffice.

The aerovern's flat snout parted, sending static bolts fizzling atop the inky mist. Irritation and annoyance. Anger brimming. It mauled *The Axe's* floor with shredded wingtips.

"Now!" she screamed, running directly for the aerovern's head. The six blades of the Strix flew right, Harlequin the Resolute to the left, both at forty-five-degree angles.

The crowd "AHHH'ed!" in unison.

The aerovern reacted to her attack as she intended. The beast drew back, curling its neck into an S shape. Mouth agape, teeth glistening in frosty saliva, lightningsac beginning to draw aether. A second was all it took, a second to gather its aether. Its *Aere*.

Calculating it would aim to end her threat quickly, Ashe put all her flagging strength into her jump.

The electrical current of *Aere* discharged from the aerovern's lightningsac, striking the footprint left by Ashe's boot. She sailed over the blast, feeling its galvanism shock her system, electricity of *Aere* surging about her flesh, raising the tiny hairs of her arms as her skin grew hot. She brought the Hammer down, slamming the green head into one of the aerovern's daemon-red, angry eyes.

A moment later, Harlequin and the Strix collided with axe and blackened blades against either flank, slashing with bluish iron, stabbing with the power of the void. The draconem shrieked, lightning crepitating all about as it flailed in pain.

The daemonized Amaranth the Pure sprang upon Harlequin, the fire-haired vicar barely bringing her bluish iron axes up to bear in time to soften the blows.

The crowd went insane with bloodlust. "KILL! KILL! KILL!"

Ashe had no time to celebrate her victorious attack as the aerovern swung its barbed tail, catching her across the breast, shearing through her cassock, biting deep into the leather vest underneath. She went flying before skidding to a stop in the center of the arena, the Hammer spinning from her grip. Out of breath, she felt pain lance her chest, multiple ribs undoubtedly broken.

The aerovern's bulk shouldered Harlequin and Amaranth aside with a swipe of its shredded wing, sending the vicar and former vicar careening into the arena's wall, bundling into a cassock of bruised bones and muscle, groaning behind her muzzle. The daemon also surprisingly dazed.

The blades of the Strix stabbed at the beast while the draconem tried to slap at the hovering blackened steel like a cornered scorpion lashing out with a barbed stinger. Minute flashes of frosty light when folded steel met scale. A crying sound in Ashe's mind, a sob coming from the Strix.

Beyond the aerovern, the godsdamned blooddrake remained watching from within Cyan's flesh. Unmoved, unbothered.

Voices waterfalled down from the tiers, the spectators jeered at her. "COWARD! LIAR! FAKE!"

Ashe screamed at the pain in her chest as she attempted to stand. Each movement was like a hot knife. She struggled to pull in a full breath, leaving her winded. Blood dribbled down her side, a wound she found rent all along her lefthand ribcage. The dirty midnight of her cassock was flush with sanguine. The fleeting light grey mist was useless as the black mist overpowered it.

But she had to do something. Probably something stupid. How she planned to do so without a weapon, her aetheurgy locked behind the Void Form muzzle, and bleeding like a stuck pig, she hadn't a clue.

She'd find a way, Lady Drakeslayer always did.

"Hey!" The aerovern stopped trying to slap the floating Strix blades and turned its one-eyed, pancake-snouted attention in her direction. "Yeah, you. Over here!" She grunted as she waved at the draconem. "That's it, you little bastard. It's me you want!"

"Ashe, no!" Harlequin yelled across the arena, trying to ward off the daemon's claws with a thrust of her axe. But the daemon swatted it away and instead caught her across her shoulder with a claw. Harlequin went down and the daemon leapt atop her, a cry echoing around the stony amphitheater.

The aerovern plowed toward her, sand flinging as it charged.

Her life flashed before her.

Ever since Drenth, the girl named Ashe had been ready to die. A past that she had never known, uncovered after seventeen long years, the impenetrable tower held aloft where nothing could harm her or her family had come crashing down that day. Her parents taken from her again, only to know them but a pittance of what should have been a lifetime in their company.

Death was but the only respite.

Going back to her training with the Scattered Shards, a place that had meant so little to the girl named Lilia before Drenth, but now was all she would ever know once more. Each case after her return she'd known it might be her last, with the draconem unsettled after her killing of the vvyrms. Danger lurked with every hunt; every lair wrought with it. And she was content with it. Even when she'd escape unharmed from each hunt, her reputation growing with every successive kill.

Death was but only the next step.

So many had she seen die over the years. Fleeting friendships before Drenth, never growing close to those training under Cyan, not even Harlequin. Long had she expected those untainted warriors of the Shards to all die and fade, axes to fall beside her should she become a vicar. Those bonds she'd formed while seeking the truth of her past. Evander. Elian. Wren. Mother. Father.

Death was but only a beginning.

But now, as she saw her taskmaster stolen from her by a hateful blooddrake and her budding lover's life on the brink, Ashe felt something else. Something she never expected. Something else driving away the specter of death like a lamp in the void.

The need to live.

A fire burned inside her; one so bright it nearly consumed every atom that was the Godsblood named Brynn Benld. The ignition was instant, as if the flames had only been awaiting her spark, harkening for a release. The black mist within the arena reached toward her, begging for her to take control. There was a familiar wailing accompanying the explosion, a piercing lament from the void, a place beyond the realm of the living. Death waiting for the realm of Life.

The black mist that swirled around the basin, borne of Nocturne's vile Void Form, she summoned to her as she did with the grey. It heeded her command, heeded her call. It cocooned her.

Noctis and Eminence colliding within her soul.

Pain no longer, reknit back to Zenith's perfection. Broken ribs broken no more. Blood-covered side sewn and unmarred, only the red stain on her cassock. A phoenix rising from the ashes unburnt. Arms spread; the fire burned a thousandfold. The torrent a firestorm, filling her with the cleansing power of Fire.

Of *Ignis.*

Of a Godsblood.

"THOU ARE THE ONE, BRYNN BENLD," said a voice she did not recognize in a slight slur. It wasn't the Strix, but more male-sounding, drunk almost. ***"USE MINE STRENGTH, COMBINE IT WITH THOU'S, GODSBLOOD."***

Ashe lowered her head, facing the charging aerovern, and she knew. She could feel the aether of *Ignis* all around her. Knew that her normally all-white eyes glowed a fiery red. She knew the feeling of a god, the same as when she felt Mother Marrow. It was Brio, the Wayward Son.

Left arm, palm up, the wailing circling like soulless ghosts in her ears. The non-hot flames of *Ignis* danced down the runes tattooed into her skin in tune with her thumping heart. The diamond in the center of her palm erupted, a familiar weight suddenly in her grip: the Hammer.

It was then she screamed.

The aetheric muzzle disintegrated as she unleashed pure aether of both crystals of Life and Death. Her shout was unbridled carnality. Essence without bounds.

The aerovern's jaws widened in the anticipated kill, only for the explosive CRACK! of shattered teeth, head wrenched sideways. The beast sailed across the arena and crashed into one of the walls, the stone of *The Arbiter's Axe* falling under its massive bulk, exploding over Port Sin in a plume of dust.

And on she screamed. Black and grey mist rising upward like a spike. Nothing would stop her now.

The first tier of suites collapsed upon itself. Guilders caught in the downslide lost in the shower of dust and stone. The higher tiers of Oldport's sinners creaked and broke, sending terrified onlookers down into the newly hewn exit. Others scrambling to a handhold, reaching for friends, anything to not fall victim. The blooddrake within her former taskmaster and the daemon of Amaranth the Pure disappeared in the melee. As did the blooddrake in her mother's flesh, as well as the blooddrake donning Klander skin. And Evzen and Roqanth.

Harlequin had been thrown by the daemonized Amaranth into the center of the arena, skidding to a stop below Ashe. She balled up as Ashe screamed over her prone form.

Ashe stood in the center of the arena, screaming. In her hand was the green Hammer of Mother Marrow, but it was now blazing crimson of Brio's *Ignis*. She felt alive like never before, the Hammer and entire left arm was a beacon of *Ignis*, like a lighthouse guiding wayward ships.

Finally, her scream ended, stunning the undamaged section of the arena into silence as the spike of mist collapsed upon itself.

And then the crowd roared. "LADY DRAKESLAYER! LADY DRAKESLAYER!"

"Ashe?" Harlequin stood beside her, dusty, a red gash along her freckled cheek. Her muzzle had been broken. "Ashe?"

Shaking her head, the aether of *Ignis* faded, the great burning within fading. She felt hale, a pulmo cough rearing its ugly head. Weakness taking over as the black mist fled from her. The grey remaining by her side. She glanced at the older vicar. "Harle-bub?"

Amidst the cries of the wounded and the cheering spectators, a gurgling roar rose.

Harlequin grabbed her by the elbow, drawing her away from Maja Carr's intense stare from across the arena, still seated in her suite. "The aerovern, love."

"Zenith's cock," Ashe said through a pulmo cough. Who was Maja? Of the blooddrake in Cyan's flesh, there was nothing. *Fuck.* "Come on."

They wove through the wreckage of *The Axe's* outer wall, passing a wounded entourage of warriors of the Scattered Shards, including an unconscious Grand Quaestor Owl, chasing after the fleeing aerovern as it clobbered into everything, its bulk ripping through stalls of the Barter Yard, pummeling through the walls of buildings, trampling people dumb enough to get in its way. Others skittered about, fleeing, crying, and screaming.

Everything crackled with *Aere*, slick with frost.

XXXVII
FINN

IT ALL HAPPENED so fast; Finn didn't realize what had happened until he was trundled into a villa's second floor bedroom.

First, the largest daemon Finn had ever seen other than the Fallen's firedrake Cinder broke through the gate at the Ceveo, sending the Legion into a bloody retreat, bodies falling every which way. The death toll of legionnaires staggering as the daemons behind the big one surged onto the upper tier.

Second, in the unfolding melee, Finn and Wick had been thrown from their feet, one of the bars from the gate striking them both horizontally, Finn in the chest and Wick in the head. The lapin crumpled to the ground. In the fall, Finn smacked his head upon a cobble, stars filling his eyesight. Titen was also struck by something, falling to the side as the daemons trampled the Legion struggling to hold the gate.

Third, Finn was pulled from the path of the oncoming horde by his chaperones, Alyx and Davel. The two legionnaires that had become his constant shadow half-dragged, half-carried him across the cobbled stones of the upper tier toward one of the nearest villas. They kicked through the front door, shoving it closed behind them, piling furniture and whatever else they could find.

Finally, they helped Finn up the grand staircase that would rival any Guilder's as the ostentatious chandelier shook as daemons raged at the doors below. They shoved him into the Guilder's chamber, sliding the bolt lock in place.

Finn, groggy from the smack to his favorite head, he turned toward the legionnaires. "I thi—"

A gurgling cry erupted from Davel's surprised agape lips as Alyx ran him through with a flaming dagger. Blood welled from the man's seared throat, only to release steam as it cauterized from within the legionnaire's flesh. Davel drooped to the floor, his daemon-killing spear clattering into the center of the room amongst piles of strewn stolae, blood trickling from the burnt wound, eyes glazed as his life left him.

Stumbling backward, Finn rammed into the Guilder's bed, backside striking one of the posts, his eyesight still seeing double from the hit at the gate. "What? Why?"

"You are to die, Finnus Dunleith." The legionnaire's eyes were trained on him, contempt filled. "The Fallen will cleanse the Dunleith line and the Peridot will be his."

The realization came to Finn in his woozy state. "You murdered Jaterral?" He plopped onto the bed, nearly slipping to the ground on the satin duvet, blackness creeping into his peripherals. He must have hit his head harder than he'd thought.

The legionnaire nodded. "And your precious optio. An inconvenience. But he'd discovered me sending word to the Fallen and had to be dealt with. Such a waste of life, but I did enjoy killing that smarmy fuck. He was insufferable to listen to each and every day of training. Always whining on and on about spear forms, sword techniques. Quite draining."

"But why the…" Gods above, his head hurt. Something inside him tingled. His parch reserves, what little remained, they itched to be used. "Why the ruse?"

Alyx prowled closer, the glowing dagger in his fist aflame. Little licks of aether, the rune of *Ignis* etched onto the blade. "Does it matter?"

"You… a scourge?" Hand to his head, Finn swayed to the side.

Alyx came ever nearer, almost close enough to smell the man's breath. "Too lost in your drunken sorrow to see it. Pity. I had heard from some of the others you were the smartest of Emre Benld's cadre. Could've fooled me."

And that's when Finn unleashed the last of his parch. It was barely more than a trickle, but he funneled his entire burn into the Four Enhancements. The fog in his brain evaporated and his fist whipped out toward the oncoming legionnaire-scourge faster than any mortal could, aimed right for the man's temple. His veins were afire as he swung.

But the blow never landed.

Alyx took the full brunt of the attack upon the fiery dagger, somehow having had raised the blade in time with Finn's punch. His fist crunched against metal, the flames kissing his fingers. Pain erupted in his hand, and then in his chest as Alyx's boot crushed into it, sending Finn reeling across the bed, taking the duvet and sheets with him over the other side.

The scourge cackled a wicked laugh. "Your aetheurgy will not work on me, princeps. I am blessed by Void Form direct from the Fallen." The man's hand went to a pendant wrapping his neck.

From the other side of the bed, Finn rolled to his side. He saw Davel's body, a fallen wheellock beside it. Rising under the waning aether in his body, Finn grabbed the bedpost, pulling with all the might of the Four Enhancements, shattering the wood apart. He used most of his Burn Form to throw that post at the scourge. Alyx ducked, going to his knee as the projectile sailed overhead. Laughing at the simple and obvious attempt.

Finn darted toward the doorway, aiming to pick up Davel's wheellock, but Alyx was somehow faster. He came at him with the flaming dagger. Finn avoided the jab by mere inches, but Alyx countered with a back stab, and it caught Finn across the back of his hip. He let out a cry as he dove away from another swing of the fiery blade.

He rolled across the plush carpet, sending shockwaves through his body. Blood soon drenched his crimson and peridot trousers. Finn rose and put his hand to stem the flow, facing the scourge anew. The flesh around the wound was sticky and burnt.

Alyx moved, his steps forcing Finn further from Davel's body, the wheellock, and the door to freedom. "I like that you aim to prolong your death, Finnus. Seeing as you were ready to die the moment I came to you." The man swung the blade, but it was half-hearted. He was toying with him.

In his hazy peripherals, he saw Emre watching him intently. Almost patronizing. Now wasn't the time he wanted to yell.

"You are weak, princeps. The Fallen took everything from you in Drenth. He knew you'd be the easiest of the Dunleiths to cull." Another half-attempt to gut Finn.

Finn's foot slipped on Davel's fallen daemon-killing spear, and he backed into a lounging chair, banging his wounded hip, causing him to cry out once more. Why was the man not trying to kill him?

"That's enough chitter, princeps, it's time for you to die." Nevermind.

Alyx lunged with the blazing blade, but Finn was already moving. A pain shot through his hip as he bent down and grabbed the dead legionnaire's spear. The fiery dagger whizzed toward him, only to glance off the raised spear. But the blade came again, slicing Finn across the forearm and he nearly dropped the weapon. He brought the spear up and blocked another stab, but the maneuver cost him his grip as the blood seeping from his arm fell into his palm, making the staff hard to hold.

"It's pathetic that a man like you were able to best the Fallen in Drenth. Or was it the Benld heir who deserves the plaudits?" Alyx unleashed a series of stabs and jabs that Finn barely fended off. It was pathetic. "You're weak, princeps. Always have been."

The scourge rushed forward, blade darting. He brought the spear up, but the scourge turned his wrist before connecting, sending the spear flailing from Finn's hands. Alyx kicked him in his wounded hip, dropping him to the ground.

Standing over him, the fiery blade held inches from Finn's forehead, Alyx smiled. "Forgive me, Finnus Dunleith, for sending you to the Meadows, but the Fallen demands it."

"You are a disgrace to Kanja."

"You think I care about the Golden Throne?" the man jested. "What has Vitus Dunleith ever done for one like me?"

"And the Fallen will?"

"Better to be on the side who would raze this world and lift it anew than to be the one standing in front of him."

"With a yoke around your neck."

"And the Golden Throne doesn't have one around yours, Finnus? The third born son who left Kalderim for a man? Tsk."

Finn locked eyes with the man, breathing heavily. "Know this, scourge, Emre Benld was tenfold the man your Lu Har is." The specter of his beloved smiled brightly. *I'm getting to it, Em, calm down.* "Not only was he the smarter, but also the better dressed."

Alyx's brow quirked at the strange comment, but he began to raise his arm, readying the deathblow. Finn didn't hesitate, he used the last of his Burn Form to harden his body, ramming his shoulder into the scourge's gut. He bowled the man head over ass, tumbling over him. He rolled to his feet and raced toward the doorway, picking up the fallen wheellock and crashing through the door as his burn winked out. Splinters stabbing into his shoulder.

Finn, the pain in his hip starting to become unbearable, raced down the stairs but could hear Alyx yelling after him. Bursting from the villa, Finn found the entire Upper City was a sprawling mess of chaos. Bodies, daemons, Fallen soldiers and fallen legionnaires. The screams were unending, unrelenting.

"There!" screamed one of the soldiers in a black tinted breather with a red skull painted upon it.

"Shit," Finn cursed as wheellock shots broke out in his direction. All around him, aethecite bullets struck the villa, dusting him in stone.

Cursing the pain in his hip, Finn ran the opposite way of the Ceveo, away from the Obelisk. Shoving the wheellock into his belt, he scooped up a pair of Legion short swords as he ran. Soldiers from the Fallen's army chased after him, as well as a handful of daemons. Closer, much closer than he would have liked.

What was he thinking? This was nothing like Drenth. As usual, his beloved said nothing as Finn raced between the villas, dodging wheellock shots and falling stone.

The ground opened up in front of him and Finn was thrown from his feet. He groaned as he rolled over, trying to regain his footing. Looking up, he saw a daemon prowling toward him with limbs ending in claws, the color black. A daemon missing half of its, no, his face, for this daemon was part man. How could that be? Summoned from the Pit, had to be. But this daemon's face was a mass of bloody flesh as if he'd been bludgeoned or flayed in death. His bald scalp covered in scars, the few planes of his once humir face were hard and angular. One red eye filled with hate, the other completely missing in the destroyed flesh as aether so pitch, so dark, so angry swam around his distended claws. A daemon who could wield aetheurgy.

That was a new one.

Descending from the villa where Davel had been killed was Alyx, the traitorous scourge. The man gazed upon the daemon-man-hybrid-thing and grinned, his own dagger blazing with fire.

Bugger him twice.

A ball of liquid *Ignis* bloomed into existence from the daemon's black claws and came his way. Finn grunted as his hip nearly locked up, slick with blood as it was, and made for the nearest alley between villas. The fire splashed across the front of the ornate home. Taking to flame, the very stone consumed by one the Tenets of Aether, but not like the *Ignis* he was familiar with, no, this was black-red. This was *Ignis* corrupted by the void.

He was almost free of the villas when a pair of Imperium soldiers nearly barreled into him unawares. Finn stabbed out with his short sword, puncturing one of the soldier's guts, sliding through the gap in his drake scale where it was clasped. But the sword stuck in the man's abdomen, yanked from Finn's grip.

The other soldier swung his blade, but Finn brought his second sword up, catching it. Both Finn's and the soldier's wrists buckled from the blow, but Finn was just slightly faster, bringing the pommel up under the soldier's breather, striking the windpipe. Down the soldier went, clutching at their throat.

"Impressive, princeps," said Alyx as he emerged in his chase.

Another blast of *Ignis* erupted from behind, and Finn dove out of the way as the void fire bathed the dying Imperium soldiers, their bodies bursting into hellish flames, the stench of burning flesh cloying Finn's nostrils. He pressed his back against the villa's wall, thinking. The scourge confidently strode forward as the daemon strafed the other way.

Think, Finn. Think. Em, could use some help here…

The spectral form of his beloved hovered nearby, his eyes glancing up.

The villa's overhead balcony cracked as the flames summoned from the void finally took hold, burning the greenery that had adorned it, aiming to destroy the building, a blackened mist seeping from between the stones. He looked up, a smile forming upon his lips. It would have to do.

Thanks, love.

With his eyes trained on both the scourge and the daemon, who stood opposite each other, almost in a triangle with he at the point, Finn gasped in pain as he lunged toward the scourge. Black fire from the daemon jounced across the expanse, heading toward the men. Finn jabbed with the sword, juking under the followed attack, ducking behind the scourge as the fire of the void struck the man full brunt. And yet, no cry of pain, no sear of flesh. The man was indeed immune somehow to aether.

But that's what Finn had intended.

With a back kick to the man's kneecap, Finn heard bone snap. The scourge went down with a yelp.

Wasting no time, he edged around the villa and found the entrance, shouldering his way inside. Flames licked the entirety of the home. Tapestries aflame, carpets nothing but burnt crisps as the black mist caroused throughout in a vibrant dance of pitch. Furniture ablaze. Smoke stung his eyes, but he raced up the stairs anyway, heading toward the crumbling balcony. He skidded to a stop at the glass doors, pulling free the wheellock. Waiting.

The scourge limped around the villa's corner. "I can feel your aether, princeps. You cannot escape your death."

Emre's shade gave Finn that special smile, the one that had sealed his heart all those years ago. Time it was.

The glass doors shattered as Finn dove through. Flipping his body, he twisted. The wheellock's dog clicked as he fired. The aethecite bullet exploded from the weapon's muzzle in a slow-motion flash, shooting forth. Between the scourge's eyes did the bullet strike as Finn crashed into the cobbled stones. Pain filling every part of him as he clattered against the ground.

The scourge's body fell, dead eyes still wide in shock. Finn spat at Alyx's corpse as he got to his feet.

But victory rang hollow as the daemon with the face of a man rounded the corner, hate and confidence filling that angry red eye.

Bugger him thrice.

XXXVIII
THE DAEMON

CHAOS, THAT WAS the word. Yes, chaos. He remembered now.

The noise was deafening, which might have made the daemon uncomfortable had he still been a man. There was broken stone everywhere from those buildings. He couldn't remember what they were called. But he knew fire. He knew death. And he knew Death.

All around was death. Blood, that thick, syrupy substance that had brought him back to the world of Life. It covered the manmade... plate? Disc? The manmade land attached to the mountain; he at least recalled the name for the 'mountain'.

Bodies lying dead, many by the Fallen's daemons. Some by his own claws. Men once living, just like he, now sleeping eternal in the Meadows. Meadows, he was there, just like these men. These women. Right, men and women were all man.

He, the once man, was there on the orders of the Fallen. O, yes, the Fallen guided him. His master in place of the other master. He hadn't heard his other master's voice in some time. Odd. But the Fallen sent him into the place with all the men and women to find one man, one who he was to hunt.

Below him, that man cowered. The man the Fallen sent him to hunt. Hunt, that's what he used to be good at, the memory true. But normally not man, no, he used to be good at hunting objects. But wasn't man merely an object as well?

It didn't matter. The man he was compelled to hunt was just below his claws, waiting. Staring.

The daemon that was once Evander raised those claws, the black, unfeeling ends that had once been fingers glinting in the void fire. All around him the fire blazed. That memory of conjuring spells from the void, that had slowly come back to him as he followed the Fallen to this city. He didn't recall the name of the city, it wasn't important. What was, he remembered aetheurgy of the void. The spells taught to him by Solanine. The spells he had only just began to play with before his death.

The man, Finnus Dunleith his name, was coated in blood from the hip down, hand pressed tightly against a wound? Perhaps. His silver, right, silver was a color, hair matted with thick redness. Gummy almost. O, yes, he was wounded.

Behind the one to be hunted was the body of a man in black… hard flesh? Armor, right, that was the word. Why was his memory so faded? The Fallen promised he'd begin to remember more. Was it the stench of death all around him? Death… death… Death, one in the same. The man was dead, killed by the one to be hunted. Killed by Finnus Dunleith.

A shard of metal came up, he thought the word for it was 'sworn' or 'sword', maybe 'sword'. It was sharp, almost as sharp as his newly formed claws. Finnus eyed him, then lunged forward, right toward him, the metal shard… sword aimed for the meat of his body, the flesh that was coated in blood.

Evander, yes, he could claim that name now that he recalled it, moved. His body contorting as he avoided the man's metal. It glanced off the protrusions piercing the flesh of his forearms. Little spikes taking the metal blow, no feeling within Evander but the sound, yes, the sound was loud. Evander brought his other arm up, seeking to strike at the one to be hunted.

Finnus, crafty that man was, dodged to the side. Even wounded as he was, the man was quicker than Evander. His body was tense, the daemon part of him trying to urge the man flesh part of him to be faster, but both sides couldn't come to terms. Perhaps this was his body rejecting the voided spells within, perhaps not. Had he been this slow in life?

"MOVE, MY DISCIPLE, TO THE LEFT. HIS BLADE COMES." There was the voice of his master, it had come back to him.

Following his master's command, Evander's body shifted to the left, the metal shard nearly caressing… a soft touch? … his gaping maw, the one he couldn't speak from. Finnus grunted as he overshot the stab. Evander brought his claws down, catching the man in the back. He tumbled. Fell to his face. Easy, too easy.

Finnus lay below him. The one he was to hunt for Snow Eyes.

"FINISH HIM, MY DISCIPLE. END THIS AEGIS."

Yes, master.

Claws together, Evander sought the void aether that was his prior to his death. The aether he had just come to learn. Aether of the void. He called to it, that pleasant feeling of Death. Up it came, he knew not how, couldn't remember why, the how. But it came. Sweet and deadly.

Flame sprung to Life, wrought from Death, upon his hardened claws. Mesmerized by the blackened fire, Evander would have grinned had he a jaw. Instead, blood gurgled from the open wound that hadn't yet healed over, if it ever would. It would end soon for the one he hunted, then he would be given his Snow Eyes.

That girl, O, yes, he remembered everything about her. Wanted her in life, now even more in death.

Before he could end the man he hunted, Evander was struck from the side, sending his entire body careening into a fiery piece of stone… building, yes, building. Down he slumped, daemon part of him hissing, man part silent despite the pain. Through his torso, pain came, something metal, something sharp had pierced his flesh. His head slammed backward into the stone, jarring him. Dipping, his unhealed, ruined face touched… landed? … upon the metal. Black blood dripped with the crimson blood, daemon melding with man, stinging his flesh.

It hurt, pain everlasting, pain neverending. There wasn't pain like this in the Pit, only torment. This was living pain. Pain of Life. He had felt this before, yes he did. Right before his death. Right before his body had been transformed by Void Form aetheurgy.

A bloodbath, he recalled that suddenly. A woman, short with blonde-red tresses. A heart-shaped face. But that was no woman, was she? No, that was Solanine.

"I REBIRTH YOU FROM THE VOID AND THIS IS HOW YOU TREAT THIS GIFT? YOU ARE PATHETIC, MORTAL."

But, master, I…

"SILENCE! DO NOT FAIL ME. DO NOT FAIL MY AGENT. END THIS AEGIS BEFORE THE GODSBLOOD FINDS HIM. THEY CANNOT COMBINE."

But the pain…

"PAIN IS FLEETING SHOULD YOU LET THE VOID CONSUME YOU. NOCTIS CAN FILL THE CUP THAT IS YOUR LIFE. LIFE IN DEATH, MY DISCIPLE. DO NOT WASTE SUCH A GIFT."

He raised his head slightly, single eye finding a snarling? beast in front of him.

Red-blue scales, yes scales, covering the entire body. Claws like his but not black, not created from the Pit and blood. In one claw was a metal shard, not as long as the one the man used, but just as sharp. Tail and angled snout. Draconem, that was what this creature was, he recalled the creatures named draconem.

"Elfir, get your ass up," the beast growled to the hunted man.

"Good to see you too, Ruane," Finnus grumbled as he rose to his feet gingerly. "Where—"

"Shut it, elfir. More pressing problems, or haven't you noticed. Daemons have overrun the Upper City. We have to fall back to the Obelisk." To the prone Evander, who twitched while he tried to follow the words of this draconem and this man. "That thing won't hold it… him. That daemon."

"You don't say?" The man winced as he stood, looking at the metal pole, yes pole, sticking out of Evander's chest, pinning him to the wall. "Lead on, O fearless leader."

The man he was to hunt put an arm upon the beast's, the beast taking his weight as they fled from Evander, disappearing between more buildings.

The chaos on the mountain's landing was growing worse, growing stronger. Buildings began to topple in on themselves. Obsidian flames burned freely, sundering everything that was built by man, built in the world of Life.

Evander, the daemon, the man, rose from the building's wall, his body creaking and gushing blood as he pulled free the metal pole. The wound remained; the pain receded. Blood flowed. It mattered not, he was dead once and wouldn't waste the gift that his master had given him. Life was his.

And so would be Snow Eyes.

After the man he hunted, Evander plodded along, remembering more from his life, more of the void aether. He called to it once more, and it came.

Terris, yes, that was what it was called.

He would have laughed had he a voice, but Evander summoned more *Terris* to him. It came, black and angry with the dark mist. The earth under his feet, the manmade landing shaking violently.

He would catch his prey. He would end his prey.

Then, only then, would he have his Snow Eyes.

XXXIX

SOLANINE

SOLANINE DUSTED OFF the cassock of the Scattered Shards servant that the blooddrake had stolen, scowling as the juvenile draconem of *Aere* fled into the heart of Port Sin.

Anger rose, not because of the surprise attack unleashed by the Godsblood, but because Ialtris had betrayed them.

In the destruction of *The Arbiter's Axe,* the Godsblood and the fire-haired vicar had raced past Solanine, thundering down the cobbled stones of Port Sin with the Hammer of the Forgemistress aflamed with *Ignis*, chasing after the injured aerovern. Hot on their tails was the Shards servant called Phlox the Faithful, the spindly humir burning his aetheurgy as he ran after.

To be true, Solanine hadn't been prepared for the Godsblood's sudden influx of aether. Had wanted it, Solanine had, but still hadn't expected it to come this full this early.

The aerovern had been a test, a way to get the Godsblood to seek her way to Noctis. But this destruction was not what Solanine had intended.

Dozens of portly, well-fed members of the Guild dug themselves from the avalanche of stone caused by the Godsblood. Confused and bloodied, they climbed. Medics called for. Wounds slathered with ointments and bound with gauze. Stones tumbled from the arena's wall, others helping search for loved ones or friends under the landslip of rock.

A towering shadow fluttered above *The Axe* on voluminous wings. Dark was the body, feathers flapping. It was the strix of Grand Quaestor Owl. The bird circled above before coming to land atop the pinnacle of the arena, surveying with saucer eyes of gold. The grand quaestor was surrounded by a gaggle of Shards servants. Fools, all of them.

By the time dust had settled, the crowd was still going crazy in their quest for blood, wanting more. Chanting the name Lady Drakeslayer as if she was the true god. How little these pissants knew.

"SHE HAS BESTED YOU AGAIN, MY DISCIPLE."

She has not! This was not what I planned, master.

"I CARE NOT WHAT YOU PLANNED, SHE HAS SEEN FIT TO PUT YOU IN YOUR PLACE ONCE MORE. I SHOULD NOT LIKE TO SEND YOU BACK TO THE PIT."

Solanine glanced up at the strix sitting contently. *Cauda is here, master. With the manacles. They will bind her.*

"WE SHALL SEE."

It will be done. I need only to get her to the guardian. Rinkhal has the Seal.

The spectators began to disperse as the soldiers in the employ of the Guilder Ifant Klander started funneling people out of *The Arbiter's Axe*. Voices grumbled as the soldiers prodded and pushed. Slow going it would be as many onlookers were still fired up with deathwant and alcohol. Their nightturn not yet fulfilled.

Within the quarter hour's turn, the medics of Port Sin began to carry the dead and wounded on huge carts. There were dozens, if not hundreds of expired souls. The amphitheater had been full during the bout and could hold thousands. The damage done was immense. Far more than Solanine wanted. This mega-city still had its use, even cowed under the Divine's rule.

Before long, none except those from House Klander were left, patrolling the tiers for stragglers. Inspecting the devastation.

A presence slid down the rubble beside Solanine. An elfirish Guilder of the High Seat, the one who smelt of aether, the one who was said to be named after the spouse of Canlon Carr. The one who'd gave Solanine fits because the blooddrake couldn't understand this creature's aether.

The one called Maja Carr.

Two mammoths climbed down the scree, standing behind Maja. Her twin titans, her orcirish bodyguards. Both were cut in more than a dozen places by strewn rock shards, their green hides flogged with dark blood. Their auras also swirled with aether unlike any normal orcir.

The elfir's gaze was upon wreckage within the city beyond *The Axe*. The side of her face facing Solanine was bleeding, her fine, golden hair stained with it. Her aether was strongly sapphire. Knowledge and ancient. Wisdom of the eons.

Solanine had a sinking feeling about that wisdom. One that set the blooddrake on edge.

Ialtris and Rinkhal—who wore a cloak to cover Cadrianna Benld's face—marched toward Solanine and the Guilder, an army of Klander's soldiers at their backs. A young humirish boy skipped beside Rinkhal. He'd been their spy on the Godsblood, a friend the Benld girl had once known, a relative of the street rat Evander, Solanine's own pet in Drenth.

Maja spoke, using the Shards' scales name. "…you hurt?" The woman had not known Solanine was within, could not have known.

Inwardly, Solanine was fine. It would take much more to pierce a blooddrake's true exoscales, but the Shards servant was the scales of man, weak and easily penetrable. Blood dripped from various wounds. Solanine shook the scales' head. "My bones feel like a rattled toy. And you, Lady Carr?"

"All in one piece," the Guilder said. "Seems like Lady Drakeslayer has earned her name wisely."

"Indeed."

"I see one of the drakes had used Lady Drakeslayer's taskmaster." The woman was pointing toward the discarded scales of the one called Cyan the Defiant left near the broken wall. The fleshy husk clung to some debris, the midnight blue cassock, horsehair bristled helm, and golden, rune-etched gauntlet lying nearby. "But the blooddrakes have failed to kill her now thrice. These rogues. What say you about them?"

A commotion distracted them both, and the orcirish bodyguards tensed. Across the arena, behind the oncoming Ialtris and Rinkhal, a boulder the size of a wagon cart flew into the air. A screech of the Pit accompanied the thrown rock, a misshapen figure flailing along with it. The boulder and the voidspawned daemon that had been one of the insufferable vicars Solanine had sent to the Pit on Gargantua crashed into the ground with a sickening thud. Both Ialtris and Rinkhal, plus the seed of a street gang leader, all instinctively ducked, throwing their hands over their faces.

But before the daemon of the vicar could rise, Maja Carr, the supposed Guilder of the High Seat, twirled her hands and aether of both *Ignis* and *Aere* swept up the daemon, hurling it into the nightturn sky. A flame erupted in the center of the daemon's armored chest, white-hot. The voidspawn howled as the flame consumed it. Then it was gone, disintegrating into motes of dust and ash.

This woman was more than a woman, Solanine jarringly realized.

It was then Maja Carr turned toward Solanine, and the blooddrake gasped upon seeing the other half of her face.

Maja Carr was no man, nor was she elfir. Maja Carr was a blooddrake. The true Maja Carr, spouse to Canlon, just as Solanine had feared.

The Godsking's blooddrake unleashed a spray of white light, aether coalescing in a fury, that encapsulated Solanine, throwing the blooddrake backwards into a pile of bricks, cracking the Scattered Shards servant's skull, rendering the blooddrake woozy.

Turning, Maja Carr's white-hot beam of aether rushed toward Ialtris and Rinkhal like a tsunami of natural magic. Solanine saw through bleary eyes the two blooddrakes react, throwing up their scales' hands and summoning their aether to form a shield.

The aether from Maja crashed upon Rinkhal's wall, like a wave crashing against a cliffside. Sparkles of clashing aether snapped at each other like two rabid dogs fighting over a kill. It clapped and blasted like thunder. Rinkhal, and the boy child, went spinning backwards into the arena. The boy howled under the strain, like he was inside of a bell when the clapper was rung.

Ialtris hadn't been quick enough.

The traitorous blooddrake erupted in a ball of white flame, searing the skin from the bikromi elfir that had been Ifant Klander. Ialtris wailed as the aether pierced their exoscales, probing deep inside to the vitals. Jaw open, screaming to Zenith and to Nocturne. To Nightingale. Elfirish flesh gone, now standing as He Who Fathered the World made the blooddrakes in the vision of the First Wife. Tail writhing back and forth before disintegrating into nothingness. Keratin horns breaking like obsidian dropped from a mountain top.

And then Ialtris was gone.

Solanine struggled to get up, but Maja Carr was already in motion as the guards in Klander's employ began firing their wheellock rifles. Lightning fast, the blooddrake in the scales of a High Seat Guilder rushed about the arena, hurling wave after wave of aether. The Guilder's two bodyguards—who were also clearly blooddrakes for their eyes flashed lavender—jumped into the fray, swinging massive warhammers coated in aether into the doughy bodies of Klander's flesh army. Corpses of men and women littered the arena floor. A scorch of blackened sand where Ialtris had been. The fleeing cloak of Rinkhal in Cadrianna Benld's scales descended into the bowels of *The Axe*, the lithe boy-spy trailing with hands pressed to his ears.

Bullets panged off the bricks in which Solanine lay, some striking the Scattered Shards servant's scales, leaving red gashes in the flesh. Solanine sat up and tried to call the innate aether to murder Maja Carr but found it difficult. The pain in Solanine's skull was too great, so the blooddrake slouched back.

Waiting until the moment to strike, for it appeared Maja had not known Solanine's true nature. Solanine rolled to their knees and crawled out of *The Arbiter's Axe* in search of the Godsblood.

"NO TIME, MY DISCIPLE, THE BIKROME YOU HATE SO IS NEAR."

Valeria? Could it be so fortuitous? Here in Port Sin, both Valeria and the Seal in Solanine's grasp. Fate worked wonders at times regardless of what Ialtris had done.

"SHE COMES TO PORT SIN. THE HATEFUL DAUGHTER HAS SEEN FIT TO BETRAY ME ONCE MORE, JUST AS THE TRAITOROUS SON."

I'll see the trap set for Valeria. Her soul is mine. You promised.

Solanine slithered through the rubble of *The Axe*, hiding behind a toppled column as more Scattered Shards tainted warriors filled the arena. But it was too late, one had seen the blooddrake, seen their scales to be precise. The quaestor called out the scales' title.

It was then the largest explosion Solanine had ever witness struck the City of Sin. To the west, down where the Beggars Chain was, the nightturn sky illuminated in a flash of brilliance. So white, the stars were lost. Following the bloom was a blast sharp as thunder, but tenfold worse. Shrapnel and debris rained down upon Port Sin. The cries of terror serenading Solanine's earholes.

Rising and composing themselves once the blast was spent, Solanine acknowledged the soldier in the red cassock as she approached and saluted nervously, no doubt wondering what orders would come. The cries of terror were drowned out now by the sounds of pain.

"I must return to the stronghold, quaestor, see to it that this… mess is cleaned up." *I will end this, master. Valeria will not be prepared to handle what I will summon.*

"SEE IT SO, MY DISCIPLE. MY RETURN IS NIGH."

XL
ASHE

THE DESTRUCTION WAS erratic, and the wounded were many.

The juvenile stopped in the Hangman's Hex, stamping on the cobbled stones as multiple quaestors and the numpties of the city watch had surrounded it. Long steel spears held in aether-infused hands stabbed at the beast while it roared and used its own aether from its lightningsac. Soldiers died while they wounded the creature of the Pentax. Even injured, the aerovern was winning. She saw the six blades of the Strix sticking out of the draconem's exoscales.

"Fucking Nocturne!" Ashe bent over yacking pulmo tar and drawing a deep breath with a struggle. Even the now surrounding mist struggled to quell her fire.

"Maybe you shouldn't drink so much, love." Harlequin was barely winded as she watched the aerovern get backed into a tailor's shop, its head low to the ground, tail held high and stabby.

"Or more." Ashe lifted the Hammer, centering herself. "Time to kill this draconem."

"No shit, Ashe, but how? We got this thing cornered like a stag, but it's still wasting them buggers out there. You just gon' run up and smack the fuck out of it again? You just unleashed the void on the thing and it's still alive."

Harlequin was right. Too much death. Too many months spent ready to die, and now she wanted the opposite. She didn't want more blood. They needed to kill this thing without hurting any others. It made her think of her father, as this path was something he would have taken. A smarter way.

"Harlequin! Ashe!"

The lovely vicar snarled as angrily as the daemonized aerovern fighting off the tainted warriors of the Shards when they turned to find Phlox the Faithful standing in the street behind them. The skinny vicar held a multi-barrel wheellock pistol in one hand, a curved sword in the other, the weapon black and jagged like a terrisvvyrm tooth. The vvyrm tooth glowed brightly in the moonlight of nightturn.

His aura was blazing crimson. Surprisingly, the normally craven man looked pitbent about a fight.

"I'm going to gut him." Harlequin crouched in a battle stance, both axes bristling.

The aerovern sent a barrage of lightning toward the dwindling gaggle of quaestors, forcing them back, giving the juvenile draconem more room to work within the Hex. The soldiers in their armor and aetheurgy-driven attacks recouped and pressed in once more. The aerovern roared.

They were between a draconem and a gutless prick-sucker.

"It's over, you faithless whores." Phlox raised the pistol and aimed it at her. A fairly stupid maneuver since Ashe was buzzing with misty aetheurgy, brought from the depths of her soul.

"Fuck you, Phloxy."

"Yeah, fuck you, Phlox."

"I'm going to enjoy killing you, Harlequin. I'll take my time. Rip you limb from limb. Skin from bone." His smile was sickening. His creepy gaze found Ashe. "You cannot beat them, Ashe. The Fallen will rule this world. You cann—"

Harlequin charged, axes aloft. The wheellock moved, firing and hitting the vicar, who went tumbling. The fastest of heartbeats.

Ashe burned her aetheurgy, the mist roaring alongside the wails of the dead beyond the veil of Life and Death, she raised the Hammer, and dove toward the traitorous vicar. The Faithful burned his Shard Form, a fulcrum of aether. The man strafed, bringing about the vvyrm-toothed blade, shooting at her with the pistol, missing.

Weapons clashed.

Normally, Ashe's Hammer did wonders on everyday blades of steel and iron, but a terrisvvyrm tooth was just as strong as the Mother's talisman, borne of the Pentax's boon. Her Hammer clanked off the vicar's draconem-wrought sword.

She attacked again.

Both were blurs, driven by aetheurgy. Speeding, swinging, dodging, strengthened by aether. Movements fast, movements dramatically graceful. Attacks blunted; attacks parried. Vvyrm tooth and Hammer glittering in aether of *Ignis* and *Terris,* of *Aere* and *Aquis*.

Phlox was every bit of Ashe's equal, and that was concerning. Either she'd always underestimated the man's Shard Form, or the blooddrakes had somehow given him a tonic of aether or some other means of enhancement. He was a simple vicar in name only, for this man now had the full control of the Four Tenets of Aether and Four Enhancements at his fingertips.

Part of her ached to summon the Strix to her, but she could sense the daemon blade continuing its attack on the aerovern, the curse of the void more somber than she expected. But, as she and Phlox crossed weapons, Ashe could sense via the blade that the aerovern was winning its battle against the soldiers of Port Sin and the Scattered Shards. The beast was on the offensive again, destroying all the buildings in the Hex. Before long, it would flee once more, killing even more, Strix or not.

She and Phlox clashed weapons, faces mere inches apart. There was pure rage in the man's eyes. That asshole smile of his never leaving his face.

"You cannot win, Ashe," he grunted as pushed against her Hammer with inhumir strength guided by aether. The vvyrm tooth blindingly bright, for the black-blue enamel glowed in the dark. "It's best to just give in."

Ashe's flaming Hammer popped. She gritted her teeth. "You betrayed us."

"The time of the Shards is over. The time of the Guild is done. The Fallen is the future. Eminence will be his. There is greater aetheurgy within it. Straight from Zenith, Ashe. You're the pa—"

Crescent of bluish iron exploded through the vicar's flesh. Phlox the Faithful dropped his terrisvvyrm tooth blade, eyes rolling back in his head as his shoulder gorily separated from arm to groin. Blood splattering Ashe head to toe. The man died at her feet; body hewn into a bloody V.

Harlequin, bleeding from the wheellock wound in her left shoulder, stared down at the corpse. "Fuck your future." She spat on the carcass. In that moment, drenched in blood and heaving, she looked even more beautiful than ever. "I'll take Ashe any day over your blooddrake who should've stayed dead in the mines."

Mines. Aethecite.

"That's it!"

"Ashe?"

Her cassock flung Phlox's blood as she turned toward the aerovern on the other side of the Hex. "I know how to kill it. We need to lure it to Dil's warehouse in the Chain." She made to move but kicked the multi-barrel wheellock that had fallen as Phlox died. Looking down, she noticed the engraved 'B' on the grip. "Hey, there it is." She scooped up the heirloom weapon, the one that was Emre Benld's. "Let's go kill that drake. Meet me at Dil's."

"I'm not leaving your side."

"Lovely sentiment, Harle-bub, but you're bleeding like gutted mammoth." Harlequin made to reply, but Ashe summoned the mist, creating a wall of grey between them. She smiled as she urged the mist to push Harlequin down an alley, away from the carnage. "Just trying to pay back what I owe you! Keep an eye for Solanine."

"You owe me thrice, Ashe!" Harlequin yelled from behind the wall of grey. "For Phlox!"

Ashe grinned at the vicar before turning and racing toward the daemonized juvenile draconem, the Hammer burned even brighter, and the mist swirled in a larger vortex. The aerovern saw her with its still-seeing red eye. It swiped the last of the struggling soldiers aside. Electricity crackled around its jaws.

But Ashe turned west toward the Beggars Chain, the aerovern barreling after, as she yelled a tantalizingly vulgar taunt.

Getting the aerovern to give chase was simple, as she could almost feel the electrical current of the young bastard's breath on her backside as she ran. Seagandr-oil and aethecite lights normally used to lure sinners to the various dens of sin now were like a series of beacons to guide her path, passing them in a blink. Buildings were a blur in her aetheric speed, the few people unlucky to be still about were specters in her vision, soon to be cursing their odds. She cut through the Barter Yard, sticking to the larger boulevards to avoid not only losing the aerovern, but also limiting the amount of damage it could do.

Still wasn't enough.

The juvenile battered about, its shredded wings causing it issues, throwing it off balance, so it skittered about the road like a crab, smacking into everything. Wagons and carriages trampled under the heavier bulk. Buildings collapsed. Havoc wreaked. Daemons just wanted chaos.

The Beggars Chain came into view ahead. Derelict buildings sprouted from the basin's floor, crumbling, unused, and disowned. It was a welcome sight. She was close.

But she was also tiring, and fast.

The initial splurge of aether whittled away faster than normal. Her pulmo raged. Had she lost the draconem, she was fairly certain her coughing would have been enough for the beast to re-find her. Ashe's legs churned acid, her dying aetheurgy giving her the slim edge to keep going, but it was fleeting. Arms pumping as she ran, bloodstained cassock trailing, hair a raven flag for the aerovern to hone on, tar spat with almost every breath.

She jumped into the bramble of broken-down buildings of the Chain, swerving between the apartment complexes, the pipeweed dens, the flophouses. The aerovern rumbled along the ground in the hunt, spewing electricity and dripping hoarfrost like the sweat beading Ashe's forehead.

Danma Dil's warehouse was unwatched, the front fence open.

Harlequin stood beside the front gate with hands on her knees, huffing and puffing. The left sleeve of her cassock was shorn and tied around her wounded shoulder, leaving bloodstained and freckled alabaster skin shining in the moonlight.

The vicar saw Ashe coming and waved her over. "Hurry!"

Ashe plunged into the warehouse grounds; the entirety of an apartment complex exploded behind when the aerovern burst from its ground floor. Stone and timber a deadly barrage. "O, shit! O, shit! O, shit!"

Summoning the last of her aetheurgy, Ashe used the flames of *Ignis* to bash in the warehouse's wall. The wailing mist did as commanded but was weakening, its grey luster dimming. The crates holding the aethecite were still stacked neatly inside in the overhead seagandr-oil lighting.

Quickly, Ashe upended a crate with an aether-enhanced shove, spilling the ore all over the ground. "Dump them the best you can, go that way, meet at the back."

"Aye, love." Harlequin groaned as she shouldered crates over with her wounded arm.

Ashe went the opposite way, toppling every crate in view, some with her shoulder, some with the might of Mother Marrow's Hammer. Thunderous cracks of breaking timber echoed while aethecite ore reverberated in the still warehouse. But outside Dil's building of deceit was silent as a moonlit nightturn over the Sea of Mist. Where was the aerovern?

She doubled back to the entrance and found the draconem warily circling the entrance, not wanting to step upon the hardened ore of aether.

"Hey, fuck face!" She dodged a swipe of the barbed tail, ducked under a slash from the wingtip talons. "Strix, we're outta here!" The six blackened steel blades made a sickening slurping sound as they retracted from the aerovern's exoscales, reforming into a single blade that whooshed across the misty grey and into her expectant hand.

"O, DEAR BRYNN, THAT WAS NOT PLEASANT FOR ME. MY CHILD..."

What? No time to care.

The juvenile roared in painful frustration. Ashe dove back into the warehouse, carefully racing through the spilled aethecite toward the back where Harlequin was waiting. The aerovern crashed into the warehouse, breaking the wall down in multiple places, slipping on the pellets of diamond aether. Raging.

Harlequin egged her on. "What now?"

Ashe brought the Hammer against the wall, rendering an opening. "Go, I'll light this."

The vicar squeezed through the gash.

"DEAR BRYNN, NOT LIKE THIS. NOT LIKE THIS."

Shut up, Strix!

Calling an *Ignis* flame to her palm, she flung the spelled fire at a crate lid, it caught, and she scurried out the rend in the wall, racing across the uneven ground toward the coast. Harlequin was waiting in the backyard of a decrepit manse.

"I lit a fuse," she said, slowing. Her Soul Form winked out, the wails returning to the realm of the dead as the once fiery mist became placid.

The wall behind buckled as the aerovern slammed against it but did not break.

"Go," she called as she dodged between the burnt-out mansions on the jutted rock. "It's gonna be big!"

Seconds passed as they ran between the destitute villas toward the cliff's edge, Harlequin wheezing. "Is it gonna be today!"

The cliff lay ahead, the plummet at least thirty feet. Nowhere else to run. One option left.

"Jump!"

They left the safety of the cliff and soared out over the VVyrm Ocean, Ashe hoping they wouldn't hit rock below. The jutting portion of the peninsula exploded in a blaze as bright as Zenith's midday sun, the stars of nightturn blotted out. Stone and shrapnel flying. Dust and earth blinding.

Ashe straightened her legs, held her arms across her chest and plunged into the dark waters of the VVyrm Ocean. Cold and vast. Debris from the peninsula splashed violently into the water. She kicked frantically, her cassock weighing her down, arms flailing as she swam upward trying to hold onto the Hammer at the same time. Her head bobbed out of the saltwater, gasping for breath as her pulmo threatened to block her airways.

Harlequin resurfaced nearby, her arms churning to keep her afloat, wet curls clinging to her face as she spat out saltwater.

Ashe saw the emptiness that had been the Beggars Chain, now it was a crater in the western side of the city. No idea how wide a swathe created by the blow of the aethecite cache. Hundreds, if not thousands of lives potentially lost. It's not what she'd intended.

The darkened shape of Mount Bastard loomed over them in taunt. Godsdamnit.

"I WARNED YOU, DEAR DAUGHTER. IT WAS TOO MUCH."

"I can't believe that just *fucking* happened," Harlequin said. Her head dunked under the weight of her cassock and her wounded arm being useless, she was struggling to stay above water. "Do you think it's dead?"

The salty sting of tears met Ashe's lips as she churned her legs to stay afloat. "I fucking hope so."

XLI

LOJEN

HIS TALONS RAKED the chains along Lemures' arms, bouncing harmlessly off the daemon's flesh.

Lemures rotated one of its limbs unnaturally, almost like a water wheel, a full rotation without disjointing, down it came and slammed into Lojen's shoulder. Pain was fleeting in his mind, as lost he was in the rage of wardkeeping. Eyes slitted, a roar rumbling within as aether built along his horns. He could feel it, the rage inside. But to control it?

He heard only the roar escaping his maw alongside Justice's Hymn, the orchestra singing loudly over the deathless beast that was Lemures' own bellow. Like two songsters out-singing one another, their attacks were the steps to the Hymn's dance.

The need to protect, the desire to ward. Not only his sister—who he knew not if she was still nearby or had fled like he'd told her—but also that of the mega-city. Gandtril had been his duty, been left in his care with his oath to the Golden Throne, and he was godsdamned certain he would give everything he could to defend it. Even against something as devilish as the daemon before him. The beast of the Pit wouldn't stop him. Only death, his or the daemon's, that would be the only way.

Lemures was fast, faster even than Lojen was in his berserker state. For all its bulk, it moved like liquid. Lojen was on the back foot with each attack. His own paltry swings caught nothing but air or the chains Lemures used like gauntlets. Claws, deadlier than ingeniator-wrought steel, scraped across his exoscales more often than not. If it weren't for the natural strength of his draconem scales, he'd long been skewered by the beast.

Slowly, ever so slowly, Lojen was being pushed backward into the center of the upper tier, further away from the safety of the Obelisk. Each swing, each parry, he backed up, trying to stave off death.

All the power of a wardkeeper, it was nothing in his arsenal. Worthy, he most definitely was not.

Down came the daemon's claw from Lojen's right, he blocked with his forearms, claws knicking his exoscales, but the other arm came in, catching Lojen under his armpit, lifting him clear from his feet. Lojen tripped over a broken bench, falling to the ground, his body jostling over trampled hedges, flipping to steady himself. A mewling yelp as Lemures grabbed his flailing tail. Tight the grip, swung like a sling overhead, Lojen was spun.

By the Arbiter, the daemon was strong.

Letting him go, Lojen crashed through the marble façade of a villa. Jagged perfection found purchase between his exoscales, piercing his flesh underneath. Dust cradled him as he flew through an atrium, coming to a screeching halt at the base of a grand staircase. Balling up, he covered his head as crystals from a large ornamental light fixture rained down upon him. Shards pelting his exoscales, clattering to the ground in a prism of sharpness.

Hurt lanced throughout his body as he put his talons to the floor, trying to rouse himself to keep on fighting. The aether within the Hymn blared like klaxons in his earholes but the fight inside him was fading. He hurt too much. He had failed too often.

As long as Ruane was safe, he could be happy with this failure. With this death.

The daemon loped into the villa, marble breaking off as its bulk squeezed through the drakken-shaped aperture. The dangling chains rattling, sending chilly reminders down Lojen's spine, reminders of death incoming.

"YOU ARE A WEAK THING, WARDKEEPER," Lemures intoned in that ghastly tone of the Pit. *"AEGIS, I THINK NOT."*

The Hymn urged him, almost like it was begging him to get up. He could almost picture his father glaring at him, too. Yelling at him to be a better wardkeeper. Demanding he be a better wardkeeper. A better drakken.

But the struggle was nearly too much.

He had given in to the Hymn, to the song of Justice, but he had been easily bested by this daemon. Barely giving it a fight. He was weak, just as Lemures said. He was so wildly unworthy of the holy horns. Mother Marrow had bequeathed a gift to a sullied drakken.

Lojen flopped onto the ground, snout first. Blood the color of orchids dribbled down his jaw. He was pathetic.

Lemures reared up over him, standing to its full height of nearly ten feet. Those daemonized eyes knowing victory. In the sundered light of the villa, the daemon's claws glinted death. Lojen's death.

He waited for it, ready to accept his defeat. Whatever this 'Aegis' was Lemures kept calling him, he did not earn it. His failure.

But before he would meet his father in the Meadows, the daemon turned as a giant blur cleaved through the villa in a blinding honey illumination. Aether crackled like lightning as *Aere* struck the daemon's side. A clap of thunder sending the beast tumbling, its chains whipping violently, knocking potted plants asunder. It skidded, the daemon, to a stop and was quickly back to its feet, growling.

Paws lifted Lojen by the underarms, a strength belying the body they were attached to. "Up, drakken," said Wick.

Up Lojen got to his feet, woozy and in pain. Wick crouched with his dueling knives held toward the daemon. Lojen picked up his longknife, held it limply.

To Lojen's left, holding the gleaming golden blade was Titen Dunlieth. His shorn, greyish hair was matted with dust and blood, it streaked his strong face. The giant elfir held aloft the Golden Sword, aether sparking along its polished surface. The peridot gemstone was brilliance in splendor.

"Back, daemonkind," Titen said. "Go back to the Pit where you belong."

Lemures let out a grunt that Lojen took for a chuckle. ***"YOU ARE PUNY TO ME, ELFIR. YOU KNOW WHAT STRENGTH I BEAR. I WAS THE VICTOR AT EMINENCE FOR THE FALLEN, FOR MY DIVINE. IF NOT FOR CANLON CARR'S LAST GASP, I WOULD NOT HAVE BEEN BESTED. NEVER HAVE I BEEN BESTED."***

"Spew lies all you wish, void kin. You were bested by Canlon, who sent you to the Pit."

"ONLY FOR MY DIVINE TO SEEK ME AGAIN. OVER AND OVER, I COME. I AM LEGION. NOT THAT WHICH YOU CALL YOURSELF LEGION. I AM MANY. I AM UNENDING."

"You are the spawn of evil. Come to me if you must, daemon. I know your weakness."

"I HAVE NO WEAKNESS, ELFIR."

Titen laughed as Lojen stood ready for the lunge sure to come. "You may be unending, but your body isn't. Each rebirth you become weaker and weaker. This is your third spawning, daemon. You are not as strong as you remember."

"PATHETIC, ELFIR, YOU KNOW NOTHING OF WHICH I AM OR WHAT I DO."

"Tell your lies, if you must. But Bliss has shown my own sister your truth. Canlon Carr defeated you once. Brynn Benld sent you back to the Pit a second time. You are not infallible, daemon. You will fail."

The red eyes honed in on Lojen, that maw of teeth frightening as it smiled. ***"AND WITH EACH PASSING I WILL HOUND YOU, AEGIS. YOU CANNOT ESCAPE FROM ME."***

The Hymn began to build once more within him. "Why me?"

The question seemed to perplex the daemon for it stopped. ***"YOU KNOW NOT WHAT YOU ARE, DO YOU?"***

"What am I?" The Hymn tingled inside, building steadily. *Father, do you know?*

"THEN YOU ARE EVEN LESSER THAN DIRT TO MY DIVINE, WARDKEEPER. YOUR DEATH WON'T BE MOURNED. WON'T BE MISSED. PERHAPS THE HORNS OF THE AEGIS SHOULD HAVE GONE TO YOUR SISTER INSTEAD OF THE PATHETIC CREATURE YOU ARE."

Something snapped within him. That rage that had built with the Hymn was no longer held back by his failure, by his unworthiness. Like a dam, he released the pure essence of all existence within him. The Hymn reaching its apex note.

Lojen wanted blood. Daemon blood.

He roared at the top of his lungs. Marble all around the villa shook, some falling from the hole in the wall. The light fixture, what little remained hanging above shattered, glass disintegrating. Aether filled his vision, fire of Life swarming his soul.

The berserker inside was let loose once more, this time unshackled. Free from being held back.

Lojen sprung toward the daemon with all the fury the Hymn gave him. He crossed the span in moments, well before the daemon could bring its arms up to block. Slamming into the beast from the void, he lifted it, almost too simply. They crashed through a stained-glass window, back out onto the upper tier of Gandtril. Lojen rolled over the daemon, his claws raking flesh, scoring the hide under the coarse hair.

The daemon's back legs rose, and before Lojen could clear himself, he was kicked. His head clattered against an aethecite-powered streetlight, bending the pole in half as it buckled under his weight. His horns skidded across the cobbled stones, his snout rubbing raw against the rock despite his exoscales.

Lojen was back onto his feet, the Hymn filling him with anger. Ignoring the pain in his body, he charged the daemon once more. Whipping the chains, Lemures caught him across the flank, diverting his attack.

Snarling, Lojen pivoted and brought his claws slashing across the daemon's body, sending tufts flying. The daemon responded in kind, swinging.

But the Hymn slowed to a pulse of heart, and Lojen's vision shifted. He saw the claw come down, searing through the meat of Lojen's thigh. The next attack striking his exposed gullet, rending exoscale and flesh alike. Down Lojen went, screaming, bloody, and defeated. Lemures standing over him victorious.

Time sped up, back to normal. The swing hadn't started.

Lojen juked to the left, confusing the daemon. Up his longknife went, piercing into the hairy hide. A scream of the Pit.

But out came Lemures' other arm, backhanding Lojen, sending him sprawling.

Lightning filled the gap, summoned from the Golden Sword. Titen swung the gleaming blade at the daemon, connecting with its shoulder blade. Black ichor arched through the air as the blackened mist that filled the Upper City pounced. The daemon spun, chains smashing into Titen's drake scaled back, sending him reeling.

Wick leapt atop the daemon with his dueling knives stabbing. Once. Twice. Thrice before Lemures shook the lapin free. Wick went tumbling across the mezzanine proper.

Lojen bound for the daemon, leaping over the whipping chain, claws aimed for the head. He tore thick tufts of hair free as he completed his jump. The wound in his side broke open, spilling draconem blood.

Titen and the golden blade came in with a whirlwind of *Aere*. Aetheric lightning sizzled into the daemon, burning its hair, smoke tendrils rising as it howled. The heir to the Golden Throne swung the blessed blade, steel kissing keratin. The elfir and the daemon slashing, parrying, dodging, cutting.

"Lojen!"

He spun to find Ruane dragging a wounded Finn. His heart was gladdened to see her, but also angry that she wasn't yet safe within the Obelisk. Finn looked terrible, bleeding everywhere. They were running toward them. Well, Ruane was, Finn was barely upright.

Behind, he spied another daemon, this one part humir. But without most of his face. Something about the humirish part reminded him of Drenth last summer, but he couldn't recall why.

"Ru, ru—" the chain caught him across the hamstring, sending him to his knees.

Wick had gotten back to his feet and raced over toward Ruane, taking Finn's other arm across his shoulders. Ruane dropped the elfirish princeps fully into the lapin's care and spun toward the half-humir daemon, her longknife stabbing.

Lojen yelled out as the second daemon unleashed a gout of flame. By the Arbiter's bloody axe, this daemon had aetheurgy!

The flames reached toward Ruane, but she was already moving away from Wick and Finn, darting across the street at an angle. The daemon dragged his aetheurgy after her but was not as fast as Lemures. His movements were jerky, almost as if he was not fully formed. Perhaps he wasn't.

Ruane brought her longknife swiping down, aiming to catch the daemon from clavicle to groin, but her blade froze stiff not even an inch into the flesh. The gory emptiness that would have been a mouth gurgled with blood, almost as if the daemon was screaming in pain. Jerking, Ruane's longknife was forced from her grip. The daemon swung his blackened claw, catching her across the snout, exoscales ripping free in a spray of purple.

The sight filled Lojen with another reservoir of anger, doubling what was already within him. His vision turned to fire, only one thing would sate it.

Forgetting Lemures, Lojen raced toward the daemon, horns lowered. The daemon slowly turned, body half-cocked in his direction before Lojen skewered the void-summoned creature. The daemonized eyes were eerily humir as they widened in shock and pain. Lojen lifted the daemon overhead, the roar of the Hymn sending aetheric shockwaves throughout the upper tier. He shook his head back and forth like a hound with a rabbit. On the fourth shake, the daemon slid off and flew, crashing into a wall, marble bricks burying him.

Lojen stood panting, his talons curled into fists.

Ruane rushed over to him, putting a claw to his back. "Brother."

He spun on her, almost mistaking her for another daemon, so lost in the dance of wardkeeping he was. Fuck, what was happening to him?

A yell brought him back to the present. Both drakken saw the Golden Sword lose his footing, going to ground while Lemures attacked. Without saying a word, only sharing a knowing glance, they leapt toward the daemon, ready to save the princeps.

But the daemon had other plans. Both chains whipped out like lashes, catching Lojen along the calf, throwing him off course, the other striking Ruane across the chest, stopping her dead. Lemures threw its enormous head abaft and laughed into the nightturn. The daemon kicked Titen, sending the princeps sprawling, the blade clattering across the stones.

"We have to get back to the Obelisk," Ruane said as she winced, staring down the daemon as it turned their way.

"Now you want to listen to me?" he growled.

"You wou—"

"Silence, Ru!" He was so angry at her; he couldn't stop the venom. "I told you to run. You're acting like a hatchling." She tried to speak, but he shushed her with a curt hand motion. "Later. Get back to the Obelisk. Now!"

She glared at him but picked up her fallen longknife and ran the opposite direction after Wick and Finn, back toward the Obelisk.

Justice, she'll forgive me. I have to stop this thing. She'll forgive me…

The daemon's massive forelimbs slammed into the cobbled stones as it rushed toward him. Lojen took a breath, then spun as the daemon careened by, barely dodging the claws aimed at his body. The daemon skidded, turning, but Lojen was already running.

He scooped up the prone elfirish princeps, as well as the golden blade, carrying the goliath of a man like he was no more than a child. The daemon screeched after, following. Lojen ran with all the haste his body could give, the Hymn supplying him strength, paltry as it were.

Weaving in and out of villas, between gardens, past private walkways, under balconies. All aflame, all basted in black mist. Bodies, daemon and man alike, lay everywhere. Blood thick. Death cloying.

And yet, Lojen ran.

One of the bridges appeared ahead, there were a handful of people still trying to get across, the few legionnaires fighting daemons and scourges, soldiers of the Fallen's army. The clash of steel and claw loud, the screams louder.

"Put me down, Lojen." Titen squirmed in his grip and Lojen released the elfir, and in a stuttered step, the man raced toward the Fallen's invaders.

Titen brought the Golden Sword to bear, slicing, killing, stabbing. The legionnaires saw their leader, took heart, and redoubled their effort. They pushed the enemy back as Lojen helped the final stragglers across the bridge. It was then he noticed Ruane waiting in the doorway between the bridge and the Obelisk.

Calmed of his earlier outburst, Lojen made to speak only to hear the unmistakable laughter of Lemures. Spinning, he watched as the beast emerged.

"PATHETIC LITTLE CREATURES. THIS IS ALL YOU GOT? ALL THAT THE GODSBLOOD CAN MUSTER?"

"Lojen, the sledge!" Titen yelled as he ordered his legionnaires back across the bridge. "The pins!"

Ruane was holding the sledge when he raced across the bridge, practically throwing it at him. He fumbled with the tool, almost losing it over the ledge as it slipped through his claws, catching it at the last moment. With a fierce blow, Lojen slammed the head of the sledge against one of the four pins, knocking it free instantly. The hammer glowed emerald as the pin flew into the smoky distance, falling into the gap without a sound. Another swing knocked free the second pin from the opposite upper side, the bridge wobbling. Two of the four now gone.

But there were still legionnaires racing across, as was the Golden Sword of Kalderim.

"Lojen, do it!" Titen yelled as he faced the oncoming daemon by his lonesome.

"What are you waiting for?" Ruane screamed in his earholes.

He couldn't, not while there were others still on the bridge. A wardkeeper would never leave others behind. Not like this. His father wouldn't, he knew it.

Shoving the sledge into Ruane's hands, he ran across the gap, turning sideways so the last of the legionnaires could pass. Titen was blocking the whipping chains as Lemures set foot upon the bridge. It wobbled, the stone underneath as the third pin went flying from Ruane's swing, emerald filling his vision.

Lojen pulled up behind the elfir in the middle of the gap, and grabbed him by the cuirass, dragging him backward as the daemon swung, narrowly missing. Titen cursed as Lojen turned, thrusting the princeps back toward the Obelisk, putting his body between Titen and the daemon. Claws raked down Lojen's back, slicing through his sleeveless vest, tearing away some exoscales.

He cried out, falling forward. Head turning, he watched as Lemures sought to end him finally. Claws coming down. Red eyes a conflagration of hatred, of anger, of Death. Of the Dark Divine. Slowly, the end was coming.

He was prepared. Eyes closing, ready to meet his father once more. Peace would come for him.

And then a grunt, a jostle, a cry.

Lojen opened his eyes and saw Ruane slam into Lemures, dead in the center of the daemon's chest. Her roar lost as her momentum carried the daemon over the ledge of the bridge.

Lojen's own cry drowned out by the sorrow filling his soul. "Nooooo!"

Down Ruane and the daemon fell, hundreds of feet between the Obelisk and the mega-city of Gandtril. His talons reaching for his sister, wanting to protect her, but she was gone.

XLII

ASHE

ASHE'S FEET ACHED and her clothing was nothing more than dirty rags streaming behind her.

She shivered from the chill of the Sea of Mist but continued onward. Mind was numb; all she could think about was putting one foot in front of the other. Nothing moved aside from the rolling mist. She thought she saw shadows within the haze, but there was nothing there. Her stomach growled at her, her mouth was so dry, she felt as if she would succumb to death at any moment.

A twig snapped underneath her muddy boots and Ashe jumped. She kicked at the branch and let out a curse, but the grey turned translucent and was accompanied by wails. In the Meadows, not the Sea of Mist. Somehow, she was there beyond the veil of Life and Death.

The shattering wails plagued her as she ran. They called to her, begged her to unchain them. They followed after her, running alongside, pestering her for release. She did her best to ignore them, but their calls grated on her sanity.

Yet, she continued.

The yearning to understand herself drew her onward. It compelled her, though she had no idea which way she went anymore. The lack of sunlight within the Meadows turned her around, there was light to be certain, but not any light she knew. A non-light. There was no way to track her path, no way for her to see which direction she was heading.

But at this point, Ashe no longer cared. She would wander until she found her destination.

"IT WON'T BE MUCH LONGER, DEAR BRYNN."

Strix?

"NO, MY TRUE SELF."

I don't understand.

"YOU WILL."

Ashe collapsed to her knees. A light drizzle began to fall as she crumpled. Her raven-black hair clustered across her forehead in thick ringlets, so life-like within the void.

The Meadows looked the same in every direction. It looked like the Sea. Pools of brown, stagnant water, only ruffled by the drops of rain pelting the surface. Dead trees reached upward from the ground seeking a distant sun that never found them.

There was something strange about the mist here in the Meadows she couldn't place her finger on. There was something… alive within it. And yet, it also felt of Death. As if Death was alive, but that couldn't be true. Could it? The mist pooled around her feet, dancing up in rivulets of grey across her skin. It was cool to the touch, but there was an underlying warmth within at the same time. A certain comfort. Ashe felt at home within the mist, at ease. It comforted her. It made her think everything would be fine. She knew the Meadows, but this, this was different.

A cough wormed up in her chest, but the surrounding mist pressed down on her, forcing the pulmo back down.

'The mist is your tool, your weapon, your existence. Harness it, be it, and it will serve you'. The words of her father, and of the Last Godsking Canlon Carr, sprang to life like a fire from a spark.

With eyes closed, Ashe sucked in a breath and allowed the grey to rush around her, prodding and touching. She opened her arms, and it pierced her skin, running into her veins. It sought out her hurts, her pains, her weary thoughts. Muscles sore from exertion softened. Aches erased. Her mind cleared and she felt rejuvenated.

When she opened her eyes, the mist in the Meadows had cleared, leaving only small rivers flowing over the non-ground. Stars shone high above her in the non-night sky as the rain fell.

"YOU FEAR WHAT YOU ARE, DEAR BRYNN. DON'T."

What am I, Strix?

"YOU ARE GODSBLOOD AND A DAUGHTER OF NIGHTINGALE. DON'T SHY FROM YOUR BLOOD. DON'T SHY FROM WHAT YOU MUST DO. CANLON DID, SO DID ZENITH. YOU CAN FIX THIS."

Zenith?

"THE MIST IS YOURS, DEAR DAUGHTER. IT IS AETHER. YOURS TO COMMAND BY VIRTUE OF YOUR SOUL. HARNESS IT. MASTER IT. AND YOU CAN FIX WHAT MY HUSBAND FAILED TO DO."

Strix? I… what are you talking about? Strix?

The voice of the daemon blade went silent. Daemon blade? Was it?

Walking toward a tree best suited to protect her from the odd non-rain, Ashe noticed something grow within the mist. As she neared, she saw the markings of what used to be an outer wall. It had been made of stones, thick and strong. Yet, the wall had looked as if it had been broken in more than a few spots, as the stones lay in piles near the base of what used to be waist-thick columns lay broken and shattered.

She rushed to the wall and began to climb over the rubble, coming face-to-face with a metal gate. The gate had been smashed inward. She crawled through and found herself inside a mega-city's outer fortress.

Littered across the ground were bones and chunks of dead skin. Dried blood caked the packed earth of the fortress. She scanned the area, but nothing moved. A queer feeling crept over her, but she didn't care, so she plunged into the darkness of the spire that awaited at the edge of the destroyed fortress. More bodies, many missing parts: heads, arms, or legs. Her eyes adjusted quickly and she limped through the building, not sure where she was headed.

Ashe entered a rounded chamber. There upon a throne made of obsidian, was a man with all black eyes. Studying her, seeing through her. She should've felt scared, but she didn't. She knew him, but he was dead. She had killed him.

Behind the throne was an enormous black crystal that seemed to suck the light in. Its facets were jagged, and inky mist seeped from it. Majestic in its horror.

Noctis?

The Fallen reached his hand toward her, offering it palm up. Attached to his wrist was a blackened chain that fanned to rings on each of his fingers. In the palm was an obsidian crystal shaped in an eye. It looked like a shadow version of the Eye of the Soul.

"COME, GODSBLOOD. EMINENCE AWAITS."

And the mist urged her to join him.

NOOOOOOOO!

Blink.

Ashe rolled over and spit out the salty water that had gotten in her mouth, opened because she had been screaming.

"Ashe, are you alright?"

Wiping the sandy-tarry-salty-water from her mouth, she saw Harlequin hunched beside her on a beach, hand upon her shoulder. The vicar was paler than normal and her red hair hung loosely over her bloodstained cassock. The concern in her eyes was palpable and in that singular moment, Ashe had never seen such beauty.

Without thinking, she rose up into Harlequin's embrace, kissing her with everything in her body. In her soul.

Lips connecting, Harlequin returned the fierceness of Ashe's kiss. Their hands tangling in each other's damp hair. A force more powerful than anything in all of nature filled the negative space between their bond. Something only dreamt of. A euphoria.

Care. Safety. Need. Love.

The mist around them cradled, it bloomed with pure aether. It filled everything that was Brynn Benld, every pore. And as had happened when she'd called upon Mother Marrow in the Temple in the sands of Drenth, the world surged into her.

Life, all life, filled her soul. The earth blossomed beneath her body, vibrating as existence ebbed through every rock, every grain of sand. Water glistened of actuality. The chilled air sparked with warmth borne of synapses between atoms. Every beat of heart from Harlequin to the rhythmic heartbeats of fish in the VVyrm Ocean to every beat in Port Sin.

But a heavy weight fell upon her as she knew not every heart still beat that had an hour's turn before.

Fighting the urge to rip the other woman's cassock off, Ashe pulled back, and even in her somber mood, she smiled as she stared directly into Harlequin's eyes. "Worth the wait."

Harlequin twined her fingers through the mats of Ashe's locks. "Yes, it was." Despite the desire in her eyes, Harlequin frowned. "We have to report, Ashe."

Ashe smirked toward the woman she wanted more than anything in this world of Life. "Business first, eh, Harle-bub?"

"You're incorrigible. No, unmanageable, love."

"O, you love me regardless."

"IT CANNOT BE, DEAR BRYNN. THE WAY TO EMINENCE WILL BREAK ALL BONDS." The voice of the daemon blade sounded different than before. Less jovial, less carefree. More serious, more grim.

It made her think of the vision. Of Lu Har in the ruins, calling to her. Of the Strix and Noctis?

Strix, we need to talk.

"VERY SOON, DEAR DAUGHTER. SHE COMES AND ALL WILL BE REVEALED."

She?

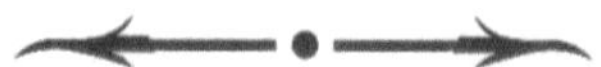

Ashe trudged up the shore, hand in hand with Harlequin, her hair and cassock jockeying for the title of most drenched.

It was a quiet procession, the pair from the Scattered Shards sloshed through the low tide on the southern end of Port Sin, down where the Guild Politic began. They were exhausted, for there had been no way to climb back up the cliffs to the Beggars Chain, so they had to swim around the curve of the peninsula.

Despite the ecstasy of finally ending her flirtatious dance with Harlequin, she was bogged down with the heavy weight of failure.

Using the aethecite to defeat the aerovern had been brash. A single-minded attempt to destroy her enemy without thinking of the impending consequences. And that's why she'd always pushed Cyan to take the hard cases, as she didn't want to have to make those quick decisions that could mean the deaths of others. It hit too close to home after the Temple of Mother Marrow.

In this case, she'd failed miserably. She'd sent many souls to the Meadows before their time, many who had not sinned enough to warrant an early demise.

O, Cyan… why?

The loss of her taskmaster would be something she would mourn for the rest of her days. She had loved him like a father. To no longer have his protective gaze upon her, to never be able to mock his bristled helm.

Gods… father…

Dawnbreak had risen, the soft glow of the sun illumining the beauty of the Guild Politic as they finally put foot on solid stone. The southern rim of Oldport Basin was full of massive mansions of Houses, the type of Guilders who weren't actively trying to screw their cohorts, figuratively for the most part. If there were any in Port Sin who simply enjoyed being fat and wealthy, this is where they lived. The beaches were kept clear of refuse and vagrants by the small armies employed by the Guilders who resorted in this part of the city. Old families with regal House names. Their homes were as large as fiefdoms, soaring as ziggurats of eons ago.

These were the Houses people like Klander and Dil wanted to burn down.

"Lady Drakeslayer?"

Ashe wearily found the halfblood giant, Clague, sitting on an expensive couch on the porch opposite none other than the Guild advisor, Roqanth. Clague, of all people Ashe didn't expect to sally forth this far south in Port Sin, was lounging esoterically. The halfblood's furry head took up a lot of real estate, his bushy beard trembled as he frowned, appearing distraught and nervous.

But seeing Roqanth here was queerer. And it was Roqanth who had spoken.

The elfirish advisor wore a waist-long coat studded in brass buttons over a dress bunched underneath them. Roqanth's flaxen hair was coiled behind their head, face painted in fine rouge, nails now lacquered black.

"What are you doing here?"

"Waiting for you, in fact," Roqanth answered as the Guild advisor leaned over and smacked the halfblood on the massive shoulder. "See, Clague, you shouldn't have worried so. With a name such as 'Lady Drakeslayer' it would take far more than a juvenile aerovern to end her. We are gladdened by your victory, Brynn Benld, for the Guild have long watched your rise."

"Let me guess, Icterine?"

Roqanth let a lilted laugh fly. "You'd expect any less? The Unfettered has plans for you, and it was ensured long ago you would reach such heights. But to the more pressing of matters." Their gaze settled on Ashe. "You've done well, Godsblood. I must admit, I didn't think much of you upon first sight, but I've been wrong before. I knew I should have trusted my friends when they said you'd be more than a match for Solanine and the blooddrakes."

Ashe wasn't certain if she should be angry or not. In fact, she was confused. "How? Why?"

Clague stood, his full height blotting out the rising sun in the east, which was now poking over the mansion of whatever House they were in the back of. He held out a hand to Roqanth, who took it and stood. Taking two steps toward Ashe. "You think you're the only one with eyes in this city, Lady Drakeslayer?"

She blinked. "No… I…"

"The Guild has eyes everywhere, Lady Drakeslayer. Especially down here in Port Sin. And the Guild pays well for one who slays the Gods."

"You're a spy for the Guild? I thought you were just sucking the prick of that Guilder."

"In a way, yes," Roqanth said. "The High Seat in Alizarin has long surmised my benefactor was up to something. And I've done well over the years keeping tabs on people the High Seat wants watched. I warned you, Brynn Benld, you'd need friends. But it is not the Guild and the High Seat in which my talents were requested for here. Instead a friend of both mine and yours."

"Prefer the sheets?" Harlequin snarked.

The spy glanced at the vicar. "You'd be surprised what you can learn between the sheets, vicar. My business is a passion of mine." Ashe chortled, but she was wondering who Roqanth was speaking of, their joint friend. "As is keeping the Mistlands free from the corruption of the Fallen. My friend sent me to be prepared should the Seal of *Ignis* be troubled."

"What's the meaning of this?" demanded a voice from a balcony in the nearest mansion. A plump Guilder stood in a velvety robe, hair askew. "You're intruding on private Hou—"

"Silence, Dagen," Roqanth cut the Guilder off. "Go back inside and tug your one-eyed cyclops before I have you silenced forever." The man was speechless. He began stuttering arguments. "Don't make me tell your mother what a deviant her son is."

"You fuckin' who—"

"Finish that sentence and I'll make sure Clague takes that wrinkled fish you call your prick and feed it to the harpies." The Guilder called Dagen huffed and slammed the glass door of his balcony, shattering the panes with a loud crash. "I hate these Guilder's sons. If I had half a mind, I'd… never mind. Where were we?"

Ashe glanced at Harlequin, but she merely shrugged, conceding the floor to her, so to speak. "Of our mutual friend."

"Of course. Clague is loyal." The spy beheld the halfblood with friendly admiration. "Once I heard you were coming to the city, I knew your taskmaster would come to Clague. Rest his soul in the Meadows. I so very dislike what those blooddrakes did to him. But I digress… I was still mildly surprised you, yourself, Lady Drakeslayer, would come to *The Parlour* while you investigated my benefactor. Alas, the poor bastard is dead now."

"Dead by your hand, Lady Drakeslayer," Clague said. "In the destruction of your aetheurgy and the aerovern. Done us both a service there."

"*The Axe…*"

"*The Axe* was unfortunate. But our friend has accepted the ancillary adverse effects of what happened there. Those who fight the Fallen accept the loss of life in the fight, although, I lament it. Call it my Calibrathian nature. Say what you will about us elfir, you can take us out of the forest, but you can't take the forest out of us."

Ashe was growing tired of all of Roqanth's cryptic half-answers. It was time for her get hers. "Klander was a blooddrake, did your friend know this?"

"She did, told me as such," Roqanth said with a smile. *She, at least that's a start,* Ashe thought while the elfir continued. "A shame really, I'd have liked to see his death. But he was incinerated by our joint friend in the aftermath of your, shall we call it, exploits in *The Axe*. Destroyed by aether."

Aether? Who could… Then it hit her. "Maja Carr?"

"I keep telling you we'd be friends." The elfir smiled. "Maja Carr is not what you think she is, Brynn Benld, but she is my friend, as is she yours. Her story is hers and hers alone to tell. However, the true source of this conspiracy of blooddrakes remains free."

"Solanine."

"Fled," Clague said.

"That's why we're here," Roqanth continued. "Not but an hour's turn after the unfortunate events at *The Axe*, Neron Hobb's glory, *Peerless*, was seen pushing out in the Bay of Fire. Maja Carr will meet you at Hobb's old roost once she finishes her business with another friend of ours. You must give chase to Solanine, end the drake once and for all. The Fallen must not gain a foothold with the Seal of *Ignis*. Port Sin will always have its detractors, but this city is part of the Guild. And I intend to keep it that way, I enjoy this mega-city."

"You saw Cyan? I mean Solanine was in Cyan…"

Roqanth gave a somber shake of their head. "Your taskmaster's… body was found. But not like you imagine. It was…" They suppressed a shiver.

Ashe already knew what it meant. The blooddrake had shed Cyan's scales. Fucker.

"I know how much his loss will come to mean to you, Lady Drakeslayer, believe me, I know."

"Do you?"

"Alas, we share many commonalities," Ro said. "Too many."

"I WOULDN'T TRUST THEM, DEAR BRYNN."

And why not, Strix?

"I... I JUST WOULD BE CAREFUL."

Suit yourself.

"You may want this." Clague had pulled Cyan's Gauntlet from the bag slung across his mighty frame. He handed it to Harlequin. She ran a finger over the runes etched into it, tears forming in her eyes.

Zenith's cock... She had to remain strong. Mourn later. Hard as it might be, that's what her taskmaster would have demanded of her. The harsh taskmaster. Her father in all but name.

"You wouldn't happen to have some wine, would you?" The spy laughed. Ashe guessed as much. "There's another blooddrake. A servant of the Shards."

Roqanth's beautiful elfirish face tilted, one side of their mouth curling upward. They reached into their waistcoat and pulled out an object, handing it over to Ashe. "Then, I suggest you be careful."

It was her golden filigreed flask. She tested it with a shake and a slosh spoke back. The grin of all grins. "Thank you, friend. I've needed this."

To Cyan... and then she drank.

Neenah

XLIII

THE REVITALIZED NEENAH LEFLEUR

THE SHITHOLE THAT was Port Sin arose from the Sea that gathered under the emerald-blue of the dawnbreak sky.

Port Sin was one of Neenah LeFleur's favorite mega-cities in all the Mistlands. There was always something to do, jobs to be bargained for, and women to toss or men to ride. It was a woman of her style's playground. Not to mention all the spirits and ale one could consume.

Neenah slapped Roland's meaty shoulder and exited the wheelhouse of *Marrow's Lover*, heading for the bow, to where Valeria Dunleith stood, her alabaster hands gripping the rail, stoically taking in Oldport Basin.

Like any mega-city, though, Port Sin had a defined area for airships to dock, but unlike those of Kanja and Altreyia, Port Sin's was nothing but an open tract of land compacted hard under the gaze of Mount Bastard. Due to the jagged foothills that surrounded the volcano's base for leagues like a wall of stony swords, only a handful of airships were moored. Though there were paved roads and stone structures lined up in imperfect order along the craggy outcroppings, people and voidspawn ran in organized chaos.

Roland deftly brought *Marrow's Lover* into landing position. Due to her low hull and lack of metal propellers, she was able to land with an ease that most transports couldn't. Many people stopped their tasks and watched in awe as the smaller airship docked.

She is a bloody beauty, isn't she? Neenah thought proudly.

Zag (or maybe it was Zig?) threw down one of the mooring lines. One of the dock workers caught it and tied it off to a stone block. Then the bugger (it was definitely Zag) jumped over the railing and slid down the line to the ground below. Zig tossed down the second line to his brother, then beamed at Neenah.

"Get back to work, you bugger!" Zig (hopefully it was Zig) ran off to fetch the ladder and Neenah heard the voidspawn laughing the entire time. *Marrow's Lover* swayed slightly as both lines were tied off and the rope ladder dropped. The captain rested her arms on the railing near to the daughter of the Golden Throne. "What's got you so puckered tightly, eh? You bloody forced us to high tail it here on the quick, hear?"

The bikrome's silvery hair shimmered in the early morning sunlight, as did the reflecting gold and silver bikromi bracelets around her frail wrists. A stray thought of how much those bracelets might sell for in the underground of Krylen fleeted through Neenah's thoughts. She shook them away.

As the Sea wilted under the growing daylight, Neenah noticed that the mega-city was not the mega-city she remembered. In fact, it appeared as if a large portion of the western sectors were either gone or drenched in smoke. And if Neenah LeFleur had to guess, she knew whose feet to lay the blame.

"The Godsblood is near." Confirmation of Neenah's suspicion. "As is Solanine. I can sense them both. Bliss has set the stage for the end."

"O?" Speaking true, Neenah wanted to be as far away from that godsdamned aetheurgist Solanine, but she knew her legend was linked to that of Brynn Benld. She just wished she didn't have to be so pissing close to the action all the time. "The little bint'll be fine, bikrome. You said it yourself."

This time, the elfir turned, her all-black eye and all-white eye bore into her, so much so that the proud Neenah LeFleur couldn't help but shiver. "It's not her I fear for." Neenah couldn't stop her stubborn legs from forcing her back a step. This caused the bikrome to smile. "Fret not, captain, I wasn't talking about you. Bliss hasn't shown me your death just yet." With that, the fourth child of Kalderim made toward the ladder.

"Bugger me," Neenah breathed.

Roland walked out of the wheelhouse and locked the door behind him. The big man passed the key to Neenah, who pocketed it. The rest of her crew appeared, awaiting her selection of those who would join them in the city. After being swindled by the Fallen in Krylen, she wouldn't dare leave her prized airship in the hands of the dockmasters. Her crew was motley to be sure, but she trusted every one of those bloody bastards, she did before, but especially after what had happened in Gandtril.

That brought another shiver. By the Pentax her stout heart was growing weak.

The escape from the Fallen and Gandtril had been clean and straightforward once they'd taken to the sky after their rescue by Valeria Dunleith. The first night, they camped aboard the airship, aloft in the sky fifty feet above the ground, still safely within the Sea's fog. They could see Gandtril burning off in the distance, the flames of the once great mega-city building a solid glow in the nightturn. It was a somber sight, and the hobgoblin twins had remained silent for once.

The next morning had brought the terror that had befallen the city. It had started as soon as dawnbreak, the clipped voices, the shouts, the steady churn of those fleeing the destruction. By the hundreds they came, the people of Gandtril did. Survivors streamed through the Sea, coming perilously close to where *Marrow's Lover* was moored. If not for Tris' keen dvergirish sense of sound, they might've been overrun. Tris had been on watch, surprisingly alone and without Doll nearby. The dvergir had raised the alarm long before the tide of flesh did.

The mist hadn't been too dense that dawnbreak, and once the forefront of the survivors spied *Marrow's Lover* anchored just above the ground, the horde made a mad dash straight for it. It was mayhem, a river of people hurrying through the fog. Babies cried as parents lugged them toward the supposed safety of the airship. Children ran beside, sniffling.

Neenah would have helped those she could, none could ever accuse Neenah LeFleur of leaving the helpless to suffer, but the worst had followed the survivors: the army of the Fallen and his daemons.

Gunshots exploded, shrieks of the void, screams of death not long after. The fleeing Kanjans raced toward her airship, begging and crying for them to wait. But Valeria told Roland to fly, even as tears streamed down her pale face.

Though truth told, Neenah's heart broke as the first mate put rudder to the slaughter.

Neenah shook the memory aside, focusing on the matters at hand. "I'll need three to watch the ship," she said. "I know you all deserve some fun and relaxation after Gandtril and all. But Neenah LeFleur will not allow some bloody prick-sucker to steal my ship from under our noses while we toss some whores and throw dice. Will she?"

Her crew acknowledged with an "Aye." Not to mention a few eye rolls and grins.

She nodded to herself, satisfied with their answer. "Right. So, Zig and Zag, you two bloody buggers stay aboard. Can't take either of you anywhere, you don't shut your godsdamned mouths for nothing! And Tris, you stay, too. I need someone with a level-buggering-head to watch over these two." The twins were about to voice their disagreement, but Neenah shushed them. "Bugger me, you two will stay here with Tris, and if I can, I'll arrange for some whores to come visit you. Port Sin usually has some hobbies willing to toss for coin."

Their eyes lit up with excitement, though Tris grimly nodded, eying Doll. No one could call Neenah unkind to her crew.

Roland knelt beside Alexina, whispering in her ear. The girl looked distressed but nodded. The one-eyed mate locked eye with Neenah and she knew he had told the girl to stay behind as well.

"You know what, Doll, you stay behind as well." That got Tris' attention. "Roland, you, too." The big man was about to protest but she put a bejeweled finger up. "We might need to make a bloody quick exit, seeing as how this place looks like a pair of mating vvyrms trounced over half this godsdamned city mid-hump." She backhanded his girth. "Wouldn't want you to find the wrong bed again."

He grinned. "Wouldn't that be the norm, eh, Cap'n?"

"'Member that time," one of the hobgoblins started but Neenah had already hopped over the rail and gracefully made her way down the ladder.

Valeria Dunleith, who had covered her silver Kanjan hair under a cloaked cowl, waited patiently, and when Neenah dismounted, the bikrome took off through the docking yard toward the eastern gate of Port Sin where it filtered into the

Barter Yard. The gate was wide open and had once been made of heavy steel bars, but nowadays the bars were either bent or rusted. In all her times to Port Sin, Neenah had never seen the gate shut. There were guards at the doors, to be certain, but she only saw one standing upright. The rest were sitting while drinking, leaning against something while drinking, or flat out drunk upon the ground that their weapons were lying uselessly next to them. The mist, itself, coated the slummy marketplace in thick waves, like a bastardized cyclone of somber death. The aethecite-powered vacuum pumps were rusted along the jagged walls as Mount Bastard looked down upon the burghal with a sneer.

And that didn't even mention the stench.

The malodor of Port Sin was so strong, Neenah wrinkled her nose. Normally, the City of Sin smelt like feces mixed with offal. Pleasant would be a word nowhere near what she'd describe it as. But now, the overpowering scent of death lingered far too closely for Neenah's tastes.

Neenah and her unlikely companion passed through the gates without a single bat of an eye or a follow-up question.

Men fought in an alley over an unmoving body in the mud. All held daggers. They stopped and stared at her before resuming their brawl over the contents of the poor soul's coinpurse.

"This used to be Neenah LeFleur's kind of place, hear?" she said after they left the gates, swallowed up by the city that was filled to the brim with the shit of humanity.

"Bliss' grace watch over these souls," Valeria said softly.

Dilapidated buildings lined rutted streets, decaying down into the ground. Walls crumbling, lying in piles that should've been stories high, but now were hardly standing. Roofs falling inward, paint nonexistent, windows busted or shuttered. Garbage and human excrement filled the aggers, smeared the walls. Dead bodies littered cluttered alleyways as rabid dogs and rats picked at bones of rotting corpses. Drunkards swaggered the ill-kempt streets of the Barter Yard, begging for anything they could get. Blood and booze-stained shirts and beards.

A shadow slunk away from one of the walls toward them. A whore by the look of her. Ill dressed, homely with missing front teeth and disheveled hair.

She looped an arm through Neenah's, the other going to the front of her belt. "Milady, care for a tongue to the privy?" Her breath was putrid, smelling of ale.

Gripping the whore's hand, the impeccable Neenah LeFleur tidily spun her away. But the strumpet was persistent. She put hands to Neenah's shoulders, guiding her off the street, away. "It won't take long, milady. Your friend won't miss you long. Though she might enjoy herself after you for a quadran."

Neenah was usually never one to turn down a proper toss, but not like this, so, she pushed the woman off again, shoving her hard. As she did, there was sudden movement within the alley behind, another shadow had lunged forward, a blade glinting. Because she was already moving, the blade stabbed directly into the whore's stomach. A thing the bint hadn't been expecting. She gasped, then screamed, then proceeded to fall to the muddy ground to writher about as blood spilled out her gap-toothed mouth as the second assailant took off running.

"Bloody godsdamned thieves," she spat, even though it was a vulgar thing to do as someone of her stature, but so was trying to plant a knife in someone's back who didn't deserve it. To Valeria, "Where to, bikrome?"

"The Parlour of Innocent Sirens."

"Now you're talking Neenah LeFleur's language."

Not even half an hour in, and Neenah was bloody bored.

She lounged upon a bench in *The Parlour's* tavern, an offshoot from the hallway behind the main stairway where Valeria Dunleith had ascended to the fourth floor, telling her to wait and not get caught up in all the 'fun' the brothel had to offer. Neenah's leg was thrown over the armrest, a mug of ale in her hand.

Normally, she would've ignored carousing as it were, but with that intrepid bikrome telling her that the little bint Ashe might show up at any moment, she was starting to get antsy. Like a ball of twine, all wrapped up in a bikrome's game.

There were plenty of handsome-looking poppets sauntering through the brothel, most wearing nothing at all, more lace and ribbon. Blonde to dark-haired and every shade in between, skin ranging from porcelain to onyx. All bosom, petite, curvy. Lots of boys, too. Even some various other species if that was a pleasure. Patrons stumbling around in drunkenness and lewdness. Flesh waiting for the right price.

The bouquet of the brothel was fragrant, a stark contrast to the smokey outside—of which Neenah had learned that, indeed, a young sprat of the Scattered Shards had caused a major calamity in the Beggars Chain. It was no doubt the Benld girl. But the roses, they were everywhere: the ground, the walls, upon the stairs leading to the rooms above. Dried roses to mask the funk of sex that permeated the entire place.

The clientele sat on plush chairs with workers naked atop them, their breasts or backsides in faces, bottoms grinding. Others stroked trousers; a few hands disappeared into clothing. Others on knees. Moaning and laughing. And buggering.

Aside from the blatant—mind, the jealous—displays of sex, a stage set two feet above the ground was near to where Neenah lounged. Two women were dancing naked to a songster playing a lute besides the stage. A soft melody, one Neenah recognized was from northern Altreyia. Both whores had paint upon their bodies, forms in no discernible manner.

"Like I said, used to be Neenah LeFleur's kind of place," she said all ho-hum into her mug of ale. Strong drink only did so much to calm Neenah LeFleur.

There was a throaty screech from upstairs on the second floor. It rippled at the walls, loud and passionate. Men stopped kissing whores; whores stopped faking pleasure at their clients' touches. All looked around in astonishment.

Then laughter.

"Someone's getting theirs," a portly man crowed, a doe-eyed, dark-haired girl upon his lap. She slapped him playfully. He tickled her fiercely.

More laughter. And the carousing went on.

Neenah drank her ale, then absently ran her tongue over her golden teeth. A bored smuggler led to bad times for all. It was one of her rules she lived by.

Finished with her drink, she rose and went to the barkeep, slamming the mug on the counter. "Give me another." The barkeep took the mug and filled it from one of the wooden barrels behind the counter. "Bloody good stuff. Got a bit of lemon in it?"

"Brew it m'self," the lanky woman said. Her hair cut straight across her eyebrows, dark with a bit of grey. "Lord Klander'd let me experiment with the recipe. Before he got roasted, that is. In *The Axe*."

"'Tis good. What you call it?"

"Lorrai's Palle?"

"Why two bloody 'L's in it?"

"Reminds me of a snake I once owned. Youse gon' be able to pay for all this ale youse be drinkin'? Clague's not one to skimp on quadrans."

"Where is that prick-sucker anyhows?" She hadn't seen the halfblood giant lumbering around the place. Maybe that was him in the back with a customer. She tried to envision someone atop that furry man-beast and stopped the thought before it took root, giving her nightmares. Clague was a good friend, though.

"Been out since… ah last nightturn. When the hubbub went down at *The Axe*. Same with Roqanth."

"'Course he was. Bloody pissing fool. Who's Roqanth?"

The barkeep shrugged. "Lord Klander's Guild advisor."

"O," Neenah said, moving away from the bar to resume her boredom—and watch two newcomer whores, a shy brown-haired lad and an olive-skinned curvaceous thing—when Roland barged into the room, *The Parlour's* front doors banging off their hinges.

The big one-eyed first mate grabbed the mug from Neenah's hand and took a drink.

"Buggers, that's mine!" she squeaked irritably.

"We've got trouble," the bald bastard said.

"Better be good, otherwise I'll have your ass caned for stealing Neenah LeFleur's bloody ale, hear?"

Roland downed the ale in a single gulp. "Scourges."

"Bugger me. Thought they were all dead as driftwood."

Valeria hadn't yet returned, but a captain of Neenah LeFleur's pedigree knew when to cut and run. And this was shaping up to be such a moment. Luckily, the bikrome descended from the stairway.

"Ease, captain." The bikrome smoothed her cloak as she stepped up toward Neenah. "All is as Bliss foretold."

"You're a crazy one, witch. You knew scourges would come?"

"I knew they'd follow us to Port Sin. Perhaps even more than scourges. That is why we are here. To draw them out."

"To draw them out?"

As if on command, there was a sudden change in the room. The warmth bled from it, leaving only a deathly cold behind. One by one, aethecite-powered and seagandr-powered lights winked out until only the stage was lit. A demented cackling came from the raised platform.

Neenah turned, a frightened gasp escaping, although she'd argue it was just the ale and not surprise.

One of the dancers had sprouted wings out of her back, arms disappearing into gossamer folds. Three appendages resembling talons protruded from her chest, all leathery and dry. Eight eyes grew from the face, almost like that of a spider. Fangs dripped from an elongated snout.

The other's hair had formed into giant horns, black as night. Her torso gaped with a maw of razor-sharp teeth. Her human head had become encased in thick plate-like pieces, her eyes missing, only the plates in their place.

Dae-bloody-mons.

The lute player threw down his lute and cravenly bolted.

"VALERIA!" both daemons roared as one.

Before the two daemons could even dive from the raised stage, liquid fire of sapphire melting into peridot struck them. Aether lifted them into the air, further aetheurgy throwing them against the far wall of the brothel.

Valeria stood with both arms outstretched, fingers twisting and curling toward the writhing creatures, her bracelets dripping with frost. Pinned to the wall, the daemons wailed as they burned. Cracks formed, the mist seeping into *The Parlour*, wrapping the daemons in a cocoon. But not protectively, deadly instead. The two shrieked louder.

A crash behind the closed outer doors, Neenah heard. Shouts and rasps of steel being drawn. A pummel against the door. A loud snarl.

"Daemons!" screamed a whore from up the stairs.

"Scourges!" yelled another patron as he staggered inside, his face full of blood.

Then the door was surrounded by glowing green aether. *Terris* formed at the edges, like mortar filling the gaps, strengthening the door, a wall building.

Neenah drew a thin dagger from her belt and pulled out her trusty multi-barrel wheellock pistol she kept sheathed in her boot. "We better bloody run, bikrome, hear?"

The bikrome had beads of sweat forming along her hairline, as one arm stretched toward the daemons, holding them in place, the other back toward the door, sewing and cementing it closed. Fingers moving and calling.

It was her doing, her aetheurgy that held the daemons at bay.

"THE FALLEN WILL NOT BE STOPPED!" the daemon with the wings croaked.

"THE PIT IS FULL OF US," the giant horned one bellowed. *"MORE OF US THAN YOU. TRAITOR YOU ARE, VALERIA DUNLEITH."*

"The Pit knows no end," Valeria said, loud enough to be heard over the screeching, even though to Neenah it still sounded like a whisper. "Wretched and forlorn you are."

The bikrome's hands blazed with *Ignis*, the work at the door complete, keeping the scourges from entering. The mist darkened and the aether pulsed in anticipation as Valeria turned her attention back on the daemons. She then yanked her hands back, the aether from her fingers dying and disappearing. The daemons fell and the bikrome waved her fingers angrily. They wailed again, the daemons, this time to a fever pitch. The mist coiled about them, binding them, cinching tight around. They struggled and fought against the aetheurgy, breaking it, they couldn't.

"Tell your master that the blood of Nightingale will break the Seals," said a gravelly voice from behind, "locking Nocturne's Pit forever!"

Neenah spun to the new voice, and she nearly shat her britches at what she saw. It was a draconem, but unlike anything she'd ever seen before.

Near black interlocking scales like a drakken formed over an elongated snout. Rounded protrusions covered the crest from the nostrils to above the blue-red eyes, where it morphed into a pair of two-foot long black, keratin horns sloping backward and upward to a point. But that's where the similarities to a drakken ended. This draconem had but two arms and only a graceful tail, no legs. Down the back the protrusions ran all the way to the tip of the tail.

The draconem brought clawed talons together. Bright sapphire brilliance erupted in the darkness of the room, yawning under the daemonic pair. A gateway opened, piercing wails meeting Neenah's ears as the mist—now black and angry—dragged the beasts into the chasm, sealing behind them.

Then there was a massive concussion in the closing of the veil between worlds. The walls of the brothel shattered as flames leapt into existence. The heat was inferno. Out into the streets beyond the wall exploded, the flames licking the entire place that was *The Parlour of Innocent Sirens*. People raced from the brothel in droves.

The room fell silent, over it was in seconds. Neenah didn't know if she'd breathed once the entire time.

"Captain," Valeria whispered, her head cocked to the side. "Captain," she repeated. "We must find the Godsblood. Solanine set this trap to snare me from meeting with Maja."

"Come!" the draconem announced in a guttural growl. This creature must be 'Maja'. "The Fallen will not waste any more time. The Seal awaits."

The draconem called upon aether once more, this time *Terris*. A quake summoned and aimed toward the outer wall of the building. Crumbling into oblivion, the Red Moon District beyond. Valeria bolted through the opening, cloak flowing behind. The draconem slithered out in undulating waves, almost like a snake but vertical instead of along the ground.

Neenah gawped, and it took Roland grabbing her by the arm before she cursed. "Shit."

XLIV
ASHE

AS ASHE AND Harlequin made their way through the Harbor of Thieves, she cursed, “O, well, Zenith’s fucking cock, not him.”

At far end of the Harbor stood Grand Quaestor Owl.

The entire area in front of Hobb’s tavern was cordoned off, quaestors keeping watch, shuttling dockworkers and fisheries onward, using wheellock rifles to prod traders and merchants, forcefully moving gawkers and pickpockets along. Many of the tainted warriors disliked the beat such as this, others looked bored, waving some through the lines.

“Ashe, love, you might want to get your ‘fuck you’ face on.” Harlequin was staring straight ahead, right at the magnificent warship *Dauntless* and the gaggle of quaestors waiting behind the grand quaestor. A giant bird circled overhead, and Ashe knew which bird it was, same as Harlequin. “Maybe that daemon at your hip can help you.”

“I LIKE HER. YOU SHOULD KEEP HER, DEAR BRYNN.”

“Yes, yes, plan on it.”

As they reached the warship, and subsequently the grand quaestor, the hobgoblin servant by the old quaestor’s side jumped from his rickety stool and scampered over, a big smile splitting his sorry face. "Lady Drakeslayer!" he said cheerfully.

She gave the hobgoblin a wink, but her gaze went to the mighty *Dauntless.*

Between the two ships formerly in Hobb's regatta, the *Peerless* was the queen bee of the seas. Fast, sleek, and unparalleled. It was no wonder the blooddrakes took the greater of the two vessels, but the *Dauntless* wasn't a bridesmaid.

Whereas the *Peerless* was designed for speed, the *Dauntless* was built for war.

The *Dauntless* was a beast of a vessel, pushing close to one hundred feet and a hundred tons. Three masts of sails. Bowsprit in the shape of a kraken butting heads with the hull, tentacles fraying out toward the sea. The steering wheel was midships, right under the mizzen, raised upon a platform with a circular stair from deck to wheel. Cannons lined the deck, piles of rounded iron stacked in small pyramids.

Ashe then bent down and cupped the hobbie's face. "Forgive me, Cadoz. I don't have time to chat with you right now, just your prick-sucker of an employer."

Harlequin sniggered.

Grand Quaestor Owl's grey-skinned, stretched face appeared slightly flushed, most likely due to the bruises formed along the mussed tundra-white beard. Part of the grand quaestor's face was covered in bloody gauze, for Owl must have taken some injury during the events of *The Arbiter's Axe*. The gangplank beside the grand quaestor had a handrail and the magnificent strix ruffled its feathers from where it perched upon it.

Digging out the small tin of lard, Owl fed the preening strix, watching with yellowed orbs. Owl's owl slurped the flakes of lard from the tin while the grand quaestor combed a withered hand down the feathers. "Where is your taskmaster, Vicar Harlequin?" Owl asked, closing the lard tin. "As official Shards protocol states, he should have reported immediately before an arrest of a Guilder. He will reap the punishment." To Ashe, "And you, acolyte, barging into a Guilder's warehouse without warrant? What were you thinking?"

"Cyan's dead, Owl," Ashe said. "He'd been taken over by a blooddrake. You'd know that if your brittle ass didn't take so long to get to *The Axe*."

A deadly grin parted Owl's beard. "Your insubordination will be Icterine's fall, girl. Provoking a grand quaestor is not wise. You'd do best to restrain yourself after what you've done in *The Axe*. It's going to take weeks to uncover the bodies."

Maybe tact would work better with this old fossil. Her voice became soft. "With all due respect, grand quaestor, time was but of the essence. There was no time to spare in following protocols when the Seal is at stake."

Owl regarded her curiously. "One should think someone in your place would recognize the need for propriety. You younglings overstep your bounds without thought. You need to remember your place. Every creature under Zenith has its place. Regardless," Owl continued, "what do you have to report in your taskmaster's stead? Bear in mind, I will send my opinion on your actions to the Conclave. I remember a time when young members of this institution had respect for the office. Were he still alive, Cyan the Defiant would be up for reparations for your behavior."

Ashe had no doubt the grand quaestor's report would be full of slander. "Nothing you already aren't familiar with. *The Axe* fell apart. I blew up the Beggars Chain. Killed Phlox the Faithful for being a traitorous prick. Standard codex stuff."

"I SENSE YOU ARE TRYING TO GOAD THIS MORTAL, DEAR BRYNN. I WONDER WHY."

Funsies, Strix. "O, don't want to forget that my taskmaster was taken over by a draconem we thought long since dead and dusted. Don't want to forget that, even though you aren't showing any remorse over his death."

Owl's bushy eyebrows rose above round spectacles. "Withholding information from a grand quaestor? A capital offense to your rank, acolyte."

Before Ashe's tongue could form a retort, Harlequin nudged her and pointed.

Behind Grand Quaestor Owl stood Maja Carr's hulking orcirish bodyguards. Arms crossed, Shon and Solly had matching scowls, which due to their underbites made it seem like someone grabbed their bottom lips and yanked up so hard, it covered half their face.

One of them beckoned with a massive, green-skinned hand.

Seeing the opening, Ashe bowed her head. "Forgive, grand quaestor, but it appears we are being summoned."

Owl blew frustration out through the snow-white beard. "By Nocturne, this Guilder is overstepping her bounds. By the by, acolyte, when you are released, come make your teams' report. I want all details regarding Vicar Cyan's death."

Red-pupiled eyes glared at her, but Ashe merely smiled before hacking up a pulmo cough near Owl's feet.

Climbing the gangplank, Harlequin leaned close to Ashe's ear. "Why do you continue to provoke the grand quaestor? What do you gain from it?"

The orcirish bodyguards parted to allow them to board the ship. Barely up to one of the oricir's belly, Ashe backhanded one of the brothers playfully. "Don't talk much, eh? D'ya sing, bub?"

The orcir growled. "Not much a voice, he." To Harlequin's bewildered look, "What? We're about to set sail, Harle-bub, don't sailors sing?"

Ashe began singing a bawdy shanty, so perilously out of key was the famed dvergirish song *'Under the mountain we drink, O'er the mountain we drink'.*

As her verse ended, she lowered her voice, "I don't trust Owl, neither should you."

"Is that what you called singing?" Harlequin said loudly, picking up the verse where Ashe left off.

Ashe grinned, then finished the last verse of the tune. "I'm just full of surprises, Harle-bub."

"I don't think that's what I'd call a surprise."

"YOU MORTALS MAKE NO SENSE. ARE YOU TRYING TO USE SUBTERFUGE OR ARE YOU TRYING TO FLIRT WITH YOUR MORTAL LOVER? I CANNOT TELL THE DIFFERENCE..."

Ashe glanced over her shoulder and saw Owl staring after them, a skeletal hand combing the owl's feathers. "Strix, that's not nice. I bet I could make her sing real nice."

Sailors scrambled all about the deck, setting mast lines, scrubbing the wooden hull, checking supplies, crawling up the mizzen and repairing the sails. Other tainted warriors of the Scattered Shards hauled crates of food and barrels of water, putting them in the appropriate places by the orders of a first mate who was suspiciously familiar looking; a big one-eyed man. But what was he doing here in Port Sin? Some quaestors sharpened blades, others oiling wheellock pistols or rolling powder, fitting bullets. It was mayhem as the ship was getting prepared to sail. Of the captain, there was no sight.

The sailors began throwing mooring lines, getting ready to push off, but stopped as a procession of tainted warriors of the

Shards marched up the plank. A great shadow flew overhead, a whooshing of wings. It fluttered down upon the wheelhouse. The strix. Grand Quaestor Owl ghosted up the gangplank, using the ancient staff of office for support. Cadoz the hobgoblin skittered behind, struggling with a fanciful chair.

Ashe avoided eye contact with the grand quaestor and was instead pulled by a voice that lifted above the noise.

"You boot-licking, godsdamned bugger better not drop that bloody crate where you were pissing planning to, you voidspawn fiend. Well, looky here, the little bint herself. That you, girl?"

Ashe put a hand to her brow to block the sun, gaze lifting toward the top of the wheelbox. There stood a woman who needed no introduction. Captain Neenah LeFleur.

"Good to see you, captain," she said. "Never thought to see you in Port Sin, but I'm sure I can count on you to have some whiskey aboard?"

"Don't know what you think you bloody know of Neenah LeFleur, little bint, but it ain't that she's not good to her bloody crew." Neenah leaned on the railing, staring down at them, her mussed brown hair fluttering in the wind, her knee-long coat snapping against her thighs. "But you know it about the whiskey. See me after we set sail, poppet, need to hear all about your trip to Port Sin, hear?"

With that, Captain LeFleur turned and began cursing at a pair of hobgoblins. Good ol' Zig and Zag.

One of the giant orcir motioned toward the hold. A stout set of steps led downward into the hull. Aethecite lamps swung from the inner beams, swaying as the ship undulated on the Bay of Fire.

There were more sailors down here doing sailor things beyond Ashe's frame of reference. There was no time to ponder as the orcir pushed deeper into the bowels of the ship, past cabins, past tangled canvas bunks hanging from the bulkheads.

A knock on a small door not much taller than she. It opened into what she assumed was the captain's cabin. It was a dank, cramped space at the stern, hardly bigger than a prison cell. She and Harlequin were bundled in, the orcir shoving the door closed. It was a tight fit.

A bed was built into the hull, curved to match the curve of the ship. Wardrobe at the foot, drawers under the thin mattress. A small writing table affixed opposite with a seagandr-oil lamp atop, the wick lit low, leaving the room in shadows.

A cloaked figure sat at the table, another upon the bed. The one on the bed withdrew the cowl of the cloak and out streamed long, silver hair over the pale face of an elfir. The elfir had one black eye, one white. Bikromi seer sight bracelets clacked as the woman put them in her lap.

"Valeria?"

"We meet again, Brynn Benld. The time has come for you to make your next move toward Eminence." The bikromi daughter of the Golden Throne held out a hand toward the cloaked figure. "Maja, if you will?"

"Godslayer." The voice wasn't the melodic articulation of the Guilder, but was more guttural, more animalistic. "The end of your case is nigh. The truth you seek is yours, should you seek it. No more secrets. No more lies. The path to the Seals to Eminence has been drawn. Your blood must seek it, Godsblood."

"YOU ASKED FOR TRUTHS, DEAR BRYNN. HERE YOU GET THEM. SOME MAY NOT BE WHAT YOU WISH TO LEARN."

Great.

A hand reached out, turned the flame up on the lamp. The cloak slipped from Maja Carr's shoulders, no longer an elfir. No longer the face of statuesque perfection. No longer a woman.

Instead of flesh, was interlocking scales. An elongated snout. Rounded protrusions from the red-blue eyes down the back of a curled tail. Black horns slopping upward.

"Blooddrake… You are the same Maja Carr, Canlon's wife, aren't you?"

"Godsblood, the truth is now ready to be told."

Zenith's fucking cock, indeed. "Why do I have a funny feeling that I'm not going to enjoy why you are here?"

Valeria Dunleith smiled. "I've forgotten what it's like to be in the presence of a Benld. I've missed it."

"I'm bet you have, bikrome," she said. Ashe eyed the blooddrake. She could feel the aether surrounding the draconem, but like other drakes, she couldn't glean an aura from them. It was eerie and annoying considering she had read the aura of the elfir woman this draconem had been hiding in. Strange, that. "And you, Maja Carr. Led us astray, didn't you?"

"No more *'Lady Carr'*, Godsblood?" There was a mild jest in the sepulchral voice of the blooddrake. The creature's smile was wicked, almost like a snake ready to bite.

Ashe barged across the small cabin, her boots stomping the warship's slats underfoot as she stood face to snout with the blooddrake. "You godsdamned blooddrake! Enough bullshit. Why me? Why Port Sin? Dragging me out here so I can, can what? Fulfill some ancient riddle you godsdamned aetheurgists sing? Cyan is fucking dead because of you. I. Want. Answers. Now!" She punctuated each word with a thrust of her finger as she stared up at the great blooddrake.

"Time is not on our side, child of Nightingale," the blooddrake said. The bikrome had not moved, she had her head tilted, watching with a serene sapphire aura. "When the tim—"

Ashe screamed, her voice calling forth her Soul Form. Her insides raged with it, her veins were ropes being pulled taut. Muscles stretching. The walls of the cabin groaned before it cut off with a pulmo cough. The mist clawed at her ankles.

Maja sighed. "I had hoped that we would have more time to discuss this. But, alas, we do not." Ashe kept her face a blank canvas like when she was interrogating a suspect as she wiped the tar from her lips. "Fair enough. Where do you wish me to start?"

Steeling herself from the raging inferno of anger within, she sat on the captain's bunk next to Valeria, her mind running in multiple directions at once. "Start with who in the Pit is Nightingale? And not give me the run around like I'm a fucking child. I'm tired of it."

"NO MORE HIDDEN TRUTHS, DEAR DAUGHTER." The daemon blade shifted on her hip, as if it was facing Maja Carr, but that was impossible. Wasn't it? *"TELL HER, BLOOD OF MY WOMB."*

"YES, MOTHER," Maja Carr's voice said in Ashe's mind.

What in the Pit?

"Yes, Godsblood, I can hear the voice of the one you call the Strix. All draconem can."

"How is that possible? The Strix is a daemon."

The red-blue eyes were portals Ashe fell into as the blooddrake wormed closer; the magnificent head bobbed. "A daemon it is not. It never has been. The soul bound to the blade is that of Nightingale, the First Wife."

All her anger withered instantly. *Strix?*

"YOU WANTED TRUTHS, LISTEN AND LEARN, DEAR BRYNN."

"The First Wife was mortal once," Maja started. "In the earliest of times, two Divines were borne of Eminence and Noctis. You know them as Zenith and Nocturne. As the world came to be, balance was forever sought. Eminence in the realm of Life, Noctis in that of Death. Two forms, two mirrors. And in Zenith, this divine was given reign over Eminence's domain, Nocturne over Noctis'." Maja paused and looked at Harlequin, but motioned to Ashe as she spoke, "I know this child does not follow the precepts of the Scattered Shards. But you, Resolute One, you're fighting an inner battle of your own beliefs after the loss of your Amaranth last summerturn." Harlequin shivered, so Ashe leaned over and grabbed her hand, pulling the woman closer. Maja continued speaking, this time to Ashe, "But what knowledge I will share will rock your beliefs to the core. Brace yourself if you can." Ashe said nothing as Maja stared long and hard at both of them in turn. Finally, "This world follows the credenda that it is Nocturne forever locked in the Pit, but it is, in fact, Zenith who remains locked within the void."

"In the quiet words of Mother Marrow, come again?" Ashe said in disbelief.

"FEEL THE TRUTH IN HER WORDS, DEAR DAUGHTER."

"It is true, Brynn," Valeria said. "The divinity you call Zenith is not the Zenith of reality. He Who Fathered the World was a benevolent divinity once. But that was long ago. Long before any of our souls were specks of light in the void."

Harlequin's jaw dropped, aghast. "That is blasphemy!"

"I told you your beliefs would be rattled," Maja said. "The Scattered Shards, and by extension, the Book, is nothing but lies. The Pentax are not what you think they are, child. The Shards you know is a fallacy conceived centuries before the Fall of Eminence."

"How dare you besmirch Zenith and Mother Marrow in such a way. Zenith is almighty. He is the Fat—"

"Who cares about the Shards right now, Harle-bub," Ashe cut the vicar off, anger still coloring her disbelief. Back to Maja, "What's this all got to do with me, then?"

"You wanted answers, Godsblood. And you shall have them." Maja's curved form retreated to the small table, almost as if to sit. "Zenith and Nocturne are more like entities rather than personified divinities like you races of man believe. They are neither confined by space nor by conscious. They simply are. But They are bound to Eminence and to Noctis. The Crystals of Life and Death are the center entity, the center of existence. And Zenith and Nocturne are the Crystals' caretakers. And with Their divine gifts, They are also creators. This world that we call the Mistlands is but one They have created."

"There are other worlds?" Harlequin's fingers tightened in hers at the revelation.

"There are, Resolute One, many in which Zenith and Nocturne reign over. But this was Their first. And the one closest to Eminence and Noctis Themselves in the universe. Because of this, the fate of this world controls the fate of the others out there."

"Are there people on these other worlds?" Harlequin asked. Ashe noted that her aura was no longer a blend of crimson and honey, but one rather of periwinkle curiosity. "Other civilizations?"

"It is not known," Maja said. "Perhaps. Perhaps not. I like to believe there are others. It gives me solace to think we are not alone in this space."

"How do you know all this?"

"From Nocturne, Brynn of Nightingale blood. The god of the void is not evil. He," she paused to think. "Neither Nocturne nor Zenith can be considered male or female, but for some it is easier to believe this way. Nocturne may be the master of the realm of the dead, but the Dark Divine can be considered kind. But even the Dark Divine does not know how fares those other worlds because all His concentration remains focused on Zenith and keeping Him contained. Ah, see, there I go again, calling Them both 'He'. It is a habit that remains hard to break, even after all these centuries of knowing Their true nature."

"NOCTURNE IS KIND, DEAR BRYNN. I LOVED THE MASTER OF THE VOID. STILL LOVE."

"Okay, so Zenith is bad, Nocturne is good. Make it make sense. And easy to understand, blooddrake."

Maja chuckled, at least the hoarse gnarr could be interpreted as a chuckle. "Zenith and Nocturne were like children once, newly birthed divines by the Crystals to oversee Life and Death. And like children, They dreamt, and those dreams became creations. Created all manners of things. Worlds. Living creatures. Animals. Man by Zenith. Voidspawn by Nocturne. Draconem. To you and I, we are bound by time and our place in it, They are not. They are eternal. But They are not static. Again, like children, They learned. In time, They learned to love. To want. To desire. Zenith and Nocturne were fond of man. Fond of the frailty of man, of their emotional intellect. Zenith and Nocturne became so fascinated with Their creations, They transferred Their eternal divine consciousness' into them so They could be amongst them. They became the living gods you know. And They tried to become like Their creations. To feel like them."

"Are you actually trying to say that these divine entities fell in love?"

Another one of those odd-sounding chuckles. "You have the right of it, daughter of Nightingale. In the earliest of man's existence, one creature was the most powerful of all Their creations. She was Nightingale, the first draconem. A truly august creature. One with the ability to touch both realms, to travel between the two as if walking through a swinging door."

"I TOLD YOU I WAS FLESH ONCE. AND YOU DIDN'T BELIEVE ME."

To be fair, I thought you a daemon, Str… er I mean, Nightingale.

"In Nocturne's own words, the living divine became besotted with Nightingale, and She with Him."

"THIS IS TRUE."

"And from Their union, the blooddrakes were born. And because of Zenith's newfound capacity to emote, the Divine of the world of Life became filled with jealousy of Nocturne and Nightingale. He Who Fathered the World craved Nightingale."

"THIS IS ALSO TRUE."

"In this jealousy, Zenith began the war eternal with Nocturne, with the fate of Nightingale in the center. Once, when Nightingale was in the realm of Life, Zenith stole Her and made Her His own. Marrying Her, making Her the First Wife."

"Stole Her. It's not like She's a coinpurse full of quadrans."

"AETHER, DEAR DAUGHTER. I THOUGHT YOU SMARTER THAN THAT."

The blooddrake smiled broadly, those elongated teeth harsh. "Remember, Zenith and Nocturne are borne of Eminence and Noctis. The source of aether, Brynn Benld. Aether is everything. Zenith used aether to ensnare Nightingale, just as She said. Jealous of the blooddrakes created by Nocturne and Nightingale, Zenith used Nightingale to spawn draconem that would be in His favor. The firedrakes, aerovern, terrisvvyrm, and finally, the seagandr. These children of Nightingale and Zenith became the four other arms of the Pentax. Mother Marrow, Bliss, Brio, and Justice as you call them. They are the first of Their orders, all draconem call Them kin. They are known as the Hatch."

"And the drakken?"

"The drakken are the children of Zenith and Mother Marrow, but that is a story for another time," Maja said.

"Wait, wait, wait," Ashe said. "Mother Marrow is Zenith's child? But She's His wife."

"In the fallacies built up by the Scattered Shards. Mother Marrow is no wife to Zenith any more than She is a true god. The Forgemistress is but a demi-divine, more mortal than divine. Regardless, She bore the first drakken by Zenith's divine seed."

"That's fucking gross." But then a thought crossed her mind. "Can you imagine Phloxy's face if he was here to find that out? I almost wish we hadn't killed the bastard to witness that."

"I killed him, love," Harlequin said softly.

Maja chuckled, well, comparatively calling it a chuckle was an insult to the act. Draconem didn't laugh so much as growl gutturally while air whistled around the thick tongue. "Don't let the idea tremble you, blood of Nightingale. The ideals are the same. The face is what is different."

"Maja," Valeria started, "we are moving off the intended target of this lesson. The Godsblood must know about the Seals and why she must break them to save Canlon."

"Yes, you are quite right, Val. Knowledge is a handy weapon to wield, but too much is like one fold too many in a blade. The history of the draconem will be best served for another day."

"To save Canlon? The Last Godsking is still alive?" She thought about the dream on Gargantua. He had spoken to her, but that was in the Meadows, not in Eminence. It didn't make sense.

"My husband remains in the ruins of Eminence, the city, with the Crystal. Do you know what the role of the Godskings were created for?"

She thought for a moment. "Lojen told me my father said they are the chosen of the Pentax to give their life to keep the Crystal revived. Giving their aether to it. Their Soul Form aetheurgy."

"There is nothing of this in the Book of the Scattered Shards," Harlequin said. Ashe turned toward her… what would she call Harlequin now that they… Her face was pale behind her breather.

"And you won't." Maja motioned to the woman's waist, toward the mist canisters. "The Scattered Shards know but a pittance to what aether truly is. And what the role of aether plays amongst your Pentax. But in reality, the Pentax is O so much more. And that's the importance of the Godsking and the Seals." The blooddrake lifted a mug from the writing table, wetting her tongue before continuing. "Eminence, the Crystal, is the doorway to Zenith's prison in the Pit. And the only way to keep the All Father locked in the deep void is by a sacrifice of life. Once Nocturne, the children of Zenith, and Nightingale won Their eternal war on the All Father, the Godsking was chosen for this task, for only a mortal can give the life required to maintain the prison. This is what is called the Breath of the Soul."

"Doesn't sound like a fun duty to me," Ashe commented.

"You've experienced the call of the Breath, Brynn," Valeria said. "On Gargantua, when you unleashed the aether in your scream. That was the Breath. You struggle to hold it, even now. It rises when you are angry."

"A great gift it was," the blooddrake continued. "One of great honor. And a taxing one as the key to Zenith's prison must forever be maintained, lest He Who Fathered the World break free and unleash unheralded wroth. Nocturne maintains the lock in the realm of Death, but the Dark Divine is growing weaker."

"How can that be?" Ashe asked.

"Because Canlon is dying. My husband grows weak." The blooddrake leaned toward her. Ashe recoiled reflexively and stupidly. Harlequin gave her a reassuring squeeze of the hand. "He is a Godsblood, like you, but my husband's last act will prove his downfall. It is inevitable."

"Canlon is doing what he must, Maja," the bikrome said. "We are all doing what we must to maintain Zenith's prison."

"What of the Seals? I thought those were the wards keeping things in place?"

"The Seals are the keys to the ruins, Brynn," Valeria answered. "Eminence, the Crystal is the key to Zenith's prison. Canlon is sacrificing himself so that the world may continue. He is elfir, his life is long, but he cannot sustain forever. We thought we had more time after last summer with Lu Har's defeat, but it appears that Zenith has found a way to rebirth both the Fallen and Solanine."

"Rebirthed? That shouldn't be possible. You never explained how."

"Souls are but, shall we call them, and forgive the pun, shards of Eminence and Noctis. They exist in infinitude. And the stronger the soul is with aether, the easier it is to pass the veil between worlds. It only takes the will of either Divine."

"But if Zenith is held in the Pit, how can He breach the veil?" Ashe shook her head, trying to piece everything together. Then it dawned on her. "The mist?"

Both the daughter of the Golden Throne and the blooddrake nodded. It was Maja who spoke. "The Crystal of Life is like a seed. And for a seed to form and grow, it needs pollination. It needs germination. That was my husband's chosen duty. All Godskings are chosen to provide germination, with their souls. But the war with the Fallen, in the name of Zenith, his master, that became the source of Zenith's influence's return."

"Lu Har hated Canlon," Valeria began. "Hated him for being the chosen servant to Eminence. And jealousy was a harsh companion. Envy Canlon, I did not. Jealous of the power he wielded, the aetheurgy of Life and Death in his hands, perhaps you can say that I was. But it would take more than Lu Har to turn me against Canlon. Even my former lover, Solanine, was resistant to Lu Har at first. You must understand, Brynn, there is no aetheurgy as great as that of Soul Form. Void, Shard, Burn, and Vision pale in comparison. They are like candles to the magnitude of the sun. Many who touch aether become consumed by it, consumed by the desire to attain more. I was no different. But I knew my place, and it was beside Canlon Carr. I had no idea of Zenith's and Nocturne's true natures until Zenith came to me, promising all the power of Soul Form Canlon had, but I wouldn't have to give my life to maintain the Crystal. All I had to do was give in. In my everlasting shame, I did. But seeing Canlon's fall, his death, was not what I wanted. Lu Har was a monster, evil even, but through Zenith's lens, I'd believed he'd right the wrongs of Nocturne. Lied to us, Zenith did. And because of my folly, Solanine was blinded by His zeal. If not for my brother-friend Finn, I would have been forever lost."

"And yet you stood by to let it all happen?" Ashe was angry again, the mist in the cabin growing surly. "While the world went to shit in a basket? That makes you somehow better than them? Because you repented after your hands were covered in blood?"

"I cannot change what I've done," the bikrome said. "But I've tried to right whatever wrongs I could. You were one of them."

"Fuck that!"

"Ashe, leave it be," Harlequin grabbed her by the shoulder. "There's nothing to be done for it. Let them finish, then you can be as mad as you wish once we defeat Lu Har once and for all."

"Fine, so Lu Har was a bastard then just as he is now. Let me guess, that bastard used Noctis to defeat the Last Godsking?" Valeria confirmed with a sad bow of her head, silver waves of hair falling over her face. "Well, fuck me."

"When Solanine lent their aetheurgy to Lu Har's and mine, all who stood before us were leveled. Even Tevun, and being pure drakken, he was overrun. None could withstand our onslaught. I thought I was doing it for Zenith, to push Nocturne into the void for all eternity. Little did I know the truth. But Zenith had now gained a foothold within the void, by our aetheurgy. Noctis became a reality, and Lu Har wasted no time in tapping into the realm of Death. The Fallen raised daemons." Ashe opened her mouth, but Valeria put a pale hand up. "Daemons are merely the souls of the dead ripped free of the Meadows, forced into servitude. Warped by Void Form aetheurgy."

"Like Amaranth," Harlequin whispered.

"Indeed, young vicar," said the daughter of Kalderim. "With daemons, blooddrakes, and some of the most powerful aetheurgy wielders behind him, Lu Har was nigh unbeatable."

"Not all blooddrakes turned, Brynn Benld. Some of us remained true to my husband's side."

"Forgive me, Maja," Valeria said.

"Nothing to forgive, dear friend. But here is the crux: the orders of the draconem were splintered. We were one brood once. All part of the Hatch, as we draconem call it. The eldest of us, the ones you call the Pentax, are our leaders, our guides. The oldest molt, the wisest of the Hatch. Though draconem are borne of aether, few can actually wield it. Those that can, they are called 'Aegis'. The shields, the protectors of aether. And by virtue, these Aegises are the protectors of the Seals. You met them, Brynn Benld, when you destroyed the Emerald Seal last summerturn."

"Yeah, I remember." Remember it she did. She wished she didn't, but she couldn't scrub the memory of Mother Marrow's voice in her mind. The vvyrms. "So, if Canlon Carr used his Soul Form to create the Seals, why weren't you able to use Noctis to break them?"

"When Canlon summoned the wards, he shielded Noctis from Eminence and vice versa," Valeria said. "The Crystals are interconnected, they cannot be cut from one another, but Canlon was able to block both from touching one another. It was something Zenith nor Nocturne could have foreseen."

"The Divines are logical, Brynn Benld," Maja added. "They are calculating, even. But They do not have the ingenuity of man. My husband was able to stymie Zenith with his spell. He needed both the Eye of the Soul and the Oculus of Apathy to accomplish it. But in the process, Eminence and Noctis both cracked. And that's what sent the Holy City plummeting through the heavens to the ground. Aether became poisoned." Maja summoned *Ignis* in the leathery palm, the runes etched into the blooddrake's exoscales blazed. "Fire begets, Fire taketh." *Ignis* extinguished into a splash of *Aquis*, a series of waves rolled above the blooddrake's palm. "Water rears, Water recedes." *Aquis* rumbled by the quake of *Terris*, leaving a statue of a tree. "Earth sculps, Earth razes." The *Terris* tree was blown away by *Aere*, a lightning blast. "Air breathes, Air stifles." Maja snapped, the aether dying. "Scales ward, Scales break. Scales are all. Scales are nothing."

"What's the Oculus of Apathy?"

Maja pointed a talon at the Eye wrapped around her wrist. "You wear the Eye of the Soul. It is the source of Eminence's aether, its key, if you will. It is what allows Life to flow. That is why you may feel everything around you. You've felt it before?" Ashe nodded. "The Oculus of Apathy is the antithesis. It is the link to Noctis. I fear Lu Har may have discovered where it lies, otherwise why would he put his plans into motion so soon?"

"I saw him in a vision," she started, "sitting atop a broken throne. He had this black stone in his palm." She touched the diamond eye. "Like this, except jagged black."

Maja shared a look with Valeria. "Then he has indeed uncovered the location of the Oculus." To Ashe, "We sought to keep the knowledge hidden from him after the Fall. Kept it in a place so obvious, he would never look there. A Temple to Nocturne in Qarthage. A wreckage built under one of Lu Har's own villas."

"Well, that doesn't sound like such a smart idea… Wait, if this thing," Ashe toyed with the golden links on her left wrist, "is so important, why did I find it?"

"I hid it for you, Brynn," Valeria answered. "Bliss gave me the foresight to know that you would come to Drenth to seek out your past."

"An aerovern apparently," she said. "Hard to believe the Ideal Daughter is a godsdamned aerovern."

"Bliss is what She is, and I do as She wills. I hid the Eye in that Guilder's home. Just as I hid the Oculus where She demanded. And you are correct, Maja, Lu Har has discovered the Oculus. He had Neenah LeFleur find it before he moved on Gandtril."

"Then we are even further into the ending than we assumed," Maja said. "We knew this was coming, just not when. This is most unsettling. And getting to the Seal of *Ignis* of even more import." The bloodrake looked at her. "If the Fallen has the Oculus, then the pieces on the board are set. You must break the Seal atop Mount Bastard. Once broken, the balance will be splintered. The final two Seals will await you. Only then will you be able to help my husband put a stop to Zenith. The Oculus might be a problem, though. Val, does your brother possess the Crown yet?"

The bikrome stiffened, her eyes closed. "No, he does not. The Crown remains broken. But he will soon have three of the tines. When Titen…" Valeria's eyes opened and her gaze settled onto Ashe with a heavy weight. The weight of the world it seemed. Ashe felt trapped. Trapped in the bind of divinities and daemons. A construct not of her own making. "The path to your destiny, Godsblood, lays before you. Are you willing to walk it?"

Zenith's bloody fucking cock Ashe was mad.

She screamed again, this time the aetheurgy roared from within. The whole godsdamned cabin shook with it. *Breath of the Soul, huh?*

Maja Carr seemed amused by her scream. "Hard to unlearn the truth you've lived for nineteen years, Brynn Benld?"

A knock at the door. One of the orcir poked its head in and spoke in a raspy dialect Ashe knew naught of. It was not orcirish, therefore must be blooddrake. She wondered if the orcir were also draconem.

Maja responded. "We will be setting sail within the hour. The rogue blooddrakes are heading straight for the base of Mount Bastard. We should catch *Peerless* by nightturn. And from there, we will need you to guide us to the Seal of *Ignis*."

"But how?"

"The conflagration you unleashed in *The Axe* was the essence of aether. Of Eminence and Noctis. Summon it again, have the aetheurgy show you. You are the Godsblood."

Str… Nightingale, what do I do?

"PREVAIL, DEAR BRYNN."

XLV
SOLANINE

SOLANINE SAT ASKEW upon the railing of the raised platform where the warship's steering wheel guided their sail with other members of the Scattered Shards. They knew not the nautical terminology, nor cared. All Solanine cared about was the Godsblood at the bow, watching the young woman for near a quarter hour's turn while the boat made preparations to set sail after the *Peerless* and Rinkhal.

It was a wonder Solanine had been able to get on board this warship without being detected by Valeria Dunleith or the intrepid Maja Carr.

To be true, Solanine hadn't been fully prepared for the Godsblood to deftly shatter their Void Form spells in *The Axe* with her sudden influx of aether. Had wanted it, Solanine had, but hadn't fully been ready for the young woman to unleash it just yet. Surprised them, drawing away the mist of the Pit from Rinkhal's Void Form summoning spell.

The girl had finally tapped into her ability to touch Noctis. And that excited Solanine. The daughter of Nightingale was edging ever closer to being ready to free Him. To free Zenith from His prison. The Divine would finally be free.

Rinkhal and Ialtris had set the stage for the Godsblood's power to come full in the bowels of *The Axe*. Where the Godsblood learned of her true heritage, listened while the woman called Lady Drakeslayer saw the ending come nigh. Rinkhal and Ialtris had done their part in this tragedy. The Godsblood was ready.

And yet, Solanine was angry.

Angry because all the careful planning had been undone by a rash power grab by Ialtris. The Scattered Shards were supposed to fall, not by blame, but by betrayal. That was why Solanine chose to steal the scales of the Godsblood's taskmaster, to show the young woman that no one was safe, everyone she knew was a target. The juvenile draconem of the greater order had not been part of Solanine's plan, nor had known of its capture. The Godsblood was meant to fight against her own team, her taskmaster and would-be lover, the blame and betrayal by one of the Shards' own. The Scattered Shards needed to fall prey to its own disloyalty. Ialtris had moved against this.

Ialtris had gotten theirs, though. Solanine mourned Ialtris not.

However, it reminded Solanine too much of Drenth, of Lu Har's folly, his unwavering belief that the Godsblood would play nice. Solanine knew better.

"HASTE WILL NOT SEE YOU PREVAIL, MY DISCIPLE. TO SET ME FREE, YOU MUST PLAY THE LONG GAME," Zenith said.

I do, master. And yet, still we wait. Give me the word and I shall end this farce.

"NOT YET, SOLANINE. WAIT AND REMEMBER. THE SEAL MUST BREAK. BRIO MUST BREAK."

I've waited long enough! I want Valeria Dunleith's soul!

"STEADY, MY DISCIPLE. THE GIRL IS NEARING HER ASCENT. YOU'VE CORNERED HER, AND WITH LU HAR MOVING IN THE NORTH WITH THE OCULUS, EVERYTHING IS GOING TO MY PLAN. EMINENCE AWAITS ME, JUST AS IT ALWAYS SHOULD HAVE. IF NOT FOR NIGHTINGALE AND MY ATRAMENTOUS TWIN. BE WARY, MY DISICIPLE, VALERIA CANNOT FORGE A PATH WITHOUT THE GODSBLOOD. MAJA CARR HAS THROWN CHAOS INTO OUR PLANS. WE CANNOT ALLOW THEM TO MERGE. THE GODSBLOOD AND THE SEAL ARE PARAMOUNT. BRIO MUST FALL."

This world is not ready for the truth, master.

"IT WILL BREAK THEM. I SHALL BREAK THEM."

But the power wielded by the Godsblood, it was impossible to fathom.

Contrary to both Rinkhal and Ialtris' desires, to Lu Har's and the Divine's, this was why Solanine was loath to end the Godslayer. There was only one path to tread, and they would need the humir to see it done.

Solanine stuffed the hatred down, soon it would be time, but still tasks remained. Just as Brio had claimed.

"THE SON IS WEAK, MY DISCIPLE. FEAR NOT."

I fear nothing!

"AND THAT IS WHY WE MUST WAIT. THE SEALS REMAIN UNBROKEN. UNTIL THE GODSBLOOD FINISHES WITH CANLON CARR'S VILE LOCKS, YOU MUST REMAIN TRUE."

Solanine had done nothing but push the Godsblood toward her path, her anger bubbling under the surface. She needed to unleash it, not anchor it. Soon this young humir would open the way to *Ignis* and the last of the noble firedrakes. And Solanine's revenge would prevail.

"Ho!" bellowed the one-eyed first mate as the man with the chest the size of a barrel of rum righted the wheel, steering them out of the Bay of Fire, yelling at another corsair skating through the water. When he noticed the grand quaestor quake on the platform, he spoke, "Be free the Harbor soon, Grand Quaestor Owl. Free waters ahead, then. Up until Mount Bastard."

If there was ever a humir that Solanine disliked more, it was the one called Owl. The grizzled tainted warrior of the Shards was dogmatic, and one Solanine would rather see in the Meadows than in life. "Very good, sailor," the grand quaestor said.

The grand quaestor's hobgoblin, Cadoz, tittered nervously about the platform besides the other quaestors. The gnarled creature of the Pit was scared witless, so afraid of the boat, he gnawed at his unclean fingernails, but did not leave the grand quaestor's side. The strix, in contrast, was asleep on the platform's rail, head buried into its feathery bed, every once in a great while, a yellow saucer would open, take in the surroundings, then back to slumber it went.

As much as Solanine hated it, the blooddrake was content to wait, content to give the humir the space she needed. Soon it would happen, and soon it would end.

Yes, Solanine thought. *This is the beginning of the end.*

The sailors of *Dauntless* hustled about the water-slick deck like they had ants in their knee-trimmed pantaloons as the massive one-eyed mate called out orders as the ship finally passed through the outer edges of the Bay, now fully entering the VVyrm. The ship lulled under the Shards servant's scales, rocking bow to stern. Teetering port to starboard as if something under the water quickly shifted directions. The wooden hull creaked as if something was testing its durability.

No, Solanine thought. *Not now. Now while we are so close to the end. Master?*

"IT SENSES THE BLOOD OF NIGHTINGALE. THIS CANNOT BE STOPPED. ALLOW HER TO SEE ITS MIGHT. IF SHE IS AS SHE SHOULD BE, THIS WILL BE NO TEST."

Solanine could smell the child of Nocturne, the cloying aether of *Aquis* permeating the sea air. The blooddrake braced.

Yes, Zenith. You are correct. A test. Forgive me.

"SERVE ME, MY DISCIPLE, AND FORGIVENESS IS FORGOTTEN."

XLVI
Ashe

ASHE SAT AT the bow as *Dauntless* set sail upon the VVyrm Ocean. Her dirty, midnight blue cassock bunched up to allow her legs to dangle over the edge. Her arms were on an oiled rope rail, chin resting on the back of her hands.

A moment of peace if there was one such moment.

Her mind was nearly bursting with information. Information about herself. About her family. Her existence. About the world. There was so much detail fighting to the forefront, Ashe felt the urge to just say bugger it and allow the chips to fall where they may for her and her future, just as she had done for the last two years.

Death had always hounded her. Her father's. Her mother's. Cyan's. Hers. Now, each was only the beginning.

"DEAR BRYNN, WHAT WOULD YOU HAVE OF ME? I AM THE SAME YOU'VE KNOWN THIS LAST YEAR. I AM THE SAME. WILL ALWAYS BE. I AM HERE FOR YOU AS I WAS FOR YOUR MOTHER."

Not now.

"SHOULD YOU WISH IT, I WILL LISTEN AND ANSWER."

I just need time, Stri… Nightingale.

"YOU MAY CALL ME STRIX, DEAR BRYNN."

And yet you refuse to call me Ashe.

"THAT IS NOT YOUR NAME."

Hypocrite.

"VERY WELL, I SHALL LEAVE YOU TO YOUR RUMINATIONS. WHEN YOU NEED ME, I AM HERE. ALWAYS."

She stared out at the pinkish waters of the VVyrm Ocean at evenfall, the Bay of Fire bathed in green as it disappeared behind the curved Thullyrish peninsula. Mount Bastard grew larger and larger in her left peripheral.

Mount Bastard, a fitting place for her to head.

Port Sin took up the first knuckle of the peninsula, where the basin became the palm of Thullyr. Like gaudy rings, foothills rose on the northwestern edge of the city above the Harbor of Thieves, creating a natural ending point where sin met death. The foothills, themselves, were not literally hills at all, but were jagged protrusions of sharp rock jutting upward like knives that extended for a hundred leagues, perhaps more. Aside from the makeshift airship landing right near the edge of the mega-city, nothing lived on the foothills, and nothing attempted to go there. Nobody had a reason to go to the volcano. Not in eons.

Beyond the jagged hills started the steady, steep rise of Mount Bastard. A singular peak that extended thousands of feet high and dozens of miles around to the end of the peninsula. It was nothing but rock; no green, no trees, no life. Snow capped the peak when leaks of living lava weren't dripping down the far side into the sea like tears every year during the high summer. All told, even though the volcano looked down upon Port Sin, it was a few hours' journey by a boat such as *Dauntless.*

The only conceivable way to attempt a scaling of the mountain was a small inlet on the northernmost part of the peninsula, the one from Cadrianna's memories. The mountain ended abruptly, almost as if Justice used Her celestial axe to cleave the crag, sending the rocky bits into the ocean. Over the centuries, the inlet had formed, leading to a cavernous opening into the heart of the volcano. Ambitious explorers have long tried to enter Mount Bastard via this cavern, but none had ever returned, as the assumption of a warren of caves and tunnels would lead the pathfinders to their impending doom in the deep dark. Or they'd fallen into pits of molten doom.

It was this inlet that *Peerless* was headed. And where Ashe must lead the search to the Seal of *Ignis*. Where her own story drove her.

She wondered where Cyan would fit in these stories. Cyan, she would miss him terribly for the rest of her days, however many were left to her.

"I AM SORRY FOR HIS LOSS, DEAR BRYNN. BUT KNOW THAT HE IS AT PEACE IN THE MEADOWS."

He's there? Now?

"THAT HE IS. HIS SOUL IS FREE, DEAR DAUGHTER. AND HE WANTS YOU TO KNOW THAT HE IS PROUD OF YOU. AND TO TELL YOU THAT HE WILL ALWAYS LOVE YOU, HIS LILIA."

Ashe put her left arm to her forehead as tears streamed down her face, the golden bangle of the Eye cold against her skin. The ancient talisman of Eminence was a fierce reminder that she was different. A Godsblood.

Cyan... Goodbye, my father. I love you.

Ashe sighed, her body gently rocking with the sway of the ship over the waves.

"Quadran for your thoughts, poppet?"

Neenah LeFleur was leaning on the rope railing, staring out at the rolling waves. There was a serenity of lightly-tinted sapphire about the smuggler. Even though this wasn't a ship in the air and instead one on water, Neenah LeFleur was in her element, where she belonged. A captain captaining her ship.

Besides, it was good to see the woman again. Reminded Ashe of a different time when she wasn't wrapped up in gods and draconem. A time of freedom.

"Just thinking about better times."

"The sea does that, little bint, the sea does that, hear?"

"Been long since you've been to sea?"

Neenah ran a delicate hand over the ropes, eyes closed. "You know, it's been bloody years since Neenah LeFleur has tasted the salted water. Kinda nice, this." She tugged at her puffed sleeves. "O, buggers, I'm getting syrupy about seagandr hunting. Ain't nobody truly misses that godsdamned job. Don't go tellin' no one, little bint. Gotta reputation to uphold."

Ashe chuckled but then a pulmo cough tore through her. Rest didn't seem like it would be for her. She wiped her lips. "I see Zig and Zag runnin' 'round, and Roland's steering the ship. But where's Tris, Doll, and Alexina? Hope there hasn't been much trouble, you runnin' with Valeria Dunleith isn't all that appealing."

"Wouldn't be the first, eh?" Neenah glanced back at where Roland steered. Ashe followed the smuggler's gaze and saw that Valeria Dunleith sat upon a crate below, the bikrome's legs crossed under her. "It's been a godsdamnable contract, poppet. One that should raise Ol' Neenah LeFleur's stock, hear? Let me tell you all about it."

"Evander? Really? Fuck me, I thought I was done with him for good. I'm sorry, Neenah," Ashe said when the passionate captain finished her story. Of Tris, Doll, and Alexina being left behind to watch over *Marrow's Lover*. "Sorry that you were forced into this mess." She shook her head. "Zenith's cock, I'm sorry we've all been thrust into this."

"I didn't say I don't deserve this, girl. Before *Marrow's Lover* collared me with her beauty and promise of freedom, I was a scavenger. I know it don't look like it, being as dashing as I am, but Neenah LeFleur was nothing once. Just a runt making her way up the chain in Krylen after fleeing Altreyia. Leaving every bloody person I've ever known to work the seagandr hunting boats. Like my brother, Merrick, when he went and joined the Shards. But myself, just caked in draconem oil, living voyage by voyage. All I ever wanted was freedom, and that's what I bloody well sought, even if it was dangerous. No godsdamned regrets, girl. What I was, what I am, what I could've been, they all make me, me. None'll ever say Neenah LeFleur couldn't see the sky beyond the clouds. Behind the wheel will always be where Neenah bloody LeFleur belongs, hear? Doesn't mean I cannot remain true to my roots."

"How do you do it?"

"Do what?"

"Deflect. You never seem to lose your head, even in a tight spot. I know elfir have this about them, but you're not elfir."

The inscrutable captain was silent a moment, considering the water. "The sea is the ultimate decider, little bint. Take this to heart, mind, for Neenah LeFleur only offers this advice but once. One day there may be endless calm, a gentle swell with a favorable wind to carry you half the world away. Or Nocturne sends vicious squalls ready to bring you and everyone bloody around you down to the Pit. Neither can you control. You simply have to hold the godsdamned line with all the strength in your fingers and hope today is not your day to go, hear?"

Dare she say it, but Ashe might have just glimpsed the true Neenah LeFleur, not the roguish façade.

"CANLON SAID THIS TO YOU, DEAR BRYNN. NOT ALL FACES ARE THE ONES YOU ARE MEANT TO SEE."

I know…

"THEN PLEASE TRY TO REMEMBER WHAT ELSE HE SAID. THE TRIALS AHEAD…"

The ship lurched to the portside and Neenah cursed. "Bloody fools. Godsdamnit, Roland's goin' be the death of me and my legend. Barely out of the Bay and he does this? O pissing great, your friend the grand quaestor, other bloody fools, and his hobbie pet are up in my wheelhouse like they've gots any godsdamned business up there." She let out a string of curses before taking a deep breath. "Don't let it anchor you down, little bint. The anger against the Shards. Against the bikrome. Your parents. Against that hunky vicar who knew how to treat a woman like Ol' Neenah LeFleur. Rest his soul in the Meadows." The affable captain patted her shoulder. "Against your destiny. You guide the ship, little bint, not the bikrome, not the gods. Not the bloody Fallen. Remember that you are your life's captain, the ship sails where you want it."

With that, the captain crossed the deck yelling further curses.

Ashe laughed. It felt wonderful to laugh again. Her mind had been slipping to that dark place again, that place where death sounded the better option. Her death instead of others. The place where Nocturne was waiting for her in the dank of the Pit, beckoning her to the endless slumber. A freedom of her worries, of her cares. Of the ties binding her to life.

She felt a stir inside her, a small flame burning in her heart. A ripple, a smoldering. Her blood rushing.

Fuck it, she needed to find Harlequin.

Getting to her feet, she made her way toward the wheelhouse, grinning at the bikrome who watched her with knowing bi-colored eyes and an aura of pure sapphire. Ashe then scowled at Owl and his ugly bird as she descended belowdecks.

Nightingale?

"YES, DEAR BRYNN?"

Am I ready for what's to come?

"ONLY IF YOU ALLOW YOURSELF TO BECOME YOU IN THE FULLEST OF MANNERS. DO NOT HIDE EVEN A FRACTION OF WHO BRYNN BENLD IS. ONLY THEN WILL YOU BE READY."

Good, that's what I thought you'd say. I need this.

"I KNOW."

Within the hull of *Dauntless*, quaestors by the score readied themselves for battle. Whether it was sharpening blades or cleaning wheellocks, they prepared. Some rested their eyes; others paced the narrow space. Still others conversed in hushed tones, some expressing displeasure, others nervous excitement. Some glanced her way, but none said anything, merely bowing their heads in respect to Lady Drakeslayer.

Ashe moved across the ship towards a cabin, not the same one in which Maja had told them the truth of the Pentax. But to one opposite, in the stern. Past dozens of empty hammocks, past stacked barrels of water and rum, past squawking fowl in cages. The chickens' squawks sounded like chiding to her ears.

To a cabin that had been gifted to Harlequin to rest before the final assault on the Seal of *Ignis*. Opposite to the one she'd been given for herself.

Taking a deep breath, she knocked on the cabin's door a little too hard, a little too hasty. Her heart was nearly beating straight out of her cassock. And all her earlier resolved fled from her.

"YOU SEEM NERVOUS, DAUGHTER OF MY BLOOD."

Fu—

The door opened and Harlequin leaned her forearm against the frame, her gaze took Ashe in while her tongue danced across her lips with a knowing smirk. She was wearing only her sleeveless jerkin and her pants, no cassock, no boots. Cyan's Gauntlet rested upon the small table next to a seagandr-oil lamp. "Need something, love?"

Ashe swallowed the lump forming in her throat. "Can I come in?"

Harlequin's brow rose but the smile never left her handsome face. Her red curls bounced as she nodded, stepping back to allow her to squeeze into the small cabin. The vicar said nothing as she eased the door shut again.

It was a tiny thing, the cabin. It was essentially big enough to take one step to reach the bed built into the hull opposite the door, while another two perpendicular paces would take her to a bench where a hand-drawn map of Oldport Basin lay atop, with hooks above, where the vicar had hung her cassock and breather. A seagandr lantern hung from a peg over the bed, giving the small room a yellowish tint.

This was right. Everything about it was right.

She faced Harlequin, who was standing with one hand delicately placed on her hip. Ashe noticed the freckles all upon her toned left bicep, her runic tattoos on her right arm gleaming in the seagandr light. "So?"

"Uh… well…" Zenith's cock, why was this so hard? This is what she wanted. Godsdamnit, she had wanted it for far too long, just too afraid to see the truth of it. Or as Neenah had said, she hadn't seen the sky beyond the clouds. "I was wondering… um…"

"You're cute when you stammer, love," Harlequin said with a grin. "You talk a big game, Ashe. But I always knew it was a ruse."

Cute? This is not how I expected it to go. Did I? She ran her hand through her hair nervously worrying about if her locks were messy. "I wanted to thank you for saving me… I mean those three times. With the Kraken's Cabal. And with Phloxy, even though I had him dead to rights."

Why was this so hard? Was she that frightened of what might happen? From her time with Wren and being betrayed? Or was she simply afraid of being hurt again?

"That's what you came here for? A thank you?" Harlequin shook her head, her beautiful features drooping before regaining her smile. "It's nothing." Her eyes narrowed, a disappointment in them. "Is there anything else, *Lady Drakeslayer*?" The way she stressed her moniker made Ashe cringe.

This is not going well. Nightingale was cackling in the void, a chiding, that. The scant mist at her ankles tickling her in mocking pokes. "I… we are sailing into an unknown situation… with all that's happened in Port Sin, I just wanted to… you know?"

"Not certain I do."

"Because I'm not sure… with what might happen… well… I don't think…" *Seriously, why can't I just say it?* "Zenith's fucking cock, godsdamnit to the Pit. I wanted to see you one last time, Harle-bub. You know? There."

"Thinking about my ass again are you?" Harlequin countered quickly. It caught her off guard. Aura blazing crimson. "One kiss, that's all it takes. You get so red when you get anxious. What would that foul-mouthed Captain LeFleur say, 'you're bloody hooked on Harlequin the Resolute, hear?'" She moved closer and pressed her body against Ashe's. "Does this make it hard for you to concentrate?" She laughed. "You are a strong-headed, godsdamned fool sometimes, Ashe. I was talking to Captain LeFleur earlier, and she told me one of her rules, you might like it."

"O?"

"'If you're gonna bloody go the way of Nocturne, fuck like you deserve it.'"

Ashe realized how beautiful Harlequin was, and not merely in the physical way. Truly saw it, truly realized it. Yes, her skin was supple despite the many scars from their training over the years. Training that they both had endured to get to this point. Harsh training that had nearly beaten this moment out of them. A moment Ashe didn't want to squander. Her green-grey, yellow-pupiled eyes opened the world, and Ashe saw the determination and grace within them. The woman teetered upon the fine balance between inflexible and vulnerable with ease and surety.

In that moment, Ashe knew she wanted her more than anything else in the Mistlands.

Life was not worth living if you don't chase your dreams. Destiny can still guide your path, but there were no guardrails, no fence to hem you in. Your steps are yours alone to take.

And by Eminence above and Noctis below, she was going to finally take her set path in the way she wanted. How she wanted. With whom she wanted.

"YOU ARE READY, DEAR BRYNN. ONE STEP AT A TIME. UNTIL THE END..."

Harlequin stared at her, blinking in brutal slow-motion as the mist around Ashe's ankles started to swirl faster, aether building within her breast. Her heart pounded as the fire within grew hot, her gaze tracing the lines of the other woman's face. Harlequin's pouty lips parted slightly, and her chest rose with baited anticipation, as Ashe's did.

A pyre within. Aether assailed by the sounds of those beyond the veil. Filling her with essence of Life and of Death.

Ashe wanted to take her, hold her and caress this alluring woman's skin. A woman forged by Mother Marrow just for her.

Heartbeats matched, then came the others upon the ship. All thumping in cadence with hers. Aether expanding, building and building until there was nothing left but a glowing sheen in the cabin. Just she and Harlequin, connected by aether.

She slowly reached out and before she knew it, their lips met in force. Harlequin's hands dug into her back, and she drew the other woman into a passionate kiss. Her mind wandered as they kissed, her body feeling relieved of all the tension she had buried deep down. This mist whorled in frenzy, in desire, in want. In acceptance. In perfection.

This was right. Everything about it was right.

Her hands went to Harlequin's waist and pulled her closer, if such a thing was possible. She breathed deeply into Ashe's mouth, and she kissed her harder. Harlequin's hand stole toward the brass studs along Ashe's flank and began to unbutton her cassock. The woman's hands deftly unlatched the armored jerkin, sliding across the hardened muscles of Ashe's abdomen, grazing the underside of her left breast as the holy garment of the Scattered Shards fell to the floor as she eased it over her shoulders. Harlequin's gentle fingers then found a wanted purchase upon Ashe's breasts, kneading. The mist and Ashe were one with their groans. Pleasure.

With precision, Ashe yanked Harlequin's jerkin over her head with the slightest pause in their kiss before throwing it toward the bench. Harlequin's breasts crushed into hers as she purred into her throat when she kissed her again, fiercer than before. Demanding by the both of them. She dug her fingers in Ashe's back and threw her head back as Ashe's tongue traveled down her chin, into the graceful curve of her neck before tracing her skin down to one of her lightly freckled breasts. Both their hearts raced, Ashe feeling the woman as if they were one under her tongue. The mist, the aether within them, within their souls, as one.

This was right. Everything about it was right.

Harlequin put her hands to Ashe's shoulders and pushed her backward onto the bunk. She went willingly and tried to pull the vicar with her, but Harlequin resisted. The mist around their knees surged up over Harlequin, the woman giggling as if tickled. Ashe looked up at her questioningly, but Harlequin smiled and bent down to pull Ashe's boots off. Ashe kicked at them in an effort to help. Within moments, her boots were off, followed by her pants, leaving her open to the woman who had cracked her code, solved her puzzle.

The mist prickled her skin, egging her on, giving her all the pleasure the world of Life had to offer. She felt it all. The boat. The water. The air. The earth far below. The creatures in the VVyrm and high above. The Four essences of Aether, the Tenets. They all pulsed with Life.

She was filled with everlasting Life.

Ashe picked her head up as Harlequin disappeared between her legs, the mist swallowing the other woman in a loving cocoon of passion, pulsing with Life. On her knees, the woman ran her hands up Ashe's thighs, then breezy kisses, reaching for her smallclothes, sliding them off before standing once more, the tease of each movement nearly blinding Ashe with passion. The devilish mist swirling in anticipation.

Harlequin's eyes grew wide as she elegantly took off her own Shards-issued vicar pants, standing completely nude, unabashedly bare. Ashe drank her body, memorizing all the muscles in her abdomen, the shape of her legs where her curves swelled from her waist. Her blood rushed; Life demanded a tithe. One of flesh. One of heart. One of desire.

"I told you, Ashe, my love." Smirking, Harlequin put her hands to either side of Ashe's hips, climbing atop and settling herself a scant inch from the warmth between Ashe's legs with a light inhale of undeniable want, the woman's aura the most brilliant form of garnet. Harlequin's hand danced between them, caressing the fire that was building in Ashe's bud with a steady rhythm. "You owe me thrice, and now I aim to collect it from you. I'm going to make you beg me to make it stop."

This was right. Dear fucking Nightingale, everything about it was perfect.

"O?" Ashe groaned as she ground her hips upward into Harlequin's tender embrace. She dug her fingers into the bunk's sheets as Harlequin moved faster and faster, only one thought filling her as she neared her end, the first of three coming: *She is a fucking beauty, and by Nightingale, I fucking love her!*

The world exploded, fiery aether bursting from her soul, filling every pore, every fiber. All that Brynn Benld was.

And that was Life.

XLVII
LOJEN

THOUGH A COLD-BLOODED draconem, Lojen couldn't stop the shiver from running down his spine as the misty breeze tingled his exoscales while he stood at the highest point of the Obelisk.

The snow had stopped some hours ago, during the razing of Gandtril, but angry-looking clouds still hung in the sky, and they threatened to unleash further gloom to add to the doom and sorrow within his breast. Smoke cast a dark shadow over the setting sun as columns of ash rose from the burning Legion fortress, mingling into the mist above and beyond.

The entire morning had passed, and the weight of the world still clung to him. The sorrow, the self-loathing. The fear.

Twelve hours would never live up to the lifetime of regret he knew he would bear.

Justice, why her? Why Ru? It should have been me. Not her…

Losing Ruane was a greater failure than anything he could have ever envisioned. His father's death, both the imagined and the real, had broken his heart. To honor Tevun, to be like Tevun, he could strive for, for his father, in life, had given him the tools to cope. To move on. To live.

But Ruane?

She was the stronger of Tevun's hatchlings. She was the fire that had kept him going. She was the reason he kept living, kept striving to find his father's horns when he had nearly given up hope. To become the wardkeeper he was meant to be. Ruane *was* his drive. His source of power when his hubris was low. She was everything he was supposed to be.

And now she was gone. Dead from the fall from the Obelisk with the daemon Lemures. Other daemons prowled the mega-city, both the Lower and the Upper, he couldn't go and look for her. His sister, she was gone, and he'd never be able to find her body, to give her the proper drakken burial. She had always been a resourceful one, but none could survive that fall. She would be remembered as a hero for saving them. He would always remember her such. But it didn't mean he could ever forget.

A gap will forever remain within his soul. One that would never be refilled.

"The gates to the Obelisk won't hold forever, Lojen," Wick said. The lapin leaned his furry elbows on the parapet of the topmost balcony jutting out from the magnificent spire. Wick was bandaged in multiple places, his fur missing in others, skin underneath puckered red and slashed. The poor creature was tired, they all were. "We're going to die in this cursed city. To think we took down the Fallen and Gargantua in Drenth, only to meet our ends in the hindquarters of Kanja. Emre wouldn't have allowed such a death." Wick's shredded ears swayed as he shook his head. "Em… O, Em… where are you when we need you most?"

Lojen put a tender claw to the lapin's shoulder. *What would Father say in this situation?* "Maybe not, Wick. Probably, but maybe not. We must stay strong." *Father, what am I to do? Guide me, please.*

This cannot be the end. I don't believe it as truth. Forgive me for failing Ru. "We must stay strong," he repeated, more to himself than to the sullen lapin. It was the only way to reconcile his loss. It's what Ruane would have told him to do.

"I'm sorry about Ruane," Wick said softly. "I know nothing I say will ease the torment within you, but we must believe the Pentax will guide us true."

Lojen bit his tongue to keep from lashing out. After their retreat from that village in the Sea, Lojen had no belief that the Pentax would do anything to stave off the horde from taking over the Mistlands, Justice included.

And why would They save wretches like them? Especially now that Ruane was gone. Why would the Pentax take his sister from him when he was the one They should take? It wasn't fair.

I'm so sorry, Ru. I should have protected you…

"Gods, will that bloody racket ever stop?" Wick growled over the parapet. "Just hurry up and break in already, won't you?"

Below, at the aether-enhanced stone gate, the ever-present hammering of a metal and rune encased ram struck repeatedly. Over and over. All through the day the daemons and soldiers of the Fallen's army had battered at the impressive gates of the Obelisk, but so far to no avail. Whatever spells of aether that were infused within the stone, they held strong. Same with the inner walls. The mortal army of the Fallen remained contained within the fortress outside the Obelisk, but the daemons were deep within the mega-city, plundering blood while the remaining residents fled the Lower City in terror. Some were even daemonized draconem.

But no amount of aether could hold indefinitely, especially against the aetheurgy of Nocturne's Pit. And when the gates did eventually breach, everyone inside would be carrion for the birds.

Not just those of the Legion, but all those who'd remained in Gandtril.

The outer walls were burning, some collapsed upon themselves. A portion of the portcullis still stood, but most of it had been ripped violently apart. Bodies up to the enemy's ankles filled the bailey between the outer walls and the middle set, many of the dead were legionnaires, some with weapons still clenched in fists, but also of the Fallen's, humir and daemon alike.

The forum within the fortress had become a slaughtering house. Every man who'd surrendered was slain and quartered. Arms and legs thrown in piles, clothing hanging to dismembered limbs, caked with dried blood and tossed to the daemons of the horde as snacks. V-shaped hunks compounded upon one another, torsos with gaping holes and deep slashes to the gullets with a web of intestines. The heads shoved upon the Legion's daemon-killing spears. Red smeared the faces of men once called friends. The women, he could hear them balling, taken into corners while crimson drake-scaled soldiers had their way with them. They would've wished they had a swift death, it was sickening. And the children. O Zenith, the poor children. Daemons had picked them clean. Lojen's stomach roiled.

It was more gore and death than he'd ever seen in his near two hundred years. Blood stained everything crimson as far as the eye could see. Mangy daemons scavenged the dead like ants.

The barracks and mess had been burned completely to the ground, only ash left behind. The armorer's foundry was a frozen lake of molten metal, tipped from the blast furnaces. Goose feathers littered the ground like snow. What little reserves of aethecite there were, was taken and sorted.

Man-driven automatons worked tirelessly organizing and lifting the stores of aethecite, the weapons, crates of food from the mess. Others, the Predator classes, used their bladed limbs to pierce the bodies of the dead and throw them into piles. Metal beasts taller than he, aethecite engines chugging black smoke, domed heads of blinking lights moving callously to do the Fallen's bidding. Chasses beeping, gears grinding. The sound unbearable against the screams of the living.

Behind the Obelisk, the mega-city was calamity. Riots had ripped the place apart at the seams as the winged daemons culled the citizens of the Lower City by the score, those who had refused to leave before the attack. Buildings in the lower tier had been reduced to little more than rubble. Fires had destroyed much of everything, and Lojen didn't know if it was the people of the city or agents planted by the Fallen. Either way, the mega-city of Gandtril was sundered. The death toll was immeasurable.

Thousands had sought protection in the Obelisk, crowding the gates seeking shelter. Thousands who had not listened to reason and fled before the Fallen's horde reached the city. Thousands who could've been a safe distance away. Thousands of fools.

The Legion had ushered as many inside the tower fortress until the great spire was near bursting before the Golden Sword and Praetor Rignork made the terrible decision to close the protective gates of the Lower City, and Lojen had destroyed the bridges between the Obelisk and the Upper City after Ruane's sacrifice.

They had warned them, but many had not fled. And now they were dead, left to the whims of the Fallen's army. Souls left unsaved.

It was tactical, Lojen knew, because the Obelisk could only hold so many, but he still felt they had failed far too many.

Finn, despite the attempt on his life by his guard, and the grievous wounds sustained, was down at the gates with the remnants of the Legion, some fifty or so soldiers. Titen was with them, as was the old praetor. After Landra's betrayal, only twenty-seven legionnaires had followed the third son of the Golden Throne and the drakken siblings into the Obelisk, plus a handful from the gates at the bridges. Roused from his bed, gout be godsdamned, Praetor Rignork and his personal guard doubled their paltry numbers.

It wouldn't be enough to hold the tower. They were a thousand souls stuck within a prison of their own making. They would all perish, and the army of the Fallen left little to the imagination of what void awaited them. Though they may have won a battle in Drenth, the Fallen's war for the Mistlands took its first casualty in Gandtril.

"I shouldn't be here," he lamented as he fingered the wound in his side, the underlying flesh was still raw. His back also ached from the number of exoscales torn free. "I never should've left Brynn's side." His snout dipped. "Ru… she'd still be…" he couldn't finish that sentence. *Was I ever given the chance? Father, would you have done the same?*

What Lojen wouldn't give to have his father answer him. Just this once. Just to tell him he'd made the right decision, even with Ru's death.

"We all should be elsewhere, Lojen." He glanced at Wick. "I remember something your father once said, after a mission. I had just joined Emre and the rebellion. Not long after Dervin's destruction this was. I was full of vengeance, wanting nothing more than to destroy everything Lu Har touched. All because I had survived. I fully believed the Pentax had forsaken me. Tevun believed otherwise. He said to me then, '*you are where the Pentax demands you.*' At the time, I cared not to be lectured." The lapin smiled wistfully. "He was like that, you know. Always lecturing."

Lojen felt the corners of his mouth curl upward despite his sadness. "That he was. It was the wardkeeper in him." *O, Father, how I miss you so. Watch over Ru better than I ever did. Please?*

"I know this isn't the best time, with what happened to your sister and all, but do you know how your father…" a tremor shook the ground, but it wasn't a strong one, just enough to cause Wick to pause before continuing, "… lost his horns?"

His talon went to one of the horns. After a year, he had never thought to ask. By Zenith, he was a failure of a drakken, and Ruane had paid the ultimate tithe. "No," he conceded, "I don't."

Wick's gaze flickered over the fortress of Gandtril. "It was that mission, before his lecture, that is. We were trying to bring a fleet of airships down. They were full of aethecite. Emre and Finn, along with your father, had devised a plan to get in and out, steal the whole fleet. I know not why the Pentax spared me at Dervin, but Zenith gifted me with the ability to pilot godsdamned near anything. This was my chance to start collecting my revenge's tithe. Tevun and me, we snuck aboard one of the airships as envoys, aiming to beat the void out of the pilots and hijack it in transit. We knew the other transports would follow, and we'd lead them back to the rebellion. It was a sound plan."

"But all didn't go according to plan, I take it?"

"By Zenith, we couldn't have been more wrong," the lapin said. "We proper fucked up, that's what happened. Wasn't no simple aethecite transport, either. Was carrying the bloody Fallen and a bunch of his scourges."

"A trap?"

"No, just unlucky. Maybe the Fallen just wanted to take a joyride, who knows. All I know is that there we were, the two of us ready to take the ship and next thing we know, the Fallen sees us. Your father, I'd never seen a wardkeeper in the dance with the Arbiter before, mind you, but I'll never forget it after what I saw."

Lojen knew what the lapin meant, for the dance to Justice's Hymn of War was a terrible and unforgiving sight. He had witnessed it firsthand, lost he had been in the Temple of Mother Marrow. With the fight with the daemon on the upper tier. It was a berserker rage.

"Tevun," Wick continued, "ripped three scourges to pieces before the Fallen could call upon his aetheurgy. He leapt at him, your father at the Fallen. Claws out. I don't know exactly what happened, as I was fighting off another scourge, but the amount of aetheurgy unleashed in that airship was immense. You have to recall, we were in the air, high above the desert. I was thrown from my paws, smacking the ship's hull. The Fallen blasted a hole through the hull with aetheurgy and we began to plummet. Your father screamed for me to jump."

"But you'd die from that height."

"Better than crashing," Wick said. "Somehow, I got up, and even more surprising, your father was able to deal a blow to the Fallen." Pride at his father's strength swelled within. "Sent the bastard flying. In a single bound, your father swept me off my paws and leapt for the hole. But before meeting free air, we hit a wall. At least that's what it felt like.

"The Fallen's aetheurgy caught us up like a fish in a net. He was there, blood dripping down his face. Your father screamed in rage and pain, for whatever Lu Har was doing to him, gods, it was unworldly. And then, a terrible crack like fierce thunder, a snap like deadly lightning." Wick shivered. "I remember seeing the Fallen's face as your father's horns fell to the ground.

"The airship gained traction, settling. The Fallen stood there, we hanging. He smiled at us. *'You've failed again, Tevun Wardkeeper.*

Should you live, tell Emre Benld it will take more than that to best me.' Your father roared again, but then we were through the hole, falling to the desert below. We survived. Maybe it was the Pentax's grace saw to it, but we survived. Emre and the others found us. Tevun was badly injured, his wardkeeper horns taken by the Fallen. But your father was one tough bastard. I didn't think he'd recover, but he did. And that was when he told me about the Pentax."

Lojen was speechless. He touched the horns again. How had his father been able to survive such a breaking? Such a fall? Would he have been able to? He didn't know if he had the strength. "Thank you for telling me."

"I admired your father, and I mourn him still. But his words remain true, even if we don't want to believe it, the Pentax has a plan for us all."

"But this," he waved his claw over the destroyed fortress, "why would Their plan involve this useless death?" It was, and Lojen mourned them. "Ru's death? It should have been…"

"All death is useless, Lojen Tevunson."

It was the commanding voice of Titen Dunleith, emerging from the Obelisk. Beside the towering elfir was Finn. Both were haggard, eyes red with sorrow and exhaustion. Finn was limping, but not as badly as before, for it seemed an augur had closed the wound on his hip. Titen's bearing still radiated strength and conviction, though. The man seemed unflappable, even under such horror.

"Any change, wardkeeper?"

Lojen shook his massive head, trying to not reach up to the horns atop his skull, for he still felt unworthy. "Nothing to report, Lord Sword."

The Golden Sword waved him off. "Enough, wardkeeper. Titen, please. I mourn for your sister-friend, she saved my brother-friend. And she saved us by knocking that daemon from the bridge. I'll never forget her bravery. She will be honored in Kalderim, my friend." Lojen glanced at Finn. The elfir giving him an answer to a question he didn't know if could be answered. "And the betrayer?"

"Still suffering." How had Ruane known it would be Landra? Gods above, she was smarter than he.

"Good riddance," Wick spat with vitriol.

Lojen's gaze moved toward the destroyed barrack and found a man pinned to the only remaining wall by a dozen daemon-killing spears, some broken into splinters. Oily hair of jet clung to his ashen face as he struggled to breathe, his lifeblood stained his ornate festival clothing, his ceremonial scabbard empty.

As if sensing them watching, Emont Landra's head rose, one eye narrowing. The other had been gouged out, claret dribbling from the socket. The former Legion primus pilus screamed, but it was hoarse and painful. Some nearby daemons looked at him with unfulfilled hunger.

"I'VE BEEN…" the coughed blood as he bellowed, "FAITHFUL… TO NOCTURNE! SAID… I'D BE… FORGIVEN!"

"Landra's a fucking fool."

"That he is, lapin," Titen said. He showed no emotion other than his left eye twitched slightly. "A fool who betrayed his own people. If such things can occur in Kanja, the Fallen is ever closer to winning. But do not allow evil men to place blame in your heart. We must remain strong."

"Don't be so dense, brother-friend," Finn started. The elfirish princeps had a gash about two inches wide above his left eyebrow and his right was heavily bruised. There was also a small cut just above the apple in his throat. All told, he looked like shit. "Our father has long allowed the rot to seep into Kanja. You think Landra and that scourge you named as my chaperone was an accident? He's done it before, not just here."

"And you forget your place, Finnus. Drenth is not Kanja. I know what trial you've been through today, but that does not bode ill speak upon the Golden Throne and our father."

Finn smiled sadly. "'Tis true, brother-friend. I wish it weren't."

A young legionnaire came from the Obelisk and saluted to the Golden Sword. She was ice blue of eye and nary older than a woman grown had she been humir, probably near three centuries plus a half as elfir age. Lojen knew her to be one of the youngest in the Legion, but her skill with a blade was renowned. Probably the best of the bunch he'd seen.

Based on the young elfir's forlorn expression, Lojen assumed the status down at the gates was less than encouraging.

"The praetor sent me, Princeps Titen," she said, "to inform you that the stores may last months. The staff has collected a detailed list. Food and water."

Titen sighed. "Any weaponry, Sanpip? Bullets, blades?"

"Some bullets, princeps," Sanpip said. "Crates stored by the praetor for just the time such as this. Though he never thought he'd have to use them. Fuck."

"None of us did, lass," Finn lamented as he delicately touched the cut on his neck. A shadow passed through his yellow-pupiled, icy blue eyes.

"Of course, you didn't, needle dick."

"What's that, Wick?" Finn pushed back his dirty, silver hair and cupped his ear. The lapin bristled. Lojen tensed for the fight that brewed, but instead, the elfirish princeps grinned. "Gallows humor, Wick. What better time than now? Barely survived the day, me."

The lapin grumbled a curse. Something was eating at the third son of the Dunleith brood, and for the life of him, Lojen couldn't figure it out. Men were odd. Gods, Ruane was right about that.

Finn recovered his genial grin, that rascally posture of his when Lojen had first met him in that underground rebel base after his father's death. It was good to see the old Finn back despite everything. "You know what I just realized? Emre will be waiting for us. And I for one, cannot wait to see him again."

Lojen amended his previous thought, men like Finnus Dunleith weren't odd, they were mad. But Ruane had also thought the same, and he'd see her soon. Same as their father. Perhaps they were all mad.

"I assume you have other news to share, Sanpip," Titen said, glaring at Finn. Although Lojen had spent little time with the Dunleith siblings since coming to Gandtril, there was no hiding the tension between these two men. Deep-seeded it was.

It stoked memories of he and Ru's relationship while banished from the Isle of Merj. That Ruane-shaped gap widening.

The legionnaire, blonde and lean, new scars across her cheeks, glanced into the forum. "The gates hold strong for now, but some of the others, the ones with masonry experience, say the gates will break before dawnbreak. And I've seen it myself, princeps, the gates are weakening. The runes of the Four Tenets of Aether fade."

A rustling amongst the daemons drew the attention of all those on the Obelisk's balcony. A blackness so black, nothing pierced it as it formed along the middle wall. Lightning crepitated within and a figure appeared. The blackness coalesced into the void, disappearing, leaving only a man in a red robe.

Lojen wasn't the only one to suck in his breath. "Broken shells," he cursed.

"The Fallen," came a whisper, from Finn, he thought, but wasn't certain.

Lu Har, even from this distance, looked nothing like the Fallen they had fought in Drenth, for this man was hunched and scarred, his hair and beard missing in multiple places under burnt flesh. But there was no mistaking the presence, for only the Fallen made his exoscales prickle thus.

The Fallen shuffled toward the pinned primus pilus, the horde of daemons scattering and retreating. The soldiers of the Fallen edged away, leaving a ring of empty ground between their master and the betrayer. A low level of pitch-black mist clung to the Fallen's bloodred robe.

Emont Landra forced a smile. "At last… the Fal…" his words died in a cough, but they were clear as if Lojen was standing right beside him. The Fallen must be projecting Landra's voice using aether. Which meant the Fallen wanted them to hear the coming exchange. Intimidation. "I've been… faithful, master. You… promised me… my oath… the city…"

"Is not yet taken, mortal," Lu Har said through the distance. The Fallen's words tickled Lojen's earholes and knew for truth the man was using *Aere*. It was frightening, this power. It was daemonry. "The gate stays barred. The Obelisk still stands."

"I…" Landra hacked blood, then pleaded, "Please, master… I did… as promised. I sacrificed my home… my honor…"

"And your blood?" Lu Har studied the man with a grin, one that Lojen could see clearly. *By Zenith, this is who we fight? We were not prepared for this, Father.*

"I served!"

"Tsk, tsk, tsk, mortal. You did not serve to completion, so I care naught for what you think you deserve. Death comes for us all." The Fallen turned his all-onyx gaze toward the Obelisk, the mist quirking. "Mors expectet."

The Fallen clenched his outstretched fist and a flame of *Ignis* bloomed, eerily reflecting off a black, jagged stone affixed to his wrist. Without removing his sight from them, the flame leapt from his hand to Landra. The former Legion captain's festival garb erupted in flames and the man's scream echoed throughout the fortress. Burnt flesh filled Lojen's nostrils by Lu Har's aether.

"By Honor and Blood, it's come to this?" Titen murmured.

A large daemon stalked forward, bent over, walking on all fours. Chains dangled from the creature's wrists, dragging through the blood as it moved toward the burning primus pilus. Its jutting jaw split in a daemonish smile, licking lips. Red eyes rose.

It was the daemon he'd fought in the Upper City. The one Ruane had died to stop. Lemures. How?

"WARDKEEPER!" it croaked, its voice so evil. *"YOU ARE MINE, AEGIS! LITTLE SISTER STOOD NO CHANCE AGAINST ME."*

Lojen turned from the Fallen's stare, away from the daemon, unable to bear it any longer.

"With the Fallen at our doorstep," Wick started, "we cannot hold him back. Those runes will not withstand his aetheurgy."

"Brother-friend, the lapin speaks true." Wick and Finn both shared a sad smile. "He does that from time to time."

As if on cue, lightning of the blackest void struck the walls surrounding the mega-city of Gandtril in more than a dozen places, the heavens crying in pain. Again and again, it struck.

And everyone atop the Obelisk inhaled as the walls crumbled all around the great spire, the roar of thousands of daemons reaching pitch as they surged from the mega-city toward the Obelisk.

The Golden Sword of Kalderim gripped the pommel of the blade of his homeland, never taking his eyes from Lu Har. Lojen saw determination, anger, and resolve, perhaps maybe even insanity. Titen Dunleith turned toward them, "Then let us finish this. For Honor and Blood."

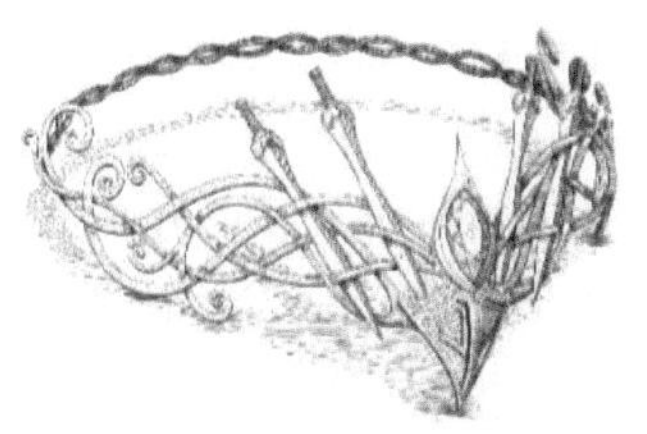

XLVIII
FINN

FINN HAD BEEN ready to die for years, been willing to pay the ultimate price for his beloved's victory. Drenth had gone their way, even with Emre's death. But today, he would see it out, see the Meadows stretch before him.

The fight with the scourge had been nothing shy of regret. Had he not been so lost in his own sorrow for so long, he would have long spotted the falseness in Alyx. Void, Finn had known Kephren had been a spy for Solanine, and Keph had been with the rebellion for years. He should have been more attuned to his surroundings.

But that was his problem, wasn't it. Ever since Drenth, he'd been lost. He had wanted to die, to go to Emre. To see Emre once more. To him, that was going to be worth the coming end, the only shame being he wasn't better dressed.

Taking two stairs at a time, Finn and the others reached the bottom level of the Obelisk—which was a covered peristyle—as the entire tower shook, and it wasn't one of the persistent tremors borne of Mother Marrow's sacrifice.

Columns surrounded a magnificent courtyard within the tower itself. There had been plants once, but now pulled free, weapons and barrels of oil filled the gaps between the uprights, aethecite globes attached to them. The vestibule of the Obelisk was elongated and had two sets of gates, both made of the finest steel and stone, and it was designed for an intended siege, which meant a second level above with killholes for archers and wheellocks. Weapons pointed down, ready. About half of the Legion still standing on the living side of the Meadows took up position near the second gate. Posture rigid with tension, knuckles white as they gripped their spears.

A loud crack followed by a heavy groan told Finn the outer gate had succumbed to the battering, its aetheric spells weakened to the point of breaking.

This is it, Em. I'll be joining your side once more. Let me join you in glory.

Finn looked toward Lojen as the piercing clang of armor and blades split the silence as the army of the Fallen rushed into the Obelisk. He was tense, but ready. As ready as one who lost a sibling could be, lost a loved one. Finn knew Lojen's pain. Hopefully it would be quick, this death.

I'm coming, Em. The specter of his beloved hovered in the space beyond his vision. Waiting. Beckoning with a smile.

That smile…

By the Pentax, he remembered seeing it for the first time all those years ago. And the memory came unbidden.

The blood, that was the first thing Finn noticed. It was everywhere.

"Why are we here, Val?" he asked, scrunching his nose at the smell of offal. He saw the stain on the leg of his trouser. "Great, now I have a blood stain to wash out." Of all the things…

It was well after nightturn, and the mega-city of Drenth was under a cloud of ash as the Fallen's army rampaged throughout the City of Sands. It was a bloodbath, destruction not witnessed since the Fall of Eminence. If he stuffed wool into his ears and began to yell at the top of his lungs, he would still hear the screams over the constant gunfire and explosions rattling Drenth.

It would be days before the mega-city would be fully under the yoke of the Fallen's floating fortress and the carnage ended.

Gargantua hovered overhead, glimpsed between the sky-reaching apartment complexes. Aethecite scree fell like rain, the many rotating cannons spewing aetheric projectiles, leveling buildings like a child toppling their blocks. The sector they were in was quiet, as the army of the Fallen had long since finished their conquest of the northeasternmost section.

Finn and his sister crept through the darkened alleys of ruin, she a ghost of pale skin and even paler hair amidst the blood. Bodies lay everywhere, broken and piled. "Because the warrior we need has taken his first steps in the void."

Stepping carefully over a very dead woman clutching her child, Finn looked elsewhere. He had seen bodies ripped to shreds during the war with the Fallen, but he didn't make it a habit to see the dead, for he would never be able to forget. "If he is such a warrior, then why is he dead?"

"You're a fool of a man, brother-friend," Val whispered as she paused at the mouth of the alley before ducking back into the onerous shadows.

A patrolling Predator automaton marched through the rubble of two crisscrossing raised mega-roads, not glancing their way. It searched through the dead with precision, checking each body with its dome-like metal skull, clicks and beeps emitted. When the automaton was out of view, she darted across the ruined street, him on her heels. This particular alleyway smelled even worse.

Ahead, a shadow was perched upon an overturned dumpster, a magnificent build, two curving horns. Its head turned their way as they approached.

"I see you survived, Tevun," Finn said with a grin. "Next time I won't bet against you. Bad for my pockets."

"And I see you haven't changed in the decades since last seen, young Dunleith." To Val, "Were you successful with the Godsblood?"

"You aren't that much older than me, drakken," Finn shot back.

"It is done," Val said over his protestations. "The Godsblood is in the hands of the Scattered Shards, on her way to Kalderim."

"And this airship captain? Is she trustworthy?"

"Unquestionably. Bliss would not send us astray. The Godsblood will be safe until her time is demanded. And our warrior?"

The great drakken wardkeeper motioned with his head toward a heaped pile of bodies. "The Fallen has not been merciful it appears. It took me a while to track him down."

Val closed her bi-colored eyes, almost as if pained. She had been there, with the Fallen when he had taken the Regent's Tower. "No, he was not."

"And Solanine?"

"Is not an issue at present, but their wingspan of treason knows no bounds. Let us reclaim our warrior's soul from the Meadows." Finn could not envision her suffering, for her betrayal to a creature loved—although heinous, the blooddrake—could not have been easy.

Jumping down from the dumpster, Tevun reached toward the tower of the dead, pulling free the body of a young man, maybe a shade over twenty summers by the look of it. His hair was curled and even in death, his face had a strong countenance to it. Handsome as well. Quite handsome.

Laying the body before them, both the wardkeeper and bikrome knelt on either side, placing talon and braceleted hands upon the unmoving breast. Finn scooched closer and realized who the deceased was.

Emre Benld, the son of the regent and regentress of Drenth.

The air around them grew as cold as the deep freeze in the VVinter Expanse. So frigid, his breaths were visible. He shivered as both bikrome and drakken summoned their aether. A glow of a soft black filmed over the body of the scion of Drenth, a shrill wail reaching Finn's ears to drown out the chaos of Drenth. The mist that danced across the bodies of the dead frolicked toward the blackness, becoming jubilant. The glow intensified, almost as if sucking the aether within the mist into the void, the wails stronger, and Finn found himself glancing around the alley in the hopes no Predators were around. Val and Tevun both began to shake, Val's normally placid face becoming strained. Tevun's wardkeeper horns bloomed a deep lavender.

There was a snap within the mist, a breaking almost, and Finn saw Emre's chest rise. Then the man's brown eyes whipped open, emerald irises dilating. His mouth opened in a scream, but nothing came forth. Both Val and Tevun slumped forward, the mist sagging around them.

Emre sat up, alive and rebirthed. Those arresting eyes searching Tevun and Val before settling on him. The man, crusted with blood from his cut throat and shorn arms, smiled. A genuineness to it, and it drew Finn in right away.

The memory made him smile. A fitting end it would be, finally, to be back with his beloved Emre, where they would have eternity together.

Soon, Em. Soon.

Wheellocks fired and archers let loose arrows amid the cacophony of legionnaires dying. A thud struck at the inner set of gates. So much death already, more on its way. A shout of *'daemon'* rattled back down the peristyle.

Titen, Finn saw, had found the grizzled old praetor leaning heavily on his cane, his feet bare and severely swollen, his stewards tightening his armor around his flabby flesh. A bedraggled augur stood nearby, a young man with curled hair to his shoulders, a kind face. His robe was no longer white, and he looked exhausted as he prayed. The Beads of Aether nearly all dark; there wouldn't be much aetheurgy from this augur.

Finn wished he had parch with him, but he'd have to suffice without his Burn Form when Death came for him.

Wick perched himself not far from the gate with a wheellock rifle resting upon the flattened part of a column's base, ready to fire. Sanpip stood off to the side gripping her blade.

"What do you think?" Lojen asked Finn as he neared.

"Why are you asking me?" Finn was surprised by Lojen's question.

"The Fallen has taken to the field, Eran," Titen was saying to the praetor, snagging Finn's attention away from the drakken. "The Ideal Daughter has done all She could for us. I suggest you fall back to your chambers, bar the door. There is no shame, you have served the Golden Throne well, old brother-friend."

"A wedge," Rignork snapped instead, his voice raspy and strained. "I will be at the head."

"Is that wise, praetor?"

The old warrior stroked his stubbled chin, grey and black peppered. "It's my duty, Titen. We'll fight in waves. The vault will survive. It always has. Gandtril must not fall."

"But this is the Fallen," Finn said. "His aetheurgy has already broken through the gate. And those we—"

"Gandtril will not fall. Or every soul of the Legion will die before that happens."

Finn was about to speak, but Titen grabbed his wrist, holding him still. "By Honor and Blood, praetor. And I shall stand beside you. Together to the end, same as it was five hundred years ago."

It was useless to argue. Not like facing Death was any reason either.

Finn was no general, but he did have some tactical knowledge from his fight in Drenth, and a wedge would work against a smaller force, but Finn had seen the numbers of the enemy. The Legion was undoubtedly courageous, but they would break the moment the Fallen's soldiers hit them. Let alone any daemons. This was to be their last stand, the praetor's plan said.

"It's been my honor, Titen," the old praetor clamped a fist to his heart. "By Honor and Blood."

A loud, thunderous boom shook the gates as a massive daemon gripped the thick metal bars. Teeth the size of its forearm, claws on sinewy limbs wrapped with chains, it wailed unearthly hymns as it bulged against the stone. Behind, soldiers of the Fallen roared in unison of the anticipation.

"WARDKEEPER! PRINCEPS! AEGIS! LEMURES WILL HAVE YOU!" It was the daemon Lojen had fought.

"Hold steady, soldiers of the Legion!" Titen Dunleith bellowed, pulling free the fabled Golden Sword of Kalderim. Aetheric light glimmered off the peridot crystal in the crossguard. "This is the day we've waited for. We've pledged our Honor and our Blood to our blessed Golden Throne," his voice rose amidst the pounding by the daemon, suddenly strong and vigorous. Finn's own adrenaline rising. "I say this is the day that we repay that debt! What say you?"

A rousing of fifty-odd legionnaires screamed, "For Honor and Blood!"

The barred gate rumbled as the enraged daemon struck it again with its bulk and might, yelling for Lojen's blood. Poor drakken. It struck again and again, the daemon did, shaking the walls of the tower. There was more to the assault than just daemon strength, there was aetheurgy behind it. The telltale sign of the Fallen's aether seeped from beyond the daemon in the form of blackened mist. It welled within the tower, coming up to the legionnaires' knees. Bloated Void Form angry within. Cracks began to blister the runes of aether in the walls and gate.

A legionnaire rushed from a side doorway that led to the killholes. She skidded to a stop before Titen and Rignork. "Princeps, praetor, the gate will not hold much longer. The Fallen's aetheurgy is obscuring our sight. We must fall back."

The two elfirish soldiers shared a look, then Titen nodded. "Fall back and regroup, legionnaire."

The woman raced the way she'd come and Titen lowered his gleaming helm upon his head as he strode behind the wedged soldiers of the Legion. The time of reckoning was upon them. Time to face the Pentax and hope they had lived well.

He found Wick grinning like a child, clenching his wheellock in excited paws. Lojen's wardkeeper horns were glowing with orchid aether, his body swaying back and forth, almost in a sort of slow dance. Tevun had once said Justice's Hymn of War played like a song in his body. No doubt this is what Lojen heard now, despite the daemon calling for him.

Yes, they were ready for the gatekeeper of the void to draw them down. For Death to take them all.

His eldest brother and the ancient praetor stood tall, the Golden Sword of Kalderim gleaming in his hand, *Aere* rippling up and down the blade's fuller. Men and women of the Legion, loyal soldiers of Kanja to the end.

Setting his feet and his jaw, Finn drew forth the curved sword stolen from the enemy after he'd lost his family's heirloom, gripping it in a steady hand.

The gate keened, dust rising as the stone holding it in place broke and chipped away. The columns surrounding the peristyle wobbled as the daemon thundered against the other side. Red eyes burned with hate as it roared with each terrible blow, drake scaled soldiers in the background, some firing back at the killholes above even though they were now abandoned, others watching and waiting for the carnage that was about to unfold. The mist of pitch swirled with cruel anticipation of the souls to consume.

It would hold, the gate would, maybe a half an hour or more if the Pentax sought fit to shine mercy upon them. But those runes would break.

Finn had never been much of a holy man, but he found himself praying to the Ideal Daughter regardless. Praying to give him the strength to die well. Praying She take him straight to Emre. There was nothing more he wanted in his last precious moments upon this side of the veil.

A tug on the tunic under his drake scale cuirass. He turned to find a humirish girl, maybe of ten summers pulling on his clothing, cerulean gaze. "Princeps Finnus, I know a way out of the Obelisk."

Shock washed over him. "Brother-friend!" the Golden Sword turned his way, "this child says she knows a way out."

A glimmer of hope surged through him as he made his way toward his brother, pulling the girl forward. Did he dare postpone his fate? The specter of Emre urged him to listen, to stay and fight. Conflicted by both paths.

"Gandtril must not fall," the surly praetor stated flatly beside Finn's brother. Was this man so eager to die?

Was he? No, said Emre's ghost. Not yet, Finn realized. Emre would never allow his people to die needlessly. The people were always the reason to fight. They had fought for Drenth's people, and Finn had to fight for Kanja.

You're always correct, Em. Always. "Hope, brother-friend," Finn said, "a child may have what we need most. We cannot turn away any hope. Not now, not ever. That is not the way of the Pentax. The people of Gandtril need this hope."

The pounding continued while Titen studied the young girl. She had a confidence about her, a steadiness a child her age shouldn't have in such a moment. Finn was awed by her strength.

"Eran," Titen started, the realization of what the girl brought. "Gandtril is not the city. It is the people inside of her."

Finn doubled down, knowing this was Emre speaking through him. "If we can save a single Kanjan, wouldn't that be holding to our duty? My father's command?" He surprised even himself in that moment. Sounded like his father, the rēx of Kalderim, he did. *Emre, you knew this the entire time, didn't you? This is what you tried to show me in Drenth?* "Thousands need not die here today if there is a way out of the city."

The old praetor looked at him dumbly, but then to the girl, face softening at seeing one so young face such a probable death. "Bliss' truth?" She nodded enthusiastically. Seeing this, he gestured toward Titen with a skeletal finger. "Princeps Titen, take ten legionnaires, find out what this girl knows. Save the people. If not, lock yourselves in a room and hole up until the time comes. We must protect those in need to our dying breath."

The Golden Sword objected vehemently. "I should be here, with you. At the gates of the void. Send Finn and his wardkeeper." Finn glanced at Lojen, the big drakken confused. *Wardkeeper? For me?* "They can take word back to Kalderim."

"Go, Lord Sword. It's an order from your father's praetor." Rignork shoved Titen back. Hard. There was strength still left in his old bones despite the gout in his swollen feet. "From an old friend, if it must be."

Finn knew his brother wanted to stay and fight beside his praetor, beside the Legion, it was in his blood to die for the Golden Throne. That's what their father would've wanted for the

Golden Sword. But Titen knew nothing but duty. And their duty was to protect the people of Kanja.

"Sanpip, Finn, drakken, with me." Titen Dunleith motioned to a few others, including Wick, then to the girl. "Lead us, child."

The small group raced after the girl, her bare feet slapping the ground as she ran, almost magically gliding instead. Deep into the Obelisk they went, corridor after corridor, storage room after storage room. Further from the sounds of protective gates, the breaking of stone, the oncoming deaths of legionnaires.

They entered a wine cellar; casks of fermented grapes stacked upon each. Dozens of liveried men, women, and children huddled down there, lowborn workers of the Obelisk, not those who'd entered during the invasion. Cooks, launderers, and squires holding bags of food, skins of water, some weapons. Breathing masks worn. Prepared, they were.

The girl weaved through the frightened people, pushing her way past a row of wine casks where behind was a door no taller than her, easily missed in the muted glow of the aethecite lights adorning the ceilings. The edges barely visible to the naked eye.

Finn knelt beside the girl and ran his fingers over the door. "How'd you find this?"

"It's called the Silent Gate, princeps. A secret kept by those in my family. From the beginning of Gandtril."

He hugged the girl, a great smile upon his face. "Thank you, child, you may've saved us all! Your fam—"

A concussion reverberated throughout the wine cellar. The gate above was barely holding. They had no time left.

"Broken shells," Lojen cursed, his horns glowing a brighter shade of purple.

Panicked people cowered as Finn dug his fingers into the door, Wick helping him pry it open with his dueling knife. Old dust filled his lungs, a cracked seal of age and disuse. Titen struck flint to a reed torch, and it sprang to life. Pushing the flame into the darkness, a tunnel led into the earth, covered in mold, not touched since the days of the Obelisk's creation. But the ground was solid stone, worn with age and built strongly.

"Hurry!" the Golden Sword ordered, beckoning for the lowborn to get into the tunnel. He turned toward Sanpip. "Go and lead every citizen of Gandtril down here now."

Wick plunged into the fore, the lapin's torch leading the way as the ragtag group of survivors fled to their escape. Titen and the legionnaires ushering the flow, waving and urging hurry.

Finn stayed near the entrance to the cellar with Lojen, listening and waiting. For a long while, there was nothing but the pounding on the gates. But then came the crash, the sounds of fighting reaching them in the bowels of the Obelisk. The army of the Fallen had breached the ancient fortress tower above them.

Within moments of the crash, Sanpip came rushing down, a steady stream of frightened people after her. Hundreds of them, scared and terrified, moving with a calm only when the end might be on the horizon. A knowledge that death stalked them. It seemed like ages, but after long agonizing minutes, the last of the citizens of Gandtril passed into the tunnel. The sounds of battle slowly died, vigorous at first, now an eerie silence.

Finn looked toward the drakken and sighed. "So much death." But then he smiled broadly as the ghost of Emre gave him an encouraging nod over Lojen's shoulder. "But we may just get out of this yet!"

Then they pulled the door shut behind them and the Pentax's mercy may have indeed shone down upon them.

Torches lined the darkness as the survivors moved ahead, Finn and the drakken at the rear. Finn wanted to ensure none fell behind. These survivors were his responsibility, and he wasn't about to fail them now. Part of him felt the guilt of failing them for so long in his misery, but no more death would be on his hands.

For the most part, the tunnel was a straight path. At one point, there was a staircase leading downward, but then the path slowly veered upward toward ground level. The end came abruptly after their long trek underground, multiple hours Finn figured, as he nearly ran into Lojen's broad back.

With the drakken beside, they made their way to the front while the ragtag group of survivors—commoner and noble alike—rested or sat on their haunches, some stretching their tired legs. All exhausted. Wick and Titen waited beside a stone doorway, of a similar height to the one they'd entered. The lapin's button-sized eyes reflected in the torchlight.

"What are we waiting for, brother-friend?"

Titen jutted his chin toward Lojen. "Need your wardkeeper strength, drakken, the door remains tightly sealed."

Lojen touched his horns, which snagged against the ceiling of the tunnel. "I can try."

Rolling his shoulders, Lojen put both clawed talons upon the stone portal, setting his muscular legs, and began to push. The drakken's booted feet skidded across the stony ground as he grunted. The stone held strong.

Lojen's bellow shook the tunnel as his wardkeeper horns blazed violet, his body straining. Slowly, the door groaned as it opened. Grey fog surged through the cracks, the smell of the Sea of Mist overpowering. The haze swallowed Lojen as the door fell forward, the great drakken tumbling.

The Sea was a welcoming sight to the weary.

The dense fog of the Sea melded with enkindled smoke, Finn couldn't make out the burning mega-city of Gandtril. But it mattered not, he knew what ruins lay beyond.

Finn was tired, but there would be little rest in his near future.

After their flight through the Silent Gate and emerging a league west of the great mega-city, Titen, along with Lojen, had led the thousand or so survivors southwest toward the Forgemistress' Blades before they would turn north toward Kalderim, using the Sea as cover. Only Wick, Sanpip, and a dozen other legionnaires held back to watch with him, a rear sentry on the army of the Fallen. They knew nothing of the Fallen's plans, but it remained sound counsel that Gandtril wouldn't be the last stop. It would take the survivors weeks to walk the hundreds of leagues to the floating mountains, and someone needed to keep an eye on the Fallen's march, to ensure the people made it safely.

Finn felt he had to do it, even if it meant further run-ins with Nocturne's champion.

"You mourn, Princeps of Kalderim," came a soft voice from behind.

Finn spun to find the girl who'd saved them all. But she looked nothing like he remembered.

She had auburn hair, eyes the color of honey, and wore a pendant of peridot around her neck above a white cassock that resembled an augur's of the Scattered Shards, a long, white robe fluttering in the Sea behind her. She appeared only ten summers, but her eyes bespoke of agelessness.

"Who are you?"

"Someone who understands what you are feeling all too well, Finnus Dunleith," the girl said. "But your journey is not yet at an end." The girl moved, seeming to grow in height, becoming a woman instead. Her skin glimmered in the mist, translucent almost. "*'Only a Godsblood can rekindle Eminence. Blood of Nightingale must bloom or aether will kill us all. Ever shall the world be broken. A protector of the Gods has been named. The Golden Sword will sing the Hymn of War.*'"

"You… a legionnaire said those very words to Lojen."

"By my command, Finnus Dunleith. To find you." The woman's cascading hair seemed to shimmer like a calm lake in winter. "Chosen, you have been, Princeps of Kalderim, as an Aegis of Eminence and Noctis. Your blood has bound you. Seek the blood of Nightingale. Then you will have your answers."

Finn stared. "Answers? What answers? My brother carries the Golden Sword. Not me."

"Answers I cannot yet give. Not until the Peridot is the last left standing. You must seek the truth on your own, Finnus Dunleith. Only then will you learn. The Godsblood is not the only one who must fight what is to come. Four warriors are to be made, the Godsblood at the head of her Aegises. Dark paths are yet for you all to tread. The true threat is for the Godsblood alone, but a threat stands before you. One you know all too well. But one you are more than capable of defeating. With this."

The woman reached into her robes and drew forth a crimson sword that was almost as big as her. At least four feet in length, shining, garnet braided crossguard where a red gemstone gleamed, and the Four Tenets of Aether were inscribed on the fuller. It looked parchment-light in weight, but sharper than any blade.

More queer, it was a mirror image to the Golden Sword of Kalderim, the one Titen carried, minus the garnet coloring in place of a peridot. Even the gemstone in the pommel looked as if it was shattered like the other sword.

"Take this Finnus Dunleith of Kalderim. The Crown of Bliss remains broken. Two other pieces remain hidden. Find them and the Golden Sword will sing. My Twin gives His blade to you. Mine own will be ready when the time comes. One lies in the west, Justice's, near Shatterstorm. The Forgemistress' soars above the mount of the Vird. Once all four blades are found, my Aegis will rise. And you will reclaim what is yours. A throne befitted of gold."

Finn took the sword into his trembling hands. He felt wearier than he had the day before. This journey was only just the beginning he feared.

When he looked up again, the woman was gone. But a flapping of great wings made him look up, and before disappearing into the haze of the Sea, Finn saw an enormous aerovern, perhaps the largest he'd ever seen. Finn was left with naught but a grinding confusion beating away at an already senseless day and more riddles than he was capable of answering.

Who was she, Em? An aerovern.

As usual, the specter of his beloved gave no answer, just a knowing smile.

XLIX

ASHE

ANOTHER HOUR TURNED and she was back sitting at the bow, pondering. Harlequin was with her, head lying in Ashe's lap, fingers roaming Cyan's Gauntlet. Fingers that had done things to Ashe Cyan would've blanched at. The glorious memory of their time together playing across the aerescreen of Ashe's mind.

Peace, that's what she felt. Peace and love.

It was full evenfall now, the stars bright in the sky above like diamonds strewn across a pitch blanket. This far from Port Sin, there was no noise, no smog from aethecite or seagandr-oil machinery. Peaceful. The moon resembled a disk bearing the guile of Nocturne, the divine entity disguised as another machination of man. The water of the VVyrm Ocean was soothing.

They were close to the inlet now. *Peerless* anchored a mere half mile away. So close, she could almost imagine the aethecite cannons on the deck had they been trained on them, but nobody moved across the ship's top. Either they were already ashore in the inlet, or they were waiting to ambush them.

Soon.

The sounds of lapping waves made her think about what Neenah had said. About her destiny and the Seals to Eminence.

Ashe held her left palm up, the diamond in the Eye of the Soul glimmered in the starlight and Nocturne's moon, a prism swirling with the ideals of the Pentax. Ideals that were nothing like those she was raised upon in the Shards. The ideals of Life and Death. She hadn't believed in them much, but Cyan sure did, and she briefly wondered how her taskmaster would've taken the revelations. Gods, she would miss him. Miss his teachings, his admonishment. His glares. His laugh.

O, Cyan…

She examined the rune of *Ignis* on her forefinger. Like a small flame, one tail higher than the other etched into the auric ring. A seesaw of tails, like power of the pyre shifting between the pair, like the balance of Life and Death.

Like the sacred oath taken by the Godsking.

Reflexively, she conjured *Ignis*, a ball of yellow-orange flame burst alive above the diamond, no larger than an apple. The prism in her palm became a conglomeration of hues. Yellow, red, orange. The sight spellbound her, drawing her in. The wails in the Pit singing their haunted hymn as the few tendrils of mist aboard the *Dauntless* hounded her.

The waves undulated aggressively, lifting the bow.

Harlequin looked up at her, but Ashe instead cradled the flame, tenderly stroking the non-heated ball with her free hand. Lovingly she beheld it. Rolling it over her knuckles like a trickster might a quadran while at the poker table. The light of it danced in her vision. The song of the Pit lullabying.

The sea heaved, the silver-emerald moon growing dark. A storm brewing, coming quickly. Harlequin drew back from her, her aura reading concern. But she ignored the vicar, lost in the call of aether she became.

Ignis called to her, nay, the power of Brio, and she heeded. The wails of the undead swarmed to a fever pitch beyond the veil. The flame grew larger in her hand, now almost the size of her head. Flames licked with the wicked snap of a crackling blaze; the center pure white. Heat began to pulse down her wrist, through her arm, tickling the runes of her tattoos.

The boat rocked vigorously.

The silent journey was silent no longer. Shouts from the sailors. Yells from Roland at the wheel to brace themselves from the squall furiously coming in. The landlubbers of the Scattered Shards rising like river-jumping trout from inside the hull. Grand Quaestor Owl poked an ugly, bearded face over the railing, demanding answers. Maja Carr, in full blooddrake form, burst from the hold, her orcirish bodyguards shouldering quaestors aside, bleating in the dialect of the lesser order of draconem. Valeria Dunleith calmly watched from her seated position on the crates below the wheel. Neenah LeFleur hurried topside, tightening her ascot.

All of it Ashe saw but she was too lost in the aether to care.

"NO, BRYNN, DON'T FALL TO THIS PREY!"

Visions of her father's death in Drenth pranced about the flames, like she was watching the tragedy from above, the choir the howling of slumbering souls in the Pit. The fight with the Fallen at the Temple of Mother Marrow. The vicious sting of black mist and aether carried by a flame's pop. The blood from Emre Benld's wounds turned the ball of *Ignis* bright red.

The bow of the boat rose under a giant whitecap, a tidal fall.

A body thrown against the wall of the Temple, her mother's body. Six blackened blades of the Strix embedded in Cadrianna Benld's, nay, Cadrianna Nightingale's body. A blade wedded to her, now the blinding pain of her death. The ball grew bigger, grew hotter.

The boat teetered, sending seawater over the rails, dousing the decks as sailors held on for dear life. Harlequin, lovely Harlequin, screamed as she slid across the soaked planks toward midships. The tentacles of the kraken bowsprit snapped, disappearing into the dark waves. Neenah's shouts deafened by the gusting wind, the now pouring rain. The moon hidden in the clouds. Thunder clapping as if Nocturne was laughing at their peril.

Or was it Zenith?

The flames grew, the scene expanded, the phantom song drowning everything else. Both Emre and Cadrianna, Father and Mother, dead in her hands. Others, a pair of drakken, two elfir, a lapin, standing in the shadows. Watching. Crying. Waiting. Dying.

Cyan, O dear Cyan the Defiant, he reached for her. His face pale in death, Death shadowing him as he called her name.

Dauntless fought the waves bravely. The masts buckled but did not break. The sailors did their best to keep the ship from capsizing. Unsuspecting quaestors lost their footing, some indeed toppled overboard, lost to the VVyrm, dragged into the deep. The living strix whooped and hollered, fought the torrent to stay perched. Owl and Cadoz fell to the wooden planks of the warship.

Anger fueled the ball in her palm. Larger now, almost standing as tall as she. The veil of pitsong shrouding everything. Revenge built inside her. Revenge against the man who did this. Revenge at the gods who allowed this. Against Zenith Himself.

Someone shook her shoulders.

The flames faltered. Shivered, shrinking. The tintinnabulation breaking apart, the souls' cries fleeing back into the everlasting void of Death.

A hollow call from the world of Life breaking the dam of fire and anger inside.

"Ashe!"

Ignis evaporated. Gone in an instant. Wails dying, returned to the land of the dead.

Ashe slumped forward; head pressed to the deck. A hand gingerly touching her back.

"Ashe?"

"Harle-bub?"

Her friend, the lover she now knew, knelt beside her, giving her a hug. "It's alright, Ashe."

The ship crested downward into the waves.

"Ho, you prick-sucking scallywags!" cried the swashbuckling Neenah LeFleur toward the sailors on deck. "Get that mizzen tight to the starboard! Bend the fore! Get me some eyes up that godsdamned nest!"

The sailors hopped to the captain's orders. Some grabbing the ropes of the masts to catch the wind. Others tactfully climbed the cargo ropes up the timber, heading toward a small half-barrel of a viewing platform high above the ship. Still others did Zenith-knows-what on the deck, for sailing was not something Ashe understood. Rigging had come loose, one of the masts was cracked in half a dozen places, still standing upright by sheer luck. The sails were ripped to shreds in more than one spot. Who knows how many had gone overboard. Quaestors not accustomed to the violent storms of the seas were hugging railings and spewing the contents of their gullets all over the place.

In the distance, below the grand peak, *Peerless* harbored, also fighting the waves.

"What happened?" Harlequin asked, reaching for Ashe's hand.

The tempest surging around the warship receded, the clouds overhead dissipating. The waves crested and died, the stillness belittling the storm that occurred. Mount Bastard, the home of the Seal of *Ignis* loomed over them.

Everything was returned to the way it was.

"I don't… don't know," she answered.

The scant mist railed at her body, frightened.

"DEAR DAUGHTER, PREPA—"

The ship lulled anew, rocking bow to stern. Teetering port to starboard as if something under the water quickly shifted directions. The wooden hull creaked as if that same something was testing its durability. Ashe grabbed the railing as the ship lurched, her head nearly smacking a nearby set of rigging. Harlequin held on to her.

In the pale moonlight, the waves parted as pitch-black, fin-like appendages rose from the deep.

"There must be a million of them!" a quaestor cried nearby, holding the railing for dear life as the ship was struck again.

The fins sunk beneath the surface. A heartbeat after, water exploded in a geyser, raining seawater down, soaking them.

And out rose the drake. A seagandr.

"Nope," Ashe said, strangely calm, blinking away the saltwater, "just one."

Prior to Maja Carr's revelations, Ashe had believed that only the nefariously vile mind of the Master of the Pit would dare conjure such a twisted creature as the seagandr, but if Zenith was truly the evil divinity, then it made more sense now.

Water cascaded down the black behemoth's glossy scales, shining like diamond tears in Nocturne's moonlight.

"Seagandr!" came the shout from many sailors' and quaestors' lips. All of them in fear.

And fear they should, for the seagandr was the hardest of draconem to kill, it took teams with specialized equipment to hunt them for their oil.

Nine heads the seagandr had. Nine triangular snouts of glistening black scales over razor sharp teeth in rows like a shark. The triangle heads were angular to a fin-like spike above equally black-orchard eyes. More fins ran down the spine of each head, a singular blowhole at the peak of each graceful neck. The seagandr's body had no arms or hind legs, only a mass of heads, a stout gullet built like a forty-foot grain silo, and a sleek, wicked tail covered in spikes, almost like a porcupine. From head to tip, the seagandr was at minimum a hundred feet in length. The body was covered in bloodred *Aquis* runes, carved into the black scales as if Zenith Himself used His holy blood to bless the drake with aetheric rage.

Aquis crepitated about the seagandr, as this drake was clearly pissed about something. The many heads shrieked a shrill cry in unison, as if chanting a magical spell. Focused gushes of seawater spewed from watersacs from within their mouths. Mighty streams of *Aquis*-infused water slammed into the masts, into the hull, into the unfortunate sailors and quaestors on deck. All three masts fractured, breaking with terrible groans, sending the sails into the VVyrm and on hapless men and women, killing and maiming those not forced overboard. The hull splintered in multiple spots; the sound as intense as the earth splitting in a quake.

Both Ashe and Harlequin held the railing, going to their knees. They exchanged glances, a fear in Harlequin Ashe had never seen before. The purest fear of looming death and no way to stop it.

She had to do something. "Nightingale!"

"I AM HERE, DEAR DAUGHTER," the black dagger said sorrowfully. Knowing what she knew now, it pained the First Wife to be used on Her children.

There is no other way.

"I KNOW."

Ashe drew the black blade, but instead of it separating into six separate blades, Nightingale wrested control from her and the magical weapon roared into life, almost like a drake itself. And in her hand, Ashe held a six-foot, slender blade of black flames, the owl-shape on the crossguard had become a fiercesome draconem with outstretched wings, its head spouting the flames up the blade.

That's new…

"MY TRUE FORM, DEAR DAUGHTER. THE BLADE OF NIGHTINGALE."

The nine heads of the seagandr reared back, readying their watersacs to discharge more *Aquis*.

Ashe coiled and burned her Soul Form, her inked aetheric runes synapsed as the magical aetheurgy burst into life. Muscles and bones alike, senses and speed, strength and thought all engorged with aether. *Aere*, *Aquis*, *Ignis*, and *Terris* crackled about her body as she leapt from the *Dauntless* onto the nearest head of the seagandr, slicing through its thick neck with her blade of flames before jumping toward another.

To live.

To fight.

For Neenah and her crew. For Harlequin.

For herself.

Father, Mother, Cyan, wait for me longer?

She cut.

The hull splintered under the pressure of the seagandr's aether as it screeched. The shorn head landed upon the deck of the warship as she severed another. The draconem was not easily defeated, for the two headless necks had already begun to rejuvenate.

The key to a seagandr is finding the prime head, only then could the drake be killed.

Of the nine heads, eight were betas, able to reform within moments of severing. Fueled by aether, the drake was relentless, and no two seagandr were alike in that the prime could be any of the nine. All the same size and shape. No distinction. And as a further bastardly move, the prime head could be shifted to any head at any moment through the beast's aether, even a newly reformed one.

So, by the time a hunter might have determined the prime, they were usually crunched in their jaws, dying a horrible death. Savvy buggers, the seagandr.

The seagandr's tail wrapped the warship from underneath, the tip slammed the deck with godslike force, splintering the wood with its spikes. The drake now had the *Dauntless* in a vice grip, its considerable bulk constricting the vessel like a python. The hull groaned under the strain. The warship objected and creaked under the continuous attack by the seagandr's many heads, regrowing as fast as Ashe cut them free with the black flames of the Blade of Nightingale. She raced along the body, leaping neck to neck, cutting and slicing with the impressive blade like a streaking flame.

But the heads kept regrowing.

One head slammed into Ashe's side while she was mid-swing, sending her tumbling across the deck. Her skull smacked wood and stars blossomed. The Blade of Nightingale clattered from her grip, the black flames quenching.

The quaestors had grown some resolve or had determined attacking was the only way to survive, as they began to hack at the tail with bladed weapons. Harlequin had been thrown back as well, her axes in hand as the hull bifurcated by the drake's pinch, bow separating from stern. Soldiers of the Scattered Shards and sailors alike screamed as they fell into the jagged gap, splashing into the seawater. Cries for help, others ordering those still on deck to launch the life rafts. Down the small skiffs went, the survivors climbing over each other to get to safety.

Cadoz dragged the grand quaestor's chair, tossing it to one of the waiting sailors before hopping into the boat. The grand quaestor was already in one of the skiffs. Of Maja Carr and her orcirish bodyguards, there was naught a sight.

The seagandr's aether struck the wheelhouse, shattering the giant steerer under a gush of water. Valeria Dunleith threw up a shield of *Aere*, the clashing magic of the gods died as they hit one another, jarring the bikrome backwards.

Curses flew from Neenah LeFleur's kissable lips as she, Roland, and the hobgoblin twins jumped overboard.

"DEAR BRYNN, GET UP."

Ashe climbed to her feet and burned more aetheurgy to clear the lingering dizziness from her head. She snapped up the Blade of Nightingale and the black flames roared back to life. Another head hissed as she cleaved it from scaly neck. But a moment later the head grew back, snapping at the irritant who'd cut it free. She slid down one of the necks, hacking and slashing. And for all the heads she'd sundered, they just kept growing back. No matter how many she sliced, she still couldn't find the prime head.

Godsdamn these beta heads.

But she was doing a wonderful job of agitating the seagandr, for it was frenzied in its attacks on the warship. The ship was split in twain like an axe wound to the shoulder blade. Sinking fast.

Harlequin clung to the bowsprit, shouting words Ashe couldn't hear over the hissing and aetheurgy of *Aquis* dousing the *Dauntless*, smashing the warship to pieces. The bow cracked under the Resolute's feet in another place, sending the vicar sprawling inches from the splintered gap, staring into the abyss churning below.

"Noooo!" Ashe screamed as she ducked under a snapping head, serrated rows of teeth clipping through part of her wet hair.

Another nipped at her leg, teeth sinking into her calf. Ashe screamed in agony, the drake triumphantly yanking her in violent fashion. Upside down she hung, swinging her blade frantically, slicing through the jaw clasping her leg, the flaming sword searing scale and drake flesh alike.

She fell twenty feet, smashing into the broken mizzen, her ribs smacking the boom in a vicious crunch, breath escaping. She tumbled to the deck, cracking her head on something hard. Stars in her vision once more.

"Ashe!" Harlequin, she thought it was. "Move!"

Ashe rolled painfully over just as one of the seagandr's heads bit into the hull where she'd landed. Another came at her, she sluggishly brought the fiery blade up and stabbed into the open mouth, the six-foot flaming blade piercing the beast, coating her in seagandr-oil. Getting upright was a chore, she slashed at the first, who was spitting out toothpicks of the hull. She cried out as another head bowled into her back, tumbling over the decapitated drake head, seagandr-oil sending her sliding across the decking.

She was up achingly, slipshod running through the suffering, dodging snapping heads, leaping across the broken bow toward the wheelhouse as her aetheurgy tried to heal her wounds. The seagandr's tail thwacked at her, but she cut the tip clear. It was the one appendage that wouldn't grow back. A small victory.

But the draconem was maddened further. *Aquis* streams pierced the hull like punching through parchment with a stick.

Harlequin stepped in front of the seagandr, issuing a challenge, but its attention found other quaestors to murder. The Resolute's mist canisters discharged; her breather full of the grey poison as she huffed it in, drawing on Cyan's Sharded Gauntlet.

"Harlequin!" She grabbed the woman by the arm. "We need to get out of here!"

The vicar shrugged out of her grip. "Not this time, love." There was madness in her aetheric aura. "I won't lose another of my family. Not again." She summoned the aetheric weapon, this one a battle axe longer than she was tall, the crescents wider than her hips. Harlequin smiled at Ashe, then turned to watch the seagandr wreak havoc on the warship. Mania drove the vicar's aura, but there was peaceful tranquility as well.

And there it was, Harlequin was prepared to die so that she could fulfill her destiny as a member of the Scattered Shards. But moreso, this was to right the wrongs of Amaranth's death. Of Cyan's. This was Harlequin's final stand.

There was nothing Ashe could do or say outside of clobbering Harlequin over the head and dragging her ass with her. But Ashe knew that was wrong.

She understood. Understood it all too well.

"Go, Ashe, my love. Go and remember that I've always loved you and you will do what you must."

Tears welled. She hugged the vicar fiercely. It didn't feel fair or right. This shouldn't be the end. Couldn't be the end. Not now, not that she had finally found a smidgeon of happiness.

"Harle-bub…" the words lost, what could she say that would tell the woman what she meant to her?

Harlequin gave her a knowing smile, then raced across the deck, the aetheric axe raised high while she shouted the prayer of their sect, "Take thy blood, the blood of man. Take thy heart, the heart of man. The fire in the soul, the forge it bequeaths. Show thy soul, let it burn in the pyre. Molded when white hot. In thy name, the vicars are yours. My soul is yours!"

Harlequin the Resolute, the girl Ashe knew as Tista, the woman she'd come to love despite everything, swerved the first head, then another, before disappearing in a swirling mass of seagandr heads all descending on her at once.

"Goodbye, Harle-bub… thank you…"

Ashe quelled her Soul Form and leapt overboard. Cold water swallowed her, threatening to drag her down to Nocturne's Pit. She kicked her way toward the pale moonlight, bobbing with the waves.

The seagandr let loose a screech so efficacious, it sent the waves crashing. A fusillade of aether lit up the nightturn with a CLAP! The *Dauntless* exploded, bits of the warship flinging far into the VVyrm Ocean. The seagandr reared toward the moon, eight heads going limp, the final head crying to He Who Fathered the World as it burst into black-scaled fragments. The full body of the drake shivered, crimson *Aquis* runes glowing, then fading.

She'd done it. Harlequin had found the prime head. Sacrificing herself to save them all. Truly resolute.

The seagandr fell back, splashing into the water, sinking underneath the dark surface along with the ship it destroyed. Something fell into the waves near her, something blue. A body.

Ashe dove under the water, swimming against the drag of her cassock, legs thrashing as she reached for the body, burning her

Soul Form so she could see underwater. It was Harlequin. She swam faster, harder, deeper.

Grabbing the woman by the waist, Ashe hauled her back to the surface. Their heads broke the water's plane. She sucked in a deep breath. Harlequin's eyes were closed, her face bruised and bloodied. Beautiful, but more importantly, still breathing.

Ashe cried tears into the maelstrom. Tears of joy.

L

ASHE

THE CAVE SWALLOWED her and the comatose Harlequin as she swam toward the seagandr-oil torches dimly lighting the grotto within Mount Bastard, holding the woman tightly.

Her arms felt like lead, but her boots finally touched solid rock underneath the still sea of the VVyrm. Her cassock weighed as much as her, and she had probably imbibed enough saltwater to fill the Bay of Fire twice over. She coughed so hard that she nearly doubled over before it finally abated.

But she laid Harlequin down as gently as she could, wiping away the sodden curls, cupping the woman's unmoving cheek. Harlequin's chest rose softly and rhythmically. Ashe was just relieved the woman had survived. She needed her.

The grotto was enormous, perchance even as sweeping as the Barter Yard. Stalactites hung from the domed rock like teeth, the rising stalagmites ready to chew all those inside. Puddles of seawater were the size of ponds under a layer of grey mist. The smell of sulfur tingled her nose. The drip, drip, drip ever present, a reassuring cadence. From where the inlet met the inside of the mountain, dozens of tunnels branched off. Ashe figured there were more, but those were all she could see from where she stood.

Even though the grotto was in the base of a dormant volcano and there was a stale warmth in the air, Ashe was tired of being wet, so, she called forth her *Aquis* aetheurgy instead of summoning a flame of *Ignis*. The aetheric runes tattooed on her arm flared as they came alive in a rush of watery magic. She ran her hands the length of her body, and the spell sucked the moisture from her robe. A few passes of magical *Aquis*, and she was dry. Her hair was still plastered to her head, but it was all she had left in her.

Tired beyond reproach, she flopped to the grotto's floor next to Harlequin, her fingers finding the prone woman's, entwining.

Deeper into the volcanic cavern, she noted the red cassocks of quaestors, plus a handful of shirtless sailors huddled around seagandr-oil torches, warming themselves, checking wheellock powder, gathering the rescued supplies, or just flat out thrilled to be alive. Not many survived encounters with a seagandr on the open sea, except for the talented hunting teams in the VVynter Expanse up north. It would be a story they'd tell the rest of their lives. They spoke in hushed whispers, their voices drowned out by the crashing waves outside the grotto.

Neenah LeFleur, Roland, Zig, and Zag had all survived, thankfully. The captain stood with hands resting on her hips as the hobgoblins were busy pouring water from their boots.

Peerless was anchored in the inlet, and as she'd swum by, she hadn't seen a single lifeforce on board. Her aetheurgy was still strong and viewing the latticework of aether, she hadn't sensed anything. The vessel was empty. With all the fuss within the base of Mount Bastard, she wondered if the blooddrake in her mother's skin was lying in wait in one of the tunnels with an army ready to attack. She almost wished Solanine would attack. For it would be the ending she craved.

An echoing whoosh filled the cavern, a shadow passing in the dim seagandr-oil luminesce. Ashe tensed, thinking it was another drake come to avenge the fallen seagandr, but then realized it was merely Owl's strix. The huge bird circled around a stalactite before settling on a mound of rock.

Out of the shadow of the rock glided Grand Quaestor Owl. Cadoz skipped behind, carrying the grand quaestor's chair, that stupid piece of furniture somehow surviving the sinking of the *Dauntless.* The bent, ancient zombie of the Scattered Shards clacked the staff on the cavern's uneven topography, beard ragged and wet.

"I see you survived, acolyte." As ever, there was no relief or joy, only seriousness.

"Grand Quaestor Owl." Ashe was in no mood for a harangue, as much as she'd rather knock the grand quaestor's teeth in.

"That was ill advised on what you did on the deck. Calling the seagandr to you. Not to mention you ignoring my presence the entire journey." He glanced at Harlequin. "I see she bears your taskmaster's Gauntlet. It's a breach of protocol to wear a Sharded instrument without being approved by the Conclave."

If she could see her own aura, she knew her milieu darkened to a shaded crimson. "I don't know if you been paying heed to current tidings, grand quaestor, but we've been getting our asses kicked out there."

"We've lost seventeen honorable members of the Shards, acolyte. Don't lecture me on losses. I'll turn the other way on your disobedience due to the nature of what brings us here. But recall your place. I hope you are certain about this. What happened at *The Axe* has not shown the Scattered Shards in the greatest of light."

"I'll do my best, grand quaestor."

"And how, pray tell, do you plan to discover the Seal?"

"Your aether will lead you, Brynn Benld."

Maja Carr curled around a stalagmite. Although the blooddrake maintained the steely gaze of lavender, there was a weariness within those purple orbs. The creature, like all of them, was tired.

Two additional blooddrakes hovered nearby. They must have been the orcir, as they wore the same armor and weapons, but they no longer bore the green goliath flesh of Shon and Solly. Instead, they were in their own scales. They didn't have the pair of keratin horns like Maja, only had flattened stumps over their eyes. Cadoz stared at the blooddrakes with the awe of a child, there was something endearing about the voidspawn's joy. The stupid chair long forgotten.

Out of the shadows came Valeria Dunleith. The daughter of the Golden Throne was dry as a pile of coals, her long, silvery hair straight and shining. Her gold and silver bikromi bracelets reflected the meager light. She stopped short of them, a strange smile on her pretty elfirish face.

"Brynn," she said with a nod of approval. To the grand quaestor, "Owl."

"Valeria." There was a coldness in Owl's response. A terseness.

"Your aether will show you the way through the mountain," Maja reiterated. "All you must do is allow it to guide you. You are a Godsblood. The Eye of the Soul is yours by blood. Seek it."

"There has to be a hundred tunnels in this cavern, blooddrake." The grand quaestor didn't share the hobgoblin's surprise, instead was passively aggressive. There was no hint of marvel, not like Ashe upon first learning the truth about Maja. Owl had seen a blooddrake before, that she was certain. But how? When? "We've tried aether in the past. It has only led to death."

The blooddrake uncoiled from the perch, towering over the bent grand quaestor, blue-red orbs narrowed. "You aren't Godsblood. None have been." Maja pointed a claw at Ashe's bangle. "Invoke the Soul."

"YOU ARE READY, DEAR BRYNN."

Ashe raised her left arm, felt the fire already burning in her blood. Her runic tattoos tingled. The non-hot flame came bidden to her call, the diamond eye in her palm igniting. Aether waited for her; all she had to do was give it life.

Instantly, a pull drew her attention toward one of the tunnels opposite from where they stood. Like a tug of the hand. Guiding.

The cavern materialized in a husky green, the brushstrokes of *Terris* a painting. A filter of emerald coating the bland rock formations. Looking through a waterfall of seafoam. The seagandr-oil torches began spitting sapphire, the essence within the oil reacting in her vision. The many tunnels were all dark juniper.

Except one. It was a full garnet shade. And the grey mist from within the cave all rivered toward it, almost as if leading her.

"What do you see?" The blooddrake was a pinnacle of aether, all Four Tenets swirling around, in, and through the draconem. It was alarmingly blinding. Heavenly.

"The way."

"Lead us, Godsblood."

For hours they walked, Ashe following the shaded hues lit by the Eye of the Soul and the grey.

They moved quickly, their party consisting only of Ashe, Valeria, Maja, and her two blooddrake bodyguards. Grand Quaestor Owl and retinue was left to follow, as one of Shon or Solly marked the path with chalk-drawn runes. Captain Neenah LeFleur, Roland, and the hobgoblin twins were all left behind, as Neenah wanted to 'check *Peerless* for rations' but Ashe knew she meant to rob the ship blind. Roland promised to look after Harlequin, and despite not wanting to leave the woman behind, Ashe was comforted by the one-eyed mate's oath.

They needed haste, not a lingering company of quaestors. Choosing which tunnel through Mount Bastard by a brightened red whereas all the wrong turns were a shaded green. One path leading toward the Seal of *Ignis*, the others false *Terris*.

Mount Bastard was a treacherous mountain, even on the inside. It was called Mount Bastard for a reason. It was a bastard of a climb.

The mountain interior was a warren of tunnels, caves, and grottos. Some were as large as taverns, others as narrow as a hobgoblins' s shoulders. Slithering rock formations borne of underground streams somehow survived the dizzying warmth of the volcanic center. Empty holes pocked with depressions extending beyond their limited sight from the seagandr-oil torches they carried with them. Dried lava beds underfoot and tail.

They saw no life within the mountain. There was a constant chirping or scraping sound of some mountainous crustacean, but they never encountered anything. At one point, they all stopped to the sound of what could be described as breathing, a hollow sucking as if the entire mountain was drawing in air. They quickly moved past that cavern; Ashe was convinced it was daemon-bred. Maja merely told her there were far worse things in the deep earth than daemons.

Darkened abysses were spanned by narrow, naturally formed bridges. The bottoms were fathomless as they cautiously stepped across the expanses, careful not to peek down. Or up, for that matter, as the sight sometimes caused dizziness. Inching along, gripped with trepidation.

The higher they climbed, the hotter it became. Which was odd considering most volcanos were hotter in the center. Down at the base, near the sea, the coolness of the seawater kept them refreshed, almost like a sauna after the heating coals cooled. But as they steadily trajected upwards, the temperature went from a muggy marsh to a steamy bath. She was sweating profusely, the three blooddrakes not showing any signs of discomfort while Valeria appeared as if she were untouched.

At points, the tunnels led them outside. It was nearing nightturn already, the day passing by in a flash. She took the respite as the wind was chilly with the wintery air of the peak. Snow blanketed the outside of the mountain as they climbed. Fresh flakes crunching under their boots and exoscales. Shivering from the cold, to this, even the blooddrakes appeared uncomfortable. There was no set path, just rocky footholds for them to traverse. They crossed a dried lava stream, obsidian glass sparkling along one edge of the ancient volcano. Black prism glinting in the moonlight and nearby snowbanks. The ground of dried molten rock irregularly smooth.

Back into the mountain they went. Back into the den of heat.

It was a quiet procession, their trek. Each lost in their own thoughts. For Ashe, this was the beginning of the end for her. The end of who she had been. Of Lady Drakeslayer. This journey had drawn the line in the sand. No longer would she be the same.

Once she broke the Seal of *Ignis* there was no stopping it; she would be barreling headlong toward Eminence. Wishes to the contrary be godsdamned.

"'Tis hotter than the Forgemistress' privy up here," Ashe complained.

They were taking a break in a small cavity, only the tunnel ahead, and the one behind. No branches, no shelf. Just rock and darkness. In Ashe's aetheric-vision, a soft crimson pulsed rhythmically with her own heartbeat.

She was dripping in sweat, her cassock soaked through, her raven hair a soggy mess, hanging down like overcooked noodles. She was sucking in breaths, her voice hoarse from the stifling heat, her pulmo stabbing at her lungs. To say she was struggling was akin to saying being mounted by a centaur was deemed a gratifying time. Or ethical.

They had to be near the top of Mount Bastard at this point, she felt they'd climbed the mountain twice over.

Ashe looked over toward Maja and Valeria. "How much more do you reckon?"

Maja was hunched, snout raised, sniffing the sweltering air. An elegance about the manner, natural and balletic. It was times like this, she wished draconem gave off auras, just so she'd know what the blooddrake was thinking. "Not far now."

"This has become a wild fae hunt," Ashe said, taking a pull from her waterskin, having long since drained her flask. "No wonder no one's ever found the Seal."

"You wish to retire back, Godsblood."

"What, after all this shit, you think I'd miss the finale?"

"Nice to know after all this tribulation, you haven't lost your mettle." The blooddrake drew up, a delicately strong pose. Graceful like the gods personified. "Nor your tongue."

"It'll take more than a firedrake at the asshole of the world to silence this tongue."

"YOU CAN COUNT ON THAT, MAJA. SHE'S LIKE HER MOTHER IN THAT REGARD."

The blooddrake chuckled that guttural laugh of hers. "I'll keep that in mind, Mother Nightingale. Shon. Solly." The three blooddrakes began to converse in their queer dialect. One of the non-horn bearers nodded, took a seagandr-oil torch and pressed ahead in the tunnel.

Ashe leaned close to Valeria Dunleith, eyeing the blooddrakes carefully. "What do you think we'll find, bikrome?"

"Fire."

"That's a shit answer."

The bikrome turned to face her. "You asked. I answered."

"Zenith's cock, bikromi humor."

The blooddrake returned, spoke in more of the draconem language, Maja nodding. "Shon says the lair is just beyond this pass. It slumbers, the firedrake guardian."

"You saw it?" asked Ashe.

The behemoth without the keratin horns confirmed with a silent nod, but it was Maja who spoke. "There is something else you must know, Brynn Benld."

"O fucking wonderful," Ashe threw her hands up. "Let's wait until we're about to ram some aetheric steel up this 'drake's cherry before giving some obviously important detail."

"The Seal is beyond, in this firedrake lair. The grand crystal is one of the Four. A shard of the Great Crystal of Eminence. The lifegiving tenets of all existence. *Ignis* is the trueborn name of the one you worship as Brio. The firedrake you will set eyes upon is the guardian of *Ignis*. The greatest firedrake to have ever lived. Remember the vvyrm at the Temple of Mother Marrow. Such is the one you call Brio. Come, let us finish this."

"O… well… fuck."

"ALWAYS A WAY WITH WORDS, DEAR BRYNN."

LI
ASHE

IT WAS SAID by the long line of pontifices of the Scattered Shards, that the inside of the world is where the Meadows resided. The eternal realm of the dead connected to the world of the living via an ethereal veil residing in the heart of the ancient city of Shatterstorm, located in what was now the Voidlands.

The high augurs believe the Meadows is where the souls of the dead go to rest, for those who lived lives in service to the Pentax met eternity with grace and comfort. A tranquil place of endless joy. For those who fell to the passionate fires which drove one to commit evil, another hellhole awaited them. A particular place in the void where the worst of humanity is forever reviled, a byproduct of the pyre of damnation down in Nocturne's Pit. An everlasting inferno of suffering and flame, the realm where the negative ethos of man stem from, such as rage and fear.

Now, Ashe didn't believe all that malarkey of the Shards' teachings, but standing in the mouth of Brio's lair, she knew there could be no hotter place in the world. The Pit be godsdamned.

It was a queer place, eerie even.

The lair itself was like any of the caverns they'd traveled through, but unlike those, this one was almost as big as the base of Mount Bastard's inlet. They were at the apex of the mountain, the highest point of the volcano, and yet, Ashe felt this cavern shouldn't exist. It was almost like an hourglass. The mouth of the tunnel they were hidden in was dwarfed by the cavern. Zenith's cock, she thought this lair might potentially dwarf *The Arbiter's Axe*, swallowing the arena in a single gulp.

Beside the heat—which was unbearable—there was a presence about the place. A feeling of being watched, probed, and prodded. A sense of foreboding, but also a sense of rebirth. A place where her sins were laid bare, and then cleansed from existence. Like a fire sweeping clean a field after seasons of poor harvest.

A crimson luminosity, the lair. Everything was coated in a layer of garnet and mist. It scintillated in a living film, breathing emotions. Anger. Rage. Warning. Passion. Danger. Lust. Longing. Strength. Every emotion normally associated with Fire. With *Ignis*.

Ashe crept closer, leaning past the mouth of the tunnel. And that's when she saw what they'd hunted for.

Brio, the Wayward Son.

The greatest of the greater draconem, the largest firedrake there ever was, the most magnificent there ever would be. This was the epitome of the gods and goddesses. Maja was right, this was Brio.

The divine drake was colossal, practically immeasurable. It lay on its side at the far end of the lair, lounging like the Drunk God He was. Four almighty legs pulled close to its body, tail curling around it, wings of leather coiled about the mass of the body, so thin, almost transparent. A rough guess by comparing past hunts of firedrakes, this beast was well over two hundred feet long, most likely much more. Larger four times over than every other firedrake, longer by a fourth over any terravvyrm ever recorded prior to last summer.

Its head was the size of a fully-grown Kanjan mammoth. With a beak-like snout ending in a point, where it curved over the protruding short swords of teeth. Eyes, closed as if sleeping, were the size of dinner plates. Arm-length spikes grew like eyebrows over the sockets, forming an intricate pattern similar to the runes of the Four Tenets. A graceful neck with a single row of progressively larger spikes until the biggest was probably three-feet tall. Scales the size of a man's head covered the body, garnet red in color. Tail ending with a stinging barb sharp enough to pierce the thickest of stone walls around Alizarin.

Bathed in ruby, in the light of *Ignis*, the firedrake wound about the illustrious crystal. If the dragon was animalistic beauty, then the crystal was agrestal purity.

Ten-plus-feet-tall, the crystal was multi-faceted. Smooth as a fresh apple, diaphanous to allow the circling aether inside. The aether was like liquid flames, snapping and popping without sound, moving never-ending inside the grand shard. Heat radiated off the crystal, the source of the mountain's incalescence. Like a heart within the volcano.

It was beautiful, unlike anything Ashe had ever seen, just as magnificent as Mother Marrow's.

"Fire begets. Fire taketh," Maja said. "This is where your path splinters, Godsblood. For once Brio is no more, only two Shards remain. The last two to hold Zenith's prison."

Ashe scanned the rest of the lair, her aetheric-vision searching for the other blooddrakes, the hateful Solanine. She found nothing but Brio and the crystal. Slowly, she stood and stepped into the lair, passing through what felt was like an invisible veil. It tingled her flesh, pulling on her cassock. It washed over her, calm, soothing, and yet, investigating, measuring. Testing her.

The others followed her into Brio's den. Each passing the aetheric veil.

"What in the Pit was that?"

Maja's taloned claw hovered over the invisible veil. "*Ignis*, pure and unfiltered."

"Is it alive?"

"Not in a way you would understand. But all aether is alive. It is the lifeblood of everything."

Drawn toward the crystal, Ashe was. She advanced closer, her arm with the Eye reaching toward it.

A rustling of leathery wings, shifting ever so slightly. She froze, staring at the firedrake. A ripple of corded muscle flexing. Massive bulk rising once, twice, thrice. Breathing. The dinner plate eyelid rolled back to reveal catlike slits of golden and garnet chroma.

"Fucking Nocturne!" Ashe involuntarily retreated a few steps.

"Fear not, the guardian will not harm you. He would not have allowed us here otherwise." Maja's voice held reverence for the enormous drake, but also an undercurrent of adoration. Love almost. "He has waited for you, Brynn Benld."

"MY SON WILL NOT HARM YOU, DAUGHTER OF MY BLOOD."

The golden-garnet eye blinked, the mouth clenching, teeth the size of blades sticking out. A tongue flicked in, licking the beaked snout. A rumbling in the drake's belly.

And yet, it did not move. Lying on its side it remained.

"What's wrong with Him?"

"He's dying," Valeria said. "The time of the firedrakes, and of *Ignis,* is at an end. Canlon Carr's strength fades, as does the Seals. This is why they must break. Knowingly."

It was true, Ashe realized with sadness. While the scales were resplendent, there was greyish decay around the edges where scale met scale. The face, while still terrifying and beautiful all the same, had a sunken quality to it. What should be a bright auric and ruby iris, was foggy and rheumy along the lids. Creases and scars lined the beak and snout. Teeth were jagged, worn, or broken.

The ancient draconem was indeed dying.

"BRYNN."

She stepped back. Tattooed runes tingling.

"BRYNN."

"Do you hear that?"

"He speaks to you," Maja said. "Listen. Open your aether. *Ignis* will sing if you allow it."

"DAUGHTER OF NIGHTINGALE. THOU'VE COME. AND THOU BROUGHT MINE MOTHER WITH THOU."

"I AM HERE, MY CHILD."

Ignis came alive inside, aether burning the tattooed rune, the auric ring on her finger. Her body felt aflush with the fire.

Brio? she asked without speaking, her aether was all she needed, sounding by instinct alone.

"THE END COMES." The firedrake's mouth didn't move, the eye blinked lazily, focused on her. ***"MINE OWN END IS HERE. WEAKENED I AM."***

What can I do?

"WE ARE BREAKING. THE HATCH. ALL WEAKENED. A REBIRTH TO COME."

The Hatch? You mean the other guardians? The other crystals? But how? Tell me, please!

"THOU ARE NOT STRONG ENOUGH YET. THE THREE REMAINING SEALS MUST BREAK LIKE THE FORGEMISTRESS BEFORE THE REBIRTH. ONLY THEN WILL ANOTHER RISE, GODSBLOOD. THE TIPPING OF THE WORLD IS NIGH, A NEW POWER WILL RISE. A NEW NATURE. A NEW DIVINE."

What of Eminence?

"EMINENCE IS SAFE. FOR NOW, BUT SOON IT WILL WEAKEN, THE CHOSEN IS DYING. ZENITH WILL WEAKEN HIM UNTIL HE BREAKS. FORGIVE US." The puissant crystal pulsed beside the ancient drake.

Ashe looked toward the Garnet, it stood taller than her by more than twice, and then some. A thousand and one reservations ran through her mind, but every single one came back to the same thought: she had already accepted her fate after her parents' death in Drenth.

Serve she had, but to the Scattered Shards.

Serve she would, this time to Life Itself.

This was her way out. Her redemption.

I accept.

"BLESSED GODSBLOOD." The firedrake's mouth curled upright, sloping into a smile, as such a draconem could smile. The beast's wings fluttered; the tail flicked. ***"HAND UPON ME. IGNIS WILL CONSUME AND PASS UNTO THOU. IT IS THOU'S BLOOD WHO MUST SEE A REBIRTH. WHEN THE SEAL IS BROKEN, SEEK THINE TEMPLE, THY MANTLE AWAITS. NEED IT FOR EMINENCE. A BOON WILL YOU RECEIVE IN MINE AEGIS."***

Aegis? I thought that was only a drakken who could use aether?

"MOTHER, MINE?"

"ONE THING AT A TIME, MY SON." To Ashe, Nightingale spoke, *"IN TIMES PAST, DEAR BRYNN, THE AEGISES WERE ONLY DRACONEM. BUT MY CHILDREN GROW WEAK, THEY GROW... FERAL. NEW AEGISES HAVE BEEN CHOSEN."*

"FEAR NOT, GODSBLOOD. THE AEGISES ARE NOT TO BE AFEARED. THEY WILL HELP THOU. THEY WILL FIND THOU. BUT YOU MUST FINISH WHAT MUST BE CONTINUED. PLACE THOU HAND UPON MINE SNOUT."

Ashe placed her hand upon the scaly cheek of the firedrake, no, of the Garnet guardian. Warm under the diamond eye of her bangle. This creature was pure fire. Pure Fire.

Now what?

Burning.

That's what it felt like as Ashe threw her head back. Burning everywhere. Inside. Outside. In her skull. Burning. In her soul. Scarlet took over her vision, took over her soul. From her toes to the tips of her fingers, fire consumed her. There was no pain. Just the burning without ash. A sensation of the essence of Fire, a theory, the practice of the natural art.

The fire ran through her blood in droves, into her heart, taking over. Pulsing red.

Aether more epic in flavor than what she'd summoned at *The Arbiter's Axe*. Greater even than at the Temple of Mother Marrow. Surrounding her in Fire. Cocooning her in *Ignis*. Dancing over her flesh, burrowing inside to where the pyre in her blood boiled. Combining, becoming one. Taking over, melding.

She roared, the legendary call of a firedrake. From deep in her lungs it originated, shattering her bones as it burst forth, reforming when it ended. Deafening her ears. The Breath of the Soul.

Her body slumped forward, head leaning upon the firedrake's scales. Breathing deep.

"IT IS COMPLETE. I FADE. BREAK THE SEAL, DAUGHTER OF MINE MOTHER."

I will see it done. Tears filled her eyes.

"I KNOW. I HAVE FORSEEN IT. I WILL AWAIT MINE SISTER."

The warmth under the Eye faded. The belly of the firedrake rose once more, then fell sallow. The golden and garnet eye rolled back, the beak drooped, teeth receding behind a tongue falling free. The leathery wings quivered and slipped to the volcanic ground of the lair. The intense heat in the cavern lowered. The brilliant red luminosity dimmed. The glorious crystal of *Ignis* pulsated, the aether within smoldering like doused coals.

"It is done." Maja Carr ran a clawed talon across the faceted face of *Ignis*. Lovingly.

"Where is the Se—"

Ashe had only a heartbeat to react before Maja went flying across the lair, clattering into the rock wall in a spray of aetheric magic. The blooddrake yowled as her exoscales burst under the strain, her body contorted as she screamed fury, then died under the strain, no chance at surviving such a blow of pure aether.

Valeria Dunleith threw her braceleted hands up, using aether to form a protective shield of *Aere* around the crystal. A shield thrown in the nick of time, saving her the same fate as Maja. A torrent of aether repeatedly struck Valeria's shield.

Ashe squinted and saw her mother, along with Evzen, standing in the mouth of the tunnel. In her mother's hand was what appeared to be an amulet of some sort. Held, cradled more like, was a circle of black, braided steel. Within were four smaller circles, each made of gemstone in four separate colors. Sapphire, peridot, garnet, and emerald. Within the epicenter of the disc, and piercing the four circles, was a six-pointed star.

The Seal of *Ignis*.

Cadrianna, no, a blooddrake thrust up her mother's hands, coated in aether they were. "Godsblood," it hissed, the voice hopefully Solanine's.

The Four Tenets billowed from drake's closed fists. Sending waves of *Aquis* and rumbles of *Terris* toward the pair of blooddrakes leaping through the air. Shon and Solly had claws and blades ready to slice the rogue blooddrake to bits, but the Divine's warrior's aether scythed through both, killing them like they were nothing.

All three blooddrakes aligned with the Last Godsking killed in an instant, their aether paled in comparison one of Zenith's brood.

Angry, Ashe summoned the Blade of Nightingale, wailing through the veil of the dead, forming the six-foot fiery blade she'd conjured against the seagandr. In her other hand, she held the Hammer of Mother Marrow. Ashe burned aether, all her runes thrummed as they came alive, her muscles flexed as she leapt toward the hateful creature wearing her mother's face.

The blooddrake threw aether at her in the form of a tempest of *Aere*. The Blade of Nightingale came down in an arc and sliced straight through it like a bolt of lightning shearing apart an age-old Calibrathian redwood. Her weapon was like Justice's sacred axe cleaving the skies. The evil blooddrake called forth a blade of aether of its own, this one billowing *Aere*.

Her blade and the blooddrake's crashed against another, sending aetheric sparks everywhere. Fire clashing with Air.

Ashe hacked with the flaming Blade of Nightingale. The blooddrake within Cadrianna parried with the gusting sword of

Aere. Their aethers clashing and breaking upon one another. The pair of them attacked, defended, retreated.

The lair of Brio was a blur. Lost in the pall of her Soul Form, mist a grey churn at her feet. All she felt was the fire burning inside her. The geyser of flames inside.

Swinging the Blade, Ashe pressed. The blooddrake used her mother's hand high on the aetheric blade, blocking. Their faces inches apart, her blade's flames snuffed by the swirling gusts of the blooddrake's aetheric sword.

Cadrianna's humirish face was covered in a sheen of sweat, but the blooddrake within smiled. "You cannot stop this, Godsblood. We will be victorious."

"Fuck," Ashe pushed with all her strength, her aether nearly devouring her, "you!"

The blooddrake hissed and pushed back with a jolt, their blades of aether separating. Ashe jumped back as the blooddrake brought the aetheric blade to bear. She stabbed out with hers, blocked by her opponent. Out of the corner of her eye, she noticed Evzen sneaking through the lair toward Valeria, a knife in his hand raised to plunge into the bikrome's unprotected back. The blade black but it gleamed like moonlight in the darkness of the cavern. A vvyrm-tooth dagger. Like Phlox had had.

Screaming, Ashe cut upward with the fiery blade, clipping the blooddrake's side, purple blood spraying all over her left hand. Her no-longer-mother screeched, yet the voice so recognizable as her mother's. But she ignored it and pressed the attack.

The Blade of Nightingale came down as the true Nightingale wept in the Meadows and Ashe screamed, aether discharging from within, a torrent of it. The blooddrake did not raise the aetheric blade and Ashe could envision where her magical blade would connect, where it would part flesh that had once been her mother. Where the fiery sword would cleave and sever. Where her inner aether would destroy.

And yet, the blooddrake did not move until the Blade of Nightingale was directly above the head of Cadrianna Benld, where *Aere* caught it a fraction of an inch from her mother's skin. She hadn't seen the electrical current building about the woman's hands. Hadn't seen the hands open and the sparkling aether release the sword of *Aere* and catch the descending sword with aetheric flurry of Air.

Across the lair Ashe flew, her aetheric scream becoming a frightened screech, the lightning in the aether of *Aere* building, thundering across her own flesh. Ashe collided with the crystal of *Ignis*. *Aere* pummeling *Ignis*, pummeling the giant crystal and aether alike. She tumbled down, near the feet of Valeria. Aether fractured the atmosphere of the lair, and the mist crackled with uncontrollable power, so much power that Valeria's shield shattered and sent her flying from her feet. Again.

"O, shit!"

CRACK!

The explosion of garnet crystal rained all about the firedrake lair, nay, the final resting place of a living god. Shards stormed, crackling with piercing wails and flames. Sizzling as they fell to the rocky ground of the cavern. Exploding through the dormant volcano into the nightturn, a phoenix of Fire busting through the southern slope of Mount Bastard, spewing rock and aether alike.

The blooddrake, in the flesh of Cadrianna Benld, Cadrianna Nightingale, burned. Screaming as they were devoured by the aetheric might of the Wayward Son and the remnants of the aether inside *Ignis*. Disappeared into nothingness did the hateful blooddrake.

Evzen cried out to Ashe. Arm reaching for the friend he'd betrayed. Legs a funeral pyre calling to his end. Tears left searing marks in the burning flesh. Gone. Ash to dust.

Valeria Dunleith summoned aetheurgy, a wall of *Aere* spun around her, shielding the bikrome from the intense *Ignis*, her long, silver hair splayed out within the wind. Her black and white eyes glowing, her gold and silver bracelets gleaming.

Ashe threw up her own hands, summoning her aetheurgy to protect her. A fraction too late. Aether preyed upon her, alighting the runic tattoos on her arms. She screamed. The Fire of *Ignis*, consumed her entire left arm in a brilliance of white. Her cassock turned to ash, but her flesh remained strong. But not that of her right. Her arm, near the whole of it, went up in flame. The flesh on the right side of her face began to melt, hair singeing away. She was dead, a moment left in life for her.

That's when she heard the voice.

"FIRE BEGETS, FIRE TAKETH."

Chanting.

"WATER REARS, WATER RECEDES."

Louder.

"EARTH SCULPTS, EARTH RAZES."

Faster.

"AIR BREATHES, AIR STIFLES."

Calm.

"SCALES WARD, SCALES BREAK."

End.

"SCALES ARE ALL. SCALES ARE NOTHING."

A face appeared in the ragged remnants of her mind. A face of a drake. A terrifyingly beautiful face wrapped in aether.

Neither beak nor true snout, the nose was triangular, a spike of keratin on the point. A lower jaw with two larger spikes jutting outward, creating a more triangular appearance. Scales of polished orchid blazed with runes of aether. Eyes large and angled, the deepest of purple, under a crown of horns. A halo shined around the drake's face, one of reflected diamond.

No?

"YES, DEAR BRYNN. DAUGHTER OF MY BLOOD. IT IS I, IN THE FLESH."

She reached for Nightingale, wanting to be with Her. For it to end. Finally, the end.

"NOT YET, DEAR BRYNN." Nightingale's draconem face hardened under the halo of horns. ***"ONLY UNTIL THE SEALS ARE BROKEN AND EMINENCE RESET, CAN YOU REST. UNTIL THEN, I'LL DO WHAT I ALWAYS DO AND PROTECT YOUR SCRAWNY BACKSIDE."***

Her death forestalled as Nightingale's aether surrounded her.

The light of Nightingale's grace receded. The last shards of Brio's *Ignis* falling, pinging off the rock of Mount Bastard. The babel of the crystal's destruction evaporating, the echo down the mountain a cry of the ages.

Ashe was thrown, body crashing against the firedrake. She slid and slumped against the dead guardian when it all ended. The pain. The fire. Gone.

Shock.

Anguish.

Tears.

Acceptance.

Ashe felt it all. Felt the phantom where her right hand used to be. From just below the shoulder to tip of the fingers, it was gone, stump cauterized, cassock sleeve hanging in shreds. She gingerly touched the stinging right side of her face with her left hand, expecting to see her hand cross over, but only darkness. Her right eye had been scalded into nothing.

No pain, she felt. *Ignis* may have ravaged her flesh, but Nightingale had healed her.

"Brynn, you've done well." In the bikrome's grasp was the Seal of *Ignis*.

"I'm fine, thanks for asking." Vocal chords tingling under the strain. Fine, she was, in a way. For the moment, that was.

Past the bikrome, the head of the guardian called Brio was unmoved, burnt by the destruction of *Ignis*. There were burns all along the flank and the gossamer wings pocked with seared holes; garnet shards had pierced them like arrowheads. The scales on both legs were blackened and wisps of smoke curled from beneath, the char of flesh strong and cloying like a roasted pig on the spit ready for a party.

A fitting memorial of the guardian of *Ignis*. The gaping hole in Mount Bastard surrounded Him like aurora. Brio was dead. A red gash in the nightturn sky, like a sword cleaving the heavens as the last vestige of the Wayward Son, adding to the eerie emerald of Mother Marrow.

"That *fuckin'* hurt," she finally said, head falling back against Brio's body.

ATOP MOUNT BASTARD

"WHAT HAPPENED TO the Seal, acolyte?" Grand Quaestor Owl's gnarled hand made a notation in the codex report with the inked quill.

"Send your servants away," the bikrome said calmly before the would-be-vicar could answer, irritating Owl.

"What's that?" Owl turned to the side, showing an ageing ear.

"The Seal cannot be seen by the unchosen." The elfirish woman's voice was little higher than a whisper, which made it harder for Owl to understand at first.

"You're the ones under my jurisdiction and protection," Owl said. "I do not take orders from the likes of you, Valeria Dunleith."

"Send them away, grand quaestor," the intrepid acolyte said.

After the story told by the young woman, Owl now understood the change that had come over her. No longer was Brynn Benld a pup. This woman was much more, a true beacon of aether. A true source of the Pentax' power. Godsblood, she.

One not to trifle with by petty games.

Owl leaned back in the fine chair Cadoz had painstakingly dragged up the dormant remains of the grand volcano, bones creaking and cracking from all the movement. Ancient body frail, but mind still sharp. Growing old was a losing battle.

"As you wish." The grand quaestor motioned for the scribes and soldiers of the Scattered Shards to fall back. Only the strix and Cadoz remained. The grizzled servant hid behind Owl's chair, shivering like a rain-soaked traveler with no shelter in sight. The poor voidspawn was afraid of the owl. As well he should be, thought Owl. "Now, where is the Seal of *Ignis*?"

Valeria's bracelets glimmered as the bikrome lifted both pale hands. Luminous aether of all Four Tenets misted towards the wall of Mount Bastard in a vortex of Fire, Earth, Air, and Water; smashing into the rock with force. There was a groaning as the stone split, revealing a hidden tomb. Lying upon a natural table of stone was an onyx disc with four gemstones inside.

Owl's grip on the staff tightened into white knuckles.

The wounded face of Brynn Benld tilted to the side, her remaining all-white eye squinting. "I'm surprised, grand quaestor, you seem more worried about the Seal and not the crumbling tower of ideals we've lived under since the Fall of Eminence."

A grim smile behind a bushy beard. "The ilk of the Pentax has not changed me in all my years. A minute change in distinction, that's all. Leave the rest to the augurs and the peasants."

In reality, Owl cared not for the dead firedrake, cared less it'd been the vessel the believers called Brio. The destruction of *Ignis* lying scattered about the lair and the side of the mountain was a loss, a shame. Of most import was the Seal.

"It's fitting you say that," the would-be-vicar said. "I was expecting a larger retort from you. If I recall, your family was deeply interested in draconem. Wasn't that so, Owl?"

Owl's jaw clenched at the lack of decorum, trying to stifle the anger. Calm, had to remain calm. "My father and mother, yes, they were interested in the children of Zenith."

"And Nightingale?" The girl shifted on the stool, her left hand gripping the chair. "Unless I'm recollecting things incorrectly, I was told that I couldn't even begin to understand what it's like to be the weakest of Nightingale's brood." The girl leaned forward. "Isn't that right, Solanine?"

Owl's hands lifted, greyish skin trying to summon aether, but the girl was faster. From the cauterized missing limb, aether burst forth in a gleaming fiery, black blade held in an eidolon arm of grey mist, the pommel with outstretched wings of a drake. The Godsblood brought the black blade to bear, searing through the table, through the man scales that had once been Owl, slicing into Solanine's own exoscales.

Draconem aether, that was within the fire of the black blade. Essence so pure, so unfiltered. Of the First Wife, Solanine knew.

Solanine's aether conjured, the skin of Owl slipping free, turning to ash under the aetheric blade. Diving from the chair, Solanine threw a wave of *Aquis* toward the Godsblood, but the young woman was already moving. Aetheric blade coming anew. So fast. So strong. Powerful with the essence of Nightingale.

The colossal strix hooted, filling the cavern with echoes. Enormous, feathered wings rustling as it took flight, divebombing the bikrome. The daughter of Kalderim blocked the curved beak with *Aere*, then reached through the aetheric dam and plucked the bird from the air with alabaster fingers. A predator the bird was, but it was no match for the bikrome. Valeria Dunleith ripped the wings apart with fingers as sharp as blades, blazing with aetheurgy. The strix crashed to the ground, forgotten.

Cadoz, the useless hobgoblin, dove behind a stalagmite, crying and screaming like a coward.

Solanine summoned *Terris*, sending a quake of earth at the charging Godsblood. The girl leapt before the quivering ground reached her, swinging the aetheric blade down. Solanine had the barest of moments to block with *Aere*. But the Godsblood punched through the defense, the Blade of Nightingale cutting through exoscale, spilling draconem blood, severing, slicing, and hacking. Draconem body crying as draconem mother cried in the void.

The Godsblood pushed forward for one last attack. Her blade of black fire bristling, striking Solanine anew with a series of fae-quick cuts. The mist surrounding the Godsblood was pure aether, angry and raw, black as the void. Solanine staggered backward as the torment of aether broke inside, rending apart all that was draconem.

"This is for my parents," the Godsblood said as she quelled the fiery, black blade and instead raised a multi-barrel wheellock pistol, firing. Solanine recalled seeing that pistol before, in the hand of Emre Benld.

Knowledge of underestimating the Godsblood crept within as bullets of aethecite struck Solanine in the breast, sending the blooddrake to the ground as piercing rounds wormed their way inside. Solanine was wounded, lifeblood leaking away, aetheurgy leeching into the void.

Across the lair, the Godsblood coughed up blood and tar, it dribbled down her chin, painting her cassock red. She was struggling to stay upright, the young woman's body spasming as she hacked. She, too, was dying.

"How?" Solanine croaked. How had the girl known?

The Godsblood ran her good hand across her chin and smirked. "You think I couldn't tell your stink from the other blooddrakes? I knew it the moment you stepped into the arena, Solanine. And why Owl had come late. Waiting on you, blooddrake."

How, master?

But Solanine's Divine was silent, and that rankled.

"Why my… parents, blooddrake?" The girl doubled over as she hacked, dropping the pistol.

The quaestors of the Scattered Shards came barreling toward the scene, wheellock weapons poised to fire upon the aggressors of their vaunted, and fallen, grand quaestor. Fools who had been marked by Rinkhal for their devotion, their unwavering loyalty, regardless of the drake within. Their ire directed toward the Godsblood.

A shot rang out, striking the ground next to the Godsblood's head. A pained yelp as the shooter was flung across the firedrake lair by a bout of *Aere* conjured by the bikrome, stopping the rest of the tainted warriors. One tried but was stopped by an oscillating wall of mist cutting the wounded or dead from the walking.

"That's a swell trick, bikrome," said the irritating Godsblood, as her coughing finally subsided. "Could've used it before, you bloody dandy."

"My brother-friend is the dandy." The bikrome turned toward the wounded Solanine. The one-time lover just stared blankly, as if their previous passion had been for nothing. To Solanine, it was everything. The betrayal still stung. To the Godsblood, "Break the Seal, Brynn. The rebirth edges closer." The Godsblood raised the Hammer of Mother Marrow, but the bikrome shook her head of silver hair. "No, Brynn. The Hammer will not destroy *Ignis*. Only Fire and blood will break it."

"What do I do?"

"The Breath of the Soul. Use it." The girl glanced at the diamond of the Eye. "It will hurt, Brynn. Life must flow. Three trials, each harder than the next. You've already faced the trial of heart. Now is mind and body. Both must suffer to be reborn."

The girl nodded. "Zenith's cock, that's what Canlon said I'd face."

"Indeed," whispered the bikrome. "Rebirth awaits. Sing the Song."

A scream rose from the Godsblood's core, aether, pure aether, ripped free from her soul. Her battered body trembled with the call of the Breath of the Soul, the Song of Eminence and Noctis. Her back arched, burned face writhing in pain. She fell to the ground, the scream never breaking.

The bikrome began to chant in the language of the Pentax, the core dialect of Vision Form. In the faint expanse between Solanine and the Meadows, the words were trailers within the mist.

The Godsblood thrashed across the cavern's floor as the scream went on unabated. Her legs kicked. Her arm beat the rock. Blood shot from her wounds like fonts.

Valeria merely chanted louder, this time in the language of Void Form. Mist of *Aere* wrapped the Godsblood up, black in opacity, she was frozen in place.

The Godsblood's chest popped, blood spraying in a fountain-like arc as her flesh parted in a ghastly runic-shaped wound. One of Void Form. She cried out even louder, a cadence so piercing, it shook the entire volcano as further runes carved their way into her flesh as Valeria chanted, the black mist digging into her flesh. It started slowly, but the blood borne of Void Form began to swirl in the air, caught in an invisible vortex of aether that spun faster and faster until it appeared as if the ball of blood was a tornado of pitch and red. Flames of blackened crimson boiled from the blood.

"Fire begets, Fire taketh," the bikrome said aloud in a voice sounding of Nocturne's Pit. A ghastly flair.

The blood Lady Drakeslayer rained from the ball of aether, splashing across the cavern in crescents of blue hurricane. The Shards of *Ignis* sizzled by the touch of *Aquis*. Her body slumped back to the ground, deflated almost. A mess of viscera.

"Water rears, Water recedes," Valeria chanted.

The ball of aether hung above the Godsblood's body, still clinging to life, her life giving the aether its existence. The ground began to rumble underneath, lifting the Godsblood off the cavern floor two feet, supported by struts of green nature, her head cradled by a halo of emerald earth.

"Earth sculpts, Earth razes."

Lightning flashed inside the ball, bright yellow aether bursting in repeating bolts. The Godsblood sagged. Blood began to trickle down the *Terris*-formed struts holding the young woman's body in steady streams.

"Air breathes, Air stifles."

Solanine watched. Solanine waited.

The bikromi seer lowered aether-laden hands, the chant ending. "Are you ready, Brynn?"

"I…" the Godsblood choked through blood and tar. "…am."

With her other hand, Valeria summoned *Ignis*, and a rope of fire bloomed, lassoing around the Seal hidden in the wall. Rising upon drifting flames, the Seal rode the rope, coming to lie directly under the Godsblood. The ball of aether brightened over the Godsblood's body, blindingly bright.

"Say the words of Nightingale, Brynn."

"Scales ward, Scales break," the Godsblood breathed. *Terris* shifted her body, turning her over, her chest now right over the Seal. Blood gushed from her wounds, drenching it. "Scales are all," the words a struggle, death but a breath away. "Scales are nothing."

"The final line, Brynn. The key. Recall the key."

"Immortality does not... come from the pr... proliferation of Life, but... up... up... upon the wave of... Death."

There was a strident SIGH! as the Aether of Life and Death borne of Shard Form slammed through the body of the Godsblood, down through her flesh, through her new Void Form runes conjured alongside Vision Form, through her Soul Form, passing with a brilliant flare of diamond. Down the aether went into the Seal, eclipsing the four circles. A brilliant flash of red as the Seal of *Ignis* exploded into a thousand or more pieces.

Zenith's voice howled in the Pit. The Divine feeling the Seal break. The next step.

A light throbbed within the lair atop Mount Bastard. The Godsblood's body lowered to the cavern's ground, unmoving.

Finally, the bikrome smiled, a smile that had once taken hold of Solanine's heart before it had withered black. Valeria, traitorous detractor of Zenith, squatted. Bikromi eyes silken with aether, as well as pity. "This was never the way of Eminence."

Solanine sneered. "What do you know of the way of Eminence or Noctis? I alone knew the way was through blood. That is what Eminence demands."

Valeria tsked. "Eminence demands grace through blood, not wrath through blood. The Godsblood was never for revenge, but for sacrifice. That is what you never understood, Solanine." The bikrome stood, a melancholic vision. "And that is why you failed."

Draconem blood spurted from Solanine's lipless mouth. Life ebbed into the realm of Death. "I've not failed. Eminence will break. They all will break, and Zenith will be freed. I will be reborn again, He will see it so. This is not over... between us, Valeria."

"No, Solanine, it is not." Valeria turned, going back to the wounded Godsblood. She summoned *Aere* to lift the young woman's body, singular arm hanging. To Solanine, "But not in the manner in which you think will be. A new Godsqueen will rise, quelling the darkness in Her light."

The veil of misty aether fell like a curtain falling from the windowsill. The tainted warriors of the Scattered Shards backed away, their weapons lowering. Seagandr-oil torches snapped loudly, that's how quiet the cavern was, it was the only sound.

Valeria stopped over Solanine, the Godsblood's fingers dripped blood upon their wounded flesh. A burning sensation, a begetting. A rebirth, if you will. "You cannot stop this fall, Solanine. And neither can I. Nor will I try. You shouldn't either. The Fall of Zenith is inevitable. But Eminence will rise anew. I will see you again soon, my love."

"I AM HERE, MY DISCIPLE. OUR PLAN REMAINS ON TRACK."

Solanine grinned in the dark. Yes, the plan was indeed working.

The bikrome's back was to Solanine, holding the Godsblood, striding confidently when there was the sound of tearing flesh. The sound of aether. The bikrome spun, but too slowly before aether borne of the Pit cocooned around her. She dropped the body of the Godsblood, the girl striking the cavern floor, bouncing. Not waking, still near death.

Valeria cried out as the black aether collapsed in on her, driving her to her knees, then down into a ball, her silver mane spread out like a blanket, her body wracked with pain. The corrupted aether pressed down harder.

"That's enough, Cauda," Solanine said as the blooddrake slithered into an S position.

From where the strix had been thrown to the ground, a blooddrake now hunched, black and brown feathers fanning around the torn flesh of the owl. Cauda stared at Solanine with gleaming black-purple eyes as aether jittered across the pair of talons, crimson runes gleaming on black exoscales.

Valeria still cried.

"Cauda."

The other blooddrake stopped twirling those talons. The aether receded, but kept Valeria wrapped in the blackened mist. Imprisoned.

Solanine, eyes hardened at the sight of a former lover shivering in pain, turned toward the milling quaestors. "The box."

Soldiers clad in the crimson cassocks of the Shards rushed forward, carrying by huckles a linen covered box. They placed it as near to the writhing bikrome as they'd chance, one pulling the cover free.

Crystal of the purest diamond shone brilliantly in the seagandr-oil lights. A box carved in aethecite. Wisps of essence burrowed through the smooth ore.

Slithering over, Solanine opened the box, pushing the lid back. Within the coffin were two pairs of manacles, also carved from aethecite. Plucking one, the blooddrake moved toward the captured bikrome, bringing a draconem head next to the pale visage of a former lover, a former friend. Now an enemy to be smote.

"You think Zenith wouldn't have known your Godsblood would know me, Valeria? You're a fool to believe Bliss would outsmart my Divine. He is Their creator. And He is no fool."

Valeria's head turned best it could in the misted prison. Her bi-colored eyes masked the pain creeping across her face. "The Godsblood…"

"Will break the other two Seals," Solanine finished. "That has been the goal from the beginning. You alone know what trial she must face next." Solanine glanced at the unconscious girl. "The trial of soul. Shatterstorm will break her, but first, I will give her unending pain. And you, dear love of mine, you will suffer just as much as she, if not more."

Reaching through the aether of Death, Solanine fought the urge to retch. It mattered not the blooddrake was bathed in the blood of Noctis, for still it seared. Batting the pain to the side, Solanine clamped the aethecite manacles upon Valeria's wrists. The bikrome shrieked in pain as the pure fire of Eminence and the virulent pyre of Noctis bonded, melding into one.

"Like Canlon did to my master, I do to you, Valeria Dunleith. You are bound to the Crystals. Your power is bound. You cannot escape me. Cauda."

The second blooddrake withdrew the aether, the blackened mist retreating back into the void.

"You are mine, Valeria. Soul and all. Cauda, the Godsblood."

Cauda slithered over to the prone girl, clamping the manacle to her remaining arm. Even without the bond of the second, her body convulsed as the spell of the device took root. The blooddrake lifted the girl and dropped her unceremoniously into the aethecite box, then looked toward Solanine.

"This will not be a fun journey, Valeria. You will not enjoy what is to come on our way to Shatterstorm and the Sapphire. But I will."

With Void Form summoned, Solanine lifted the bikrome on black mist. She flailed but couldn't fight. Into the box Solanine commanded her. The bikrome slammed her fists against the clear ore-wrought wall of the box as Cauda closed the lid. The Godsblood lay unconscious behind the bikrome.

"Let us be gone of this place," Solanine announced to the frightened quaestors, who then jumped to lift the box.

Valeria continued to hit her manacled hands against the inside walls, her mouth screaming but her words were silent without.

"YOU HAVE DONE WELL, MY DISCIPLE. TWO CHILDREN LEFT, THEY WILL BOTH FALL."

The blooddrake known as Solanine plucked the Hammer of Mother Marrow, then the wheellock pistol from the ground, handing them to Cauda. Solanine beckoned the hiding hobgoblin forward. The hobgoblin nervously peeked toward Solanine, but tittered after Cauda as they marched away, disappearing into the sweltering heart of the volcano.

"SHATTERSTORM AWAITS."

And I will have my revenge.

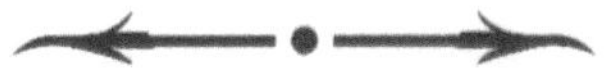

EMINENCE

THE CAUSTIC AETHER tousled Canlon Carr's waist-long, bone-white hair as he undertook his daily shuffle through the ruins of Eminence. His prison, a prison of his own making. A solitary figure doomed.

"RELEASE ME, MORTAL, I CAN REMAKE WHAT WAS BROKEN BY YOUR DISLOYALTY. FIX IT ANEW AND YOU CAN FINALLY REST."

O Zenith, I'm not in the mood today, so why don't you just go bugger off?

"I AM ETERNAL!"

The words weren't truly words, for a Divine spoke not like man did, but instead were imprints of language derived of a lesser creature's attempt at conversing via vocal communication. Pictures and feelings were more accurate. The true language of Zenith and Nocturne was not for the faint of heart.

But for a man such as Canlon Carr, he knew this argument, for it had been eons in the having.

Yeah, I get it. We've had this conversation for nigh on seventy thousand dayturns. It's tiresome.

"YOU DARE MOCK ME? I WILL SMITE..."

Canlon Carr, the man once known as the Godsking, forced the voice of Zenith from his mind as he did to the best of his ability for nearly five hundred years since Eminence fell from the heavens. It was growing more difficult as he weakened, and the voice came to him louder and more demanding in the time since. A mortal man Canlon was still, which meant he felt emotion, temptation becoming harder and harder to resist.

But the morality of his choice raged inside of him, knocking back the feeling of letting go, of finally giving in. It had coalesced into apathy. A detachment that had grown more prevalent as the years passed.

Once, he was tall and broad shouldered. Now, his body carried a myriad of aches with every movement; stooped and frail. Once, he'd kept his beard short to his strong jaw of delicate brown Calibrathian elfirish tones. Now, there was just sickly grey blotches marring his flesh and his beard scraggly. Once, he'd been the chosen one to protect the balance between Life and Death, an unparalleled master of aether. Now, he was a husk, drained almost to the point of death.

The end was nearing. Finally.

The ground under his bare feet trembled greatly, causing him to put a hand to a nearby cluster of stonework. It had been a statue of one of his forebears but now was faded to rounded shapes under the unyielding assault of corrupted aether. The quake was furious, they all were this past year since the Seal of *Terris* had been broken. The ground heaved, almost renting in twain what was once the greatest city in the world. Canlon squeezed his eyes shut until the quake finally passed, for he felt the sorrow of pained aether keenly within the tremor. The hurt of the world collapsing on itself.

Then, just as swiftly as the quake had gone, a blazing inferno swept through the poisoned aether filling the ruins of Eminence. Not a true blaze, but a fiery pyre within the aether itself. A fire so engulfing, so strong, Canlon knew there was only one way to yield such a force.

The Seal of *Ignis* had been broken.

But inside, in his soul, his heart of hearts, a light bloomed and then faded. Another ending, one he both feared and knew would come eventually. They both had.

"Poetic," the Godsking whispered as he forced himself another step through the ruins, the voice of Zenith ranting at him, but Canlon ignored it. "The blood of Nightingale is fulfilling their destiny. Rest is indeed coming for me. Maja, my beloved, you've done it."

"THAT DEVIANT BLOODDRAKE IS DEAD, MORTAL. DID YOU FEEL HER SOUL PASS INTO THE VOID?"

Canlon sighed. "Yes."

Connected as he was to Eminence, the life-giving crystal, he felt all of it everywhere in the entire world. Every life, every ending. Not just of man or beast, but everything. All existence. Every infinitesimal spark, he felt its pulse, its demise.

He had felt Maja die. Which also meant Brio was gone as well.

Once, there would have been tears. Now, only acceptance.

"RELEASE ME AND I CAN BRING HER BACK!"

Let me mourn her in peace, daemon Divine."

"I WILL NOT BE SHUT..."

Canlon closed off the Divine known as Zenith, resuming his aimless drifting through the ruins of the Holy City of Heavens.

He was deep within the once grand quarter known as Luminous, where the permanent dwellers upon the floating city had lived. Homes and villas stacked next to each other, rich and poor alike. Once, teeming with life under the glow of aether-filled lamps. Now, crumbled stones within the poisoned mist, specters of souls watching a once-noble man shuffle past.

This was Eminence.

Canlon stopped his routine trek through the ruins at the threshold of Luminous and the quarter beyond, the former beautiful gardens of White Oaks. It always pained him, each day's turn, as he came upon the residuum of White Oaks, for this tranquil slice of heaven had been where he and Maja had professed their undying love to one another centuries ago, lifetimes ago. Once, this garden had been the culmination of *Terris.* Now, a wasteland of broken visions, of shattered truths.

"ALL THIS CAN BE ONCE AGAIN, MORTAL. YOU MUST MERELY RELEASE ME."

Maja was dead, and so was his heart. *Five hundred yearturns, Maja. I can wait a little longer… You've work still to do, my beloved, but this from the realm of the dead.*

"SHE CAN BE ONCE MORE. I CA—"

On, Canlon went, reminiscing.

Even to this day, Canlon could recall the first time he had laid eyes on the magical godsblessed city of Eminence. Aside from when Maja had come into his life, it was the most beautiful thing he had ever seen.

Not a perfect circle by any means, but close. The city, that is. Maja was perfection. The city was near two full leagues in diameter at the base. The bottom of the floating city was roughly hewn, solid stone, as if the giant divine hand of Zenith had scooped it from the ground and had placed it in His heavens for all to witness His glory. O, what a fallacy that had been. Three tiers, three sections of the city, all with roads pointed inward and upward toward the Great Crystal, the city's namesake: Eminence.

Where Canlon now walked, the first tier was for all the souls who had called Eminence home, as well as those who had visited in pilgrimage. The homes of Luminous, the gardens of White Oaks, the merchants and vendors of Lamplight Markets, and finally, the Temple of the Pentax—comprised of the Inner and Outer Sanctums.

At the height of Eminence's grace, thousands had called the floating city home, and still a hundredfold more journeyed to the Holy City of Heavens yearly.

"MY CITY CAN BECOME GRAND ONCE MORE, MORTAL. FREE ME AND YOU SHALL RESUME YOUR PLACE UPON MY THRONE."

Every day, the bombardment was the same. Rote promises; recycled and reworded. For five hundred years it was the same.

Canlon carried on, the diseased, stagnant aether his only true companion. Dawnbreak was an hour's turn hence, so he quickened his gait.

Connected by a broad, arched gateway called the Godsking's Gate, the second tier of Eminence was a walled fortress called the Strata. Once, twenty thousand legionnaires manned the Strata, souls of all nations, not just of Kanjan, sworn to their Godsking. Now, an emptiness crying out for life to resume its watch.

At each cardinal point, a tower stood. While crumbling due to the deterioration of time and disuse, the towers still stood high. One tower each for the Four Tenets of Aether. A hundred feet tall, each tower was topped with a ten-foot crystal. Sapphire, Peridot, Emerald, and Garnet. Once, these Shards were as bright as the midday sun. Now, Sapphire and Peridot were dim, the Emerald and Garnet completely dark.

But Canlon's destination was the Tower of Zenith, a pitch-black pillar punching straight upward from the center of the Strata. Once, a three hundred food tall spire with a screw-shaped dome of solid glass at its apex, a single entrance guarded by a score of legionnaires and aetheurgists. Now, inky, depraved aether seeped from the tower like let blood.

"IT NEEDN'T BE LIKE THIS, MORTAL. THIS IS NOCTURNE'S DOING. HE HAS DONE THIS TO US. NOT I."

The Godsking placed his skeletal hands upon the Tower of Zenith's entrance, his fingers glowing with the Four Tenets as he opened himself to it. The Four Tenets surged within his breast, from deep within his ageing soul. The door to the Tower groaned as it opened, the black misty aether crying as if in pain. Beyond was a platform, as there were no stairs to the top of the Tower. Even with the corruption overtaking all of Eminence and the lands beyond, the platform still bloomed a brilliant diamond as he stepped upon it.

Whispering the words of the Breath, the platform—silently and without pulleys or gears—rose.

At the apex, the door opened into the corkscrew glass dome, where a singular pathway wound around the tower toward a great, rune-inscribed door, which beyond was the Chamber of Eminence.

Canlon again put his hands upon the door, saying the words he had every day since the divine Crystal had chosen him a lifetime ago. The door opened under his aether, although it screamed as the corruption fought his touch. Black mist poured from the portal as if releasing a dam, filtering down the corkscrew and into the hollow Tower. Walls of glass at the pinnacle of all heaven. The fleeting stars of waning nightturn spread above.

And as it had the first time, so did Canlon's breath catch in his throat as his dimming eyesight took in the Crystal of Eminence.

It was beautiful. Magnificent and striking. As tall as the tallest of giants, twice the width. Smooth as Thullyrish silk, hard as the Forgemistress' Blades. Clear as a prism, but up close, the veins flush with the Four Tenets, swirling as if living and breathing. But at its base, perfection was rotted, clawing its blackness upward toward the unmarred structures. It bled from a two-foot crack in the Crystal's surface.

"RELEASE ME!" The Divine's words echoed within the chamber, within his eardrums, almost too harsh a price to bear.

"Never, Zenith!" he screamed back. "I am Canlon Carr, chosen of Eminence and Noctis. And you have no will over me!"

Zenith ranted as the Divine locked within Eminence radiated with aetheric rage. Canlon merely chuckled to himself, as his response was unnecessary and a bit over the top. He just enjoyed a good probing retort every now and again. It's what kept him sane.

But alas, another day, another chosen duty.

Canlon knelt before the Crystal of Life, placing his hands upon the base of the life-giving entity. The blackened aether curled around his wrists, as if dragging him toward the void of Death. He could hear the wails of the dead beyond the veil, could hear the pleas of Nocturne, calling to him so that he remember his oath.

An oath he'd never forsake. Not even to bring Maja back. It was not his place to do so anyway. But this, this was his duty. This was when he must break another oath.

The Four Tenets, corrupted as they were, came alive under the tips of his fingers. Fire. Earth. Air. Water. His duty, his sacrifice. To give life, one must bleed life. The Godsking leaned forward, shoulders tense, head bowed at the base of the broken Crystal.

It was time.

Maja, my beloved, wait for me just a little longer? Maybe Nocturne can… no, don't think on it.

Then, Canlon drew up his sleeve to reveal intricate runes tattooed into his left arm from wrist to shoulder. Each rune bound into his flesh with aether, pulsing underneath his skin with the Four Tenets. Attached to his wrist was a thin, golden chain with no clasp. In the center of his palm was a diamond in the shape of an eye. The golden chain connected to his fingers via solid, auric rings, each with a Shard of Eminence encased.

The Eye of the Soul, the boon and poisoned chalice of the chosen.

Softly, the Breath of the Soul, the words of the Divines—and the lock in which Zenith remained bound—left his lips. "Fire begets, Fire taketh."

"RELEASE ME!"

"Water rears, Water recedes."

"I CAN BRING HER BACK!"

"Earth sculpts, Earth razes."

"YOU CAN HAVE IT ALL BACK!"

"Air breathes, Air stifles."

"YOU CAN REIGN OVER EVERYTHING, JUST BOW TO ME!"

"Scales ward, Scales break."

"YOU CAN BE THE TRUE DIVINE IF YOU BUT SERVE!"

"Scales are All. Scales are Nothing."

"I WILL BREAK YOU, CANLON CARR! I WILL SEE YOUR SOUL BURNED INTO THE VOID WHERE IT CAN NEVER RETURN. I WILL GIVE YOU THE FINAL DEATH!"

"Immortality does not come from the proliferation of Life, but upon the wave of Death."

And then it started as he said the words over and over.

Eminence's brilliancy quickened first, always blooming with neutral energy from the Eye of the Soul, flitting toward the Great Crystal in tiny tendrils of aether. The aether wrapped around the Godsking in tune with the chanting of the Breath. The aether drawing from Canlon's own soul.

Soul for soul.

His blood turned cold, and his breath became a sharp intake. The energy rushed into him as if the very essence sought to claim what was for the Divines only.

The magic of the Four Tenets came next. Surging from the connection between the Godsking's soul and the Crystal's aether. The Fire of *Ignis* igniting the chamber, heating the glass walls in a blazing presence, sending the blackened poison reeling. Calmness of *Aquis* draining the heat back like a cresting wave of Water, drawing into the Godsking's body, siphoning his energy with serenity. The stimulation of Air, strengthening and contorting his flesh, twisting and turning in pain like the tempest of *Aere*. The earthly balance of *Terris*, relaxing and revitalizing the angry energy, creating stability.

Billowing out from Eminence, the Four Tenets churned in a dance of ancient magic borne from the Twin Divines, colliding into Their chosen, eating away at his lifeforce, striking at each nerve, prodding and stealing away his soul, binding his essence to that of the world. The Godsking pulsed with the rainbow force of each Tenet, a tormented grunt escaping his gritted teeth as aether ripped through him.

"I AM ETERNAL, MORTAL! THIS LOCK WILL NOT REMAIN FOREVER!"

He waited for it to end, for the Tenets to bleed back into the Great Crystal, another day of Life extended to the world. Awaited the quake of the world around them to signify his gift. Once, as it had each day before the Fall of Eminence, he would sag expended and tired. Drained and spent. Eminence would glow fiercely with his strength, as the aether within collected their due, his blessing and curse.

But not this day. Not since *Terris* had been destroyed.

Now, the Four Tenets of all and none, the power of Life and Death exploded from his body, filling the glass Chamber with such ferocity, Canlon fleetingly worried the dome would shatter.

It never did.

A resounding crack reverberated within the inky aether, sending shudders along the Chamber's panes. Hot and cold filled him at once, anger and calm, empty and filled. An emotional gamut washed over him as the rainbow of the Tenets illuminated the Chamber like a prism.

He cried out, a shrill sound.

Pain. Harsh and strong.

Torment. Searing and killing.

Canlon's blood raced, his entire being felt like it was being torn apart from the inside, greater than anything he'd ever felt. His heart threatened to explode, blood burning like an inferno, flesh rendering like a rift. His muscles shook and stretched. His very soul wailed.

And then it was over. The corruption had taken its tithe, Zenith locked within Eminence for another day.

Canlon Carr, the Last Godsking, crumpled at the base of the Crystal, head in his hands. Canlon numbly stared at his sacred duty, questioning words on ragged breath.

I await you, blood of Nightingale. You cannot come soon enough.

"SHE NEEDS HELP, CANLON."

Canlon sighed. "I know, Nightingale. Maja told me in the Meadows before her death. There is only one who can help her now. Can it be done? Is this the price she is willing to pay? Does she even know it, or have you kept that from her?"

"SHE DOES NOT KNOW."

"Then you would make her suffer anew?"

"THE AEGISES MUST RISE. KNOW THIS, YOU DO. THE WARDKEEPER AND THE PRINCEPS ARE IN MOTION. THE GIRL'S LOVER WILL CLAIM MY SON'S MANTLE WHEN SHE WAKES. THE LAST MUST BE OF HER BLOOD. MY BLOOD."

"It will break her, the Godsblood."

"I KNOW. IT IS THE ONLY WAY."

Canlon put his head in his hands. It was the only way. It would be his end. Finally. "Then take your tithe, Nightingale. Bring her back. For the Godsblood. Maja sacrificed her life for this. I will too. A soul for a soul."

Pain blossomed within Canlon's breast, just as strong as before when he reset Zenith's prison. Aether engulfed him. And just like before, he allowed it. Drowned in it. Accepted it. Welcomed it.

Soon, Maja. Soon.

The mist in the Chamber gleamed bright ruby. The Crystal faded into the mist as a figure approached from within. A woman, raven-colored hair, curled in waves. Skin the color of caramel. But her eyes were not all black as they had been for the past seventeen years before death took her, instead were a soft brown. A woman not expected to be seen in this realm ever again.

The blood of Nightingale.

The woman stopped before the Last Godsking, looking around the Chamber of Eminence, eyes narrowing at him. "Where is my daughter?"

"She's been captured by Solanine and is on her way to Shatterstorm, Cadrianna Benld."

Here Ends Passage Two of the Divine Godsqueen Coda

The Coda Continues In:

Shatterstorm

Appendicis

The Divines

The Divines [dih-**vahyns**] – The ultimate deities of Life & Death.

Zenith [**zee**-nith] – The divine of Eminence & the realm of Life. Also known as He Who Fathered the World and the All Father.

Nocturne [**nok**-turn} – The divine of Noctis & the realm of Death (the Meadows). Also known as the Master of the Pit or the Dark God.

The Pentax Gods [**pen**-taks gods]**, also known as the Hatch** borne via **Nightingale** [**nahyt**-n-geyl] & Zenith:

Mother Marrow [**muh*th*-er mar**-oh] – Goddess of the east, guardian terrisvvyrm of the Emerald Shard. Patron goddess of creation, healing, & life, as well to the ingeniators of the Scattered Shards. Associated with *Terris*. Holy artifact is the Hammer of Mother Marrow. Also known as the Forgemistress of Creation, the Forger of Life.

Justice [**juhs**-tis] – God of the west, guardian seagandr of the Sapphire Shard. Patron god of peace, law, & war, as well to the vicars of the Scattered Shards. Associated with *Aquis*. Holy artifact is the Aegis of Justice. Also known as the Arbiter.

Brio [**bree**-oh] – God of the south, guardian firedrake of the Garnet Shard. Patron god of desire, stimulation, & lust, as well to the quaestors of the Scattered Shards. Associated with *Ignis*. Holy artifact is the Mantle of Brio. Also known as the Wayward Son, the Drunk God.

Bliss [blis] – Goddess of the north, guardian aerovern of the Peridot Shard. Patron goddess of purity, order, & time, as well to the augurs of the Scattered Shards. Associated with *Aere*. Holy artifact is the Crown of Bliss. Also known as the Ideal Daughter, the Virtuous One.

THE ORDERS OF DRACONEM

Draconem [drey-**koh**-nem] – Greater & lesser orders of drakes.

Firedrake [fahy*uh*r-**dreyk**] – Greater order. The smartest, as well as the cruelest, grand of size, & notoriously violent. As such, these savage beasts tend to lair on fiery peaks far from the races of man. Their scales are near impossible to breach, thus are used in body armor manufacturing.

Seagandr [see-**g*uh*n**-dyr] – Greater order. The bane of every sailor, for they possess multiple heads & rise from their gloomy depths only when cargo ships are bulging with drake essence or aethecite. Their oil offers an alternative fuel source to aethecite, as well as a suitable machine grease.

Aerovern [**air**-oh-vern] – Greater order. The smallest in size, with a wingspan half the size of their firedrake cousins but possesses a healthy dose of claw & lightning breath. Their scales drip poison & frost, but once past their exteriors, they make for excellent food seasoning.

Terrisvvyrm [ter-**uhs**-vurm] – Greater order. All have perished during the destruction of the aethecite mines & Temple of Mother Marrow. The largest drake, but simplest of intelligence. These subterranean behemoths had slimy scales & no eyes. Instantly after death, vvyrm corpses become fetid & rotten, making a perfect source of fertilizer.

Drakken [drey-**k*uh*n**] – Lesser order. Anthropomorphic, these drakes live amongst men. Renowned for their warrior-heart, some become wardkeepers, or counselors & generals to rēgis & rēginae.

Blooddrake [bluhd-**dreyk**] **–** Lesser order. Cunning & secretive, most owing allegiance to the Divines. These loathsome drakes utilize aether to wear the flesh of men, stealing their identities to further the Divine's endeavors. Wily & hateful.

Aetheurgy Forms

Soul Form [sohl fawrm] – the purest form, borne only in those with Godsblood, the world's essence via Eminence theirs to command. Marked by pristine, white pupils & irises. Manipulation of all Forms.

Vision Form [**vizh**-*uh*n fawrm] – the voice of the Pentax Gods, Bliss & Brio. Marked by one all-white eye & one all-black eye. Manifests in prophetic visions of past, present, & future, as well as manipulation of the veil between Life & Death.

Burn Form [burn fawrm] – borne in the essences of the Four Enhancements of Aether. Burned via injection or ingestion of distilled aethecite, called parch. Marked by a colored pupil; colors of garnet, sapphire, peridot, or emerald. Enhances senses, speed, strength, & stamina.

Shard Form [shahrd fawrm] – borne in the essences of the Four Tenets of Aether. Burned via inked runes in the flesh sparked by inhalation of the poisonous mist. Marked by a colored pupil; colors of garnet, sapphire, peridot, or emerald. Enhances strength, speed, & senses, as well as allows manipulation of the four elements.

Void Form [void fawrm] – from the darkness of the void beyond the veil of Life via Noctis, scarred runes upon breast & spine. Marked by all black pupils, irises & sclera. Manipulates the body by use of blood, as well as manipulation of the mist.

THE RUNES OF AETHEURGY

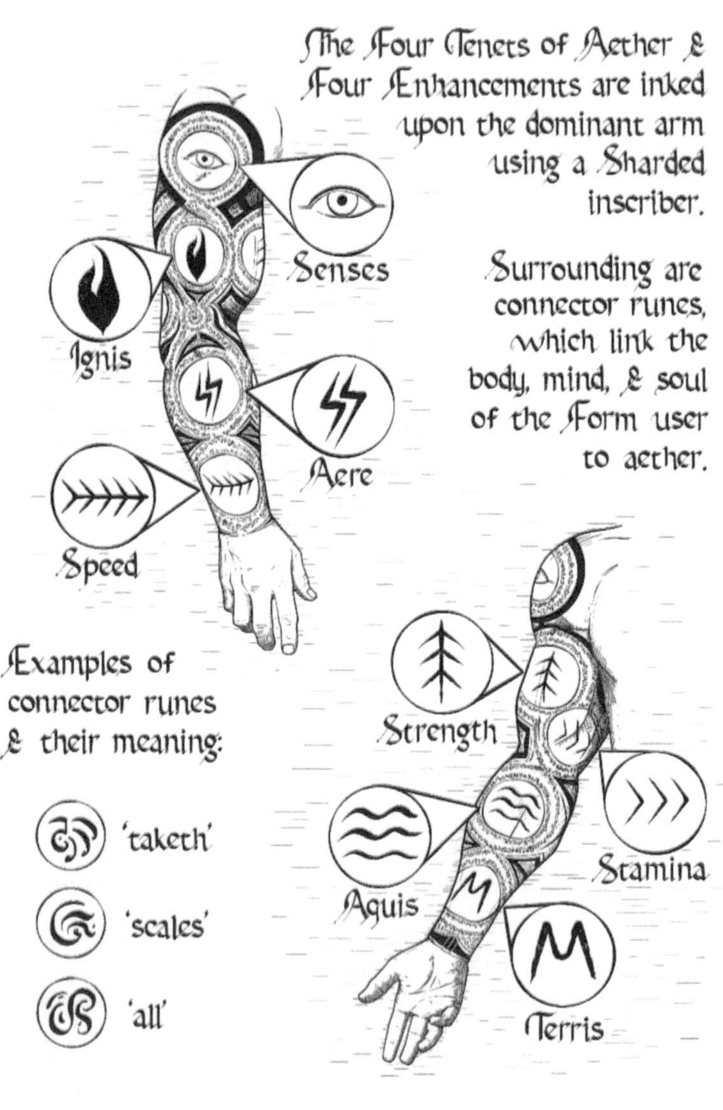

The Auras of Soul Form

Aura [**awr**-uh] – the art of reading a person's emotions and/or intent by a color. Used solely by a wielder of Soul Form aetheurgy.

Blue – the ideal of Trust.

Tints – Serenity, Wisdom, Stability, Contentment, Intimate, Nurturing
Shades – Distancing, Aloofness, Inferior, Apathetic, Bored, Guilty

Green – the ideal of Awareness.

Tints – Health, Fertility, Faithful, Confident, Eager, Powerful
Shades – Greedy, Sickness, Jealousy, Wanting

Red – the ideal of Stimulation.

Tints – Loving, Passionate, Lusting, Strengthened
Shades – Anger, Danger, Warning, Critical, Hateful, Hostile

Yellow – the ideal of Energy.

Tints – Joyous, Optimism, Playful, Daring, Amusement, Excitement
Shades – Cowardice, Fear, Anxious, Rejected, Submissive, Bewildered

Factions of the Mistlands

The Scattered Shards [thuh **skat**-erd sharhds] – the religious order formed after the Fall of Eminence. Broken into four sects, each branch devoted to one of the Pentax Gods. Headed by the Conclave & pontifex maximus in Kalderim.

Augur [**aw**-ger] – the preachers of Bliss' words & healers of the ill. Denoted by a pristine white cassock. Upon attaining the cassock, an augur receives a new name, determined by their Shard preference. An augur's Shard Form is held within the Beads of Aether wrapped around their wrist, each sharded Bead contains one of the Four Tenets & will crack upon use. Untainted by the corruption in the mist.

Ingeniator [in-**ge**-ni-ator] – the followers of Mother Marrow, creators & scientists using aether. Denoted by an emerald cassock. An ingeniator carries a smaller version of the Forgemistress' green-iron hammer but are not warriors. An ingeniator's Shard Form is tattooed upon their arms, which allows them to combine aether with science. Untainted by the corruption in the mist.

Quaestor [**kwes**-ter] – the tainted warriors of Brio. Denoted by a crimson cassock. Former criminals allowed to repent. Upon attaining the cassock, a quaestor receives a new name, determined by their crime. A quaestor's Shard Form is tattooed upon their arms & is only accessed by inhalation of the corruption in the mist, thus their tainted bodies wither & die. A quaestor carries a red-iron mace. All Shards strongholds are headed by a grand quaestor.

Vicar [**vik**-er] – the untainted warriors of Justice. Denoted by a midnight blue cassock. Upon attaining the cassock, a vicar receives a new name, determined by their Shard preference, plus given an honorific denoting a physical or emotional attribute. A vicar's Shard Form is tattooed upon their arms & is only accessed by inhalation of the corruption in the mist. They are, however, untainted by the corruption.

The Imperium of the Fallen [thuh im-**peer**-ee-*uh*m ovh thuh **faw**-l*uh*n] – the physical embodiment of the Fallen's coven, in both lands conquered & soldiering force.

Scourge [skurj] – the assassins of the Imperium. Broken by torture, they are the blade of the Fallen. Some scourges are trained in Void Form.

Oracle [**awr**-uh-k*uh*l] – aged aetheurgists living in a basilica in the ruins of Illigan. Blind, these seers paint one hand in whitewash, one in blackwash in a corrupted Vision Form. Led by the Matron.

The Guild [thuh gild] – the growing affiliation of Houses within each mega-city, each pledging fealty to the High Seat in Alizarin.

The Golden Throne of Kalderim [thuh **gohl**-d*uh*n throhn ovh kald-**er**-im] – the imperium & formal seat of power in Kanja. Led by the rēx & rēgīna.

The Legion [thuh **lee**-j*uh*n] – the soldiering force of Kanja. Legionnaires are trained in hand-to-hand combat as well as artillery. Each stronghold is led by a primus pilus (captain) & serve under the guidance of the praetor (general).

The Golden Sword [thuh **gohl**-d*uh*n sward] – a title & a weapon held by the eldest heir.

The Holy Order of the Vird [thuh **hoh**-lee **awr**-der ovh thuh vurd] – a sect of devout believers in the Shards of Eminence & Noctis. Found upon the highest peak of the Forgemistress' Blades, they are the creators of the rune inscribers for the Scattered Shards.

The Matriarchy of Krylen [thuh **mey**-tree-ahr-kee ovh krahy-len] – the leadership of the free city of Krylen.

The Wardkeepers [thuh wawrd-**kee**-pers]– drakken chosen. They bear the horns of the Pentax & sing the Hymn of Justice. They are the generals, counselors, & protectors of a ward's bloodline until their death, then the honor is passed on, along with the horns.

The Isle of Merj [thuh ahyl ovh murhj]– the homeland of the drakken. Each wardkeeper bloodline can be traced back to Merj & the first wardkeeper.

The Broken Quarry [thuh **broh**-k*uh*n **kwawr**-ee] – a forgotten bloodline found in the Voidlands near Shatterstorm. Led by the Goldkeeper, these wardkeepers are the guardians of the Sapphire.

ACKNOWLEDGEMENTS

Where to start? Family first, probably. I suppose I should start with my parents because they showed me that nothing is better than burying myself in a good book. To my sister, who reads far more than I do, this is probably too big and dark a book for you. To my extended family, you rock! To my BIL, I'll get you to read indie fantasies soon enough. To my lil goblin, you tire me out, but I wouldn't change it for the world and to my biscuit, your happy smile gives me life. To my wife and biggest cheerleader, you probably won't read this book, but I still love you.

A huge shoutout to all the writing friends. Amanda, my first writing friend. Claire, my voice of narrative reason, guardian of stakes, and pusher of bettering my craft. Sam, my ever-present ear, always listening to my crazy ideas and reading everything I send your way. Dewey, my grumpy brother, my great friend, my fellow quester, I couldn't have gotten to this point without you. To AJ and Mario who beta read this chonker, your feedback was ever helpful. To Mike, Tim, Andrew, Dave, Greg, Alex, Zack, Pete, Nick, the FanFi Addict Team, the Silverstones Books gents, the Secret Scribes, and the rest of the indie community rockstars who've adopted me into their tribe, you are simply the best!

Finally, to those who read this coda, I hope you've enjoyed following my stabby, sarcastic little bint. Without you, none of this is worth it. And I'm not sorry if I killed off your favorite character…

Love you all!

About the Author

During his collegiate days at the turn of the century, he began to develop his passion for writing, especially within the epic fantasy genre about unlikely heroes. It was there, Bill began to formulate the story that would eventually become Ashe's unwanted journey and *The Divine Godsqueen Coda*.

Aside from writing, Bill loves movies and reading, especially SFF B-movies. He likes to know all the useless trivia, like who played who, and what the stories were behind the curtain. He is a master at Scene It. Bill's few other hobbies include soccer, good whiskey, a slice of pizza, and growing a beard. It is the little things he enjoys most.

Bill currently lives in the greater Chicago, IL area with his wife, young goblin, and biscuit.

Gentle Reader, my eternal gratitude goes to you for taking the time to read Passage Two of the Divine Godsqueen Coda. I sincerely hope you enjoyed this tale. Self-publishing relies on word of mouth and reviews/ratings on sites such as Goodreads and Amazon.

If you can find the time, please leave your thoughts on Lady Drakeslayer wherever you can, good or bad, every little bit helps. My thanks.

Scan the QR Code above to be taken to Lady Drakeslayer's Goodreads page.

Willow Wraith Press is a collective of nerds who write the types of books we want to read. If you have enjoyed this book, please check out the other Willow Wraiths.

Dewey Conway & Bill Adams:

The Tenacious Tale of Tanna the Tendersword

Andrew D. Meredith:

Deathless Beast
Bone Shroud
Gloves of Eons
Dread Knight

Thrice
Four Scored

Quaint Creatures: Magical & Mundane

Michael Roberti:

The Traitors We Are
A Grave for Us All
The Revenge of Thousands

Timothy Wolff:

Platinum Tinted Darkness
Tears of the Maelstrom
Age of Arrogance

The Whisper that Replaced God

To visit the Willow Wraith Press website, scan this code

The Secret Scribes are an affiliation of independent fantasy authors. If you have enjoyed this book, please check out the other books from some great authors & show them some support!

L.N. Bayen

The Wingspan of Treason

Tom Bookbeard:

The Corsair (Early '25)

E.H. Bradley:

The Ranger

L.M. Douglas:

Gharantia's Guardian
Gharantia's Fury

Bella Dunn:

The Dreams Thief
Blood and Dreams (Spring '25)

The Sorrow of the Wise Man (Spring '25)

Damien Francis:

The Tome of Haren

Dave Lawson:

The Envoys of War

Sean O'Boyle:

The Ballad of Sprikit the Bard (and Company)

R.E. Sanders:

A Path of Blades
Tann's Last Stand
Demon's Tear

R.A. Sandpiper:

A Pocket of Lies
A Promise of Blood

Alex Scheuermann:

The Odyllic Stone

G.J. Terral:

Bloodwoven
Bloodbound

www.ingramcontent.com/pod-product-compliance
Lightning Source LLC
Chambersburg PA
CBHW020243030826
48979CB00030B/2501/J